Zigomar

Zigomar

by
Léon Sazie

translated by
Michael Shreve

A Black Coat Press Book

Acknowledgements: André-François Ruaud.

English adaptation and introduction Copyright © 2019 by Michael Shreve.
Cover illustration Copyright © 1928 by Georges Vallée.

Visit our website at www.blackcoatpress.com

TABLE OF CONTENTS

Advertisement by Leonetto Cappiello (1909)

Introduction

Zigomar? What's a Zigomar? Well, it's a character dreamt up by Léon Sazie in 1909. An evil, nefarious character, a criminal genius who was so popular in his heyday that his picture could be found on bags of bread, pipes and matches. Alas, the poor devil has since fallen into obscurity.

"In Paris this morning a cry of public indignation, terror and anger rang out." So begins this epic of crime, this action saga replete with tragic women, grieving mothers, working girls, showgirls, heroines and heroes fighting side by side in all the breathtaking, breakneck adventures to conquer the hooded, blood-thirsty gang of Zs. True to the cliffhanger narrative, every episode leaves the reader in suspense, but not always resolved in the immediate sequel. There are characters that come and go, stories interwoven with each other, a pace that races, slackens, then shoots off again... all part of the great panoply of Paris, from high society down to the dregs, that is put on display behind the battle between justice and crime. Here we also find the epitome of modern action stories maybe for the first time in fiction: the car chase. It wasn't until more than a year later that the Bonnot Gang was credited with inventing the "getaway car" in their bank robberies.

Gypsies, Gitanos, Tziganes, Djinns also called Ramogiz—spell it backwards—is the narrative's explanation for the origin of the name Zigomar. It could just as likely come from "zig" or "zigoto", slang for a guy on the street who likes to show off, to boast and brag and amaze, to go so far as to be considered a freak. But then again there was also an old fashioned sword that was inscribed with a Z, the same mark that the gang uses to identify themselves. And there comes the Z in the heart of the author's own name. In any case, Zigomar is the leader of a gang of outsiders, miscreants, rebels, gangsters and thugs, a secret society emerging from the underground world of Paris. Everybody knows about Zigomar, everybody feels his presence, but nobody knows who he is. He is a mystery hiding in plain sight.

On December 7, 1909, Zigomar saw the light of day for the first time. He would lie and cheat and murder his way through *Le Matin* in 164 different installments until November 13, 1910. He was resurrected by the publisher Ferenczi in 1913, 28 installments this time of 128 pages each, with covers by Georges Vallée. Then in 1916 two big volumes come out under the titles *Zigomar* and *Zigomar Works with Germany* in which he betrays France, thus entering the world of spy fiction. Once again in 1924 we get a new adventure with *Zigomar vs. Zigomar*. After a long hiatus he makes his final appearance in *Le Petit Parisien* in 1938, just before the author's death, under the title *Zigomar*

Strikes Again, which was published posthumously in book form by Tallandier in 1948. But Zigomar did not just haunt the print media, he invaded the silver screen as well. Victorin Jasset created a serial film in 1911, *Zigomar, roi des voleurs.* He went on to make the sequels *Zigomar vs. Nick Carter* (1912) et *Zigomar, peau d'anguille* (1913).

Masked, hooded, or in disguise, Zigomar constantly confounded the law. Very probably he was the first of the masked criminals who faced off against a heroic detective, as we find later in Fantômas. But not just a hidden identity, it was also the taste for gratuitous crime and the style of almost automatic writing, typical of serial fiction, that found emulators who would replace him in the public adoration. It was the power of his unusual crimes (typhus-bearing mosquitoes for example), his appalling but imaginative atrocities, murder, kidnapping, robbery, torture, and his inevitable escape from the clutches of the law, his perpetual evasion of justice that made him so popular with the public for a time and that left his mark on the history of crime fiction.

As with his most famous character, the name of Sazie is also a mystery and his life was full of its own tragedies and adventures. Of Basque origin, Léon Sazie was born in Algeria in 1862. He suffered an accidental death in Suresnes in 1939. When he was still a child his father committed suicide after being ruined in a bank fraud—real life setting the scene for fiction perhaps. His widow was left to raise six children. She remarried an ex-captain of the military, Charles-Ange Laisant, who would become a politician, then an anarchist, for a while a newspaper editor and finally a mathematician. Sazie, too, wore several hats. Socialist and Dreyfusard, he started writing for newspapers before turning to theater where he found little success, so he tried his hand at various serial fiction. He created Martin Numa, king of detectives, in 1908. And a year later he introduced his most famous, most successful character, the king of criminals, Zigomar, anti-hero, criminal genius, incarnation of evil. And like his fictional nemesis, Sazie was a passionate fencer who fought several duels. For a time he gave up writing to devote himself to the art, eventually inventing an innovative safety tip with Paul Mahalin to avoid accidental injuries while wielding the sword.

Rocambolesque is a word used to describe wildly fantastic adventures. It comes from the character created by Ponson du Terrail in the 19th century. Zigomar certainly deserves this sobriquet. But even more so, with horrific crimes that would make hardened criminals balk, traitorous political intrigues, an array of identities from common grocers to noble gentlemen, disguises that make you constantly question who's who and what's what, with its cliffhanger episodes and melodramatic love affairs, hooded tribunals in secret lairs, for the fear and confusion that shook up the public, for its influence on popular literature and film, it's high time we rescue Zigomar from oblivion and perhaps introduce a new word into the language: *Zigomatic.*

Bibliography:

Zigomar (1910)
1 Le Maitre Invisible [The Invisible Master]
2 Les Lions et les Tigres [Lions and Tigers]
3 L'Heure de la Justice {Time for Justice]

La Femme Rousse (1910) [The Red-Haired Woman]
1 Le Bras Marqué [The Marked Arm]
2 Dans l'Au-delà [Into the Beyond]
3 *My Darling*

Peau d'anguille (1912) [Eel Skin]
1 L'Homme Inattendu [The Unexpected Man]
2 Au plus fort ! [The Strongest One]

Zigomar au service de l'Allemagne (1916) [Zigomar Works for Germany]

Bouche en Cœur (1917) [Heart-Shaped Mouth]
1 La Fée d'Amour [The Fay of Love]
2 L'Homme d'Amérique [The Man from America]
3 Chiffons [Rags]

Zigomar contre Zigomar (1924) [Zigomar vs. Zigomar]

Un Nouveau Coup de Zigomar (1939) [Zigomar Strikes Again]
Anthology of short stories
Le « Z » au menton (1938) [Z on the Chin]
Les Corps Inattendus (1938) [The Unexpected Bodies]
Livré au Fauve (1938) [Thrown to the Beast]
Les Pipes en Or (1938) [The Gold Pipes]
Le Volcan Fantaisiste (1938) [The Accidental Volcano]
Les Tueurs d'Ombre (1938) [The Shadow Killers]
Le Pendu sans Figure (1938) [The Faceless Hanged Man]
Le Train Gazé (1938) [The Asphyxiated train]

Poster for first Zigomar *serial (1911)*

Filmography

Zigomar (1911)
Director: Victorin-Hippolyte Jasset
Cast: Alexandre Arquillière (Zigomar)

Zigomar contre Nick Carter (1912)
Director: Victorin-Hippolyte Jasset
Cast: Alexandre Arquillière (Zigomar), Charles Krauss (Nick Carter)

Zigomar peau d'anguille (1913)
Director: Victorin-Hippolyte Jasset
Cast: Alexandre Arquillière (Zigomar), Josette Andriot (Rosaria)

BOOK ONE : THE INVISIBLE MASTER

1. Signed in Blood

In Paris this morning a cry of public indignation, terror and anger rang out. In everybody's hands, in the streets and on the tramway and buses, were newspapers being feverishly scanned, flashing their sensational headlines.

The paperboys were running around screaming, "Extra! Extra!... Read all the details... The drama on Rue Le Peletier! The mysterious crime... Murder of the banker Montreil!"

Last night the office assistant Michel had found his boss lying on the ground in a pool of his own blood with stab wounds in his chest. Terrified, Michel sounded the alarm...

They ran to find the police who were quickly on the scene with a doctor. By telephone they informed the police headquarters and the prosecutor's office.

Monsieur Montreil was lying on the floor. He had lost a lot of blood from his gaping wound. The doctor, however, found the victim still breathing, his heart still beating.

One of the bank employees was sent right away to Rue Chalgrin where the banker lived with his family in a magnificent house. They wanted to inform the banker's two sons: Raoul the lawyer and Robert the doctor, who used the utmost delicacy to tell their mother and their sister Raymonde about the great tragedy.

The Montreils were very close, a loving and affectionate family. The children adored their mother and father and always showed them the greatest respect. The two brothers were always together and not only seemed to be of one mind but of one will.

With his head burning up, his heart wrenching and his soul in turmoil, Dr. Robert rushed into his father's office. He fell onto the banker and covered him with tears. "Oh, what a tragedy! What a horrible crime! Our good, tender father... Murdered! Why him... such a great man!"

The authorities arrived right after the doctor: Monsieur Urbain, examining judge, and Monsieur Baumier, the police chief. They gave him a few minutes to pour out his grief, then the judge went to him and said, "Monsieur, be strong! Call on all your energy, all your courage... The first hours are the most valuable for justice. Please let us do our job."

Behind Monsieur Baumier stood Paulin Broquet, the finest, cleverest inspector on the force, and the most famous police detective in France. At first he let the others pursue their investigation, to launch it officially. His time to jump in had not yet come.

Broquet stayed completely calm, utterly indifferent until Robert Montreil and the doctor took off the banker's coat to reveal the wound and put a make-shift bandage on it. He approached the two and asked to see the wound, to examine it. It was on the right side of the body, just under the collarbone.

"Uh huh," Paulin Broquet muttered. "A nice clean stabbing." Then he added, "As for the killer, he's left-handed."

"Left-handed!?" they were surprised. "How do you know that?"

"The victim was stabbed in the right by the left hand of the killer."

"That's not proof," the investigating judge said. "The murderer could have struck the victim with his right hand holding him off to his right... or from behind."

The detective bowed slightly and answered, "That's true, but that's not what happened and here's the proof." He pointed to the banker's neck. "The murderer was holding Monsieur Montreil by the neck with his right hand. See, on the left of the neck, the four bruises from fingers... and the thumb is to the right. Therefore, he had to stab him with his left hand."

At that moment the anthropometric officer started taking photos of the room, the crime scene.

Broquet asked him, "Could you take some to get a really good look at the bloody traces we can assume are on the safe."

The photographer said that the door of the safe was brown and the traces of blood were very dark so nothing would show up on the plate.

Paulin Broquet did not press him. But he asked for a sheet of copy paper that he dampen and prepared carefully. With great care he laid it against the safe and pressed hard with two blotters to get the good print that he wanted. After two or three minutes, he took off the blotters, one by one, and on the door of the safe, in the middle of the big sheet of white paper, to the astonished eyes of all those present, there appeared a big, bloody mark in the frightful form of the letter Z...

"The killer's mark," Broquet said gravely. "Guard it closely, judge, like a treasure. Guard this Z because you're going to see it again. It's a deliberate sign, a sign left here... for us."

In a whisper, so that Robert could not hear, he added shrewdly, mysteriously, "Just for us this Z... for us, the law... for a few others, our partners... and maybe also for the victim."

2. The Last Visitor

When the bandage was on, they had a better idea of the banker's condition. He was seriously wounded but not dead and he was strong enough, according to the doctor, to be transported now without too much danger to his health.

The police continued their investigation by examining the layout of the bank. They came back to the director's office to proceed with their first interrogations. They brought in the head accountant and the teller.

Paulin Broquet stepped away to give the police and employees more room and freedom to talk. He wandered over to the fireplace in which a coke fire was burning. He squatted down and poked through the ashes until he could pick out some torn pieces of paper, half-burned, which he scrutinized.

"Oh, oh," he said, walking back to the chief and the judge, "here's something weird. Some papers... promissory notes... I've never seen anybody burn stuff like this before, the most valuable papers in a bank. In fact, if these notes were paid, whoever had issued them would have been sure to take them away. If they weren't paid yet, the holder would've been even surer to keep them safe. You never destroy them like this."

"Exactly right," the head accountant said.

"Furthermore," Paulin Broquet concluded, "we will know the reason for this strange behavior because here are some fragments of the address that with the cooperation of your accounting books will help us find who signed them."

The detective carefully put the papers into a portfolio. Even though they insisted that he participate in the questioning, Broquet said nothing more. He went and sat in a corner of the room as if he wanted to be alone but in perfect sight and hearing of the interrogation.

The head accountant and the teller could give the authorities only some technical details about the bank operations and information about Montreil's habits. The safe, a huge room built into the wall, strong as a fortress, really seemed to be able to withstand any attack by robbers. And yet the massive door, reinforced with bars and locks, stood ajar. They could open it easily. The police saw the shelves and strongboxes, some rolled gold and a handful of silver coins. But they did not see a single bill.

In the neatly arranged boxes were other promissory notes and papers that the accountant denied knowing anything about. One of these boxes, unlike the others that were locked, was turned over, its contents spilled out, indicating a hurried search... rummaging... even pillaging.

They closed the safe, locked it up and then called Michel, the office assistant. Michel was an ex-soldier, decorated, who had worked for Monsieur Montreil for many years. He entered in tears, deeply disturbed.

After a few words of consolation, the investigating judge questioned him. "You're the one who brought in the visitors who wanted to see your boss. Can you tell us who were the last people you led into Monsieur Montreil's office?"

"The last visitors? Yes, your honor…" But the old servant hesitated, confused. "Uh, who was it? Who… Oh, your honor! That's strange… quite disturbing… But, I can't say who I brought in last. I'm sorry, your honor, but my poor head got such a blow that my brain's a scramble, my memory's failing me. I know there was Monsieur Laurent… and the Count de la Gueriniere…"

On hearing this name Paulin Broquet, although he had extraordinary self-control, could not help sitting up in surprise.

"I'm sure," the old man continued, "I brought in Monsieur Laurent and the Count de la Gueriniere, but who came first? I don't know… I don't know…"

"Look, my friend," the judge insisted gently, "this is of the utmost importance for us. I understand but try to remember."

Paulin Broquet broke the silence that he had kept since the start of the interrogations. "It's no use, judge," he said, "to torture this good man's mind."

"But…"

"Since we know who the last two visitors were, we only have to ask the Count de la Gueriniere and Monsieur Laurent who was first and who was the last to see him."

"True, that's logical."

"Yes. Now we just have to see," the detective whispered to his boss, "if they'll tell us."

First thing the next morning Paulin Broquet entered Baumier's office. "Hello, boss. I managed last night, not too easily mind you, to piece together the document from the scraps found in the fireplace of Montreil's office and I think it's going to be a key for us. Here, it's signed by Monsieur Laurent… worth 5000 francs, payable in fifteen days."

"Great."

"Now, I've also learned that Laurent is a little hard up at the moment and will certainly have trouble meeting the deadline."

"Good to know all this. And do you know anything about the Count?"

"The Count de la Gueriniere spent two hours last night with his mistress, Lucette Minois, the star at the Lutetia. Then he went as usual to his club where he bet big and lost a little fortune."

"That he paid?"

"That he paid! Did you think he couldn't?"

Baumier thought quietly for a moment. Then he asked the detective, who was staring at him the whole time, apparently waiting for a new question, "Who is this Count de la Gueriniere?"

"He's the Count de la Gueriniere."

"I see… But what's he like… as a man?"

Paulin Broquet, unblinking, answered, "A gentleman."

"Genuine?"

"Like so many others."

"Meaning?"

"That with certificates and papers he can prove it, justify his name and title…"

"How's he live?"

"Like so many others."

"Gentlemen?"

"Or not… who live it up with no guaranteed income."

Broquet's composure was annoying Chief Baumier who barked, "Come on, out with it, you know more than you're telling me about the Count."

Without being disturbed in the least, the detective continued in his calm, even voice, "I'm telling you, boss, I'm telling you. He's a dandy, a member of the most popular, chicest who's who of Paris. He cuts a fine figure riding in the Horse Show. He's a wonderful hunter, a fierce boxer and a formidable swordsman. With his muscles of steel, last year at Molier's he fought Patouchny, the Cossack, the champion of casino fights, and he took him down."

"Oh, come on, aren't you exaggerating a little?"

"No, boss, not at all. And there's more… a real charmer, well educated, an exquisite dancer, good-looking… and he spends a lot, his wealth is famous."

"Lucky man!"

"His mistress, Lucette Minois, recently lost… or had stolen from her a diamond necklace."

"Right!" the Chief said. "Now I remember. The Count came here to make a report about this stolen necklace. I met him… Oh, good, good…"

Broquet said nothing for a minute. Then he asked his boss very simply, "Should we arrest him?"

Baumier was taken aback. "What? Are you kidding? You're asking me if we should arrest the Count de la Gueriniere?"

"Yes, Chief."

"Arrest the Count de la Gueriniere?!"

"Either him or Monsieur Laurent. Because one or the other was the last to be with Monsieur Montreil. So, one or the other must have killed him. It's obvious."

The police chief looked very puzzled. "Don't arrest anyone just yet. Don't do anything stupid. I'm going to go over all this with Monsieur Urbain and I'll let you know what to do very soon."

"Okay, Chief."

"I sent for news about the banker. I'm still waiting…"

"I've got the latest… The banker had a very quiet, peaceful night. He recovered his senses and recognized his wife and children."

"Good."

"If this continues, it's likely that tomorrow we can bring in Monsieur Laurent and the Count de la Gueriniere before the banker…"

"You don't think it's too soon?"

"No, Chief. It's worth a try."

"We'll be taking a great risk."

"I figure that we'll get to the bottom of this nerve-wracking problem at the wounded man's bedside…"

The day passed. The evening papers were snapped up just like in the morning. The crime was captivating the public, piquing their curiosity, whetting their appetite for headlines.

Naturally the police and the prosecutor's office were assaulted by reporters who had to be given news for the next edition. But they could only be told what was already known. Nevertheless, despite the judges' defense, trying to keep them secret so as not to obstruct the wheels of justice, the papers printed the names of Monsieur Laurent and the Count de la Gueriniere.

Monsieur Laurent suddenly became very famous. They went to talk to him but the businessman, in a strange coincidence, had suddenly left Paris. Therefore, they made do with the Count de la Gueriniere, the other last visitor…

The elegant gentleman had not just friends in Paris. All his success had earned him a good number of jealous rivals, if not outright enemies, at the very least people who were delighted today to see him finally get mixed up in trouble.

The Count, however, in this situation like in so many others, proved to be a good sport and was kindly available for all interviews.

Summoned before the investigating judge, he readily admitted being with Monsieur Montreil around the time when the hateful crime was probably committed, which, he stated, he found out about only later, like everyone else, in the evening papers.

"Was I the last one to see him," he said to the judge, "or the next to last? I really can't say. What I can say is that Monsieur Montreil showed me to the door of his office and shook my hand like always."

But while describing the Count's visit to the judge, a reporter who wanted to strike a hard blow at the illustrious gentleman said at the end of his article that a rumor was running around the courts about the probable arrest of the Count de la Gueriniere.

Now, in public this news was more welcome than the Count really could have imagined. The Count thought it good, necessary, imperative to face the storm head-on and turn public opinion in his favor. He declared himself offended, a victim of defamation, and he sent two faithful friends to demand the journalist retract or defend his accusation with arms. Then, like every morning, he went to the woods to ride his horse. When he came back his butler told him that someone was waiting for him.

"Who is it?" the Count asked.

"The gentleman did not give his name. But he said he had an appointment with the Count about this morning's affair."

Very intrigued, the Count headed for his study. He could not hold back a shudder on seeing the unexpected visitor. And he could barely stop himself from crying out in surprise: it was Paulin Broquet!

3. The Accused

"Please excuse me, Monsieur, for the liberty I took in waiting for you in here," Broquet said, "but I thought it would be better if your friends didn't see me at your house."

"Why? Who do I have honor of addressing?"

"I'm Paulin Broquet... from the police."

"Ah, very well then, the famous detective! I remember hearing about your exploits. What can I do for you, monsieur?"

"Follow me."

"To the station? Again?"

"No, to Montreil's."

"What for?"

"Monsieur Montreil has recovered his senses... he's clear-headed."

"You want me to see him face to face?" Smiling he added, "I hope you don't think I'm guilty."

"I came to see you privately," the detective responded in the same tone. "This should reassure you."

"No matter, I'll gladly do as you wish." Then the Count asked, "What time should I go to Montreil's?"

"Immediately."

"Right now! Just like that! You'll give me time to change my clothes, won't you?"

"Every minute counts. Despite the doctor's opinion I fear he could relapse any second and it could end in tragedy."

"I'll follow you then..."

The Count was holding his hat in his right hand.

"Your riding crop," the detective grabbed it from the table where the Count had laid it on entering.

The Count took it but it slipped out of his hand and fell to the floor. He bent over, picked it up and said to Paulin Broquet, "I'm all thumbs with my left hand."

The detective said nothing. But he remembered that he had proved that Monsieur Montreil had been struck by a left-handed person.

When they got to the front steps of the elegant house where an automobile was waiting for them, a servant gave the Count a telegram that he opened on the spot. On reading it the gentleman's face suddenly changed, which the detective noticed instantly.

The Count raised his eyes and looked confidently at Pauling Broquet, with a smile on his face, maybe even a little sneer. "Great," he said, "I've been waiting impatiently for this note." He read aloud for the detective: "Meeting prepared. Matter to be handled as you want. Regards. Jacques." Then he added, "It's one of my friends whom I sent off with second to a certain gentleman who took the liberty of offending publicly."

An anxious crowd was parked in front of the banker's house. Among the public, who love these kinds of dramas, it is believed that a witness confrontation is the first sign of guilt. In the present case, this opinion was even stronger because in the morning papers they had mentioned the names of the two last visitors, Monsieur Laurent and the Count de la Gueriniere. They already considered one or the other as guilty, mostly hoping that it would turn out to be the Count.

His glamorous personality, his name, what they knew of him, of his adventures, of his conquests, of his horses, all this made him the favored hero, spiced up the drama in a weird way and really excited the romantic itch of the impressionable, impulsive crowd.

When the automobile turned onto the street, when they recognized the Count next to the detective—who was popular as well—they believed he was arrested. At first they just whispered, "The Count de la Gueriniere! Here he is!" Then they said out loud, "The murderer!" Until finally, like in so many other cases like this, they started shaking their angry fists and screaming, "Death! Death to the killer!"

The Count shuddered. He wanted to jump into the crowd with his riding crop, which he still held in his hand, but Paulin Broquet held him back inside the car. At this moment, a heavily bearded man wearing a dirty, shapeless cap broke through the police barrier and clamped onto the car door. He yelled in a gravelly voice, stinking of alcohol, with the thick accent of the suburbs, of the outskirts, "It's none too soon for justice to deal with the rich! Yer number's up, Count! You can go to the showdown... it's all over for you!"

At first surprised, the Count de la Gueriniere stared at this man, listened to him and he who a minute ago wanted to charge into the crowd swinging his riding crop did not even try to push away the foul mouth that was drooling insults on him.

Paulin Broquet, however, reached over and tried to grab him by the collar, but could not manage. Then he shouted out to the policemen there, "Arrest this man! Arrest him!"

But the man who had slipped out of the detective's hands was quicker and disappeared into the crowd.

Right after this incident the automobile pulled up to the banker's house. The Count jumped out and skipped up the steps leading to the entrance hall, as relaxed as could be.

Paulin Broquet, on the other hand, looked gloomier—his brow was furrowed, his eyebrows almost touched each other and a strange fire burned in his eyes. When his colleagues and boss saw him, they thought, "Uh oh, there's something wrong. Broquet does not look happy at all!"

In the little salon, behind a Louis XV table, Monsieur Urbain sat next to Monsieur Baumier. At another table the stenographers were ready to record the interrogation. They came in and the Count sat down across from the investigating judge. Broquet remained standing behind him.

"Monsieur," the judge began, "please tell me your name and your profession."

"Faustin, Count de la Gueriniere, a person of private means."

"Is that your real name, verifiably?"

"It's my name and my authentic title."

"Okay. Have you ever been arrested?"

The Count jumped in his seat. "Your honor," he almost shouted in indignation, "your question is truly, deeply shocking to me."

"You are in the presence of the law, you will please answer the question."

"My record will speak for me. Still, I must protest vehemently. It is not, as far as I know, usual to ask such questions of witnesses."

"That's right. But you, monsieur, are not brought here as a witness."

"As what then?"

"As a defendant."

The Count jumped out of his seat this time and cried out, "A defendant! Accused of what?"

"Of the attempted murder of Monsieur Montreil."

"Oh, come on, that's crazy! Me, accused..."

"It's a formal accusation."

"It's crazy, I'm telling you. Absolutely crazy!"

"Calm down, calm down," Paulin Broquet put a hand on his arm and tried to make him sit back down.

"Calm down? You think you can do whatever you want with a man's conscience, with a gentleman's honor, without him reacting, without protesting?"

"Quiet down," the judge told him. "Stop shouting, I beg you."

"But my head is on fire... my heart is racing... my entire being is outraged... Accused, me, of murder... because I just happened to come into the bank on the day of the murder! Good reason! You see, gentlemen, to accuse me like this you have to have some firm basis, some serious, irrefutable evidence... on what are you basing your accusation? Who dares to accuse me of being a murderer?"

"Monsieur Montreil himself."

"That's not true. That's a lie... Montreil is lying."

"Excuse me, Monsieur Montreil gave us a long deposition and signed it." The judge added, "We'll read it to you in a minute... in his presence. Basically it says that you went to see him, tried to borrow a large sum of money and he refused..."

"That's correct."

"Monsieur Montreil got up and showed you to the door of his office..."

"And I left. So I couldn't have killed him."

"But you came back."

"Came back... me, came back?! No, there was another visitor. I won't accuse that man but I'm telling you and I can prove I didn't go back."

"That's precisely why we want to bring you in front of the banker, to clear up this very important point..."

"Good, good, your honor. Like that I'll have no problem proving my innocence."

The Count seemed to be getting a hold of himself now, calming down and lowering his voice. His attitude changed. He sat down and in a quiet voice, although still trembling a little, he spoke to Monsieur Urbain:

"I'm sorry, your honor, for losing control and letting my temper loose like that... But what man of good conscience wouldn't do the same under such circumstances. Do you accept my apology?"

"I do and I'm listening, monsieur."

"When I said this outrageous accusation was unfounded, I reacted harshly... Now I know the true source and I'm calm... believe me. Far from being afraid of confronting Monsieur Montreil, I welcome it... I demand it. I'll remind him exactly what happened during our visit and I swear that he will recant his deposition, every word of it."

4. The Secret of the Document

Since the tragic return of the banker, Madame Montreil, his daughter Raymonde and his two sons did not have a moment's rest. Today they were joined by Captain Fabien de Rennebois, Raymonde's fiancé stationed at Fontainebleau. He had rushed over when he got news of the crime.

When the doctors and Robert announced that the patient could go through a demanding interrogation, the authorities arrived. They asked Madame Montreil and Raymonde to step out of the room, not wanting the unfortunate woman and the poor girl to have to face more trials and tribulations. Captain de Rennebois took them away, leaving the sons Robert and Raoul with the banker.

Monsieur Montreil, whose mind appeared to be as sharp as ever and whose memory was coming back clear as day, told the investigating judge that he had seen several clients before the Count de la Gueriniere and the last visit with the businessman Laurent.

"I couldn't see the Count," he said, "and I sent off Monsieur Laurent after a rather heated argument, without giving him what he wanted... It was when I was putting Monsieur Laurent's papers back in the safe that I found myself suddenly face to face with the Count de la Gueriniere... The Count grabbed me by the throat to keep me from screaming and then stabbed me in the chest..."

"And you clearly saw that it was the Count de la Gueriniere?" Judge Urbain pressed him.

"Perfectly! Absolutely! I have a clear memory of everything until I fell to the floor."

The banker gave a long statement about the details of the attack. After they read back his deposition, he nodded and signed it with a steady hand. So, a warrant was put out for the Count de la Gueriniere and Paulin Broquet was put in charge of seeing it through.

The interrogators had barely finished the sensational deposition when they were visited at the banker's house by his two old friends, Messieurs Bejanet, the long-standing notary of the Montreil family, and Grillard, who had been in charge of collections and liquidation at the bank for many years.

After the introductions that the banker made and the congratulations they gave him for having, as they said now, "survived" the murderer's knife, the notary and the law clerk asked Montreil for a moment of privacy. The authorities left. Robert and Raoul, however, wanted to stay with their father.

"No, my friends," Bejanet said, "you can't..."

"Why" Robert objected, "can't we stay here? Me as a doctor and Raoul as a lawyer?"

"Impossible, my friends. Nobody can hear what we have to say. It's strictly confidential."

"It's all right, my sons," the banker was intrigued and forcing himself to smile at his children, "don't worry. My good friends Bejanet and Grillard have no intention of finishing off what the murderer could not accomplish. Go on, I'll call you when you can come back in."

Robert and Raoul felt anxious but left their father's side nonetheless. The two old friends, therefore, were left alone in the patient's room whose door was firmly closed behind them. For even more security Bejanet leaned over the bed to whisper in the banker's ear. In a solemn and sad voice he read off an officially stamped paper.

While listening, the patient started trembling all over and his eyes filled with tears. "Oh, it's dreadful! Absolutely dreadful!"

The notary and the law clerk tried to comfort him the best they could.

"My friend, come on, be strong! Think of your children... Keep your chin up... You'll get over this new hurdle... Buck up!"

As the judge let them know discreetly that the Count had just arrived and asked if they could proceed with the interrogation, the police called back Robert and Raoul. The two brothers found their father totally despondent, making a great effort to keep a hold on himself... and tears were starting to roll down his cheeks.

They wanted to postpone the confrontation for another day but the banker insisted that it take place immediately. "Except," he told them, "stay here now. My sons, don't ever leave your father..."

When the Count showed up the banker sat up straight in bed. He examined the gentleman with an eager, curious and enigmatic eye... and breathlessly, feverishly he stared at him for a long time without blinking.

The Count de la Gueriniere coldly, calmly, without a twinge of emotion on his face, a little more pale than usual maybe, was disturbed although he did not show the slightest trace of anxiety as he entered the room. Standing straight and tall in his riding suit, as comfortable as could be, he planted himself before the patient's bed.

Monsieur Montreil, leaning forward as if to get a better look at the Count, as if drawn to him, fascinated by him, could not take his eyes off the elegant gentleman. And he shuddered when he whispered so quietly that no one heard or understood him.

His sons on either side were supporting him, holding his hands, encouraging him gently. With bated breath they were waiting anxiously for the end of the emotional scene where they could not begin to describe the inscrutable look on the face of the man whom their father had categorically accused of attacking him.

The judge and officers were also keeping a close eye on all the phases of the horrible, mysterious and passionate drama unfolding before them.

Paulin Broquet, one step away from the Count and the patient both, saw every twitch and shudder of the patient and all the quiet composure of the Count.

"Do you recognize this gentleman?"

"Count Faustin de la Gueriniere," the banker answered slowly, quietly. "Yes, I recognize him."

"Is this the man who came to see you in your office at the bank?"

"Yes, he came... indeed, it was him."

"It was the Count de la Gueriniere here present... whom you identified in your deposition?"

"Yes, yes... it's him."

At these words the Chief of Police made a sign to Paulin Broquet who put a hand on the Count's shoulder and said, "In the name of the law..."

But the banker cut him off, shouting, "Wait! Wait a second!"

The Count had not moved an inch, had not even flinched. Everyone turned to look at the banker.

"I spoke about the Count de la Gueriniere, yes, and I named him... I pointed him out... but I was mistaken."

Everyone present was startled. Only the Count did not budge and behind his thin, black moustache a strange smile crossed his face. But in his eyes a flame was lit and he automatically looked at Paulin Broquet.

Then the banker resumed, slowly, as if every word coming out of his mouth was causing him pain. "I was mistaken... yes... I made a false statement..."

"And yet," Monsieur Urbain jumped in, "we read and reread to you your deposition. You signed it in full knowledge... of sound mind... with your memory intact... You signed it."

"Gentlemen, yes, but I was mistaken."

"We pressed you when you identified the Count... You insisted..."

"Gentlemen, believe me, what I told you was wrong..."

"And yet..."

"Yes, I named the Count de la Gueriniere because his face was stuck in my memory... yes, he came to my office. We talked... without reaching an agreement. But I showed him to the door, shook his hand and... yes, gentlemen, he left."

"And he came back!"

"Came back? No, he didn't come back."

"It's at the end of your statement. It's what you were very precise about... it's the basis of your deposition, of your accusation."

"Gentlemen, I'm telling you, I'm stating right now that he did not come back."

"So who hit you? Who grabbed you by the throat? Who attacked you and hurt you?"

"I can't say... I can't say..."

"Why can't you say now?"

"Because even though I said it was the Count, I was wrong. But now that I see Monsieur de la Gueriniere, standing right here in front of me, I see that I was wrong. No, he didn't come back... it wasn't him who tried to kill me... I swear it! It's not him!"

"Oh, monsieur," the judge commented, "such a retraction is not normal, it's very strange. Justice will draw the most dangerous conclusions... We have the right to hold you to your original statement and arrest this man..."

"No," the wounded banker broke in, "I have the right to be mistaken..."

"Isn't it just that you're tired, maybe a little disturbed... overwhelmed by the sight of your murderer... your mind's wandering..."

"No, no, I'm perfectly fine and I retract my first deposition. I was wrong. I made a false accusation. I declare it before everyone... before my children, my old friends, you judge and the police... The Count de la Gueriniere cannot be my murderer."

Monsieur Montreil was trembling all over. In a panting, feeble voice he said, "Sign it! Quick! I want to sign this retraction, sign this statement... the good one, the true one... Affirm that the Count de la Gueriniere is innocent, that it's not him, not him... Quick, quick, let me sign!"

They handed him a piece a paper with his statement. He took the pen... With difficulty, with great pain, he put down his signature, reading out loud everything that was written:

"Not him, he's innocent! It's not him... not him... not him."

The pen dropped out of his hand. He chin fell on his chest and he sank into the pillows.

"Father! Father!" his two sons cried out at the same time, in a panic. "Father!"

They raised him up, thinking he had just fainted, that he was feeling too weak. But he did not respond to the desperate appeals of his sons. With that final signature, he died.

Amidst the chaos that this dramatic end caused in the room, the Count turned to the judge and said, "You see, I'm innocent."

But Paulin Broquet jumped over to the Chief of Police and asked, "Should we arrest him now?"

The Chief did not answer. He turned to look at the investigating judge who had also heard the detective's question. Between these two authorities who held the honor, the freedom and the life of a man in their hands this question hung in the air:

"Should they or should they not arrest the Count de la Gueriniere?"

They hesitated to resolve the issue. Their instincts as men and their conscience as authorities collided and suggested a different solution.

But the investigating judge was the first to pull himself out of the bewildering dilemma. He pointed at Montreil's corpse, still holding the statement he had just signed proclaiming the Count's innocence, and said to the police chief, "We can't... legally... after that!"

The Chief turned to Paulin Broquet, who was waiting like a hunter holding his prey at bay, ready to strike, and said, "No!"

Broquet lowered his hands, reluctantly, and obeyed. All he said was, "Too bad."

During this brief moment, which seemed long to everyone present, the Count stood absolutely still. He, too, was waiting for their decision without showing the least fear or anxiety.

"You're off the hook," the judge told him. "You can go now."

The Count de la Gueriniere bowed slightly and without saying a word strolled slowly toward the door. Before leaving, he turned around and cast a taunting look of triumph and defiance at the detective. Broquet answered this bravado with a steady, cold, steely eye, shooting daggers at the challenger. In this dramatic moment between the two men was born one of those implacable hatreds that push men into merciless battles!

5. The Brothers' Vow

From the moment they had brought the wounded banker to his home the front door had remained closed and guarded. Only four people were allowed past the strict watch. Irene de Valtours, daughter of the Count de Valtours, and her fiancé Captain de Cazeaumont and Alice de Brialle, daughter of the Marquis de Brialle, as well as the Marquis' nephew, the Count de Marnais.

Irene and Alice were friends of Raymonde. The three of them were very close and even after leaving boarding school they had remained intimate, writing to each other as often as possible since Irene and Alice did not live in Paris.

The two friends were informed by telegram and came to Paris only to learn that the banker, on the verge of a brilliant recovery, had died. Alice de Brialle was in deep mourning.

"No one better than I," she told Raymonde, "can share your sorrow."

"Yes, my dear Alice, you know what heartbreak we experience when we lose someone we love. It's a little of our life we lose with them, a little of our soul that their soul steals from us, oh the beloved whom we lament."

Two years earlier Alice's mother had passed away just a few days after contracting a strange sickness that frightened everyone and stumped the medical authorities. A year later her older brother, who had been strong and stout, died of the same mysterious illness that a very short time ago also carried off her younger sister...

The constant mourning that tragically struck the Brialle family caused not only great sorrow in the region but also a serious anxiety. Dr. Montreil wanted to perform an autopsy on the girl but Alice refused what she looked upon as a desecration. The Count de Marnais firmly supported his cousin's refusal.

But the doctor, in secret, had taken away the last bandages that were used on the little girl.

I want to study them under a microscope," he told Raymonde. "I think I can know what sickness it is but I need scientific evidence to support my diagnosis before announcing it, a horror whose name alone will spread terror in the hearts of men..."

Raymonde wept with Irene and Alice. "Today a grief just as terrible has entered our house."

Alice, who had pieced together the details of the death through Raymonde's sobbing. Asked her friend nervously, "Is it really Count Faustin de la Gueriniere?"

"There was only one..." But Raymonde was surprised and asked in turn, "Why do you ask me that, Alice?"

"Because I know him."

"The Count de la Gueriniere?"

"Yes. He came several times to hunt with us in Sologne. He's a good friend of my cousin de Marnais who introduced him to my father and invited him on our hunts."

At this moment Marcelin, the brother's valet, came to ask if Mademoiselle could see the employee from Maison Perkins on Rue de la Paix for the mourning dresses.

"Show him in," Raymonde said, "and tell me mother."

The dress designer from Perkins, whose reputation was widespread, had sent its finest representative, Monsieur Portet. He was accompanied by a young woman, one of his workers who had been carefully chosen and specifically appointed for this assignment. Her name was Henriette Menardier, whose friends at work called Riri... Pretty Riri, whose friendly smile also got her clients to call her Riri, (meaning smiley in French).

Riri's beauty was delightfully astonishing, such that her friends admired it without feeling a bit of jealousy. It seemed to them that no one but Riri could be as pretty as Riri. Her face was so perfect that it was idealized. But it was not cold, frozen like happens to too many pure kinds of beauty. It was very expressive and lively... A head of golden hair formed a marvelous frame and her blue eyes, sometimes almost deeply purple, cast an exquisite radiance over her pink cheeks. Overall she looked rather grave, serious, even sad when her soul shown through, but when her mouth opened on her pearly white teeth the adorable face lit up with an embracing, captivating smile.

Rather tall and graceful, with nothing of the artificial figures of dressmaker models, the young woman who was barely 20 years old still had a young girl's beauty enshrouding the woman she was becoming. Her boots, made of leather that was a little too thick, could not make her feet look any bigger than a child's and her slender hands with long fingers, more satiny than the satin they folded, silkier than the dark silk they tucked away, came out white, almost transparent, like the tapered hands of madonnas in the paintings of old, devoted believers.

Riri lived in a poor lodging in the heart of Batignolles with her elderly, paralyzed mother and her older sister who was hunchbacked and sick. She loved both of them and gave them a little relief, a little wellness from her work, restraining her own desires, her own hopes, her own pleasures. Her situation was no secret and it was why Pretty Riri never worried about her comrades' friendship, her manager's admiration, her clients' sympathy and everyone's respect.

By choosing her to accompany him, therefore, Monsieur Portet, the great dress designer, was confident. Riri would be well received.

He also thought that with an important client like the Montreils Riri, in her difficult circumstances, could show more tact, say the right thing, be more gentle and sincere, in a different way, indeed better than Monsieur Portet who would have to be very formal in presenting his condolences to the family.

Madame entered the salon on the arm of her son. Raoul supported his mother all the way to the wing chair where she sat down. Then he stood behind her. But on seeing Riri, he could not hold back his reaction... He quivered, turned pale all of a sudden...

While she was talking, he listened with passion, then when she started opening the boxes in front of Raymonde, obviously not wanting to reveal his heated emotions, he scurried out of the room.

"Her," he mumbled, "Riri! Her, here!"

Over the long night of the wake, the two brothers stayed in the salon between their two bedrooms in their father's house. They were joined by Paulin Broquet who had asked to come see them as soon as possible.

"Don't you find," Raoul the lawyer asked him, "our father's sudden turnaround in front of the Count de la Gueriniere really weird?"

"The sick sometimes say strange things like that," the detective answered.

"So, what should we think about his odd denial?"

"From the legal point of view there's nothing we can do... We have to accept it. But from the medical point of view, we have to ask the doctor what he thinks."

The doctor answered, "There's no plausible explanation... It could have been an effect of the trauma, a fit after the cerebral shock... A man wounded like your father can make statements that he'll have to rethink later on..."

"That's true."

"But our father doesn't make snap judgments like that... first declaring that it was the Count and then denying it..."

"But that's what happened."

"I don't believe it. We know our father's always clear-headed... extremely logical... too intelligent to let his well-organized mind get shaken up." He added, "Besides, since the attack he's given us ample proof that he was lucid, that his mind had suffered no damage..."

Paulin Broquet nodded and concluded, "So, we have to admit that your father's about-face started during the short discussion he had with Messieurs Bejanet and Grillard."

"I'm sure of it."

"It's possible, yes. In that case, gentlemen, in that secret meeting they could only have been talking about the Count?"

"Yes, and that confirms what we are thinking."

"Which is?"

"That the Count de la Gueriniere is guilty."

"Oh, do you really think so?"

"But you, too, come on, Monsieur Broquet, don't you believe it too?"

"Me?!"

"You were asking... we heard you... if you should, despite our father's retraction, still arrest the Count... aren't you sure he's the killer? Admit it, you think the Count de la Gueriniere is a brazen, wily, menacing criminal."

A spark flashed in Broquet's eyes, but he looked down right away and whispered his answer to Raoul, "Well, go see who's listening to us in the next room…"

Raoul headed for the door that Broquet pointed to but the detective stopped him.

"The snoop left… Look over here," and Broquet pointed to the door to the hallway.

Raoul opened it.

"It's me, Monsieur Raoul," a voice said right away.

"Oh, you, Marcelin! Okay, okay."

Raoul was reassured and came back to Paulin Broquet. "False alarm. It's our valet doing his chores."

"Oh, your valet…" the detective repeated.

"A good guy who's very devoted to us."

"He's been with you a long time?"

"Six or eight months… We're very happy with him. He was well recommended and sent by one of our friends, the Count de Marnais."

"The Count de Marnais," the detective repeated in a curious voice. "Well, that's great."

Paulin Broquet knew that the Count de Marnais was a close friend of the Count de la Gueriniere. But he did not tell the brothers. Dropping the subject he spoke again in a low voice, "You were asking my opinion? It's the same that the law imposes on my boss and the judge, after what your father confessed… I have no other opinion, officially. But this could change."

"How's that?"

"The paper that Bejanet and Grillard showed your father contained the truth about this man… That paper alone will tell us if he's a criminal and let me collar the guy for good…"

"You're advising us, then," Raoul said, "to go and ask Monsieur Bejanet to hand over the document?"

"He should do it."

"Okay, right after the funeral we'll go over to his office on Rue Notre-Dame-des-Victoires."

Robert objected, "But what if he refuses to hand it over?"

Paulin Broquet spread his arms, saying, "In that case your heart will guide you. As for us police, we can't do anything. We can't even legally obtain the paper. We need some new evidence to reopen this affair."

"So it's up to us to do something!" Raoul declared.

Broquet nodded. Soon after this he bid farewell to the two brothers.

One more upsetting fact was added to their grief, to their distress, that was bound to push them actively toward their goal: their father's burial was a source of surprise and alarm…

Because of his financial situation and his many socialite friends, Monsieur Montreil was one of the who's who of Paris. At the parties he gave everyone who counted for something in literature, art, finance and politics showed up. However, the newspapers announced Montreil's death and reported only the facts. They also gave the time and date of the funeral. That was all!

Robert and Raoul looked through all the papers, expecting to find something else, some consolatory words, a few lines of eulogy about his life. They read nothing but polite and friendly sentences about his young sister, about themselves, the lawyer and doctor, their mother whose spirit and good grace was praised... Nothing about their father, or at least very, very little.

They called him the common and unremarkable epithet, "The famous banker on Rue Le Peletier" or "The well known financier" and such like clichés, but no sign of sympathy, no kind memory, nothing.

"Why?" the two brothers asked each other. "Why?"

Robert and Raoul had sent thousands of letters to announce it. They were expecting a huge crowd at the funeral. But when the two brothers along with Captain de Rennebois, Captain de Cazeaumont and the Count de Marnais got ready to follow the luxuriously decorated hearse that carried the remains of their father, they saw a big crowd in the street, of course, but only curiosity-seekers, bystanders, passers-by... and they recognized almost nobody in the procession.

The employees of the Montreil bank were there, the mandatory representatives of the credit firms that dealt with their unfortunate father; Messieurs Bejanet and Grillard, then a few lawyer friends of Raoul and some people from Robert's hospital; a handful of merchants whose names they did not know...

But all the guests at the parties thrown by their father, the people who lived in their mother's salon, all the famous who's who of Paris who used to visit their house all the time—not even ten of them. And they looked bored to be there, really miserable, like they were doing some unpleasant chore.

The church was full of uninterested or nosey people, just like in the street. People who came for the show, to hear a free performance of the Opera singers who would melodramatically implore the Eternal on behalf of the murdered banker. At the cemetery Raoul and Robert watched a line of around 100 people file by them but they only shook the hands of a few friends.

"Why is this?" they asked each other. "Why is our house in mourning suddenly so empty?"

Raoul was getting worked up and concluded, "We've been slapped in the face by this desertion amidst our grief. We have to find out why they've committed this awful offense against us, why so many people who used to visit us are now ashamed—that's the word—to show up at the funeral of the banker Montreil!"

More solemnly than ever the two brothers vowed to find out.

The evening after the burial, the two brothers left their mother, intending to go back to their usual routine. One said that he had to pass by the court and the other to see a patient who was expecting him. Raoul went downtown and Robert went to Passy. They parted, therefore, in opposite directions.

Around 7:30 pm at the corner of Boulevard des Capucines and Place de L'Opera, an elegant man was walking, slowly, in full mourning, heading for Rue de la Paix. It was a time when this street was full of fashion designers, models, pretty, giggling women workers who are like the female sparrows of Paris, sassy and taunting, the seamstresses leaving the workshops, chattering away, laughing, grouped together to go back to the suburbs.

As the young ladies were heading back up toward the Opera, toward the boulevards, the gentleman in question was watching all of them, trying to recognize one of them... All of a sudden he met another gentleman, also elegant, also in mourning, who was also searching for a girl among the groups of giggling workers.

The two gentlemen almost ran right into each other. They stopped, stared in surprise and then cried out, "Robert!" "Raoul!" "Fancy meeting you here!" "What a pleasant surprise!"

The two brothers shook hands warmly and smiled. But their smiles concealed something cold, something held back. There was an inexpressible but clearly uncomfortable awkwardness between them.

"I was just visiting a patient," Robert said. "Now I'm off to another."

"Well, I'm going to see my colleague who replaced me during these past few painful days."

"Which way are you going?"

"Towards Rue Drouot."

"Me, I'm headed to Madeleine."

As the two brothers were about to say goodbye, their handshake turned into a strong but nervous hug.

"Look," Raoul whispered to his brother.

"I see," Robert answered.

Coming toward them down the street was a gentleman with a handlebar moustache, a monocle in one eye, his head held high, dressed in the latest fashion, and a rare flower in his buttonhole. He was smiling, self-confident, swaggering, eyeing boldly the groups of young ladies walking up the street.

The girls fell under the charm of the domineering moustache, the chic smile and in spite of themselves they turned around and watched him eagerly. For these little brains, this gentleman represented the perfect type of fictional hero whom they read about in the workshops; the Prince Charming of the serial novels, the one each of them dreamed of, whom they all desired, whom they all hoped for, were waiting for, the one they could all give themselves to, body and soul...

And when the Don Juan was lost in the crowd, the two brothers anxiously looked at each other.

"Him! The Count de la Gueriniere! Whose house is he going to curse now?"

At this very moment, a nice older man who looked like a professor from the countryside, with white hair peaking out from under his wide-brimmed top hat, wearing blue-tinted glasses and a loose-fitting frock coat, came up to the two gentlemen, uncertain, a little clumsy.

"A thousand pardons, gentlemen," his shy voice said, "would you be so kind as to point the way to Rue Notre-Dame-des-Victoires."

"Rue Notre-Dame-des-Victoires?" they both shuddered, "But, Messieurs, it's quite simple. It's at the end of Rue 4 Septembre, behind La Bourse..."

"Oh, thank you immensely!" And then in a firm, self-assured voice the old professor added, "Indeed, it's quite simple to go to Rue-Notre-Dame-des-Victoires." With a bow he went away and hurried into the crowd.

The two brothers were a little shocked by the voice change and when they got over their surprise they cried out, "Paulin Broquet!"

"Yes," Raoul said, "Paulin Broquet who shows up just when the Count de la Gueriniere passes by, gloating, to remind us of our mission, our duty..."

"Oh," Robert certified, "we haven't forgot."

The two brothers stood there in silence for a moment, nervous, before the lawyer told the doctor, "Broquet is taking this matter very seriously.

"I feel the same."

"He's a marvelous detective, really smart, oddly clever and braver than the bravest..."

"He's completely on our side, our most valuable ally... So, we have to make his job easier."

"As far as we can. You felt the gravity of his declaration, didn't you? He's expecting us to find the secret of that terrible document... the evidence that can allow him to act."

"Yes, Raoul."

"Okay. And you've made up your mind like me, to help him, to get that paper that cost our poor father his life?"

"Yes, Raoul. We have to help Broquet... We have to know the secret. Now it's about our father's memory, about our honor, maybe our peace of mind and our mother's tranquil heart... the future of our sister..."

"I believe so. It's our duty. We have to do it, no matter what, no matter how, even if we have to resort to ways that we might otherwise consider criminal..."

"Agreed! Let's swear on it!

"I swear!"

6. Pretty Riri

At this time of day on Avenue de Clichy between Montmartre and Batignolles, the crowd was not as elegant as on the boulevards that the two brothers sauntered down, but it was bigger and busier. It had changed: it was the petty bourgeois, the male employees who made up the crowd now. Everyone was getting off the Metro and the tramway, hurrying home where dinner was waiting after a hard day's work at the office or the workshop or the store.

In this crowd, one hard worker with his cap cocked to one side, dressed simply but respectfully in a coat and big corduroy pants, was strolling down the street. He was holding the hand of a little boy and in his other hand a string bag full of groceries with bread and a bottle of wine sticking out. At his side, his wife was still young and fresh, quite pretty, with that bright Parisian smile that you can find nowhere else in the world. She was carrying a little girl in her arms.

All of a sudden the worker cried out in surprise, "Oh, hey, doctor! At this time of the day in our neighborhood?!"

"Oh, Fernand! How's it going?"

"Good, doc. Excuse me if I'm a little surprised to see you here. It's really because I'm glad to see you... because if you're in this neighborhood it's probably 'cause you're taking care of some poor soul like you usually do."

The doctor shook the worker's hand, bowed to his wife and patted the little girl, smiling.

"She's your patient, doc," Fernand said. "Doesn't look like herself, eh! You cured her, you saved her..."

"Yes, doctor," the young woman said, "if she's still with us it's thanks to you."

"No, my friend, doctors only help nature. The proof, you see, is that she's doing fine even though I'm not coming to see her anymore."

"We're still eternally grateful to you, doc."

The doctor was about to protest when a gang of rowdy children ran by screaming, "Carabosse the hunchback! Carabosse the hunchback!"

Fernand swung around and shouted, "Those little hooligans again!" He handed his bag to his son. "Hold this. Sorry doc, I'll be back in a minute."

He ran after the boys and slapped a few them around before they ran off, still yelling, "Carabosse the hunchback!". Then he took the hand of a poor, lame, hunchback girl dressed pitifully and standing scared out of her wits against a doorframe.

"Don't you be scared, Marie," he said. "You go home now. They won't bother you again today."

"Thank you, Monsieur Fernand," the girl said. "Thank you... You're kind..."

He walked her over to Ganneron Alley, watched her limp away and when he was sure she was all right he went back to his wife and the doctor.

"Sorry, doc," he said, "you know... oh, my wife told you. They're good people and we like them. They don't deserve all this bad luck. One girl hunchbacked, the mother paralyzed, on her deathbed... or almost..."

The doctor asked, "Who's taking care of the mother?"

Fernand raised his voice, "Who's taking care of her?! Who wants to take care of her? She's too poor to pay..."

But Fernand cut himself off, seeing that he was about to say something stupid... And the doctor had a sad smile on his face and simply said, "Would you show me where she lives?"

"What? You? You, doc? Really? You think you... Oh, excuse me, I'm a little dumb. I forgot that Dr. Robert took care of my child, me a simple worker... and your heart is as big as your brain... Sure, I'll show you where this nice family lives. When do you want to go?"

"Right away. You must never make a patient wait."

"Ok, doc. I thank you for them. Thanks..." Fernand turned to his wife, "Go home with the kids. I'll see you there."

The young lady thanked the doctor again for treating their little girl and for the good work he was going to do. Then she went down Avenue de Clichy while Fernand led the doctor down Ganneron alley.

When they arrived at their destination Fernand said to the doctor, "Sorry, doc, I didn't see before that you were in mourning."

"I lost my father a few days ago."

"I'm sorry to hear that. Please accept my condolences."

The doctor was surprised to see that Fernand did not know about the death of Montreil the banker even though it was in all the papers. He asked the worker, a little embarrassed, "Don't you read the papers? About the death of my father... or do you not know my name?"

"Sorry, uh, your name, I'll never forget... You're Dr. Robert!"

"Yes, yes," Robert said, "that's right. I'm Dr. Robert."

That was how they called Dr. Montreil at the hospital where Fernand had brought his sick child. It was to be friendly, familiar, like with nurses or friends whom they called by their first names.

He had become Dr. Robert. For the poor whom he cared for, it seemed better, simpler, easier for them to call him this and his name stuck in their thankful hearts. They did not know Dr. Montreil, but Dr. Robert was very popular among the poor and suffering.

And at this moment Dr. Montreil thought it was better like this, that they not know his family name, that he remain Dr. Robert.

Ganneron Alley is dark and gloomy. It is one of the old streets destined to disappear... Black, dismal houses lined it. In front of one the most depressing Fernand stopped.

"That's it. See how miserable it is!"

"Very sad, indeed."

"Especially since Madame Menardier was a woman of substance once, rich, you know... Her husband was an important businessman... Banking... The Stock Market... But he lost everything, swindled by a friend. He died of sorrow... They even say he killed that old friend of his... Since then, this is what happened to his wife and two daughters. See, besides the hunchback you saw, there's another girl who's working."

"Let's go up," Robert said. "Introduce me."

Fernand and the doctor entered the house and started climbing the grimy, musty staircase whose stench scratched his nose and stuck in his throat.

On the sixth floor landing Fernand said to Robert, "I'll go in first, doc, to see Madame Menardier and tell her about you. I'll just ask you to wait a few minutes with Marie."

"Do as you think best, my friend."

Fernand knocked on the door in a particular way and presently it was cracked opened.

"It's you, Monsieur Fernand!" the hunchback said.

"Yes. Now shush and don't be alarmed. This is Dr. Robert with me, the one we've talked so much about."

"Dr. Robert! But Monsieur Fernand, you know very well that we can't..."

"Don't worry about that. I want to talk to your mother first... to tell her he's here."

Fernand knew the layout of the house and led Robert into the girls' room before going to see the sick mother.

The hunchback said to Robert, "Oh, doctor, we've heard from Fernand about your skill and kindness as a doctor. Let me thank you for coming into our shabby house... for taking an interest in poor people like us... like our unfortunate mother..."

"Now wait a second there, Mademoiselle," Robert smiled at her. "Wait until I've at least had a look at the patient before you thank me." He instinctively looked around the small bedroom and was quite surprised.

It was a tiny, cramped attic room with only one small window in the low ceiling. But the charm and grace that the girls had bestowed upon the hovel were brave attempts to hide their poverty. With nothing, a few scraps of fabric, waste cuttings from the workshop, a little spare lace, the two sisters had cleverly fashioned half-curtains, a bedspread and small cushions that covered the straw seats of the simple chairs. The hunchback was painting on porcelain and on candy bags: she had painted pictures of flowers framed in ribbons and hung on the wall to hide the peeling wallpaper. Everything in the room was neat and straight and meticulously clean.

Robert's eyes were drawn to a plaster medallion hanging on the wall inside a garland of artificial flowers. Robert stepped over and examined it. And he felt deeply moved. His heart skipped a beat. He seemed to lose his breath for a moment. He looked almost shocked.

"That's a portrait of my sister," the hunchback said.

"Your sister!" Robert squawked. "This is your sister?!"

"My sister Henriette, but everyone calls her Riri... Pretty Riri."

"Riri! Your sister... Riri..."

"One of our good friends... a young sculptor, Paul, a neighbor... kind of a relative... he made that. Me, I think it looks a lot like her, but Riri is prettier in person."

Fernand popped in and cut short the conversation. "You can come in, doc," he said. "I've convinced Madame Menardier that it's no problem."

He stepped aside for Robert, whose head was burning and heart racing, mumbling to himself, "I'm in Riri's house... Pretty Riri... Riri whom I love..."

In a room like the other, decorated the same, on a low, iron bed an old woman, wan of face with jutting cheeks and bulging eyes that glistened with fever, was sitting up painfully on her pillows. It was the mother, Madame Menardier, the mother of Marie the hunchback and Pretty Riri...

An oil lamp was lit by the bedside.

It did not take Robert long to see that the woman was in a sorry state and her days were numbered.

"Oh, doctor," her voice was barely audible, "our good friend Fernand is abusing your kindness and charity. And he's forcing me to owe a debt of gratitude to you that I'll never be able to repay..."

"Come now, Madame Menardier," Fernand broke in, "I told you that Dr. Robert doesn't want to talk about charity else he'll get mad."

"Madame, my friend Fernand would be right if he's calling charity what every doctor simply calls his duty."

Fernand shook his hand, squeezed the patient's hand while wishing her good luck and after a friendly farewell to Marie he left, happy to have taken part in this scene. With his cap cocked to the side, sure that the doctor would perform a miracle for the mother and her daughter, he ran back to his wife and kids.

Robert got down to studying the patient. But he did not want to stay long in this house... He had a weird feeling here that he had never felt anywhere else, a feeling both awkward and pleasurable, impossible to pin down but as disturbing as it was delightful.

Of course he had been with many patients in as pitiable state as Madame Menardier and he had seen rooms more miserable, more destitute and barer than this... So, it was not the setting nor the hunchback nor the dying mother that troubled him.

What affected him was inside the wreath of artificial flowers hanging on the wall, the medallion, the plaster medallion like a radiant star shining in the dark night of this sorrowful house... That gorgeous face, those pure features... It was also the golden tint given to her hair, the violet sparkle put in her eyes and the pinkish smile on her mouth where the sculptor had to express all the charm...

Then, listening to the feeble voice of the sick woman, Robert told himself, *Now's the time when Riri will be coming back from work.*

He could not see her here. Riri... He did not want to be here when Riri got back, walking down Rue de la Paix where Robert had just been looking, searching anxiously, passionately, for someone among the laughing girls...

He had come to this house without knowing whom he would see, without any idea that Fernand was leading him to Riri's mother. And yet, with a twinge of conscience, he did not want Riri to see him here, to imagine that he was using his role of doctor to get into her house. He shuddered at the idea that Riri might believe that he was offering his services with ulterior motives, that he was caring for this poor woman in the hope of being rewarded by her daughter, Pretty Riri.

No, he did not want to be here when she got home, but at the same time he would have given up a year of his life for her to walk in right now...

Cruel choice!

Like any man in similar circumstances where his will faltered, became fatalist, Robert gave himself up to chance. He decided to leave, although he delayed his departure as long as possible. He took a notepad out of his pocket and wielded a pen.

"I'm going to give you a prescription."

"But doctor," Marie protested, "I can't..."

"Yes, mademoiselle, you must. A doctor who doesn't give a prescription... doesn't look like a real doctor. Besides, it's for you."

"For me?"

"It's only some instructions... how you should give the medicine to your mother. As for the medicine, don't worry, they'll bring them over."

"But doctor, I'm not sure..."

"All that concerns you, mademoiselle, is taking care of your mother. I'll be back tomorrow. Be strong."

And not wanting to hear the hail of thanks, he headed for the door. He went down the sticky stairs and back up the alley that had looked so glum to him before but now seemed sparkling with gold... gleaming with violet... brightened by the hair and eyes... and the smile of Pretty Riri.

He was walking in a dream when he ran into a man whose cry of surprise pulled him back to reality. "Robert, why it's you!"

"Raoul!"

Like shortly before on Rue de la Paix, the two brothers stared at each other speechlessly for a moment.

"What a nice surprise!" Raoul finally said. "We're seeing each other all over Paris today."

"So it seems."

"What are you doing here by Ganneron alley?"

"I was just seeing a patient. And you?"

"I was dropping something off with a client."

"Oh."

Robert was telling the truth but it was not so for Raoul. Lawyers do not usually drop things off at their client's house. But Robert was still too confused to notice his brother's unlikely response. He took his arm and led him away, glad for any excuse to forget his stifling distress.

Without saying another word the two brothers were strolling toward Place de Clichy when they stopped and shivered on seeing three young workers heading for them. Two of the girls looked nice and sweet, no doubt, but except for their youth there was nothing particularly attractive about them. The third, however, was thin and graceful and with her elegant gait seemed to radiate her marvelous beauty over her two companions. Under a simple but stylish hat, as only Parisian hands can create, was a face of ideal purity framed by soft, golden hair, illuminated by big, purple eyes...

When they got to Ganneron Alley the three friends kissed and parted.

"See you tomorrow, Riri."

"Yes, see you tomorrow."

And while her friends went on their way Riri hurried down the alley, anxious to get home to her sick mother and her sister, Marie the hunchback...

Robert and Raoul watched the charming little scene. They stood mesmerized in the same place, staring down the dark alley where Riri had just lightened with all that youth, all that beauty, all that charm. All of a sudden they jumped and a shout was ripped out of their throats: "Him!"

A car had just pulled up to the sidewalk a few feet away. Out of this car hopped the Count de la Gueriniere and he headed straight down the alley that Pretty Riri had just taken!

Just then, a worker came out of a nearby bar. He was wearing a smock under a drab coat, loose pants and a zinc roofer's toolbox slung over his shoulder. The man had apparently got his two-weeks and was celebrating the occasion by stopping in every bar on the street. Right now he was singing a song whose refrain told more hard truth than good sense:

It's for all the workers of zinc

That they line the streets with drink!

Stumbling by the two brothers he stopped, looking surprised to see well-dressed bourgeois in the common crowd. No doubt spurred on by some drunken idea he took off his hat very formally and bowed elaborately. Then he went on his way and shouted out a marching song:

Victory with a song

Will carry us along...

Waving his arms, reeling from side to side, he staggered down Ganneron Alley, belting out, "Victory with a song..." And he disappeared in the shadows that had just swallowed Riri and behind her the gallant Count. His raucous voice kept repeating, "Victory... Victory..."

Just like on Rue de la Paix after the old professor had passed by, the two brothers shook themselves out of their astonishment and said together, "Paulin Broquet!"

They had just recognized him, or thought they did.

Raoul said, "Broquet was warning us again that duty calls us to Rue Notre-Dame-des-Victoires."

The two of them were thinking separately but at the same time, *And we have to finish our mission before thinking about these girls, as pretty as they might be, like lovely Riri.*

7. The Fatal Document

The next morning Robert and Raoul got under way to clear up what they were calling the mystery of their father's death.

First, following the course of action that had been interrupted, they went to see their father's notary, Monsieur Bejanet, on Rue Notre-Dame-des-Victories. The city official greeted them warmly as the sons of his oldest and best friend. He had known Robert and Raoul since they were children, had seen them grow up. He liked them a lot and was very casual with them.

After shaking their hands he gushed over their dearly departed, eulogized his late-lamented friend.

"It's because you were such close friends with our poor father that we've come to see you," Raoul said. "It's all the affection you showed to him that brings us here..."

"My dear boys, I'll do whatever I can... You have my full support... I am at your service."

"We came to ask you to give us the papers that you and Monsieur Grillard had our father sign."

The notary sat up straight in his chair. He was obviously not expecting this request.

"That's what you came to ask me, Raoul?" he almost shouted. "What am I supposed to say? I don't understand!"

Raoul answered coldly, "Let me explain. Listen carefully. Our father was the victim of a murder attempt. He survived the knife attack, seemed to be recovering, about to get back on his feet, was clear-headed, reasonable... and his memory was as accurate and faithful as ever..."

"True."

"And in this condition our father stated formally to the authorities and signed a statement declaring that his murderer was the Count de la Gueriniere."

"Yes, I heard that, but..."

"Allow me to continue... The authorities sent detective Paulin Broquet, carrying an arrest warrant, to bring the Count to face the accusation of his victim..."

"I know... I know..."

"Wait! In the meantime, between my father's official statement and the Count's arrival, you and Monsieur Grillard asked to speak with your friend, to speak with him in private, to give him and him alone a terribly important, urgent message..."

The notary broke in, "But, my boy, what's so surprising about that? It's completely normal. Monsieur Grillard and I are not only the oldest friends of your father but we take care of his business. We have a lot of confidential papers to deal with..."

"Okay! But the one you gave our father, the urgent one, before the Count showed up, was so serious, so special that... after listening to you for a few minutes, our father, whom we had left in perfectly good health, smiling and cheerful, looked totally defeated, overwhelmed... and he broke down in tears..."

"But I assure you, Raoul..."

"One more thing, please. After your little meeting, our father who had just formally accused the Count, fully aware, fully informed, came back and denied his previous statement. He retracted his accusation... and everyone was astonished... except you..."

"Me?"

"Yes, that's what I said. Except you and Monsieur Grillard standing next to you. Our father declared that the Count was not... was no longer... could never have been his murderer!"

The notary looked nervous and tried to answer, "But my dear boys, there are reasons for that... explanations..."

Raoul cut him off, "We've imagined all of them. There's only one way to settle the issue, to convince us... by showing us, his sons, whatever it was you gave to our father."

"Impossible! Impossible!" Bejanet shouted. "Don't even ask me! I can't do it!"

"Then we'll be forced to take the matter to court."

"No court will make me give up the document. I've done my duty for whom I had to... Now I'll just hide behind professional confidentiality... I'll never give it up."

Raoul was shouting now, "Fine! That's what we wanted to hear. You've just confirmed our suspicions. It's that paper that caused our father's death. And you refuse to show it to us... Your choice! Now we'll see what we can do to get a look at it..."

"But, my boys," Bejanet took a no-nonsense tone to convince the two brothers, "what do you imagine? What monsters are you fabricating? You know how I felt about your father, the friendship that bound us... Could you for one second imagine that I would do anything to harm him? That under such tragic circumstances I would give him this weird, mysterious, shocking document that you're fantasizing about?

"So give it to us to see."

"I can't... and I don't have to..."

"Is that your final decision?"

"To act otherwise would be a violation of my duty in the legal profession... and of my conscience as an honorable man."

Faced with this categorical refusal, the two brothers sat there stunned for a minute. A heavy, uncomfortable silence hung in the air of the notary's study. The three men stared at one another nervously. Robert and Raoul were furious but Bejanet was cold and inflexible, in total control of himself.

The painful silence was broken by the arrival of a clerk who handed Bejanet a card. When he looked at it he had to hold back his surprise, his worry... but he shuddered nonetheless. He said to the clerk, "Very well, be careful." And very gingerly he slipped the card under a file...

Then he got up to leave and held out his hand to the two brothers. "Goodbye, boys. I'm sorry to cut our visit short... Goodbye. Believe me when I say that you have no better friend in the world than me, no ally more sincere... There's no one more than me who wants to guarantee your happiness and respect the memory of your poor father."

He showed them out through a door leading to some stairs so that they would not have to pass through his house. And he went back to his study to receive the visitor whose calling card had disturbed him.

As the two brothers were going down the stairs, Robert said, "Raoul, did you see how scared he looked?"

"And since he rushed us out... It's like he was afraid we'd run into his unexpected visitor."

"Yes, it couldn't be a regular client but still someone who has something to do with us."

At the same time the two brothers blurted out, "It's him!" And they added, "We have to see if it's really him. This is important. We must know for sure."

The only possible way, without looking too suspicious, was to keep an eye on the building from the outside. Almost directly across the street was a small café, nothing fancy, one of those neighborhood places scattered around the city that are like old country taverns.

Raoul and Robert entered and sat by one the windows looking out on the street. By opening the half-curtain they could see the door of the notary's house. When it is too early for the regulars to show up the cafes are deserted...

In this one there was only one customer in the back of the room who had his back to the door and was reading a newspaper. The customer did not react, did not even turn his head when the two brothers came in. He just raised his eyes from the paper to look in the tilted mirror over the counter where the waitress stood and where he could see the whole café reflected.

Around 15 minutes passed. The customer paid for his drink, put down this paper and started rolling a cigarette very calmly. And at this moment the two brothers jumped in their seats. On the notary's doorstep the Count de la Gueriniere had just showed up.

Standing on the sidewalk the Count looked in both directions, then after a few seconds of hesitation he started walking down the street, briskly, urgently...

Then the customer who had lit his cigarette also decided to go. He walked calmly out of the café and stepped onto the sidewalk where he sped up, hurrying down the street.

And although he passed very quickly by the window, the two brothers were able to see him, to recognize him. And they said in unison, "Broquet!"

8. The Safecrackers

Astonished by the sight, the two brothers threw some coins on the table and without waiting for change they ran after the detective. But they did not succeed in finding Paulin Broquet or the Count who were both lost in the crowd that was getting thicker and thicker around La Bourse.

"It's useless following them," Raoul said.

"Yes. We're wasting time."

As Robert and Raoul were talking about the issue and thinking about it, they were also wondering whether they should go to the prosecutor's office to get them to force Bejanet to turn over the document. But Raoul figured that it would probably turn out to be another useless endeavor. Nothing would come of it.

"The best thing in this case," Robert said, "is to use the most extreme methods available before we lose courage and give up."

"Okay, brother... and without delay... We'll have to get the document that Bejanet refuses to show us right out of the safe."

"Right, brother, whenever you'd like."

"Tonight."

"Okay, tonight."

They spent the day organizing the plan, quietly, secretly. Then in the evening, using different excuses, they split up before they would meet at dinnertime with their mother.

Robert went to Ganneron Alley to see his sick patient, Madame Menardier. Like the day before he struggled against the desire to wait for Riri to come back from her job but still he left before the pretty worker made her radiant appearance. However, desperate to see her despite everything, he stood in the shadows by her house where he could watch the gloomy alley without being seen. Presently Robert had the painful surprise of seeing Raoul, off in the distance, discreetly following and ogling Pretty Riri...

After Riri kissed her two friends goodbye as usual, as she was swallowed like a ray of sunlight in the darkness of the dreary alley, Raoul stayed on the sidewalk, anxious and thrilled, watching the attractive figure of the charming girl drift away into the night.

When Raoul got hold of himself and decided to leave, he did so with a heavy sigh that pulled him out of his reverie as he plodded off. From his vantage point Robert had seen everything. And his heart felt a weird pang.

"Oh," he said to himself, "no doubt about it... he loves Riri... like I do... What a curse! What an awful curse! We're both in love with the same woman!"

Knowing his brother's secret, Robert tried to bury his pain and disappointment in the depths of his heart. But as strong as his love for Pretty Riri was, as smitten as his heart was by the charm of the lovely girl, despite all the suffering that this painful effort must have caused him, Robert still saw this rival as his brother whom he loved so much. In his pain, in his sacrifice, he started wanting his brother to be happy, with only one fear in mind, that Raoul might find out about his own love and suffering and then feel the same pain on his part.

Therefore, from now on he would make sure that Raoul never saw him around Ganneron Alley and that he would have no worries, not the least suspicion. With total self-control, repressing his pain and suffering, he forced himself not to care, to think about more serious matters than a love that he must henceforth forget.

He would devote himself completely to his patients and get back to work on his bacteriology. He would also look more deeply into the traces left on the bandages of the young sister of Alice de Brialle. And he would start searching for the mysterious microbe that he suspected, whose name he dare not pronounce aloud lest the sickness spread terror throughout the city.

Furthermore, nothing more must distract him from the sacred mission that he had undertaken. Nothing more must prevent him from reaching his goal!

Besides the rooms they had at their parent's house, the two brothers also shared an apartment on Rue des Mathurins which included the Doctor's office, where he saw patients three times a week, as well as Raoul's where he could meet with lawyers every evening after court.

In this apartment the two brothers met every evening at seven o'clock to go home together to the house on Rue Chalgrin. Sometimes the banker would meet them after leaving his office. Madame Montreil and Raymonde often stopped by on their way back from shopping or from the dressmaker before going home.

Robert and Raoul, therefore, on this evening, both left Ganneron Alley and went back to their rooms on Rue des Mathurins. Coming from two different directions they arrived still almost at the same time and together they climbed into a cab and reached Rue Chalgrin at the usual time.

Both of them were preoccupied and barely said a word to each other during the whole trip. Robert preferred it this way. He needed silence because although screaming and shouting sometimes gave a certain release in some crises, silence had a calming effect in heartaches like the one he was suffering at the moment.

After dinner Robert and Raoul stayed a little late with their mother and sister. When it was time for their mother to go to bed, the two brothers kissed her and Raymonde, wished them a good night and went up to their rooms. Marcelin, the butler, was waiting for the final orders for the night.

"Bring up some coffee for us," Raoul said.

The butler was surprised. "So late? Monsieur doesn't want to sleep?"

"Don't you worry about it. Once you've brought it up, you can go to bed."

"Oh, Monsieur, I'm not worried about myself. But really, after all these tragic events both you and Monsieur Robert need some rest and coffee at this hour..."

Raoul waved him off and the butler left without saying another word. A little later Marcelin was back with a tray carrying a steaming coffee pot and two cups.

"Put it in the salon," Raoul said. Then he added, "Now you can go to bed."

"You won't be needing me anymore tonight?"

"No, Marcelin, good night."

The two brothers were alone now in the small salon that connected their two rooms. They were sitting in armchairs, drinking coffee and smoking cigars. Slowly, one by one, all the sounds in the house went quiet and all the lights went out. Masters and servants were in their rooms and sleep was creeping over every floor but this one.

The deep chime of an old Norman clock in the entrance hall cut through the silence.

"Midnight," Raoul said.

"Yes," Robert said in turn, "midnight."

And the old clock invaded the silence with its twelve slow, sonorous tolls.

Raoul suddenly jumped up from his chair. "Come on Robert, let's go… It's time. We have to do it."

But Robert put his cup down slowly. "Do it? Do you really think, Raoul, that what we're about to do is reasonable?"

Raoul looked at his brother in surprise. "Are you having second thoughts?"

"I'm scared that we're doing all this for nothing… that we're off on some ridiculous wild goose chase…"

"Why?"

"What are we doing?"

"We going to find out about the document that Bejanet showed our father and that caused such a weird reaction, a relapse… really the cause of his death!"

"Yes, but…"

"But since Bejanet doesn't want to give it up willingly and we need to know about it, we're going to do what everybody does when they want something that somebody else has and doesn't want to give."

"Simply put, we're going to break into Bejanet's office and steal it."

"Correct. I see no other way…"

But Robert stopped his brother from continuing, "Wait, listen."

"What? What do you hear?"

"I don't know… I thought… I heard something in the hallway, a floorboard creaking or a footstep…"

"In the hallway? Like that night when Paulin Broquet was here with us?"

Raoul crossed the salon and opened the door. He looked out in the hallway and listened. "Who's there? Marcelin, is that you?"

But he got no answer. The hallway was dark. Switches to turn on the ceiling lights were next to every door. Raoul pressed the one by him. He looked both ways but saw nothing. When he turned off the lights the hallway sunk back into darkness. After carefully closing the door behind him, he went back to his brother.

"No one. It was nothing."

"Good thing. And yet I really thought…"

"Now who would want to be listening to us? And why? No one suspects anything. Mother certainly wouldn't be out there   nor Raymonde."

"Marcelin?"

"Oh, Marcelin was too happy that I let him go to bed early. Besides, what good reason would he have for listening at our door?"

"Yes, indeed… yes… no reason at all."

But as Robert was muttering these words, another loud creak was heard in the hallway.

Robert kept his voice low, "There, again… did you hear that?"

"Yes," Raoul answered, listening hard. "Yes I did." He waved to his brother to stay quiet and tiptoed to the door.

Once again a creaking floorboard broke the silence.

Raoul threw open the door of the salon, shot his hand out to the switch and turned on the lights. It was all done so quickly that if anyone was in the hallway it would have been impossible for them to escape. But Raoul and Robert, who had joined him, saw nothing. They walked opposite ways up and down the hallway but came back without anything to report.

"Okay," they agreed, "it's just the wood settling down for the night. And the weather's changing. These old house make noises."

Therefore, they went back into the salon and resumed their conversation without thinking anymore about the incident that did not recur, which should have made them even more wary.

"As I was saying," Robert went on, "I was telling you just now, before the phantom of the hallway interrupted us, that I'm wondering if we're being reasonable in undertaking such an operation."

"And why not?"

"What are we doing? We're going to break into Bejanet's office, which will probably be well guarded, and try to open his safe."

"We're got keys for that and a crowbar."

"Of course. We've got the gear of any good burglar. Okay, we've got the tools and the courage, right?"

"Right."

"But what about experience? You see, Raoul, we're society people, playing lots of sports, sure, but in no way prepared for an operation like this and we're about to embark on an adventure that even professional burglars would consider daring, difficult and dangerous… We're about to rob a notary's safe."

"Well, I hope we're successful."

"Do we know how to do it? Do we even know how to break into the office? Can we even get to the safe?"

"Why not?"

"Okay, let's say we get in there. What if a guard catches us? If someone sees us and sounds an alarm? What do we do then?"

"We'll see when the time comes."

"Should we silence the guard? If so, how? Kill him? We didn't think about murder... Will we go so far as to kill someone?"

"There are other ways to silence a man. You can bring some chloroform."

"Yes, but if despite all our precautions we're caught in the act... if we're arrested for burglary, what'll we say? In Paris tomorrow, where will we stand, you a lawyer and me a doctor, when they find out we were caught red-handed?"

Raoul answered, "I understand your objections, and you can be sure that I've asked myself the same thing... I've imagined all possible mishaps and I've ruled them all out. Robert, dear Robert, nobody will believe that you and I, sons of the late banker Montreil, as rich was we are, with our well-known and long-established reputation as gentlemen, that we're petty thieves..."

"The facts will be there nonetheless..."

"Sure, the facts... but they'll know we weren't there to rob the notary's cashbox, especially since there wouldn't be much cash, or to steal from a friend of our father... No, they'll know we wanted something else and when they remember the scene before our father's tragic death everybody will guess what our real goal is... and nobody will blame us for it since Bejanet refused to hand over the fatal document. And that's it. If we succeed, as I'm hoping, everything will be all right. If we fail, our reputation won't suffer for it. We'll just be considered clumsy... or unlucky."

Robert made a few more objections that Raoul shot down.

The lawyer concluded, "In the end, this document that caused our father's death is so important to us that we have to do everything in our power to see it. And who's to say that this deadly document won't cause even more grief in our house? We're fighting for our mother's peace of mind, for Raymonde's, and for ours... We're fighting for the reputation of a man who was murdered, for his honor and for ours... And it's worth taking a few risks for all this."

Robert finally gave in to his brother's enthusiastic plea. "Okay," he said. "You're right, Raoul, we have to do it. Yes, we have to... Let's go and may heaven help us."

So, the two brothers changed into the dark, loose-fitting clothes that they usually wore in the country for hunting. They donned woolen caps and rubber-soled tennis shoes. They dropped their key rings and pliers in their pockets in such a way that they would not clang against each other when they walked.

Equipped, unrecognizable, ready and willing, firmly resolved to run any risk, to face all dangers, to succeed in their bold mission, they stepped cautiously into the hallway where they had heard the floorboards creaking.

The hallway was lined with wallpaper. Coat hangers and benches, a few old chests and palm plants in big pots cluttered the hallway where paintings, statues and displays of exotic objects or sports paraphernalia hung on the wall, transforming it into a kind of museum where the two brothers used to play as children.

It was very easy to see someone hiding in there. As Robert and Raoul snuck down the hallway they were sure of it. Just like earlier, the floorboards creaked under their shoes. They stopped. The creaking stopped. They now had proof that someone was there just now, had spied on them, listened to them... This was troubling.

They looked at each other anxiously. But they could not stop at the first sign of danger. They got back on the move.

And under their rubber soles, under the carpet, the floor again made itself heard. Disturbed and nervous the two brothers stopped again.

"Now," Raoul whispered, "I'm sure that when we were talking just now there was someone in the hallway."

"I knew it."

"But who could it be? Who?"

"Who and why?"

"We'll try to find out tomorrow."

"Yes, we can't waste time on it now."

Cautiously they went down the stairs, step by step, listening, anxiously, but hearing no sound but the tick-tock of the big Norman clock that sounded like the house's heartbeat. They finally got to the front door and opened it.

Sneaking down the stairs and getting the door opened was like a warm-up exercise for them. Before leaving they listened once more. Nothing was stirring in the house...

So, the first stage of their expedition, but not the most difficult, had gone off without a hitch.

"It's a good sign," Raoul said.

"I think so too. We make really good thieves."

Once on the street they could breathe freely.

Raoul smiled, "As long as we don't run into Paulin Broquet on the way."

They went up Avenue de la Grande Armée. A taxi was passing by, headed back into Paris. They hailed it, climbed in and were taken to Place de la Bourse. There they went straight to Bejanet's.

The notary's office on Rue Notre-Dame-des-Victoires took up the entire floor of the huge building but Bejanet did not live there. There were two stairways: a big, wide one in stone with an iron railing that dated back to the Sun King, Louis XIV, when they built these houses around Victoires; the second was in the courtyard, a service stairway. Both went up to the office, the first to the clerk's room, the second to a hallway that also, ultimately, led to the clerk's room. Only one night watchman guarded the office.

But Robert and Raoul had to face the fact that this endeavor was looking more and more difficult... You don't become a thief on the spot... and to open a safe quickly without raising the alarm takes a lot of practice… As for taking care of a night watchman there were many and varied ways but they all needed a special type of person to put them into action.

The two brothers who had, as we know, imagined all possibilities, all the while knowing that they would face serious problems, did not stop or even hesitate for an instant. They were nearing their goal.

"What others can do for evil," they told each other, "we will do for good, for a just and righteous cause."

To get the street door open by tossing out the name of another occupant as they passed by the sleepy doorman's booth was simple. The difficulty started in front of the office door. Robert and Raoul had decided to go up the service stairway because there was less risk of meeting anyone, and also the night watchman would be set up in the clerks' room, therefore farther away from this door.

Raoul, who was feeling the thief in him really come out, found a key to the door very quickly. And so rather easily they found themselves in the hallway. Their rubber soles made no sound. They headed straight for the clerk's room.

Since they had often come to the office, they knew the layout pretty well. Therefore, even in the darkness, they did not run into any obstacles. When they got to the door to the big room, they stopped and listened.

They only had to push the door open, which they did without so much as a creak. The heavy, regular snoring of the guard reassured them and proved once again the old saying that nobody sleeps better than a night watchman.

Robert and Raoul slipped into the clerk's room. Big, tall windows let in a pale light that was just enough to move around the huge room cluttered with boxes piled along the wall and long tables covered with files.

Full of confidence now the brothers headed for Bejanet's office. The door here was also cracked open and only need a push. They figured that it was probably the guard's habit who was maybe hoping to hear someone entering the room better this way. Without worrying about this minor detail Robert and Raoul pushed the door open. As it swung open it revealed a sight to the two brothers that froze them to spot, stupefied, astounded!

In Bejanet's office they saw three men leaning over the notary's desk, which was completely covered with papers that they were searching through. The three men were all carrying flashlights with blue bulbs. Blue, in fact, is a cold color, as painters say, that does not strike the eye too hard, does not attract attention as much as white light or especially red. In this very soft, blue light, bright enough for their purpose however, the three men were busy at their mysterious work. They had no fear that the cold light would be seen by a passer-by or another tenant who would be surprised to see anyone in the notary's office so late and therefore alert someone.

The fright that the two brothers got on seeing this unexpected sight lasted only a few seconds. They could not stand there doing nothing for a long time.

Moreover, one of the men leaning over the desk was turning around to the safe whose door was wide open behind them. As the man swung his flashlight, it briefly lit up his face and the brothers saw who it was. At the same time they cried out, "The Count de la Gueriniere!"

As soon as they said this they ran in to jump on the man they had just recognized. But at that moment, a dark veil fell over their eyes. Their heads were caught in black, cotton sacks that were tightened around their necks.

Robert and Raoul wanted to scream out but the cotton was sucked into their mouths and choked their voice. They tried fighting but their arms were held tightly and being tied down.

At the same time they were slapped hard on top of the head, which broke something in the sack. Right away a jet of cold air and liquid gas shot out and shrouded their face with cold. Knowing they were in danger, Robert and Raoul struggled furiously, kicked out desperately as they choked, suffocated, feeling the horrible torture of drowning...

The struggle lasted only a few seconds. Their arms relaxed, their legs went limp and they fell into a deep sleep. They were now at the mercy of the mysterious men whose work they had interrupted. And they dropped to the ground, still and silent, like corpses!

9. Car versus cart

Never had the singer Lucette Minois, who made all of Paris fall in love with her glow and grace and her marvelous smile, never had she been as cheerful, captivating and charming as she was this evening. She was playing the role of a vixen in a cabaret show that was opening at the the the Lutetia Theater. It was on the same evening that the dramatic events at Bejanet's office were unfolding.

The show "Only in Paris" by the masters of cabaret Loujot and Alevay was very witty. The songs, a bit racy perhaps, accentuated the delightfully funny scenes that the audience whooped and cheered. Lucette Minois was at the head of the bevy of pretty girls and carried the show, receiving bravos and encores.

One stage-side box seemed more enthusiastic than the others. It was occupied by the Count de la Gueriniere with a few close friends, the Count de Marnais, Baron Dupont, Baron Van Cambre and the financier Guttlach. He had brought them here to support Lucette Minois, his mistress and latest conquest.

After the show the Count de la Gueriniere, to celebrate the triumph, invited the playwrights, a few friends and the prettiest actresses from the show to dine in one of the most fashionable restaurants in Paris (for frisky business) where he had reserved a big room.

In a private room nearby Mad Muguette, one of the prettiest extras, was eating alone with a rich businessman from the country, Monsieur Cendron, whom she had very recently hooked. She was not yet ready to "ditch" him but she was getting bored all alone hearing friends laughing next door. She was waiting for Lucette who had come up with the idea of inviting her and her new friend, but it was the Count de Marnais who was in charge of the negotiations.

Among the revelers word spread quickly. The private dinner guests were soon in the big room making a noisy entrance. The Count de la Gueriniere congratulated the country businessman on his Parisianism and introduced him to his friends and the young ladies. He offered Monsieur Cendron a seat between Lucette and Mad, on the other side of himself and Baron Dupont. And the party resumed with even more festivity.

Monsieur Cendron turned out to be a cheerful and charming guest. And he had great fun. The Count was surprised by his sense of humor, his quick wit and his dandy spirit.

"We'll call you up to collaborate on our next show," Loujot and Alevay said, who were, however, throwing around their praise rather freely. "You won't wriggle out of future couplets…"

The sunrise was making the electric lights turn down, as well as some of the laughter around the Count de la Gueriniere. In fact, there had been more and more dull moments falling among the guests, but there were enough pretty girls and good cheer for the party to continue.

54

"My dear friends," the Count said, "dawn is upon us... As honorable folk we must go see it rise..."

The cars were waiting at the door. Soon they were helping one another inside, some of the waiters even carrying guests whose legs were on strike. In the Count's car they piled in Lucette Minois, Mad Muguette, another girl friend, then the Count de Marnais and Monsieur Cendron, the provincial businessman who seemed as lit up as the others.

The cars lined up.

On a whim the Count de la Gueriniere took the place of his chauffeur and sat next to Baron Dupont who was in front to get a little fresh morning air. He grabbed the wheel and stuck his head out the window to make sure the festive parade was following.

Everything went well. The cars jaunted up the Champs-Elysées, which was almost empty at this time of day. But when they got to the Place de l'Etoile, the Count clipped—who knows how exactly—the arm of an old grocer woman. The dame was heading up to Les Halles. The car swerved away but the poor woman fell to the ground, more out of fear no doubt than from the minor collision.

Still, the Count stopped the car right away and jumped out onto the sidewalk. He ran to help the old girl who was panicking, rolling around on the ground among all her vegetables, probably imagining that she had been crushed, broken, cut into pieces by the infernal machine.

The Count's party guests also jumped out, ran up and surrounded the good old woman who was now feeling neither dead nor wounded but was shrieking in fear. It was no easy job calming her down but everyone pitched in to help.

Now that the good woman was over her fear, she wanted to hear what they had to say and she was apprised of the situation. Seeing who it was she was dealing with, she was hoping to squeeze a little profit out of the adventure.

By pure chance, two police officers who had apparently had nothing better to do were in the vicinity and saw the accident. They ran over and immediately pulled out their pens to write a ticket. The Count was very compliant and gave his name, address and position.

"I have no intention," he declared, "of shirking my responsibilities. Ticket me, officers. Do your duty. Follow your orders. I will fully compensate this good woman." He paused before adding, "But we're in a hurry right now, my friends and I... Would you let us leave..."

"What about my vegetables?" the merchant cried. "And my morning sales? How am I gonna manage? Me, I live day to day. I can't wait for a judge to get me money..."

The Count cut in, "You're right, Madame." He pulled a 100-franc bill out of his wallet and handed it to her, saying, "Take this, in the meantime."

Monsieur Cendron, the businessman from the country, added five louis to the blue bill on behalf of his friend Mad Muguette.

Then the merchant woman thanked them profusely. It was a good day for her.

Just for fun the Count's friends gathered up the leeks and tied them to the car lights like flower bouquets. They put the carrots as trophies on top of the hood. To every passing woman they offered cabbage like a rose.

"A flower festival" they laughed loudly.

And with the cars decked out they got back on the road under the watchful eye of the officers while the vegetable merchant shouted after them happily, "Well, at least there's some good people still left in this world!"

10. The Letter of Sand

But it was not, unfortunately, a never-ending party.

After a tour of the Bois, the businessman convinced his new girl to go home. He accompanied Mad Muguette to her apartment on Avenue de Wagram, did not say good night but rather good morning, and promised to see her again that evening. Then he went home. Monsieur Cendron had barely taken off his coat when he was called to the phone.

"Come quick... Rue Notre-Dame-des-Victoires, to Monsieur Bejanet's office..."

Monsieur Cendron threw off his clothes, squeezed a cold sponge over his head and washed up quickly. Presently, forgetting all about how tired he was from the night out, the businessman from the country disappeared, came back as Paulin Broquet, and went to answer the police chief's summons.

The office boy Alfred had arrived half an hour before the clerks to sweep up, mop and do the cleaning, which was really only moving dust from corner to another. He was heading into Bejanet's office with feather duster in hand when he dropped everything in the doorway, stood aghast for a second, then turned and ran away screaming, "Murder! Murder!"

His screams woke up the whole building and the neighbors came running out of all the doors.

On the floor, lying in a pool of blood, they found the night watchman's body, still alive, and next to him two men, wounded and unconscious.

They immediately went to inform the local police who arrived with a doctor. The investigation was started, as usual, before the chief arrived from headquarters. The coroner stated that the three men were wounded in different ways, more or less seriously, but luckily none of them were in danger of dying.

It was made sure that nothing was touched before the rest of the authorities could get there. So, when Baumier and Broquet arrived, they could start their investigation under the best conditions.

In the office, near watchman's body, they found a big cane that he kept in arm's reach every night, as well as a finely chiseled blade covered in blood: the "murder" weapon.

Paulin Broquet leaned over the two men, examined them carefully and bolted upright again. He went straight to the chief, drew him aside to a corner of the room and rattled something off in a low whisper. Baumier shuddered and looked shocked. Then he, too, went to lean over the two thieves.

"You're right," he said to Broquet. "How very strange!"

Orders were given. Ambulances arrived. Three stretchers were brought up.

They laid the three men on the stretchers. On the first two they carefully put a sheet that covered their faces to hide the identities from journalists and photographers. The night watchman, however, they left uncovered. They could look at him and take as many photos as they pleased.

The ambulances left with not only a nurse and a doctor in the back but also a policeman with strict orders.

The night watchman was transported to the Hotel-Dieu as was proper. But the other two injured parties were brought to the prison infirmary and put in a special room. The Chief of Police asked the local captain to proceed with interrogating the office boy, the doorman and the neighbors who first got to the office.

In Bejanet's office the only people left were Monsieur Urbain, the investigating judge, the notary, the chief and detective Paulin Broquet. Broquet asked the chief to get everyone to sit down as far as possible from where they had found the wounded bodies. He himself got down on all fours and examined the wood floor, his usual method for starting an investigation. They let him do as he wanted without paying any more attention to him. In the meantime, they judge started asking questions of the notary who had recently arrived.

After quite a while Paulin Broquet suddenly raised his voice and asked the notary, "Don't you have electricity here, Monsieur Bejanet?"

"No, we use gas."

"Okay. So, there couldn't be any broken light bulbs."

"Obviously not."

"The gas jets have covers, glass covers, which support lampshades made of rather thick glass. Could this be some…"

Broquet used a calling card to sweep up some pieces of glass that he dumped on a sheet of white paper and showed the notary.

"Do you know where this came from?"

"No," Bejanet answered. "Looks like from a watch… it's so thin… but it's oval or spherical… like a tiny light bulb…"

"It doesn't remind you of anything?"

"I can't give you any more information than that."

"Thank you."

Paulin Broquet delicately folded the shards in the paper and put them in his coat pocket. Then he continued his search. Finished with the floor he got started on the chairs and table.

"This cap," he asked, "who does it belong to?"

It was a gray, English cap.

"It was one of the wounded."

"All right. It's got spots of blood."

They had picked it up off the floor and put it on the notary's desk. Broquet grabbed it, examined it, scratched at something with his fingernail, looked in the fold that formed the visor, unsnapped it… He took out a few scraps of cotton, then some pieces of glass that he compared with the ones found on the floor.

"All right! All right!" he said.

And he delicately rolled the cap in a big sheet of paper that he slipped into his coat pocket with the other evidence. Then he went to the safe, examined it, studied it for a long time, meticulously.

Now everyone was quiet, including Bejanet who was nervously watching Broquet. The room was absolutely still, solemn, dazzled.

All eyes were fixed intensely on Paulin Broquet who was calmly using a bright flashlight to carry out his examination of the safe and walls around it, going from right to left, then left to right, like a reading a book line by line, slowly descending inch by inch...

Broquet got to the bottom of the safe door, which had been found closed in the morning. He stopped for a long time, turned off his flashlight, but kept sweeping his eyes over the whole door. At last, he broke the silence and in an emotionless voice, still studying the door, he said, "Monsieur Bejanet, could you bring me a large sheet of white paper and some glue."

The notary called over his head clerk and asked him to bring what the detective required. With a nod from the latter he went off in search of the materials. When the head clerk, who was hoping to watch this operation underway, saw that his curiosity was not to be satisfied, he left. Broquet quietly coated the four corners of the paper with glue and as carefully as possible he put it against the door, held it for a moment and let go only when it could stick.

Then he turned to the notary again, "You were not only the friend of Montreil, right, but also his notary?"

"For many years, in fact."

"All right. Everything fits together. Your safe has been opened and searched."

"But I didn't have any money in the safe. Everything of value that I get I put in the bank since it's far safer there than here with me."

"Without a doubt. But there's more than just money that has value. Cash is all important in the eyes of some people, but for others there are papers, deeds and certificates that are just as precious."

The notary shuddered, "What are you saying? Do you think I've been robbed?"

"I don't know. It's a fact, however, that your safe has been skillfully opened even though there's no sign of a break-in."

"You really believe my safe was opened?"

"Opened and searched. I know for sure that when you go through your papers in here you'll find that some documents concerning the Montreil bank... or Montreil himself... are missing."

The notary was shaking now. He put a trembling hand on his sweaty brow and said, "Oh, what are you telling me! What are you saying? It's awful! It's dreadful! It's impossible!"

"But it's true," Broquet answered simply.

The notary turned to the detective looking astonished and nervous. "So, you know, don't you?"

"I only know that yesterday morning you got a visit from Robert and Raoul Montreil, the sons of the murdered banker..."

"That's right."

"I also know that almost at the same time you got a visit from Faustin, Count de la Gueriniere..."

"Yes, yes."

"That's all I can know... and I can't make any conjectures based on these two visits. My boss has told me as much."

The investigating judge broke in, "But if Paulin Broquet believes that they stole some documents from your safe, Monsieur Bejanet, documents concerning a client of the Montreil bank, it should be very easy for you to see whether it's true... and tell us.?

"I hope so."

"It would make our job a lot easier."

Broquet said, "Monsieur Bejanet can open the safe without disturbing my work, which will be explained in good time."

The upset notary trembled as he approached the safe. "The lock," he said, "is secret. How could anyone open it?"

This remark brought a smile to Broquet's lips. "If we had the time, I would show you how easy it is and you would feel that all these so-called secret locks that are made by Polichinelle et Cie... But it's a waste of time right now. Besides, the door is only closed, not locked in secret. You only have to use the key... and without even saying 'Open Says Me' it'll obey you."

The notary did, indeed, open the safe quite easily. On the steel shelves were lined up files upon files. Right away he grabbed a rather fat folder, strapped closed and with the words "Montreil Family" written large at an angle. He unfastened the strap, rifled nervously through the papers... and sighed in relief.

"The Montreil file isn't missing anything," he said, strapping it closed again. "It's intact, absolutely complete."

The investigating judge asked the notary, "That paper is really there? You can declare definitively that the precious document is present?"

"What paper are you talking about?" Bejanet looked surprised. "What document?"

"That document you showed to Monsieur Montreil... the one whose contents were so serious that they caused the astonishing change in his body and mind, which we were all, even his sons, so startled to see. That document that made Montreil, after his precise and formal accusation, suddenly retract his statement and deny his former charges. That document, Monsieur, that we judges firmly believe caused the banker's death more assuredly than being stabbed with a knife."

Monsieur Bejanet turned pale... and started trembling nervously. He tried to give the judge some explanations and clarifications:

"You're exaggerating, Your Honor. The significance of the document which I gave to Monsieur Montreil in the presence of Monsieur Grillard informed him... It was a kind of confidential document, of course, but simply concerning an ongoing and urgent affair. I'm the poor man's oldest friend and you have to believe that I would never do anything to hurt him... I told this to his sons..."

"We have no doubt. But, well, I'm going to ask you to hand over the document for the murder case."

"Impossible!" Bejanet shouted. "Absolutely impossible!"

"Can you at least give us the title of the document?"

"No, Your Honor, I am bound by professional confidentiality."

"I will force you to tell the secret about this matter."

"Only Monsieur Montreil could authorize me to release the document... and he's dead. I rest on my conscience as a public official... on my duty and I say that I cannot reveal this document."

"Your statement is duly noted," the judge said gravely. Then he added, "Can you tell us now if anything is missing from the file of the clients of the Montreil Bank?"

"That's easy, messieurs. I keep here only the files that I can't leave with my clerks for... various... delicate reasons."

"We understand."

"There are only three or four of these special... confidential... intimate files..." Bejanet gave a few names that made no particular impact on those listening. Then he named, "Count de la Gueriniere and Monsieur Laurent..."

The investigating judge asked the notary to check the last two files.

"Count de la Gueriniere," Bejanet said, "gave Montreil, as security for a rather substantial loan, some property titles that my friend Montreil had me verify... examine."

"The Count de la Gueriniere," the judge asked, "was a client of the Montreil Bank?"

"Yes, Your Honor."

"As far as I know he's not a salesman or trader or speculator or businessman, so what was he?"

"The Count is a very busy socialite, a big spender, and sometimes finds himself in need of Monsieur Montreil's kindness."

"For borrowing money?"

"Yes, Your Honor... friendly loans... loans to finance a man of the world..."

"I understand. Can you check the file?"

Thumbing through the file the notary declared, "The Count's file hasn't been touched."

The authorities present made no comment on this statement. They passed no judgment, formed no opinion.

In the meantime, Paulin Broquet was sitting in one of the armchairs very calmly. He was listening and watching every movement that the notary made. No detail of the scene escaped his notice.

"And here's Laurent's file," Bejanet said but when he opened the folder he yelled out, "Ah! There are two very important documents missing!"

"In Laurent's file?" the judge asked.

"Yes... Messieurs... I owe you an explanation here. Monsieur Laurent was... still is... I think so at least until proven otherwise, a good, honest man. He owns a chemical factory on Rue des Lombards that did good business in the past. Unfortunately, Monsieur Laurent was bitten by the demon of speculation... He dove into the stock market, in mines and other things, and lost a lot of money. In hard times he had recourse to Monsieur Montreil... He owed him a large sum but he gave the banker various titles, different securities that came out of his wife's dowry... Madame Laurent is the daughter of a big rancher from Laigle, Monsieur Bilmat. The father, Normand, had planned for his daughter to marry the son of one of his friends, another landowner, and he struck a deal between the two families. But the young girl fell in love with Laurent, a travelling businessman from Paris, and she forced her father to consent to the marriage by using a rather extreme method... and the father agreed so as not to fall into dishonor. But he would never pardon his daughter or son-in-law. As dowry he gave his daughter what had come from her mother... and kept to himself around his properties in Laigle, having very rare contact with his son-in-law. Naturally, the losses suffered by Laurent exasperated Normand to no end. Monsieur Bilmat had a large fortune but he was very tough... not miserly, mind you, but he held onto his money and didn't give anything up easily."

"And in this matter he was never approached by Monsieur Laurent, who must have known what his father-in-law was like?" Paulin Broquet asked.

"Yes, Laurent approached him several times."

"And Monsieur Bilmat refused?"

"Not exactly."

"He gave him money?"

"In truth, no."

"That's a little ambiguous," the judge said, "and for our investigation we'll need something more precise."

"I have to tell you this, messieurs, because among the papers that Laurent confided to Montreil for his loans, there were several that had been given by Madame Laurent's father. Now, knowing the father-in-law's feelings on the matter, Montreil had a few doubts about the authenticity of the documents, at least on the way they were acquired by Laurent... and he gave them to me to deal with it..."

"Excuse me," Urbain, the investigating judge interrupted. "But had Montreil already loaned Laurent some money?"

"Yes, Your Honor… and a rather large sum."

"With these documents as guarantees?"

"Yes.

"Even with his suspicions?"

The notary did not answer right away. The judge's question seemed to upset him a little. Still, he ended up saying, "Monsieur Laurent was so insistent. It was a favor to him… and I was to check the documents."

"Afterward? This means that Montreil was a generous man, a good man with a kind soul whom we rarely meet in the business world or finance."

"That's right. That very well may be."

"So, this means that Montreil paid dearly for the favor he was granting Laurent."

Bejanet did not respond.

The judge did not press the point. He said, "'Let's see what's in Laurent's file."

"It's missing two documents."

"So, two documents from Laurent's file are missing, that's a fact. Now, you don't know if Laurent was at Montreil's office the night of his murder…"

"I know he was."

"He was there as well as the Count de la Gueriniere…"

"I know that too. But Montreil called the Count innocent."

"Which means that we can consider Monsieur Laurent guilty."

"No!" the notary shouted. "I'm not accusing anyone! I told you that until proven otherwise I'll consider Monsieur Laurent an honest man."

"Monsieur Bejanet is obviously unaware," the Chief of Police spoke up, "that we also found some documents missing in Montreil's office, from the safe that was robbed."

"There too!" the notary cried out. "Oh, there too some documents were missing?"

"We will ask you to tell us what the missing documents are from your file and with your help try to find out what they took from the Montreil Bank."

"I believe," the notary said, "we won't be able to know for sure, absolutely, without the help of Monsieur Laurent."

"So, we should wait for him to come back."

"Come back?"

"After the Montreil murder, since the very day of the tragedy, Laurent has disappeared."

"Disappeared!" the notary almost screamed in torment. "So, well, but then he killed Montreil! He's the one who came and robbed my safe!"

The Chief of Police did not answer but Paulin Broquet stood up and said, "In any case, there's one thing for sure… it's that Montreil's murder, the attack tonight, the death of the watchman, the theft of the banker's documents and the robbery of the safe here were all committed by the same hand."

"How can you know?" the notary asked.

"And this hand, for some unknown reason, each time, as a challenge or perhaps just showing off, left its signature."

"Its signature?"

"On Montreil's safe," the detective said, "written in the victim's blood we found the letter Z. And here on the door, under the paper that I stuck to the safe, we will be finding a Z."

"A Z?"

"Except instead of blood this time he used your jar of gum arabic and a brush. After brushing the Z with a little glue and throwing on some sand from your bowl over there, we'll have our Z in sand."

This statement caused a stir. It opened the field to all kinds of crazy, fanciful theories.

This Z of blood and Z of sand that were like a signature of the author of these crimes, just like Paulin Broquet said, took on a terrible, disturbing, chilling character.

But Broquet went on, "Therefore, messieurs, we have to consider as certain that we are faced with a bold, well organized, powerful gang that will do whatever it takes to fulfill their mission... that goes from robbery to murder with frightening ease... and that, we cannot doubt, is holding more surprises in store for us." He paused before adding, "Now we must ask Monsieur Bejanet whether he recognizes the victims of this tragedy played out in his office."

"My night watchman."

"And the other two?"

"No, really, I didn't see their faces... I don't think I know them."

"And yet they are Robert and Raoul Montreil!"

This statement by Broquet stunned the notary.

"Robert and Raoul! Here, in my office... at night! What were they doing?"

"Probably," the detective said, "looking for what you refused them yesterday morning."

"Oh, that's not possible... They would never..."

"We found them near the open safe where the secret document was kept."

"But they didn't see anything or read anything or learn anything..."

"That's what we'll find out later."

"Oh, the poor boys!" the notary was overwhelmed. "The poor, poor boys!"

11. Wounded without knowing it

The night watchman had been stabbed in the back. The deep wound had spilled a lot of blood but it was, in truth, not too serious. The blade went in at the shoulder, slid along the scapula but did not touch any organs. The victim, however, when he woke up, looked very astonished to be in a hospital and feeling pain in his shoulder.

Paulin Broquet was at the good man's bedside when he recovered his senses. He wanted to be present when Urbain, the investigating judge, questioned him.

"Like every night," the guard began, "I made my rounds in the office, checked all the doors..."

"And you saw that they were locked?"

"Sure... Then I went to lie down, nothing to worry about."

"You didn't hear a noise? Didn't suspect anything? Didn't see anything unusual?"

"Nothing at all. Otherwise I wouldn't have been so relaxed... I wouldn't have gone to lie down, you know..."

"Indeed."

"Now I'm in this hospital bed and I'm hurt... You gotta believe that no one's more surprised than me."

"So, you didn't see anybody in the office last night?"

"Nobody."

"You don't remember being woken up at any time... standing up?"

"Not at all."

"You didn't get into a fight, hit someone with your nightstick?"

"No, no one. Even though I'm feeling pain, even though you're telling me all this, I feel like I'm dreaming... like I'm in some kind of nightmare."

They could not doubt the man's statement and that everything happened as he said. So, the judge left, wishing him a quick recovery. On the way out, Monsieur Urbain asked Paulin Broquet what he thought about it all.

"My opinion," the detective said, "is that the night watchman is telling the truth. He couldn't see anything because he was dozing off... and perhaps forced to doze off."

"But afterward... his injury... and the two others?"

"All the rest is purely for show, a beautifully executed deception."

"So you think that Robert and Raoul Montreil attacked the night watchman?"

Broquet had a strange smile. "With the two of them they could easily have got the better of a man surprised in his sleep."

"Indeed."

"Moreover, all three of them were hurt. That's too much." He thought for a second and concluded, "We're dealing with very strong, very clever people here... fearless... but they forgot the old proverb: that which proves too much, proves nothing."

Broquet's purpose was very firm when he told the Chief of Police to get the two brothers away without reporters, photographers or even the public being able to know their identity. He was absolutely sure that he wanted to keep their involvement secret.

However, Robert and Raoul were not hurt as badly as the night watchman. In their hospital beds they were in a deep but peaceful sleep.

"Okay," Broquet said, "no doubt about it, they, too, just like the guard, were put to sleep."

Broquet had been leaning over the two wounded men, or rather the two sleepers, for a moment and examining them very closely. But they knew that the detective did nothing in vain, even when his action seemed extremely simple or without importance. He always had a goal in mind, known only to him... and whose results were surprising all the time.

It was thus that after looking at Robert he went over to Raoul's bed and like he had just done to the doctor he started studying the lawyer. Raoul had a full, brown beard, neatly trimmed into a point. Broquet combed his fingers through the beard and gingerly pulled out a few white strands, a little snow-flake...

"Cotton!" he said.

"Cotton in his beard," everyone blurted out in surprise.

"Yes. I wonder what this cotton's doing here? Anyway, here we have a few strands of cotton."

He laid the fibers aside carefully, then continued studying the patient's head.

"Ah! Now this is even weirder..."

Between his thumb and index finger he was holding something shiny but so small that they could barely see it.

"What is it?"

"A piece of glass."

"In his hair?!"

"Exactly." Then he added, "A piece of glass that looks strangely like what I picked up in Bejanet's office." And he concluded, "Well, all this makes me believe that Raoul Montreil was suffocated with some cotton and the bulb was broken over his head."

Urbain listened to the detective with great interest. Monsieur Baumier was smiling. He, the Chief of Police, was used to his detective's amazing feats, his magic tricks as they said. But the investigating judge was in awe.

Paulin Broquet continued, "As for Robert Montreil, he only has a moustache and it didn't catch anything. I also didn't find anything in his hair because the doctor kept his cap on during the attack. But the cap that I picked up also had traces of glass and cotton."

"Great!"

"Which tells us that the two brothers suffered the same fate."

"Meaning?"

"They were put to sleep."

"Put to sleep?"

"Knocked out, plain and simple. And here's the proof!"

Paulin Broquet took the cap out of his pocket and showed it to the judge.

"See that spot or rather that stain there near the visor?"

"I see... it's kind of round."

"Right. Robert Montreil was very conscientious about how he looked and kept his hair neat and shiny with some pomade, slicked back with some kind of cream or gel... and it left traces on his cap... not much I admit but enough for us... for us to see it."

"You have to have sharp eyes."

"Most of the traces were completely removed here."

"Indeed."

"Now, there's only two products capable of cleaning greasy stains so thoroughly: ether and chloroform."

"Yes, okay, ether and chloroform."

"So, I'm thinking now that these two sleepers and maybe the watchman too were smothered with a cotton pad and they broke a bulb full of chloroform on them."

The investigating judge shook the detective hand. "You're one in a million, my dear Broquet."

"Hold on, judge," Broquet shot back. "Just hold on... We've only just begun. We're only in the first stages of this affair. Everything I just said is barely a start. What remains to be discovered is much more serious!"

"Indeed, we have to find out why the two brothers were at Bejanet's at such a late hour."

"First of all, yes."

"We also have to find out how they could be taken by surprise... who did this to them... and why?"

"They alone can tell us how they were caught off guard," Broquet said. "As for the reason, the purpose, the motive that brought them to the notary's office, we already know it."

"What?" Urbain asked.

"Yesterday morning Bejanet refused to show them this famous document in the safe, just like he did to us today. The banker's sons, and this is easy to understand, wanted to know about them in spite of the notary... and to finally find out about the strange mystery surrounding the sorrowful end of their poor father."

The Chief of Police backed up his detective's deduction. In his opinion there was no other reason that motivated the break-in by the two brothers. "And yet," he added, "there's one thing that's escaping us, Broquet, and it's of the utmost importance."

"What's that, Chief"

"Well, it's weird that the guys in this Z gang, since we must be dealing with an organized gang here, that these Z guys who tried to kill the banker Montreil so ruthlessly, these same guys were caught last night in the middle of their robbery by the Montreil sons and they didn't try to eliminate such dangerous witnesses. It's weird that they set this whole thing up... and that's all! It's inconceivable that a gang of professional thieves would be so careless as to leave themselves to the mercy of an inevitable witness. Why didn't they kill the two brothers?"

"That is weird. Why indeed?"

"They could have done it. No, they should have done it... to save themselves! But they didn't. They stopped short, didn't finish the job... didn't commit murder... Why?"

The judge and the chief were looking at Paulin Broquet as if seeking his insight.

The detective simply said, "I shouldn't say aloud what I've got in mind."

"Tell us anyway."

"No, Chief. No! It's too risky!"

"Come on!'

"Well, Chief, I'll just say that the key to this bloody tragedy, to this whole mystery, is in the document that Bejanet refuses to show us."

"The secret document?"

"The paper will tell us both why Montreil retracted his accusation of the Count de la Gueriniere and why they didn't kill the Montreil boys last night."

The judge and the chief were startled. "But, Broquet, you're accusing..."

The detective cut them off, "I'm accusing the one who signed these crimes with his initial... I accuse Zigomar!"

The authorities jumped again, "Zigomar? What's a Zigomar?"

Instead of answering Paulin Broquet pointed to the two brothers and said, "Shush, you'll wake them up."

12. *An alibi too good to be true*

In fact, almost at the very same minute the two brothers were coming out of unconsciousness.

Just like the night watchman they looked extremely surprised to be in a bed in an unfamiliar room. When they saw the men standing around their bedside, they looked even more anxious.

"Monsieur Urbain! And the Chief of Police!"

"Paulin Broquet!"

They sat up straight, sounded scared.

"What is this? Where are we?"

"What do you want with us?"

The judge spoke gently, quietly, managed to calm them down. And without losing valuable time the interrogation began.

Robert and Raoul now had all their senses back, all their presence of mind, all their memory and just wanted to talk, to tell everything they knew about the strange adventure.

Raoul began, "Neither my brother nor I have any intention of hiding the truth from you. We accept full responsibility for what we did after pondering the consequences for a long time... and we will put our honor in your hands, messieurs, trust in your good faith..."

"We want the same thing. Go ahead and talk freely."

"My brother and I, messieurs, feel that it is our duty, for the honor of our family, for the memory of our father, for the safety and security of our family, to know about the document that killed... yes, that's the word... that killed our father."

The judge listened with great interest. The young lawyer had just corroborated, in no uncertain terms, the opinion expressed a few minutes ago by the detective.

Raoul went on telling those present that he and his brother had sworn to find the document and learn the truth, even if it meant going to extremes and if necessary going beyond the law. Therefore, dressed as they were now they set off after midnight for Bejanet's office.

"Now" the Chief of Police said, "you have to be clear about what you remember."

Raoul told the story of how they got into the office and found the night watchman dozing off and even snoring.

"What's that?" the Chief pressed him. "He was sleeping deeply enough to snore?"

Raoul said that he and his brother had been surprised by a sour smell that they took for rum, that the guard must have been drinking... or maybe some medicine that he had rubbed on his sore muscles...

The young lawyer continued his story about how they were stunned when they opened the door to the notary's office... and what they saw in front of the open safe: three men using blue flashlights to search through the papers...

"Did you see their faces? Did you recognize any of them?"

"At least one of them... only one... and it was enough for Robert and I. We recognized one of them, messieurs. Oh, we recognized him right away and the two of us, at the same time, shouted out his name and pounced on him."

"Who was it?"

"The Count de la Gueriniere!"

On hearing this name Paulin Broquet did not say a word, did not budge. But he did smile. Which was not the case with the others there. The investigating judge and the police chief both jumped.

"The Count de la Gueriniere!" they cried out. "Are you sure? You're not mistaken? It wasn't someone who just looked like him?"

"No, messieurs, we are absolutely, positively certain that it was the Count."

"And after that?"

"After that, messieurs, I can't say more."

"Me neither," Robert piped up.

"Why not?"

"Because it was just when my brother and I jumped on the Count that I was stopped... they grabbed me..."

"Me too," Robert said.

"They threw a sheet over my head, a hood or a bag, filled with cotton... it stifled my cries."

"The same for me," Robert agreed.

"I wanted to fight but they held me tight and almost right away I felt something break on my forehead, glass or something, then it got very cold inside the bag... but I was breathing in fumes... of chloroform, I think. Well, after a few fruitless attempts to get free I lost consciousness. And that's all I can tell you."

"I have nothing to add to my brother's statement," Robert declared. "What he just told you is exactly what happened to me."

There was a moment of silence. Then the judge spoke up.

"You're sure, messieurs, that you're not forgetting anything?"

"No, Your Honor, that's all. And that's the truth."

"You didn't have to fight with the night watchman?"

"No, of course not. We're sure of it, aren't we, Robert?"

The Chief of Police asked again, "And you swear you recognized the Count?"

"Yes, we swear! It was him!"

Then the Chief said, "We'll take down your statements... but I think it's my duty to tell you something..."

"We're all ears."

"The Count de la Gueriniere spent the night at the theater, the Lutetia, enjoying a show in which his mistress Lucette Minois was in the leading role."

"But after midnight," Raoul stammered, "he could have... The Lutetia is on Boulevard Montmartre and Bejanet's office is Rue Notre-Dame-des-Victoires, really close... The Count could have... just hopped over... and in a few seconds been back."

"That's true but after the theater the Count took his friends, his mistress and a few pretty girls out to eat at a restaurant around La Madeleine."

"During the meal he could have slipped away."

"He didn't leave the festivities for a single instant... and he was the life of the party." The Chief explained, "My information about this is infallible. One of Broquet's men was serving the meal and there was a guest at the table, a businessman from the countryside, a Monsieur Cendron, in whom Broquet has total confidence. After dinner, so in the morning, just a few hours ago, the Count brought his merry band of partygoers to the Woods in his car... I have on my desk a report telling everything... To spice up the little party he knocked down an old lady selling vegetables... I have the statement taken by two policemen... and the report of Cendron who was in the car of his gracious host."

"So?"

"So, gentlemen, minute by minute we know the whereabouts of the Count de la Gueriniere during all of last night."

"His alibi," Raoul groaned, "is air-tight."

"Yes, perfectly."

Then the young lawyer cried out, "Don't you find this alibi a little too perfect, messieurs?"

The question made a deep impression on the others. By asking it Raoul was saying out loud what each of them was no doubt thinking to himself... what nobody could or would say...

The investigating judge and the police chief looked at Paulin Broquet. The detective did not blink. He was listening but showing no emotion. Nothing in the world could have changed his attitude, broken his stoicism... He was listening!

But the two brothers, one last time, shouted out, "Whatever the case, whatever evidence you've gathered up, however strong it may be, and even with you saying the opposite of what we're saying, we will stick by our statement no matter what! It was the Count de la Gueriniere we saw in Monsieur Bejanet's office!"

The judge turned to Paulin Broquet and asked, "What do you think of all this?"

"I think," the detective answered gravely, "that we're dealing with people who are a lot more powerful than we imagined. With this Z, we're jumping from one surprise to another and I think my friend Cendron, the businessman from the country, was played for the fool."

"How's that?"

"The Montreils swear they saw their Count de la Gueriniere, but my friend Cendron was just as sure of his. Now, while Cendron was at the party with his Count, drinking champagne around La Madeleine, the same Count, at the same time, was robbing the notary's safe on Rue Notre-Dame-des-Victoires. It's very good... very, very good!"

Broquet's statement fell like a ton of bricks. Everyone felt the mystery was becoming more and more enigmatic.

After a moment the investigating judge spoke up, "You also swear, messieurs, that you didn't fight with the night watchman?"

"Absolutely, we swear it!"

"Well, in that case I ought to tell you that we found you two passed out and injured in Bejanet's office... and the night watchman was nearby, gravely wounded by a knife." The judge presented a knife to the two brothers. "Do you recognize this weapon?"

Raoul cried out, "That's mine!"

"I also have the same knife."

"It's mine... my initials are engraved on the handle. Look, JRM, Jean-Raoul Montreil."

"Perfect."

"How did you get this?"

"We found it in Bejanet's office."

Raoul jumped, "This knife? No, it's impossible... impossible... It's mine and my brother has the same one... but it was hanging on the wall in my room... We didn't take any weapons with us. I wasn't carrying this knife... So I couldn't have lost it at Bejanet's. I repeat, I had no weapons on me. This knife is mine, I admit it, but yesterday it was hanging in my room and I didn't take it down."

"And yet," the judge declared, "this knife didn't walk to Bejanet's all alone. Someone had to bring it there and use it."

"Use it?"

"It was this knife, your knife, that the night watchman was stabbed with."

13. Tom Tweak

A few days later Baumier, the chief of police, arrived in the morning to go through his mail. The bailiff handed him a visiting card.

"Well, well" he said after reading it, "yes, by all means, show him in."

After a few seconds the visitor entered. He was around 40 years old, very well dressed, with care and elegance, looking like a typical North American. Clean shaven, sharp-boned, with wide jaws indicating boldness and energy; a strong, hooked nose sticking out between two bright, inquiring, very intelligent eyes; the mouth slashed over a prominent, determined chin.

In a guttural but nasal voice like Americans use who have a deep voice, after saying hello he told the chief, "I'm Tom Tweak from New York."

The police chief motioned to an armchair in front of his desk.

Tom Tweak sat down, then with the usual abruptness of American businessmen he asked, "Do you speak English?"

"No, sorry."

"Too bad. Me, I don't speak French too good."

"I think we'll manage just fine."

"Well, I'm glad you think so." The American continued, "My card can tell you my name but not what I do. I'm Tom Tweak, the greatest American detective."

"I am familiar with your name."

"Yes, I'm sure... I'm the most famous detective in the United States... and the highest paid..."

"Congratulations."

"Yeah... I worked with Sherlock Holmes at the start. He was really a very great man... very great... for his time. Now we can do better."

"And yet..."

"Yeah, we do better."

"Indeed, it seems that Nick Carter..."

"Oh, Nick Carter!" the American smiled. "Nick Carter is my student. Yeah, he's a great bluffer. He tells the press what he did... and what others did he kind of passes over... If true, it would take a hundred years to do all alone everything he said he did... Nick Carter is now working for Barnum, with his cousin Buffalo Bill... Yeah, it's now Bluff and Co."

The American did not stop there.

"My reputation isn't in little books for children but in the memories of men. I forbid them to write anything about Tom Tweak. Plus, I work especially for banks and high finance and only get involved in a crime when it's too much for the likes of Carter." He concluded, "Now that you know who I am, here's my badge, a letter from the Attorney General in the US and a recommendation from the American ambassador in Paris, all of which accredit my qualifications."

Tom Tweak put everything Baumier's desk. As the police chief cast a quick glance over the documents, out of respect, Tom Tweak pressed him.

"Please check the papers, examine them very carefully to verify my skills, to give me, without a moment's hesitation, the support I need."

Baumier looked over the documents more carefully before handing them back to the American, waiting calmly to see where all this was headed. "It's fine," he said. "The papers are authentic and certified. You're qualified in my book…"

Tom Tweak stood up and held out his hand. "Yeah," he said. "I'm glad to meet you." Then he gathered up the papers, folded them carefully and put them away. "Now, I'll ask you to put me in touch with Paulin Broquet."

"That's easy," the chief pressed a button on the telephone sitting on a table next to his desk.

"In America," Tom Tweak said, "we have a lot of admiration for Paulin Broquet. His ingenuity, his boldness, his courage—it's amazing to us Americans."

On the telephone someone said that Paulin Broquet was not at the station or at home, that he had left at the crack of dawn and would not be back all day.

"Until tomorrow, Mr. Tweak. Leave me your address and I'll tell Broquet to stop by and see you tomorrow. Is that okay?"

"Sure. No problem." He gave his address, shook the chief's hand very hard and left.

The next morning he waited for his French counterpart whom he was very excited to meet. The American detective was staying in a little apartment in a "family house" on Avenue de la Grande-Armée that was regularly occupied by Americans. He had with him his Chinese valet who knew all the habits and particular needs of his specially complicated service.

Around ten o'clock Tsin announced Paulin Broquet.

Tom Tweak was sitting at a table, writing. He stood up and looked at the door where the French detective had just showed up. Broquet stepped into the room while Tsin closed the door behind him. Then he stopped and cast a steely look over the figure of Tom Tweak.

The two men stood there for a moment like that, staring at each other, studying each other, trying to probe each other's soul.

"Paulin Broquet?" the American finally asked.

"That's me."

"All right!"

"Tom Tweak?" Paulin Broquet asked.

"It is… I!"

"Very well."

Then the American approached Broquet with his hand held out, paying him compliments in English.

Paulin Broquet smiled and said, "I don't understand."

The American was obviously very surprised, "Oh, I thought you spoke English very well."

"I can babble a few words like all the French..."

"And yet you stayed in England for a long time as well as in America?"

"That's right, but I had one of my lieutenants with me who spoke impeccable English. Thus the mistake."

"No doubt."

There was a moment of silence during which the two men stared at each other some more. A cold, awkward, nervous air hovered around them. As Broquet was playing the passive, impenetrable Sphinx, the American broke out laughing, very loudly.

"Okay, okay, we'll get along just fine."

"Let's hope so.'

Tom Tweak stopped laughing abruptly and motioned to an armchair while offering Broquet a cigar. The two men started smoking in silence, sneaking peeks at each other now and again.

The American was the one who broke the silence. "Baumier saw all my papers of accreditation."

"I know."

"He checked them and verified my identity."

"He told me. You gave him undeniable proof that you are Tom Tweak, the American detective."

"Yes... but here in this house and in Paris I'm incognito... under the name of William Donald... for my work."

"I understand."

"And for this work I need your help."

A flame lit up in the gray eyes of the French detective but he lowered his eyelids right away and as if to hide them even more he let out a few big puffs of smoke.

"Yes," the American continued, "I need your marvelous talent... the fantastic skills and admirable courage of Paulin Broquet."

"You flatter me."

"No, I'm telling you the truth."

"Well, no compliment will make me more valuable than Tom Tweak, the greatest, most famous, most respected American detective."

Tom Tweak held out his hands to Paulin Broquet. The latter stretched out his own but instead of putting them into the American's, by reflex he grabbed the other's hands and shook them vigorously, American style, hard enough to dislocate a shoulder.

Then the two detectives sank back into their armchairs and went back to smoking in silence, all the while spying each other.

After a moment of silence and stillness, it was the American again who had to strike up conversation.

"Well, here I am, sent to Europe by two big banks in New York. These institutions were getting a big transaction ready and had sent some securities and very important, secret documents to the Montreil bank for the big launch."

Broquet listened. Tom Tweak went on.

"Mister Montreil was murdered... It's a double tragedy because the securities in his safe, since the transaction wasn't finalized, haven't been indexed. So, we can't stop them... If these securities are thrown onto the market in Paris or London or Berlin, it will cause a terrible plunge, a crash, a loss of millions of dollars for my clients. Plus, the documents might fall into knowledgeable hands and could derail other deals that could cause my clients very serious damage."

Although speaking with his American accent Tom Tweak expressed himself in very correct French. Sometimes, however, the French word escaped him and he had to search for it or he said it in English hoping that Broquet would give him a translation. But Paulin Broquet just listened. He let Tom Tweak search and he waited, emotionless, inscrutable, until the American found the word he was looking for.

"It is my duty," he continued, "to get all these papers back." And he concluded, "That's the problem posed, as our master Sherlock Holmes would say."

Here Broquet said, "Yes. It is posed. But you don't need me to fix your problem."

"Sorry but I can't do anything without you..."

"Why?"

"You're the one in charge of the investigation onto the murder of Montreil. I know all about the affair."

"We're not aware of a theft of these kinds of documents."

"I've got proof. Offers of sale were made through the regular channels of fences and thieves."

"This is your concern and I can't do anything about it because we haven't identified the theft. As for the murder, it will no doubt be closed..."

The American almost jumped out of his chair. "Closed! You, Paulin Broquet, you will let an affair like this be closed! You!"

"It really must..."

"No! It really must not!"

The American detective flung his cigar butt into a far corner of the room.

Paulin Broquet calmly placed his in the ashtray.

Then Tom Tweak pulled out his case and was about to offer him another but Broquet put up his hand. He quickly whipped out his own case and held it out for the American to take one. The two detectives lit their Cubans and shrouded themselves with smoke.

Paulin Broquet was back in the same position in his chair, leaning back with his arms on the armrests, this legs crossed casually.

Tom Tweak suddenly slammed his fist down on his armrest and asked, "Tell me, what do you think of this Count de la Gueriniere?"

"Nothing," Broquet answered softly.

"Oh, nothing... what do you mean nothing?"

"Nothing, that's all."

"Is he guilty or innocent?"

"One or the other, that's for sure."

"But what do you think? What's your opinion?"

"I don't have one."

"Oh."

"The one who knew better than anyone, Monsieur Montreil, declared that he was innocent."

"Well, there's this Laurent?"

"Nothing to prove it."

"And yet," the American was shouting, "one of them has to be the murderer."

Broquet shook his head and said, "No."

"What do you mean no. You're saying no pretty confidently."

"Very confidently."

"You know who it is?"

"Yes."

"Yes?"

"Zigomar!"

The American detective was startled. "Zigomar!" he shouted. "Who's this Zigomar?"

Paulin Broquet answered calmly, "It's Zigomar."

Tom Tweak jumped out of his chair. "That doesn't tell me who it is or what it is..."

"It's Zigomar. That's all I can tell you."

The American detective was pacing the floor now, nervously, his head hung down, puffing away on his cigar, hands behind his back, snapping his fingers.

Paulin Broquet had not budged or blinked. Calmly, quietly, he watched his American counterpart furious repeating, "Zigomar! Zigomar!"

When the American reached the end of the room he stopped short, turned around and asked, "How do you know that it's Zigomar? Who told you?"

"He wrote it himself."

"Aha! Yes, the Z on the safe door... the Z!" The American resumed his pacing. "Zigomar! The Z!"

He marched by Paulin Broquet several times, then all of sudden stopped right in front of him, planted himself squarely and asked, "And that's enough for you, Paulin Broquet?"

"What's enough for me?"

"To know that it's Zigomar…"

"No."

"So why don't you arrest him?"

Paulin Broquet started laughing. "Wouldn't that be great!"

"Oh, really… So, this gentleman's too powerful…"

"I'm afraid so."

Tom Tweak went back to pacing, then came back to Broquet and raised his voice again, "Well, you have to arrest him anyway!"

"I'd like nothing better."

"And as soon as possible, because of the securities he's got… you understand. I came to Europe for this. You have to hurry."

"Yes, let's hurry."

"Yes, we'll both work on it together. You want to?"

"So be it."

"All right! Have you started anything?"

"No."

"You have no plan, no clue? Really?"

"I'm relying on luck."

"You have to force luck… push things along… When can we meet again?"

"When it's necessary."

"Where? Not here… because I'm incognito… At your place?"

"I'm never there… but here's what would be best: send me a note with the day and time and we'll meet at Baumier's office."

"Why there?"

"You have nothing to fear, I imagine?" Broquet laughed again. "There are all kinds of ways to get to the station without raising any suspicions… A Zigomar won't come spying on us in there."

"You're right. So, it's agreed. See you soon."

Paulin Broquet stood up. He said farewell to the American detective and went away as calmly as he had come in.

When he had gone, Tom Tweak stood for a moment lost in thought, unable to move away from the doorway where he had just said goodbye. Then, at last, he shrugged his broad shoulders.

"Zigomar!" he said loudly. "Paulin Broquet! The Zs! The police! Good Game!"

He lit another cigar, then he sat at his table and started writing a letter. Tsin entered a little later and whispered a name into his ear.

"Show him in," the detective said, continuing to write.

The Chinese valet introduced an elegantly dressed visitor who came into the room looking astonished and intrigued. Tom Tweak was still writing and smoking without even looking up at the newcomer who was very surprised by the lack of attention.

After a brief instant he approached the American and in a haughty voice asked, "William Donald?"

"Me," the other answered without moving an inch. "Yes, that's me…"

"You asked me to stop by to see you about a confidential matter of the utmost importance."

"Yes, yes."

"Your odd form of welcome is terribly surprising."

"No… I'm finishing up… Wait a second…"

"No one ever makes me wait."

"I'm sorry to be the first."

"I dare say, monsieur!" the visitor shouted, extremely irritated, furious and taking a threatening step forward.

"Please sit down."

"I don't tolerate anyone treating me…"

"Please sit down," Tom Tweak was still writing.

"I am the Count de la Gueriniere."

Tom Tweak looked like he did not understand.

"I am the Count de la Gueriniere," he repeated more loudly, taking another step forward and standing now right next to the table.

The American shrugged his shoulders this time.

"Did you hear me?" the Count demanded, brandishing his cane with a trembling hand, ready to strike.

"Come on, calm down," the American said calmly.

The Count started to repeat for the third time, "I am the…"

"Zigomar!" the detective cut him off.

The Count looked stunned, as if he had just been hit hard in the chest. But he quickly got a hold of himself.

"Mad! You're mad!"

"No."

"Well, you insult me…" The Count raised his cane to smash it over the other man's head.

"Zigomar!" the American looked up.

And Count, seeing him, cried out, "You!"

14. The Forger

The chief of police had told the investigating judge that he had to wait for Monsieur Laurent to return. The chemical products manufacturer had, in fact, been absent for a few days, but on the morning of his return he went to work and was back home for dinner.

From his serious, preoccupied attitude, Madame Laurent knew that her husband had some big worries, big problems. For years she had seen him come home like this, worried, serious, even sad sometimes, when deadlines were due. Madame Laurent tried to cheer him up, to encourage him. She helped with the books and wrote letters. Above all she gave him moral support and showed him all the affection and tenderness she felt.

They had married for love.

And love, that rare thing, had stayed with them. They loved each other and each of them was as affectionate as the other.

Monsieur Laurent was around 35 years old and his wife barely 28. She was a beauty in full bloom. A healthy, graceful, brunette beauty. She had big, black, very gentle eyes and a lovely smile.

Monsieur Laurent was strong and sturdy, very intelligent, very bold, quite handsome with his full, dark beard in which not a single gray hair dared to grow. A good talker, with the Parisian wit of a man who has traveled for work and knew how to turn clients of his business into personal friends.

He used to go into Normandy and stop at L'Aigle for a few days, selling his products to the landowners, farmers and factory managers in the region. He was also the supplier of Monsieur Bilmat, a huge property owner and majority stockholder in a pin factory as well as mayor of the town of Itonville on the banks of the Iton river.

Naturally, he was Bilmat's guest, invited to lunch and dinner with him, which was considered a great honor because Bilmat was not generous with his invitations to people nor with anything else.

Bilmat hoarded his profits and income with a severity that astonished the Normans. He kept all his money and stocks locked up in a massive, heavy safe, as big as a fortress. He had lived for a long time in a big house inherited from his parents, a house surrounded by a vast garden and enclosed by walls that were too high to climb and were protected by big dogs constantly on guard.

In this big house, with its big, solid doors that were locked on the inside by iron bars, Monsieur Bilmat, a widow for a long time, lived alone with his daughter Octavie. A woman served as both cook and maid. Her husband was the chauffeur, gardener, bodyguard and right-hand man.

Octavie Bilmat was pretty. Many suitors paid visits, seduced by her beautiful eyes and her dowry, which they imagined would be very rich. But Octavie turned them all down… to the great joy of her father who planned to marry his daughter to the son of one of his friends with whom he did business. This young man would accept Octavie with almost no dowry, just a little annuity. On the other hand, he would have to manage his father's properties and make them even more profitable. It was a marriage of convenience in every penny-pinching way possible… and it had been decided.

But he was not counting on Octavie to refuse her father's choice, declaring her love for Monsieur Laurent and not wanting to marry anyone but the chemical products salesman.

There is no need to describe the anger that burned inside the mayor of Itonville… but it was terrible! When Octavie told him, after a few months of wicked fighting, that he could not oppose her marriage, Bilmat thought he was going to explode in a fit of rage.

He married his daughter to the seducer but he gave him no dowry except what came in from her mother, a small amount… and he threw his Parisian son-in-law and his daughter out the door.

Monsieur Laurent took his wife to Paris and had only a distant relationship with his father-in-law, the kind that must be kept up between family members, even enemies. Moreover, his business prospered. He bought out the business where he had been a traveling salesman and lived happily with his wife.

But Laurent had the misfortune of not being happy with his lot, as enviable as it was. He dreamed of better things for his wife, luxurious things… and he speculated. It was a failure. He was not made for this kind of business. So, in order to put a plug in the flood of losses, he had to find help from the outside. He was spotted among moneylenders and crooked middlemen… and loan sharks.

He had to deal with the banker Montreil, who held some of the outstanding debt, give him guaranties, submit securities, furnish the signature of his wife… and even of his father-in-law, yes, of Monsieur Bilmat!

On that day Monsieur Laurent was headed for disaster.

By using all his skills and not a little sacrifice he managed to postpone the day of reckoning… but only postpone it, not cancel it.

This evening, therefore—it was the day after the mysterious burglary at Bejanet's office—he went home more worried, more troubled than ever. And more frantic than when he went nervously and angrily to see the banker Montreil on the night he was found murdered.

During the day he had to make one last ditch effort with the Montreil bank. Even harsher than the banker himself, the chief accountant, whom the director of the bank had asked to clear up outstanding debts, refused Monsieur Laurent any extension or delay.

After the heated argument with the accountant at the Montreil bank he went back home, furious and desperate. His wife demanded he tell her why he was so upset.

"It's just because," he answered, "even though that thief Montreil refused to postpone a due date… his replacement is strangling me and this time I'm lost!"

"Lost! Come on, you always think like this, that everything's lost," his wife said affectionately, "and it always ends up working out."

"But up until now I could always juggle things around to pull through. Now it's impossible, I've got nothing left. I'm lost!"

"What do you have to pay?"

"10,000 francs in eight days."

"10,000 francs!"

"The amount due is 10,000! And I don't have a 100-franc bill to even start paying it off. And if I don't pay, it's over. I'll have to kill myself…"

"Kill yourself!"

"I'm ruined! Totally ruined… Worse than ruined… Dishonored… It'll mean going to court… and prison!"

"Oh!" Madame Laurent was shocked, "What are you saying? You, Albert, going to court? Why? Why prison?"

"Because of that crook Montreil!"

Laurent was pacing nervously now all around the room, grumbling, "Crooks… crooks…"

Then he decided to tell his wife the problem, understanding how worried she was.

"To pay off the other debts I asked Montreil to lend me the necessary amount. He wasn't satisfied with the collateral I usually offer…"

"Why?"

"Because I needed this money more than ever and he claimed that he was taking too much risk in lending it to me."

"What was the collateral?"

Monsieur Laurent stopped pacing. He did not answer.

His wife asked him again, "What collateral? Wasn't it any good?"

"Sure it was."

"Why did he refuse?"

"He wanted collateral for the collateral…"

"I don't understand."

Laurent hesitated once again.

Then all of a sudden, trying desperately to control himself, he shouted out, "Enough! It's time, I have to tell you everything… because a little later, in a few days, you will learn about everything anyway."

"Yes, yes, tell me. You know you can trust me and my affection, my love for you will never wane."

"Even if I committed serious mistakes?"

"Of course, my love. But what mistakes are so serious, so bad that you won't tell me?'

After struggling, Laurent ended up telling his wife, "I committed forgery!"

Madame Laurent shuddered woefully. "Forgery! You committed forgery! You, Albert! You forged something... Oh, you poor soul!"

"Wait, my dear, let me explain. You'll see that I'm not as guilty as you might believe."

"Tell me... now that the blow's been struck... I can hear everything."

"Counting on your love... on your affection, whose assurance you just gave me once again, I was trying to stay out of trouble... out of danger. I was hoping that you'd never know... that everything would work out and to Montreil, who was demanding it, I gave him your assets, yours, for my collateral."

"But you did the right thing!"

"No, my dear, I gave him your signature... meaning I signed for you... I forged it."

Madame Laurent went to her husband very quietly and said, "Is that all? Well, the forgery wasn't really one because I would've signed anything you wanted. Therefore, when the signature shows up, I'll say it's mine."

Laurent squeezed his wife's hands. "Thank you, thank you."

"So don't worry. I'm not the one who's going to send you to prison because of a signature."

Sorrowfully Laurent added, "There were others."

"Others? You imitated other signatures? Whose? Tell me! Whose signatures?"

"My dear Octavie, your whole dowry... without you knowing I used it all."

"My dowry! Oh well, it's yours as much as mine. But what other signatures?"

"Oh, just one."

"Whose?"

"Montreil was demanding it..." Then he admitted, "Your father's."

This time Madame Laurent was horrified. "My father's! You forged my father's signature?"

"When the whole dowry was put up, I was committing your entire future... your part of your father's inheritance..."

"So?"

"Montreil required your father's signature for it."

"But my father would never accept..."

"I know! I know all too well. You father never forgave us for our love. But his fortune is yours... What he wouldn't give us at our wedding was due to you at his death. It's that future part that Montreil agreed to advance me what I needed."

"Well, didn't you ask my father?"

"No, I signed for him."

"Oh, my poor Albert..."

"I signed the papers that Montreil gave to his friend, the notary, Bejanet. They are the forgeries that allowed me to delay paying everything off for a while... I would get back on my feet again, little by little, and get everything back, pay everything off... And your father would never know... you too. But luck was against me. Then Montreil refused not only to give me new loans but even to roll over the ones that are coming due. If I don't pay in eight days he's threatened to hand everything over to his friend Grillard in collections. Grillard will show everything to your father since I can't pay... and you can imagine what your father will do... You see, I'm lost, ruined!"

15. Aunt Melie

Now Madame Laurent was weeping, faced with this disaster.

"I'm so sorry," her husband said, "I told you why I did it... how I did it and you know what came of my mistake. Now all I can do is ask for your forgiveness for all the trouble I'm going to cause you."

But Madame Laurent was an admirable woman. She did not even think of opposing her guilty husband who was ruining her, destroying her life and once again, in a most tragic way, incurring the wrath of her father.

After spending a few moments lost in sorrow, she dried her eyes and told her husband, "I don't have to condemn you... or forgive you... What is done is done. Right now we have to try to reduce the damage as soon as possible."

"How? There's nothing we can do."

"We have to find a way. A way exists, surely."

"There's only one person... and he is beyond our reach."

"To pay?"

"To pay, yes. Where do you think we're going to get 10,000 francs in eight days?"

"We have to find it. At least look for it."

"Where? Who can we ask?"

"Don't you have friends?"

"Never count on friends when you're in need of money."

"That's true."

"You see, after that wretched banker refused an extension, not only did I call my friends but I took a little trip... to visit relatives. I got nothing. Nobody was willing to help me out of my predicament."

Indeed, Laurent had been absent for a few days, which had made Paulin Broquet think that he had left Paris after the death of the banker.

"Nothing! Nothing!" Laurent complained. "No friends or relatives!"

"Well," Madame Laurent sounded decisive, "we'll just have to get more aggressive."

"How's that?"

"Let's go to my father."

"He won't see me. He'll throw me out and we'll just be insulted even more."

"Maybe not. Anyway, we have to try. Of course my father is going to kick up a storm, yell and scream, rant and rave... but there's one thing that's more important to him than his love of money—it's the protection of his honor!"

"You want me to admit the forgery?"

"No, not that. You will only tell him how desperate you are. I think... I hope... I'm sure he'll listen to you. After all, a man's life is at stake... and the honor of his daughter, his family in fact. My father will consent. I'll write to him. I can't talk about business with him, about money, that's for you two to figure out, but I can smooth the way for your visit."

"You think he'd see me?"

"Yes, after I write to him."

"Oh, what a painful process."

"Come on, be strong. Of course, you're not going to get along with my father but our salvation depends on this meeting... Be strong!"

She took some letterhead and started writing. It was a long letter, difficult to write, and she had to restart several times. It was sprinkled with tears. Then she read it to her husband.

"Yes... it's humiliating to plead," she said, "to beg like this, but now it's done. Basically, when you go see my father, all you'll have to do is get an answer to my letter."

She put it in an envelope, sealed it and told her husband to take it personally to the post office so that it would arrive the next day in Itonville. Overwhelmed, Laurent obeyed his wife without thinking.

After he left Madame Laurent fell into despair for a moment, devastated by her nerves which she had kept under control before her husband. She broke down weeping. But when Laurent came back half an hour later she had washed out her eyes, wiped away all traces of tears and showed her husband a calm, tender, smiling face.

"You leave tomorrow evening for Laigle," she told him. "The next day you'll see my father. You'll spend the day with him... Stay calm... Don't get carried away... Listen to him and try to convince him..." After a moment she added, "We've got another safety line."

"What?"

"If my father refuses, I'll take care of it myself... I'll go see Aunt Melie."

"Aunt Melie! She's a worse miser than your father!"

"We'll see when you get back from my father's. If you succeed, great. If not, I'll go see Aunt Melie."

Monsieur Laurent was sure now of his wife's support and feared nothing more but guilt, or at any rate the cause of the forgery he had committed... He slept rather peacefully.

The next day he went to his office, prepared for his trip, which might last two or three days, and did some shopping in Paris. He figured he would take the train, which would arrive at Laigle at 11 p.m. He wanted to give his father-in-law time to get Octavie's letter. Even if he happened to be travelling in the area on business, which was common. He also wanted to let some time pass, a day at least, between the arrival of the letter and his visit. Like that the mayor of Itonville could lash out, lose his head and have time to calm down. Laurent was hoping, then, to have a little less severe reception.

In the evening, therefore, he headed out for the Montparnasse station. His wife went with him to give him some final encouragement on the platform. Monsieur Laurent was carrying only a tan leather travel bag.

As he was leaving his house, holding the bag and heading for the carriage that his maid had hailed, a porter sitting near his front door promptly jumped up, came over to him and grabbed his bag. The porter opened the carriage door for Madame Laurent and handed the bag to the coach driver. Then, taking off his cap, he asked Monsieur Laurent, who was sitting next to his wife now, what he ought to tell the driver.

"Gare Montparnasse," Laurent answered, handing a few coins to the porter.

The carriage started off. The porter watched it head down the boulevard, then he himself headed for a little café-bar nearby. Right away, to a customer who was drinking at a table, he whispered, "Gare Montparnasse."

The customer paid for his drink immediately and left the café while the porter went to the counter to pay for a drink with Laurent's money.

Once outside the bar the customer jumped into a car that was parked a little farther down the street. All he said was, "Gare Montparnasse."

The car drove off and of course arrived at the station before the carriage with Laurent and wife.

Just as the train was closing its doors, a man carrying a small suitcase jumped into the compartment that would be occupied by Laurent and sat in the corner.

One of the seats opposite the open door and looking directly into the corridor was already taken by a passenger who was wrapped in a blanket and sunk in a pillow, preparing to travel as comfortably as possible.

This man was the one that the porter had talked to at the café. As for the other, the one who had barely caught the train, he was coming from Boulevard Sebastopol.

On the sidewalk across from Laurent's house a peddler had been standing for three or four days, all day long, trying to sell his wares to passers-by. He droned and chanted about his dog chains, key rings, shoestrings and the fragrant Nubian paper... The merchant—was it by chance?—stopped hawking his merchandise when Monsieur Laurent climbed into the carriage. You might say he closed up shop.

He crossed the street and jumped into another carriage that was parked there. Without saying a word to the driver who whipped the horse, which looked like a thoroughbred under its cheap harness, he started following Laurent and his wife.

At the station the carriage in which the peddler had got in let out a well-dressed, if not elegant, man who was carrying a small suitcase. He went up to the ticket counter at the same time as Laurent and bought a ticket for Laigle.

While waiting for the train to depart, this passenger had time to write something in his notebook before stepping onto the platform. Then he ripped out the page and carried it to the carriage driver who was waiting for him. Finally, he hurried down the platform and got on the train as we have seen...

Soon after, the train was rattling down the tracks, carrying Monsieur Laurent and the two mysterious passengers. Standing on the platform after the farewells and tender hugs, Madame Laurent waved goodbye with her dainty handkerchief between spells of drying her beautiful eyes.

Then the train disappeared into the distance and Madame Laurent left the station. She went to the nearest post office and filled out a telegram that said:

"André Girardet, Ville-d'Avray. Albert is gone for two days. Tell me if I can see you tomorrow. Best. Octavie."

She brought the telegram to the counter where the employee counted the words and gave her the price. Staring at the pretty customer he said, "This telegram won't leave before tomorrow, Madame."

"Tomorrow? Well, I'll just have to fix it," she said.

The employee gallantly handed her his pen. Madame Laurent crossed out the word 'tomorrow' and wrote in 'today'. For peace of mind she named the day.

Then she paid and left, saying "Tomorrow I'll see him for sure."

Was this André Girardet... was this the fearsome Aunt Melie?

16. Hotel thieves

For many long years Monsieur Laurent had not seen Laigle. He was once well known there. His marriage to the daughter of the mayor of Itonville had made him popular. But although he had not been back to Laigle, his clients had not abandoned him. They continued to give him business and to give a warm welcome to his salesman after he bought out the company.

However, he had no desire, especially today, to taste the fruits of this popularity and suffer the endless questions of these good people, always eager for news and for a good long conversation.

He used to stay at the Hotel du Grand Laigle. He had to stay there this time as well but luckily the manager had changed and most of the personnel were new too. It was perfect for him. Without stirring up any curiosity he could get a room like any traveler and sleep easy.

The two other travelers were given rooms on the same floor.

In the countryside they go to sleep early. At the Grand Aigle they were just waiting for this train so they could go to bed.

Moreover, when the three travelers had closed their doors, the hotel doors were closed too, the lights switched off and the night watchman (just like Bejanet's) looked forward to a good long nap like you only get in the country. Soon the building was quiet.

The travelers, of course, were probably not asleep when the bell at the front door stirred the watchman awake. It was some motorists having car trouble who wanted to spend the night at the Grand Aigle rather than risk a breakdown on the way to Paris. Making as little noise as possible, they put their car in the garage, then went to the rooms that the night watchman assigned them.

As they went down the corridor where the other guests were staying, they could not help laughing. One of the guests had thought it wise—probably so nobody would trip over them during the night—to hang his shoes, which would be shined in the morning, from the door handle instead of putting them on the floor like everyone else.

"A weirdo," one the motorists said, "either a maniac or a practical Englishman."

Soon there was silence throughout the hotel again.

But one of the guests did not seem able to sleep. He had left his door cracked open and the light from his candle filtered into the corridor. You could even see him passing in front of it from time to time. It looked like he was pacing in his room like a caged jackal.

Maybe he was sick? Maybe he was just smoking one last bowl of tobacco before going to bed...

Nonetheless, very quietly, without a sound, the door of another guest cracked open. Oh, just barely, as if to spy into the corridor. And it closed right away on seeing the light.

But then from another room a shadow slipped out, a man in a tight-fitting gray-blue outfit and rubber-soled shoes—a thief no doubt. Without worrying about the light from the door or the pacing guest, he slipped into the corridor and snuck down to the door with the hanging shoes.

The door opened right away. Obviously, the arrival of the thief was expected on the other side of the door. The man in dark clothes entered the room like a shadow, without a sound... and the door closed behind him.

The other man, at the end of the corridor, continued his pacing after opening his door a little bit more.

The thief—we shall keep calling him this for clarity's sake in this game of doors—the thief stayed only a few minutes in the room. While he was there, the door of the room with the guest carrying a small suitcase once again cracked open but the man still saw the light in the corridor and closed his door again.

A very strange night indeed in which none of these travelers wanted to stay in their room... except Monsieur Laurent who was sleeping soundly and, with all due respect, snoring up a storm.

After four or five minutes the door with the hanging shoes, which was almost exactly across from the man with the small suitcase, opened again... The thief left... But this time, instead of going back up the corridor toward his room, he headed in the other direction toward the stairs and he disappeared, melted into the shadows...

Then the guest at the end stopped pacing. He finally closed his door with a little click... and the corridor was plunged into such deep darkness that the meager gaslight in the middle had almost no effect.

The night would have been completely silent if it were not for the snoring of Monsieur Laurent upstairs and of the watchman downstairs.

A few minutes passed, long and peaceful, and then a third snoring joined in with the low, steady harmony of the other two. The guest who hung his shoes on the door had just dropped off to sleep.

The door of the man with the small suitcase opened for a third time... he heard no strange noises except for the snoring, which was a good omen, and saw nothing suspicious, no more disturbing light in the corridor. He slipped out of his room, went to the hanging shoes and with amazing dexterity he opened the door and entered the room where the thief had just snuck out.

When he was in the room, the thief hiding in the shadows of the stairs popped out in the corridor. With a few swift, agile steps he went to the now empty room of the man with the small suitcase who was paying a visit to the room with the hanging shoes.

At this moment the guest who had just stopped pacing nervously started up again. He must have been very worried. He lit his candle again and went into the corridor, on tiptoes, but still making the floorboards creak and giving himself away.

The door with the hanging shoes cracked open anxiously and shut again right away.

Soon the thief came stealthily, silently out of the room he had snuck into.

The worried man who had reached the stairs and was going to ask for something to drink from the night watchman, turned around and went back to his room, this time locking the door. And once again the trio of snoring bore witness, calmly and innocently, to the blessedness of sleep...

Then the guest with the small suitcase left the room with the hanging shoes and hurried back to his own room where he was soon fast asleep...

This coming and going, this game of doors that transformed the quiet corridor of the old hotel into a wing of the royal palace finally settled down, once and for all, into a peaceful rest.

At the crack of dawn the night watchman came to wake up the traveler with the small suitcase. He got dressed quickly, swallowed a little breakfast and with his suitcase in hand headed out for the station.

A few minutes after he left, the door with the hanging shoes opened, then the door of the worried man who had been pacing and these two guests slipped into the room of the one who had played the role of thief.

The thief was dressed now as a tourist and was sitting at a small table, hunched over a pile of papers that he seemed to be studying very carefully.

"How are you, boss?" the man with shoes asked. "You didn't sleep!"

"Sure I did, of course. I slept until they woke your burglar." And Paulin Broquet started laughing. "You did good work, Gabriel. My compliments." He held out his hand. "You, too, Baiter," he said to the other. "You acted like a pro in your role as worried traveler who bothers everyone and keeps his neighbors up at night. It was great."

Here was Paulin Broquet and his two partners: Gabriel, his best student, and Baiter, whose nickname comes from his marvelous ability to lure people in. He was better than anyone at making others talk, making them trust him or setting things up so that they only needed a little bump to explode.

To explain the presence of Broquet here in the hotel along with his faithful partners, we have to remember that the detective was intending to ask Laurent some questions when he got back to Paris. Broquet knew all about the business trips. One of his agents was constantly watching the short-tempered client of the Montreil Bank, the client whose compromising papers were stolen both from the murdered banker and the notary Bejanet during the mysterious break-in.

At Laurent's doorstep, therefore, was an agent pretending to be a porter. And in the café-bar another agent from the Broquet brigade was waiting for him. The precious evening Gabriel came in person to see how things were going.

Chance, which is sometimes responsible for many things, would have it that he was there for the porter to report to. The car was waiting for him and he just had to jump in and get driven to Montparnasse while giving the driver instructions about what to tell the boss. It was a car in the detective's service and built according to his plans, for his work, answering all his needs...

In the trunk Gabriel found everything he needed to look like a traveler: a small suitcase, a blanket, etc. He could play the role and show up on the train without raising any suspicions. Therefore, following the instructions that he had received, he started following Laurent. But seeing what train he boarded at Montparnasse and suspecting that he might be heading out to see his father-in-law, he thought it better to warn his boss.

Paulin Broquet, in fact, knew all about Monsieur Bilmat and Laurent's marriage to the Itonville mayor's daughter. He knew about Bilmat's hatred for his son-in-law, whom he would never forgive for forcing his hand. He also knew that in the safe at the Montreil Bank and in Bejanet's office there were official documents bearing Bilmat's signature. And Broquet figured that Madame Laurent's father would have proved to be the most generous man in the world if he had signed all those papers for a son-in-law he detested.

If, then, Monsieur Laurent was going to see his father-in-law now, he must be in very dire straits and Paulin Broquet wanted to know the outcome of the meeting on the spot.

The detective, therefore, had driven to Laigle with his partner Baiter. They used a breakdown as an excuse to stop in Laigle.

Gabriel had got word to him about where he had got off and how he could recognize his room without having to ask for him at the hotel. Everything worked like a charm. And Gabriel wanted to see his boss even more because he thought the presence of the traveler with the small suitcase was a little odd.

Broquet's men had learned their lessons so well, they knew their roles so thoroughly that without even planning it they carried it out to perfection.

That was how Baiter, while his boss was with Gabriel, managed to keep the small suitcase from leaving his room, giving Broquet plenty of time to talk with his partner. And Gabriel could give his boss a lengthy report and bring him up to date.

"Good," Broquet said, "we'll know who this guy with a suitcase really is... if he's after you or Laurent..."

"But why Laurent?"

"After what happened at the Montreil Bank and Bejanet's office, all for the sake Laurent's papers... we can't say anything for sure... we have to see. As for you, you're my team, my brigade. That says it all. We have to expect anything. By the way, do you have anything compromising on you?"

"No, not even identity papers."

"Good. Here are two or three letters, papers from a business in Havre. Your name is Guiboiseau. You work there. These are letters taken yesterday from some guy who's going to spend a few days in jail for public drunkenness and insulting police officers. See any problems with being Guiboiseau?"

"None at all, boss."

"Good. I'll put the documents in your coat pocket. If *the suitcase* comes to search it, he'll know everything he needs to know. Let him do it. Get a good night's sleep. See you tomorrow, Guiboiseau!'

Paulin Broquet left his partner and played his role of thief, while *the suitcase* went to search the room of the so-called Guiboiseau. Broquet the thief went into the room of this mysterious character and searched his little suitcase, his pockets and his wallet, getting a good haul of documents. Back in his room he studied the papers for a while and was reexamining them when his two partners came in the morning.

"This gentleman," he told them, "is careful. He's taken precautions that an honest man with nothing to fear would never think of if he didn't want to complicate his life. His cards have different names but no address... The two or three letters I've got here aren't in their envelopes... Two of them don't say anything and the third is all in numbers."

The detective showed them to his men.

"See, what's interesting is that the first two letters look meaningless, harmless... but they're marked in blue pencil with this sign..."

Gabriel and Baiter shouted in surprise, "A 'Z'!"

"Yes, a 'Z'. Just like we found with the murdered banker and the burgled notary. I think I got lucky last night."

"Sure did, boss."

"But here's the most interesting... the weirdest thing... Look."

Broquet held it out, still folded, showing them only half the letter. Gabriel and Baiter leaned over the table. It was a typewritten letter.

"But it's all in numbers!" they were flabbergasted.

"Yes," Broquet answered simply. "I'll decipher it when I have time. What's really important right now, really amazing, is less the hidden text than the signature..."

"The signature?"

"Yes, the signature."

"A 'Z'? Another 'Z'?"

"No, a complete signature?"

"It's complete?"

"Take a look, read... read..."

The detectives cried out at the same time when they saw the name:

"Zigomar!"

Broquet held the letter over his head in triumph and raised his voice in joy, "Yes! It's Zigomar! At last, Zigomar!"

17. At the Mayor's

As evening approached Monsieur Laurent requested a car and was driven to Itonville. Itonville is a small town in the middle of fields around a five or six miles from Laigle.

However, while Laurent was heading off to see Mayor Bilmat, Paulin Broquet and his partners were not sitting idle. Moreover, it must be imagined that the mysterious traveler with the small suitcase was not sleeping on the train either...

Soon after Laurent's departure in the rented car Broquet climbed into the car he had driven down with Baiter. As for Gabriel, who was Guiboiseau now and keeping faithful to the role, they had to pick him up farther down the road.

The car driven with great skill by one of Broquet's agents first made a tour of the town, came back to where it started, cruised around the mayor's property and seemed unsure which way to turn. When Broquet and his men had studied the place enough, seen what they needed to see, they decided to talk to a farmer who gave them the directions they asked for. Then they sped off.

But just as they were taking off, another car arrived with five people inside. It was 5 pm now and night was starting to fall. These travelers were certainly from Paris. They stopped at the only café in town, then two of them headed for city hall. They asked to see the mayor but his office was closed. Nevertheless, they were given directions to his house on the edge of town.

A boy showed them how to get there... receiving a small silver coin for his troubles.

Monsieur Bilmat, we know, was expecting a visit from his son-in-law who had not yet arrived. He was in his office reading the morning papers that had only just been delivered to him. The sound of the door bell made him look up... He thought it was Laurent and was surprised to see someone with him.

The old maid, after opening the garden gate, calmed the two giant guard dogs, Pataud and Miro, who were barking loud enough to wake the whole region. The travelers were also trying unsuccessfully to hush them up. They crossed the yard and entered Bilmat's house, led by the old maid.

"We're very sorry, Monsieur Mayor," one of them said—a young man who looked friendly and elegant with a thin black moustache—"we're very sorry to disturb you by showing up unannounced like this."

"Messieurs," Bilmat was surprised not to see his son-in-law, "please sit down, I am at your service."

"Your countryside is very, very pleasant. We've been told it's full of game... and we'd like to know if there are any hunting grounds open."

The mayor gave the tourists the information they required and after a few minutes chatting about the area and hunting in general... the land they could buy... the tourists did not want to overstay their welcome and bid the mayor farewell, thanking him for his kindness and generosity. They also complimented him on his garden and dogs, being connoisseurs they could appreciate them, and they left.

They went to fetch the two other tourists who were in the café. As they were all getting into the car the latter two said, "Well?"

"It's okay, the dogs got their snack."

"And the house?"

"Easy pickings, like all these dumps. The door no problem, the stairs solid, the rooms on the second floor... It'll be child's play."

But the motorists who were discussing this issue did not get back on the road until they saw Monsieur Laurent ringing the bell at the garden gate of his father-in-law.

After seeing out his visitors, figuring that there was no point in lighting his lamp to read the newspapers, Monsieur Bilmat decided to stay in the garden and smoke his pipe quietly while waiting for dinner and the arrival of his son-in-law, which was certainly less appetizing than the cauliflower soup they were preparing for him at the moment.

When the bell rang, he went in person to open the gate. "Ah, it's you Laurent. Come in... come in."

Monsieur Bilmat thought of his honor and the honor of the town he governed when he avoided showing family disputes in public. The mayor had to set an example for the people. He asked, therefore, about the health of his daughter and answered politely all the questions asked about his own.

"Fine, fine," and he added very naturally, "We have time to smoke a pipe or a cigar before dinner."

He walked with Laurent, talking about grain and cattle and the needle business, about whatever... apples, cider... except what his nervous son-in-law was really interested in. But the mayor of Itonville was of Norman blood as pure as his apple juice and as strong as his cider. He remained impenetrable.

"Oh, my son-in-law," he said sitting at the table, "you've caught me a little off guard. You're not going to have one of those nice little meals you're used to in Paris. Here it's cabbage soup with real cabbage and bacon, real bacon! It'll be a nice change from the food in Paris where everything is artificial. Go on, taste it... you've already had it and enjoyed it... in the past..."

After the soup, they served the bacon. After the bacon a Camembert that came from a neighbor, thus certifying its authenticity and quality. Then they took away the silverware.

The maid, who was a real jack-of-all-trades and took care of the whole house, the kitchen, dining room and bedrooms, brought in a bottle of old hard cider. The mayor of Itonville took out his pipe. Laurent snipped the end of a cigar and the two of them sipped their drinks in silence, starting to smoke.

After quite a long while during which Laurent suffered like the saint whose name he bore, the mayor decided to break the silence, "Generally, after dinner, I don't talk business because heads tend to be a little groggy. I only talk politics because if you say something stupid it doesn't matter... However, with you, being my son-in-law and coming all this way, I'll break my habits."

"I am truly grateful."

"No need. Look, your wife, my daughter, wrote a long letter to me about your affairs. It was very disturbing. So, things are not going well?"

"Unfortunately no."

"Come now, don't get discouraged... don't beat yourself up... it's not worth it. You're a very intelligent young man whose expertise I can appreciate... Your business is working, I know. You must be making good money. You don't have a lot of debts. You don't womanize or gamble... you love your wife, your home, I know all this... So, I don't see how you could get yourself in trouble. Octavie was talking about being ruined... dishonored. I think that's the worst thing possible. Octavie was exaggerating..."

"Not at all," Laurent cried out. "Octavie told you the sad truth."

"Oh, well, what did you do?"

"I tried to speculate, which should have worked out..."

"All speculations ought to work out... and yours, like all the others, have got stuck in a rut..."

"That's it."

"It's forgivable. We can make mistakes."

"Yes."

"I'd like to believe that in the aftermath you didn't sink into a spiral of loans and debts... in which case it would be absolutely unforgiveable."

"I have to say that..."

"A real businessman would never bury himself like that."

"That's true but..."

"When you have to rely on the dishonesty of others to pull through, it's because you yourself are shady."

The mayor of Itonville stopped talking. He poured another glass of liquor and offered it to his son-in-law.

Finally, out of the blue, Bilmat came out with, "How much do you owe?"

This time Laurent shuddered. Was he wrong? Would his father-in-law show pity? He felt self-confident.

"10,000 francs," he muttered.

"10,000 francs! That's a lot... or it's pathetic... it depends."

"For me right now..."

Bilmat asked, "There's a deadline?"

"Yes."

"Well, you'll just have to postpone it."

"Can't."

"But... but if your creditors know you, even like you... They know that you're good for it. they wouldn't want to get you in trouble for 10,000 francs."

"There's only one creditor. He's inflexible."

"Only one! That's more serious. But if you pushed him..."

"He died... suddenly!"

"Damn... That's a problem."

"And the appointed administrator won't agree to anything... he won't budge an inch."

"I understand. It's a big problem but really, among your family, your friends in Paris, you must be able to find someone who could lend you the money?"

"I don't want anyone to know about my troubles."

"I understand that too. But you can certainly get a loan for 10,000 francs in Paris. Didn't you ask around?"

"I couldn't find one."

"Couldn't get 10,000 francs?"

"No!"

"Ah, it's because you're not worth 10,000... and since you've been forced to come to me, which must be really hard for you, and since my daughter wrote to pave the way..."

"You're the only one who can save us."

"So, you're hopeless."

"Absolutely."

"A man like you, who has what you have, if he calls himself hopeless for 10,000 francs he's not a man who can be saved with 10,000 francs."

"I guarantee you..."

"Nonsense. After this 10,000 there will be a whole flood of others that will pour forth... I can see it. Giving you 10,000 francs would be like pouring a glass of water in the desert... useless."

"But what do you mean?"

"I refuse, damn it! What's the use? You don't think that I'll pay all your debts? I won't pay your first any more than the ones that will inevitably follow."

"But monsieur," Laurent cried out in desperation, "it'll be my ruin!"

"I'm afraid so."

"I beg you in the name of your family."

"That you entered in spite of me."

"In the name of your daughter."

"She chose to be your husband over being my daughter."

"For the honor of us all!"

"Yours alone is in jeopardy. Mine here is safe from slander."

"But if my name is dishonored, my wife will also be blemished by my shame."

"She can divorce you. That'll fix it."

"And if I kill myself?"

"She'll be a widow… and can mend her broken life."

"You're heartless, merciless, relentless…"

The mayor of Itonville cut him off by raising his hand. "Come now," he said, "don't be rude. It disturbs me. I'm a simple man from the country… who needs to be told things straightforward… like I say things."

"I was just saying that if I'm not saved from ruin I'll kill myself."

"I told you that the idea of it, death and mourning, won't make me do what I think is foolish. My daughter is my only connection to you, but if you disappear, in one way or another, my daughter will come back to me. So, you can figure it out…"

"Oh, you're a monster!"

"No, just a Norman. A Norman whom you cheated… once! You exploited his kindness, his friendship and stole his daughter. With no more love around he turned pitiless. His heart hardened because you kidnapped what made him tender… So whatever happens to you is your own fault."

He stood up and concluded, "There's nothing I can do about it today."

Then his attitude changed and he said very calmly, "It's time for me to go to bed. I need rest. Tomorrow I have to go supervise some workers. I've had a room prepared for you. I hope you're sleeping here? Okay, I'll leave you. Good night."

He left coldly after shaking the ashes out of his pipe into the fireplace.

18. The car chase

Monsieur Laurent knew that it was useless trying to plead his case, trying to make this stubborn man change his pitiless mind. Soon after his father-in-law left he decided to go to bed and was shown to his room.

He had to pass by Bilmat's room on the way. Thinking of the thick, massive safe that was in his bedroom and that he knew was always stuffed with money and valuables, he could not help sighing and then expressing signs of anger, rage and hatred...

As for Monsieur Bilmat, he fell into that good, deep sleep that seize people who live all day in the open air. He would not have stirred if a bomb exploded next to him.

And the sleeping man was watched over by another man standing at the foot of the bed, ready to act on the slightest movement, holding a rubber mask stuffed with cotton.

In the meantime two men were going through the famous safe that Laurent knew about and in which he knew he could find ten times enough money to save himself. The two men, dressed in dark, tight-fitting clothes, were working calmly but quickly and were completely relaxed.

They chose what they wanted to take away, wedged the stacks of bills between the piles of gold and silver and wrapped up everything, to keep it quiet, in a canvas bag. The bag was strapped shut and slung over the shoulder, leaving hands and arms free to move.

The operation was done and the men closed the safe, stepped away silently, carefully, just like they had come, and left the house without leaving a trace of their visit. They did not cross the garden leading to the road, avoiding the front gate, but instead headed for a kind of little pine forest that stood behind the house. They came up against the wall surrounding the property that was built in the middle of the fields. A thin but strong rope ladder was hanging down. Two men were holding it fast on the other side.

When the thieves had climbed over the wall their partners started pulling in the ladder but froze for a second when they heard a loud whistle nearby. Speechless and surprised they finished their job nervously, trying to understand what the noise meant. Then a man suddenly jumped out of the shadows and stood alone in front of the group of five men.

"Paulin Broquet!" the robbers cried out, immediately pulling their black hoods over their heads.

But they were not fast enough with the hoods. Broquet's piercing eyes had seen their one of their faces... and recognized it.

"Count de la Gueriniere!" he shouted. And he pounced on him, fighting through the others who tried to get in his way.

Facing five men in a fight was not about to stop the detective whose courage was phenomenal. Paulin Broquet had bravely rushed the two men carrying the loot and started fighting. Broquet was a talented boxer so his first punch sent one of the men dressed in black straight to the ground. Now the second was attacking him, the one whom he had recognized as the Count, and he was trying as hard as he could to get him in a hold. The two of them were rolling on the ground…

While wrestling he was yelling out to his men, "Over here… Over here!"

But the partners grabbed him, pulled him off and freed the thief who ran off behind them. The Count de la Gueriniere was escaping from the clutches of Paulin Broquet…

But the detective broke free right away and jumped on him again, punching off the ladder men who were defending the Count. He fought even more fiercely, more passionately. He grabbed the Count so violently that a piece of clothing was ripped off.

But one of the men stepped back and pulled out a club and swung hard at his head. Broquet tried to block it. He only half-succeeded and was hit on the temple. He fell to the ground with a bloody face and passed out. Then his enemies fled.

One of them, however, before running away, leaned over him, looked hard for a second and said in English, "Dead!" And he ran off to join his partners.

Broquet's men came running. Each of them had been watching a part of Bilmat's vast property and had, of course, heard the whistle. They answered by coming as fast as they could. But they were far away so it took them a few minutes to run to the spot. When they got to the scene of the battle it was too late.

The robbers had fled, taking with them the guy that Broquet had hurt badly during the fight. They had not even left the piece of the Count's clothing that the detective had torn off. They jumped into their car, which was parked nearby under some trees, and sped off.

But Broquet's driver had also heard the whistle and had come to lend a hand. As a result, their car was nearby as well, sitting on the road.

Gabriel and Baiter did not waste time checking out their boss. He was breathing and that was enough for them. They carried him to the car and the driver floored the gas after the thieves.

There was only one road the car could take so it was a race to see if they could catch up. It all came down to the engine and tires.

On the road, Gabriel and Baiter pulled out everything they needed to take care of their boss, to bring him around.

The road was straight, perfect for this kind of chase, with rolling hills so that the car ahead would disappear in the distance, then reappear… It was a thrilling chase. They followed the car by its headlights. Soon it looked like the detective and his team were gaining ground.

"We're catching them," the driver said. "We're winning…"

In the backseat Gabriel and Baiter had cleaned Broquet's face with some water. The cold did him good and a little pick-me-up brought him around. Then Gabriel put on a makeshift bandage. Luckily it was only a bad cut.

"I've got a hard head," were the first words out of the detective's smiling mouth. And he asked, "What's going on?"

They gave him a quick rundown of the situation.

"Good. Let's catch up to them… Nab them… We'll have our men, the men who robbed the notary and who killed the banker. We'll have the famous gang of Z and one of those men is the Count de la Gueriniere."

The road continued to stretch out. The two cars continued to eat up the miles.

Now they could see that it was a matter of minutes before the detective's car was even with the thieves. All of a sudden from the back of the car someone started shooting at Broquet's.

"Ah!" the detective said, "They're pelting us!'

He grabbed his pistol right away. Gabriel and Baiter did the same and fired back from the front of the car. But with the rumbling engines and the bouncing tires the gunshots went flying off target. It was bound to be a waste of effort.

A hundred bullets must have gone back and forth in this duel of cars. For naught, as they say.

However, one time when Paulin Broquet took careful aim and fired, one of the thieves fell backward.

"He was hit!" they shouted around the detective.

The shots from the bandit car ceased. They must have run out of ammunition. And the distance between the two cars was getting shorter and shorter.

"Hurry! Hurry!" Broquet was urging on his driver. "Floor it!"

It sounded like the detective wanted to board the auto, like a pirate ship in times of yore…

But with no more bullets for their guns, the thieves were not looking at Broquet and his men. Now they were paying attention to the car. Instead of nails or shards of glass that they knew would do little damage to the tires, they threw out scraps of metal in the shape of a Z, twisted so that one sharp edge was always facing up.

The driver saw the ploy, understood that the thieves were tossing out some kind of weapon, but in the night it was impossible to see exactly what it was… and impossible to swerve around them.

"Keep going!" Broquet told him. "It doesn't matter, we have to catch them."

Luck was on their side. They did not run over any of the Zs that were, in the end, not very numerous.

Then they saw the lights of the first houses of a city. Although at such an hour the city must have been asleep and its streets deserted, they still had to slow down, both because of the pavement and because of the clutter. For, no city, no town in France had decided to stop the annoying habit of considering the street as an extension of the house.

But if they reached the city, they would win. They would surely catch the Count and his partners in crime.

"There will be a fight," Broquet said. "And a hard one... probably..."

"It's okay, boss," the other detectives encouraged. "It's okay. We'll get them back and they'll pay for that wound of yours!"

To prepare for the battle Paulin Broquet and his men armed themselves with mallets, which the thieves were probably doing as well. They could not make the same mistake as before and face the shameless scoundrels unarmed.

In the bandit car were five men and the driver who would no doubt take part in the fight. Broquet had with him only three men, including the driver. But the two-man advantage was evened by the fact that Broquet had injured the guy he had knocked down. And they had seen one of them drop in the car, certainly hit by a bullet.

Now the cars were only 10 or 15 feet apart. The battle, the race was getting heated...

"Don't close the distance," Broquet told his driver. "Stay back. Get ready to slam on the brakes."

Sage advice, in fact.

They had to be ready for the bandit car to stop suddenly, to crash or run into some obstacle, like all car chases end. They needed time to brake, space to come to a stop, without hitting the obstacle themselves, and without crashing into the car they were after.

It was clear now that the thieves knew they were about to be caught and would come up with a new strategy to stop the detectives. Consequently, they needed room to protect themselves.

But the Count's imagination was obviously much less creative than Paulin Broquet believed. Because the fugitives only threw out of their windows some tacks and nails. This time the cars were so close that the bandits, instead of scattering them haphazardly on the road, could lay them, so to speak, right in line with the tires of Broquet's car so that they were unavoidable. It was a good plan... or evil rather... It worked.

When the detectives heard a loud explosion they knew that their tires had been bit and blown out. The driver swore in anger.

"Drive! Keep driving!" Broquet yelled. "Catch them even if you have to ride on the rims!"

Unfortunately, as often happens, the dumbest things can make the best plans fail.

The tire that had just blown went flying off under the car and slapped into the back tire. It was a miracle the car did not flip over. The driver reacted quickly, cutting the ignition and slamming on the brakes.

The two back tires went skating over the road. They left dark skid marks and started smoking but they stopped.

The thieves were sticking their arms out the window and waving their handkerchiefs as a goodbye, shouting in joy and honking their horn, but not slowing down at all.

Broquet's driver jumped out of his car and went to take stock of the damage, shaking his furious fist at the escaping car and shouting, "Bastards!"

Gabriel and Baiter were steaming mad. They turned to their boss...

Faced with this disaster that nothing at the moment could fix, Paulin Broquet was very calm. He pulled out a cigarette, lit it and started smoking silently.

19. *A decorative witness*

"Are you ready, Messieurs?" the fight director asked, holding the adversaries' swords by their tips.

"Yes," the combatants answered.

"Okay… Allez, messieurs!"

He stepped back, opening the strip that had been carefully prepared by a dutiful gardener, and with a cane in hand he watched over all the lunging and parrying of the combat.

This fight director, the first witness of the Count de la Gueriniere, was a man around 55 years-old, well-groomed, with a white beard, a full head of curly hair, dressed in a perfectly tailored frock coat and pants that covered light-colored gaiters. He wore a rosette in his buttonhole.

He was a very decorative witness. They called him Baron Dupont and he was well known in high society and the sporting world.

The duel was taking place on a private property around Ville-d'Avray. Although the meeting was, according to custom, absolutely private and nobody was allowed to watch except the witnesses and doctors, there were 100 spectators hiding (to some degree) behind the curtains in the villa and even peaking out of the attic windows.

In fact, the duel was sure to be sensational. It was pairing two fine blades with hard-earned reputations: the journalist Marc Collas and Count Faustin de la Gueriniere.

While writing about the murderer of the banker Montreil, Marc Collas had hinted that the Count might be guilty. The journalist had said that the Count was present at Montreil's when he was murdered and had been summoned by the court. He added insidiously that there was a potent rumor that he might be there for a long time, that they should not be surprised if the judge kept him very late…

It was a way saying quite clearly, even for those who could not read between the lines, that he believed the Count was going to be arrested. The column made a big splash when it came out.

The Count sent two of his friends to the journalist right away. As it happened, it was the morning when Paulin Broquet was at the Count's waiting for him to return from his walk in the woods.

Marc Collas, whose bravery was unquestionable, had witnesses who declared that he had not overstepped the rightful boundaries of a reporter and they refused any compensation or reparation for the Count until a formal statement exonerating the Count could prove that Marc Collas was wrong in his allegation.

Moreover, when Montreil's sudden and baffling reversal claimed the innocence of the Count de la Gueriniere, the accused was eager, or so one would think, to give this news as much publicity as possible, by any means possible, and so he had sent his friends to the journalist a second time.

The duel was set. It would take place in the morning.

Marc Collas and the Count de la Gueriniere, after the solemn "Allez, messieurs!", were now engaged in a valiant battle. Although they had never faced each other before, they both knew each other's strength and that they had to use not only all their courage but all their knowledge and skill as well.

They were an equal match, both being excellent swordsmen. At first they felt each other out, studied and sparred, if you can call it that. The first bout was spent like this, studying, without either side attacking outright, just darting in and out. They parried each other's strikes like it was a game and pulled back every thrust that might have led an attack.

The second face-off was the same although the Count seemed to be more on the offensive... Still, the result was the same.

Thus it went for three or four rounds.

The journalist was now putting more energy, more daring into his attacks. He was gaining ground. The Count blocked him, held him at bay with remarkable agility and resilience, but was kept on the defensive.

The battle was truly passionate and attracted the admiration of all the amateur spectators. After every skirmish they applauded.

Marc Collas was soon attacking fully and, seeing that he was gaining ground, more fervently. He made the mistake of wanting to push his opponent to the limit and he was using up more and more of his strength and energy. The Count answered with the same alertness and the same calm as at the start.

They gave back some lost ground according to the rules.

Marc Collas attacked furiously, hastily. It was obvious that the nimble defense was upsetting him, annoying him, and he wanted to finish him off.

The Count stayed calm, smiling, blocking the feverish blows with the greatest of ease. But he lost ground again. With every attack he got closer to the edge. And now they would not give it back to him.

Marc Collas made the same mistake as at first in trying to push the Count to the edge and if not being able to strike him, at least to throw him off balance.

The duel had already lasted almost an hour without any other result but a few scratches. The Count had no more than five or six feet behind him now. Baron Dupont was warning him.

Even though Marc Collas was lunging hard and swinging furiously at his enemy who stayed on a straight line in front of him, he was also showing signs of fatigue. The Count looked as fresh as at the start, dodging, blocking, keeping his thin moustache formed into a cold, cruel, enigmatic smile.

Collas charged. He wanted to finish this with all his might. He tried to hit the epée and lunge forward. The Count did not parry the blow, his epée went down with his enemy's, offering no resistance, but it came back up swiftly and once horizontal, freed, alone, it lunged...

The Count only had to stretch out his arm and Marc Collas, left open by his wild swing, did not have time to get back en garde, to parry the blow and defend himself. He had got himself caught in a trap of his own making… fatally.

The Count's blade, which should have pierced the chest, stuck in the arm thanks to an instinctive move by Collas. It went through the biceps and came out the other side. Collas dropped his epée and was carried away by his witnesses.

As for the Count, he had drawn back his weapon from the wounded arm and was calmly, still smiling, holding the bloody blade out to his second who was throwing a coat around his shoulders. Then he saluted the witnesses and the curious onlookers who slowly moved in around the battle. With a discreet nod of his head he went to get dressed.

The gardener who had prepared the strip and watched the combat started, very philosophically, to rake the gravel back where it belonged. When everyone, the winner, the wounded, the witnesses and the onlookers had gone, the gardener shuffled out through a small door in the wall that exited directly onto the street, which was deserted of all the cars now. Well, almost deserted. For, one car was parked near the small door.

The gardener looked right and left. Seeing no one around he jumped into the car, which started up right away. Inside was a man who excitedly asked the gardener:

"Well, boss?"

"A magnificent battle!"

"Who won?"

"The Count de la Gueriniere."

And Paulin Broquet took off his gardener clothes, saying, "He's too lucky."

"For now, boss," Gabriel said, "but you'll have your revenge."

"Let's hope so." He lit a cigarette. "The most surprising thing in this matter is not the Count's victory, since he's an excellent duelist, but the duel itself."

"What do you mean?"

"I'm not surprised that he got the better of Marc Collas, which I'm truly sorry for because he's a good swordsman too and a really nice guy—so, it's not so much that the Count won but that he was even there in the first place."

"Why's that?"

"Because last night the Count and his men were in Itonville, paying a secret visit to the mayor, Monsieur Bilmat."

"Exactly."

"And because around two or three in the morning I gave the Count a good thrashing… I can swear I hit him hard… I knocked him down, gave him a black eye, a bloody nose…"

"I know, I know."

"My punches should have left traces."

"No doubt, boss."

"He should have been marked up… So, this morning, a few hours after our fight, the Count de la Gueriniere should have shown the signs it all over his face."

"Very likely."

"Well, that's what's surprising, really astonishing, what I can't understand. The Count who just fought the duel looked completely calm and fresh, rested and relaxed… and not the slightest trace of our fight."

"Impossible."

"He was a little pale, like always when someone steps onto a dueling field. So the 'wallops' should have really stood out more than usual."

"Absolutely right."

"But even though I looked hard where I knew I socked him, I didn't see anything… nothing! As if the Count's face had never touched anything harder than cold cream! His face showed no signs of my fists. And because I'm sure I thrashed him and even more sure that it should've left marks that would last for days, I have to admit, that the Count has another face… that he has a spare head!" He let that sink in before concluding, "And that's what really surprises me."

Then he kept silent for the rest of the ride.

20. Showdown at the gate!

Paulin Broquet got taken home. He lived in a house on a corner, one side looking onto Avenue Trudaine, the other onto Rue Rodier. For years he had lived in an apartment here that he kept up with good taste, comfortably furnished.

Broquet was a new kind of detective. Policemen like Lecoq or Vidocq and others who had their time in the spotlight had completely disappeared. Today in France, just like in England, a new race of detective had been born.

No longer the violent, vulgar policeman, sometimes ex-criminal whose only difference from the culprits he arrested was that he was holding the handcuffs. Detectives like Paulin Broquet are completely different. Today they are educated, polite and friendly.

The bonding of police does not exist now like in the past. It cannot. It would be out-of-date, inappropriate in modern life which makes demands that are much more imposing, multi-faceted and complex than 50 years ago. Outside the job, which he has elevated by the way, which he has turned into a real art, the modern detective is a perfect gentleman.

As for Paulin Broquet, the most famous of all, the model that others look to as a guide and try to imitate, he was a man of taste, an artist and accomplished sportsman. He wielded a sword like a master. He always won the city competitions with ease where all the great fencers came from the world of the press and the arts. For two years he was the champion of the individual challenge in "Combat Arms".

He lifted weights like a professional. And in boxing he had, during his stay in London, fought honorably against the most famous pugilists. Thanks to him the Japanese fighting style, the famous jiu-jitsu, was spread among the police. He rode a horse like a cowboy, knew how to drive all kinds of steam-powered vehicles on rails or water, and had walked off with cups in both automobile and yacht racing.

Besides all that he was refined, well acquainted with literary movements, with the theater, and an enthusiast of music, even accomplished at piano playing and painting. He knew several languages and above all spoke English like a native.

He had chosen Gabriel, Baiter and a few other officers that he trained because they met his criteria and he wanted to make them ready to act on all levels of modern society, from the highest to the lowest, without anything giving them away—lack of taste and polish in clothes, manners or conversation.

"We can find scoundrels everywhere, not just among the rabble," he said. "Sometimes we have to make the rounds of the grand dukes." Here grand dukes meant society people, party people, the glossy and glamorous...

108

Jules was a good kid, devoted body and soul to him, who was naturally considered one of his agents but worked as his butler. Jules' mother did the cooking. Paulin Broquet trusted his servants like his lieutenants. His house was well guarded and perfectly maintained, run like the military.

When Broquet, who had put his city clothes back on in the car, arrived home, it was noon. The duel had started at ten. His lunch was waiting for him.

"Anyone come by?" the detective asked his butler.

"No one, boss."

"No news, no calls, nothing?"

"No, boss."

"Okay, we'll wait. Let's eat."

The table was set for two. Broquet and Gabriel sat down and ate a hearty lunch.

"Nothing builds up an appetite like a good duel!" Broquet laughed.

Afterward they went into the sitting room where Jules served them coffee. Broquet held out a box of cigars to his partner, choosing one himself. He leaned back in a rocking chair and sipped his coffee, which he drank a lot of.

Savoring his cigar, he said, "While I was the gardener and hiding behind bushes, I saw every twist and turn during that excellent duel. One thing in particular interested me: it was the fight director."

"Baron Dupont!" Gabriel said.

"Yes, Baron Dupont. Very chic in his frock coat and gaiters... decorated and decorative... very much the director of the matter of honor... Where have I seen him before? Where have I seen those sharp, penetrating eyes? That's what I'm asking myself, what I've been trying to figure out this whole time."

Paulin Broquet furrowed his brow and started rolling his eyes up slowly toward the ceiling, following the trail of cigar smoke as if he might see the name of this ideal director, this elegant gentleman who participates in such sensational fights of honor.

Jules came in and interrupted the reverie that Gabriel was careful not to disturb. He announced Simon.

"Oh, good, show him in."

Soon afterward Simon, one of the detective's main agents, a stocky man with strong hands, a thick neck and a hard, bony head—everything about him exuded strength. But above the big, brutal chin his face was brightened up by two sparkling little eyes, a terribly stubby nose and a mouth that constantly looked like it would break out in a smile. Simon had been a clown and a fighter. He lifted weights, boxed when he had time and played like a pro in all the roles his new profession demanded.

He came in smiling and looking straight at his boss with those devoted puppy-dog eyes, capable of devouring anyone at a simple sign from his master.

"Sit, sit," Broquet told him. "Have a cigar and a cup of coffee, then tell me what you found out."

"Okay, boss," the former clown said, "it's simple. The Count de la Gueriniere, who you told me to get an eye on after you took off in the car, didn't…"

"Right, you never lost sight of him?"

"No, boss, not for a second."

"Good, go on."

"He didn't do anything different. He did a little shopping during the day. He went to an armorer in the afternoon near Bastille where he picked out a couple of epées. Then met his witnesses, Baron Dupont and the Count de Marnais at the club. Around eight o'clock he went on his usual walk around Rue de la Paix. He went all the way up to Avenue de Clichy…"

"Ah, again!" Broquet blurted out. "Still after that working girl?"

"Riri. Yes, boss."

"Do the Montreil brothers know about this?"

"No, boss. I didn't see the lawyer… but I know the doctor had been to see his patient, Madame Menardier. They told me at the pharmacy that he had ordered some medicine for the poor woman whose days are numbered."

"Let's get back to our gentleman."

"At Ganneron Alley he watched Riri, a really wonderful girl, gorgeous…"

"Okay, okay, just tell me about the Count. He's the one you're supposed to be watching and not the pretty girl."

"Sure… and that's a pity, boss. I'd rather… but the Count, okay. He took a cab and went back to the club. He had dinner there with his witnesses…"

"He didn't leave the club?"

"No, boss. A guy took over for us and waited on him until he went to the theater, to the Lutetia. So, I was in an orchestra seat in front of his box and I swear that he couldn't have made a move all evening without me seeing."

"Okay. And after?"

"After the show he went to eat in a restaurant around Madeleine. I was sitting right next to him there and couldn't lose sight of him."

"You like these stakeouts where you get to eat?"

"Sure, boss… except you don't always get to digest the meals. In fact, I followed the Count and pretty Lucette Minois all the way to the star's home. And was there until four in the morning watching the house… from the street."

"It does you good to get some fresh air."

"Sure, boss… At 4 am the Count went back home and straight to bed… and his witnesses came to wake him up around 10. You know the rest."

Broquet replied, "So, you're sure, absolutely sure, that it was really the Count de la Gueriniere you were following all night… all the way to the site of the duel?"

"Yes, boss."

"No way you were wrong?"

"No, boss. I swear to you, it was him! It was really him!"

"Okay. The thing is, my dear Simon, while you were ogling Lucette Minois on stage, for whom you have a soft spot..."

"Me, boss?"

"Yes you. Just like for Pretty Riri..."

"But boss!"

"Women are going to play you some dirty tricks... but forget it. While you were dining with the Count, because you're as big an eater as you are a lover..."

"But boss..."

"Be quiet. Gabriel, Baiter and I were chasing the Count up in Normandy, in Itonville."

"No..."

"Yes! I even had the pleasure of serving your dinner partner my own kind of punch, which knocked him out, floored him, passed out, even tore up some of his clothing."

Simon looked stupefied. His beady eyes blinked, his nose was quivering and his gaping mouth was the funniest thing in the world. So clownish indeed that Paulin Broquet and Gabriel could not help laughing out loud.

But the detective put an end to the old clown's astonishment. "You carried out your mission beautifully, Simon," he said. "You told me what I absolutely needed to know. See, while you were whooping it up here in Paris with the Count de la Gueriniere, I was over there knocking the lights out of the same Count. Plus, I noticed that the Count I hurt in Laigle showed no signs of it in Paris... Now we just have to find out how he did it?"

The three men fell silent. Broquet started blowing smoke rings with his cigar. Suddenly he cried out.

"That's it!"

The detectives jumped and looked anxiously at their boss.

"I've got it!" Broquet told them. "I've got it! I know who it is!"

"Who, the Count?"

"No!"

"Zigomar?" Gabriel asked. "You finally figured out who this mysterious Zigomar is?"

"Maybe... Maybe I've found out who Zigomar is... This Zigomar who the criminals of Paris whisper about with admiration, veneration... But Zigomar's time has not yet come. Right now I'm talking about the guy who looks like a worker without a job, the bearded, dirty guy who looks like a drunk, all shabby and foul... remember when I brought the Count to the banker's for his confrontation, this guy was at the door, insulting the Count, shouting, 'Yer number's up! It's all over for you!' I wanted to arrest the guy but he disappeared in the crowd. Well, the old boozer was none other than the upright, well-dressed, very decorative gentleman Baron Dupont!"

Simon blurted out, "Baron Dupont?! The Count's second at the duel? He dined with us!"

111

"Exactly. The witness, the director of the duel, the friend of the Count, the Baron Dupont and my drunken thug are one and the same."

This statement the detectives stop and think. Paulin Broquet, however, remained very calm as he stood up.

"Let's talk about something else." He went to his desk, opened a drawer and pulled out a letter. "This is the ciphered letter. It's been translated."

"Oh, boss, what's it say?"

"This."

With a pencil on a big sheet of paper Paulin Broquet wrote two lines, letter by letter. His men stared at him, spelling out the words as they came out.

KEEP... LOREN

SUNDAY... KLAF

Broquet translated out loud: "Keep Laurent... Sunday Klaf!"

"Klaf?" the detectives questioned.

"Sure. Klaf... meaning Clafous."

"Clafous!"

"Clafous. No doubt about it. Klaf is an abbreviation for Clafous."

"You're right, boss."

"Clafous... the owner of the café... of the bar "Les Enfants de l'Aveyron" that's on Boulevard de la Chapelle. You know that Clafous' is where all the most notorious criminals meet. They make their plans there. And they wrap up business, make their payouts."

Simon said, "Hey, boss, I should also tell you that I found out some of the Zigomar gang was meeting at Clafous."

"That's great, Simon." Broquet continued, "As for the KEEP LORAN, here's what it means: it's the order that Zigomar gave to the man whose pockets I picked. His mission was to watch Laurent... KEEP an eye on him..."

"The Laurent who..." the detectives started to say.

"Yes, Monsieur Laurent, the last one in the Montreil Bank at the time of the murder... the last one or at least at the same time as the famous Count."

"Aha, now we're starting to get it."

"Good, because it's obvious. Monsieur Laurent was at the Montreil Bank at the time of the banker's murder. He was the one who went into the office before or after the Count, but certainly one of the last two."

"It's Laurent whose papers, oddly enough, were thrown into the fire and half-burned in the banker's fireplace. It's Laurent whose file was the only one found taken out and rifled through while all the others sat undisturbed in the safe."

"Indeed."

"It's Laurent whose file was looted again in Bejanet's safe. And Laurent, finally, who left traces everywhere we found a Z marked in blood or even only in sand..."

Broquet added, "Notice also that Monsieur Laurent was sleeping at his father-in-law's, Bilmat, who he doesn't get along with, on the very night we were chasing the people who, as we'll learn very shortly, certainly robbed the mayor's fat safe."

"So, keeping Laurent meant…"

"It's Zigomar's order to the man with the small suitcase… the man who was the hotel thief and whose papers I decrypted. It's the order that they gave this man to keep an eye on Laurent, not to lose sight of him, to follow him, just like our good Simon had a mission to keep an eye on our glamorous, carefree Count. That's what it means."

Paulin Broquet stubbed out his cigarette or rather the butt of the spent cigarette that was about to burn his lips. He rolled another, lit it and went on.

"But the letter from which I transcribed those two lines was full of other surprises, as I told you. Those two lines were not the only ones on the page. On the back was another document that I didn't see at first because it was written in pencil and very faint… These other lines were of great use to me, as I said, allowing me to form a table to decipher everything easily. Here's what I read. I'll translate it but I'm afraid that this time I only deciphered the statement of a problem… or a puzzle that'll be harder to solve than figuring out what it says. Here goes."

Again on the big sheet of paper Paulin Broquet wrote out in big letters with blue pencil:

BRING… BARON… NEKL…
NIGHT… BALL… MAHON…

While writing he said, "Putting it into full words reads: Bring the Baron necklace, tonight, ball, Mahon. Which doesn't tell us a whole lot."

"That's true, boss."

"The words can be interpreted in all kinds of ways. Here are some that I think are the closest to the truth. We'll probably have to choose which one of them we prefer. Listen."

Then Broquet recited: "Bring the Baroness to see the necklace or for the necklace or because of the necklace… the night of the ball on Avenue MacMahon.

"Another version: Bring the Baroness her necklace or with her necklace to Avenue MacMahon the night of the ball.

"A third version: Bring her to Avenue MacMahon for the necklace that she will give or buy… or that they'll take from her the night of the ball.

"In brief, there are all kinds of versions but basically they all have a Baroness, a necklace, a ball and Avenue MacMahon.

"Knowing the man who possessed this curious paper, in what world he lives, to what category of special citizens he belongs, we can pretty much guess, with no fear of being wrong, what it's about."

"We're thinking the same as you, boss."

"It's about a Baroness or a woman called the Baroness who has a valuable necklace that she's wearing to a ball… and they want to take from her."

"Yes, it's gotta be that, boss. It's what we're reading in it too." The lieutenants agreed.

"Right. But how are they going to get the necklace from her? That's where I'm stuck. Is the baroness going to bring it to Avenue MacMahon? Is the ball on Avenue MacMahon? Does the Baroness live there? This is what I really can't figure out. It's not enough to just decipher the words, we need the key to what they mean."

After a pause Paulin Broquet almost shouted, "And yet we have to clear up this mystery! We have to foil their plans… find the key… uncover the true meaning of this document. My friends, we have to do whatever it takes to defeat Zigomar!"

"Yes, boss. Just tell us what to do."

"Well, my friends, I need your advice. I don't know what to do."

"Oh. It's not gonna be easy."

"I have no doubt. But when it's too easy, it's not interesting." Then he concluded, "My friends, let's search. Search everything, everywhere. Remember the note."

The detectives repeated, "Bring Baron Nekl Night Ball Mahon."

"That's it."

"Okay, boss. Now, let's go."

21. Raymonde the partner

While these events were unfolding both in Normandy and around Ville-d'Avray, there was another scene developing in Montreil's house that, although not so dramatic, was no less important.

After being questioning in the prison infirmary the two brothers had been set free. Despite the damning charges against them, it was judged unnecessary to keep them in custody. The judges were convinced and the allegations of Paulin Broquet were coming to light one by one. Robert and Raoul were no doubt guilty of intending to rob the notary's safe—we know why—but they did not get there in time and became themselves the victims of more daring, more skillful and certainly more experienced criminals.

Paulin Broquet got a car brought up to the courthouse. Without anyone seeing them the two brothers climbed in. They had to get home in good time so that no one would notice they had been gone all night and they could have breakfast with their mother who would thus be spared any unnecessary anxiety.

Without attracting the attention of the servants or anyone else, Robert and Raoul managed to sneak back into the house on Rue Chalgrin. They went to their rooms. But waiting there for them was a big surprise. In their salon, sitting in an armchair and reading, was their sister who looked like she had been waiting for a long time.

"Raymonde!" they blurted out, astonished.

The young lady jumped up, threw down her book and ran to her brothers. "There you are! Oh, I'm so relieved! Are either of you hurt?"

"Hurt?"

"Did you kill him?"

"Kill? Who? Who do you think we were supposed to kill?"

"The Count de la Gueriniere…"

The two brothers were startled. "The Count de la Gueriniere!" they repeated. "Why do you think that? What could make you think such a thing?"

"It wasn't him? You didn't go to fight him?"

"Of course not, Raymonde."

The young lady stared at her brothers, not believing a word. "You can tell me. I'm with you all the way."

"We swear to you that we had no point of honor to settle with the Count."

"Oh," Raymonde was disappointed. "I don't know then… I don't get it. I thought… I was hoping… and seeing you come back so late I just imagined… but since that's not it, I won't ask you anything else."

Robert and Raoul replied, "Excuse us, Raymonde, but right now we're the ones who are going to ask you why you thought that, why you were hoping that we challenged the Count."

Raymonde Montreil was a very pretty girl, elegant and absolutely charming. Her black eyes had a velvet caress, as the saying goes, but sometimes also when she lowered her brown eyebrows, they sparkled like black diamonds. In these moments her mouth, which was generally smiling, narrowed slightly, her chin lost its cute little dimple and her whole face was possessed by a cold, untamable energy that recalled her father's willpower.

Willpower and energy that, as we have seen, her two brothers had inherited as well.

Raymonde had heard the question that Robert and Raoul had asked her, staring at her anxiously, fervently, but she did not answer. Instead, she went and sat calmly in an armchair by the fireplace. Casting her gleaming eyes at them once again, she finally decided to respond.

"I was thinking... I was hoping that you were fighting the Count," she said in a calm, firm voice, "because one of you has to kill him."

"But my dear Raymonde," Raoul cried out, "why would you say such a thing?"

"You know very well why..."

"Let's see if we're thinking the same thing."

"Well," the young lady declared coldly, "I'm sure that the Count de la Gueriniere murdered our poor father."

Robert and Raoul jumped.

Raymonde went on, "It's my conviction and it's yours! I don't know exactly what happened in our father's room when the judges were there... but I do know that our father, whom we all saw getting better, had formally named the Count as his murderer. That's right, isn't it?"

"Yes," the brothers agreed.

"I also know that after a short conference with Messieurs Bejanet and Grillard our father denied his declaration and then suddenly fell sick again, very sick and he proclaimed the Count's innocence... before he died, murdered by whatever happened during those few minutes... on top of the stabbing."

"We believe so too."

"Moreover, our father's funeral was not what it should have been, I believe. People were afraid to show up, to be recognized. Why? During those days of grieving, all the people who had come to our parties stayed away. Why? I thought you'd gone to find out the reason for this offense..."

"You're right."

"I thought you went to Monsieur Bejanet to get the secret..."

"We did."

"And he refused to reveal it to you as he should have. So, you went to take it by force, with sword and pistol in hand, from the Count de la Gueriniere who should have known it..."

The two brothers shuddered. "What's this? You suspected us too? You also believed that?"

"I'm your sister. I share your filial love for our poor father. I want as much as you to save the memory and honor of his name... whatever the cost. Listen, we have to find the key to this agonizing mystery..."

Just then a sound from the door cut her off.

She turned to her brothers and said, "Go see who it is."

When Robert went to open the door, someone knocked on it. The doctor was startled but said, "Come in."

Marcelin appeared. "I just came to see if the messieurs needed anything before breakfast is served."

"No, no, we're fine. You should only come up here when you're called. Leave us alone."

When Marcelin left Raymonde and her brothers looked very curious, even worried for a few moments. The two brothers were thinking of the night before when they felt the same anxiety and also of the meeting here with Paulin Broquet when the same thing happened with this strange Marcelin.

"He was listening to us," Raymonde said. "He was standing at the door for a while and listening to us!"

"You really think so?"

"Yes!"

"What for? Why would he do that? He's a loyal servant..."

The young lady shook her head. "I don't trust him. I don't know why but despite seeming to be loyal he makes me makes me nervous, suspicious."

Raymonde's misgivings only deepened her brothers' suspicions.

"We'll keep an eye on him," Raoul said. "Besides, if he was listening, he'll be disappointed... He couldn't have heard anything..."

"I hope so." And Raymonde continued, "So, I caught you... last night, I was watching."

"You were watching? Did you see us?"

"I was watching and I saw you leave."

"What did you think?"

"I knew you were going to fulfill the sacred mission that has fallen upon us."

"That was what we planned, true."

"And this morning I managed to distract our mother's worried thoughts when she started wondering where you were. And I waited for you to come back."

"That's good, Raymonde. Nothing gives us more hope and courage than your approval. Nothing can assure our victory more than your support."

"I still need to tell you that you have an ally."

"An ally?"

"My fiancé."

"Captain Rennebois?"

"He's got a good heart. He's a good man! I gave him my love because I admire his soul... It's equal to yours. Therefore, I shared my worries with my fiancé about the death of our father. I told him that I would only become his wife when we have torn away the veil of mystery, when we have received justice and vengeance for our sorrow, which ought to be considered a public insult, a disgrace."

"And how did the captain respond?"

"You can count on him like a third brother."

"Thank you, thank you, Raymonde."

"Now I'll leave you. Get dressed. Don't make mother wait any longer and don't let the noble, saintly woman suspect anything or know anything about our plans. Don't cause her any more suffering!"

After Raymonde left Robert and Raoul discussed how they felt about what their sister had just told them, then they searched the whole room.

"Are you sure, Raoul, that you didn't take your sword yesterday?"

"Absolutely. And you didn't take yours."

"No."

"And yet there's a sword missing."

"And it's ours... The blade was used on the night watchman."

Raoul concluded, "So, someone took it yesterday after we'd left... to frame us... and struck when we were knocked out in Bejanet's office. Therefore, our enemies got one of their men inside our house here last night."

Just then Marcelin showed up at the door and announced, "Breakfast is served."

22. Two great detectives

In the morning Paulin Broquet entered the office of Monsieur Baumier, the chief of police. "I got a message," he told him, "from Tom Tweak, the grand American detective, asking to meet me here in your office this morning."

"He sent one to me too."

"We should only be meeting if one of us has interesting news to give."

"So, he must have something."

"No doubt. I've already said that if he finds anything that we don't already know, he's better than we could ever say because without blowing our own horns too much, chief, we've done good work in this affair... and if it were only up to us, a long time ago we would have..."

"Sure, but Montreil tied our hands."

"And since nothing else has happened, we can't do any more than we've been doing."

"Maybe the American can bring us something?"

"We'll find out. Here he is."

Tom Tweak had just shown up. He was beaming. He shook the chief's hand and gave a warm, vigorous but rather rough handshake to his colleague Paulin Broquet.

"Oh, chief," he started, "you're about to hear more praise for your marvelous Paulin Broquet..."

"Coming from you will make it twice as sweet."

"Too bad if he's here to hear it. I have to tell you what I think of him."

Broquet was standing by his chief's huge desk, leaning against the wall, one foot crossed casually over the other. He was carefully (as usual) rolling a cigarette, which he lit when finished. Then he looked at the American, who was still talking, and stared hard at him, smiling all the while.

"My dear friend," the American detective was saying, "your international reputation is not mere legend. You are more than astonishing... you're fantastic... yes, yes... sure enough."

"What makes you say such a thing?" Baumier asked.

"Whenever I got a lead I thought was worthwhile... Paulin Broquet had already explored it. Whenever I got on a trail I thought was hot... Paulin Broquet had already been over it. Whenever I thought I'd found some indispensible clue... Paulin Broquet had already investigated it. When I was about to get my man... Paulin Broquet had already rejected him. Everywhere, all the time, Paulin Broquet was ahead of me... he'd searched and scoured and without saying a word, without looking like it, without a sound... He's holding all the cards. I'm telling you, it's unreal, colossally stunning!"

During this flood of compliments, Broquet was smoking calmly, without changing his position, without moving an inch, looking like a sturdy statue with lively eyes and a strange, enigmatic smile.

The American went on, "They talk about Sherlock Holmes... he's a master, sure, but I think, with all these complications, he couldn't do what you did very simply, without any tricks or games. As for Nick Carter, Nick the blowhard, he ought to be your student... to learn about logic, willpower and truth."

Tom Tweak stopped talking and turned to look at Broquet who was still smiling his cryptic smile which you could not tell if it was ironic, skeptical or glad to be hearing such praise.

The two men stared at each other for a moment, just like they did the first time they had met.

Then the American said, "My dear Paulin Broquet, I declare you the greatest, strongest, most astonishing detective in the world."

After another moment of silence Broquet replied very softly, "My friend, you flatter me."

"No, no, I'm telling the truth... exactly what I think."

"You're really too kind."

"No, just fair. You're incredibly fantastic!'

"In that case, I can return the compliment and say the same about you."

"How's that?"

"Well, you, too, did what I did and what you think is so fantastic... and in your eyes it's even greater because it happened here in Paris, my city, and not in New York, yours."

"Yes, exactly. I'm also a great detective..." After a big laugh the American concluded, "So, we're both the greatest detectives in the world."

Paulin Broquet asked him, "So, something happened to you?"

"Yeah... a big thing... it'll astonish you."

"I'm sure."

There was another short moment of silence.

Then the American resumed, "I retraced the whole Montreil investigation starting with the banker's murder."

"The result?"

"Great! I know where the stolen documents are."

"The documents that we didn't know about," Broquet remarked. "See, you're even better than we are."

"No, wait... I also investigated the men who were with the banker last... the night of the crime."

"The Count de la Gueriniere," the chief of police said, "and Monsieur Laurent."

"Yes!" The American detective started to smile and shrugged his shoulders. Then he scowled, "Poor fellows, to pull off such a trick! Oh, just to think of it... The yellow bellies!"

"But the Count is a renowned duelist."

"Yeah, yeah, duelist... in public before an audience, pricking the arm of his enemy, super... it's all a show but to fight well in a duel doesn't mean that you can kill a banker in his office."

"No, true enough."

"Basically the Count likes parties, the night life... very much in love with Lucette Minoir... and that's all."

"And Monsieur Laurent?"

"Him, the poor guy who's fighting over a few thousand francs? He's very much in love with his wife... very middle-class, manufacturing chemicals... ridiculous." And he concluded, "Yes, neither one of them is a killer."

"Ah," is all that the chief said.

Broquet asked, "In your opinion, who was it?"

"The other."

"The other?"

"Yeah, the guy's big, tall and with some weight on him... he's the real adversary of Paulin Broquet."

Baumier the chief sank back in his chair as if to listen better, to follow more closely what the American was so proudly declaring. As for Broquet, he had not moved, was still smoking and staring at his beloved, transatlantic colleague.

Tom Tweak was talking directly to Broquet now. "This other guy's powerful... strong... yes, a lot stronger and extremely bad."

"Really?"

"This guy... is Zigomar!"

Baumier and Broquet reacted at the same time. "Zigomar!"

"Yeah, Zigomar," the American repeated. Then he said, "The other day when my friend Broquet was talking about this famous Zigomar, I didn't understand..."

"And yet..."

"Sorry but I thought it was... how should I say it... a Parisian catchword, slang, for someone unknown... a fiction, made up, like Whathisname or Thingamajig..."

"Or John Doe."

"Exactly, John Doe."

"But now you know..."

"That Zigomar is real."

"Oh, come on," Broquet looked completely unconvinced. "You're joking. It's a bluff, an American prank, right?"

"Not at all... no, not at all. It's true, absolutely true."

"Zigomar exists?"

"Yes."

"You astound me!"

"How's that? Didn't you know?"

"I didn't want to believe it."

"But the signature, the Z on the safe was an obvious perfect clue."

"Precisely! I thought the thieves put the Z there to fool me, to throw me onto hunting for a Zigomar who doesn't exist... an imaginary Zigomar."

"Well, Zigomar is real. I have proof."

"Proof? You've seen him? You've talked to him?"

"Seen, no. Talked, no. But I know he's the one who has the documents... the papers that I need to bring back to America. He's the one I have to get them from."

Paulin Broquet finally kicked off the wall and stepped over to Baumier's desk. Tossing the butt of his cigarette into an ashtray he boomed out, "Chief, when I told you that Tom Tweak was the best of us all, me and everyone else...when I told you that Nick Carter, his student, was a child compared to him and even the great Sherlock Holmes couldn't touch him..."

"Yes, yes," Baumier said, "it's true."

Paulin Broquet turned to Tom Tweak and stood before him, staring for a moment, fixing his piercing gray eyes on him. Then he went on.

"Well, well, you've discovered Zigomar! Thanks to you what I figured was most unlikely is now becoming true. And you have proof. Oh, my dear colleague, you'll never know how happy I am for your success. You've done us such a great service! I'm so full of joy! Let me congratulate you on your astonishing generosity and your staggering talent!"

"No, my friend," Tom Tweak said, "no, I was just lucky."

"Yes. Humble geniuses always say that. But I know a little something about this job... I know how much intelligence and imagination you had to use... not to mention the diligence and courage to succeed where, despite all my efforts, I failed. I can't give you enough compliments, truly sincere compliments!"

Tom Tweak thanked Broquet for his praise, then said, "But discovering Zigomar, my friend, in short, is nothing."

"You think so?"

"Yeah. The most important thing is to catch him."

"To catch him... yes indeed... that won't be easy."

"No. And that's where you're going to have to do the work, my friend. Because me, in France, I don't have the right... Oh, if we were in America it would be done lickity split... but in Paris it's your business."

"I can't do anything without you, Tom Tweak."

"Well, I'll give you everything you need to catch him..."

Paulin Broquet cut him off abruptly, loudly, "No, no, I don't want to step into your spotlight. We have to work together, the both of us, to arrest Zigomar."

"No good, my friend."

"Excuse me? Everyone has to know that if Zigomar is caught it's because of you."

"Why?"

"To each his glory... Let's not argue about it. if you don't want to work with me, we can break it off right now. I won't hear another word from you. And since you guarantee that he really exists, I'll go out alone looking for Zigomar, who has so far escaped me completely."

The two detectives were about to outdo each other in generosity and self-sacrifice but the chief of police broke in. "Tom Tweak," he said, "look, let's be logical, you can't refuse."

The American bowed, "Okay, very well." Then he asked, "How are we going to do it?"

"I don't know," Broquet answered. "I don't know who Zigomar is, where he is, how he lives... Therefore, I don't see how we can get to him. You're the only one who can lead the expedition."

Tom Tweak thought about it for a few seconds before saying, "We have to nab the pigeon in his nest."

"How so?"

"I'll tell you where the nest is and you swoop down and catch him off guard."

Paulin Broquet shook his head. "A good method but it can't be done."

"Why not?"

"The law doesn't let me enter houses at any old time. Zigomar will have time to escape. Or the day we go to get him he won't be at home... Anyway, he's a man who knows how to fight back..."

"But if we surprise him?"

"I can't count on surprise. I'm too well known not to be seen right away... They're spying on me... Zigomar will always be warned."

"Yes, that's possible. However, we have to hurry because the papers, the documents he's got... So, what can we do? Some advice..."

"Here's what seems logical to me... a surprise, like you said, but not in the same way."

"Go on."

"We have to lure Zigomar away from his home, into a place of our choosing."

"An ambush? No good. He's too smart. He'll never come."

"Sorry but he'll come."

"You think so?"

"Absolutely. Because you have to negotiate with him about the documents."

"Okay, so?"

"With you he won't be suspicious. We'll prepare everything. We'll set up a meeting in a house with several doors, alternative exits, where we can get in easily..."

"Like here," the American detective laughed.

"But where you can't get out without going through us."

"Like here again."

"Yes, like here."

"Okay, and after?"

"After?" Broquet repeated. "After? When you, Tom Tweak, the greatest American detective, when you figure you've completely succeeded in your bold, brilliant plan and triumphed in your risky, fearless pursuit... after... when Zigomar thinks he's fooled the idiot Paulin Broquet once again..."

"Oh, come on," the American protested.

"Then Paulin Broquet will appear out of nowhere."

"Yes."

"He will go up to Zigomar..."

"Yes!"

As if he wanted to make Tom Tweak better understand what he was saying, Paulin Broquet started acting out the scene as it would happen.

Tom Tweak, for his part, to play along and make it look more real, had got up from the chair he had been sitting in. He stood up and with a strange look in his eyes watched the movements of his colleague.

Broquet stepped up to him saying, "At that moment Paulin Broquet will give him... sorry for this, but... on the shoulder a blow like this..."

He illustrated by shoving him violently, making the American detective stagger back and he instinctively shot his arms forward to catch his balance. In a lightning quick movement Paulin Broquet grabbed the outstretched arms and slapped his handcuffs on the wrists.

He shouted out, "And Paulin Broquet will shout: Zigomar! You're caught!"

What happened next lasted only seconds but was completely unexpected, unbelievable, crazy... Monsieur Baumier was watching but understood nothing. He was dumbfounded.

A fight ensued, a violent struggle, howling and screeching like wild animals tearing each other to pieces, furniture smashed to pieces...

Then, finally, thrown down on the couch, his eyes popping out of his head, blood all over his face, his clothes ripped up, his wrists still in chains, Tom Tweak...

Paulin Broquet was holding him by the throat, kneeling on his heaving chest and shouting out, in rage and triumph at the same time, straight into the American's face:

"You see... you don't do that to Paulin Broquet! It's over! I've got you, Zigomar!"

23. *Zigomar everywhere*

After a moment of stunned disbelief the police chief shook himself out of it. He went up to Paulin Broquet, who was still holding Tom Tweak on the couch and squeezing his throat harder and harder, leaning more heavily on his chest and saying, "No, my friend, no... you don't fool Paulin Broquet everyday! Doesn't matter if you're American and the greatest detective in the universe, you don't do it to me twice. I've unmasked you... I've exposed you... I've got you now, you crook... thief... Zigomar!"

Tom Tweak was choking in his tight grip. He was turning red. His eyes were bloodshot and blood-streaked drool was seeping out of his twisted mouth.

"Come on, Broquet," the chief said, "what's got into you?"

Paulin Broquet broke out in a nervous laugh, "Got into me? No, chief, it's me who's got him."

"You're making a mistake."

"No, chief, this thug..."

"Come on, you've crazy!"

"Crazy? Look, chief, just look at his face... Look at the rage... the fear... and tell me if I'm crazy... if I'm making a mistake, if I'm wrong about this guy! Tell me I'm not holding one of the worst criminals we've ever chased."

"It's possible but don't kill him... Give him some air..."

"And the keys to the cuffs? No, chief. We have to watch him close because he's strong and clever... We have to watch him very, very close..."

"But, my friend, we can't... He's caught. You've got him. Let him explain. At least let him breath."

Broquet made sure that the handcuffs around the wrists of his dear colleague were fast and tight. He let go of Tom Tweak's throat and lifted his knee from the American's chest.

Tom Tweak took a deep breath, then looked at Baumier. "Thank you, really thank you, a lot." He took a few more deep breaths before turning to Paulin Broquet, "I compliment you sincerely. You've got a grip that could crush an elephant."

And he started laughing. Then the most astonishing, most unexpected, and most typical thing happened.

The American whom Baumier, with his big heart, was helping out, sat up on the couch, very calm and collected. "Oh," he said to Broquet, "I feel really sorry for this Zigomar when he falls into your hands."

Paulin Broquet, still trembling, looked at the guy and could not help not admiring his self-assurance, his energy, his presence of mind, his marvelous self-control.

"Chief," he finally said, "we have here if not the boss at least one of the main leaders of the Z gang. We have Zigomar... or the very soul, will and brains of what is called Zigomar."

The American tilted his head, "Paulin Broquet has a wild imagination."

The French detective went on without paying any attention to him. "Tom Tweak is really Tom Tweak. The papers that he showed us... and that he wanted us to be sure to check are verified, legal and authentic. He really is the famous American detective but what he is first and foremost is the king of cosmopolitan criminals! He's the one who organized the thefts in the banks and houses of the rich... by the gang... and he's the one whom the victims are going to come to to search for the thieves."

The police chief said, "What you're telling me is very serious, Broquet. We need proof."

"We'll have it."

Baumier turned to Tom Tweak, "Are you listening to this?"

"Yes."

"What do you have to say?"

"Nothing. It's very amusing. I'm just disappointed that I ended up as the hero of this very ingenious story."

Broquet continued, "Chief, you understand that I'm not just acting on a whim. I've followed the man. I've seen the Count de la Gueriniere meet him at his house. I've seen him with the Count and Baron Dupont and others."

"Excuse me," Tom Tweak interrupted. "Are the Count de la Gueriniere and Baron Dupont known criminals?

"We don't have to answer that."

"Sorry but for my own protection you must tell me. If they're criminals you failed your duty by not arresting them. But since they're free, I guess they're perfect gentlemen and you can't fault me for talking to them."

The police chief cut in, "None of that change's Paulin Broquet's accusation of you. What do you have to say?"

The American shook his head, "Nothing. Nothing at all."

"And yet..."

"Yes, nothing. I don't even have to defend myself."

"In that case I'm forced to keep you in custody."

"If you'd like. But, chief, I will respectfully remind you that I gave you authentic documents that validate me... by holding me like this you're abusing your power."

"I have an important reason."

"Yes, but I'm an American citizen."

"Our international treaties authorize me."

"Yes, I know... but I showed you a letter from the American ambassador in Paris. So, he'll stick up for me. You can't hold me without notifying my ambassador."

"It will be done."

"Yes... but I beg you to do it right away."

"One telephone call..."

"No. My car's out front. Get someone from your office to take it and explain my situation to the ambassador... and I'll only leave if they come back to get me."

Paulin Broquet dragged his boss into a corner of the spacious office and the two men had a heated discussion in lowered voices.

Then Broquet told Baumier, "Okay, I accept."

"We have to do it."

"I hope it works out like you want but it's still tough luck for us."

The police chief called in one of his men and sent him to the US Embassy. After seeing this move Tom Tweak thanked Baumier, then very calmly, still smiling, he asked if he could light a cigar while waiting.

Puffing away serenely on his cigar he said to Paulin Broquet, "My dear friend... yes, you're still my friend... I never wanted this kind of competition between us. Oh, I understand what you feel and what's happening to me right now. You've got a fixation, an obsession... You see Zigomar everywhere. Yesterday you were thinking that Zigomar was the Count de la Gueriniere and today you believe he's your colleague Tom Tweak... Tomorrow you'll be taking your boss, Baumier, for Zigomar!"

In answer to this, Paulin Broquet, who was back to his normal self, just smiled and lit a cigarette in silence.

Baumier very courteously asked the American, "Would you like me to take off the cuffs?"

"No," Tom Tweak shot back. "No, I want to keep them until you set me free." He looked at the steel chains like an expert and said, "Well done. Strong and tight. I challenge any criminal to get out of these."

The wait was not long. The car was back soon with an attaché from the US ambassador who gave Baumier the necessary explanations and all the required guarantees. Tom Tweak, therefore, could go free.

He jumped off the couch and as one of the detectives who had brought the attaché from the Embassy came up to him on a sign from Baumier to unlock the handcuffs, the American detective smiled and thanked him.

"No need. See..."

And without the slightest effort he shook off the cuffs and placed them on the chief's desk. Then with a little bow he bid them farewell and followed his compatriot out of the office. As he passed by Paulin Broquet he gave him a smile and said, "No hard feelings, old friend."

24. *"Enfants de l'Aveyron"*

"Hey! Antonin!" Clafous shouted cheerfully. "Antonin and Gushtave! How'sh it going?"

Clafous was standing behind his counter, holding out both his huge, hairy arms from his rolled up sleeves. At the end of his arms his big, bony hands hung like vises in the air. Antonin and Gustave each put a trusting, friendly hand in his and were crushed, which was the usual greeting to start their conversation.

"What can I get I sherve you?" Clafous asked. "We'll make a toasht! Ish been a long time shince and I'm sho glad to shee you."

Clafous had a bar on Boulevard de la Chapelle that was well known in the neighborhood. For a dozen years he had been running the place: The "Enfants de l'Aveyron". Even though he always claimed to have made a fortune and that he could retire into the countryside if he wanted, he stayed there behind his counter pouring drinks, playing Zanzibar with the dice on the counter and giving his well-respected opinion about news, politics, whatever... crimes and even high society. Sometimes he also had to give a few pokes with his fists, which were even more respected and decisive as they generally left whoever disagreed with him in a state unfit to argue.

The clientele of the bar respected his strength, revered his hands, which were real clubs of flesh and bone, and held Clafous in sincerely high esteem.

Clafous was the best guy in the world and nowhere else was a little glass of absinthe less watered down. Without even looking you knew it was good stuff he served... top shelf stuff that scoured the throat going down and really knocked you out. You would get your fill and the drinks at the Aveyron were famous beyond the bounds of the neighborhood.

He also knew his people. When he honored someone with his precious respect, that someone could say, "Clafous, hold on to this for me." Clafous would say, "Ish good, kid." This "Ish good" was worth more than all the sworn oaths for clients. Whoever got credit with Clafous could hold his head up high in the neighborhood and go anywhere without paying.

Except that Clafous never forgot to collect his debts. Sometimes, most times, maybe even all the time, he bumped up the number of drinks that were ordered... and had to be paid... But you could never argue. Clafous would refuse you any more credit and every bar around would do the same. And if you could not pay upfront for drinks... impossible to live!

As for fights, Clafous did not allow them. Especially not brawls. You could do anything, drink, get drunk, play cards, scream, yell, bicker, whatever, no problem, but with the first punch thrown Clafous left his counter, jumped into the fray, grabbed the foes by the collar and threw them out into the street.

This was absolutely necessary. He wanted his bar to keep its dignity, its tranquility and friendly atmosphere.

In fact, the Enfants de l'Aveyron had more than the two rooms that one could see from the street. After passing through the back room, where the pool table was, there was a little dance hall. Twice a week they danced to accordion music.

The people who came to the dance were the weirdest of all. Only in Paris could you find this untroubled mishmash, this uncompromised promiscuity...

The girls from the street came with their men to the languid waltzes to warm up their tender affections before going elsewhere to do something nasty... to carry out their charming work. The pimps and thieves, everyone who lived off of evil and crime, showed up. But there were also the friends of Clafous, his compatriots. These good people who worked as masons, bricklayers and construction workers came with their wives and children. The younger folk, still just engaged, danced to the sound of a squeaky violin and the accordion accompanying a piano on the festive nights.

Clafous had principles. He never put up with any indecency during the dance at his establishment... as long as there were families there. Afterwards they could do as they pleased. And a scandal never broke out; the tiniest snag never got between these two worlds. Everyone knew each other and minded their own business without any contempt or hatred on either side.

The prowlers knew the names of all the young ladies and where they worked and the young ladies also knew the names of the guys they bumped into on the dance floor, and the girls they were with... They said, "Excuse me, mademoiselle or madame" and gave them a knowing smile.

But when the dance was over, everything else was finished. In the street, during the day, the same women never even looked at each other, refused to recognize each other.

But all these simple, honest, good people of the Aveyron became sacred in the eyes of Clafous' worst customers. It was understood that the friends of Clafous would never be targeted, never accosted, solicited, seduced, mugged or robbed. And if once in a while, which rarely happened, one of the good family men succumbed to the arousing charms, to the spicy appeal of the loose girls, it remained a secret and nobody would ever reveal it to cause a domestic quarrel.

As for the girls, they were given the upmost respect. Clafous would clobber anyone who acted improperly toward them and he would shut them out of his bar with no hope of pardon.

Now, Clafous' meeting house was, so to speak, indispensable to people. They met up there, ran into each other, gave news and heard gossip. Trusting Clafous, sure that he would allow nobody in whom he did not vouch for, nobody suspicious or who might cause trouble for one of his customers, people whose lives depended on chance, on making preparations and weighing the consequences... pimps waiting for their girls, thieves counting on the perfect time, criminals hiding, unable to leave this refuge, this shelter, this place of sanctuary… They were at home there, better, safer than at home.

From time to time Clafous, a good and honest man himself who loved his special customers a lot, pulled a fugitive out of a tight spot… hid him, guarded him, fed him and saved him! Nobody was ever arrested there. However, right outside the Enfants de l'Aveyron a number of customers might very well be collared. Still, inside the establishment… never! Outside, he was responsible for nothing.

Clafous did all he could to save his customers, but if one of them got caught, was clumsy or careless, just plain unlucky… even when the arrest was a surprise, completely unexpected, unforeseen, incomprehensible… Clafous was sorry about it but said he had done all he could to save the guy. Everyone believed him and inevitably his customers remained faithful.

Also when he saw friends like this Antonin and Gustave, whom he greeted with his thundering voice and awful Limousin accent, the customers did not have to budge; they could peacefully go on with their game of cards or conversations about their little affairs.

Clafous—this was a great honor that he showed to these customers—came out from behind the counter, leaving a waiter to watch the bar, grabbed an old bottle of wine with three glasses in his huge hands and went to sit down at the table where his friends were sitting.

The conversation began, "Howsh it been sho long that we haven't sheen each other? Traveling probably? Bushinesh going okay? Heresh to your health!"

The glasses clinked and the conversation started. The three men talked about this and that, about the country, the new houses being built, the potholes all over the Paris streets…

"Nish time for ush. Pitted roads, fenshes everywhere… Great!"

Then suddenly Antonin clinked Clafous' glass again and whispered, "Zalamor!"

Clafous answered in kind, "Zalavi!"

Then the three men drank their wine in silence.

These two words, Zalamor and Zalavi, which the friends had just mysteriously whispered to each other like a password, a special code, was one of the traditional jokes of the old melodramas in the theaters on the Boulevard of Crime. When the heroes of the play cried out "I'm yours unto death!" the others answered "Me, I'm yours unto life!"

And it was shortened to "Z'à la mort" and "Z'à la vie".

After this brief exchange the three friends drank their old wine and a few minutes later resumed their conversation. They talked about construction, building in cement, stone or plaster… Clafous started up a discussion about reinforced glass because he had just put some in a transom window.

"Generally," he said, "they put in normal glash and a grill. Okay but when the glash breaksh the little pieshes fall on peoplesh headsh."

"And the reinforced glass?"

"Got itsh own grill inshide! Sho, when it breaksh the little pieshes don't fall out and you can shleep like a baby right under it."

The conversation about this thrilling subject could have gone on forever. But at the table next to where Clafous and his friends were sitting two new customers had just sat down. Clafous obviously knew them because he said hello.

Then the barkeep, being summoned by the demands of the watering hole, stood up, shot down one last drink with his friends and went away saying, "You're going to pay a little vishit to the dansh hall... Good... Shee you later."

The waiter behind the bar, meanwhile, came out to take the order of the new customers. "What'll it be?" he asked.

While the two men made their order they waved hello to other customers playing cards in the back of the room, shouting out in a familiar way, "Salu...e!"

The gesture they made in the air, a kind of zigzag with their hand, was answered in kind by their comrades who yelled back in the same rowdy tone, "Salu...e!"

Now, these friends spoke with a particular accent from the streets, the shady streets, the outskirts of Paris where they lay a heavy accent on the "s" so that it sounds like a "z". Thus, it was more like they said, "Zalu..e!"

As the waiter set the foaming mugs of beer on the table one of them shouted out jokingly, "It-zee best head in town!"

And he really stressed the dangerous liaison "It-zee".

Then he took the glass and as if he wanted to dry the bottom he rubbed it on the table. While looking at the table next to him where the two friends, Antonin and Gustave were sitting, he made a motion with the glass from left to right, down to the left and back to the right, then stopped... In short, he had just made a big Z on the table.

His partner did the same.

Antonin and Gustave took their little wine glasses full of ole Aveyron and traced the same sign in front of them.

The two new customers looked more relaxed after this. They started talking about the races, about horses, about their various little jobs.

And the dance kept spilling in its melodies of waltzes and polkas.

Antonin and Gustave stood up and said to Clafous, "We're going to dance."

"Good, good," the barkeep said. "Shee you shoon."

As they strolled through the back of the room where the men were playing Manille, they saw them shooting looks back and forth at each other and saying, "Iz my turn?"

"Yeah, iz your play..."

The guys watching the game said nothing, but either with their cigarettes, as if shaking off the ash, or taking their glass, they all made a sign that looked like the Z...

Antonin and Gustave were delighted to see all the girls and ladies. They made a tour of the room.

One group of people who looked especially happy attracted their attention. Around the table the father, mother, a girl and a boy, then a young lady around 18 years old and a young man around 24 or 26… The boy and girl, brother and sister, had just danced a polka and come back to their parents' table red-faced and a little sweaty, which did not keep them from giving their progenitors an affectionate hug.

But the orchestra was starting up a waltz. The young lady stood up along with the young man.

"Again?" the father tried to sound grumpy. "Again? But these kids are too much!"

"Leave 'em alone, Arsène," the mother said. "Let the kids have their fun."

"Okay, okay, but listen up. I've got my eye on you, boy, and on your cousin!"

The young couple had already turned their backs and was heading to the dance floor as their happy parents admired them, sharing their joy.

The mother, a good-sized woman, held her dishwasher hands in her lap as she sat in the chair a little too stiffly for her corpulence.

The father, a construction foreman no doubt, with his white beard that his children had mussed up by hugging him, wore a soft felt hat on his big head. He looked like an ordinary, simple fellow with a kind of frock coat and a vest that only had one button over his striped shirt and a cheap, pre-knotted tie. Big, calloused hands that wielded tools, a well-rounded belly after a copious Sunday dinner in some fixed-price restaurant in the neighborhood, a wooden pipe in his mouth…

Antonin watched this group, then leaned over to Gustave and pointed at the family man. "Keep an eye on him. That's Baron Dupont!"

Antonin slipped into the crowd, abandoning Gustave, and soon had left the dance. But this time he did not go through the bar. He snuck out through a narrow corridor that led into a small courtyard where a man dressed like all the others in Clafous' bar stepped out of the shadow in corner of the wall.

"We can go now," is all he said.

"Okay, go get Gustave."

25. The triangular room

Antonin pushed open a small door and entered the same building as the Averyon. He climbed a spiral staircase and waited in a little room lit only by a gas lamp that was aflame when he came in.

He was there only three minutes, barely, when the staircase creaked under the weight of a heavy-set man. In no time at all Clafous appeared. He closed the door behind him then stepped into the little room.

"Hold on boss," he said, "until I hook up the alarm."

He went and plucked out of the wall an electrical wire that connected the stairs to a bell that was hanging on the wall. Nobody could step on the stairs without their presence being signaled.

The little room was part of Clafous' apartment, built into a corner. It had two blank walls and the only opening in the third wall was the door they had come through, which was usually sealed off so that no one knew about it.

The walls were made so that no one could hear or see into the room, which allowed this strange, triangular room to hold the kind of serious meeting that the two men were about to engage in.

Antonin turned back into Paulin Broquet after leaving his loyal Gabriel in the role of Gustave to follow Baron Dupont, the father of the family at the Aveyron. The man waiting at the small door downstairs was Baiter.

Clafous was Clafous but he was part of the gang, part of the Broquet Brigade. He was one of the most valuable agents.

The Enfants de l'Aveyron was, after all, the meeting place of all the people whom Pauline Broquet was after. Clafous was trusted by his customers, sometimes helped them out, or so it seemed, protected them, guarded them in order to catch them more easily, to find out their secrets and without even asking them he always knew what new jobs were done or to be done.

But Clafous was so clever that not only was he never caught as a traitor but he was never even suspected of being in cahoots with the police.

Paulin Broquet had warned his agent about his visit on Sunday. He ran less risk and could work more easily if he were in the crowd.

"So," the detective said Clafous, "you knew about the murder of Montreil?"

"Yes, boss, I heard all about the safe marked with a Z."

Now when talking with his boss Clafous lost his strange accent.

"Okay," Broquet said, "and you also knew that the notary's safe had been robbed?"

"And marked with a Z."

"That's right."

"And I know that in the countryside, in Normandy, they pulled off a nice job."

"So, there is a strong, well organized gang here."

"Yes, boss. The gang uses the Z as its sign and when it pulls a job it leaves a Z behind to tell all the members that it's been done successfully and there will be some money to share."

"Okay… I suspected as much. I also saw just now that like all serious gangs, Z has chosen your bar to meet up at."

"And nowhere else."

"I noticed that they trace the Z in all kinds of ways to be recognized… and when they talk they stress the Zs, on purpose, everywhere."

"That's right, boss. I saw you just now downstairs responding to the signs to the guys next to you. It made them feel better."

"Good," Broquet said. Then he asked, "Who's that Arsène with his family at the dance?"

"Arsène's an old workman who's got some construction business going on now… He's made a little fortune."

"An honest man?"

"In appearance."

"Suspicions?'

"I think so."

"He's part of the Z gang?"

Clafous spread out his big hands. "That, boss, as hard as I tried to find out, I can't tell you. Arsène comes here with his family but never gives the Z signs. Still, that doesn't mean anything."

"Why?"

"Because the chiefs of the Z gang are unknown. You never see them. Nobody knows who they are."

"Ah."

"They give orders, the orders are followed, and that's it."

Clafous went into some details about the Z group. It was recently formed and seemed to have very powerful members. They were recruited from all levels of society or rather they had titles that allowed them to enter into the highest, most closed, most difficult circles to penetrate.

The Zs were divided by classes, by ranks, according to their qualities, their skills, their accomplished missions. But except for the Zs of the lowest levels who might know one another, who needed to know one another to do their jobs, i.e. robbing and looting, the other Zs remained unknown and could meet each other at any time without knowing that they were part of the same organization, the same gang…

As a result, they could imprison one or more Zs who were informed on or caught and this would not matter in the least. These Zs could say that the gang was real but they could do it no harm and cause no interruption in its actions.

"Yes," Broquet said, "it's very clever." Then he added, "And yet, I know that their boss is Zigomar."

"Zigomar!" Clafous barked. "That's right, that's what they call their chief."

"But who is Zigomar?"

Clafous shook his head, "There's no way to know, boss. They know Zigomar exists and they obey him blindly... but nobody's seen him, nobody knows who he is. Zigomar is veiled in the deepest mystery..."

"And you couldn't find out anything?"

"No, boss. You know I've done things for the Zs to earn their trust. They all just tell me, "Zigomar, it's Zigomar.""

"And the American? Do you know the American?"

"The American?"

"Tom Tweak?"

"No, boss. They haven't mentioned him yet."

Paulin Broquet kept silent. He thought about things for a moment, then asked Clafous, "Is there a Z meeting tonight?"

"Yes."

"Where's it being held? At your place?"

"No, boss, it's at the Barbottiere."

"The Barbottiere in Guelma Alley near Pigalle?"

"That's right. The Barbottiere is the favorite dive bar of the worst criminals, the most notorious gangsters of the area, hence it's name."

"I know... after that murderous captain Pierre Le Diable from the Barbot family."

"But the meeting's not in the Barbottiere itself. It's in a one of the dumps next door. There's a workshop right next door, an old statue maker."

"Good," Broquet said, "I'll see..."

"They enter through the workshop and when the password is given a trapdoor is opened in the back of the room and they go down into a cellar. That's where the Z gang is meeting."

"I'll go see it tonight."

Clafous was startled and scared. "No, boss, don't do it!"

Broquet looked at him in surprise, "Why do you say that?"

"Sorry, boss," Clafous sounded upset, "but I'm telling you not to do it... not to go to the Barbottiere."

"You're scared I won't fit in with that noble company?"

"Oh boss, don't laugh. This is serious. It's your life at stake."

"That happens to me every day. Why would the Barbottiere be more dangerous than any other den of thieves?"

Clafous replied, "Boss, if I'm not out of place... it's not on behalf of your lieutenants or your partners that I'm speaking, but on behalf of everyone who cares about you, who admires you, who has a sincere love for you..."

"My friend!" Broquet shook his hand warmly.

"Look, boss, I'm telling you it's not only reckless but totally useless to throw yourself to the lions in the Barbottiere. So, you know the main purpose of the Z gang. You know that it first meets at my place and holds its secret conferences at the Barbottiere. But, boss, it oughta be enough to tail them, to nab them when you figure the time's right... Why go expose yourself like this?"

Broquet answered, "I don't want to just make a few arrests. You, my dear Clafous, just told me that the Z gang was so organized that if we arrest some of the members it'd do nothing to the gang as a whole."

"That's right."

"Therefore, I have to strike at the head. I have to find out who the boss is. I have to see Zigomar! He's the one I have to get."

"Boss, we all know how incredibly brave you are, but I can still tell you about the dangers you'll be facing, the risks you'll be taking, the fear you should be feeling..."

"I'm listening, Clafous."

"The Barbottiere has a basement where the Zs meet."

"Okay, go on."

"But the basement is not just for the Z meetings... it's also used as a court of justice and a place of execution."

"That's very practical," the detective smiled. "I'll be interested to see their set-up."

Clafous begged his boss not to go and risk his life for nothing. His supplications were in vain.

Paulin Broquet had decided to attend the next Z meeting and nothing in the world could change his mind.

"At least don't go alone," Clafous ended up saying. "Take Gabriel or Baiter with you..."

"No, my friend, I think it'll be better, I'll have a better chance of success if I'm alone. With two of us we couldn't remain incognito, which is absolutely necessary."

"But boss, I'm begging you."

In a tone that closed the discussion for good, Broquet said, "That's enough! The battle has begun between Zigomar and Paulin Broquet, between crime and justice... this justice that I serve, that I fight for, it has to be victorious! In any way possible, even if it costs me my life, I, Paulin Broquet, must bring down Zigomar!"

Clafous could only nod.

Then Broquet asked him, "The password to get into this wicked Barbottiere, is it the same one we know about... Zalavi."

"Zalamor... yes, boss."

"Perfect."

"And they add 'Zigomar'."

"While signing a Z with their hand?"

"That's right."

"Thanks."

26. The Barbottiere

Before going back to his bar, when Paulin Broquet had left, Clafous, being justly alarmed, went to the dance. Pretending just to be making sure that all was well, he wanted to see if he could find either Gustave, alias Gabriel, or Baiter on the dance floor or with the parents watching on tenderly as their kids waltzed.

Paulin Broquet had spoken of Arsène during their meeting in the triangular room. Clafous logically figured that the detective must have put one of his men on the tail of this character who worried him and who was the object of his investigation. He was hoping, therefore, to see one of his boss' partners near the construction entrepreneur.

Arsène, his wife and his two children, his older daughter and the young cousin, all of them had disappeared.

And naturally, on their tail, Gustave and Baiter as well.

Clafous was crestfallen. He wanted to tell one of the loyal lieutenants about the great danger their boss was recklessly about to confront. He wanted to warn them so they could take the necessary, urgent measures that the crazy actions of Broquet desperately called for.

Despite feeling confused and helpless, not knowing what to do, unable to leave his bar to sound the alarm, he had to go back and with a heavy heart, keep filling the glasses and joking with his customers.

It was only after knowing all the advantages, after a thorough study of everything the sinister lair offered that the Zs had made it the site of their secret meetings and fixed it up for this purpose. It was organized magnificently.

Even knowing the Barbottiere, even entering the old workshop of the statue maker, even going down the hallway that led to the basement, you would not reach the room that they used, as Clafous had said, for the crooks' council, court and execution room, unless you were initiated.

By entering through the bar you would go down a dead-end alley and get into the workshop without being seen from the street. Once inside, if you were initiated, you could easily get into the underground maze, a kind of inevitable trap where you could never leave unless the Zs allowed it.

At the end of the maze of hallways that snaked around and criss-crossed to form a tangled web of alleys there was a pretty big room, deep underground, where you could talk loudly, scream and shout, and not the slightest sound would escape into the street.

This huge room was actually on old gypsum quarry that was still used last century but had been walled up and long forgotten ever since. It was by pure chance that someone had found it and given the secret to the Zs.

One of the hallways that led to the quarry was once used by the public works department when the houses of Paris were encroaching on the Butte

Montmartre which had been outside the city limits and still in the countryside until then. This hallway was used to make the temporary sewers for the district. Since in France what is temporary lasts forever, this sewer was still in use. It ran under the present Place Pigalle and along Rue Blanche, a few feet underground, of course, continued behind Trinité all the way to the Opéra and ended at the Seine near Tuileries.

They were sure that the Zs carried out their death sentences there and threw the corpses in the sewer, but they could never prove it. The poor devils, in fact, drifted slowly down to the Seine. They would find the mutilated, decomposed corpse only months later, floating in the river. No one could say where it had come from. No one could trace back the route it had taken… and certainly not imagine that it had come all the way from the top of Montmartre to be fished out at Point-au-Jour, if not even farther away!

There was no doubt that Paulin Broquet remembered all this. But even though the thought and prospect of a walk in the sewers would be enough to discourage any other man, even the most daring, it would not for a second stop Paulin Broquet from fulfilling his mission, from following his plans through to the end. Nothing could deter him from what he considered his duty.

Therefore, he entered the sinister bar, the Barbottiere…

Paulin Broquet was dressed like one of Clafous' customers. So, here he looked like a lot of those guys who finished their drink at the bar and went through the back door of the Barbottiere in Guelma Alley.

He was clever enough to slip out at the same time as a guy he had seen at Clafous' and, by chance, was in the Barbottiere. He made the Z sign and was answered in kind.

Broquet stepped into the workshop after his companion, whom he followed like a guide. From the workshop they went into the next room that was used as a bedroom. A man, probably the statue maker, was lying on the iron bed.

"Z'à la vie," he said.

"Z'à la mort," Broquet responded.

"Pass!" On saying this, the worker pulled a cord.

A wooden panel camouflaged as a wall lifted up revealing a stairway lit by a small gas lamp. Broquet went down the stairs into a hallway that he followed until he ended up in an intersection of other hallways. He would have had a hard time deciding which one to take if a new member posted in the shadows had not spoken up.

"Z'à la vie!"

The detective answered the call. The voice came from the hallway that he was supposed to take. He went towards the man who was talking to him and saw in the distance another hallway lit by another lamp. Without a doubt they put the lamps at the crossroads to point the way, to serve as markers, like lighthouses for the members.

Long ago the sound of clopping horses and tramways on the street had disappeared.

At the end of another hallway another man stepped out of the shadows. This man planted himself right in front of Paulin Broquet. Silent in the semi-darkness, standing still, he waited.

"Z'à la vie," Broquet finally said.

"Z'à la mort," the man responded, but he did not move. He was still waiting, blocking the path of the detective.

"Zigomar!" Broquet said, remembering Clafous' directions.

"Zigomar!" the man said and he stepped aside, disappearing into the shadows again, simply saying, "Pass."

Paulin Broquet went on and followed the hallway unobstructed now. Suddenly he found himself in a huge space. Men were standing around waiting, in rows, almost without moving and keeping absolutely silent.

Broquet stood among them, imitated them, did exactly as they did. Nobody looked at him or took any notice of his presence.

Other members arrived and lined up like him, paying no attention to the others around.

They waited for a long time, then all of a sudden, in front of them, a light flashed on. A door had just opened. The big door of the conference room. Slowly, the members went in. Broquet followed suit.

Two gas lamps were hanging from the cross beams that held up the vaulted ceiling. They threw just enough light in the room for Paulin Broquet to examine it at will. It was nothing remarkable. Just a gallery, a room in a mine, damp, gray, plain, no furniture at all except in the back.

On a big, wooden platform accessed by a few steps was a kind of podium covered by a black sheet that clashed with the gray walls. On this black sheet were woven big Zs in red.

In front of the podium, on the platform was a table with a candle. The table was also covered with a black sheet. On the table lay a notebook and a blue pencil.

Behind the table stood a man dressed in a red hood pulled down over his head with two eyeholes. And behind the podium were five other men, also dressed in red hoods, but one of them, the one in the middle, also wore a big, golden Z on his chest.

On the wall behind them hung a large, black coat of arms on which a big, red Z was crudely carved.

The men guarding the podium stood absolutely still, just like the one in front, at the table.

The gang members, the Zs crowded into the room and likewise stood as still as possible, all the while keeping a religious silence. This stillness and silence was necessary. The slightest noise echoed loudly under the vaulted ceiling like in a cathedral.

The ground was covered by rough timber, beams of thick wood laid over the water that dripped off the walls and seeped out everywhere, drop by drop, incessantly.

The flooring kept the members from slogging through the gray, sticky mud but every footstep sounded like a little explosion.

Paulin Broquet, therefore, making a quick assessment of the room, catching every detail, squeezed in and waited with the others, silent and still. The surroundings and the wait were hard and stressful because his life was at stake. But he set his worries aside. It took a mind like Broquet's, strong and secure in his body, not to shake and tremble, to stand there calmly amidst his enemies, in the heart of their lair, in their hands, completely at their mercy. It took a heart like his, solid and stout, to wait for the coming events, one of which was probably going to be his torture and his death.

But Paulin Broquet had real courage, unshakeable, that thrust him into situations like this, seemingly simple and innocent but in reality quite astounding.

The lamps hanging on the pillars gave off only a dim light and they were behind the members. In fact, there were only two, cheap lamps, like they used at fairs or on the little wagons of travelling salesmen. A reflector cast their glow before the podium. The rest of the room, therefore, was lit only by what was reflected off the walls and behind the pillars it was totally black. Therefore, it was impossible to recognize the faces of the people there, even those standing right next to you.

All of a sudden, without any movement from the podium, a bell rang out. Right away, the man dressed in a red hood standing at the table in front of the podium raised his hands as his sleeves floated in the air like giant, red wings.

"Zigomar!" he shouted.

The gathering repeated, "Zigomar!"

And the shout rolled like thunder under the subterranean vaults. Then there was silence once again, even deeper and more disturbing.

After a rather long moment, a voice spoke out. The voice came from one of the hoods at the podium, the one in the middle... Broquet believed. And this voice, despite the inevitable distortion because of the red mask, despite the special tone it had under the echoing vaults, this voice sounded familiar to Paulin Broquet. And he was not terribly surprised to recognize it because he was almost expecting to hear it.

"Friends," the voice thundered, "dear friends! Zigomar has brought you here this evening for two reasons. The first is good news. The second... listen carefully... is serious, very serious... but it, too, will be turned into good news, into victory!

"You have heard, without us needing to notify you specially, that we succeeded in several, profitable operations. The mark of our association, the dreadful, mystifying Z, has shined forth in dazzling brilliance. But it's nothing compared with what we still have to do... with what we are going to do! For our future projects this first success is like a guarantee of a grand, glorious victory."

The speaker paused for a few dramatic seconds before continuing.

"Zigomar wants to tell you again, my friends, to remind you here of what our association means, what it wants, what its goal is. We are not an association like all the others that sprout up by chance, all of a sudden, like mushrooms on the dunghill of modern civilization! Those associations are just common gangs and die off as soon as they've got what they deserved.

"We, however, are on solid ground, we have unshakable foundations and we rely not on chance encounters but on the tradition passed down through the ages! We have our past battles, glories, trials, tribulations and triumphs. We have our history like any brave people. Our ancestors came out of India, the mother of the world, the cradle of religions, the source of ideas. They lived in colossal Egypt, in the Promised Land of Israel, in artistic Greece, in sovereign Rome, in the spectacular Spain of the Moors and in gentle France with its infinite riches, in England sparkling with gold and in Ireland with its tender heart, in Germany where heavy arms clash and in Bohemia where the air is full of music, in China and America! Everywhere! Everywhere!

"We are the descendants of the sons of the Universe! The people whose fatherland is bounded by no mountain, no river, no simple marking post... we march before them and as masters of the world, as lords, we collect the tithes from the slaves whom they let occupy the lands!

"We are the Djinni, the Tziganes, the Gitanes and Gitanos, the Gypsies, the Romany, the Ramogiz!

"We are the Ramogiz!

"Ramogiz that by tradition, read backwards, we call Zigomar!

"Zigomar! That's the cry of the Ramogiz down the centuries! It's the symbolic name of the chief, the king. The name of him whom no one has seen or known but whose power everyone has felt. It's the name of him who, immortal like the sun, can rejuvenate every day, become different, all the while staying the same, die without ending his life, snuff out and keep shining... That is Zigomar!"

Everyone shouted out fervently, "Zigomar! Zigomar!"

Paulin Broquet raised his voice with those around him, "Zigomar!"

The speaker went on, "Our goal is to take possession of the gross opulence, the deranged riches that should belong to the one who lives by intelligence, boldness, strength and courage, who has been judged worthy of being Zigomar!"

After a short silence, giving his dramatic words time to sink in and take effect, the speaker continued without moving an inch, just like the four masked men around him and the one in front of the little table, standing absolutely still.

"However, dear friends, Zigomar did not call you here today to remind you of our origins, our goals or to talk about our glory. No, he did not gather you to tell you what you already know, all the successes we have accomplished... He

141

brought you here to tell you that a grave danger is threatening us and to ask you to act as a court and pronounce a sentence."

A murmur ran through the audience. Now they were expecting something very serious.

"Dear companions, listen up! Listen carefully because Zigomar speaks these solemn words but rarely.

"Zigomar cannot flourish without everyone's devotion, everyone's loyalty, everyone's total self-sacrifice on behalf of one another. We've already found traitors among us. This is fatal. There are bad seeds in every society, double-crossers in every party, betrayers in every religion… But you have seen how we can flush them out. We have judged them here. And we have executed them here when need be. Well, my friends, there is a traitor among us. He has given the secret word to our enemy… not only the name of Zigomar but the password and the sign of recognition."

Another murmur and shiver ran through the audience.

"Our enemies," the speaker continued, "now know how to slip in as one of us! They know how to find out about our projects, our moves, our latest efforts. They can get in our way, cause us great harm, maybe even arrest a few of our cleverest, bravest, most useful companions.

"Yes, the danger is pressing. And Zigomar's duty is not to hide it but to recognize it so as to fight it better… Zigomar's power is great but he who has gotten the secret is the only one who can make Zigomar anxious, even fearful. It is a man to whom we must bow with respect. He is as courageous as a lion, as sharp as a fox, as keen-eyed as an eagle… He puts the hero in heroism, is as bold as he is brave and as strong as he is bold.

"This man can take up the challenge against us, which is the highest praise one could say of him. This man has earned this great honor by forcing us all to meet here in order to organize our defense against him. This man is the only one in the world who can challenge us, who can confront us face to face. This man," the speaker shouted, "is Paulin Broquet!"

There was a nervous, agonizing movement in the crowd. This name had an effect on criminals. Many of them, if not all, just hearing the name, could not help trembling.

Paulin Broquet did not lose his calm. In the midst of his enemies he was living proof that Zigomar, in praising him so highly, was telling nothing but the truth. And strangely, as if it all had to do with someone else, he stood and waited for the end of the speech, wondering where it was going, but already smelling a trap, already for a long time sensing danger.

"That's the man we're up against," the voice rose again. "They've thrown Zigomar to Paulin Broquet! Friends, we have been betrayed. What punishment do you demand for betrayal? What punishment do you demand for the enemy?"

Everyone present, in unison, answered, "Death! Death!"

Broquet chanted with the others, "Death!"

This was very disturbing, really tragic. A man pronouncing his own death sentence...

After the shouting rolled like thunder, heavy and low, under the sinister ceiling, there was an even heavier silence, more agonizing perhaps than the roar of voices calling for death.

Then the speaker resumed, "So, you voted for death!"

"Yes, yes, death, death!"

The speaker, "Good! Friends, you are going to take responsibility for your vote and according to our laws each of you will sign the death sentence that the assessor is holding."

One by one, silently and solemnly, as if participating in some sacred ritual, the members stepped onto the stage from the left and approached the table. They all made the Z sign with their left hand, then took the blue pencil, signed the sheet of paper, set down the pencil and walked off to the right, passing behind the others who were slowly advancing in line.

One by one, they paraded by.

Paulin Broquet's turn came. He could not escape the formality. Squeezed in, nudged forward by the companions, he had to step up and approach the table. This was the critical moment for him. But whoever might look at him during these brief minutes when his life was at stake, would not see the slightest sign of worry on his face, not a single nervous twitch. He kept his composure and marched forward with exemplary courage.

Of course he suspected that this ritual was a trap but he still thought he could avoid it, sidestep the danger.

He watched closely what the others before him were doing. He climbed the stairs and drew the Z in the air with his left hand. So far, everything was going fine. But the fear of failure surged up at the sight of the white paper. When they signed, they leaned over and Broquet could not see what they wrote. Nevertheless, when his turn came he bravely grabbed the pencil.

The sheet of paper looked to him like it was covered in nothing but Zs. It was the only signature that the members had put down. The detective leaned over and wrote a Z.

At the very moment that he finished signing the paper, the voice of the speaker shouted out in triumph, "Thank you, Paulin Broquet! You just signed your own death sentence!"

This outburst caused a wild cry of response, "Death to Paulin Broquet! Death! Death!"

The men suddenly unleashed against him, a man who was now at their mercy and whose name had made them tremble just moments before. They raised their fists and shook them in the air, threatening, menacing, wanting vengeance for their fear and their cowardice.

"Death!" they howled. "Death!"

Paulin Broquet turned around and looked at all the criminals. He was alone against this howling pack but he remained calm, impassive, as if all these people were just a curiosity, as if the cries for death were not targeted on him.

And then a sound rang out in the room.

Straightaway everyone quieted down and the mob that was about to jump on him turned still and silent again, as if by magic. These people could truly boast of admirable discipline.

In no Parliament in the world, in no gathering of politicians or financiers, and not just in books, during a stormy, passionate meeting like this one, would you ever see such calm fall at the sound of a simple bell.

The speaker spoke out again in the midst of the silence. "Paulin Broquet, the praise you heard just now of your bravery and courage... Zigomar stands by it. It is the expression of his profound and sincere admiration for the exceptional man that you are... But it is also a farewell! It is your eulogy that just tickled your ears. It is praise spoken over the grave where you are going to lie forever in just a few minutes."

Paulin Broquet, still calm, looked around at the men at the foot of the platform and at the red hoods who called themselves their judges. He crossed his arms and smiled.

The speaker went on, "We pay due respect to your keen intelligence that led you to discover our secrets and to your audacity that led you to attack us and to that astonishing courage that has brought you here among us... You, alone, facing all of us, it's admirable! And now that you know you are going to die, you still have the power to smile. Paulin Broquet, you are a hero! Zigomar salutes you!"

Then the speaker ordered, "Friends, hats off!"

All the members doffed their hats.

"You voted for your own death," he continued, "you yourself signed your death warrant, ratified the sentence... To bring yourself to do that, you who are so astute, you have to be very strong. Now that we're out of danger we can tell you that even though you managed to steal our password, you didn't get everything. One tiny detail betrayed you. Since you have a taste for these kinds of puzzles and deductions, we'll satisfy your curiosity one last time.

"Listen... You saw on the paper all the Zs written in blue... Each of us wrote his own Z... And you, too, wrote yours... Except that you didn't really see how to do it. They didn't tell you that. You wrote your Z down from top to bottom like normal, but the secret is to write it from the bottom up. That's something you couldn't guess. With an enemy like you we can never take too many precautions.

"It was a duel unto death between us. Zigomar or Paulin Broquet. One or the other had to go. It's you who has played out your role, who has finished your mission. Zigomar, once again, comes out on top, the master, the victor. Zigomar is gloriously immortal!"

All of a sudden Broquet yelled out loudly but clearly, "You're wrong, Zigomar! I'll die but I'm only a soldier falling on the battlefield. There's a power that towers over yours... It is the law! There is a glory that is truly eternal and it will crush yours... It is justice! You have won easily tonight but the time of punishment is at hand! Kill me now, friends of Zigomar... Execute me! Your heads are already pledged to the gallows!"

The crowd started howling again, "Death! Death! Death to Paulin Broquet!"

"I'm not scared of you, thieves and murderers! I deny you all!"

"Execute him!"

"Wretches! You're not my executioners, you're just my murderers!"

"Death! Death!"

"Before dying, Broquet will also salute you and take vengeance!"

On saying this he took out his pistol and aimed at the judges. Then he pulled the trigger.

Now, we know that Paulin Broquet is a good shot with the pistol. His bullets, as always, hit their targets here. They bore into the red hoods right between the eyes, exploding their skulls.

But cackling laughter answered his shots.

The hoods were torn off. Paulin Broquet saw the mannequins that the bullets had struck. And a bell tolled loudly again.

The floor under Broquet suddenly opened up.

"Cowards! Murderers!" Broquet shouted.

And he fell into a pit that dropped into the sewer. His body thudded on the ground in the shallow pool of water. Then under the vaulted ceiling of the sewer, everything became silent.

Up above, while the criminals closed the trapdoor, a laughing voice spit out a little joke, in English:

"Broquet is broken!"

27. Clafous in a stew

While serving all the drinks, large and small, and pouring all the liquor, as strong and sundry as possible, Clafous was keeping a close eye on his customers. He was not worried that they would leave without paying... but he was hoping that by chance—that fickle benefactor of policemen—he might see someone from Broquet's squad.

His hope was futile. Clafous had to stay behind the bar and with a heavy heart let precious time slip by, every minute losing the means of bringing help to his boss. But then, how could he help him?

Even if he could warn the squad, how could they get to Broquet? Was it already too late? Was it already over? Would they find only his corpse?

Clafous, however, could not stand it. He thought that it was his duty—even at the risk of revealing his true identity, his connections, of ruining his bar, incurring the vengeance of all the criminals who had been fooled by him for so long—Clafous figured that he had to warn Broquet's men at any price.

Finally, he decided to close the bar just when a group of customers came barging in the door. Clafous had known them for a long time. They had just been at his bar... just now... during the dance... while Augustin and Gustave were drinking with him... Then these customers had left when he went to meet the boss in the triangular room and give him directions to the Barbottiere and the information on the Z gang...

Now these customers were back.

They were in a good mood, having a good time, celebrating as if they had just pulled off a big job. Shouting and banging on the table they ordered drinks.

Nervously Clafous went to take their order, with a bad feeling about the cause of their celebration.

"Come drink with us, Clafous!" they whooped.

"Gladly, but why are you sho happy?"

"We've got good reason!"

"A big job?"

"I'm telling you... and the means to do more, nice and calm."

When the waiter brought their drinks they clinked glasses and toasted, "Z best for you!"

"And Z best for you!"

They all started laughing and shouted together, "Z best for him!"

Clafous felt a chill run through his blood. His fears were confirmed. But he wanted to know for sure so he laughed with them and asked, "Z besht for who?"

The laughter died quickly.

"We'll tell you later, old Clafous."

"Doeshn't matter to me," Clafous said.

146

One of the men said to the others, "It's better drinking here than at the Barbottiere."

The friends laughed at this joke.

"Yeah, the water's less salty! The drinks are smaller but at least they won't drown us!"

"Come on, another round to Z best for him!"

Clafous, who wanted to cry instead because now he was certain of his chief's demise, Clafous who made a heroic effort to force himself not to jump on these villains, not to strangle them, not to revenge Paulin Broquet, Clafous who was laughing with them, clinking glasses with these wretches, finally shouted out:

"Sho, Z, besht for him again!"

Now he did not need to ask anyone, he knew what it was about... He knew Broquet's fate.

But he stayed faithful to his role despite his profound grief. He went back to the counter, watched other customers come in showing the same joyful face... A joy that meant: "We've executed Paulin Broquet!'

Clafous told his waiter, "You close the bar. I'm going to bed." And he left.

His departure was nothing unusual. He happened—oh so rarely!—to retire early in the morning. Then the waiter took his place and with the hope of one day taking over for good, he tried to carry on like normal.

Clafous would have like to have a man working for him like Paulin Broquet had in his squad but the boss talked him out of it. It was better, safer, that his waiter and other help be real workers... and nothing but...

When Clafous had something to tell his boss he always found a way to do it without getting his staff mixed up. It was only in very special case, like to-night, that this posed a problem.

So, Clafous put himself on the line.

Soon after, through a secret door, Clafous left the building without any one of his usual customers, even his closest ones, aware. They would not even recognize him if they happened to meet him in the street. The owner of the Aveyron was incognito. He had transformed.

Clafous had taken care to put on a rarely worn suit that was an eyeful. Of course Clafous had no intention of rivaling the demeanor, elegance or chic of the fancy Baron Dupont... No, he simply put on a sergeant's uniform. And he added a beard to his chin. Like that, big and stout, with his belly bursting the buttons of his uniform, he looked like any other police sergeant strolling through the streets of Paris. One of the good people, the terror of handcart merchants but who wished no harm on anyone and were really sorry when they had to arrest an offender.

But once in the street Clafous was no better off. Where should he go? What should he do?

He scratched his head trying to trigger an idea. But nothing came.

While standing there scratching himself, searching for an idea, undecided, Clafous realized that he looked a little ridiculous. So, he started walking. Without thinking he turned down Boulevard Rochechouart.

While he had been getting dressed Clafous considered he might go to see Gabriel or Baiter... or even Simon... nearby on Rue Rodier. But he figured rightly that with the boss out of the city his lieutenants would not be at home. So where to go now?

"Okay, I give up!" he thought. "I'll come up with something..." But on the sidewalk he came up with nothing.

However, at any cost and as soon as possible he had to find out exactly what they had done with Paulin Broquet, where they had tossed him in fact... and also to know how to save him right away. Knowing that the whole thing took place at the Barbottiere was not enough.

The mysterious Barbottiere... with its uncharted underground passages... booby-trapped... would not reveal its secret, even if he searched all the surrounding buildings for the tunnels.

No, it was absolutely necessary that one of the members who had attended the tragic ceremony give not only the password but also precise directions to the room, the prison, the sewer where Clafous was afraid they were holding Paulin Broquet. Because in spite of the criminals' good mood, he could not admit that they were reckless enough to have put the detective to death.

He imagined, on the contrary, that the Zs had seized him but they would not be so careless as to kill him. They would hold him hostage in exchange for a pardon, an acquittal or freedom.

Clafous did not want to consider the frightful idea of his boss' death!

But how could he find out what happened to him? How could he find out if there was still time? There was only one way. Make the villains talk!

Yes, that was it. That was what was crucial. What was needed. What he had to do at all costs.

But how to make a Zigomar member talk?

Clafous had stopped scratching his head but the solution had not come to him. Hunched over, gloomy and grumbling, furious at the situation, he was walking down the street when all of a sudden, almost at the corner of Rue des Martyrs, he bumped into two men coming in the opposite direction. Lost in his dark thoughts Clafous had not noticed them.

"Hey look!" one of the men said, "what's wrong with the copper?!"

The street was deserted. The men acted like they owned the place and feared no punishment. It was the perfect opportunity. What a windfall to be able to get a little vengeance on a lost officer without worrying about others coming to his rescue.

The other man seconded his partner with a violent punch to approve of the cheap insult.

But hitting Clafous was about as effective as hitting a brick wall. He felt nothing and the attacker hurt his hand. But the punch, the brief skirmish did have the effect of snapping Clafous out of his thoughts and back to reality. He raised his eyes, looked at his attackers who were just getting started and he recognized them.

Right away the idea that he had been searching so hard for was awakened by the blow… which proves once again that there are countless and unsuspected ways to stimulate the imagination.

Here was the way, the perfect way standing in front of him!

Quick as lightning Clafous hit one of the men square in the face, which threw him to the ground, bleeding and passed out, as good as dead, maybe even really so.

As for the other, he had slipped out a knife and was ready to revenge his comrade but without wasting a second Clafous kicked him in the shin, which hobbled his left leg. The man cried out in pain. But the howl ceased right away because Clafous punched him in the stomach so hard that he lost his breath.

The man fell down. Clafous picked up the knife like he was gathering evidence and put it in his pocket. Then he searched the man lying still on the sidewalk and took possession of a revolver, another knife, some keys, a dagger and a few papers. Coming back to the second man he picked him up off the ground and dragging him like a drunk brought him to the closest police station on Rue de La Tour d'Auvergne.

At the station he talked briefly with the officer on duty before going into the chief's office and throwing the prisoner on the floor. The poor guy looked like he was breathing his last.

The officer sent someone to fetch the chief back to the station. Then he brought Clafous the first aid kit and prepared to help him take care of the wounded attacker on the rug.

"He has to come to right away," Clafous said. "We have to bring him around and get him ready to talk so that when the chief comes…"

Clafous and the officer on duty got to work on the prisoner. After loosening his clothes they started rubbing him, hard enough to sand off his skin, and pressing his ribs. They forced him to swallow a drink they concocted that would help their massage. It was a mix of alcohol, arnica, lemon water, ether and caffeine, which they spooned down his throat.

With such treatment, not to mention the ammonia rubbed on his temples, it was hard for the man to remain unconscious. In fact, the gentleman was fully awake in no time.

28. Ripard the traitor

When the chief got to the office the wounded man was swearing up a storm, insulting Clafous and the officer, which proved that everything was all right. Just to be careful they had put him in chains.

Clafous made sure that he was recognized by the chief before telling him who the prisoner was and what information they had to get out of him. The guy was one of the most dangerous ex-convicts who had served out his sentence but was still supposed to be in exile. Being in Paris was, therefore, a serious offense that he was guilty of.

The chief did not mince his words, "Bipard, we have to understand each other."

The prisoner wanted to object, to deny everything, even that he was Bipard, but the chief was informed by Clafous and cracked down. He proved that he could not deny being the criminal.

"Well? So what!" the man yelled. "You have no right to keep me here. I've done nothing wrong."

"Excuse me, my good man, but first of all your visit to Paris is prohibited. Then you hit a police officer and threatened him with your knife. Well, that's enough to justify your arrest and keeping you locked up."

"I didn't hit him... I didn't..."

"Enough! If we throw you in front of the judge you'll be back behind bars for years to come."

"I'll get a good lawyer and we'll see about that."

"You'll be seeing a good judge and the law is clear. We won't argue about it. You know very well that you were caught and you're going down for it."

"Too bad."

"Don't say that... You're just angry and in a really tight spot."

"I'm used to prison. The penal colony will suit me just fine."

"Sure, sure, except you'll be far away from the Swinger."

A tremor ran through Bipard at the mention of this name. The chief was pulling the right string... the only one that vibrated in this brute.

The Swinger was a pretty girl with whom Ripard had fallen crazy in love. It was for her, to satisfy her material needs, that he was leading a life of crime and had become the dreaded criminal he was. For her he had gone to prison, for her he was willing to die on the scaffold. He loved the Swinger with all his huge, heavy heart and was violently jealous. He had suffered a great deal...

The girl got her name because she loved to dance, so on the streets they nicknamed her the Swinger. She was the best, the most graceful, unflagging, dauntless and adept, the girl who knew how to be the most enticing, the most lascivious, how to show her lecherous body to the oglers, to give herself completely to the man who could make her twirl...

Speaking to Bipard about the Swinger was a sure way to get him to listen.

"That's it," the chief went on, "if you put up a fight, we'll lock you up and the Swinger will go dancing without you."

Bipard flew into a rage.

"And there are plenty of good dancers who are just waiting for her."

"I'll kill them all."

"No, no, good man, no... this time you'll be gone for many long years... and exiled again. When you come back, if you ever come back, you'll be old, washed up, and the Swinger will have had many other dance partners. She'll be swinging with so many men... so many that she won't even recognize you as the man she loves today."

Bipard was rattling his chains, furious. He started screaming as if he were being tortured, scalded with hot iron... he was trying desperately to break his chains now.

The chief let him exhaust his powerless rage, get out all his anger and curse the world.

Then he continued, "Whereas, Bipard, if you want to be reasonable, just a little bit, well, we could come to an agreement."

"Who me?" the tortured man shouted. "Me? An agreement?"

"You're not hearing me. I'm saying that if you want to be reasonable you could walk and go find your Swinger who's probably waiting for you right now... while all those guys are trying to make her forget all about you not being there."

Once again the poor guy fell into a jealous rage.

"Listen up, Bipard," the chief said, "you can go free."

"Free?" the felon asked. "Free?"

"Sure. You can leave."

"When?"

"Very soon. There's plenty of time to find the Swinger and keep her from dancing off with someone else."

"You'll let me go? I'll be out of here?"

"Not only out of here but we'll close our eyes and will forget that you ever were in Paris. So, you'll be able to... go dancing all you want."

The wretch was quiet now. Still aching but calm, he was all ears, waiting. Then he spoke in a serious, almost bashful voice. He had decided to ask, "What do I gotta do?"

"Not much. You were at a meeting tonight at the Barbottiere..."

Bipard broke in before the chief could finish. He almost yelled, "If you're asking me to betray my friends... no deal! Never! I'll never squeal. Keep me here. Lock me up but you won't make me say anything about my comrades."

"It's not about them."

"I see where you're going. Still, I'd rather never see the Swinger again, I'll never say a word."

A formal statement like this did not lack grandeur for a wretch like him. The chief and Clafous could not help admiring this pitiful nobility but they were not the type of men to be effected by it.

Very calmly the chief resumed, "We know perfectly well that you won't betray your comrades."

"So?"

"Again that's not what we're asking."

"What do you want?"

"Some simple topographical information."

"Topographical?"

"Yes. We know where the meetings are held at the Barbottiere and the passwords, Z'à la vie and Z'à la mort. We know all that already."

"So, you can learn nothing new from me."

"We want to get to the meeting room and we want someone to take us there."

"Good luck."

"It's you."

"Never. Never!"

"No… Okay, say goodnight to the Swinger."

"Goodnight Swinger."

"And congratulate her lovers who'll show her the good times that should be yours."

Bipard jumped. He wriggled and writhed on the floor, on his knees, almost managed to get to his feet. He was in the midst of a violent, internal struggle between his animal passion, his love for this woman and his primitive consciousness, his special point of honor.

Should he give in for the Swinger, the girl for whom he had stolen and killed, for whom he had gone to prison and suffered? Or should he sacrifice her for his friends, forfeit his love for the sake of loyalty?

The chief knew the side he had to take in this battle that he caused in the criminal's savage soul. And he knew that it was to his advantage to press him hard.

"No, no!"

"Otherwise it's the paddy wagon for you and you'll be in jail in an hour."

"No, no!"

"A quick trial and conviction, then the penal colony… and at least 20 years without seeing the Swinger again."

Bipard was no longer fighting. He was overwhelmed, vanquished. There were even tears of rage slowly draining out of his eyes.

"You'll set me free?" he finally asked.

"Immediately."

"And not come after me?"

"And not come after you. You can go back to Clafous' or pick up the Swinger anywhere else before someone else gets a hold of her."

Stiff and ghastly but resigned to his fate like cattle seeing the butcher and knowing what was going to happen to them, he said, "Let's go." But he asked, "How are we going to get there? Not like this. The members can't recognize us. Otherwise it won't be you keeping me from seeing the Swinger... it's them who'll kill me."

"Don't worry, no one will recognize either you or us."

The chief threw a big coat over the bandit's shoulders and gave him a floppy hat along with a scarf. Now it was easy to hide his face. Besides, rain had been pouring down for a long time.

Clafous and the chief also changed clothes. The chief put on corduroy clothes like zinc workers wear and Clafous changed into a coach driver on his way to work. Since a parking lot was nearby it was simple and logical as a disguise for corpulent Clafous.

Two other officers in disguise followed at a distance and some uniformed officers were posted around the Barbottiere.

"The trap is set," the chief told Bipard. "If you try to escape, you'll be caught. And right now the Swinger is being guarded by two of our men. In case you want to play a dirty trick on us, she'll be whisked away and gone from you forever."

"Come on, let's go!" Bipard said. "Since I've agreed to betray my comrades, I have no desire to give you the slip. I'm your prisoner. My liberty and my happiness are in your hands, at your mercy... Let's get walking!"

The chief and Clafous undid the chain around Bipard's feet and took off the handcuffs. But Clafous slipped his rough hand around the prisoner's arm like old friends and Bipard could feel his powerful grip. Anyway he had already felt it and was still aching from it.

"Let's hurry," Bipard said. "There's no one left at the Barbottiere now except the statue maker, who's probably sleeping."

So, the three men left the police station in a hard rain, moving as quickly as possible. Bipard was still feeling pain and limped. Clafous holding his arm looked completely natural. He looked like someone helping his drunk friend get home. Both in front of them and behind walked the plainclothes officers.

From Rue de La Tour d'Auvergne to Guelma Alley is not a long way. Despite their handicap the three men were there in no time. They took Rue Victor-Massé, Rue Frochot and reached Place Pigalle, which they only had to cross.

Clafous was afraid of meeting one of Bipard's partners, a member of the Z gang who might recognize the prisoner, give the alarm and ruin the whole plan. Fortunately, this did not happen. Besides, Clafous and the chief were careful not to pass in front of the Barbottiere when they entered the alley. They went all the way around, came back up the street and entered through a door that led into a courtyard that ran down into Rue des Abbesses.

The pouring rain had chased away the last night crawlers. Therefore, being absolutely certain that no one had seen them or followed them, Clafous, the chief and Bipard went to the statue maker's workshop. They swung the door open.

"Take a good look at this," Clafous showed Bipard a revolver. "Any sign of betrayal and I shoot you in the head."

"Okay, okay, it's all good," Bipard said.

And they entered the workshop. The statue maker was sound asleep. Nevertheless, when the key in the door rattled a little, he woke up.

"Who's there?" he shouted.

"Z'à la vie!" Bipard threw out.

"Z'à la mort," he muttered back.

"Good. Don't worry. I'm just getting something from down there."

"Eh? Down there? All right, go ahead."

Bipard asked, "Is there light?"

"No, but they're filled. Just got to light it up."

"Okay, okay. Go back to sleep, I'll do it, I'll light it."

Clafous and the chief listened very carefully to this conversation between the two men.

Bipard told Clafous, "We have to take this lamp for light because the ones in the hallways are out." He pointed to a small table.

The chief picked it up. Clafous was holding Bipard now with his right hand and the revolver in his left.

"If you're playing us, if you're leading us into a trap, you're a goner."

Bipard just shrugged, "If you're scared, you shouldn't have told me to bring you here." He pushed open a door and showed the way taken by the Zs.

The three men went down into the basement, then through the old mine shafts and corridors. The farther they went, the harder Clafous' heart beat inside his chest. He felt that every step was bringing him closer to Paulin Broquet. But the minutes felt like centuries and everyone was keeping them away from the meeting room, the courtroom, the execution room.

"Now you're going to tell us where Paulin Broquet is!"

The three men walked for quite a long time in the tunnels, trudging through gray, sticky mud. The lamplight made their shadows dance wildly on the walls.

"Left... right... that corridor, the one in the middle," Bipard would bark directions from time to time.

The three of them trudged on, bogged down here or sliding around there, staggering, tripping, almost falling down constantly.

"Are we almost there?" Clafous asked, becoming worried by their lengthy journey.

"Almost," Bipard said. "After this corridor..." And just then he slipped and fell to the ground. He cried out in pain, "I twisted my ankle! Just what I need for this Sunday stroll. It's the same foot you hurt before."

"Lean on me. Come on, show a little backbone," Clafous was becoming more and more impatient.

They slowly, painfully got back on their way.

"Luckily we're there," Bipard said. He pointed down a long, dark corridor in front of them. "It's at the end of this corridor. But give me a second, my foot is killing me."

He leaned back against the wall in apparent pain. Clafous had let go of his arm and was thinking about the time ticking away, every second that kept them away from Broquet. He was sure that the wounded man could not escape them here or even dream of it, so he let him go, giving him a little room to recover.

The chief was standing right next to them. "Catch your breath and get a move on since we're almost there."

"Yes!" Bipard shouted. "We're there! Just a few feet away is the room where Broquet was so brave and reckless to enter... where he was judged... and where we threw him in the hole!"

"Bastards!" Clafous yelled.

Bipard was bent over, rubbing his injured foot. Suddenly he straightened up and ran off. He had knocked the lamp out of the chief's hand. It fell in the mud and went out. And someone cried out in pain. Clafous had just got stabbed in the back with a knife that Bipard had snuck up his sleeve when he grabbed the lamp.

In total darkness now Clafous was wounded and the chief was confused. They heard loud fits of laughter.

"Well now, gentlemen," a hoarse voice was trying to control its laughter, "you're just not up to fighting against Zigomar. You wanted to know where Paulin Broquet was? Nothing simpler... you're going to join him."

Applause and bravos echoed through the chambers.

"Long live Zigomar!"

At the same time, a purple glow lit up the vaulted ceiling. Then a peal of thunder shook the walls and an explosion went off... part of the tunnel system collapsed into rubble. The rogues were blowing up their lair.

Of course, this decision could not have been made without regret because the place was safe, convenient and practical. But it was their policy that any hideout that was discovered had to be abandoned and destroyed.

Moreover, from the first day that they occupied the Barbottiere, they had started planting bombs, meaning they were preparing to blow up the tunnels that they were so carefully cleaning up for their use.

Dynamite was set around the mines in strategic locations to get the maximum effect. The bombs were hooked up to electrical batteries in the workshop where the statue maker or someone else was always on guard. Other electrical posts were spread around the tunnels but only the superiors knew their secret. They were installed in case of a surprise attack, a chase, to blow up individual tunnels to stop an invasion or aid an escape. The bombs were examined every single day. And before any meetings they were double-checked.

When Bipard spoke to the statue maker he was careful to use specific words to ask certain question that would sound normal to Clafous and the chief of police but that meant something completely different in their secret communication.

"Is there light... just got to light it up... etc." Obviously they were talking about the bombs. But the tunnels were not empty like Bipard claimed at the station. The "they're filled" probably meant there were still members down there. And they were warned when Clafous and the chief entered the corridors.

Now they understood why Bipard had taken so many detours. He wanted to give his partners time to get ready to escape. When he figured they had enough time, he thought of his own race to freedom. He pretended to fall, to twist his ankle...

When he leaned against the wall, complaining that he could not walk, could go no farther, there was good reason for it. This part of the wall, which looked no different from the others, especially in the dim light, was in fact made of wood but painted gray to hide the door that led to another corridor.

Bipard leaned on it where there was a narrow slit between the planks that looked like any other crevasse in the rock. But through this slit was stuck a small, flat piece of wood like a knife. Bipard leaned on this because it was pre-planned that the Z members hiding behind the door could use this to signal to him that everything was ready... and he could act.

It was then that Bipard, after saying what the Zs had done with Broquet, lunged, knocked out the light and stabbed Clafous. Then he escaped through the wooden door that was being wedged open for him and now he was with his companions after playing his role admirably and successfully.

The explosion produced its expected results.

The columns supporting the ceiling of the meeting room collapsed, cut down by the dynamite, and the ceiling caved in, crushing everything, leaving no trace, no clue of what the room had been, and plugging up the pit opening where they had thrown Paulin Broquet.

Clafous and the chief were not crushed. But behind and in front of them piles of rubble blocked them in, condemning them to die slowly of suffocation or hunger. The total darkness in which they were plunged only added to their torment.

And Clafous was hurting from his wound.

Their situation was desperate. And they knew it. For, there was no hope that someone could reach them except after many days of long, hard digging. They would be dead by then!

Nevertheless, they tried everything that men of action in their situation would try. They went at one pile of rocks, trying to dig a hole through the corridor. But they only had their hands to work with and they quickly saw how useless they efforts were. They just ran up against unyielding rocks and walls and all the willpower in the world, all the energy of hardened men like them was futile against this lifeless matter.

For them this was the most frightening way to die, this slow, hideous agony...

They were going to die only a few feet away from the man they had come to save. They were going to die next to the tomb of brave Paulin Broquet.

29. Conquering Riri

Morning came and like always after a long, rainy night, it was radiant. Beautiful and cheerful. Paris was washed clean, smiling under a blue sky that was scattered with a few white clouds as fine as silk.

The houses were tinted pink and the charming odor that was spread by the flower merchants seemed completely natural, just part of the street scenery. You would have thought that there were violets growing under the pavement like in some field of pasture.

With a bright sparkle in their eyes and a smile on their lips the Parisians headed to work, to the office or to the shops. Laughing and giggling, the living flowers of Paris, the working girls hurried to the factories, sometimes hiding their little pink noses in their muffs, their imitation furs, because it was cold this morning.

In Place Pigalle and around Place de Clichy, on Rue Blanche and Rue de Clichy, however, teams of workers were setting up roadblocks, starting to tear up the pavement, opening up big gaps in the sidewalk.

A few hours earlier, at the break of day, a big explosion had been heard underground. In several places the ground had cracked and water was spewing from a few broken pipes. They thought a gas main had blown up. But they did not know exactly where to look for it.

As one of the young working girls was passing by Rue de Clichy on the sidewalk, scurrying on her tiny feet, a road worker who was laying a protective iron grill over a manhole called out to her, "Better off on the other side of the street, mademoiselle Riri."

Riri stopped short. She looked at the road worker who had just called her name. His beady little eyes and turned up nose were totally unknown to her. He looked nice enough and was smiling, but she could not remember ever having seen him before.

"You know me?" she asked, genuinely surprised.

"Yeah... sure... mademoiselle Riri," he stammered, a little embarrassed. "Of course."

"How so?"

"I live in the neighborhood. Avenue de Clichy. Near Ganneron Alley."

"Oh, I see."

"Well, if I may... you should use the other sidewalk because... the gas line runs under this one... and we're making some repairs... because of an accident... there might be more explosions."

"Oh, thank you. That's kind of you to warn me. Thanks."

And Riri crossed the street, reached the other sidewalk and continued on her way, with a light and charming step.

One of the road worker's colleagues came up to him and said, "The boss is right, Simon, you're always bungling things because of women."

"It just came out, Gabriel. Sorry. I said her name without thinking. But it doesn't matter. She won't ever guess why I really know her... how I could know her name..."

"Okay, okay, let's get to it."

And Gabriel, Simon and the team of men got back to work.

When Gabriel and Baiter had not seen their boss return, they suspected he was under the Barbottiere. Agents from Broquet's squad who were on watch around it had seen him go down Guelma Alley. Gabriel and Baiter were in a panic, fearing the worst from their boss' reckless move. They went back to Clafous' to get some information because the owner of the "Enfants" was the last to talk with Broquet, so he should know something.

But Clafous was not there. Then they understood that Paulin Broquet had gone alone, maybe with Clafous, to try to infiltrate the bandits' lair.

"He was obsessed with the idea," they told themselves. "He didn't want to tell us so we wouldn't try to change his mind... which would've been nearly impossible anyway. You know, when Paulin Broquet has something in mind a cannonball can't knock it loose."

Gabriel, Baiter, Simon and a few men from the squad came up with a plan. They decided to get into the lair themselves either by force or by stealth, to search it from top to bottom and not to leave until they found Paulin Broquet.

But even though they knew that the meetings were held at the Barbottiere, they did not know exactly how to get into the bandits' hideout because they had no idea where the actual entrance was. They expected, however, that getting the information would be a big waste of time while their boss was probably hurt and in grave danger.

The policemen they met, the ones they knew, told them about the latest adventure of Clafous and the chief going into the Barbottiere with Bipard. Broquet's partners, therefore, for the moment at least, could only wait to lend a hand, to run to the aide of those who were right now doing what they wanted to do.

All of a sudden there was an explosion and they knew for sure that something serious had just happened in the Barbottiere. For, they did not believe for a minute in a gas main blowing up. They immediately thought that the criminals had very likely been surprised and cornered and were defending themselves by collapsing the tunnels that led to their hideout, thus burying the detectives under the debris.

Now crestfallen, they joined the workers who were starting the search. They wanted to be there to go down first. In anguish they wondered how they were going to find their boss. If he was still alive...

And Simon, in spite of the panic in the air, still found time to fool around, to flirt with the girls going to work, to strike up a conversation with Pretty Riri!

But it must be said that Simon was not just out to have fun. He went back to work harder than ever without paying any more attention to any girls, with nothing on his mind but his suffering boss.

As for Riri, she was back on her way to work.

She had already forgotten about the little incident that had just surprised her so much. The worker who claimed to know her as a neighbor had already, almost completely slipped her mind. She had other, more important, more serious matters to think about. While managing to keep a sparkle in her eyes and an exquisite smile on her lips she strolled down the street with a heavy heart and tortured soul.

During the day, in front of her co-workers, Riri, the poor girl, played a hard and painful role. She looked happy and laughed with the others, but once alone, when nobody could see her, on her way back home in the darkened Ganneron Alley, she fell into a gloomy mood that reflected off the houses that hid so much sorrow and grief. Her smile disappeared and a dreary veil covered her radiant face.

She was thinking of all this as she went to work on this bright and beautiful morning. In the workshop, out of pride, she did not want anyone to know about her worries but on the street her anxiety, her anguish, the hard reality of misfortune that weighed on her, came crashing down in spite of herself.

Barely out the front door she was already thinking of the terrible return in the evening and the cheerful streets could do nothing to dissipate her sorrow. Oh, the return home… how she feared it! How painful it was for her!

Every night she started trembling the closer she got to the house where she lived, where her sister suffered, where her mother was dying. And she knew that behind the glass door, the merciless concierge was waiting for her to come back. When she said hello the look in her eyes said: "You already owe two months to the landlord. The third is due in a few days. Can you pay three months back rent? Can you even pay one?"

Riri was responsible for paying for this run-down apartment. And for a long time she knew that she could not afford it alone. She could not even pay in installments. It frightened her to see the concierge hovering over her, ready to pounce. Of course this concierge, Madame Thomas, was not an evil woman. If she could, she would always have given extensions to the tenants, but she got orders from the landlord and had to carry them out.

Riri knew. Madame Thomas, rather bluntly sometimes, had warned her that if three months went by without rent, the eviction process would start… Evicted from this small apartment under the roof, chased out of the two attic rooms, thrown into the street with her dying mother and sick sister!

The landlord is letting you stay out of charity, she said, out the generosity of his heart because even though a 'for rent' sign had been hanging outside the building for a long time, nobody was offering to rent the place, no other poor family was so desperate to live in this hovel.

But what would happen to her and her family if they were tossed from these rooms that turned into a freezer in winter and an oven in the summer, under the thin sheet of zinc that was called a roof? Where else could they find shelter?

This morning, more than ever, out of some dark foreboding, the painful return home, which she was already thinking about, seemed even sadder and more woeful to poor Riri. But at the same time—was it because of the ominous foreboding?—she was engrossed by an event that happened recently and was feeling more distressed in her already desolate heart.

For a while either coming out of the factory or especially in the morning when she was alone on the street she had been running into an elegant gentleman. This very handsome, very well dressed young man had managed first just to attract her attention. Then he smiled at her discreetly as if he knew her. Then he waved. Finally he gathered the courage and spoke to her.

Without fail, as if it were the most natural thing in the world...

Riri met men who flirted with her all the time, giving her compliments, trying to strike up a conversation, not to mention the real womanizers who were bolder or the brutes who barked crude propositions. That was normal for the streets. Every woman, if she is even slightly attractive, faces this when she steps onto the sidewalk. Now Rirette was, as we know, gorgeous. And she was inevitably told so. She whetted men's appetite and unconsciously stirred up their desire and love. But Riri knew how to defend herself and turn them down so roundly, so bluntly that any indecent advance made by audacious men was cut short, crushed for good, and the louts sulked off.

This gentleman, however, appeared so discreet and so attractive that she could not brush him off like the others. When he finished talking, she could not bring herself to reject him. Besides, his voice was soft, captivating and she felt like some strange, enchanting caress was stealing over her.

"Mademoiselle," the gentleman said, "do not take offense at this audacity of mine. I know who you are... I know who I'm talking to. And I'm not out to conquer or seduce you. I am truly, madly in love. It is my impassioned heart that forced me to approach you... and to beg you to hear me out."

Rirette tried to walk away, to hurry down the sidewalk, but he followed her and went on saying, "Let me just say something very brief to you. You're very unhappy at home... your mother is sick and well, if you'd like, all your worries, all your pains could disappear. You're beautiful, Rirette, like no other woman in the world. I love you! I'm rich and..."

This time Rirette did not let him finish. Her eyes flashed with indignation, making them even more beautiful, as she cut him off and said, "Enough, monsieur! Enough! Since you pretend to know me, you ought to know that I can't listen to you any longer!"

"But..."

"Leave me alone! Goodbye, monsieur!"

161

"I assure you, Rirette, you're making a mistake by not listening to me. You're wrong about my intentions. Let me explain to you..."

"Please, leave me alone!"

Rirette ran this time across the street and left the gentleman on the opposite sidewalk, a little irked it must be said.

But without Riri suspecting, a co-worker of hers had seen the whole thing, the whole drama. Naturally she ran off to tell the other co-workers. Word spreads fast among young women and they had long discussions about Riri's behavior. Especially since all the girls knew the gentleman. He was the one they all called the Count.

It was none other than Count de la Gueriniere who himself had seen the two brothers in Ganneron Alley and hanging around Riri's workplace in Rue de la Paix and figured that the banker's sons must have been madly in love with her.

The Count, therefore, so that his rivals not best him in this lovely conquest, was determined to make his move. But he was not counting on Riri's honor and integrity. He was used to seeing women surrender to his first propositions, even those that seemed much harder to seduce than this little working girl. He was sorely mistaken. This was, perhaps, his first defeat, his first downfall as a Don Juan.

His pride as much as hatred for the two brothers urged him on, despite the initial failure, to keep after Riri, whom he really did desire and whom he wanted to conquer at any cost. Besides, maybe there was something else for him in chasing after this girl, something more than a simple satisfaction of a passing fancy.

The Count de la Gueriniere was not the type of man to launch himself on such adventures, to risk being drowned in ridicule without a stronger, ulterior motive. But what else could he expect from Riri, whose mother was dying of poverty in an attic room? And yet he was determined to break through Riri's resistance.

"A little patience," he told himself. "A little more nerve... and you'll get a hold of Pretty Riri whose virtue will end up being tamed."

Furthermore, the Count could not leave it like this, being snubbed and insulted on a public street!

"I've got other ways of making her see reason. If the usual, simple ways don't work, there are better, more forceful ways I could use." And he repeated to himself, "Riri, my dear Riri, you have to be be mine! It's inevitable! It's unavoidable! By hook or by crook, Pretty Riri, you will be mine!"

Poor Riri! Ill-fated Riri!

30. Two love letters

In the workshop, however, her co-workers supported or criticized her for denying the Count according to their own tastes and their own nature.

"You shouldn't have done it! You shouldn't have denied him!" some of them said. "A rich man! No more poverty! No more working! It's all comfort and happiness! Come on, just think about it! You're crazy not to accept him. In your shoes I know what I'd do. Tomorrow I'd be sitting among my own furniture in my own house... with horses and a car... and easy street for the rest of my life. Wedded bliss! You shouldn't have missed your chance!"

They went so far as to say that she had no right not to listen to the Count if only to save her mother who was dying because she did not have the care she needed.

Others, however, supported Riri, praised her honesty, agreed that it was not necessary to listen to smooth-talkers to be happy and help your parents. They remembered many others who surrendered to the promises of slick gentlemen, counts, barons and more... who did not find the happiness they dreamed of or were promised. These girls could say and prove that what they called the easy life, wedded bliss, was really a painful experience and in no way desirable.

And yet Riri, caught between these two opposite opinions, kept telling herself, "To take care of my mother. To have a little money for her, for poor Marie. To bring a little sunshine into the sad house where they have suffered for so long. Where they have wept!"

And she wondered, "Should I listen to the Count? Should I deny him again?"

With her heart in dismay, her loyal, honest soul in upheaval, coming back from work after a day that had started so strangely, when she went down Ganneron Alley and stepped onto the stoop of her building, she was asking herself, "What new misery is awaiting me tonight?"

The concierge saw her and stopped her in the hallway. "Mademoiselle Riri," she called after her. "Wait, I have some letters for you."

"Letters? For me?" Riri was surprised. "For me or my mother?"

"For you. Since it's written 'personal' on the envelope I didn't think I should bring them up and give them to your sister. I was waiting for you. Here."

Madame Thomas handed the girl two letters. She looked at them but did not recognize the writing. One of the envelopes was framed in black—a letter of condolence. The other was written on fancy paper with a golden wax seal in the form of a count's crown and bearing a coat of arms.

The concierge gave Riri a few words of explanation, "This letter is from a young man in mourning. A nice-looking young man who made me swear I'd give it to you personally."

163

"He didn't give his name?"

"No, mademoiselle, but he looked a lot like Dr. Robert who comes to take care of your mother."

"Oh, Dr. Robert!"

Rirette had still not seen him. She only knew him from the descriptions of her sister, mother and good Fernand who constantly sang his praises.

"Maybe you know him."

"Maybe."

"I'm sure he put his name on the letter because he was a real gentleman, from a good family, a man of the world, I could see that. As little as we see that around here, it's obvious from the start."

"It's probably some business for mama," Rirette said, "or a job offer for my sister or me."

She blushed, trying to find an excuse, feeling embarrassed at the thought that Madame Thomas might think her capable of receiving love letters. She wanted to find some explanation to give her, some reason for this letter whose contents were still unknown to her.

But the concierge lowered her voice and said, "Oh, I haven't told you everything. Another gentleman came by. Well, this one was a lord for sure and good looking, very distinguished... a count."

Riri jumped, "How dare he come here!"

"He said he only had one thing to say to you."

"You didn't answer I hope. He can keep his one thing to himself."

"That's what I led him to believe."

"Well done."

"I told him he was wasting his time with you."

"Yes, certainly."

"I know."

"If he comes back, be so kind as to tell him that chasing after me like this is very painful, very unpleasant for me. I'm lucky that he talked to you who are a good woman and have known me for a long time... otherwise what would people think of me?!"

"That's what I told him, too. But he answered that he had no intention of causing you any trouble, that he wasn't trying to compromise you, that he thought very highly or you and your family, your mother... that he was hoping, therefore..."

Riri cut her off, "In that case, he shouldn't be writing to me personally or speaking to me but to my mother. But please, Madame Thomas, if he comes back, tell him to leave me alone. There are plenty of pretty girls in Paris who would be happy to hear him out. Let him go find one of them and leave the others like me in peace with all the worries we have to deal with."

Madame Thomas agreed, "You're right, mademoiselle, righter than rain. It's always good to hear an honest girl like you talking like that." Then she changed her tone and added, "I've got another message for you."

"What now?"

"From someone else… and unfortunately a lot less pleasant."

"Go on."

"The manager has been coming by and he told me to tell you that you promised to pay up… and he wants to know if he can count on you?"

Rirette turned pale. Slowly, grievously, she answered, "Yes. I think so, Madame Thomas… I hope so."

"The manager doesn't want to give you any more time. He can't wait any longer."

"Okay, okay."

The concierge went back into her apartment. Rirette started plodding up the sticky and slippery stairs. She felt sick at the thought of going back to the cramped, unhealthy rooms that she had so much trouble keeping.

Back in her own apartment, Madame Thomas gossiped with her friend, Madame Bochu, a neighbor who came over to drink a glass of Curacao with her, "Well, you're a witness to it. You heard what I told her."

"Every word."

"I gave her the message."

"Without a doubt."

"It's that the count gave me 100 francs. Yes, 100 francs to say that to Riri!"

"100 francs for what you told her? Well, what would he give to make her accept!"

"Oh, when these people are in love, money is no cost to get what they want."

"You can say that again."

"A real nobleman that one. 100 francs… Five Louis for a letter!"

"Oh, if Mademoiselle Rirette would just listen to him… well, there's someone who could certainly pay her back rent and medicine for her mother… and all the rest…"

"Yes, but Rirette's an honest girl."

"No doubt!" Madame Bochu chirped. "But she's too pretty."

"She's very virtuous, you know. I'll vouch for that. Pure as the driven snow."

"She hasn't got any money."

"Not a cent."

"Well?" Madame Bochu raised her glass of Curacao and said, "Virtue, you see, is a luxury when you're poor." And with this stab she emptied the glass down her throat.

Riri entered her apartment, grievously troubled by what the concierge had just told her, and threw herself around her mother's neck. She hugged her long and tenderly. She needed some comforting, some support and strength, to not be beaten down, to purge her ears of those hideous words, to keep her thoughts free of bad advice.

"Oh mother, dear mother," she said, "how much I love you! You have no idea how much I love you!" Then she asked about the visits of Dr. Robert.

"He came again today, my child," the sick woman answered. "He's such a charming man. Such a good heart, so kind and affectionate."

"And," Marie the hunchback added, "he's starting to think mama's getting a little better."

"Really?"

"Yes. For the first time he pronounced the word healing."

"Oh, what good news!"

Then Rirette went to help Marie to prepare the meager dinner. Later, left alone for a moment in her room, she decided to open the two letters that Madame Thomas had given her. The one framed in black and the other sealed with a coat of arms... She started with the latter.

"Mademoiselle, allow me to urge you once again... You were upset this morning... because I didn't know how to tell you my feelings... But I was flustered by the great, unexpected pleasure of talking to you... By writing to you I can keep my head about me and tell you more calmly what I wanted you to understand. I suffer to see you so unhappy and I want to see your beauty in the light it deserves. I am very rich and I can..."

Rirette stopped there. She crumpled the letter.

"It's always the same thing. You're beautiful... I'm rich... I can pay... Sell yourself! Oh, how nauseating!"

She stared at the other for a moment, not sure she wanted to open it, afraid of finding even more words like what she had just read and it would make her angry, fill her with shame... But she remembered what Madame Thomas had said: "Yes, a very nice young man, very proper... in mourning... who looked a lot like Dr. Robert."

She opened the envelope and read the letter. The tone of this one was very different. Rirette read it through to the end, very slowly. For the first time among the many love letters she received and that she tore up right away, she found here one that she could read without feeling sick at heart.

"Mademoiselle, allow me first of all to excuse myself for being so bold as to write you. Please do not be offended or feel that my sincere respect for you is in any way diminished. I would like you to allow me to say all this in person. But since I dare not approach you on the street and out of respect for you and my own dignity I can find no other way to do this. I would be satisfied, however, if I could make you see that it is not some clichéd love I feel for you but it is a powerful attraction, an inexpressible feeling of deep and sincere affection that constantly drives me into your path. You are alone in life with a sister and a sick mother, without support, without help, without relatives. I come to ask you to do me the pleasure of trusting me, of believing me, of treating me with these two whom you love so much as if I were an old friend, a relative, a brother. I ask nothing in return. Later, when the time is right, if you judge me worthy, you can show me a little affection. I make you no golden or false promises. I can only tell you that I will be infinitely happy when your eyes stop crying and you can finally smile at the future…"

Rirette was astonished by kept reading this letter that was so different from all the others that she had ever received. Those last lines were especially striking:

"I ask nothing of you… Later… when the time is right… I will be infinitely happy when your eyes stop crying and you can finally smile at the future!"

This letter she did not crumple up. She did not tear it up. She held it in her hands, dreamily, and repeated, "Your eyes stop crying… you can smile at the future."

But shaking herself out of her reverie, she shrugged her shoulders and moaned, "Bah! A liar like the others… just a more clever liar… Worse than the others! What does he want? To be here at home with me… to plead his case… he asks nothing because he figures he can demand everything! Oh, it's always the same story in different words… You're beautiful, I'll pay, be my mistress! It's disgusting!"

But she still hesitated to tear up the letter like she did the count's. Unconsciously, calmly, she knew not what speculation, what intuition made her keep it, place it in the box where she kept her souvenirs from childhood.

And when her sister called her to her mother's side, those last words kept drifting up in her memory: Stop crying! Smile at the future!

31. Wealth and poverty

To smile at the future. In a few days Rirette could imagine a time when this might be possible... In the sick room, bent over a small folding table, Marie the hunchback had set the table in front of her mother's bed. A very simple setting that consisted only of a napkin, two plates, two glasses and a pitcher of fresh water.

As for dinner, the hunchback's ingenuity made do. She called them by the pompous names that she had read on the menus posted in the restaurant windows. Some dishes were just vegetables and she was rarely able to add some discounted tripe.

Now, tonight, on a plate triumphantly called a dish, was a chicken decorated with watercress.

Riri was absolutely stunned. "What's this? It looks like chicken... It is chicken!"

"Yes... yes," the hunchback smiled at Riri's wide eyes. "Yes, it's a chicken."

"A chicken... a real chicken?"

"A real chicken. Two feet, two wings and a whole bunch of white meat."

Riri was flabbergasted. She stared at the chicken without being able to understand how this fowl could get into their home... and be so generous as to offer itself to them all golden and cut up on the table.

"What kind of miracle..."

"Watch this," the hunchback said. "Look, Rirette!" And she put down another plate, also called a dish, the sight of which made Riri cry out in joy.

"A pastry!"

She clapped her hands, leaned back in her chair and sat there, looking from her mother, who was smiling, to Marie, who was gloating, and the pastry, which was sparkling.

"A pastry? Real as well?"

"A real one with crust and delicious things inside."

After holding her breath in surprise and wonder, she gasped and asked, "Where did this marvel come from? Tell me!"

"Fernand, our friend Fernand," the sick woman said. "He sent all this over to us."

"How did Fernand manage it?"

"Apparently," Marie answered, "they had a lottery at his factory and he won two chickens and two pastries."

"What luck!"

"Since he figured it would be just make extras at his house he gave half of it to us because the chicken has to be eaten fresh and the pastry isn't any good the next day."

"Good old Fernand! An excellent pastry and a magnificent chicken."

The hunchback continued, "I'm keeping the white meat for Mama and the rest is for us."

"There's enough to feast on for a week!"

Happy Riri, a naïve gourmet, bit into a slice of pastry and declared it tasty, delicious. Then she shared a chicken wing with her sister and found it no less exquisite.

All this was truly too good for Riri to believe every word her sister had told her and she wasted no time trying to figure out where it all really came from. In truth, half of what was said was true. But her mother and sister knew no more about it than she did.

Here is what happened.

To bring a little light into the dark home Dr. Robert had thought up this story of the lottery. Not daring to show up in person at the apartment he went to find Fernand and had given him the mission under this pretext so the mother and young ladies would accept the gift without suspicion or offense. The strategy worked perfectly. A little joy entered the home where sadness usually held sway.

However, Dr. Robert, as delighted as he was, did not want to leave it there. He was thinking, not without reason, that the hardship in the poor apartment must be much greater than one could imagine. He knew how important the question of lodging was among the poor and he wondered if Madame Menardier and her girls were also facing serious problems.

He questioned Fernand about this very delicately.

Fernand did not hide the fact that although he knew no details because Riri and the hunchback were very proud and never talked about their troubles, still he reckoned that they were late on their rent and bills.

"Well, my friend," the doctor said, "here's what you're going to do: You're going to tell Marie and Riri that for some reason, which you can figure out yourself, you got a little advance from work and since you don't need it right now you'd like to loan it to them."

The worker shook his head, "Not a good idea. They'll never believe me."

"Why?"

"They know all too well that workers in my factory barely make enough to live on and when we've got kids there's never enough money. And good fortune falling from the sky slips right off the roofs of the poor! It just doesn't hold water."

"And yet..."

"Sure, the story of the chicken and the pastry, that one worked. But real money is too much. It's less easy to swallow."

169

"So, what do we do?"

"Maybe there's a way."

"How?"

"Monsieur Paul, who's kind of a relative, who they trust a lot... I think he wants to marry Riri."

"What?! He wants to marry Riri? Who is this Paul?"

"A really talented artist who makes sculptures... statues..."

"What does he have to do with us?"

"Well, suppose this money you want to give me for Madame Menardier was given instead to Paul... I mean you buy a statue from him. With the money he'll want to help out the people he loves, so of course Riri, who he loves a lot."

Good-hearted Fernand had no idea how much pain he was causing the doctor with his simple statement. He did not see that he was digging a wound in this heart and by insisting on it he was hurting him more.

But Dr. Robert managed to say, "Maybe that's the way. You're right, yes, we have to do it to get our friends out of misery. How much do you think is needed?"

"I don't know exactly. But since Paul is really strapped and so that everyone gets their share, maybe 1,000 francs? Is that too much?"

The doctor responded, "No. Tomorrow I'll give you 2,000."

"2,000 francs!"

"That you can do with what you think best."

"But the statue?"

"You make the decision. You can say it's for an amateur collector who wants to stay anonymous and you can bring it to where I tell you."

"Why not choose it yourself, doctor?"

"Me?! But I can't show my face. If the artist knows it's the doctor, everything will be ruined."

"That's true."

"Not only can he not know it's me but I also don't want to know him."

"I understand, doctor. I understand... we're doing this for the best."

The doctor walked away, moaning to himself, "With every step I take I feel pain and every time I do good I hurt more! If I hadn't come to the help of these poor people I never would have found out about the sculptor's love for Riri. I already knew he existed, this relative of sorts, but I knew nothing about Riri's drama or her love for this guy..."

And the doctor wondered, "Does she love him like he loves her? Have they confessed their love? Whispered to each other? Are they engaged? Just waiting for a little relief in their poverty to consummate their happiness?"

Despite his new anxiety Robert let nothing show when he went so generously, so kindly to look in on Riri's mother... Riri whom Paul loved... who maybe loved Paul... and whom he, Robert, adored!

Pretty Riri whom Raoul also loved.

A few days later, when he went to get news from his accomplice Fernand, he was very surprised to learn that his good intentions remained unfulfilled.

"Why?" he asked anxiously. "Did Paul refuse?"

"Oh, no, not him. He was happy to sell the statue, which is wonderful by the way, really pretty, you'll see."

"So?"

"So, when Paul, who had shared the secret with Marie to make a surprise for Riri, went looking for the concierge, they told him that the landlord had declared that the rent was temporarily, meaning definitively, taken care of."

"Oh."

"That's what she told me."

"The landlord's a good man then."

"I don't know. But it was a surprise to everyone. Because if he forgave the rent, that means he wanted to help out his tenants in need."

"Obviously."

"And he had already ordered them to leave the Menardiers alone for three months."

"Who is this marvelous landlord? Do you know his name?"

"Baron Van Cambre."

"Baron Van Cambre?" Robert repeated. "I've heard of him. He's a banker, I think, a financier. He's well known around the stock market."

"He's the one, Monsieur Robert. And well known around the racetrack too. He's got stables. They talk about him at the factory. He's got horses that aren't too bad. Some friends who hang around jockeys, who get tips, guys who bet on horses know him... by sight of course... and hear about him."

"Is he a good man?"

"I don't know. It seems that he's got a wife, the Baroness Van Cambre, who thinks she's the fashion queen of Paris. I think even Riri has done work for her. That'd be strange. She's big woman who might've been pretty once. They also say—but it's a friend who bet on one of the baron's horses and didn't win who says this—that the Baroness is as romantic as she is fat... and that she got some verses dedicated to her by a young poet with got long hair who wanted to get into the Académie Française."

Dr. Robert smiled and said, "All this talk about the baron and poetry but I just want to know about the rent that's been put off and since it has been, I guess we can't do anything but wait." Then he added, "But, Fernand, don't let your guard down. Don't get caught napping. If there's some kind of trap that we don't know about yet, we've got to be ready for it."

"Got it."

"You keep informed and let me know right away..."

"Yes, doctor. But what about the 2,000 francs?"

"That the sculptor kept? Take the statue where I tell you."

"You're a good man, Monsieur Robert. Good to everyone. Thank you for my friend Paul… it'll get him back on his feet."

The same idea had crossed Raoul's mind. He, too, was obsessed by the thought that in this time of trouble Riri's mother could not pay the rent. He knew that the landlords in Paris, even the best of them, did not like or often could not stand waiting long for their payments.

He feared the poor family would be evicted.

When he decided to take the letter to the concierge he had seen the note about the due rent and he had no doubt that it concerned Madame Menardier. Then he came up with a plan.

Not being able to carry out the plan himself he gave the job to his butler whom he wanted to trust despite recent incidents. He was, in fact, the only person he could trust with this mission. He was still a young man, clever and smart, who had worked for him devotedly for several months now.

"Marcelin," he said after giving specifics about the apartment in Ganneron Alley, "you're going to go to this place and rent the room. Rent it in your name, of course. And you'll tell the concierge, after paying two months in advance, that you can't move in right away. Therefore, she can leave the tenants alone at least until the next rent comes due."

"I understand, monsieur. And the next rent I'll say the same thing?"

"You got it."

"Okay. It's good work that you're doing."

"Well, in no case whatsoever should you mention my name."

"Okay."

Marcelin carried out his mission. But he did not take the trouble to go all the way to Ganneron Alley. He simply went over to Avenue de la Grande Armée, into the bar where the chauffeurs and mechanics hung out. And strangely enough there he met the chauffeur of the Count de la Gueriniere.

The next day, when he told his employer about what happened, he told him that the note had already been torn up and the rooms rented.

Raoul was upset. But logically he could not be too upset. Since he had written to Riri once already he would write to her again… and be more explicit about certain things that he had not yet dared to mention. He would state his case in a clear and friendly manner. If need be he would ask to come over in person to better and more faithfully offer his aid.

Moreover, with a few coins slipped to Madame Thomas he was not only confident to be kept informed about what went on in the house but he could make sure that no harm would come to his beloved.

Plus he was hoping he could meet with the new tenant and arrive at an understanding so that he could finally fulfill his dreams.

"A good man rented them," the concierge told him. "An older gentleman who works during the day and sometimes at night doing who knows what… He's a friend of the landlord…"

A friend of the landlord. That would make it a little harder but Raoul had what was necessary to tame the wildest... to calm the most restless: money, master of all! Money!

At the club Baron Van Cambre had been dragged into a corner by the Count de la Gueriniere who almost forced him to sit on the couch next to him.

"My dear Baron," he said, "I have a big favor to ask of you. You must do me a great service..."

"My dear friend, whatever you desire. What's it about? Money problems? A thorn in your side?"

"No, nothing to do with money, thank you. When I say a great service... it's because you will make someone very dear to me very happy."

"So, twice as good."

"And who is also one of your friends... of Lucette Minois."

"Ah, the beauty, yes, for her... like for you of course... whatever I can do. I'd be delighted to prove my friendship."

"Okay, let's talk clothing."

"All right. I know a little about it. I've certainly paid enough for it..."

"They're making a lovely dress for Lucette right now at Perkin's I believe."

"Probably. Perkin's is the king of dressmakers. Or so says the Baroness who gets her clothes made there."

"I know. Now, the sleeves have to be sewn by the same hand... And it just so happens the worker who's doing it has serious problems because of you..."

"Because of me?"

"She's one of your tenants."

"Oh, one of my tenants. What do you need for the pretty girl working on the sleeves of Lucette? Some new wallpaper? A coat of paint?"

"I want you to forget about the back rent she owes you."

The baron jumped. "What? So, I'm supposed to pay for Lucette's sleeves myself?"

"Not at all. I'll pay it."

"Oh well, in that case... where does the girl live?"

"Ganneron Alley."

"Ganneron Alley. Oh, sure, the young girl, the hunchback and the sick old lady? I know them. I even gave order to my manager about them." Then Baron Van Cambre added, "I'd love to let you pay the back rent but since you're so interested in them, try to get them to move out. The mother's going to die soon and you understand how things like that can lower the value of a building..."

The Baron gave the Count a note for his manager and the next day the Count not only paid the back rent but took responsibility for the future as well. And he introduced the tenant who was supposed to replace the Menardier family: a good man who was a partner of his and who, when the time came, would ask to move in and force the Menardier family to get out right away.

They would have to leave, be out on the street, and accept the home that the Count, out of his generosity, would offer Riri.

Thus the Count had once again got the better of the two brothers. More clever and more daring than them, he also made up his mind more quickly and tiptoed around details of propriety that sometimes stopped Robert and Raoul. In the race for Pretty Riri, he had taken a big lead.

There just remained to see if it would really work and if he would win over Riri for good, as he hoped and as he was betting on.

The trick was not to throw Riri, her sister and the dying mother out of their hovel because it was still necessary that Riri, in her distress, in her panic, accept the Count's hospitality offered so graciously. Here it was Riri who had the last word!

"And yet," the Count de la Gueriniere told himself, "it's absolutely necessary that Riri be mine. It would be so stupid for me to lose this treasure, yes, all these riches of the Montreils."

The Count, who was not in the habit of wasting time on trifles, of compromising for nothing, must have been powerfully motivated to launch himself into this adventure. With a man like him, it was more than likely that in so intently pursuing the conquest of Riri he had another motive besides the simple satisfaction of love.

In what sense were the words of the Count to be really understood: "It would be so stupid for me to lose all these riches of the Montreils".

Surely the Count de la Gueriniere was not just talking about the treasure of beauty or the riches of Riri's charm. But what other treasure, what other riches could be at stake when it came to the adorable girl whose mother was dying of poverty in a hovel...

32. Death fever

Robert was alone in the rooms he occupied with Raoul on Rue des Mathurins. The young lawyer had not yet come back from court. The doctor had just seen his last patient on this day of consultation. He had arranged some notes and was getting ready for his daily visit to the patient in Ganneron Alley when the butler announced the call of Mademoiselle Raymonde.

"Am I disturbing you, Robert?" the young woman asked on entering what the doctor used as a consultation room.

"No, my dear Raymonde. I'm glad to see you. At least it's a nice surprise for me." He smiled, led her to an armchair and added, "Unless it's not your brother you've come to see but the doctor?"

"I've come to see my brother."

"Who is delighted."

"And the doctor at the same time."

"Oh, well…" Turning more serious, like when he gives a consultation, he said, "Go on, mademoiselle, tell me how you're feeling? Stick out your tongue… Let me feel your pulse."

Raymonde smiled. "Oh, I'm not the patient."

"Well, well. You've come to consult me on behalf of another. I have to tell you that I don't work like this… nor by correspondence. I'm not knowledgeable enough…"

"I just came to see you for my friend Alice."

When Dr. Robert heard this name he stopped joking around. "Alice de Brialle?"

"Yes."

"She's sick?"

"No, not her."

"Oh, what a relief. Dear sister, you gave me quite a fright there."

"You were thinking that Alice got that terrible, unknown illness that struck down her mother, brother and younger sister?"

"Yes. Reassure me… She is not sick, is she?"

"No, it's her fiancé."

"Captain Cazeaumont?"

"Yes. Alice, you see, is in such a state. She's seen so much death around her that she's wondering if she's not going to go through another mourning…"

"We mustn't jump to conclusions… but I understand why your friend Alice is scared."

"She's got plenty of reason."

"Indeed. Captain Cazeaumont is sick… Did she tell you what it is? Give you some clue?"

"No. She just said that her fiancé was in bed, that he couldn't leave his room, that he couldn't go back on duty and since he came back he's suffered from the worst fevers…"

"That is worrying. Captain Cazeaumont, for his love for Alice who is your friend, with sympathy for your fiancé Captain de Rennebois, who is his best friend… he came from Orleans to attend the funeral of our poor father… He's a good, honest young man, very nice, very kind."

"Absolutely. A good heart. A man, Robert, like we love."

"Yes, but this sudden fever. Let's see… he seemed in good health to me, strong, full of energy. What happened? What did his doctor say?"

"His doctor said that it's the fever."

"What fever?"

"The fever."

"How do you know this? Did Alive write to you? Did she give you any details?"

"Here's the letter. Take it. Read it. You'll know as much as I do."

Raymonde held out her friend's letter.

"Look at that part there… I say part but it's almost the whole letter… where she talks about her fiancé. Read."

Robert read through the letter. Then, at Raymonde's request, he read it again out loud.

"My dear Raymonde, I'm sorry to disrupt your immense sorrow with my own problems, with my personal worries and cares… But to whom else but you can I go with my troubles. What heart better than your own can understand my heart?

"I am crying while writing this. And I am writing as if talking to you, while crying. But you know how to read me and you can imagine.

"Maybe, after all the sorrows that have befallen me, one by one, I'm more scared than reason demands. That's what I tell myself. That's what I want to believe. But I'm still scared. Alas! I'm frightened to death!

"My fiancé came to see me the day before yesterday when I arrived in Paris with my poor father who is more and more dejected… I found Jacques so worn down, so tired that I couldn't hide my anxiety. He tried to reassure me. He said it was nothing, a little fatigue, stress. He was trying to break in a horse and it threw him. It was nothing.

"But I saw his face turn pale. He shivered, trembled and almost at the same time was boiling hot and sweating a lot. Then he shivered again. His legs wobbled and he almost fell down.

"'I'm such a wimp!' he declared, trying to smile. 'I look horrible. I should go home. A fiancé who has any self-respect and wants to stay in the good graces of the girl he loves should never show up looking so dreadful in front of her.'

"I wanted to do something for him, to take care of him because I saw how much he was suffering despite his courage and all the effort he was making to hide his pain. All he wanted was a hot toddy.

"Then he said to me: I'm sorry, Alice, for not staying here with you longer but I'm really feeling too... under the weather, as they say in the ranks. I'll go home... call a doctor... or the veterinarian from my squad if need be. A few quinine pills ought to do the trick and tomorrow I'll be rearing and ready to come back and apologize for my weakness... for my little drama as a contender for Invalides.

"When he tried to leave he couldn't get back on his horse. He almost fell on his face. Father and I begged him stay with us but he didn't want to, claiming that the next day there was some military maneuver that he couldn't miss.

"As compensation, he said, I'll leave you my horse.

"He climbed into the car and left, leaving us standing there so worried, as you can imagine. When the chauffeur got back he told us that he Captain had trouble on his own so they had to help him into the house and up to bed.

"You can understand how anxious I was that night. I didn't sleep a wink. I prayed all night for him. In the morning my father came to see me.

"He said, I'm sorry, my poor child, to come so early but I imagined that you, too, were suffering and I came to see how you were.

"He saw my tear-stained eyes and the candles whose wicks had burned down and he didn't have to guess that I hadn't slept. He gave me a big hug. His eyes were also red... and during the night I had heard him pacing up and down, like the slow and regular ticking of a clock, as the floorboards creaked in his room. Poor father, so good, so gentle, so caring. What sorrow was crushing him... what despair was weighing on him! I felt I was the only thing keeping him attached to life.

"My dear child, he said, I don't know what evil I could have committed unwittingly for the heavens to strike us like this, but this punishment, which I don't want to discuss with the Eternal for fear of making it worse, goes beyond all bounds when it falls upon you! I don't dare cry out that it's unjust because I don't want to sound impious, but it reminds me of the cruel God of the Old Testament and it makes me tremble... Still, although I've lost hope for myself, I want to believe that the fatality will stop at your life... and that you will be spared the retribution that you deserve so much less than your unfortunate father...

"My poor father was overwhelmed and dropped into an armchair. His elbows lay on the armrests and his face was buried in his thin, trembling hands. He wept. And on seeing this my heart that was once so brave and satisfied, always so happy, became burdened with pity. More than ever I felt at that moment the merciless hand of a cruel God weighing down on our house and both of us in the clutches of the tangled web of hideous fatality.

"Then my father finally looked up: Like you, he said, I happened to see Captain de Cazeaumont yesterday. I recognized the symptoms of his high fever. I didn't think it was very serious. At his age, being strong and sound, you don't fall victim to a fever; you always get over it... But what the chauffeur told us worries me. I want to convince myself... and calm your anxieties, so I've got the car ready. When you're dressed, we'll go together to get news about your fiancé.

"I didn't know how to thank him as he was fulfilling my most ardent desire. Then he said: I want the Captain himself to reassure us and dispel our worries.

"May heaven hear you, father!

"Let's go, child, get dressed. We're just waiting for you.

"He hugged me again or rather it was me who cuddled his head in my arms and covered him with kisses. You can imagine how quickly I got ready. I barely had time to eat breakfast. From Brialle to Orléans only takes 20 minutes. I felt like it took hours. We finally arrived at the house where Captain de Cazeaumont had his little apartment...

"Wait for me, my father said, in the early morning it's only proper that I go up alone... but I'll be back right away to reassure you.

"My father, I saw, the poor man, didn't want me to get shocked by any bad news if my fiancé was getting worse like we both feared. And alas, my intuition was right.

"The Captain is very sick... very, very sick, he said as gently as possible. The Captain is in the grips of a dreadful fever. He was delirious all night long. The doctor from his regiment and other doctors, friends, came by during the night. Everyone was alarmed. The doctors are dumbfounded. They don't understand how the fever broke out or why their doses of quinine can't control it. And he's got even more disturbing symptoms. They found indications of malaria and at the same time it looks like typhoid. Now, Jacques already had typhoid in school and it's extremely rare that you catch the awful thing twice."

Raymonde interrupted her brother's reading. "Does it happen? Can you get typhoid fever a second time after such a long time?"

"Yes, yes," Robert answered, "it's possible."

"And is the second time as dangerous as the first?"

"It's always dangerous."

Robert resumed his reading in a quiet voice.

"Indications of malaria... looks like typhoid..." He thought about it for a moment before mumbling, "Malaria, typhoid, yes, that's right. It's still the same thing." And he concluded, "Strange, very strange."

He went on reading poor Alice's letter:

"Since he was supposed to see another doctor in the morning my father didn't want to leave without knowing the results. So, we stayed in Orléans where, as you know, we have a little house that we use when we're in the city.

178

But didn't want to wait for the outcome of the visit that could only aggravate my troubles, so I came to my room and wrote this letter.

"Now that you know all about my suffering at the moment, my dear Raymonde, you will no doubt be sharing my anxiety in spite of your own grief. I know your heart and I'm not ashamed. I have no qualms in calling upon it.

"Although you can't take away my worries you can at least reassure me. You see, I don't dispute the ability of the doctors around Jacques. I have total confidence in their dedication... but I'm placing my hope in only one man whose intelligence and knowledge are infinitely higher... He's the one who, I'm sure, will be able to diagnose the exact illness, recognize the peculiar affliction, the mysterious calamity that has befallen Jacques. He alone can pinpoint the malady and heal my fiancé.

"This man, I'm sure you've guessed, is your brother, Dr. Montreil. Oh, if you could convince him, if he could come..."

Robert did not finish reading. "Raymonde," he handed the letter back to his sister, "we're going to send a telegram to your friend Alice to tell her I will be there."

Raymonde threw her arms joyfully around her brother's neck. "Oh Robert, you're so good, such a good person. I didn't want to ask you this... but your heart echoes my own. Thank you so much for my dear Alice."

Robert answered his sister solemnly, "Raymonde, there's no need to thank me."

"Why?"

"We owe a great deal of gratitude to your friend Alice and to her fiancé, Captain de Cazeaumont."

"How's that, Robert?"

"Alice and the Marquis de Brialle, her father, came to our father's funeral! Captain de Cazeaumont helped us with your fiancé in our hour of grief. They stayed by our side when everyone else shunned our house. We can never forget that."

"That's true, Robert, very true." Then Raymonde asked, "When do you think you can leave?"

"On the next train of course."

Raymonde told her brother, "And if I come with you? "

"I'd be delighted."

"I'll be with Alice in her new ordeal like she was with us in our time of need."

"I couldn't agree more. But you'd be leaving our mother all alone."

Raoul will be here. Mother will understand the situation and approve of our mission of gratitude."

"I'm sure you're right."

"How should we do it?"

"Look, you go back home to pack your bag and get mine prepared as well. Me, I have to see one or two patients who are expecting me. I'll make sure they can do without me for the two or three days we'll be staying over there. Then I'll come get you at the house."

"And Raoul?"

"Raoul will find a note telling him to join us as soon as he can."

"Okay."

"You take care of the telegram."

"Perfect."

"Good, I'll have time to send word to Irene de Valtours to tell her everything."

"Irene de Valtours is no longer in Paris?"

"No, she only came for the funeral like Alice. She left the next day. She's up in Brittany with her father who lives like a bear in his mansion, as you know... Enough talking. We're wasting time. You choose the train, I trust you. See you later."

Raymonde shook her brother's hands, calling him her good Robert, and she got taken back to her mother quickly in her car.

Left alone, Robert scratched a few words on a sheet of paper that he was planning to leave in plain sight in his brother's office. Then he wrote a telegram for the Marquis de Brialle to announce his coming with Raymonde and give him the arrival time of the train they would take.

Next he wrote a second telegram: "You must come immediately to the Brialle mansion near Orléans. You are needed. I'll explain. Cazeaumont gravely ill." He signed it "Dr. Robert". And this telegram was addressed to Fontainebleau, to Captain de Rennebois.

To make certain that they would be sent, he brought them in person to the post office on Boulevard des Capucines. Then he got a car to take him to Place de Clichy. In short time he was at the bedside of Madame Menardier, who was surprised to see him so early.

"I came to order you, madame," he told the sick woman, "to take good care of yourself for three or four days."

"Why, doctor?" she looked worried.

"Because I'm going to be away and I won't be able to see you."

"But doctor I've already told you that you're too good and you shouldn't be spending so much time coming here to see me every day."

"In theory, madame, doctors should visit their patients as often as possible. That, it seems, is how they heal. Me, I think that it's when the doctor is away that the patients get better. I'm not disappointed to make another experiment here. Besides, a sick man in the countryside needs me. I have no qualms leaving you for a few days and when I get back I'll come to see how much better you're doing with my new treatment."

Nevertheless, he gave Marie strict instructions. Reassured by the poor woman's stable condition he knew that outside of some sudden, unexpected crisis he had nothing to fear. Just to be sure, however, he sent word to Fernand whose devotion he could count on.

With peace of mind he left and went to Rue Chalgrin. Along with Raymonde he took the first train in the evening that was heading to Orléans.

When Alice de Brialle ran off to Paris after getting the telegram announcing the murder of the banker Montreil, she threw herself into the arms of Raymonde and said, as we might remember:

"No one better than I can understand your sorrow. I was burdened with three deaths, one after another. I lost my mother and my older brother, struck down by a mysterious, dreadful illness that all the science and all the devotion in the world were powerless to help. And lastly you came to me when my younger sister was herself lost to this implacable evil."

The doctor had no chance to see Madame de Brialle nor her son because their deaths came so quickly. They were swept away, so to speak. With his brother Raoul and Raymonde he barely had time to arrive from Paris to attend the funeral. He was, however, able to be present for the hideous death of the young sister.

So, today the sudden onset of sickness for Captain de Cazeaumont looked to him like the same thing, alas, that had already brought death into this house three times.

Dr. Robert was in a hurry to arrive, not only as a friend of the Brialle family, but also as a doctor wanting to see, to study this mysterious malady that he suspected but was still unable to pronounce the name. He was hoping, if it really was this sickness, to be able to specify it, prove it scientifically and finally relieve some of the pain.

They did not in fact know what caused the death of Madame de Brialle. The doctors decided on a decomposition of the blood that they attributed to albuminuria, to uremia, to a general morbid condition, to a latent sickness that the patient had not told them about or did not know about.

The death of the son followed symptoms of tissue mutation, swollen muscles, rotting sores and rapid decomposition so that they diagnosed tetanus. But without any appearance of truth. In fact, the young de Brialle helped his father in the farm work and taking care of the livestock. He was constantly in the fields, in the barns or in the stables. Therefore, an insect infected with anthrax could have stung him. Moreover, he remembered that when he was showing the horse groomers how to change the bandage on a sick horse he had scratched a finger. Maybe this was the cause of the awful disease that would lead to his death.

As for the girl, she was in good health, fit and firm. However, unlike her brother, she did not have anything to do with the farm work. All her time in the countryside was spent riding her pony with a basket lunch and the only time she went to a farm was in the afternoon to drink a little fresh milk. She did not touch the farm animals or any equipment. Moreover, she always protected her pretty face under a big hat with a veil and wore gloves. Therefore, she was safe from stinging insects.

The doctors were baffled by the malady that struck her in turn. The symptoms were so strange, so puzzling, so unusual for France that they hesitated to call it by its name. Nevertheless, after long consultations the opinion they came up with was that they were confronted with a case of typhoid fever, that cruel sickness that takes such weird forms. This one showed all the signs of typhus fever with complications of meningitis. The girl could not be saved. Her youth fought hard but death, in the end, despite all the care, despite all the help that modern science could bring, ended up being dreadfully victorious.

Dr. Robert Montreil was at the Brialle mansion by then. He had come with his sister Raymonde. But he had arrived too late to take part in the doctors' consultation and could only stand over the corpse and observe the damage done by the sickness.

Dr. Robert was strangely affected. He, too, had never seen such a case among his patients or in the hospitals. But since his professor, his master had been called to the consultation and pronounced his opinion, he could not, out of respect, voice his own view. Still, he asked for authorization to study the sickness a little more and for permission to perform an autopsy, not from the Marquis de Brialle, who was devastated and barely seemed aware of what was happening around him, but from Alice.

Urged on by an understandable sentiment, by the scruples of a loving sister, Alice de Brialle, believing that it would be a useless profanation, did not want a scalpel to cut open the poor little body that was already so tortured, so deformed and so afflicted by terror. The Count de Marnais, the Marquis' nephew, shared his cousin's opinion.

Robert Montreil, therefore, respected the relatives' will. He did not touch the girl's body. But he attended the funeral and while helping in the final preparations of the body, which had only a few days before been full of life and laughter but was now repulsive even to the religious nurses, the doctor's experience with the spectacle of death allowed him to study the body a little more.

Not satisfied with this he was able to hide away some of the bandages that were stained with puss from the wounds. In complete secrecy he set them aside, folded them up in a leather cloth and snuck them out in the bottom of his trunk.

When his sister Raymonde asked him about this he answered, "Even though they refused to let me perform an autopsy, I think I know what killed the poor girl."

"It wasn't typhoid fever?"

"No! But my professor and the other doctors were close to the truth. This death is so bizarre that it's no surprise that these experts in their field didn't think of it or ruled it out as impossible... unreal."

"And you, Robert, you believe?"

The doctor, as we know, gave this answer: "First I want to analyze what I've got under a microscope. I'm hoping to find in the rags and bandages the bacillus that I think is there... to support my conviction and give me irrefutable proof before naming the disease, which is too terrifying."

When Dr. Robert got back to Paris he got down to work. But he did not want to say anything about the results of his research. He just said that it was taking longer than he thought, all the while asking Raymonde to keep his studies a secret.

Now we can understand his rush to answer the desperate call of Alice de Brialle.

The next morning he was in the room with Captain de Cazeaumont. To avoid questioning the authority of the officers and doctors who were in charge of his care, the Marquis de Brialle had come to introduce him as a friend of the family who happened to be a famous doctor. For, the name of Dr. Montreil was renowned among his peers. They were kind enough to welcome him with no hostility, no jealousy, recognizing his scientific authority and appreciating his simple manners and sincere modesty.

They were all eager to hear his opinion in this most intriguing case and unhesitatingly gave him all the information they had, all the observations they had made during the last two days.

Then Robert stepped over to the bed. The captain barely recognized him. He looked gravely ill. At times he shook with fever. Then he would lie motionless in a coma-like state. Sometimes he shivered and at other times he was stifled by heat, covered with sweat that was rancid and foul. Discolored patches appeared on his body while under his arms and in his groin swollen cysts erupted like fat nails trying to pierce through the skin.

Robert studied all this and said to the doctors: "Your diagnosis is correct, messieurs. We are looking at malarial fever that the Captain must have caught during some excursion, a hunting party near a swamp perhaps... It's rare, indeed, to see such a violent case in our country but exceptions must be made, unfortunately, in medicine as in everything else. However, as rare as it is in this country, we can find a reason for it or at least an explanation that I will offer up to your judgment without wanting to impose my own. In my opinion, what makes this normally benign fever look so much like the violent effects of malaria... is that it is complicated with a sudden relapse of a typhoid fever that the Captain already had once. And a relapse in such conditions is always more serious. Hence this fever that is not only very violent but doubly so, as it were, by all the aggravations of typhoid."

The military and civil doctors were quite ready to agree with this statement, which did nothing but corroborate their general opinion. They informed Dr. Montreil of the treatment they had given the patient. Robert nodded. He just recommended that they increase the dose of quinine.

"He must do everything we can," he said, "to bring down this fever. The rest will take care of itself."

Alice and Raymonde were waiting anxiously for Robert to come back after the consultation. Whatever he said would be like an infallible oracle to their ears.

"Well?" they asked him when he stepped into the room.

Robert thought it best to hide the gravity of the patient's condition from the eyes of the young women and the Marquis.

"Well," he pretended to be calm although he felt far from it, "it's not as bad as all that."

Alice cried out, "Oh, doctor, talk to us. Tell us the truth!"

"I just told us. I understand how you feel but I think you were mistaken to get so alarmed."

"So Jacques is better?"

"You're not going to see him riding a horse anytime soon but..."

"But you'll cure him?"

"I hope so."

"You swear you'll save him..."

"A doctor never swears."

"Then promise me."

"I promise you. Mademoiselle, I promise to do everything I can to get him back on his feet."

"Oh, from the moment you arrived, from the moment you took charge..."

"Don't give me any magic powers that I don't have."

Raymonde said to Alice, "My brother never swears to anything. If you knew him you would know that he's gone further here than he usually does. The moment he told us that he would probably save your fiancé... that means that you can consider the Captain out of danger."

Alice suddenly relaxed. She wanted to speak, to thank Robert, but she could not utter a sound. She fell into Raymonde's arms, sobbing.

Smiling this time Robert had to offer his care... to save the young lady now.

Nevertheless, hope and confidence had returned to the Brialle family. Raymonde and Alice went back to the mansion.

33. The right shot

Robert and the Marquis stayed in Orléans to see the patient a second time. At his request the Marquis got Robert a room in the house so he could be close to the Captain. Robert also asked for one for Captain de Rennebois who, no doubt, would soon be here after receiving his alarming telegram.

In fact, when the young ladies got back to the mansion they found Captain de Rennebois climbing out of a car. He had lost no time. Getting permission to leave, jumping on a train and arriving at the mansion was all done as quickly as humanly possible.

Raymonde, who knew nothing about it, was highly but happily surprised to see her fiancé. Robert in turn, who kept secrets like this, must have been just as surprised when he arrived later with the Marquis because along with Captain de Rennebois was the Count de Marnais, whom nobody was expecting.

After paying his respects to his cousin Alice and Raymonde the Count de Marnais greeted the Marquis. "Uncle," he criticized affectionately, "once again you're in a dilemma, my dear cousin here is torturing herself with worry and you didn't say anything to me! You didn't inform me!"

Alice asked the Count de Marquais, "How did you hear that Jacques was sick?"

"I have my police," he answered. "I have my police who tell me everything."

"What do you mean?"

"I simply read about it in a Orléans newspaper. It was pure luck. I must have had some intuition, some premonition of it to glance at the few lines reporting the sickness of Captain de Cazeaumont. And do you think, dear Alice, that I could find out you were troubled and not come running to offer my help and support?"

"Thank you," is all Alice said.

"And," the Count de Marnais added, "I had the good fortune to meet Captain de Rennebois on the train, so we traveled together."

Robert felt scared as he thought to himself, "I only hope Rennebois didn't show my telegram to his companion!" He got obsessed with this point.

While the Marquis was giving details to his nephew about the curious illness of his future son-in-law, Robert took the Captain aside and asked him the question that was nagging him.

"Don't worry, Robert, I was careful not to the show the telegram or say anything at all to Marnais."

"Oh, what a relief."

"He's the Marquis' nephew, Alice's cousin, both of whom are loyal, trustworthy people, but I know all too well that the Count de Marnais is a friend of the Count de la Gueriniere, a witness in his duels. That's enough for me."

Robert shook the Captain's hand warmly. They had no need to discuss the matter further. They understood each other perfectly.

After breakfast the Count de Marnais, who had pretty much the only subject of conversation, once again said to the Marquis:

"Yes, uncle, I would have been so heartbroken not to know that Captain de Cazeaumont was sick, not to be here in his suffering, especially since he was so recently my guest in Paris."

Robert and Rennebois shivered involuntarily when they heard these words.

The Marquis asked his nephew, "What do you mean that he was your guest?"

"When you came to Paris, uncle, with my cousin, to attend the funeral of the dearly departed Montreil, Captain de Cazeaumont came with you."

"Indeed."

"To avoid the trouble of finding a room I offered him a guest room with me. He did me the honor of accepting."

"Ah, yes, that's right. I remember," the Marquis said. And the poor, trusting man added naïvely, "In that case, we're lucky. You can give us some information about the trip to Paris. Maybe you can tell us if he did anything... imprudent. Did he eat something bad or drink who knows what that could have affected him..."

"I don't know, uncle," the Count de Marnais responded. "The Captain always ate at the club with me and my friends, Baron du Jard, Baron Van Cambre and Baron Dupont."

"That's a lot of barons!" Captain de Rennebois commented.

"Yes," Marnais smiled, "but from good and noble stock. There was also the financier Guttlach."

"What? Not a baron? He must have stood out. The title of baron today is like an academic prize... everyone has one." He paused before adding, "Sorry for this little digression but I'm wondering... Jacques ate with you and your friends, right?"

"Yes. The kitchen at the club is famous. And as you see neither I nor my friends were in the least bit sick."

"But at night?" the Marquis asked, "The coffee, perhaps?"

"The Captain stayed with us. His lovely fiancée, my charming cousin, was with her father and their grieving friends. The Captain, well, my God, I'm making an act of contrition here... I debauched him... Oh, not too seriously. I brought him with us to see the show 'This is Paris', which was a big hit in the city and shaking up the towns. We were cheering on the star, Lucette Minois."

The Marquis was surprised. "But... Wait... Isn't this Lucette Minois... Oh, excuse me Raymonde and you too Alice for talking about this in front of you but... Isn't this Lucette Minois the famous mistress of the Count de la Gueriniere?"

"I can't deny it, uncle."

"In that case, my friend, you have committed a serious error in discretion. When his fiancée is with Mademoiselle Montreil, you don't bring the Captain to cheer on the mistress of the Count de la Gueriniere. The Count who is facing a terrible accusation at the moment."

The Count de Marnais responded, "Which was completely cleared up by the banker himself. I consider the Count de la Gueriniere, who is my best friend, to be the most honest and the most charming of men. He was a victim of unfortunate events in that tragic affair, that's all. As it happens I'm sorry for bringing it up but it seemed called for while talking about the Captain."

It was Captain de Rennebois who spoke up next, "Did Cazeaumont, at some point during the night, talk with your friend Gueriniere?"

"Never. And I have to admit that the Captain made me aware of the error in discretion, as you put it, dear uncle, that I committed by bringing him to the Lutetia. Gueriniere was not with us... but when the Captain heard one of my friends say that he would inevitably show up... when the Captain, who didn't know him, found out that Lucette Minois was his mistress, why he stood up saying he was tired, he had to get up early and he left."

"Bravo!" Rennebois applauded. "That's the good old Cazeaumont I know."

Then he added, "Well, no offense to you, Count, but I'll take sides with my friend Jacques. The Count de la Gueriniere was declared innocent by Raymonde's poor father, so be it... but it was bad enough that such an accusation could even be leveled against him and quite disastrous that all of Paris would believe it could be true!"

And he quickly changed the subject, "So enough talk about this monsieur. Let's get back to our good and loyal Cazeaumont. I'm eager to see him. Is it visiting hours yet, doctor?"

"Sure," Robert answered. "Are you coming with us?"

"Absolutely."

During the tumult of preparations, Raymonde found a moment alone with her brother. "Robert," she sounded on edge, "we're alone. No one can hear us. Just between you and me, tell me the truth."

"What truth, Raymonde?"

"Alice's fiancé is stricken with the same mysterious illness that's already carried off three poor souls from this house, isn't he?"

Robert looked at his sister in surprise.

She went on, "When Alice's sister died, I was here, with you, and I remember that you wanted to do an autopsy but you were refused... and you snuck out some bandages so you could analyze and study the disease."

"That's right, Raymonde."

"Well, is it the same awful disease that you haven't named that has attacked the Captain?"

Robert could not lie. "I can't say for sure, Raymonde. I have to see him again. Besides, I haven't finished studying all the material I brought back to Paris."

At that moment Alice showed up and Robert could say no more about it to Raymonde.

Presently a car came to pick up the Marquis, his daughter, Raymonde and her fiancé. A second car followed with Dr. Robert and the Count de Marnais. Like the first time the girls would wait in the house for the men to come back after visiting the patient.

With the Captain there was an assistant major who was helping the nurse. To study this case the civil and military doctors who were caring for him wanted to observe every second of the patient's sickness so that they could write a report for the Academy of Medicine.

He seemed to be feeling a little better or at least when his friends arrived the Captain was resting. He recognized everyone and was extremely touched by the presence of Dr. Robert and his partner in arms Rennebois. Then he asked for news of his fiancée. Robert promised that he would arrange a visit for the next day.

"In a nutshell," he asked the doctor, "what have I got? What the hell's wrong with me?"

"Fever," Robert said. "That's it, with a relapse of typhoid."

"So, you're going to pull me through?"

"Of course!"

"Thanks."

The Count de Marnais acted very friendly and showed the greatest sympathy to his cousin, as he called him.

They stayed for as long as possible with the patient, then they went back to the house to give the good news to the girls.

The Marquis de Brialle, Raymonde and Alice returned to the mansion while Robert and Rennebois stayed in Orléans. The Count de Marnais chose to keep them company.

Over the course of the evening Robert managed to get a moment alone with the Captain when the Count de Marnais left, saying he wanted to smoke a cigar and drink a hot toddy before going to bed.

After making sure that no one was listening in, Dr. Robert told the Captain, "My dear Fabien, I wanted you to come here because something serious is going on... and I need your help."

"I'll do whatever I can."

"I know. In short, your friend Cazeaumont is a goner?"

"A goner," Rennebois was startled.

"Yes, unless we give him a quick and ready cure."

"But what's wrong with him?"

"The fever is obvious... but he's also got blood poisoning."

"Poisoning!"

"I'll explain everything later. For now the details don't matter. What's important is to save him."

"Of course. So what can we do?"

"Listen carefully. By upping the dose of quinine I could have beat the fever and stopped the effects of the disorder... but only temporarily. Tomorrow it would be back, twice as bad, and in the evening... you hear me... in the evening he would be dead."

"Oh my."

"A dreadful death."

"But that's awful. We have to save our friend. You can do it, doctor."

"Yes," Robert declared firmly. "Yes I can." And he resumed, "Just for this, for what I was expecting to see here, I've brought the cure."

"Great!"

"The cure is here in my pocket."

"Why haven't you given it to him?"

"Hold on... The cure is going to save him for sure, but I can't give it to him."

"Why not?"

"Because I don't want anyone to know that I'm using it."

"It's a secret?"

"Not at all."

"So?"

"I don't want to use it in front of my military or civil colleagues... because they would talk about it... and it's important, you hear me, it's important that nobody, especially the one I won't name here, find out that the Captain is going to be saved."

Rennebois and Robert looked at each other in silence. Like before, they understood without saying a word more.

Robert went on, "Therefore, I'm counting on you to give him the medicine for me. They don't watch you like they do me. You can do things without them asking questions, without causing any alarm."

"Got it. Tell me what I've got to do."

"It's as simple as can be. Here, in this case is a Pravaz syringe all filled up. You just have to push the safety button and the plunger will work. So, you stick the needle pretty hard into the patient's thigh and get the medicine under the skin, into the muscle... good and deep... as much of the medicine as you can and that's all."

"Okay, sounds easy."

"Yes, but you have to be alone in the room and let nobody see. It's important."

"Got it."

"If you can go give it to him now that'd be perfect. The Captain ought to be sleeping or really exhausted. I gave him a drink with some opium. He won't budge an inch. And he won't even feel the prick. Let's go."

Robert opened the small, black leather case and showed his future brother-in-law how to use the syringe. Then he sent him off to his friend.

The Captain had understood. Soon he was in Cazeaumont's room. A nurse was on duty, staring at the patient with orders to watch out for any unusual movement and to inform the major who was resting in the room next door.

Rennebois stepped up to the bed to look at Jacques. "He's sleeping soundly."

"Yeah," the nurse was sitting right next to him, "it's the concoction he drank. When he wakes up and asks for something to drink, I have to give him a glass of water with a spoonful of that concoction… it puts him to sleep."

"Very good."

Rennebois was thinking of a way to get the bothersome witness out of the room so he get use the syringe. He saw the glass of water that the nurse was talking about and while pretending to turn around to leave he knocked it with his elbow.

"Oh, clumsy me," he apologized.

"It's nothing, Captain," the nurse said. "Easy enough to fix. I can get another from the kitchen."

"Thanks. I'll watch the patient while you're gone."

The nurse left.

Quickly the Captain pulled the case out of his pocket. He took the syringe and freed the plunger. He lifted the blankets and planted the needle firmly, boldly, militarily in the patient's thigh and pressed the plunger all the way to the bottom. The prone man only flinched a little.

"Okay," the Captain put the syringe back in the case, "you got it all… that's great!"

Three minutes later, when the nurse came back, there was no way to tell what he had done.

"My friend," Robert told him, "when he wakes up later on, Captain de Cazeaumont will owe you his life."

Indeed, the next day he looked better. Two days later the doctors and majors could declare that their patient was pretty much out of danger.

"It's great," Robert told Rennebois. "It's perfect. But now we've got to keep a close eye on Alice de Brialle!"

34. The secret friend

While these events were unfolding in Orléans and at the Brialle mansion, in Paris Monsieur Laurent was terrified to see the fatal due date of the first debt he had to repay, which carried the backing by the mayor of Itonville, meaning the forged signature of Monsieur Bilmat.

Laurent saw his hour of ruin and dishonor rushing toward him too fast...

When he got back from Laigle, after visiting his father-in-law, his wife did not have to ask a single question. She understood right away from his defeated, disheartened look that he had, as she had feared, failed in his difficult task.

"Good Lord!" Laurent told her, "That man has a heart of stone!"

Madame Laurent knew all too well about her father's implacable malice. She knew that he would never forgive Laurent for the way he had forced himself into the family. On letting her husband try to soften her father's heart, she had only a slim hope. Even after the letter, after knowing that the desperate situation would spell ruin, her father would not relent. She knew it. She had, therefore, no illusions. She felt only a little sadder when she heard the trip had failed.

"He refused," is all she said. "He didn't want to see you?"

"In fact, he was kind enough to see me. He even listened to me, but he told me that he couldn't do anything for me, that he had no desire to pay my debts. He said that since I was already ruined it was better to let everything go and face the facts without dragging my feet, which was doing no good."

"What about me in this disaster? Did he think about his daughter?"

"Oh yes... He says you have to follow the husband you chose against his will. And if you don't like it, you just have to divorce me."

"Divorce you when you're in a bind?"

"Well, either a divorcee or... a widow."

"Widow?"

"Yes, widow. He'll accept you with open arms. He'll rebuild your life and guarantee your happiness."

"But what you're saying is horrible!"

"That was the outcome of our meeting. Otherwise your father was charming."

"He was nice to you?"

"Yes. He gave me some soup with cabbage, real cabbage and real bacon like we don't see in Paris. He gave me a glass of his old liquor for special occasions... and then he went to bed. That was it."

Madame Laurent was bewildered, lost in thought. She dried two tears that were trickling down her cheeks. "Don't you think," she told her husband, "Don't you believe for one second that I share my father's opinion... that I could listen to his advice. Oh, divorce! Abandon you!"

"I don't believe it… or, well, my dear Octavie, you would be very different. I know your heart is good and affectionate. I trust you…"

"You'd better! You can trust me completely. It's at times of crises that we know who truly love us. And I love you sincerely, deeply, today as much as the first day of our love. I wanted you… I married you because I loved you. I will follow you everywhere and I will stand by you always because I love you…"

"My wife, my dear wife, oh how your life that fills me with joy also revives my sorrow… because of my fault, because of me you're going to be so unhappy."

"Never with you… never if I'm by your side."

"Maybe it'd be better for you to follow your father's advice… and divorce me."

"How can you say that!"

"You can see the darkness I'm dragging you into…"

"It doesn't matter!"

"It's total ruin."

"Well, we're young, we're strong, we can start all over again…"

"All this because I couldn't be satisfied with the happiness in front of me, because I wanted more money, a lot of money, and then more, to get rich, really rich, so that you would be the happiest of women just like you are the most beloved."

"My dear, be strong, you'll see, we can rebuild our life."

"It's impossible now."

"Why?"

"We don't have enough time. In a few days the first loan with your father's signature is coming due… and I can't pay it!"

Madame Laurent answered firmly, "Calm down. We'll pay it."

"How? Only your father could have saved us. He refused."

"There's still Aunt Melie."

Laurent shook his head, skeptical, "Aunt Melie… She'll refuse too."

"That's my problem. I'll make sure she'll do it."

"Poor girl, you going to fail just like I did with your father."

"It's not the same thing. My father can't forgive the past. Aunt Melie bears no grudge against us. She loves me a lot. I'm her goddaughter. I'm sure she'll say yes… You'll see… I promised you I'd go see her and I'm going."

"A pointless journey."

"No, I'm going."

"Well… you seem so sure of yourself that you're starting to give me some hope."

"More than hope, it's certain."

"When do you plan on seeing Aunt Melie?"

"Since it's an emergency I'll leave tomorrow."

"Tomorrow… You want me to come with you?"

"Oh, no," she almost shouted. "No, let me go alone. You... you have to stay here. Being at the office is absolutely necessary... and it's better if I go see her alone."

"As you want."

The next day Laurent went with his wife to the train station at Montparnasse. Only this time it was Madame Laurent who got on the train and he waited on the platform. The train left carrying two passengers in the compartment next to her. One of them we know and without waiting for him to hang his shoes on his door to recognize him we can name him here: Baiter.

At Laigle Madame Laurent hired a car to take her to see Aunt Melie. She stopped at the post office wearing a thick veil to hide her face she sent off two telegrams. One was to tell her husband that she had arrived safe and sound. The other was addressed to Ville-d'Avray and said:

"Wait for me tomorrow at five."

Then Madame Laurent went to Aunt Melie's where she lived at the end of Rue de Bécane in an old Norman house, alone with an old servant, collecting rents from her properties and never leaving except to go to mass at the nearby church.

Aunt Melie was the sister of Octavie's mother. But she was worthy of being part of the Bilmat family—she could have taught them a few things about greed.

She had a considerable fortune, living off the profits of a small stretch of land behind her house, a chicken coop and rents paid in potatoes, cider and lard brought to her by the farmers. She spent nothing, went to bed at sunset so as not to waste candles and kept warm by sitting next to the weak fire in the kitchen. As for clothes, she had only been extravagant three times in her life: One for her sister's marriage when she had a new dress made. The second time was for her niece Octavie's first communion when she got her first dress refitted. The third was when she remodeled this same dress for her sister's funeral. That was plenty, in her opinion, for clothes.

To tell the truth, knowing her aunt, Octavie held no hope of success. But she was determined to make the effort all the same, for her husband.

Therefore, she rang at the small door of Aunt Melie's house. It took a long time to open it and after turning the locks and unhooking the chains the hinges creaked. Behind the door stood two old ladies, Aunt Melie and her maid. But the door was stopped by one last security chain.

"What do you want?" they asked sourly.

"It's me, Aunt Melie."

"Who are you?"

"Octavie!"

"Oh, Octavie, it's you."

Faced with this joyless, cold welcome, Madame Laurent was wondering if Aunt Melie was even going to unhook the chain and allow her to enter the house.

On the other side of the door, always on her guard, Aunt Melie was wondering: "Why did she come here? What does she want from me?" But she wondered this with no anxiety because she was sure of herself and she knew that whatever she asked she would give her nothing. Finally, she decided to let her niece, her goddaughter into the house.

I feel no need to describe the complete lack of heartfelt effusions.

"What brings you here?" Aunt Melie asked.

"The pleasure of seeing you."

"That's all?"

"That's all, yes."

"Oh. And just for that you paid for a trip to Laigle from Paris!"

"It didn't cost me anything. Otherwise... you can imagine..."

"What do you mean it didn't cost you anything? You travel for free on the train?"

"I wouldn't travel otherwise. My husband is a big supplier for the company and can get free tickets. He made me take advantage so I came to give you a hug."

"Well, well... How long are you staying?"

"Oh, just a few minutes. I'm leaving on the next train."

"Yes, that's good," Aunt Melie said with relief. "If I were ready, if I could, I would gladly have you stay until tomorrow... but with just this one old maid, I'll have to refuse the pleasure."

"I couldn't accept anyway."

"Your husband's business is doing well?"

"Oh, yes, very well. He's making lots of money."

"Is he saving some I hope?"

"He's doubling it."

"Good! Because earning money is one thing but keeping it, that's better. So, you're happy?"

"Very."

"You still love each other."

"Very much."

"No children?"

"No."

"Just as well. You know what they say: Children do nothing but irritate when they're young and inherit when they're grown."

There was a moment of silence. Madame Laurent thought of her husband who was expecting so much from this visit.

Aunt Melie was expecting, suspiciously, that her niece, after all this beating around the bush, would finally reveal the real purpose of her visit because she did not believe a word of this story about free tickets.

But Madame Laurent looked up and said, "Aunt Melie, I'm very glad to see you're in good health. Unfortunately I have to say goodbye."

"All right... goodbye, Octavie."

She walked her niece to the door.

"I would have offered you something but I have nothing here but bad cider and now that you're a Parisian, you're used to better than that..."

"I don't need anything, Aunt, thanks."

"I would have also liked to give you a little souvenir, like in the past, to have bought you something... a little something for yourself. But I'm still waiting for the rents to come in. Besides, you don't need anything from me. Your husband is earning money and doubling it! All right, then, goodbye."

And with the same paucity of emotion, she bid farewell to her niece.

Madame Laurent left. With a heavy heart she struggled not to break down in tears.

It was too late to take the train. It was already getting late and she had told her husband that she would be staying in Laigle. Therefore, she went down to the hotel Grand Aigle and spent the night.

In the morning she went to the post office and sent a telegram to her husband. "Saw Aunt. Surprise success. Happy. Back at 11 tonight."

Then around 1 p.m. she took the train. She got off at Versailles a few minutes before four. From Versailles she got a car to Ville-d'Avray and rang the bell at the gate of a handsome villa, bright and cheery, framed exquisitely between old trees and blooming flowers.

At the sound of the bell two fox terriers ran up barking furiously but when they saw her they became happy, crazy, jumping around, wagging their tails, giving her, it seemed, the most affectionate welcome.

"Hello, hello," Madame Laurent bent down and petted the dogs. "Yes, yes, okay, good Tintin... good Plym... okay, okay... good doggies."

A footman was standing before here. He accompanied her to the villa while the dogs ran around her feet all the way up the house.

Standing on the front steps but leaning on a cane was a young man with a lean face, emaciated, sickly. On his wooly jacket was pinned the thin red ribbon of the Legion of Honor. He was Andre Girardet.

At the sight of the young lady the young man's face lit up with joy. "How nice of you to come visit this sick old boy, my dear friend." He kissed her hand tenderly.

"Let's go inside," Madame Laurent said. "I'll scold you for getting up and being so reckless as to come outside."

She offered her arm. Slowly, painfully, they went into the salon. Tintin and Plym had already jumped onto the cushions of the big sofa and were waiting shamelessly with their muzzles in the air to be asked to make room.

Madame Laurent sat Andre Girardet on the sofa, his usual place and helped him stretch out his weak legs, supported by the big cushions.

"Oh, you're too kind, my dear Octavie," he said. "I'm so glad to see you."

Laurent pulled up a small armchair that was nearby and sat across from the young man.

"Well," Girardet asked, "tell me all about your trip to Laigle... and that magnificent Aunt Melie..."

The young lady, with tears in her eyes, recited her meeting with the old miser. She also told him how her father had treated her husband and the outcome of all his effort. She revealed the mistakes he had made and the forgery he had been so weak to commit. Finally, sobbing, she told him of her great sorrow and despair.

Andre Girardet pulled her toward him. "You're a child," he said tenderly. "Why go to Laigle? To fool your husband? To send him a telegram from there to cover for your visit here? I can only hope so! But if you'd listened to me before, you would've avoided this grief. Come now, dry your eyes. I don't like to see you suffering. I want you to come here bearing smiles not tears. Your husband, whom I don't know, is in trouble. I love you. I should be jealous of him... but he makes you happy. So, I've got a big soft spot for him. Therefore, if everyone he thinks is a friend has abandoned him, it's up to me, whom he's never seen and probably never will... since it's the only way to make you happy... Octavie, I love you with all the strength of my broken heart... of my shattered soul..."

"Dear Andre, if there wasn't this question of money between us right now I would tell you, too, how much I love you... and how much I care about you."

"I know! I know! We're victims of maliciousness and human hypocrisy, of social treachery... Nobody will ever believe that, loving each other like we do, you the honest and irreproachable wife that you are and me your loyal friend, nobody will ever believe that you came here to comfort and console me in my suffering and to rub the balm of kindness on my wounded heart... We're forced to hide our fidelity like others hide their sin. And even though I'm nothing but a big brother to you, we play this detestable game of forbidden love and adultery... It's awful but we have no choice."

"And yet only one man would understand this."

"No doubt, but he's the very one who can't find out." After a pause he went on, "Look, let's drop this mushy talk and discuss serious business. I've got a huge fortune that I don't know what to do with and you would be doing me a big favor by letting me be of some use to you."

"You're a good man, so good, Andre."

"Okay, you told me about the difficulties. Well, when the loans come due... so that the hard-hearted mayor of Itonville know nothing about them... you come here the day before... it'll be your trip to good old Aunt Melie. And that's that!"

"I don't know how to thank you!"

"You always know better than you think. When it's only a matter of coming to see your poor cripple from time to time... bringing him the sunshine of your beauty, the radiance of your smile... showing him that he's not completely alone on this earth, that another soul knows his painful secret, understands him and will comfort him by showing that although he has suffered and died for a woman, a woman is trying to assuage his suffering and will manage to do it."

Then, as tears were welling up in his eyes, he cradled Madame Laurent's head, as she was also crying, and he forced himself to smile.

"Let's not talk about this anymore. It'll ruin our appetite. They're going to serve us... here... and I think they've made a nice little dinner. Do you enjoy gourmet food?"

"You know I do."

"My, my, you have all the faults... like a true angel woman. Although we don't have cabbage soup with real cabbage and real bacon... I think you'll have some of that wonderful foie gras that you love so much but that they rarely eat in Itonville... Okay, little gourmand, I'll ring for dinner."

While Madame Laurent was leaving the Versailles station in a car and heading towards the strange, flowery house, another car was taken from the station and also heading toward Ville-d'Avray. In this car sat Baiter who had not lost sight of Laurent since the day before.

Not far from the Andre Girardet's villa Baiter stopped the car, paid the driver and sent him away. He watched Laurent pass through the gate, noted the reaction of the fox terriers and saw a young man leaning on a cane waiting for her on the front steps. He watched him kiss her hand, take her arm and together enter the villa.

Baiter figured he had seen enough and he did not need to waste any more time there. But suddenly a car went screaming by at full speed. Baiter jumped back in time... and even though it had sped by quickly he had time to recognize the car of Count de la Gueriniere.

And in the car was a young blonde whose big, violet eyes were staring frightfully out the window. Baiter had recognized her... and he cried out "Riri!"

35. The hideous trap

It was indeed Riri.

On the express demand of an important customer, the dressmaker Perkins had sent Riri to her home with a box containing various fabric samples among which the customer, who was too busy to come into the shop today, wanted to make an immediate choice.

A car was waiting at the shop to drive the young lady to the customer's home. With no ulterior motives, therefore, with no fear at all, although cautious as always, Riri climbed into the backseat, quite pleased to be taking a drive in a comfortable, elegant car. She did not know where the customer lived, so she was not surprised when the car cruised into the Bois de Boulogne. She only started to get a little worried when it came out of the Bois and climbed up the famous Côte de Suresnes.

At that moment she wanted to ask the driver where they were going. She looked for the ear trumpet but there was nothing. It surprised her a little that a luxury car like this had no way to communicate with the chauffeur.

Then she tried talking through the glass partition but there was no way to lower it, to roll it down, and she had the feeling that as hard as she tried she would not even be able to open the door.

Then Riri understood that she had fallen into a trap. She looked through the door window, calling out, waving her arms but at this speed no one could see her.

The car screeched through the gate of a villa without slowing down. The gate closed behind them immediately. And the back of the gate was covered with sheets of metal to hide whatever was happening in the yard or in the house.

The car stopped at the front steps and the door opened.

A footman, stiff as a board, very proper, was waiting. "Madame is expecting you."

"Here?" Riri was still worried.

"If Mademoiselle would be kind enough to follow me."

From inside the villa a voice yelled out, "Bring her into the little salon." And a short, heavy-set woman whom Riri believed she recognized as the customer stepped into the shadows in the back of the entranceway. From this dignified person came a voice addressed to Riri: "I'm all yours. I'm coming... two minutes."

Feeling a little reassured Riri followed the footman who opened the door of the salon. Riri entered, still holding her box.

She looked around the room that seemed lavishly furnished. But even in the light of day the curtains were drawn and only the electric lights of the crystal chandelier lit the salon.

Riri waited a few minutes. Presently a curtain rustled and someone came in. Riri cried out in surprise, "Count de la Gueriniere!"

The Count stepped forward, smiling, and approached the young lady.

"So, I really scare you, my dear Riri?" he said.

"No, monsieur," Riri responded, trying to sound confident. "No, I'm not scared."

"Glad to hear it."

"But I came here for a customer of the shop."

"She'll be down shortly. She wanted me to take care of things in the meantime."

"I brought some samples here... I can leave them. It's not necessary for me to stay here while she chooses. Anyway, they didn't realize at the shop that I'd be taken so far away... I should be getting back."

"Wait a minute."

"No, monsieur, I want to leave."

"So you really don't like talking to me?"

"Please let me leave."

"Be kind enough to give me just a few minutes."

"No, monsieur, I'm begging you!"

While speaking Riri was walking slowly around the room until she found herself in front of the door where she had come in. She tried to open it but the door did not budge... It would not open!

Riri knew then that she could no longer pretend. She had fallen into a trap! But under her fragile and charming appearance Riri had a brave soul. She saw the danger and was ready to face it.

"Open this door," she told the Count.

The Count smiled and came up to her. "Excuse me, Pretty Riri, I've had to resort to this ploy so we could have a heart-to-heart."

"It's no use, monsieur, I won't listen to you."

"Did you read my letters?"

"I want to leave..."

"In my letters I told you about the deep love I have for you..."

"Let me leave!"

"I tried to make you understand when I spoke to you on the way to work, but it was really not the place at all... I thought that here in this house we would be more comfortable and I could tell you what I want to say..."

"I don't have to listen or answer. And, this cowardly, vile trap is not going to force me to hear anything that is unkind or hurtful..."

"My dear Riri..."

"Enough!" Riri shouted as she recoiled from the Count.

"I love you. Oh, don't run away like this. Believe what I say... This is not a common love... not just some whimsical fancy... It is love in the purest, most passionate sense of the word. It is a love that possesses my entire being and will hold on until I die."

The Count followed the girl. She was running away from him in the little salon, dodging between the chairs, behind the furniture, trying to keep some obstacle between her and this man. But the Count was chasing. He was closing in on her, pushing her into a corner of the room, toward the sofa.

"Monsieur, your behavior is despicable! The only feeling I can have for you after this will be hatred... so it's no use keeping me here any longer."

"No, beloved Riri, you'll change your mind about me when you know me better, when you truly know how much I love you, when you learn to appreciate the strength of my passion for you..."

He reached out to grab her.

"Don't touch me!" Riri screamed. "Don't touch me!"

"Come on, don't be cruel... don't play the shrew..."

And suddenly changing his tone, unveiling his taunting, mocking self, sure of his victory now, he went on:

"What good is this doing you really? Think about it! You're here with me, in my house... it'd be better just to give in, willingly... to listen to me..."

Riri was stuck in the corner where the Count had trapped her. She started screaming, "Help me! Help me!"

The Count sneered, "It's no good. No one can hear you and no one will come. Listen to me! Resistance is futile... I can force you, physically, but I want you to do this on your own..."

"No, you're awful!"

"Love forgives everything. And my love is infinite. Listen to me, Riri, I don't want you to be just a mistress... I want you to be my wife. Do you hear me... my wife. Yes, you'll be a Countess, the most beautiful, most beloved, most celebrated countess..."

"You're a wretch! I'm a poor girl and I have a sister who's sick, a mother who's dying... I have no father to defend me, no brother to avenge me and you have gone too far... to dishonor me, to ruin me! It's vile and sordid and coward-ly!"

"I will fix it! You will be my wife!"

"Let me go! Let me leave!"

"What good would that do now? Everyone knows that you got into my car and came here in the country with me. Everyone will believe that you're my mistress. Like it or not from now on you're mine, yes, you're mine!" Taking a step closer, almost touching the girl, he said, "So, my dear Riri, stop fighting against it."

"Let me go!" she repeated, "Let me go! I deny you! I hate you!"

The Count grabbed her, "Come on, you're just blabbering, wasting time... I love you... I want you... I will have you..."

He dragged Riri to the sofa. The poor girl was screaming, calling out for help and struggling to break free. She bit his hand, planted her pearly whites so deeply, so strongly that the Count yelled in pain and let go.

Riri dashed away, trying to escape, calling out for help. But the Count came at her again in a rage. His eyes were flashing anger as he shouted, "Enough of these tantrums! Let's get this over with…"

In his hand he held a handkerchief and in the handkerchief was a small, glass vial… full of chloroform.

But Riri suddenly pulled herself together. She stopped screaming, calmed down, but bravely and aggressively she was wielding her pair of work scissors like a sword. She was ready to defend herself!

The Count was surprised. He stopped short, hesitating. Then he burst out laughing. "Ha, ha, nice weapon. The thorn of the rose… that never kept the rose from being plucked."

But as he was about to step forward again, it was Riri this time who made the move. She jumped at him and with all her strength, with surprise on her side, she stuck the scissors into his throat.

The Count howled in pain and staggered backward, dropping the handkerchief and its contents on the ground.

Riri stabbed the bloody scissors once more into the Count, then ran to the window. With one strong punch she broke one of the panes and started screaming for help.

Outside a voice answered her, "Hey, hold on. Where are you?"

"Here, here," she yelled.

She tried to open the shutters but they were locked. She pounded on them with her fists, but all of a sudden they were being attacked from outside. A couple of blows from a hatchet and they flew open.

A man jumped into the room. But at the same time the Count had taken advantage of the brief respite to get up and despite the pain he had grabbed his revolver. He fired.

The man who had entered was rather tall, well dressed, and wore a black, pointy beard, perfectly trimmed. He jumped in front of Riri to protect her from the Count's bullets. But Riri was standing firm, head held high, proud and calm, triumphant, smiling at the Count whose sudden, unexpected defeat filled her with joy. She did not show any fear of the Count's revolver. She was superb, both in beauty and bravery.

But the bearded man still stood in front of her just in case, protecting her from the gun, and he pushed her back hard against the wall. At the same time he swung the hatchet in his hand and hurled it at the Count.

The hatchet whistled through the air and hit the Count as he was emptying his firearm and backing away toward the door. It stuck in his head and the wretch wobbled a little before dropping to the floor.

The bearded man ran to him. But he had to skirt around the furniture that Riri had overturned in her defense. When he reached the door the Count had just disappeared behind one of the wall hangings. The man searched quickly and found a hidden door in the wall. A big pool of blood was the only trace left of the Count.

Another man (this time it was our friend Baiter) climbed into the salon through the broken window. He went up to Riri. "Are you hurt?"

"No, no, monsieur, thank you... You saved me... thank you!"

The man who went after the Count had picked up the hatchet and was about to smash through one of the doors when he stopped himself all of a sudden, turned to his partner and shouted, "Get away! Fast! Against the wall! The wall!" He broke away from the door and jumped onto the sofa.

It was good advice because almost right away they saw a big rug get sucked into the floor. A big trap door had just opened onto an abyss... a dungeon.

Baiter and the girl had to stay plastered against the wall in order not to fall into the pit. The bearded man leaned over the sofa and gingerly picked up the handkerchief with the vial that was left behind by the wounded Count. Then he jumped over to his partner and the girl near the window. Another swing of the hatchet and the lock was smashed.

They opened wide the window and Baiter hopped into the garden, revolver in hand. He took a quick look around, then went back to the window. "We can go."

The man with the hatchet stepped in front of Riri and slipped out. The two men helped the girl out and kept her between them to protect her, shielding her with their bodies, guns sweeping the grounds, ready to defend at all costs. They ran to the gate without incident.

The house and the grounds looked totally deserted now. A car was parked in front of the gate.

But once out of danger Riri, who had shown such admirable courage and charisma so far, saw herself covered in blood, let out a little shriek and fainted. After such a violent shock the sudden calm was too much for her delicate organism.

Baiter and his partner saw the blood covering her hands and clothes and figured she was hurt, wounded by a stray bullet from the Count. They did not want to risk driving her in the car. However, someone from a neighboring villa had heard the shots and come running to see if help was needed. The man with the hatchet accepted. He swept up Riri in his arms and carried her to the next villa.

On the front steps, leaning heavily on the arm of a charming young woman stood a young man. He ordered his servants, "Quick, bring the wounded girl inside. Get whatever you need for the first aid and take my car to find a doctor... quick!"

It was Andre Girardet and Madame Laurent whom the gunshots had alarmed during their peaceful meal.

"Oh," Madame Laurent, said, "the girl's hurt! Oh, poor thing! Maybe she's... dead?"

"No, Madame," the man carrying Riri answered. "No, she's not dead. But I'm afraid she's seriously injured."

"We have to take care of her, save her. Quickly, monsieur! Carry the poor girl into this room... Put her on the sofa, gently now, very gently."

At Andre's bequest, Madame Laurent took charge, becoming the head of the household in the grievous circumstances.

After laying Riri on the sofa the man stepped away, telling Baiter, "You do what needs to be done."

36. The big brother

Andre Girardet came into the salon a little later and sat down in a deep armchair. He called over Baiter and asked him about the weird event. As usual, while appearing to answer the questions, Baiter got more information out of Girardet than he gave.

"This villa next to yours is really... odd... unusual... Surely this isn't the first time that a scene worthy of the theater has played out there."

"But of course it is," the sick man answered. "Since I've been here it's the first time I've seen anything strange happen at my neighbors."

"You've never heard fighting like today, calls for help or screams?"

"Never. Of course a lot of people are over there. The owner of the villa is an old woman, a widow I'm told, whose name I forget... but she has a lot of friends and entertains a lot. We can hear the parties, piano music, singing, even gypsy orchestras sometimes."

"Like a music hall... or casino."

"They do play a lot of bridge, apparently. I suspect there are other games as well. It's more like a pleasure house, to be honest... than just a simple country house."

"Like a flower boat... just window dressing." Baiter could see there was something else going on behind the façade. That would explain the trap doors in the salon. In case of an alarm, a police raid perhaps, they could make all the game tables, roulette and such, disappear and the salon would look like a nice gathering of honest folk playing bridge.

However, Andre Girardet asked his own questions of Baiter about the adventure while Madame Laurent washed off the blood covering the face and hands of Riri with warm water.

"This matter," Baiter told him, "is as simple as can be. In short, this young lady, you can see how simply she's dressed, her worn shoes and such, is not a regular there, not one of the widow's friends, one of the elegant guests at the 'flower house'."

"Indeed."

"This young lady, as you will see in a moment, is very pretty. She's a simple worker from a poor but honorable family... and with her needle, her work, she provides for the needs of her sickly sister and her paralyzed, dying mother."

"Really?"

"It's the darkest misery at her home but their honor is intact."

"Oh, the poor child," Andre Girardet exclaimed. "In that case, monsieur, notice that I am very rich and it would please me very much to help her out. Use me, I would appreciate it."

"Thank you, monsieur. This young lady is as virtuous as she is pretty. You can imagine that she gets plenty of compliments and propositions and inflames passions... It's because she never responds to the most alluring temptations that she fell victim today to a horrible trap."

"You're sure of this?"

"You want proof? Very soon when Riri, that's her name, wakes up, she'll give it to you."

"Are you a relative?"

"No, monsieur, I'm not a relative nor a friend. She doesn't even know me."

"So how do you know... that her name's Riri and that she got trapped here?"

Baiter leaned closer to Girardet and whispered, "I know it like I know that this nice, charming lady who is so kindly taking care of the girl at the moment came from Laigle."

"What's that?!" Andre Girardet gasped.

"That she's going back to Paris, Boulevard de Sébastopol, on the 10 o'clock train."

"Monsieur!"

"That her name is Madame Laurent."

Andre Girardet was stunned and distressed by this stranger. "Who are you? And what are you doing in my house?"

Baiter answered quietly, "Don't worry, I'm here for good people, with good people, with brave souls... I'm here with you like with this kindly lady and this charming girl... To tell you the truth, I belong to the Paulin Broquet Brigade."

"The great detective?!"

"Yes, Monsieur, but speak more softly."

"That's why you and your friends, your colleagues were in the villa next door during the attack?"

"That's right, yes, my partners and I were lucky enough to arrive on time to save this girl."

Andre Girardet held out his hand to Baiter, "Allow me to shake your hand, monsieur, to congratulate you sincerely... Now, I'll have to remind you of what you just told me... You made me very happy to be able to help out this young lady and her poor family, who hold some interest for you..."

Riri was waking up.

Madame Laurent had washed off the blood from her hands and face and was looking for the wound where, she figured, the blood had come from. She could not find one. With the help of Baiter, who was more experienced in this kind of thing, she made sure that the girl was not injured in the least. It was a great relief to everyone.

Soon afterward Riri opened her eyes. And was shocked at her surroundings.

"Don't worry, Mademoiselle," Baiter told her, "you're safe here. You're with friends. These are good people who are glad to see you safe and sound."

Riri was relieved. She looked at the man speaking so kindly and the others around her. Their decent faces, honest eyes and genuine smiles assured her that what she heard was the truth.

She smiled back at them. "Thank you, Madame, thank you, Messieurs... But how did I get here?"

Madame Laurent explained very briefly what had happened. She held her hand and caressed it gently, trying to comfort her in the sudden awakening, to distance her from the anguish that had made her faint.

"We no longer need a doctor," Girardet had told the servants. He asked everyone to leave and ordered no one to be let into the villa.

Then he turned to Riri and said, "Mademoiselle, we were about to eat, Madame and I, when you paid us this surprise visit... now an agreeable surprise I must say..."

"Monsieur, I'm sorry... excuse me... It wasn't my fault..."

"You will join us nevertheless, you and your rescuer."

At this Riri turned to Baiter, "Oh, yes, monsieur, I'm so grateful... yes... oh, thank you... You're the one who came in through the window... you and your friend with the hatchet... You saved me from that wretched man! Oh, thank you, thank you!"

She held out her hand to Baiter and he shook it amiably. Just like Simon, the old clown, he had a soft spot for this girl who was just as brave in danger (he now knew) as she was in the moral struggle of life, just as loyal and honest...

It was a rare nature, precious virtue in a woman. In Paulin Broquet's school they learned to recognize and respect noble souls.

Riri was simple, charming, exquisite... Without even knowing her very well yet, only out of a sense of duty, Baiter would take a bullet for her. Now that he was seeing her up close, getting to know her better in reality, he felt ready to face a whole gang of criminals all alone just to see her smile... he would walk through fire!

Oh, now it was going to become dangerous just to touch one golden hair of this girl's head... Baiter, Simon and the rest of the Broquet Brigade would guard her from now on.

Andre Girardet smiled, "I was telling you, mademoiselle, that we were about to eat when you arrived here... You came, perhaps, a little involuntarily but I hope that you will stay of your own free will now.

But Rirette, who was back to herself, stood up. "Stay here! Oh, monsieur, I'm so grateful for the offer... but I can't accept your gracious offer. I have to get back. I don't know where I am. They brought me in a car and it was going so fast I couldn't recognize anywhere we passed by."

"You're in Ville-d'Avray."

"Ville-d'Avray! So far! Now I think is about the time they'll be leaving the shops. I have to get back home. My sister and mother will be worried... and since I'm out of danger thanks to you, I'd like to make sure my home doesn't get alarmed..."

"Don't worry, mademoiselle, you'll be driven back right away. This gentleman who pulled you out of danger will be able to keep your family from worrying. A car will drop you off at your front door at the usual time."

"Oh, monsieur, thank you so much! But I must be causing you so much trouble..."

"None at all, none at all... So, if you don't mind, we can get back to dinner."

"Please do."

"But since you're my guest, you'll do me the honor of sitting next to Madame... your savior will sit next to me."

"But Monsieur, really..."

"Yes! Yes! You will be served... I've rung... Here's your silverware... Madame now has you under her courteous protection... She's the one who will know better than I how to comfort you and get you back to normal after such a terrible shock. You just have to obey her. You'll see how easy it is to follow her orders."

Madame Laurent, therefore, took care of Riri.

Baiter also accepted... not dinner but a few cookies and some Spanish wine that they brought out for Rirette.

While nibbling with her pretty teeth and sipping politely the Spanish wine, Riri told her hosts about what happened next door.

"Do you know the name of the wretch?" Andre Girardet asked her.

"Yes, monsieur, at the shop everybody knows his name..."

"What is it?"

"The Count de la Gueriniere!"

At the sound of this name Madame Laurent could not help shivering... in deepest dread.

But Andre Girardet was watching Riri, so did not see her reaction. He simply said, "I don't know him. But I'm sure he's a scoundrel. And if I weren't... sick, I'd give him a piece of my mind."

Baiter said nothing. But he did second Girardet's opinion with a nod of his head.

The time had come, however, when Riri had to leave Ville-d'Avray to arrive home without worrying her family.

Girardet spoke to her: "Mademoiselle, chance, which is so often just the manifestation of heaven's will, has given me the pleasure of meeting you. I wouldn't like to leave it here. You're alone in this world and despite your bravery, your courage, which I know now, you could still face some serious problems. One should anticipate everything... I want to declare myself your defender, if you would do me the honor of accepting. Alas, I'm sick! But one word to a friend in Paris... a brave and good man there... and he'll be at your side as if it were me. If ever you have a problem, you see, if ever you're in the slightest danger, contact him just like you would, if hope, contact me."

"Yes, monsieur."

"In him, just like in me, you now have a sincere and loyal friend, an older brother."

Andre Girardet wrote a quick note and on the blotter that Madame Laurent was holding for him. Then he addressed the letter and handed it to Riri.

"Guard this dearly and promise me you'll use it."

"I promise, monsieur, and thank you very much."

He gave her his calling card and added, "Here's my name and address... I'd be happy if you could give me a telephone call tomorrow... just to tell me that you got home safely and are doing okay."

"I promise you that as well, monsieur, but I'm really confused about all this kindness. I'm just a poor worker. You've only known me for a few minutes and you're treating me as kindly, as warmly as if we'd known each other for years."

"One minute is enough," Girardet said, "to like and appreciate someone who is worthy. No number of years would be enough to earn respect when you don't deserve it. From now on you have a friend in me, yes and what's more—my condition allows me to speak to a charming young lady like this—a big brother who loves you."

Rirette went to thank Madame Laurent who hugged her affectionately and promised to come see her at the shop, not to lose sight of her.

For Andre Girardet, giving thanks to him, Rirette held out her hand, but after seeing Madame Laurent making a sign and smiling, she offered her blushing cheek to be kissed.

In no time at all she was riding in a car with Baiter down Avenue de Clichy. Baiter let her off at Place de Clichy and started to follow her, mingling with the crowd, keeping her in sight, until she entered Ganneron Alley and reached her gloomy dwelling, the dark house where Marie the Hunchback and her mother becoming weaker and weaker, both of them waiting for her to come back.

In her room Rirette placed the precious letter given to her by Andre Girardet into her little treasure box. The letter that was supposed to be such a great help for her, that would give her the support of a good, loyal and brave man, a big brother... this letter that was addressed to a name: "Raoul Montreil, attorney."

37. The giant grave

While these events were unfolding in Ville-d'Avray, in one of the rooms at the club, around a table holding all kinds of drinks, aperitifs and a bottle of Vichy water for Baron Van Cambre, there were gathered some peaceful smokers: Baron Van Cambre and another baron with a trimmed beard and a flower in his buttonhole, a splendid, decorative attitude—Baron Dupont. With them were the financier Guttlach and Count Faustin de la Gueriniere!

Baron Van Cambre was telling his friends about the trouble he was having at the moment with the Paris public works that were forcing him to renovate his house, to shore up his building in Ganneron Alley after an explosion of a gas pipe.

"How's that!" the Count de la Gueriniere shouted out. "They're still talking about that explosion? They shut down Rue de Clichy and Rue d'Amsterdam all the way to Trinité... It's madness to close all the roads. They did the work, fouled up the traffic and it's still, always going on!"

"And it will be," Baron Dupont added, "since Alphand[1] is dead."

"Well," the financier Guttlach said, "speaking of the dead, they reported that at the time of the explosion there were sewer workers underground... and two of the unlucky fellows were killed."

"Poor devils!" the Count de la Gueriniere.

"They pulled out two corpses up around Rue Moncey. It was the firemen from the station on Rue Blanche who brought back the bodies."

At this moment the server came and told Guttlach, "Monsieur James Twil just telephoned. He gave his apologized for this evening because he won't be able to attend. He's working at the factory and he can't break off. He will see you tomorrow morning."

"Okay, okay," the financier said.

The server walked away. He looked like an intelligent young man with bright, mischievous eyes looking over a funny, turned-up nose and a mouth that twisted in the strangest manner—he looked like a clown. There is no need to drag out the mystery. Let's go ahead and say that it was Simon, one of Paulin Broquet's men.

When he left the room, Guttlach told his friends, "This James Twil whom I invited to dine here to introduce him to you and who just sent word that he can't come, is an American, a quite astonishing man...."

"Like all Americans!" the Count interjected.

"He invented the airplane."

---

[1] Adolphe Alphand, French engineer considered the father of green, open spaces of Paris.

"Again! Him too!"

"Yes, his machine is based on completely new principles... never even thought of. It looks like nothing we've seen so far."

"Great!" Baron Van Cambre exclaimed. "And you're thinking of starting a company to make this machine?"

"Exactly. I wanted to talk to you about it so we could do it together. What do you think?"

"We'll see. First we have to see the thing."

"Whenever you want. Any day at all..."

"Okay..."

And they spoke of other things. Dinner time came, then time for the theater where Lucette Minois was getting her usual ovations. The friends ate together and when the cigars were finished they each went their way to their own particular pleasures.

The Count and the elegant Baron Dupont went to the Lutetia having a nice, quiet talk...

Thus, then, while they were looking after Riri in Ville-d'Arnay, washing her hands of the blood that had spurted from her scissor attack, from the stab wound in the Count de la Gueriniere, the Count himself was at the club with his friends!

He was with them, talking about one thing or another... the explosion, the bodies found in the sewer on Rue Blanche, the problem of aviation by heavier-than-air craft. Then he went to the show and got ready to have a night of fun...

However, in Ville-d'Arnay, in the villa next to Andre Girardet's, it was the Count de la Gueriniere who had set the wicked trap and who had attacked Riri in the salon. It was Gueriniere who was seriously wounded by Riri. It was Gueriniere who had shot at Baiter and his partner coming to help the girl. It was Gueriniere who was struck by the hatchet of the bearded man, who had collapsed, gravely injured...

And yet, there he was at the same time on Rue Royale, then on the boulevards and strolling into the Lutetia. There he was in plain sight, strutting around, smiling, saying hello to his friends just like he was there in the same Lutetia theater cheering on Lucette Minois on the evening when they robbed Bejanet's safe and Robert and Raoul recognized him as one of the notary's robbers!

The banker Guttlach had spoken of two corpses found in the sewers. Two corpses brought up to the surface by the firemen on Rue Blanche...

Indeed, they found underground, not far from Place de Clichy, two bodies—that of the Chief and of good old Clafous who were identified under their muddy disguises. They were carried immediately in a city ambulance to the Lariboisiere Hospital.

An hour after the transport, with his wounded shoulder quickly patched up, Clafous was back to himself and behind his bar since Bipard's knife had glanced off his huge shoulder blade. As for the Chief, in the morning he was reading his mail and checking the evening reports.

The explosion that was supposed to bury them had in fact saved them, so to speak. They were stuck in the rubble between two huge piles of stone but the men who came to check the damage saw that it looked recent and knew right away that they had found the source of the explosion. Therefore, they went at one of the recently collapsed walls to make the necessary repairs, to see what pipes were damaged, and they found the two men.

Smoking a cigarette, the two of them were waiting philosophically for someone to pull them out of the cavity that could have been their grave. It was not long before they were able to make the workers clearing the rubble aware of their presence on the other side of the collapsed wall.

Gabriel, Paulin Broquet's second-in-command, who was overseeing the work and guiding the research, was informed right away and ran over, hoping that it might be his boss. He found only Clafous and the Chief who could not (you can understand), to their great regret, give any information about the fate of Paulin Broquet.

Nevertheless, since they had to be on guard against spies that the Z gang would certainly be scattering around, Gabriel decided to fool everyone by making them believe that they had pulled two corpses of sewer workers out of the wreckage. So, they carried out the stretchers and brought them to Lariboisiere Hospital. Clafous and the Chief, however, had no serious injuries, luckily.

Thus the Zs were fooled by their spies' report and believed that their attack had succeeded, that the agents led by Bipard into the Barbottiere tunnels had gone to join their boss in the underworld as they wanted. But this ruse, which was undoubtedly very useful, prudent and ingenious, still gave Gabriel and his men no news about what had happened to Paulin Broquet.

Gabriel, who had taken control of the special search, left the technical aspects of the work to the city employees. He was satisfied with joining in on the different teams of road and sewer workers or even firemen. One man from each was tasked with informing him if they found something.

Moreover, still on guard, following Broquet's method, he had asked the directors of the public works to use only men whom they knew well, whom they could fully trust, whom they could count on to be discreet.

Gabriel, in fact, had good reason to fear the intrusion of a Z among the city workers. He therefore took all necessary precautions and kept a close eye on the work.

He was given a map of the sewer network, the pipes and the works in progress in this part of Paris. This was not enough: he went to look at the old maps, the original documents about the contracts made in the past with entrepreneurs who wanted to mine the quarries around La Butte Montmartre. These maps showed him—only in a very basic way, to tell the truth, but with a positive attitude it was quite sufficient—the underground topography of the abandoned quarries that were walled up but should have been filled in.

Gabriel took a blue pencil and traced the lines from the old map onto the map of the modern sewers. Thus by looking at the new map, he could see the ancient quarries and their routes.

He was able to recognize the tunnels that were temporarily (meaning, in the French language, always) being used. He matched up the landmarks and noted the points where the entrances had been dug by the public works department, especially the points where these entrances led into one of the old tunnels.

At each of these points Gabriel set up a team of his men to wait. As was their custom, each team surrounded the entrance with a metal barrier to keep pedestrians away. This precaution would prove very useful.

The underground passage that extended out of Place Pigalle, out of the cellar in Guelma Alley, was very long. Remember how long Clafous and the Chief felt they had walked with Bipard... Paulin Broquet, as he was going to the Z rendezvous, had to go on and on, from tunnel to tunnel, guided by the gas lamps, stopped at the intersections by the gang members who asked for the password.

This particular tunnel extended under Place Blanche all the way up to Rue de Clichy. The construction of the Metro ran into it and followed along for a rather lengthy segment. Today the various works had destroyed it. The tunnel had collapsed, closed off, and only the new rails of the municipal service used it. The explosion and the minor cave-ins on the Metro line required the reinforcement and fortification of the ground, which had made them close down the underground in a way, let us hope, that would be as permanent as the temporary work.

Now, the big room, the criminals' Parliament, though they called it the Barbottiere, was actually very far from the Barbottiere. It was located almost right under the garden of a religious community on the corner of Boulevard de Clichy that ran all the way up to the little Place Vintimille. In the past, apparently, the monastery even used part of the tunnels as a crypt for its church and buried their dead brothers there.

It was, therefore, almost at Boulevard de Clichy that Paulin Broquet was thrown into the hole that opened onto one of the tunnels maintained and used by the city for its works. Broquet fell into about 20 feet of water...

He could have hit the bottom and broken some bones, got knocked out... The Zs were counting on this just as much as on him drowning, which should have ensued so that they could be sure of the certain death of their formidable enemy.

Having already used this method, they knew that no one could get out of the hole alive. For the victims it would be either an instant death, short and sweet, the best you could hope for, or else a long, painful agony. But inevitably the body would be found at some time along the Seine, dragged away by the sewer water into the river.

However, it had rained in Paris over the last few days and the sewers were flooded. The place where Paulin Broquet fell was almost full up. All the water from the gutters around Montmartre was pouring in, oily, yellow, filthy and ice-cold.

Oh, there was an ugly death awaiting the condemned man in this abyss.

But it was this very deluge of dirty water that would save him. It cushioned his fall. And although he was dazed at first, shaken up, at least he could feel no broken bones. This alone was a big advantage.

The icy cold, moreover, kept him from passing out, which would have proved fatal. For, being unconscious, weak and helpless, Paulin Broquet would have drifted in the water and certainly drowned.

The detective, however, was shocked back to his senses.

"Not killed. Not dead!" he told himself. "That's good... nothing broken, nothing hurt... good! We're going to pull through this after all." And he added, on purpose in English, "All right!"

Then, shaking his fist at the ceiling he cried out, "See you soon, Zigomar!"

Zigomar

20ᶜ
LE
VOLUME

par LÉON SAZIE...

BOOK TWO: LIONS AND TIGERS

1. Back to Life

Paulin Broquet got back on his feet in the hole where the thieves had tossed him after sentencing him to death. He shook his fist at the ceiling formed by the trapdoor that had opened under his feet and closed up again over his head after the fall.

"See you soon, Zigomar!" he had shouted.

Daring to shout under such circumstances, in this situation... in this grave, was proof that he either had a lot of guts or was raving mad.

Now, Paulin Broquet had not an ounce of arrogance in him and he was perfectly aware of his situation. After pronouncing his death sentence his enemies had just executed it so that the punishment would take full effect... would be irrevocable. The executioners knew through experience that their victim could not escape his grim fate.

In the hole, in the sewers, there awaited certain death for everyone. An awful, undeniable, foul death that might be quick or drawn-out. In their refined cruelty they did not want their victim to die immediately. They took pleasure in hearing desperate shouts and cries for help echoing up the pit. In the end it was a good lesson, an excellent warning for anyone in the Z gang who might try, for one reason or another, to betray Zigomar or risk his anger and fall under their stroke of justice.

This time, with Paulin Broquet, no plea, no cry for help, no painful groan rose up the sinister well. The Zs did not hear his defiant shout, his promise as he stood up. They were likely to believe that the detective had fallen to his death.

"Too bad," some of them thought. "We should have lowered him gently into the filth."

Still, they congratulated each other and celebrated the victory, shouting out louder than ever the glory of their invisible, terribly powerful master... the glory of Zigomar!

While they were rejoicing up above, happy, confident, fearlessly planning their next lucrative enterprise, their enemy Paulin Broquet, down in the hole, was already planning his revenge.

What extraordinary energy, strength of character, courage and will! No one had ever got out of this pit alive!

Paulin Broquet was walled in, surrounded by water, and he could expect no help from outside. Even if his men were running to help him, they would arrive too late to snatch him from the clutches of death. Without a miracle he would not escape from his dreadful fate.

Well, Paulin Broquet was no infidel but he did not believe very much in miracles. He did, however, believe very strongly in justice. And despite everything he still represented the law here. Up above were criminals boasting of their victory... without being absolutely sure of their success.

Justice was down below, crime on top.

"Come on," he told himself, "this unnatural situation can't last! Something has to happen to even out the balance. The scales of justice, all askew right now, must be set right. The side of crime, gloating for the moment, has to be pulled down, forever, into the depths.

Paulin Broquet had faith in this.

Now, if faith could move mountains, it could certainly show the way to pierce through the few feet of earth that separated him from the rest of men, that cut him off from the living. And since he was not counting on a miracle from above he started right away to work on what could be called a miracle.

First of all he stood up as tall as he could. The water was at waist level. But in his fall he had become completely soaked and he felt the cold weighing on his shoulders.

"Okay, this is nothing. Let's get organized."

First he slipped his hand into his side pocket and pulled out his tightly shut, water-proof, silver cigar case and the matches in the same kind of case, which he held in his teeth. He had these cases specially made for such adventures as this—falling in water—after which it was always nice to have a smoke.

"If die we must," he thought, "let's die sweetly... and have one last smoke to while away the final hour."

But he was in total darkness. And this black night in an underground full of freezing water was awful. It made this most frightful of punishments even more terrible. However, although Broquet certainly realized that it was very dark and cold, he did not find the situation so critical or desperate.

He was thinking of how sweet life was and dreaming of once again enjoying simple little pleasures, which were maybe the best of all—having a good smoke!

With the silver cases safely held between his teeth, he dug into another pocket.

"I need some light first of all... Let there be light!"

He was searching all his pockets for something to make light while looking up at the ceiling. As his eyes became accustomed to the darkness he could tell that no light was coming from up above, from the hole he had fallen down. His ears heard nothing but lapping water, the constant flow of water entering... and a few loud squeaks to tell him that he was not the only living creature in this tomb.

"Rats! Great! At least they won't die of hunger."

But the underground remained without light from above, without the sounds of voices. Paulin Broquet figured that after his fall the bandits had closed up the pit, replaced the cover and forgot about him, considering him already dead and gone. Therefore, convinced that he was not being spied on, he pressed the button on the object he found in his waterlogged pocket and as he had said, there was light. It came from a small flashlight that was lucky enough not to have broken in the fall.

Now he could see and his situation did not look so dangerous.

First of all he dealt with what was in his immediate vicinity. With his flashlight he could examine his cigar case.

"Bravo! The water didn't have time to leak in."

He plucked out a cigar, bit off a little of the end and held it between his teeth. Then he opened the silver case with his matches. He was sure that it, too, had suffered no damage because it was hermetically sealed. Indeed, the matches were fine.

"A good cigar and dry matches! It's perfect... but now comes the hard part."

How to light it? Hard indeed. More than hard, almost impossible.

Having a good cigar and matches was one thing, a great thing, but lighting a match is the most important of all...

More than for anything else it seems that the French government, industry and manufacturing had covered it's matches with its permanent seal of "temporary"... By fabricating matches that you could handle safely and put in boxes the French government had made them, it seems, for its workers, inflammable... "temporarily". Now, this "temporary" was lasting forever for the public because the matches never lit!

If they never lit up on the surface, using the box, in dry weather, no wind, what would they do down here in the humid underground, in water so to speak... on a wet striking surface?

Broquet pondered this... anxiously.

The problem weighed on him: how to light his cigar without anything dry to strike his match on and holding the match in his wet finger to boot? It was hopeless.

But Paulin Broquet was not the type of man, as we know, to be discouraged by such obstacles, as formidable as they might seem. Everything on him, including himself, was wet. Everything around him was damp or dripping with water.

"It is, however, in this water that I have to light my match!" he told himself.

He looked at the walls. Well, he was not hoping to find a dry stone, a striking surface to save him. He knew this was impossible because even if he found the ideal stone, he would have to hold the match, push it with his wet fingers... and here the old saying "by rule of thumb" seemed a bit tricky...

217

"Come on," he thought, "this would be a really bad joke if I'm under the City of Lights and can't even get a spark!"

The walls of the old gypsum quarry held pieces of flint. With his flashlight Broquet searched for one that would serve his purpose. He pried it loose with his knife, shook it out and dried it as best he could, taking great care to touch as little as possible. Then he held it fast over a match. Using the back of his blade as a lighter he struck the flint. A spark flew out. Then another…

After a short period of useless tries, one lucky strike produced a more generous spark that fell right on top of the match and heated the phosphorus. Wonderful! It lit up! First a sizzling then a flame.

And the cigar was burning voluptuously.

"Great! Now let's get going!"

For protection he tucked his cases into his collar to keep them out of the water. Then with the help of his weak flashlight he inspected his prison.

It was, as he expected, a tunnel… a big pipe. Among his accessories, as a lucky charm, Broquet carried a small compass attached to his watch chain. He looked at it, calculated the layout of the duct and fixed his position like a sailor at sea. Knowing Paris like he did, he easily got a rough estimate of the direction and even the location of the underground. He figured that by following the water, the only thing he could really do, he should reach one of the streets leading out of Place de Clichy.

"That's fine," he said. "The worst that can happen now is for the tunnel to get too small for me to climb through."

But this seemed impossible. The pipes began at the big streets like this and the network was kept up by the public works department to allow employees, sewer workers, electricians and anyone needing to work underground to pass through.

And he knew that there were manholes all over the sewers. He thought, "Let's try to find one of these manholes."

He switched off the flashlight to conserve its batteries and lit only by the end of glow of his cigar he advanced cautiously through the water, moving downward, step by step, careful not to fall into a hole.

He walked like this for a long time. But he took pains to count his steps. Measuring each step as a meter, he calculated that he must have been around Rue de Clichy or D'Amsterdam. However, it seemed that the water was flowing a little faster than before.

"There must be a dead-end… or a sudden turn… a sharp angle that's holding up the water."

Broquet turned on his flashlight to find out. He was not mistaken. He was in front of a wall that closed off the tunnel. The water could escape only through a small opening in the bottom… and probably into one of the sewage ducts built by the city.

This was the danger that Broquet was afraid of because he was not stupid enough to dive into the water and try to worm his way into the duct. It would be a deliberate suicide attempt.

"Hell," the detective said, "this complicates things."

Just then he thought he could feel the water rising, that it was higher and faster than a minute ago. He decided to go back up because the water was pouring in so fast that if it could not empty through the spillway it would inevitably rise all the way to the ceiling... he would be drowned in no time.

The water was already up to his chest. It was hard, however, to wade back... and the water was getting higher.

We might remember this was the moment when an awful storm had just hit Paris and turned its streets into raging rivers. All the water poured into the sewers and quickly filled up the ducts.

Broquet saw the danger and thought that he would have to start swimming to get back to the pit where he started from, to stay safe in a place where the water could not totally fill up. he would wait there for the flood to end... until he could go back down and see if he had a chance of escaping somewhere at the end of the tunnel.

He was also afraid of putting out his cigar, his only beacon in this ghastly dungeon because he knew now that it would be absolutely impossible to light another in the same way... the only way he had. And without his cigar, without this little red glow that showed him the water, the dirty, ice-cold water, he would be a goner for sure. As long as his cigar burned, he felt like he was following a star!

But nature is sometimes stronger than the will of the most blessed man. And lifeless matter can get the better of the most hardened soul!

The water surged suddenly, so fast and so abruptly that Broquet was swept off his feet. He had to start swimming.

At first he swam on his back to save his precious cigar. And his cigar was now reflecting its faint glow off the ceiling, which was only a few inches away.

Broquet was putting all his effort into outswimming the rising water to get back to the hole where he would still have a little air to breath. But soon his cigar sizzled... the water had touched it. Then it went out.

At the same time Broquet hit his head against the ceiling. In a few seconds he was going to drown! Stuck against the ceiling now it was impossible for him to swim. All of a sudden everything started shaking. The ceiling caved in and water rushed out, roaring like a waterfall, sweeping the detective along with it.

The bomb that the Z gang had exploded to kill Clafous and the Chief caused this. One of the walls of the tunnel collapsed, creating a passage for the water to escape and pour into one of the corridors leading to Rue d'Amsterdam, thus flooding the sidewalks and gutters and causing a general alarm.

Broquet the fatalist let himself be swept along. There was nothing he could do, anyway, against this turn of events. Then the water subsided. He found himself in another duct, if not dry at least with some room to breathe, to revive, to continue the fight.

Tired, banged up and a little bruised, he sat in the water, in the mud. He could not stand up under the low ceiling. Turning on his flashlight he looked at the compass.

"Damn!" he said aloud. "I'm on the right path! Come on, stay strong!"

Crawling now he started forward. Next to him he saw cast iron pipes and cables that told him that he was in one of the big tunnels maintained by the city. Now, in these tunnels, for the needs of the workers, there were shafts with manholes scattered all over the sidewalks of Paris. If he could find one of these manholes, he would be saved.

"Look hard! Look hard!" he told himself. "I'll find one for sure."

Now he no longer feared for his life. In fact, after hours of this painful progress he ended up reaching one of the shafts. He was exhausted but seeing the iron bars that were used as a ladder for the sewer workers gave him back all his courage, energy and vitality. He could grip the iron rungs, pull himself up… but he did not have the strength to climb the ladder even though it was only a short one.

He was not alarmed. Salvation was at hand!

Through the manhole he saw light. Day, freedom, life for him. Dawn had never looked so radiant.

He leaned his back against the wall, looked up at the manhole, caught his breathe, tried to recover some strength, then after a few minutes once again attacked the climb. This time he could do it.

His hand reached the cast iron cover that was the only thing separating him from the living. He did not try to lift it, knowing it was impossible for him. He just looked out, touched it, caressed it so to speak. It was no longer a tombstone but the gates of life! He heard footsteps. He heard voices. He saw carriages rolling by, the sound of horses. This was encouraging, telling him that he would be discovered in no time. Then he started searching for a way to make his presence known, to let them know that he was there.

Shouting, calling out… vain efforts. With the sounds on the street they would not hear. He had to find a way to make the passers-by see that there was someone in the sewer under this manhole. The metal was thick. Broquet had to find something that could stick out far enough into the sidewalk to be noticed. He stumbled down the ladder and sat down.

Oh, if only he had a cane or a stick, he could have signaled them quickly! But he had nothing of the sort and had to find something to do the trick.

He searched himself and found a pen, a pencil, a notepad, his knife and his cigars. Each of these items could obviously pass through the slot in the manhole used to lever it open by the workers, but none of these objects were big enough to draw attention on the street. Then Broquet figured that if one was not enough by itself, he could put together two of them… and possibly three…

Here is what he did: He opened his knife and stuck the pencil on the tip. Then he tore out a sheet of paper attached it to a cigar like a flag and jabbed the cigar onto the pencil. Now he had himself a wonderful signal.

He climbed back up the ladder and nervously, fearing a haphazard footstep that would destroy all the hope he was putting in the piece of paper on his cigar, he slipped his signal flag through the slot.

We know that Gabriel, Broquet's partner, had placed men at all the manholes around Rue de Clichy and D'Amsterdam. Therefore, the detective's signal could not go unnoticed. It was seen right away. And soon one of the men stationed there leaned over and called out, "Who's down there?"

Paulin Broquet did not answer. First, to be certain, he asked, "Who's that?"

The man gave his name.

"Okay," the detective responded. "You know Gabriel?"

"Gabriel, Baiter and Simon. Yes, boss. Hang in there! Two seconds... I've got you..."

The man had recognized Broquet's voice and sent his partner to Gabriel as they were ordered to do. Then he opened the manhole cover and saw Paulin Broquet.

"Boss! Are you hurt?"

"No."

But what a state he was in! No one would have recognized him. His face was hidden behind a mask of mud; his hair was stuck together with chunks of hardened sludge; his torn clothes were even dirtier and more unrecognizable than his face.

But Paulin Broquet did not crawl out of the hole. He said, "Get me some worker's clothes. Throw them over here. I can't draw any attention when I come out."

The agent gave him a sewer worker's uniform that they had nearby in case they had to go down into the sewers. Broquet slipped into it and with the man's help managed to crawl out just as Gabriel was running up with Simon and Baiter, who were also dressed as workers.

They were overjoyed to see their boss whom they had thought they had lost for good. Tears were shed, but this was not the time nor the place for a show of emotions. Broquet leaned on their arms and after closing the manhole cover he walked slowly with them as if work time were over and the team were heading home. Then all three entered a wine shop on Rue Blanche.

Presently a car stopped in front of the door and collected the three men who looked nothing like sewer workers. The car sped off toward Neuilly.

Paulin Broquet went to get a little rest, not in his house on Avenue Trudaine—an apartment that everybody knew about—but in another place unknown to the public. At 1 Rue de Neuilly (I am not allowed to call it anything else) Broquet had a small house set up for his professional needs and very artistically decorated. He went there sometimes to get away from the noise and action and maybe have a few days of rest after a tiring adventure.

The house was in the middle of a pretty big garden, squared off and protected from prying eyes by tall trees, which were the remains of an old park now parceled into more or less pretentious houses. Here, then, two big men, rock solid, retired police officers but still strong with sharp eyes and ears, guarded the dwelling and defended it like watchdogs. Paulin Broquet was brought here.

At first he went into the bathroom. After a good cleaning he got something to eat because he was dying of hunger.

Well rested, back on his feet, smoking a cigar and sipping his coffee, he told his lieutenants the story of his visit to the lair of the Zs in the kingdom of the Zigomar. Then he added, "Now they think I'm dead... killed... drowned. That's good. I'm going to stay dead... until further notice. It'll make our work easier."

Therefore, Paulin Broquet was no longer seen at his home on Avenue Trudaine. But he was still searching for the solution to the big problem that lay before him worse than ever:

"Who is this Count de la Gueriniere?"

That was how he had ended up around the gentleman's home and saw the Count's car leaving the garage and instead of waiting for the master in front of the house it headed back to the center of Paris. Broquet wanted to know where the car was going.

"Let's go see," he told his partner.

They jumped into their car, which was parked nearby, and followed the Count's car. It stopped on Rue de la Paix in front of Perkin's, the famous dressmaker. Soon afterward Broquet and Gabriel were surprised to see Riri come out and climb into the car. From that moment on they had the feeling that the young lady was being lured into a trap. They were sure of it when they saw the car flying through the Bois and entering Ville-d'Avray.

It goes without saying that Broquet's driver did not lose sight of the Count's car. The driver stopped only once along the way to pick up Baiter in front of Andre Girardet's house. Besides, the house in which the Count's car had entered was a neighbor, as we have seen.

But the house was shut off from prying eyes by high walls and a gate. Broquet and his men disguised themselves with black beards and tried to enter the grounds where they had taken Riri. They walked around the property and jumped over a back wall where they could not be seen from the house. Gabriel stayed near the wall as a lookout. It took time.

Paulin Broquet was armed with a hatchet that was kept in the car for such occasions. Baiter had his gun out. They were lucky enough to arrive at the right time and save Riri who, despite her brave defense, was about to fall victim because someone was coming to help the Count.

We know how the Count was gravely wounded in the neck by Riri's scissors and was hit in the head by Broquet's hatchet and thus fell down covered in blood. He was deftly carried away by his accomplices. Broquet could not grab hold of him but he knew that he had been hit and seriously injured.

Nevertheless, almost at the same time as all these dramatic events were happening in Ville-d'Avray, the Count de la Gueriniere was seen bright and cheerful, a good old boy, at the club with his friends Baron Dupont, always so dapper, Guillach the financier and Baron Von Cambre. He was talking with them about airplanes and about the American James Twill.

2. A mother's anxiety

Robert went to Ganneron Alley every evening. His patient, Madame Menardier, seemed to be getting a lot better since he had started treating her.

"Oh, doctor," she told him one evening holding out her thin, frightfully bony hand, "I think you've brought joy into our poor home."

"How's that, madame?"

"First of all you with your knowledge, with your dedication you perform this miracle of prolonging my life. Then there's Riri, my pretty Riri, who's made friends with a client at work whose husband, I believe, has business with your brother the lawyer."

"That is fortunate indeed."

"This lady's got a big heart and was brave enough to come into this house here, all the way up to our poor apartment. If I remember right her name's Madame Laurent."

"Madame Laurent!" Robert was taken aback.

He knew that the name Laurent had been given along with the Count de la Gueriniere as one of his father's last visitors on the day of his death. Why was this Madame Laurent coming to visit Madame Menardier who was a patient of Robert Montreil? What purpose was driving her friendship with Riri? What was hiding behind all this?

Robert promised himself to consult Paulin Broquet because he was intrigued.

Madame Menardier, who had not seen any of the troubling effects in the doctor caused by her remark, went on, "Oh, I was so happy to see a nice lady again whom I could talk with a little... It took me back... to happier times. I lived a little of my past again... carried back to the time when this poor patient you're caring for out of charity..."

"Not at all, madame! You can say out of sympathy if the word affection is still too strong for the short time we've known each other."

"You're nice, doctor. Then I'll say affection."

"That's right."

"When this poor patient who's lying on this pallet was a woman of the world... beautiful, happy, an object of envy... I was very rich, doctor. I had a smart, handsome, strong husband who loved me and whom I loved. I was the mother of two girls, one of whom, alas, was my only sorrow, my only woe, the bitter price to pay to fate for the rest of my fortunate life."

Robert listened intently to his patient who was struggling to talk, slowly, faintly, almost in a whisper.

"Sadly," she continued, "despite the cost of my daughter Marie coming into this world deformed, my happiness was still not paid off... because one day disaster hit. They brought me my husband's body. He was killed at his best friend's house. They said and I believed that he was killed by this friend who stole our fortune..."

Madame Menardier raised her hand and cried out, "Oh, curses on that man!"

Then she got hold of herself and said, "I'm sorry, doctor, to lose control in front of you amongst these painful memories and this desire of mine for revenge. Oh, vengeance... I only want justice from heaven for all this because me... alas... me..."

She shook her gaunt, pale head. Her bones could be seen through the leathery skin... and only a smile that cracked through the aged folds of suffering and the flame that sometimes glowed in her fading eyes gave sign that this was a living body and not the remains of a mummy.

"Let's forget all that," she said. "I don't want to talk to you about sad things, Dr. Robert. It's quite enough that you're not discouraged by the sorry sight you see here... Let's talk instead about the nice time I had with the wonderful Madame Laurent. I experienced the magical enchantment of an oasis for travelers crossing the desert. Obviously I'm surrounded by good people. Fernand and his wife are always so nice to me, but despite their comfort, their encouragement and their consolation, they're too simple and uneducated and I only feel the depth of my decline... below my position... and my misery.

"Oh, when I lost my fortune, when the high class people who came to our home suddenly forget where the ruined widow lived... when the society ladies, my good friends, turned a cold shoulder, I was certainly very hurt but I consoled myself, I knew that it was completely natural, that it was always like this. In the mad rush of this world, like in a stampede, you can't fall down because whoever falls is trampled on mercilessly, crushed under foot without pity... Whoever has no money has no friends."

Robert listened gravely, not wanting to interrupt the poor woman who was baring all the bitterness in her soul for the first time.

She went on, "I was quickly abandoned by the world but I knew that everything was a charade with these people, everything was superficial, that the smiles were fake, painted on a knowing mask, that not one word was sincere, that the finely gloved hands held out were ready to grab you or push you away, never to support you, prop you up or help.

"But I didn't wait to be abandoned. I left. I who had become poor withdrew and without waiting to be betrayed I cut them off.

"Then into this poverty came sickness and I caused pity in the humble commiseration of the poor and oh, my friend, if only you knew how much I suffered! Yes, I knew I was beaten and lost all hope forever...

"Poor me, I thought my life was over after becoming a widow. I was a body without a soul... but I suffered for these two children who alone kept me attached to this earth. I suffered for these girls who were meant to live happy, adored, who should have seen every day of their life as a celebration starting with a radiant sunrise and ending in a grand finale of golden twilight...

"I was blotted out from the world, me, but my children were going to be used by the world, to work for a living. One got a job in a dressmaker's shop; the other, the cripple, painted fans, candy boxes, postcards... and they had to earn a living and could live, alone, without help, exposed to the countless dangers, confronting life in Paris. Of course, work is good and honorable and it sanctifies your hands, as the Book of Prophets says, but my poor Marie is deformed, so weak and Rirette is so pretty, a jewel, not a tool... Oh, my children, who should be rich, surrounded by friends, happy, my dear little girls, what will become of you?"

Madame Menardier wiped away tears. "There was a ray of sunshine, a little hope in my misery when Dr. Robert walked through my door."

"Madame..."

"There was a second day of joy when Madame Laurent came here... earlier... to say: 'Madame, don't worry anymore about the fate of Rirette and Marie. Riri has made a sincere friend in me and I love her a lot. I don't have children and all my maternal love will go to Riri as she deserves. From now on you must forget all your anxiety, all your worry about the future. In me and my husband and our friends your children will have good, honest friends, support and defenders. They are no longer alone in this world. With their charm, their virtue and their filial love they have gained a new family."

"That's great! Yes, that's wonderful..." Robert murmured.

"Oh, doctor, if you knew what a relief it was to hear these words. And I who was starting to doubt God, I thanked Providence first for sending me Dr. Robert to bring me back to life and giving me the strength to see that my children will know a little happiness, will be surrounded by love, guarded against poverty, supported against Paris... they are going to live to be twenty, enjoy their springtime of life, smile finally at this life that has reduced their mother to worry and tears."

"You can believe," Robert said, "that Madame Lauren, whose big heart and beautiful soul I do appreciate, by making you these promises, has only told you before I could what my brother Raoul and sister Raymonde already decided a long time ago."

"Oh, thank you, doctor, I knew that your kindness was not reserved for me alone."

"My sister also knows Rirette. Her interest in her became more affectionate when she found out through me what kind of daughter she was and what kind of mother she had."

"Oh, Doctor!"

"I couldn't tell you this but my good friend Fernand should have said something."

"Doctor, since we're talking about this, let make a confession that will show you how I had a feeling. I know that despite your knowledge and good care, my days are numbered now. I decided... when I felt death approaching... I decided to tell you: Dr. Robert, I'm going to die but before going to join their father I want to entrust my two daughters to you. Dr. Robert, will you watch over Marie and Riri?"

The doctor took the patient's hand, "You knew the answer that I would give, didn't you, madame?"

"Yes. And that's why I am trusting you with my children."

"Thank you."

"It's me who is thanking you, doctor. But what can I do? I have no way to show you my gratitude."

"Yes, madame, by helping me... by showing me that my treatment is useful by getting well as soon as possible."

"Oh, doctor, that doesn't depend on me. It doesn't even depend on you."

The long conversation was too much for Madame Menardier. She squeezed Robert's hand hard and affectionately. Then, still smiling, she sank back into the pillows that Marie the Hunchback, who had just come into the room, was fluffing gently behind her head.

3. Where does the money come from?

Robert and Raoul were in the office that once belonged to the banker Montreil, their father. The bank naturally had not stopped doing business since his death. But neither Robert nor Raoul, without the slightest inclination to finance, had wanted to take control. The Montreil Bank was going to pass into other hands, merge with another. Bejanet was dealing with this matter.

In the meantime the two brothers had asked Brunet, the head accountant, to go through the documents found in the banker's safe. Documents that he, even though as head of accounting and of litigation he should have had some knowledge of, nevertheless was totally ignorant of their existence.

It was a long and delicate task. He had started on it only a few days before. The seals put on them the day of the crime had barely been taken off.

The two brothers had implored Brunet to start with the file of Monsieur Laurent. As we remember it was the only one found out of order among the meticulously arranged files that stood neatly on the shelves in the banker's safe.

Brunet had made good headway and could now give a little information to the brothers. Therefore, they had come to meet him in their father's office and were ready to hear his explanations.

"I checked the Laurent file just like you asked," the accountant said. "I tidied it up the best I could... I had to rebuild it in a way."

"Thank you, Monsieur Brunet. You have taken on an important task. You are our most valuable collaborator. This reconstruction must have been hard work and taken a lot of time."

"Quite so... yes, indeed, quite so... Because as you know on that fateful day of the awful attack on your father, he was robbed by very skillful criminals."

"Yes."

"It is absolutely impossible for me to say how much money was taken because I found no form, no receipt."

"That doesn't matter to us right now," Raoul said. "We want to know what the secret documents were. We want to know why they didn't go through you like they would normally do."

"I understand what you want, messieurs."

"And so you have been kind enough, clever enough to piece together Laurent's file."

"Yes. Here it is pretty much complete... with a note on how to complete it."

"Great!"

"I have to tell you first of all that I found a bill for 10,000 and 15,000 francs... due now."

"Ah! And the bills?"

"Have been paid."

"Laurent's account is clear then?"

"Not quite. According to my calculations, Laurent paid over several installments a sum totaling around 400,000 francs. Now in reality Laurent... according to Montreil's papers Laurent owes a lot more but in fact received only..."

The head accountant hesitated. He cast worried eyes on the two brothers asking not to continue.

"Go on," Raoul said. "We're here to learn everything, to see everything... above all to fix everything."

"Okay, messieurs. So, Laurent, in truth, only received 50,000 francs from Monsieur Montreil."

"And he paid back?"

"400,000."

The two brothers looked at each other nervously. Then they waved to Brunet to continue.

"Here's what Montreil did with Laurent... and with almost all his clients. It was easy to figure out. Montreil loaned a first amount at an annual interest of 3%."

"That's the legal rate, normal..."

"Yes, but he never agreed to a loan for more than three months."

"Oh, that would end up at 12%..."

"When the client paid off it was no problem. He paid only the interest on the money borrowed under these special conditions, formally agreed upon."

"If he didn't pay?"

"Monsieur Montreil granted an extension, if the client accepted."

"And for the extension?"

"He doubled the interest rate."

"But after a few extensions the interest must have become impossible... and legally..."

"Excuse me, but he always kept it at 3%."

"How's that?"

"Montreil added a new note with the amount of interest due as the capital loaned... plus the amount of the new interest at a new rate."

"That's usury, exploitation, out and out thievery!"

"Now Monsieur Montreil never went beyond four extensions, which for the clients meant a loan at 12%, still acceptable in unusual, difficult times for clients who had collateral."

"And after these four extensions?"

"If the client didn't pay? The matter went to Monsieur Grillard."

"The collections department."

"Who did what was necessary, ruthlessly. Foreclosure and auctions. When the auction went well, meaning when the store, factory, farm or house was worth more than the bids, Montreil had them bought by one of his men and speculated on selling later."

"Oh, that's despicable!"

"Perhaps, messieurs, that gives you an idea of the tragedies, the losses, the deaths that result from a loan taken in this office. Pardon me for saying so... but looking at these documents I was shuddering, trembling... and I feel really sorry for you."

"Please, Monsieur Brunel, just do your work. We are counting on your loyalty and your conscience. You have to tell us everything... we have to know everything. Go on."

"Among Monsieur Montreil's clients I found the names of people in all ranks of society. I found some surprising names, that you'd never expect, even some famous names, and people who get into a difficult situation, as happens, and come to their friend Montreil, also a society man, charming and thoughtful, who was a friend, who invited them to his house..."

"It's awful!" The brothers were in agony. "Now we understand why none of his friends came to our father's funeral. We understand! Yes, now we understand!"

After a painful moment of silence Raoul said to the accountant, "Let's go back to Monsieur Laurent."

"Laurent," he said, "as the file shows, got a loan for 50,000 francs that accumulated the rate you've seen and went up to 500,000 francs."

"The poor man!"

"He was like other privileged persons, meaning Monsieur Grillard did not show up at his house at the due date. Montreil agreed to split up his debts, to put them off... but only with the backing of Monsieur Bilmat, Madame Laurent's father, a very rich landowner."

"We know."

"Now Bilmat never wanted to secure the debts of his son-in-law. They quarreled a lot, which Montreil was well aware of. But he took it on anyway and accepted the forged signature as genuine."

"Now we see why."

"Today Laurent is under threat of being arrested for forgery and theft if he doesn't pay."

"So, Monsieur Brunel, for Laurent and the other clients you are going to register their debts as paid. You will make the sum available to them."

The head accountant said, "If I may make an observation that my age, my experience in such matters, my long employment in this bank and my affection for you should allow?"

"You may."

"If I understood what you want, you are going to give back the money that Monsieur Montreil earned under these conditions that..."

"Say the money taken. Since we're talking about our father we can go ahead and say stolen! But words do nothing. There's only one thing we can do: repair the damages as far as is in our power."

"Okay, messieurs, but I have to tell you that you will be ruined."

"But we won't be dishonored!"

Brunel nodded his head.

"This money," Raoul went on, "doesn't belong to us. We have to give it back. What we're asking you to do now is to help us find who it belongs to and reimburse them as promptly and discreetly as possible."

"That should be easy enough with our means and with the help of Bejanet, the notary who dealt with buying and selling the properties, and with Grillard in collections who took care of legal proceedings."

"Did you call in Grillard like we asked?"

"He said he was available anytime."

"Great."

The two brothers looked more closely at some of the files with Brunel. They had started on what they were calling their project of restitution, of compensation. From this colossal fortune, from all this money collected in this way, they did not want to keep any one cent.

They meant to clear their name, to redeem the memory of their father, to leave nothing could sully the respect that their talent and hard work would deserve and had already earned. For this, even though it pained them greatly, they were determined to search through their father's life. And they had decided to make the necessary sacrifices, to give back whatever money seemed suspiciously acquired. As Brunel had said, they were headed to ruin.

But this would not stop them for one second in their firm decision. Until now they had felt the greatest, deepest love for their father, total veneration. They saw in him not only the best father but a highly intelligent man, one of the most remarkable bankers and they took him for an honorable man with scruples.

It was heartrending (as we saw) for them to see nobody around the coffin of a man they believed would be surrounded by friends on the journey to his final resting place—a large, emotional crowd...

The mystery bothered them as they sought in vain for an explanation. They imagined everything possible but not for a second did they think the truth was what they now saw as irrefutable proof under their teary eyes.

4. Sage advice

Two of the files that the brothers examined with Brunel attracted their attention more than the others. One was not very thick. There were only a few sheets of paper. But what was found on these sheets was of utmost interest in the eyes of the banker's sons.

First of all there was a promissory note for 10,000 francs with one word written in a corner, "Extended", and a date.

Then a letter written a few days before the due date asking for an extension on a second note for 12,000 francs. A copy of the banker's response was attached stating that another extension was absolutely impossible. On this copy was a word written in blue pencil: "Paid".

That was all. Except that the date of the second note was close to the date of the banker's murder. And the name on the note and the signature asking for an extension was Count de la Gueriniere!

"Well then," the brothers declared, "the Count de la Gueriniere did have business with our poor father just like he said during his interrogation."

"Yes, messieurs," Brunel said.

"His presence on the day of the murder, therefore, might have a reasonable explanation."

"His justification, yes. But what makes less sense is what's in the other file."

"The mysterious file you told us about?"

"Here it is. Judge for yourselves. See if I'm wrong, if I exaggerate by calling it mysterious."

Raoul opened the file.

In a thin cardboard sleeve with no markings, bound by a rubber strap, were some faded, yellowed letters and a few pages from the banker's notebook. On the letters he written an R in blue pencil to mean "Response sent".

The notebook pages had numbers and dates. The numbers must surely have meant the amount of money sent and the dates matched with the letters... and the amount was the same as that requested in the letters.

But the letters had no signature, no postmark and no address. Moreover, the writing looked rather simple, common, most likely from a woman.

It was the only one of its kind... the mysterious file.

"Do you have any idea what it's about?" the brothers asked the head accountant.

Brunel said that he was completely in the dark. In his opinion the file did not seem to belong to the bank but rather to Montreil's private life. It was not his job, being a bank employee, to investigate it.

"So," Raoul said, "our father might have had a weakness, like every man, and this file contains a piece of his past."

"An expensive past," Brunel observed, "because the amount of money adds up to more than 200,000 francs."

"Should we try to find out what that's all about too?" Raoul asked his brother.

"I think so. Nothing should remain in the dark. Any negligence, any oversight might compromise our work of reimbursement."

"You're right but who can tell us about it?"

"Our father's old friends... Grillard and Bejanet probably..."

"Will they talk about this more than about the document that caused our father's death, whose grim mystery we still haven't solved?"

At that moment an office boy announced Monsieur Grillard. They called him in right away.

After shaking all their hands Grillard took a seat and started in, "I know, my friends, why you brought me here. Brunel informed me about your intentions, your projects..."

"Good. We're counting on you to help us in this difficult but necessary work."

Grillard raised his arms to the heavens, "But what you're doing, my boys, is pure madness!"

"What do you mean? You really think so?"

"I say that before undertaking such a project, as hard as it is useless, you should have asked the advice of people who have more experience in life and business than you... to guide you. You should have first consulted your father's oldest friends, Bejanet, and myself."

"Why?"

"Because we could have definitely discouraged you from undertaking this absurd plan."

"My brother and I have consulted our conscience..."

"You're young, my boys, your blood is boiling. Your wild imaginations and your generous hearts are deluded. You're off chasing fantasies."

"But for the sake of honor..."

"Sorry... I'm sorry... Let's not use such big words. We're here in a banker's office... We're going to talk numbers... and in business you have to talk simply, not be blinded by pretty turns of phrase like larks being dazzled by a spinning mirror. Business is business. The point is to succeed."

"By honest ways, so be it."

"Honesty in business is whatever doesn't fall foul of the law. You're honest as long as your speculations, whatever they are, don't get you convicted. Take that as a principle. It's the truth, the only way to make a profit."

Raoul raised his hand, "We've read the 'Gazette des Tribunaux'."

"You've read!" Grillard raised his voice.

"We know all the court cases our father had to go through. From the suit that poor Monsieur Menardier filed against him…"

"He won them all!"

"Yes…"

"So, you shouldn't go back into them… you, his sons."

"On the contrary. We, his sons, have to do the work of justice and right the wrong that the law, the cleverly sidestepped law, allowed to happen."

"You think you're better than the judges?"

"Judges have a code whose text is explicit. They pronounced according to the code… on the evidence that was before them. They couldn't do otherwise. But the judgments finding in favor of our father are more dishonorable than a conviction."

"What are you talking about?"

"Our father was clever, very influential, merciless… His victims…"

"His clients," Grillard broke in.

"No, his victims had to meet his demands and he knew how to fix everything to suck them dry within the law… which could only judge him later."

"But that's how we have to do it."

"That's not how we feel."

"Because you know nothing about life."

"We're proud of not knowing it like that. It's hard enough to admit that our father, who you think was smart and powerful, was in truth just a loan shark."

Grillard jumped again, "Loan shark… he said loan shark… your father…"

"At the rates our father lent money, under those conditions he demanded, it was even worse… it was robbery."

"You have to understand… let me explain it to you."

"Go on."

"Your father lent… or rather sold money because a loan is really just a sale of money. He had the right to sell it as he liked. His clients didn't have to accept it."

"That's not the issue."

"On the contrary, it's everything. They came to him… asking. He gave… but he would've been crazy to give it away for nothing."

"There are limits."

"Not when it comes to money."

"There's a legal rate established by law."

"It's unjust… an anomaly… a defect in our penal code that must be rewritten." Grillard was getting stirred up. "How can they! They don't fix the rates for merchandise that's being sold, only for money, which is merchandise like anything else. Let me give you an example. You go to a jewelry store and buy a pearl necklace… it costs you 30,000 francs. You pay without saying a word. That's the price, accepted. This 30,000 francs necklace, ten minutes later, you want to sell but they tell you it's only worth 10,000! So, the jeweler stole 20,000 francs from you. That's good business, accepted, avowed, loyal, honest! Now you want 10,000 in cash so you go to the money seller who wants to give it to you with interest, at a rate and, if you still want it, a commission. But all of this will never add up to the 20,000 francs difference for a necklace. Moreover, though the pearls have an imaginary value that varies and even disappears, money has its own value that will never vanish. So why call this bank operation usury, exploitation, dishonor when you don't criticize it where it's 100 times more scandalous?"

Raoul responded, "Monsieur Grillard, we thank you for trying to prove that our father acted correctly..."

"Completely... He made very good, very wonderful deals... and no one can find fault with him."

"We thank you but we asked you to come here not to make us renounce our decision but to make this job of reimbursement easier... which we're going to follow through despite everything, all the way to the end."

Without allowing Grillard to voice another plea of defense on behalf of the banker, Raoul asked, "Could you tell us if you know about anyone our father dealt with who might have sent these letters and perhaps received some money?"

Grillard glanced at the documents that Raoul pointed to. Then he looked through them, reading a few. There was a moment of silence during which Grillard examined the mysterious file.

The two brothers looked at each other. They were thinking the same thing: "Grillard knew but he didn't say anything." They were not mistaken.

Grillard looked up. He had taken time to get over the surprise that the documents had caused him and to find an answer to give his friend's sons.

"Wow, in your place I'd consider them useless and unimportant and I'd toss them in the fire."

"You would do that?"

"Without a second thought. All these papers don't mean a thing."

"And yet... our father kept them for such a long time..."

"You want to know what I think?"

"Please."

"Well, they're letters from beggars, from deadbeats, from people abusing your father's kindness. Your father, who'll end up getting his just rewards, was extremely generous. He gave a lot, easily, always, to all sorts of people..."

"Our father did some good, we know, but his generosity, as great as it was, didn't go so far as to give away a simple demand for 10, 30 or certainly 50,000 francs... as is duly noted. If it's a deadbeat like you say, he knew how to beat back... and he beat back for a long time because there are letters dating back 30 years."

"Maybe it was charity work."

"Stop right there. This is a woman's handwriting."

"Even more reason…"

"Surely you don't mean…"

"Ask me anything you want about the bank but don't question me about your father's private life… I don't know… I don't know anything."

"Then thank you for coming."

Grillard stood up. "My friends, believe me, one last piece of advice: Give up your project right now. Money earned is money earned. It'll be the devil to pay and the verge of madness. Nobody will thank you and people will talk… That's how it is in life. When they need money, they come to you on hands and knees. When they have it, they laugh at you. And when it's time to pay it back, they scream 'usury'. When you force them to pay, they treat you like a criminal but it doesn't take them long to come back. Moreover, in doing this, not only will you not exonerate the memory of your father, who doesn't need it, but you will make it worse because you're saying nothing else but you know about his faults… if you want to make things better, you, his sons, shouldn't be calling him a usurer and a thief!"

"When we've paid, they won't be able to say anything."

"No, it'll be worse than before."

"No matter!"

"You don't want to listen to a wise and aged man who's more experienced than you, so be it, I'll go. Me, I've earned a lot of money thanks to your dearly missed, venerable father and nothing in the world will make me take one cent out of my account. It's mine, I've earned it and I'll keep it! Goodbye!"

The two brothers let him leave. The man was worthy of being Montreil's right-hand-man in his operations.

There was still Bejanet, the notary. What would this second friend say and think? Would he say the same as Grillard?

Raoul and Robert did not think so. They had a completely different opinion of the notary. But their first experience with him had taught them a lesson. They assumed that for this new mystery they would find no more clarification than they had for the first document. It was not even worth trying.

So they decided not to question Bejanet whom, it was very likely, Grillard had visited after leaving the bank to tell him about the brothers' plans.

For the time being they left the file alone and started going through the others with Brunel. In the evening, however, they brought the mysterious file home with them to Rue des Mathurins in order to examine it more seriously in private.

236

5. The weight of infamy

Robert and Raoul did not want to limit themselves to just studying these files. They wanted to pursue their investigations to the end, leave nothing in the dark, leave nothing out in order to right the wrongs of the past.

In the files they found some notes written by their father saying only this: "Case pleaded... Won..." This provided them with a new source of information.

"Obviously," Raoul said, "our father had to deal with a lot of lawsuits. Such matters don't last long without the courts getting involved. So, we'll find some traces at the courthouse. I'll take care of getting the documents about our father."

"Are you going to ask the lawyers who pleaded the cases to give you their files?"

"No, Robert, my colleagues won't give me anything but incomplete documents. We'd be hearing only one side of things."

"So what can we do?"

"We've got one better. We've got the complete record of the arguments, pictures of the audience, the rulings, the sentences... I'm going to look through the *Gazette des Tribunaux*."

"Ah, sure, that's the way to go."

"We'll find a record of... if not all the cases at least the big ones. And we'll know what the cases were really about, even those that were won."

"That's it... maybe we'll also find some documents that that will exonerate our poor father, that'll speak in his favor, purge his memory and lift this weight of infamy from our heavy hearts."

"Let's hope so, Robert. Let's hope so."

Therefore, Raoul went to the courthouse archives and checked out all the cases in which his father's name appeared. Then he pulled out the *Gazette des Tribunaux* and other legal journals that mentioned the cases. He had some bulky piles of papers, which he obviously did not send to his parents' house but rather to his office.

The two brothers, therefore, started to examine the documents, to read the reports. Raoul read aloud to Robert the speeches and analyzed the grounds of judgment. Every time Montreil came out on top... but the reading of the cases was too much for him. The declarations of the plaintiffs were still tortuous after all this year to the sons of the banker. Their father, now, seemed different, even considering the worst, they had no idea how bad it was.

"Crook, pirate, usurer! The plaintiffs said.

"Murderer!" One of his enemies went so far... "You didn't just steal from your clients, that would be understandable, even excusable, but you robbed your best friend... You denied the deposit that he was foolish enough to leave with you. And this man whom you pulled out of a rut—you ruined him. You cast him into poverty, him and his family. You caused his death... Come on, let's say it like it is, you're a murderer!"

Raoul shivered as he read this part of the defense speech. He stopped.

"Keep going," Robert said, troubled.

"Yes, yes, you could prove that he committed suicide, but you're the one who put the weapon in his hand even if you didn't fire it yourself. You killed him. You were the murderer if not physically at least morally responsible for the death of Monsieur Menardier."

Together the two brothers cried out, "Menardier!"

They looked at each other in disbelief. "Menardier!"

Raoul dropped the journal. "No, no, no! Everything else can be true but this... not this... it's not possible... not possible."

Holding his head as if he were afraid it was about to explode, he paced around the room, blindly, bumping into furniture, into the walls, crying and repeating, "No, no, not this, not this... It's awful... not this."

Robert watched his brother with sorrow in his eyes. Finally Raoul collapsed into an armchair in the back of the room, bawling out, "No! It's too cruel! No, my father did not kill Menardier. No, no, it's impossible... it can't be..."

Robert picked up the journal. He found the article and read out loud quietly, "And that's your work here. You ruined an honest man whom everyone remembers with kindness and respect. You threw his young wife into poverty and stole everything, even the bread, from his children. Ruin and suicide... or murder... a widow and two orphans... That's what the banker Montreil has done."

Robert now dropped the journal. He did not cry out like Raoul. He did not grab his feverish head. He did not pace the floor. But he did sink back into the armchair and for a long time, in silence, he wept.

Raoul stood up and went to join his brother. "The journal lied, didn't it? It's not true. It can't be true. It's just a lawyer talking. It's false, inadmissible... impossible!"

Robert shook his head.

Raoul looked at him, "You think it's true, don't you? You can accept it..."

"I already knew... before reading the journal."

Raoul was surprised, "You knew! What did you know? How could you know?"

Robert answered softly, "I knew that Madame Menardier had been ruined. I knew the story but I didn't know the name of the banker who caused the tragedy."

"Who told you about it?"

"Madame Menardier herself."

Raoul jumped, "Madame Menardier? She's the one who... She... but how could she? Do you know her? You talked with her?"

"I see her every day."

"Where?"

"Madame Menardier, after being crushed by this tragedy, is dying. A doctor is caring for her, trying to keep her alive day by day for the sake of her children. This doctor is called Dr. Robert among the poor..."

"You?"

"Yes, Raoul, it's me."

"You're the one caring for the widow of the man whom our father..." Raoul broke down in tears again before continuing, "But you don't know, Robert, you can't imagine how horrible, how terrible this is. You have no idea what new calamity, what great and incurable sorrow this is going to cause now..."

Robert stood up. He hugged his brother affectionately and said, "Yes, I know. I know that you love Riri."

He did not give his brother time to ask questions and rocking him in his arms like a sad child he said, "I saw you in Ganneron Alley. I saw you in love. I know how much you adore pretty Riri. Cry, my dear Raoul, cry. Empty your heart of tears. Cry."

Faced with his brother's tragic sorrow, Robert forgot his own love for Riri, forgot that he had suffered in secret for a long time what Raoul was feeling now, forgot that it was for Raoul that he had broken his own heart... and he tried to comfort Raoul, to console him, to support him. It was a beautiful scene of generosity and brotherly love... of human grandeur.

6. Broken windows

Paulin Broquet was just getting over his adventure in the Barbottiere basements. He was starting back to training, as he called it. He had not yet started back to work, officially, and nobody in Paris knew where he was. His friends, who were used to seeing him disappear like this then reappear all of a sudden when an important arrest was made to wrap up a sensational case, were waiting calmly for his return.

His enemies, with whom he started a fight that could only end in absolute defeat, in the death of one side or another, seeing that he was nowhere in sight, could believe they had beat him in the first round.

So, Zigomar had won!

Their mysterious chief, who had presided over the spectacle, who had spoken and pronounced the death sentence against the bold detective, the Zigomar who claimed to be immortal, who boasted that Zigomar would always be victorious, whose voice, despite being distorted by the red hood, Broquet had recognized... the Zigomar who seemed to rule over that gang of criminals, was still on alert, keeping watch, trying to get evidence that they had succeeded as he had hoped. He wanted proof that the Zigomar gang would never again have to fear their formidable enemy.

Moreover, around Avenue Trudaine, on the corner of Rue Rodier—where we know that Paulin Broquet has his official residence—very often when coming home Gabriel and Baiter—who were staying in this house on Rue Rodier—saw passers-by, casual strollers, curious-looking people, people who stopped in front of the house during the day, who took long walks under the trees in the Square d'Anvers or stood on the sidewalk as if in the middle of a heated discussion.

All these people were only spies. There was nothing easier for experienced men like Broquet's lieutenants than to spot them.

Until now it seemed that Broquet's villa had escaped Zigomar's investigation. Did they still not know about it? Did they think he had not come there? Impossible to have the slightest idea. The spies, for the moment, were centered solely on the officially recognized house in Paris.

However, Paulin Broquet, after a stay in the villa during which he carried out a little study on the trees and flowers (we know how excellent a painter and musician he was), feeling better now he wanted very much to go back home to Paris and get back on duty. But he wanted his return to stay secret from Zigomar and so he would try to slip under their noses without raising suspicions.

Broquet had not chosen the location by chance. The house, recently constructed, was pretty and—something quite precious—Broquet's rooms, on the side of the entrance by Avenue Trudaine, had no neighbors across the street. In fact, facing the windows was the Square d'Anvers and the Rollin elementary school. Therefore, no neighbors could really see what happened in his rooms.

Gabriel and Baiter were living between Broquet's house and another on Rue Rodier just next to it. A wall was between them and in this wall, by a special, justified favor, the two house had agreed in secret to put a hidden door. Thus you could get from Rue Rodier into the house on Avenue Trudaine and vice versa. This was a huge advantage, even just in theory.

Every day and night, depending on their duties, Baiter and Gabriel went home as if they had no idea they were being watched closely from all sides.

Paulin Broquet as well. But he had to wear a disguise and play a role every time. It bothered him a lot that he was forced to submit, in a way, to his enemies and fight them stealthily for such an unimportant thing. Nevertheless, so that nothing might give him away when he stayed at his house, he turned on no lights in his bedroom and ate with one of his men who kept the kitchen light off all the time.

But since he came to work, to examine the files and papers, he was obliged to light up his office. So that the light not be seen from the outside even with the curtains drawn, Gabriel had pasted black photography paper on the windows. Thus, from the street it was impossible to see a speck of light. And Paulin Broquet could work in peace as usual during most of the night.

But he was dealing with a formidable enemy. Certainly he was not betrayed by the lights but the smoke was another matter…

Broquet was a heavy smoker. He chain-smoked cigars and only put them down to burn his pipe. As a result, when he left his office early in the morning you could, as the saying goes, cut the air with a knife. And as soon as he left his faithful butler ran in and opened the shutters to air it out.

Well, one morning when good old Jules was finishing up his work, a street merchant was on the opposite sidewalk pushing her cart to sell cauliflower and carrots in the neighborhood. She proudly displayed the bronze plate on her left hip that gave her the right to sell on the street. An older man with a bushy white beard, wearing a cap and baggy trousers, was pushing the cart. The merchant and her helper stopped to rest for a minute on the sidewalk in front of Broquet's house and while pretending to arrange their goods for sale they snuck peaks at the windows.

As chance would have it, Paulin Broquet just happened to glance outside before going to bed and naturally he saw the little cart, the merchant and the good man.

A merchant on this street at this hour seemed a little unusual to him. It was not the way these modest traders usually took and it was still too early to be making sales. Broquet was naturally very suspicious and kept a close eye on the two pedestrians. And he saw them looking back, too often, too intently, which betrayed them.

Broquet had eagle eyes and a rare gift of recognizing people behind any disguise. "Aha!" he said, "I've seen that woman before... without her bronze plate."

He looked more closely at the man and laughed, "Why, it's Baron Dupont pushing a cart!"

As long as they were parked on the sidewalk Broquet watched them. "It's the same guy who looked so downtrodden with his shaggy head and came up to the car window when I was bringing the Count de la Gueriniere to Montreil's for his confrontation. It's the same eyes as that very proper gentleman who supervised the duel with the journalist Marc Collas. It's the same face as the family man, the entrepreneur who brought his children to dance at Clafous'. And Good Lord, this vegetable seller was the same woman playing his wife that night."

As he was mumbling these things he saw the two of them flinch. At the same time he heard his faithful butler opening the window of his office. Then he saw the man sneak one last peak at the house, smile behind his unkempt beard and grab the handles of the cart. They got back on their way, chatting together, and the woman, too, cracked a smile.

"Well, well," Broquet said, "they saw what they wanted to see. They found what they were looking for. And they're happy about it." But he wondered, "What exactly did they found out?"

He went back to his office and saw Jules waving around a towel to chase the smoke out of the room. The smoke, however, lingered heavily against the fanning towel.

"Not to complain," the butler said on seeing his boss, "but you smoked quite heavily this evening. Your office looks like the tunnel of Batignolles after a train chugged through it."

But Broquet was in no mood to laugh at Jules' joke. He crossed his arms and tried to sound severe when he asked, "So that's it! You've switched sides and are working for Zigomar?"

Jules froze. He stared at his boss with big eyes, his mouth hanging open, completely flabbergasted.

"Yes," Broquet repeated, "I'm asking you if you're working for Zigomar?"

"Me... for Zigomar?" Jules stammered, "Me?"

"Exactly."

"But boss, how could you... why... where's this come from?"

"You're giving me up at this very moment."

"Giving you up? By doing what?"

"By waving that flag."

"It's just a dust rag."

"You're signaling them."

"Here... in the office?"

"Outside. You're pretending to clear out the smoke but you're telling Zigomar, your accomplices who are sitting across the street and spying on us, you're telling them 'Hey, the boss spent the night in his office and all this smoke proves it'!"

"But…"

"Well, it was totally useless putting all that black paper on the windows and keeping all the lights off if you're telling them I'm here during the day."

But seeing Jules's astonishment Broquet took pity. He laughed and said, "It's okay. What's done is done. It won't get them anywhere. Continue your work. Go on, Jules."

"So you don't think, I hope, that I'm a Zigomar?"

"Of course not." Paulin Broquet had figured it out. He understood what had happened, what Jules had told his enemies without meaning to.

In fact, as they were walking away the man in the cap was saying to the merchant woman, "Someone spent all night in Broquet's office."

"Sure, we already know that."

"Maybe this someone was alone, maybe there were several someones… There's an awful lot of smoke."

"But it doesn't tell us who it was."

"Who would go into his office?"

"His lieutenants."

"Or Broquet himself." After thinking a moment he added, "If it's Broquet, it means he escaped from the Barbottiere, from the flood and the explosion. It means he got out alive."

"That's big news," the woman said.

"Yeah, it seems unbelievable, really unlikely, but with a guy like him you have to expect anything." He paused again, pushing the cart along. "If Broquet escaped, it's a disaster for us. The chief will want to know. At any rate, we have to find out for sure."

"We're sure now that someone was in his office all night… but who?"

Paulin Broquet, meanwhile, was talking with Gabriel and telling him about the incident.

"Okay, boss. We'll be more careful."

"It's obvious that they want to know if I'm still alive, if I'm back home. But it bothers me not to have some elbow room, to be forced to play hide-and-seek with these devils."

"In any case, what they might have learned this morning can't get them very far."

"You never know. Have to wait and see."

From this moment on it seemed to Broquet and his partners that Zigomar's spies doubled around the house. They were closing in their lines of surveillance.

"Of course," Broquet said, "they're preparing to strike."

"Good, let 'em do it. We'll see. With you, boss, we don't have to worry about the enemies plans because they always backfire."

"They just have to succeed one time."

Gabriel, Baiter and the clown Simon, for their part, became more watchful and imaginative to protect their boss and further his plans against anything Zigomar might come up with.

Now, a few nights later Paulin Broquet was working in his office. Gabriel and Baiter were with him. Broquet had turned on his lights since the black paper was protecting the window. It was 2 a.m. On the street, in almost the same place where the vegetable merchant had stopped her cart, a car was parked.

Wrapped up in their discussion neither Broquet nor his lieutenants suspected anything or were worried. They kept talking, smoking and drinking beer. All of a sudden, without any sound of explosion, one of the windows shattered to pieces. The black paper was torn open by a projectile, the windowpane broken and the light from the electric bulbs shined through into the street.

"Quickly," Broquet ordered, "Show yourselves, both of you. Open the window and make sure they can see you."

Broquet himself ran into his bedroom which was down the hall. From there, hidden in the dark, he took up his post where he had watched the cart the other morning.

Gabriel and Baiter threw open the window and leaned out, making sure they were in full light and clearly seen. And they spoke loudly.

"What's going on? Who thinks it's fun throwing rocks through our window? Some kids playing tricks probably…"

Gabriel yelled out at the imaginary kids, shaking his fist at the empty street. "You just wait, you damn brats! I'll show you how to play with rocks! I'll rip off your ears! Aren't there any police in this city to stop this kind of thing?"

In the street, of course, there were no kids. For a minute Baiter and Gabriel looked around as if trying to find who could have broken the window, saying it must be kids… brats, delinquents…

But the whole time they had one eye on the nearby sidewalk.

On that sidewalk two men passing by heard Gabriel and Baiter talking loudly, cursing the invisible brats and shaking their fists out the window. They stopped and watched, curious, for a minute, then they went on their way.

A little later Broquet's lieutenants closed the window, still grumbling about reckless, thoughtless kids who were pretending to throw rocks at the sparrows sleeping in the trees only to break windows… and they complained about the police who were never around when you needed them…

At that moment the automobile pulled away from the curb. Broquet saw it stop a little farther up the street at the corner of Rue Say and pick up the two passers-by who had just witnessed the drama played out by Baiter and Gabriel.

Broquet went straight back to his office, laughing, looking perfectly satisfied. "Bravo! Bravo! We just won a great victory over Zigomar without them even knowing!"

"How's that, boss?"

"You see how our enemies are absolutely set on knowing if I'm dead or not, if the corpse of Paulin Broquet, sentenced to death by Zigomar's tribunal under the Barbottiere, is floating through the sewers of Paris and slowly making its way to the Seine along a probably very pretty but very undesirable route…"

"Sure."

"Well, in spite of all the precautions we've taken the goons saw something, we have to admit it."

"Probably."

"And the other morning, that damn Jules got the stupid idea of opening my office window to air it out, just when the vegetable seller was across the street with that clever Baron Dupont behind the cart."

"So they found out we were working long and hard that night."

"Yes, but that wasn't enough. They wanted to know for sure who was working in my office."

"Paulin Broquet or his lieutenants?"

"Exactly. Even with the black paper stuck on the windows it's more than likely that they were aware of someone in this room tonight."

"No doubt."

"And they tried this ploy, not too shabby I must say, of breaking the window to find out if anyone was really in here… by seeing the light come through."

"That's right."

"Moreover, they were hoping that whoever was in the office would run to the window to see who had broken it, which is what happened."

Broquet's lieutenants burst out laughing. "Got it, boss. Zigomar knows we've been working here since you died, since they killed you, and seeing us caught off guard, they naturally believe that we're here alone, that we're working maybe to put your papers in order for replacement."

"I hope that's the case and they believe that I'm dead now… and far away. Because they could never imagine that we guessed their plan and didn't fall into their trap at the moment of surprise."

"These people don't know Paulin Broquet very well yet," Gabriel said.

The detective lit another cigarette and said, "We didn't hear an explosion, so it wasn't a gunshot they fired."

"No, boss."

"And a gunshot wouldn't do what they wanted to do." Broquet explained his idea. "For this trick to work, it had to be between them and us alone. Now, a gunshot, which can never really be mistaken for a blown tire, would've brought some neighbors to their windows and become a little spectacle, which would be a problem for them. Besides, a gunshot at that distance would only make a little hole in the windowpane, not enough for them. They wanted to break the window, smash it to pieces. They didn't throw a rock because we might see them do it. They didn't use a slingshot because they might have missed and hit the wrong window… So, they used an air rifle, which is powerful enough and they could aim and it's weak enough to only break the window instead of shooting through it."

While Broquet was explaining this, Baiter was searching for the bullet. He found it and put it on the desk.

"I was right, see, it's lead and long with no cone-shaped end… from an air rifle."

"That's right, boss."

"Okay, now that they know I'm dead, let's get back to work." But the detective added, "It's been two days since Zigomar's been playing with us… two attacks… now it's our turn to strike back."

While this was happening in the office, the car parked across the street, which had driven away, continued cruising toward the outer boulevards, toward l'Etoile.

In the backseat was Baron Dupont and next to him a younger-looking man whose cap lowered over his eyes and turned-up coat collar completely hid his face. In the front seat were two young men—the passers-by picked up on the corner of Rue Say—Baron du Jard, who was one of the Count de la Gueriniere's witnesses in his last duel, and the great American detective Tom Tweak.

The man whose face was, so to speak, masked was sunk in the corner, holding the air rifle between his legs, the peashooter he had used to break Broquet's window. Baron Dupont was still clutching the long lorgnette that he had used to spy on the men leaning out the broken window. The man sitting motionless in the corner said nothing. But the others, Baron Dupont and Baron de Jard, were talking.

"Now they're working at Broquet's, but it wasn't him. It was his lieutenants putting his papers in order, getting the documents to follow through on all the cases he started."

"Right. No doubt about it, Paulin Broquet is no longer…"

"Hmpf!" Tom Tweak groaned.

"Otherwise he would've come to the window with the others since they don't suspect anything."

"Maybe."

Then all eyes turned on the man in the back who said, "I wonder if we haven't been a little careless now."

"How's so?" Baron Dupont asked.

"Yes, because what did we end up learning? Nothing… or at least very little. We're sure that they were working in Broquet's office at night, which we already knew…"

"But we didn't know who," Dupont said. "Now we can say for sure that it wasn't him. And I'll admit that I feel a lot more relaxed seeing my suspicions not confirmed. For a few days I really thought Broquet was back home at night."

"Us, too," the other Baron agreed. "And we're thrilled to find out it wasn't our formidable enemy in there."

"There's no proof that it wasn't him!" the American detective said.

"He would've shown himself."

"Maybe not. A broken window can make someone look outside..."

"And it did!"

"Yes, yes, but at Paulin Broquet's it should've had the opposite effect. There are no surprises with him, no weak points. If he were there, he would've known right away what we were trying to do. He would've guessed it as soon as the glass shattered. And clever as he is, he would've been very careful not to fall into our trap, which wasn't so complicated."

"We don't think so. No, we don't think so... we're really hoping that we got rid of him so we can carry on with our projects in peace."

From behind the upturned collar the man said, "I would be delighted to share your confidence, my friends, but, in any case, we'll know soon enough if Paulin Broquet or his men were aware of the trap we laid."

"How will we know?"

"They'll inevitably try to get their revenge."

"So, we just wait for them?"

"Yes, my friends. Except I advise you to be especially careful, to watch closer than ever the corner of Avenue Trudaine and Rue Rodier."

At home Paulin Broquet seemed more than a little upset. "This Zigomar, either a lack of imagination came up with nothing better than this crude trick to see what was happening here or else they really think I'm stupider than I am to think that I could be caught so easily." He paused before concluding, "He will have to know he's wrong!"

With no open display of his indignation he went back to his routine, coming and going when necessary, using disguises to stay incognito and letting the people wander around in the neighborhood despite their nefarious purpose.

7. The Baroness' necklace

The party that Madame Guttlach, the wife of the rich banker from Amsterdam (with a branch in Paris), gave in her splendid home on Avenue du Bois was such a tremendous success that it became an annual Parisian event. Whoever was somebody in the arts, literature, finance and foreign colonies was found in her rooms.

First of all there was the show. A special performance written for the occasion starred the beautiful Lucette Minois. A few charming dancers from the Opera did a pantomime composed by the lady of the house. Then they applauded a symbolic play from the young poet Anthime Soufret. And a singer from the Opera-Comique sang a few poems from the same poet put to music by Baroness Van Cambre whose talent as a composer was well recognized.

After the show the ball commenced.

Lucette Minois was an item with the Count de la Gueriniere, so they congratulated him on the success of the pretty star.

As for the Baroness, they praised her music as wonderful, masterful. They dared not say monumental because of the author who would find such a reference in bad taste.

The Baroness fanned herself gently, coyly, playing up her modesty, "Oh, well, it's not really me, I just followed the verses of the poem."

It was not really empty praise because the verses with its feet running in all directions could have made a very odd march. As it happens, no one understood a word of the poem. Anthime Soufret called himself a pioneer! They lavished him with an adoration here that would have been roaring laughter elsewhere.

He, the poet, deigned to accept the compliments.

One hand in the pocket of his vest, dignified, a long neck and long hair pulled back, his eyes staring into a void, he accepted the praises with the self-assurance of superior people who are never surprised to find the human race at their feet.

But someone overshadowed this poetic glory and kept the sun from shining with all its splendor on this pioneering genius with his incomprehensible verses: it was an American, James Twill, who would soon be famous.

James Twill was the inventor of a new airplane that was supposed to be better than all existing planes. The banker Guttlach and Baron Van Cambre were setting up the company that would allow him to proceed with trials as soon as possible and prove the superiority of his flying machine. Guttlach had invited him to the party to introduce him to some shareholders.

James Twill was a little tan, rather tall, well built, a redhead with a sharp chin, liked to live it up, typically American, a serious mouth cut into a deadpan expression with scintillating, penetrating eyes. He spoke French but American style and could at least make himself understood.

Seeing everyone congratulating Anthime Soufret he did not want to sit in the background so he, too, complimented the poet on the dancers' grace. He thought he was the manager, the dance master. They had some trouble explaining to him that it was just for the poetry.

Anthime Soufret, although very annoyed, had the good graces not to bear a grudge against the inventor of a flying machine that had nothing in common with Pegasus. "These Americans," he sneered, "have great brains for mechanics but they'll never know anything about poetry."

As for the Baroness, she was indignant and could not understand how this man did not know about the marvelous and universally renowned genius of her poet. To render unequivocal honor to the brilliant verses of her poet she had worn her best jewelry and sparkled like a shop window on Rue de la Paix on New Year's Day. On her shoulders, on her ample breasts, around the low-cut front of her dress, a river spilled over... like a flood... a river of diamonds. It looked like millions of them.

On her arms she wore huge bracelets, loops of precious stones and diamonds and her fingers were armed with overwrought, torturous rings that the pioneer had got made in the art of the future, without, of course, having to pay for them. But he had celebrated the rings in a poem addressed to the swooning Baroness:

Your fingers are heads of kings
And each deserves a crown.

Discreetly—everyone was smiling when they whispered so as not to seem to notice—the Baroness left quite early from the ball. The poet, naturally, went with her. The Baron had left long before with one of the dancers...

But the poet did not bring her to her home nor to his. He lived in Montmartre, on top of the Butte, near the Moulin de la Galette, in a small house in the 6th arrondissement but one of the tallest in Paris... the Baroness would never have made it.

It was to a friend's home, one of his supporters, one of his most fervent admirers, one of those who weave crowns and prepare to erect statues. This friend, the Count de Marnais, had a bachelor's apartment on Avenue MacMahon, on the ground floor and splendidly furnished in the latest fashion as befit a pioneer poet.

The Count de Marnais often invited the pioneer to breakfast, even to dinner, to hear him recite his beloved verses. And he bestowed as much affection as admiration on his poet, this genius. He gave him countless gold coins... He was more than an admirer, more than a disciple—he was a brother!

He also knew all about the love life of this poet of the future and about the Baroness, a woman of the past. Very graciously he put his small apartment at the disposal of these two artists of beautiful verse and music. He had even convinced the poet to use the excuse of Guttlach's ball to spend an inspiring night with his muse in his apartment. It was accepted. Therefore, the poet had the silver key that would open the heavenly room.

He climbed into the car after the Baroness. She did not slide over too much because she wanted to stay close to her poet. Anthime Soufret was, naturally, skinny and angular, as any respectable budding genius. His belly would grow later when he would be in the Academie, if he deigned to enter! But the Baroness was fat enough for two and compensated for him.

The car stopped in front of the building on Avenue MacMahon. The pioneer poet got out first and gave his hand to help the Baroness squeeze out. Just as he was about to ring, he found himself standing in front of James Twill, the inventor of the flying machine.

The American was surprised to see the two of them together here. "What's this?" in his Americanized French, "You live here? That's strange… I lived here too with a friend. So, I'm delighted because I'll have a chance to say hello and listen to your poems."

The poet and the Baroness looked annoyed by this meeting. But what could they do? Besides, the door was open. The American very politely stepped aside to let the Baroness enter. He went in second and the poet third.

After a brief hesitation the poet went to open the door on the ground floor. And he was surprised to see the American—he was really far too friendly— follow them to the door.

Nevertheless, not wanting to stay in the hallway, he opened the door. The American entered with them while complimenting the Baroness on her music. The poet closed the door, completely astonished.

But the Baroness was not so shocked by this casual friendliness. She told the poet, "We'll ask him to be silent. We'll make him understand that nothing must be said about all this… to tell no one."

"You're right."

The three of them were standing now in the little salon. A cold dinner was waiting on a small table. The Count de Marnais did things right when he was being hospitable.

The American continued acting without a thought to French manners. He looked all over the salon, even under the furniture, behind the pictures, knocked on the walls, then he went to peek into the bedroom. The key was in the door. He locked it and slipped the key into his pocket.

The poet was starting to think the American was exaggerating now.

James Twill came back into the salon. He spied a small game table and opened the drawer. "Cards! We can play bridge. What do you think?"

"It's really not the time for games," the pioneer remarked.

"You're right, Sir Poet. First, serious matters. Here's one: a pistol. Beautiful weapon. You're familiar with it, Sir Poet, with a pistol?"

"I'm against all sports. I hate muscle… I exercise only my mind."

"Very well. Me, I love sports… weapons… good pistols."

While listening to the poet the American had picked up the gun, turned it over, examined it.

"Nice weapon," he said, "very nice…" He put it back in the drawer.

The poet was annoyed by his casual attitude. "Monsieur Twill," his voice was animated, "the habit of being high in the air must not put you above good manners."

"Yes, yes," the American dropped into an armchair and lit a cigar. "You're so right."

"You are astonishing."

"Not yet absolutely."

"You think so?"

"Now we can start." He made a sign to the Baroness, pointing at the necklace. "Give me that!"

The Baroness did not understand or was pretending not to understand what the American wanted. She looked worriedly at Anthime Soufret. The pioneer figured he ought to intervene.

"What do you mean?" the poet asked.

"The necklace."

"What about it?"

"It's very beautiful."

"Obviously, but…"

"I want a closer look."

"That's just not done."

"Undo it then," the American laughed at what he thought was a play on words. "Undo it, Madame… Sir Poet, help the lady take off her necklace."

The poet raised his voice and his arms at the same time, "Now Monsieur, patience has its limits!"

"Yes, especially when you're in a hurry. And I'm in a hurry."

"That's enough! Please leave immediately!"

"I'd like nothing more. So, take off the necklace, Madame."

The poet wanted to show the frightened Baroness that he was not just a pioneer but that he also respected the traditions of ancient chivalry. He pointed to the door for the American. James Twill pointed too but at the poet's shaggy head and with the hand holding the gun.

"Do you understand now?" he asked the poet. "The necklace, now, please…"

The Baroness screamed out in horror. "A thief! He's a thief!"

"Madame, no screaming," the American said. "It's no use. And stop wasting time talking. I'm sorry to bother you but I like your necklace a lot… and I'm a little pressed for time. Quick!"

The poet was trembling all over now. He hated firearms. Still, he tried to stand firm. "But it's disgraceful! Cowardice! It's… thievery… a theft…"

"Yes, yes, I know exactly what it is."

"But come now, monsieur, you can't," the Baroness stammered, "you can't steal like this."

"Excuse me, I know all about stealing. I'm the inventor of a flying machine. I steal away into the skies all the time, see. Besides, one of the founders of the company, one of my most ardent supporters, is Baron Van Cambre, your husband..."

"But monsieur," the poet tried to break in.

The American pushed the gun closer to his head. "Silence! Or else a bullet. And all those poems nesting in your hair will fly off."

The Baroness was terrorized now. She unhooked her necklace and threw it on the table in front of the American.

"Thanks," he said. "Now the bracelets, the rings..."

"Everything?"

"Your charms have no need of these vain accessories."

The Baroness did as told. She slipped off the bracelets and rings and all the rest of her jewelry.

James Twill picked everything up and stuffed them in his pockets. Then he waved to them as he was leaving. At that moment, however, they heard the front door opening and someone entered the apartment. The Baroness and the poet started shaking.

"Maybe it's a robber," the American joked coldly. Then he smiled, "Or it's your husband coming to catch you. If it's him, tell him you're in my place and we'll have no trouble. Here, put your necklace back on so he won't suspect anything."

He went and hooked the necklace around the Baroness and straightened out the river of diamonds around her throat.

Someone knocked softly at the door.

"Open it," the American told the poet. "And don't be scared, I'm right here."

More dead than alive the poet stumbled to the door. The American ran to side of the door so that he would not be seen.

A man was there, formally dressed, very elegant. When he stepped into the salon to greet the Baroness politely, James Twill kicked the door shut. The man was surprised by the noise and swung around. He saw the barrel of a gun pointing at him and staggered back in fear.

"Hands up!" the American ordered. "Get them up!" He spoke coldly. "Not a word. Not a sound or I'll kill you."

The man had no choice. He had to obey.

8. *A thief and a half*

Looking upset now he raised his hands over his head.

James Twill spoke to the pioneer whose teeth were chattering and limbs shaking. "You, Sir Poet, get the gun that his gentleman has in his right pants pocket under that nice coat."

"I... I... I can't," the poet sputtered.

"Yes... yes... you can. Hurry up, he's getting tired holding his arms up like that. Go on, get the gun."

Anthime Soufret did as he was ordered.

"Take the wallet from his inside pocket," the American said. "Take it, take it."

The gentleman was about to protest, to defend himself.

The American smiled and raised his gun. "Good. Now, Sir Poet, search his coat, on the left... there, inside, a little higher... there's a dagger, take it."

Anthime Soufret searched the vest, all the while apologizing profusely.

"Great!" James Twill said. "My dear poet, stick all these souvenirs into my coat pocket."

The poet obeyed again.

"Very well," the American beamed. "You have good hands, Sir Soufret. If poetry doesn't work out, come and find me at my pickpocket school. I'll make someone out of you."

Then he turned to the man.

"Now you can lower your arms. Sorry for making you keep them up for so long."

And to the Baroness:

"Madame, please ask this gentleman and myself to sit down. You and Sir Poet can do so as well."

When everyone was seated the American asked the gentleman, "To what do we owe the pleasure of your visit?"

Instead of answering with words the gentleman made signs that James Twill watched curiously, but that he did not understand.

"Have you suddenly become mute?"

The gentleman leaned over close to the American and whispered, "Zigomar."

James Twill then cried out enthusiastically, "Oh, so you're Zigomar?"

The Baroness and the poet started shaking all over again at the sound of this name. Who wouldn't tremble in front of Zigomar? Zigomar, the famous criminal, the chief of the Z gang who committed such reckless, terrible crimes!

"So you're Zigomar," the American went on. "My sincere compliments. We've heard a lot about you in America. I think you've set up some posts out there, some branches, no?"

The gentleman finally decided to speak. And in fluent English.

"Oh la la," James Twill snickered, "why didn't you speak up right away? At least we can understand each other." Turning to the Baroness he asked, "Do you understand English? No... too bad. Excuse me for speaking in a foreign tongue before you but it's the easiest way to deal with this honorable gentleman. Besides, Madame, if anything concerns you I'll let you know."

The conversation rattled on quickly... in English. While talking James Twill kept his gun and his eyes trained on the man.

"Go on, I'm listening," he said.

"I just whispered the name Zigomar because I saw what kind of man you are and I thought the name of the famous bandit might create a connection between the two of us, which I would very much like."

"Are you Zigomar?"

"No. Nobody is Zigomar."

"What?"

"No one man can claim to be Zigomar because Zigomar is the invisible force that orders and acts, that others obey and serve, that all is sacrificed for..."

"But you're here for Zigomar?"

"Yes."

"Me, I'm here for myself, just myself."

"Zigomar is all-powerful."

"I'm not so lucky but I do all right with my little jobs, as you see. And I've got a few friends close by who help me out and aren't complaining too much either."

"You had the same idea as Zigomar."

"Which means it's a good idea."

"To steal this lady's jewels."

"Yes. I tried during the ball but it wasn't possible. I followed them here and you came in right on time."

"I'm sorry, believe me, but..."

"The risks of the profession."

"What should we do?"

"Being the first-comer I could, as is usual in America, tell you to get lost. But out of consideration of your boss Zigomar, who is in fact a leader whom I respect..."

"You're going to give me the job?"

"Ah, not so fast. It's too late."

"So?"

"We're going to play for the necklace."

"What do you mean play for it?"

"Play for it. Whoever loses will walk away. Okay?"

"Okay. What game?"

James Twill called over Anthime Soufret. "Sir Poet, do you have a coin? Don't worry, I'll give it back. It's to play heads or tails."

Then Zigomar's gang member spoke out, "Excuse me but the stakes are too high to risk everything on one lucky flip of a coin. We must fight for our luck."

"With revolvers?"

"No. I know this place a little and I know that there are some cards in that table."

"Cards! Well, okay then. Bridge?"

"That might be a little long. Plus it has to be between just you and me. Let's play écarté."

"Ecarté it is. Like euchre, no problem. Get the cards."

The man went to the table and with his back turned to the American quickly searched the drawer. The revolver that James Twill had recently discovered and complimented was slipped into his pocket.

In the meantime James Twill was lighting another cigar next to the fireplace with his back turned to the man who then carried the table to the middle of the room and fanned the cards out on the green felt.

Twill sat across from him and suddenly pointed his gun at the man. "Before beginning," he said, "would you kindly hand over the revolver you took out of the drawer."

"But..."

"Don't deny it, I saw."

He nodded toward the mirror on the wall where he had lit his cigar and on the opposite wall a Louis XV medallion that reflected the exact spot where the revolver lay in the drawer. James Twill had casually watched every move his adversary had made.

"If I had room I would put the gun in my pocket but they're full. I have two revolvers on me, one of them is yours, and a dagger... I can't turn myself into an armory so place the gun on the floor."

The man had to do as ordered. Right away James Twill kicked the gun under the sofa where the Baroness and poet were sitting, anxiously watching the scene.

Seeing the gun sliding across the floor, both of them let out a scream. The Baroness tried to lift her pudgy feet but rolled off the sofa onto the floor. Anthime Soufret kicked up his legs and knocked over a table full of porcelain statuettes. Then he gathered all his strength to help the groaning Baroness back onto the sofa.

Meanwhile, without paying any attention to them, the two gentlemen started their card game seriously, silently. James Twill kept his gun in hand to prevent any attempt at escape... or a surprise attack from the other.

The hand started.

After a while James Twill lay down his cards. "I've lost," he said. "Zigomar won. We must keep honor among thieves, so I'll leave and congratulate you."

He stood up and addressed the Baroness.

"Madame, I'm sorry I won't keep a fonder memory of our meeting. My lucky colleague here will have the honor of paying his respects... Farewell."

Walking backwards and waving briefly, he left.

When he was out of the room the man who was standing like a statue next to the card table dove onto the floor by the sofa, shoved it hard so that the poet toppled over to the other side, and found the revolver.

"You don't get away from Zigomar so easily," he said.

With gun in hand he ran toward the door, threw it open and saw James Twill just opening the front door.

The American remained calm and asked, "Did you have something to ask me?"

"Yes. This is from Zigomar!" He pointed the gun at the American's face and fired.

The hammer clicked six times but no shot was heard.

"It's a very pretty weapon," the American said coldly. "I know, I already saw it. I might try it later with the bullets I've got in my pocket."

He puffed on his cigar and strolled out the door.

The man stood there furious and frustrated for a second. Then he went back into the salon where the poet and Baroness were in a panic. The Baroness awaited the man like an executioner coming for her. She had no strength to put up any kind of resistance.

The man walked up to her, trying to keep a little calm, trying to hide his anger and disappointment. He wanted to get this over with as soon as possible.

"Madame, give me your necklace."

The Baroness was already unhooking it. She handed it over.

He took it and thanked her. "You're free to go now. Monsieur Soufret, be so kind as to show the lady home so that she can recover her senses."

The Baroness took the pioneer's arm and they stumbled away.

But when they reached the door the man called out, "Madame, is this really your necklace? Your famous diamond necklace?"

"Why of course."

"You're sure? It's the same one you had at the ball?"

"Certainly. I only have one like it."

"And yet... see, this necklace... it's fabulous... Didn't James Twill try to take it from you?"

"Yes, he even had it in his pocket."

"And he gave it back to you?"

"When you came in."

The man shook his head, "There you go. That explains everything. He conned us."

"What do you mean?"

"James Twill has the real necklace, that river of diamonds, and switched it with this."

"And this is…"

"A fake!"

8. The trail

Paulin Broquet woke up late in the morning. He wiped his face with a sponge soaked in fresh water, put on his long bathrobe, rang for his breakfast and walked into his office. His two lieutenants had been waiting for a long time.

He shook their hands. "Want to eat breakfast with me? Some coffee and milk or a hot chocolate? No? Nothing? Well, how about a glass of port since it's almost time?"

Good old loyal Jules served the meal.

While dunking his buttered toast in hot chocolate Paulin Broquet said to Baiter, "Take that little box on the mantle. Open it and show Gabriel what's inside."

Baiter took the box, put it on the table in front of Gabriel and opened it. Both of them hooted in admiration, surprise and amazement.

"The Baroness' necklace!"

"Yes," Broquet picked up another piece of toast. "You guessed it. The diamond necklace of Baroness Van Cambre."

"How'd you get it?"

"I stole it last night from her excellency. Right under Zigomar's nose."

You can imagine how curious Gabriel and Baiter were to hear all the details of the adventure. Broquet finished his hot chocolate, drank a glass of water and then lit a cigar. He stretched out in a bamboo lounge chair and smiled at his partners as he recounted the drama that played out in the Count de Marnais' apartment. They laughed and congratulated their boss.

"You understand," Broquet said, "we have a lot of revenge to take out on Zigomar until we've unveiled the mystery surrounding him and trapped him for good. We have to get revenge for the bath they gave me in the sewers… where they think I'm still floating. And for crushing good ol' Clafous and the police chief who were trying so bravely to rescue me. From now on it's a fight to the finish between us and Zigomar."

"We're ready and willing, boss, and glad to be on your side instead of Zigomar's."

"We'll see about that. In any case, I can assure you that we're going to have trouble. We're up against a bunch of thugs."

Broquet paused for a minute before continuing.

"You remember the papers we found in Laigle, in the hotel thief's pocket?"

"Sure, boss."

"We found one document that was particularly interesting…"

"The one with all the numbers."

"That's right."

"Hold Laurent, Sunday Claf."

"Exactly."

"Baroness necklace evening ball Mahon."

"Yes, my friends. We immediately understood the first part about Laurent and we went to Clafous."

"And even to the Barbottiere," Gabriel said.

"Yes. And the second part of the document intrigued us."

"It's just been solved and in one of Paulin Broquet's more clever exploits."

"My friends, most of the success in this affair is due to you."

"You mean you haven't done anything, boss?"

"Bah. I just pulled off a simple robbery that anyone could've done. You, my friends, you showed extraordinary ingenuity in unveiling the mystery of the document, which allowed me to do what I did. I got this idea that I thought was kind of funny, since Zigomar had tried to make my fall into the trap of Tom Tweak, to answer in kind, American style, with James Twill."

Despite all his energy and determination Broquet was feeling the effects of his fall down the shaft and his struggles in the sewers where he should have died. He had been pulled out of what should have been his grave and brought, as we know, to his house in Neuilly that no one knew about. For days on end he rested and recovered. But for Paulin Broquet resting does not mean doing nothing. He did not go off on adventures but he was preparing for new ones.

He had said to his lieutenants, "It's time now to try to find out what the second part of the cipher means."

Gabriel, Baiter and Simon went out in the field and inquired discreetly about the balls being given on Avenue MacMahon. It took some time but was easy enough to find. They went to florists, bakers, electricians, anyone who usually works when big socialite parties are taking place. Baiter even managed to get fairly complete guest lists.

As it happened, there were not many balls scheduled in the season on Avenue MacMahon and most were much later.

"It can't be that," Broquet said. "I think we're on a false trail."

"We think so too, boss. But we don't see any other meaning for the document. We don't know what other trail to follow. Where else should we look?"

"In my opinion, it's not a ball being given on Avenue MacMahon but rather to bring something like the Baroness' necklace there on the night of a ball given somewhere else."

"Boss, you're probably right."

"Maybe. We still have to find out who this woman is called the Baroness... If we're dealing with a real Baroness or a nickname."

One afternoon, therefore, Broquet was with his lieutenants on the veranda under the tall palm trees that he was so proud of. It was two or three days after the Barbottiere expedition. He was lying on a kind of bamboo lounge chair like they have in India, soft and flexible, which made an ideal cot.

The others were sprawled in big, rattan armchairs. They were facing him across a table on which sat a steaming teapot, some toast, hot chocolate, rum, port, dried pastries, something for everyone... and a box of cigars.

Paulin Broquet put down his cup of tea silently. He picked out one of the cigars, snipped the end off carefully and lit it with a wooden match... because to light a good cigar with a wax match was sacrilege to a real smoker. The wax from the French manufacturers was made from stearin and this give the cigar a horrible taste of burned pork chops!

Having thus lit his cigar Broquet lay back in the lounge chair. He posed his arms on the armrests and let his long but somewhat nervous hands droop down. With his head tilted back, the cigar firmly held between his teeth, he savored the taste as he watched the bluish smoke float slowly into the air and drift through the palm leaves.

His lieutenants had also lit cigars and were watching their boss, waiting. Knowing Paulin Broquet they knew that when he was silent and still and gazing at the smoke, it meant something serious was about to happen. When Broquet was like this they would say, "The boss is doing his cat."

In fact, the cat, that mysterious animal that remembers being a god in by-gone days, also gazes attentively at smoke with its gold-flecked green eyes. The cat thinks, meditates, studies. Maybe it remembers being worshipped in the past and... (why not?) being a god unrecognized today, like so many others, it muses sadly seeing the smoke rise up like the incense they once burned for it.

Paulin Broquet, therefore, was doing his cat. Watching the smoke rise he was thinking.

After a little while, he slowly lifted his right hand and removed the cigar from his mouth gently so that the ashes would not break off. Still deep in thought he said, "Who is Zigomar? Who is Zigomar?"

He fell quiet again.

And a little later said, "Who is Zigomar? Who? We will find out! We will know... All in good time."

His lieutenants listened religiously.

After taking a few more puffs on his cigar Broquet continued, "The Z hit the Montreil bank, then Bejanet's office, the Mayor of Itonville's house... At every scene we find the Count de la Gueriniere. So, the Count is one of the main Zs. Is he their invisible chief, the one who played the role of the Grand Zigomar? The one who sentenced me to death? And carried it out? Is it him? Or Tom Tweak? The rub... but anyway I'll bet he's also involved in this plot against the Baroness and her necklace and the affair on Avenue MacMahon."

His lieutenants nodded silently.

"So, we should be looking in the Count's social circle for this Baroness. She has to be an acquaintance for them to act like this so easily... Who is she? Is it the wife of that haughty Baron Dupont? Officially he's a bachelor and only the father of a family at Clafous'... and that woman was no baroness. She was the good Madame Arsène and probably never owned a decent necklace in her life. Besides, as Madame Arsène her husband (otherwise the luxurious Baron) wouldn't have thrown her into the hands of the Zs. Or else it makes no sense!"

He spoke quietly but very clearly for his lieutenants who saw the logic of this reasoning.

"No," Broquet went on, "it's someone else, meaning someone in their social circle. Their most intimate friends are Baron du Jard, but he's not married and since it seems he's got not parents he can't have a mother Baroness. There's Guttlach the financier, very rich, but even with his millions he still hasn't bought himself a title... soon enough I'm sure. So, we're left with Baron Van Cambre, even richer and a baron to boot. A good, safe and solid barony, not a single problem since he got the crown... and he's got a wife. The Baroness is solid, too, as expansive as their lands when she sits down. She believes herself to be very sophisticated, gets her dresses made at Perkins, where Pretty Riri works... The Baroness has well-known artistic tastes... She writes music... and her diamonds are famous."

Paulin Broquet looked at his lieutenants.

"The document is talking about the Baroness Van Cambre. We've got it!"

"Yes, boss, we've got it."

"Okay, boys, since I can't leave here and I have to stay dead, it's up to you to wrap up the mystery."

Gabriel, Baiter and Simon went straight into the field. It did not take long to find out that Guttlach's wife was organizing a big party. They would enjoy the show, drink and dance and applaud the music of Baroness Van Cambre.

"But," Broquet asked Gabriel, "where's the party going to be?"

"At the Guttlach's."

"Do you realize that the Guttlach mansion is one of the most lavish on Avenue du Bois-de-Boulogne?"

"Sure."

"So we still don't know anything about Avenue MacMahon."

Gabriel answered, "Right, boss, we'll keep looking."

It was Baiter who discovered the key to the mystery. As usual Baiter had spoken very discreetly with the Baroness' servants and learned that the substantial woman had a heart as plentiful as her charms and she was as dreamy as she was chunky.

They even told him a few juicy anecdotes about her trysts. And they named the poet Anthime Soufret as the lucky mortal on whom she lavished her magnificent favors.

Baiter wondered where the Baroness and her scrawny pioneer found a nest to coo their love. To find out Baiter got intimate with Anthime Soufret.

He was also a poet, but a shy poet, inferior, who had boundless admiration for Soufret's genius. He was dazzled by the blinding sun that was going to enlighten the world. The pioneer poet listened to him indulgently. Intoxicated by the crude incense of flattery he assured his disciple that he would be there to support and encourage his efforts.

Baiter saw from the start that Anthime Soufret was a complete idiot, a ridiculous nitwit puffed up with unfathomable vanity. They met a few times in a small café on Rue Lepic where the poet allowed Baiter to buy him a beer that he drank very prosaically while talking about himself or listening to his own praises. In this café Baiter heard from the poet's own mouth that they were soon going to hear his latest verses put to music by Baroness Van Cambre. Baiter poured on the praises. And he learned that it was going to cause a great stir in the artistic world where the pioneer poet had already received such warm compliments from one of his ardent admirers.

"A man who understands me, who admires who... the man... the Count de Marnais..."

As you can imagine the name awoke the interest of Broquet's lieutenant. A few beers later Baiter ended up hearing all about the Count de Marnais being so sweet and supportive of the project. Meaning he was helping the collaboration by lending his apartment where the Baroness could show him her music more comfortably than in her house. The apartment, besides being very elegant, was making it much easier for the poet and the musician to work at their leisure. And it was located on Avenue MacMahon.

When Paulin Broquet got the key to the mystery, when he knew where the Baroness would be on the night of the ball, he himself hit the streets.

To get close to the Baroness without raising any suspicions of his vigilant enemies, he used his great talent as an actor to play the role of James Twill, the airplane inventor, which would also get him close to the famous American detective Tom Tweak.

He met with the financier Guttlach who naturally introduced him to Van Cambre and his other friends, Baron Dupont and the Count de la Gueriniere. James Twill was invited (one imagines) as a curiosity, an American marvel, to the Guttlach Ball, which was bound to be one of the highlights of the social season... and probably also the night when the Z gang was counting on stealing the necklace.

Paulin Broquet was not mistaken.

We saw him congratulating the poet over the course of the evening. We also saw him working his charms in the apartment on Avenue MacMahon.

"I was hoping," he told his lieutenants, "to steal the necklace during the ball, so I took a fake one to momentarily replace the one I stole. Thanks to my fakes the theft wouldn't have been noticed right away because even if they looked and admired the jewels, no one was going to examine them up close. If the diamonds were switched... and done correctly, the Baroness wouldn't have noticed it until much later."

Broquet recounted the scene that unfolded in the apartment and added, "Now this partner of Zigomar is going to have a hard time with that river of fake diamonds. But I'm sure the Zs won't take the defeat sitting down. They're going to want revenge, to show that Zigomar is still all-powerful. And I have the feeling that the gentleman I tricked is going to try to redeem himself. I guess the Baroness is done with the Z gang and the poor poet is going to be used in another big job. You'll see... you'll see."

Gabriel spoke up, "Boss, something surprises me in this funny story. Why didn't you slip on the handcuffs when you had the Z in your hands? Why didn't you arrest him?"

"I couldn't. Impossible. First of all I would've revealed myself. And arresting someone in that place, under those conditions, would be compromising the good Baroness and creating a scandal for no good reason."

"You're right, boss."

"Besides, I got what I wanted. I wanted to save the diamonds, to face off against Zigomar and protect one of his victims. I did it and won. Why go further?"

"Very true. Never try to overstep your goals, that's a wise saying."

"Even more so, my good friends, because while I was fulfilling the mission I had set out on, I noticed something very important for us."

"What's that, boss?"

"In Madame Guttlach's ball I saw the Count de la Gueriniere."

"Oh!"

"He's a friend of the financier as you know. Plus, Lucette Minois was in the show. Now, the Count left at the same time as Lucette just after the Baroness absconded with the poet, whom I followed and interrupted their poetic rendezvous."

"Right, boss."

"Okay, Simon's confirmed the Count was at the Lutetia Theater. He's confirmed that as usual the Count went out with Lucette afterward and then took her home."

"Exactly."

"Good. But I'm sure that the gentleman thief who wanted the Baroness' diamonds was the Count de la Gueriniere."

Broquet's lieutenants were startled.

"He had a great disguise that was hard to see through but I could tell in his eyes, in certain gestures and in his voice... and, listen closely friends, I noticed that this man I thought was the Count, this man who came to steal the necklace, who tried to kill me with a gun, this man was left-handed!"

Gabriel and Baiter repeated together, "Left-handed!"

"That's right. He held the gun on me in his left hand. He was left-handed just like the murderer of the banker Montreil."

This observation had a profound effect on the listeners. It opened new horizons and established a certainty that until now was only a hypothesis proposed by the detective during the investigation into the dramatic attack on the banker.

"If this man," Broquet went on, "who played cards with me, who was furious at being held captive by my gun, whom I kept there docile, powerless and full of rage so I could study him, if this man really was the Count de la Gueriniere, then there's no doubt that he, being left-handed, killed Montreil."

The detective laughed and added, "And since in every good drama there's a little comedy mixed with the tragedy, I have to tell you that in the bedroom of that apartment, hiding in the shadows, apparently getting ready to lend a hand to their friend, was the dashing Baron Dupont and the great American detective Tom Tweak. I locked them in and kept the key... here."

Everyone broke out laughing as they imagined the look on the Baron's pompous face locked in a bedroom so ludicrously.

"On the other hand," Broquet said, "I don't think the Count, or whoever he was, could recognize me as James Twill. Otherwise he wouldn't have given himself away by slipping me the Zigomar password. Moreover, the Zs must be sure I'm dead. They must be dead certain that Paulin Broquet is floating around as a bloated corpse under the streets of Paris in some foul sewer waiting to pop out some day into the sad, gray waters of the Seine."

Then Broquet changed the subject. He said that the Count had already been defeated once in Ville-d'Avray by his enemies (and he must know by now that they were the agents of the famous detective who foiled him) and he was not a man to take a second defeat lying down.

"As for the river of diamonds, this necklace here, since he didn't recognize me he'll probably figure he's dealing with a thief who's smarter than him... and just write it off."

He started laughing again and said, "In fact, I wouldn't be at all upset if he knew he was dealing with Paulin Broquet and he realized that I had tricked him. Zigomar tricked me good with that Z signed from the bottom up... Me, I signed it stupidly like anyone would, starting from the top. It earned me the sewer. So, I wouldn't be upset if they knew I was the one holding the diamonds."

Then in a more serious tone he said, "But he will not want to admit being beaten twice... and he'll try to get his revenge for what happened at Ville-d'Avray. What do the Zs want with this girl? The love that the Count is showing for Riri is a front, I'm sure. There's something behind it. I still can't see what! But I'll bet anything that Riri hasn't seen the last of her troubles... that Zigomar is going to strike again."

He paused before concluding, "How they're going to do it now I have no idea. But we have to keep a close watch on that adorable girl."

9. A healthy patient

Paulin Broquet went to Rue des Mathurins to see the banker's sons who were working more closely with him now. He admired their courage, their loyalty. He agreed on their project of compensation. He supported them. He helped them in their difficult, delicate task all the while remaining incognito to the rest of the world.

Raoul and Robert, for their part, held Paulin Broquet in high esteem. They appreciated his dignity, his loyalty and his bravery. They admired him as a soldier with mad valor, a kind of paladin for good... a knight of justice.

Therefore, the two brothers showed him the mysterious file that they were obsessed with. "We both think," Raoul said, "that these crumpled old papers are hiding a big part of our poor father's life."

Broquet looked them over, page by page, studying every note, scrutinizing them, analyzing them and after a long silence he asked the young men, "You want to know the key to these documents?"

"Yes."

"You've decided to learn everything, no matter how painful it might be? No matter how unsettling?"

"Yes," they said firmly.

"Okay then, we'll find out." Broquet addressed Raoul, "I see here the last pages seem more recent. So, your father was still involved in this blackmail that started so long ago."

"It seems so."

"For a shrewd, powerful, clever man like Montreil not to be able to wriggle out of blackmail..."

"He must have been really afraid of a scandal. The secret held by the blackmailer was really serious, right?"

Broquet did not answer. He told Raoul, "I will ask you to bring me a few pages from the notebook on your father's desk. It's still the one your father used?"

"It is indeed. Brunel told me that our father got it just a little while ago."

"Good. Be kind enough to ask Monsieur Brunel to try to remember exactly what day he got the notebook."

"I will."

"Finally, you will tell your father's driver to come here tomorrow around this time without him knowing, of course, that I'm involved in any way..."

"Of course."

The next day Raoul gave him some pages from the notebook. Broquet compared them with the latest ones tacked on to the last letter demanding a payment. This letter, like the others, had an R written in blue. The banker, therefore, had answered and sent the money almost right away. The amount sent by Montreil was 10,000 francs. And the date above the sum was May 15.

"So," Broquet said, "Last may 15, Montreil paid 10,000 francs to an unknown party." He smiled and added, "The problem for us now can be put quite simply as follows: Given a sum of 10,000 francs paid on May 15, how was it paid... and to whom?"

"Exactly."

"Solving this problem is not as easy as stating it. We have to search the whole world for this stranger who received the money. And the world is big!"

"Maybe," the brothers said, "it would be better to drop this lead and not waste our time, which can be spent on more pertinent matters."

"I'm sorry," Broquet responded. "Aren't we looking for your father's murderer?"

"Yes."

"Don't you want to know what the document contains that was shown to him by his friends Bejanet and Grillard?"

"Certainly."

"To find this out you turned into thieves and almost got yourselves killed by real thieves. You almost fell victim to Zigomar. Today we know this for sure."

"That's true."

"Well then, to show you that solving this mystery is worth the time and effort we will spend on it... I tell you that the solution to this problem lies here and we will find out not only what that secret document said and why your father was killed but also the name of his murderer."

Raoul and Robert looked troubled.

Broquet sounded excited. "Therefore, we just have to find this unknown party, the 'X' in the equation!"

A servant came in to announce the arrival of the driver.

"Show him in," Raoul said.

Paulin Broquet was disguised as a police inspector. He had powdered his hair, put on big gray eyebrows and wore a bushy white moustache like an old veteran. The driver, who had seen him at Montreil's house without a beard, with brown hair and black eyebrows did not recognize him.

"Don't worry, Joseph," Robert said. "The inspector here just wants to ask you a few final questions."

"I'm not worried, monsieur," the driver said. "I'm ready to tell you whatever I can."

"Can you recall," Broquet asked, "where you went with Monsieur Montreil last May 15?"

"Around that time... on that specific day, you understand, I can't remember. But I can tell you the usual stops I made with him. There wasn't anything extra."

"Meaning?"

"Stops at the house on Rue Le Peletier, the bank, then to the stock market, in a few loan offices or at Monsieur Bejanet's office..."

"So you didn't make any extra stops with him around that time?"

"None. But there was one thing that was kind of strange at that time."

"Ah, you see!"

"It's that one day after Monsieur went to Bejanet's I took him to Rue Notre-Dame-des-Victoires."

"You can't remember the exact day?"

"No, sorry, but it must have been around May 15, a few days before or after maybe, but around then."

"That's fine," Broquet said. "You can go now." But he stopped him, "Wait, Joseph. We don't need to tell you that this is all strictly confidential."

"The messieurs can assure you that I am very discreet."

"Wonderful. You shouldn't mention this to anyone in his house, especially not Marcelin."

The driver straightened up excitedly, "Oh, not him for sure."

"Why?" the two brothers asked.

"Because I don't trust him. I probably shouldn't say anything... but messieurs know how fond I am of the house... And all the others there except for him..."

"Yet he does a good job."

"Sure, but he's a little too busy. You see him in the hallways all the time, wiping down doors behind which people are talking... and he offers to help when they clean the other rooms..."

"Like he's planning something... a robbery?"

"I don't think so, no. He just wants to know what's happening in the house." Joseph balked for a minute, then said, "And then, well, there's something else."

"What is it, Joseph?" Raoul asked.

"I don't want you thinking I gossip about the staff."

"We've known you for a long time and we respect you too much to think badly of you."

"I hope so. Well, anyway, I've seen Marcelin several times in a bar on Avenue de la Grande-Armée."

"He doesn't seem like a drinker."

"It wasn't for drinking that he was there. I've been told he meets friends there. There's one guy with a white beard who takes all the bets on horses and then two other younger ones, servants like we don't see around here but we all know what they're like... I was surprised... one of them, apparently, is the butler of the Count de la Gueriniere."

Robert and Raoul shuddered.

"Yes, messieurs, and you can imagine how I, as well as the guy who told me this, found it all a little... too much."

"The guy who told you this is reliable?"

"He's a guy I've known for 30 years. He's like me, for about the same time working in the same house. He knew about the tragedy that hit my house and that the Count was mixed up in the affair. So, he found it strange, not quite right, that the butler here is friends with the Count's butler... and he warned me about it."

Robert and Raoul thanked the devoted driver for giving them the information, which they would put to good use.

Joseph looked relieved to tell his masters. He went on, "I have to add that just now when I left the house to come here, in a curious coincidence Marcelin also had some errands to run. He offered to go with me. I thanked him and took the Metro toward the outskirts. He said he was off to Vincennes. I transferred at Villiers and got off at Rue Caumartin, right close. Now, I'm not absolutely sure because he was slipping between cars... but I think I saw, I recognized Marcelin across the street."

"Do you believe it?"

"I would almost say for sure but Boulevard Hausmann isn't on the way to Vincennes."

"Indeed!" Raoul said. "Joseph, my brother and I thank you for the devotion you've shown us. You discreetly as possible."

As Joseph was leaving he told Dr. Robert that two people were waiting for him.

"Okay, I'll be there," Robert said.

Raoul looked a little taken aback, "Aren't your consultation hours over?"

"Yes, but they might have been waiting a long time before I was told."

Robert went to his office and had the patient shown in. A middle-aged man with a trim white beard, very spiffy, complaining of a stomachache.

The doctor was surprised to notice that only one visitor was in the waiting room and not two like Joseph had said.

Paulin Broquet crushed the end of his cigarette in the ashtray. "I'll bet," he told Raoul, "that the visitor in Robert's office is no sicker than you and in a lot less pain than me." Then he shook the lawyer's hand and said, "Don't walk me out. Don't move from here. I'm going to see who it is."

He left the room without making a sound and snuck down the hallway.

At this moment Robert was opening the door to his office saying goodbye to his patient. In the waiting room a servant was ready to open the door for the departing visitor. After one last handshake with the doctor, the patient apologized again for coming so late. He crossed the waiting room, went through the door held open by the servant and started down the stairs.

The visitor was barely taking the first steps when the sound of a man running, a scramble, overturned furniture and broken objects came from the office. Then a man jumped into the hallway and ran for the exit.

"Close the door!" a voice shouted from the end of the hallway. "Don't let him leave!" Broquet came rushing forward.

The servant had gone back into the office after showing the visitor out. On hearing Broquet's shouts he came back into the waiting room. But the man who was escaping ran past him and punched him in the face, knocking him to the ground.

The man got out the door, which shut behind him.

When Paulin Broquet got to the door almost right after him he heard a key turning in the lock from the outside. And he burst out laughing.

"Well played!" he told the two brothers who were panting and alarmed. "Well played, indeed. We're prisoners, locked in... very clever."

But without wasting a second he ran to the window of the small salon facing the street. He threw open the window and clapped his hands. Then he waved into the street before closing the window. He sat down calmly in an armchair and lit a cigarette.

Then he said to Robert, "Doctor, you should see to your servant. The poor guy got hit pretty hard."

As he saw the brothers looking at him perplexed and anxious, he added, "The two healthy patients were from Zigomar."

"Zigomar!?"

"Yes. Tipped off by Marcelin that Joseph had come here, they wanted to know who he was meeting. And why. So they set up this scene. While one of them was in the office the other prowled around the rooms and listened in on what was being said in the salon."

"Unbelievable!"

"Not really. I'm sure of it. If I knew this house better I would've caught him. He apparently knew it better. I'll bet he's been many times before. And he had the key. Did you see that?"

"Yes..."

"I think we can assume that they came not only to know what Joseph said, which they couldn't have heard, but also who was questioning him. Now, I know it's really hard to recognize me in my disguise and I look like Inspector Legret, who is well-known by all the Z gang, so they probably took me for him... even though..."

And Broquet stopped as if he did not want to finish his sentence.

"Though what?"

"Even though I know by the voice that the so-called patient with the trim white beard that would make Baron Dupont jealous was my dear colleague, the American detective, Tom Tweak. And the other..."

"The other?"

"The gentleman thief who tried to steal the diamonds from the poet's muse on Avenue MacMahon while his worried partners Tom Tweak and Baron Dupont got locked into the other room... This gentleman thief who was taken in by the pickpocket James Twill, who had been strolling around in the Guttlach mansion earlier and who is now called the Count de la Gueriniere."

Robert and Raoul jumped. "The Count de la Gueriniere!"

"Exactly. His incarnation as a gentleman thief did not fool the keen eyes of James Twill. Of course, James Twill was none other than myself, so... today the police inspector recognized him again as the partner of the very curious Tom Tweak, the healthy patient."

10. The Breton nanny

The revelation put all kinds of ideas into the minds of the brothers.

"The Count is always popping up. He was there before us at Bejanet's…"

"When will we ever get rid of the wretch!"

"Oh," Broquet said, "he's a formidable enemy."

Before leaving he gave them a few instructions. They were to ask Brunel for the mail receipts from the money sent by the bank, which they had to keep. Just the receipts dated around May 15.

"Among them you might find one for 10,000 francs if Montreil sent it registered mail through the bank. That would make it easy to trace it back to the recipient and know the name of this person whose file we have… and find the key to the mystery."

Raoul went through the records with Brunel at the bank and the next day told Broquet that they found no receipt for 10,000 francs sent around the date.

"Too bad," Broquet said. "Well, there are two explanations for it: one, Montreil sent it himself, personally, in which case we'll have to give up the search since we haven't found any receipts at all with his files."

"That would be the worst case scenario. But the second?"

"The second seems more likely. Montreil had an accomplice in the affair."

"An accomplice?"

"Yes. And in my opinion it's with this accomplice that we'll find not only the last receipt but all of them from the start. I think the file we're dealing with here has a double… or rather a supplement held by the accomplice."

"And the accomplice?"

"Is none other than Monsieur Bejanet."

The two brothers listened nervously to Paulin Broquet. They sounded troubled when they said, "So, we'll never know anything because he won't speak, he won't betray his friendship any more than he did for the first document that caused our father's death."

"I'm sure. But we won't rely on his cooperation."

"How's that? You think you'll get luckier than us and rob the notary's safe like the Count de la Gueriniere?"

"No need. It would do no good now."

"Why not?"

"Because the file isn't in the safe."

"Where is it?"

"The Count de la Gueriniere has it."

Robert and Raoul looked absolutely stunned.

Paulin Broquet took his time. He rolled a new cigarette and lit it carefully.

Then he went on, "I am convinced that one of the reasons why the Zs, or if you will, the Count de la Gueriniere, robbed the notary's safe was not only to get a look at the document that you want to see that they certainly knew all about, but especially to make the file it belongs in disappear so we can't find the real trail... that file with the names and purpose and proof that will finally bring the criminals into the hands of justice.

"But," Raoul said, "if the Count stole the revealing, incriminating file..."

"Well, I'll let it go... that's it." Broquet added, "Besides, we've already got the start of an answer."

"Where do you see that?"

"There in the papers. Not all of them but a few, particularly the last one."

"Show us."

Broquet pointed to the corner of the paper. "See next to the 'R', which means 'Responded', that sign. It's a letter too."

"That?"

"Sure, look closely, it's a 'V'."

"A 'V'? What could that mean?"

"A lot of things. We still have to figure it out. It could mean: View or viewed, value, venture... who knows? Or victory! And victory is the end of the thread in this maze."

"Victory?" the brothers exclaimed.

"Exactly... or rather victoires. Rue Notre-Dame-des-Victoires where Bejanet's office is."

"That's right. Which supports our opinion."

"First of all, it could also be the first name of the recipient, the name we're looking for, that we want so badly to know..."

"Maybe."

"We'll see," Broquet said. "So for now, as soon as possible, I have to know where Montreil sent the money in such an unusual, mysterious way. Where... to whom and how. Then we'll know why and the problem will be solved."

"Undoubtedly. But how can we find out?"

Broquet smiled, "Allow me, gentlemen, since it concerns a secret document, to have my own secrets."

A few days passed.

Robert and Raoul naturally kept their butler. They did not fire him because they did not want to raise any suspicions among the Zs or worry their mother or sister who would want to know the reason. Therefore, everything looked normal and peaceful in the Montreil household.

The same went for Broquet's house. The detective and his lieutenants tried to keep Zigomar in the dark. They succeeded brilliantly.

Now, one afternoon this apparent calm was shaken up in the most unexpected way by the city street cleaner in charge of this part of Avenue Trudaine and streets around Anvers Square where there is a corner that became a strange but amusing site.

Along the Rollin school, which creates a nice shade, on the wide sidewalk of Rue d'Anvers and Avenue Trudaine, every day when the weather is nice you can see all kinds of baby strollers. It is the meeting point of the mothers and nannies of the neighborhood taking their babies out for a walk. While the older children play on the sidewalk or on the road where there is little traffic, the women, sitting on folding chairs, watch the babies in their strollers. They chat, read or do a little sewing, some embroidery, sharing gossip and neighborhood news.

Around 4 o'clock a street cleaner normally washes the pavement with great care, sprinkling the road and, maybe for the amusement of the children, giving the fox terriers a little shower as they chase after the jets of water.

The street cleaner was an old man, a fine old man. For many years he had done his job dutifully, punctually, never missing a day. Now, on this particular day, as he was washing there on Avenue Trudaine, all of a sudden, after an un-explainable movement, by some unheard-of accident, the jet of water showering the street suddenly turned and fell on the sidewalk, right on top of a stroller of a young nanny who had just started coming to the corner. The jet of water shot under the leather canopy and straight into the stroller. All the women cried out in a panic. They thought the baby would drown and they feared the same fate for their own, so they all grabbed their babies and started pushing their strollers away. It was a mad scramble, a stampede…

Even more than the women, the street cleaner looked horrified by the clumsy mistake he had just made. He turned off the water, dropped the hose and ran to the nanny to apologize and do whatever he could to help her.

But the nanny was in a panic, yelling, "Help! Help!" She grabbed her drip-ping wet baby and stuffed him under her arm. Then, hiking up her skirt, still screaming, she started running as fast as she could, faster than you would think possible for a chubby Breton nanny.

When the street cleaner got to the soaked stroller it was empty and the nanny was already far down the street toward Rue Gerando. The street cleaner saw her and started running after her, faster than anyone could have suspected from an old man.

But the mothers and other nannies and the scared children were bumping into each other in their flight, crying and shouting. They made it impossible for the old man to get through. So while the Breton nanny was getting away, the others were grabbing at the street cleaner or stumbling around. The police in the square and some concerned passers-by figured it was their duty as honest citi-zens to stop this man although they had no idea why.

The old street cleaner was jumping around like a boar caught by a pack of hunting dogs, shaking off the wild women as best he could. "The nanny!" he shouted. "Quick, get the nanny!"

He had to push them off him forcibly. He tripped a few, kicked some in the stomach, threw the most persistent ones on the ground and finally managed to get out of the crowd. But by then the nanny had stopped a car that happened to be cruising down Rue Gerando. She threw open the door and jumped in the back with her baby.

The car was about to speed off when the street cleaner jumped on the running board and tried to grab the nanny. The extraordinary young Breton had not only solid legs and a solid build, she had solid fists too. Her fists rained down on the old man's head and he did his best to answer in kind.

The strange battle, this weird, shocking boxing match would have went on for a long time if the car had not shot off, making the old man lose his balance and fall on the road, screaming and shouting. But as he fell off he had snatched away the baby still dripping wet.

A cry of horror rang out!

They saw the baby fall out of the car with the old man. The little one rolled under the car as it screeched off at full speed.

When the panic and fear that had caused this accident had calmed down a bit they ran to help the old man and prepared themselves to pick up the baby that must have been crushed, flattened, left in an unspeakable condition…

But the old man stood up by himself. He reached out and before anyone could get to him he snatched up the baby by one of its lifeless hands. As two policemen were coming up he said, "It's okay, let's go to the station and I'll explain everything."

He took the crushed baby, folded it in two and stuffed it under his arm, very calmly.

The initial fear and anguish and horror of the crowd in this tragic scene turned into utter stupefaction.

The Breton nanny who had run and boxed so well… was a man.

And the baby she had in the stroller, the baby soaked by the street cleaner, the baby run over by the car… was a doll.

As the two policemen led the street cleaner to the nearest station on Rue Bochard-de-Saron, they told the crowd, "Go on! Keep moving! Can't you see this was just for a movie… It was all a set-up for the cameras!"

Then the people all started laughing and poking fun at each other for being taken in by the show.

Later however, while taking off his disguise at the police station, Paulin Broquet told the two officers along with Gabriel and Baiter, "I think that after that shower Zigomar will know that we'll figure out all their tricks and they'll leave us alone."

But he added, "What I wanted, you know, was to rip off the disguise of that nanny to see if I'm right in thinking that the Breton dish was none other than the Count de la Gueriniere."

11. The new Barbottiere

Three tables were put up front. The table in the middle, the smallest, was raised up a little higher than the others. Black cloth covered all three, hanging down to the ground, in the middle of which was a big Z in red cloth, like blood against the blackness.

On the middle table was a revolver, a dagger and a rope with a noose.

The room where these tables stood was an attic. For light there were gas lamps hanging from ceiling with metal shades. Scattered around were some broken furniture, bedraggled mattresses, piles of clothes, empty bottles, a cracked bathtub, two bicycles and other domestic ruins, suitcases, crates, all the junk that clutters the attics in Paris.

This attic was 25 to 30 feet long and barely 15 feet wide. It had a window but black curtains covered it, preventing the light from escaping outside. There was only one door to the strange attic that recalled the set-up in the Barbottiere. It was, in fact, the new site that the Z gang had temporarily adopted while waiting either to renovate the Barbottiere, which had not yet been decided, or to find a new refuge with as many conveniences as the Montmartre underground.

The house under the attic was in Grenelle. It no longer exists today, at least in the same state because a modern rental property has replaced the old rundown house where we are entering.

This house had three stories plus the attic. On the ground floor, on either side of the door, was a wine-seller and restaurant to the right and an antique dealer or rather junkshop to the left. The house was owned by a retired officer from the supply department who had spent his life between the barracks at La Tour Maubourg and the storehouse of military beds and could not bring himself to leave the area.

When Monsieur Melidon retired he married Zulma. From the time she was 18 years old Zulma had done laundry in the neighborhood. Her customers were half-military, half-civil. She was 45 years old now, meaning she could have worn the golden stripes on her rolled-up sleeves like the veterans of old. Oh, she had done her duty well and her love for the army had never waned.

However, Zulma could no longer do the ironing herself. Years ago she had taken over the shop where she used to work so she did not have to deliver the laundry. Melidon could not stand this.

Zulma had been a spicy brunette. Apparently it was a real treat to see her carrying the laundry basket with bare arms, bent over exposing her ample bust, and it was a delightful pleasure to check the shining white laundry with her. She made a fortune from the house he lived in, where she would also live by and by.

Monsieur Melidon had been a customer since he got his corporal stripes, since he was able to buy a white-fronted shirt that was non-regulation but that

Zulma brought back every two weeks white as snow with its little iron buttons sparkling.

Melidon went up to sergeant and bought two white shirts. Instead of every two weeks Zulma came by every Sunday. Around this time Melidon let Zulma know that she should let the apprentice carry the laundry to the other houses.

When Melidon became a major he talked about making an official union of what had started from the first washing of his first shirt as corporal. He thought, either naïvely or he was just being smug, that it was only in his house that Zulma forgot about her ironing for an hour or so when delivering laundry.

As for him, just as he was loyal to his duty and nothing in the world could make him reveal to the enemy the number, formation or placement of the military beds, so he would never betray Zulma. He gave himself to her almost a virgin and when he married her he was pleased to believe that she was the same.

Zulma had always been a little plump, which is charming when it is kept in check. But her generous soul and tender heart were too liberal to control it for long. Watching Zulma's development Monsieur Melidon often thought that to make Madame Melidon comfortable it would take at least three military beds. For himself, to wrap around his belly that had profited from a life behind a desk, he needed two belts.

They were a beautiful couple, a perfect match. When all is said and done, good people, reliable friends who you could always count on. They were well respected in the neighborhood where they knew everyone and everyone knew them. They had a little savings. Zulma still had the laundry business. They were happy.

Then Zulma sold the store. They took possession of the house along with the furniture. They rented out rooms to some of the foremen from the factories in the area and to a few officers whom Monsieur Melidon welcomed as young brothers-in-arms and whom Madame Melidon greeted like in former times when she strolled so elegantly down the street with her laundry basket under her arm.

To take care of all the rooms the Melidons hired a maid and young man who would act as a night watchman because at bedtime Monsieur Melidon was snoring like a bassoon and Madame Melidon accompanied him as an asthmatic soprano.

On the third floor of the house were four rooms. Two were empty after the departure of a sublieutenant and a lieutenant whom Madame Melidon sorely missed. But she had some consolation for her grief. A young man who had been in the military, a lieutenant or captain at most, came and rented one of the rooms. That same night an older man, old enough to be a colonel at most, rented the other room.

The colonel said he was working for the railroad at Molineaux; the young man was an engineer photographer... so, he also asked for the attic to set up his darkroom and do some work. After he swore that he would do nothing involving fire and would do no damage to the building, the Melidons agreed to rent the attic to him. He could set it up as he wished and he had the only key because there were plates and paper and products that could not be exposed to sunlight.

The two other rooms that had been left vacant were immediately rented by two young employees from the education department.

The four tenants on the same floor met each other and got along famously. They were very conscientious, coming and going without a sound and always respectful of the owners. But it was not just because the Melidons were good people that they were friendly or that this was the only nice house in Paris, so to speak. No, it was especially because behind this house was a huge empty lot not far from the Ferris wheel where the Swiss village had been built during the exposition of 1900.

Now, on this empty lot, by lifting a board in the fence you could come and go without being seen at night. The Melidon house had the kitchen on this side with rather high windows. A foldable wooden ladder was used to get to the third floor by the Zs who were given the secret or who were summoned by the chiefs to a meeting like formerly in the Barbottiere. The ladder was let down from the window and from there it was easy to get to the attic where the photographer was thought to be working hard.

But not many Z members knew about this new Barbottiere. When someone was summoned one of the chiefs went to pick them up at Clafous. He was put in a car and blindfolded until he was on the second floor. Thus he had no idea where he was or what the house looked like from the outside.

Tonight, therefore, the grand council of Zs was taking place. Zigomar was behind the small, raised table and the four assessors stood on either side. In the center was a chair.

Zigomar made a sign with his hand... because tonight under the robes, under the hoods, there were no mannequins like in the Barbottiere, but real men... and two new people who were also wearing hoods, but black. Between these two was a another man dressed like the customers in the "Enfants de l'Aveyron".

We know this third person—it was Bipard, the violently jealous lover of the Swinger.

"Sit down," Zigomar told him. "Sit, Bipard, take a load off."

Bipard bowed to Zigomar, then to the assessors on the right and left and finally sat in the chair.

"Zalavi!" Zigomar said.

"Zalamor!" the assessors responded.

"Zigomar!"

"Zigomar! Zigomar!"

And silence fell over the room.

The rule of the Zs is that you never talk to Zigomar, you only answer the questions he asks.

Zigomar spoke, "Don't worry, Bipard, Zigomar is not here today for a trial but rather for a supreme council. Zigomar didn't want to wait any longer to congratulate you for your clever and courageous behavior. When we have a new temple, a new palace where all our friends, all the Ramogiz, all the Zs can gather together, you will receive commendation publicly and the honors you deserve. For now, know that soon you will get a special bonus reserved by Zigomar for those of his children who, like you, are particularly helpful and devoted for life."

"Zalamor!" the assessors raised a hand and traced the symbolic Z in the air.

Zigomar was silent for a moment before resuming, "Now Zigomar needs some information. Let's see, you told us that you'd started a fight with a police sergeant on the street. That was a mistake. Zigomar doesn't want to take any risks that have no payoff for the association and especially that could lose a member. Zigomar wants to fight only when there's something to gain... Skip it. So, what station did they take you to? There are two in the area. There's the one on Rue de La Rochefoucauld and another on Rue de la Tour d'Auvergne. There's even one over on Rue de Saron... So, can you remember and tell us exactly which of these stations you were brought to?"

"No, boss," Bipard answered. "They already asked me about it and, well, as hard as I try I just can't remember."

"Why?"

"Because I was hit so hard that it rattled my brain. I was laid out on the street..."

"Let's see, they knocked you out good, I can understand... but you came to after. You came back to your senses."

"Sure, boss."

"Okay, so when you were showing those people where to go, in order to accomplish your act of initiation, you knew where you were going?"

"I should be able to remember, boss, but in the state I was in, my head pounding... and I also got kicked in the shin that was hurting bad when I walked..."

"Did you walk for a long time?"

"In that particular situation it seemed a real long time."

"Did you recognize any streets? Did you look?"

"I did notice that we crossed Place Pigalle."

"Aha!"

"It wasn't until I was back in the Barbottiere, so on home ground, that I finally got a grip on myself. The rest you know."

"Yes, that's fine. So, you can't give any more details after you were arrested... You can't remember anything else, not even what station you were in?"

"No, boss."

"Okay." Zigomar raised a hand. "Bipard, you can go."

Bipard stood up. He saluted Zigomar, then the assessors and escorted by the two men in black hoods he left the attic that the Zs were temporarily calling the Temple, the Palace.

When the door closed Zigomar spoke again. "My friends, the situation is bad for Zigomar." In the dead silence he added, "It's too bad that Bipard, whose actions deserve the utmost praise from Zigomar, can't tell us anything else. He's putting us in a very tight spot. We blew up one of the tunnels in the Barbottiere, we destroyed our meeting place that was so practicable, so convenient... we applauded this sacrifice because we thought that the police chief and another office who had arrested Bipard were buried under the rubble. Now, Bipard's partner's been keeping a lookout to spot all the policemen in the district. Among them he hasn't seen the one he and Bipard ran up against.

"This partner has sworn that he can recognize the officer but he hasn't seen him, which makes us believe that he perished in the explosion. But what bothers us is that no police chief has disappeared, no captains from the stations have gone missing... or missed a single day of work. However, one of them was with the other officer and must, logically, have shared his fate. If one is dead, the other can't be alive. If one of them is alive, the other must also have escaped death. And that, my friends, is what Zigomar was hoping to figure out tonight. That's what we have to know. We have to find the answer to this frustrating puzzle."

12. The good lieutenant

Bipard was blindfolded and brought out of the house. They led him down the ladder, into the car and drove him all the way to Boulevard Ornano. There the Zs took off the blindfold and stopped the car. In no time they all entered the "Enfants de l'Aveyron" and got drinks from Clafous.

All possible precautions were taken to keep the new meeting place a secret. Generally the bandits chose basements, cellars or grottoes as a lair. The idea of meeting in an attic was unusual. But despite the uncommon choice, despite the precautions to keep it a mystery, Paulin Broquet was bound to learn all about it very soon.

The very evening when Zigomar had summoned Bipard to its High Court of Justice, a man who was certainly less suspicious than ever, heard about the trip to Montmartre while serving drinks... all about to the visit to Zulma's house.

Zulma's name starts with a Z and was fated for Zigomar.

After pouring drinks Clafous left his bar for a second without attracting any attention. It happened often enough for his business and his short absences surprised no one. This time Clafous stayed outside for only a minute. Just enough time to tell Gabriel, who had chanced to come by, the news:

"Watch out, two or three of them are going to take Bipard out of here. They'll take a car and go to Zulma's."

"Zulma?"

"It's the name of their new Barbottiere."

"Great."

"Get ready to follow them and tell the boss."

"Perfect. Thanks."

Behind the car that was carrying Bipard and the Zs another car was following at a safe distance. Gabriel was in this second car, which was one of Broquet's. He saw Bipard and the others get out of their vehicle. His own driver, nicely dressed as a chauffeur, passed by and parked a little farther up the street.

Gabriel jumped out of the car and tailed the Zs. He saw them lift the board in the fence and climb through into the empty lot.

Then he saw them climb the ladder and one by one, slowly because Bipard's blindfold made him clumsy, scramble through the third-floor window.

He also saw the ladder pulled up and into the house.

Gabriel, who had infinite patience, waited. So as not to raise any suspicions, he plopped down in a shady corner like a passed out drunk.

Bipard and his companions reappeared. Gabriel kept waiting. He spent the night there, through a drizzling rain. It was not until early in the morning when he was sure no one else was coming down the ladder that he decided to leave.

Soaked to the bone, shivering from the cold, he got driven to Neuilly. The boss was terribly worried that his devotion would cost him a long sickness, so he had him undress, put on something dry and climb into a warm bed. While drinking a hot toddy, feeling much better, before taking a rest, Gabriel wanted to tell his boss everything he had learned. Broquet understood it was important.

"So, we've got a new home for the Zs," he said happily. "Zulma! Zulma!" He shook his lieutenant's hand, "Now get some rest... and sweat as much as you can. Good night and good morning."

He closed the curtains and went back outside.

Under palm trees, stretched out on a lounge chair, a cigar in his mouth, he started, as usual, to think long and hard, blowing smoke up toward the light clouds.

"Zulma," he repeated, "Baiter will find out all about it."

When his lieutenants, Baiter and Simon, came as usual, one after the other from different directions, to get news from their boss, Broquet told them about what he had learned from Gabriel, who was still sleeping.

And he told Baiter, "You, my boy, are going to shed some light on this, find out what this house is... in Grenelle... around the old Swiss village... this Zulma. Sort it out."

"Got it, boss."

Baiter had a talent for making people talk, gaining their confidence.

"Grenelle-Invalides," he said, "factories, the military, okay, I can see that already."

In the morning an infantry soldier was sitting in a small café near Avenue de La Motte Piquet. Several other soldiers and some workers were there. Someone pronounced the name Zulma... and Baiter pricked up his ears.

One of the soldiers, a former secretary of a lieutenant who had been sent far away from Paris, was telling a buddy about the good times he used to have.

"Prevalant... He was a good guy that lieutenant of mine. He lived in a place where the owners were special to the military. The old man was a former supply officer and never forgot the men still in the service. And his wife, even more than her husband, loved a man in a uniform... she had a soft spot for the secretaries of her tenants, I can tell you. Oh, you don't often good folks like the Melidons... like m'am Zulma."

Baiter already had a good picture. When the soldier left with his friends he got the owner of the café talking, which was the easiest thing in the world.

The Melidon house, as Baiter had expected, was almost right across the street. Therefore, the owner was very familiar with Monsieur Melidon and Zulma. He knew their stories from the start of their love affair, step by step, stripe by stripe so to speak, up to the retirement of the supply officer and his marriage with the well-endowed Zulma.

It was a pleasure for him to tell everything to Baiter who listened intently to every word of the interesting story.

The next day a young lieutenant, well built, rather handsome, self-assured, with blue eyes and a smile under his handlebar moustache, showed up at the Melidon's house... at Zulma's.

"I'm a friend of Lieutenant Prevalant," he said. "He gave me your address because I'm going to be stationed in Paris."

Melidon gave the lieutenant the friendly welcome all older brothers give to younger brothers entering a career in the army, the welcome older brothers give when the new kid becomes a guest.

But M'am Melidon, on seeing the dashing officer, young, smiling, muscular and full of life, felt the heart in her ample chest start beating like a 20-year old again.

She sighed, "Oh, here's one who'd have his collar starched like porcelain... like delicate porcelain."

"So," Monsieur Melidon said, "you're saying hello on behalf of that good Lieutenant Prevalant."

"Not just saying hello but giving you his best wishes, his warmest regards, compliments to Madame Melidon, and he told me, 'In Paris there's only one house where a like you could live. It's the Melidon's.' So, I came to live here."

Zulma raised her short, pudgy arms, then let them fall back down with a bellowing sigh and an asthmatic whistle.

"Unfortunately," Monsieur Melidon said, "my dear lieutenant, unfortunately..."

"Don't tell me," the lieutenant cried, "you're going to refuse me a room!"

"No, no, not at all... but we can't do it."

"Why?"

"All our rooms are taken."

"By servicemen?"

"Servicemen on the second floor."

"And civilians on the third?"

"Yes."

"Well," said Lieutenant Baiter, "that won't be a problem."

"Why not?"

"You can send the civilians on leave and I'll set up camp."

A chauffeur stepped out of the car in which the lieutenant had climbed in. The car sped off and the chauffeur jumped into the front seat of another car parked nearby. He settled into the seat next to the driver who put the car in gear and started off toward Neuilly.

A few minutes later, after an aimless tour of the streets, the car entered one of the villas whose gates opened at the sound of the horn. It only took a few seconds for Baiter to tell Broquet the results of his investigation.

He concluded, "As for the guy the Melidons call Grandel the photographer, I recognized him right off by his voice, then his attitude and finally his eyes. The photographer is the Count de la Gueriniere."

Broquet smiled, "That's what I thought. The Melidon's house is the new Barbottiere." And he added, "After the basement, the attic! It's logical. Come on, boys, let's go see about this."

It was still risky. Broquet's lieutenants had a long talk about it, but they finally decided that they would have to catch the Zs in their lair.

This time, because of the location, the expedition seemed a lot less dangerous. Unlike the disastrous Barbottiere, they did not try to talk their boss out of coming. On the contrary, they encouraged and supported him.

They were hoping that it would be easy to surround the house and catch everyone in a well-laid trap.

13. At Zulma's

Baiter went back to see the Melidon couple. He had a long talk with Zulma who told him nothing new. She only corroborated the information he had got from their first meeting. His mind was made up now, along with Broquet's and Gabriel's.

The photographer Grandel was the Count de la Gueriniere in a new incarnation, the railroad engineer was Baron Dupont and the locked up, religiously guarded attic was definitely the new Barbottiere.

And Paulin Broquet was determined to try carry out an expedition. He prepared it as he always did with utmost care, assigning the different roles that his men had to play, giving each detailed instructions about what to do.

The orders were transmitted by Gabriel. He and Baiter were in charge of rehearsals, so to speak. Their boss was absent for everything... absent for a certain time.

Because the Barbottiere affair had never been fully exposed and the Broquet brigade had not seen their boss since the event, they did not know what to think. Was Broquet dead like the Zs claimed in their muttering conversations at Clafous? Had he been saved but gravely injured like his men preferred to believe?

So many mysteries for them that Gabriel and Baiter decided not to clear them up when asked.

"The boss is dead," they said, "and we're going to avenge him."

Because following Broquet's advice, they let the men believe that they were out for revenge. This would avoid any indiscretion, any leaks reaching the ears of the Zs who were constantly on the lookout. Because the Zs had a surveillance on Broquet's men that was as thorough as the brigade was famous for.

Broquet had confidence in his men but even his most faithful allies, his most devoted supporters could let a word slip out. If they knew nothing, they could say nothing. It was far better this way.

As for his lieutenants, Paulin Broquet told them not to acknowledge him until he gave a signal, a special whistle or a gunshot. Otherwise, don't move, don't try to contact him for any reason whatsoever, however long it might take for him to show up.

It might happen, in fact, that the expedition would end up in a simple stakeout the first night, that it would be nothing more than a practice run and they would have to postpone the attack for another, more auspicious day.

With their roles understood, each man assigned a post, they were waiting for nothing else but the date. In the area, the men of the brigade, whom they called the Broquets, were suddenly everywhere in disguise, making reconnaissance excursions around the battlefield, spying on the comings and goings of the good, trusting Melidons who suspected nothing amiss from the tenants in their gracious home.

Clafous had given a date for another Z meeting in the new Zigomar palace. Paulin Broquet decided to act that night. Around midnight, Broquet and Gabriel, dressed as simple workers, after spending the evening in a crowded bar, stumbled onto Avenue de Suffren and headed for the place where Gabriel had sat in the rain for long hours.

Broquet shook his friend's hand, "See you later." And he went down the alley that led to the fence around the empty lot. He saw two or three men lift the board that dropped into place after them, covering their tracks so that they could sneak into the lot unseen.

Broquet approached the fence. Through a crack in the old boards he could easily see the men crossing the empty lot and waiting at the back wall the Melidon house. On the third floor a light was shining, then went out.

Then from the window at the end of the hallway on the third floor he saw a ladder come down. Everything was happening just like the night when Gabriel had followed the Zs with Bigard. The men waiting at the foot of the wall climbed up the ladder and it was pulled up after them. We know that it could easily slip back into the house as it was folded up.

"Good," Broquet thought. "They're starting the meeting. And they don't suspect a thing. They haven't seen us, have no idea that we're here. So far so good."

Broquet thought correctly that the Zs hoisted up their ladder like that because they did not suspect his presence in the area. Otherwise, they would have left the ladder to try to lure... not Broquet, whom they thought was dead and gone, but one of his lieutenants who might be less cautious than his boss and easily fall into a trap, climbing up the ladder and straight into the lion's den.

He, of course, would never have thought of entering the house this way. Therefore, he took the disappearance of the ladder as a good omen.

So, with nothing more to do on this side of the fence he went back to Avenue de Suffren, then to Avenue de La Motte-Picquet and finally reached the front of the Melidon house. Since he was constantly wary of Zigomar spies and could not for a second risk revealing himself, he pretended to ring the bell. But at the same time he slipped a key into the lock.

Baiter had taken advantage of his visits to the house to sneak an impression of the key to make a copy. With this copy Broquet opened the door silently and stepped calmly into the house as if he had been invited in.

Now, in the dark alley he had taken a minute to change disguises. He was a worker wandering around the fence but now he was a nice middle-class man from the neighborhood.

Thus Paulin Broquet found himself inside the Melidon house whose attic, called a workshop by the pseudo-photographer Grandel, alias the Count de la Gueriniere, was being used by the Zigomar gang as the new Barbottiere. Once in the entrance hall he stayed close to the door and listened. When he heard no suspicious sounds he figured that no one had heard the door opening and closing.

"Okay," he said, "Let's go."

Paulin Broquet had never been in the house but Gabriel had described it for him clearly enough so he was not completely lost. Besides, he was not walking in the dark. There was a small gas lamp on the wall in the staircase that served as a nightlight. And from the office that was used as a bedroom by the watchman who opened the door for tenants at night there was also some light spilling forth. Then on the sill of a small window that formed a kind of niche, there was another gas lamp with candlesticks under the room keys hanging up on a numbered board. Thus the tenants could light a candle to see their way back to their rooms. But most of them kept their key with them and did not take a candle. They went straight to their room. Broquet knew this because Zulma had told Baiter in person.

Therefore, he did not take a candle and as he passed by the watchman's room he mumbled an incomprehensible name. Like others of his kind, the watchman was fast asleep. It was a habit, instinct, an automatic response like all doormen in Paris that if you rang you would not wake them up or if they were only half-asleep the bell would plunge them into the deepest slumber. So, Broquet slipped by without a problem.

He did not come here to live through another experience like at the Barbottiere. He had no intention of making the same mistakes. For, this time he knew that Zigomar would make absolutely sure that this enemy was dead and that no miracle would come to save him.

Moreover, Broquet did not feel recovered enough to start another fight so soon after his first adventure. He did not want to throw his brigade into an affair that could easily turn into a ridiculous blunder. No, before "broqueting" the bandits, as they said, he wanted to be sure that the "broqeutage" would not come up empty and that the criminals they were looking for were really here.

Once he had seen for himself what he wanted to see, when he figured it was the right time, he would get to a window and give the signal. Immediately, all the "broquets", with Gabriel and Baiter at the head, would come running and pull the trap to make the arrests. Everything was set up for this. Everything was ready. The men were there waiting for the signal to invade the house.

Therefore, Paulin Broquet snuck up to the second floor like a shadow. He listened, studied the silence, then decided to move up to the third floor. On the third floor were the rooms of the photographer, the engineer and the others who were certainly members of the Z gang. It was here, then that Broquet was entering the danger zone.

After listening carefully for any suspicious sounds, he walked up the stairs, one by one, step by step, until he arrived on the dreadful third floor. Before stepping onto the landing he stopped again to listen... and look. He only decided to continue when he was sure that it was safe.

He went down the corridor to the next set of stairs. At the foot of the stairs he swung around to see if anything was moving in the hallway, if one of the closed doors had not opened up, which would cut off any chance of his escape. Nothing looked at all suspicious.

Broquet continued his climb. In the middle of the staircase where they started turning to reach the upper floor, the attic floor, was a door in the wall. Baiter had warned him about it... this door on every floor. It was painted to blend in with the walls in fake marble and was noticeable only by a lock and two glass doorplates.

Broquet approached cautiously and used his key to lock it. If there were, by chance, anyone inside, certainly a Z, he would be a prisoner. At first Broquet thought of opening the door to see if anyone was behind it but then he would be forced to fight and the plan would be ruined. Whereas by keeping them locked up, if anyone happened to be there, he felt safer. The prisoner might hesitate to act, to sound the alarm.

Having locked the door, therefore, Broquet continued climbing the stairs. He had not gone two steps when the door he had been so careful to lock opened up and two men stepped out. Before he had time to even turn all the way around, a woolen sack was thrown over his head and yanked from behind. He lost his balance, tried to hold onto something but found only empty air and he fell down. Someone grabbed his arms and he was tied up, arms and legs, in the blink of an eye.

Then they picked him up by his feet and shoulders and carried him away.

They did this all in only a few seconds... and in complete silence.

14. A hare's heart

When he fell into his enemies' hands, his entire body shook with terror. A shiver of fear ran through him from head to toe. Under the thick, heavy hood, you could hear his teeth chattering. He did not try to fight it. It would have been useless. Besides, there was nothing he could do. He did not have the courage... not a single thought of resistance or revolt.

The two men carrying him entered the workshop. They took off his coat, his vest and his shirt and tied him bare-chested to an instrument of torture. The Zigomar court was in full swing, as we have already seen.

Paulin Broquet knew he was sitting in a chair, that a stronger rope had been tied around his chest... and that some kind of unknown machine was connected to this rope. It made him tremble all the more, assuming that they were about to extract their revenge.

Zigomar made a sign with his hand. One of the men untied the hood and lifted it off the prisoner's head. Broquet looked around, but his sight was blurred by the sudden light and by fear. He opened his mouth. He wanted to cry out, to call for help, but no sound escaped his trembling lips.

He saw next to him two men wearing black hoods... and in front of him other men behind the tables covered with black drapes... they, too, had hoods on but theirs were red. He saw the symbolic Z slicing across all the black, across all the red. Nobody moved.

He felt like he was living through some feverish nightmare.

Now Paulin Broquet was staring at the hood with golden stripes that towered over the assembly. And his eyes seemed to panic again.

The stillness and silence was agonizing.

Never had a man sentenced to death woken at dawn to a sight more frightening, more tragic...

The Zs seemed to be enjoying this drama of fear, of dread that had delivered them the detective. Through the holes in their hoods their eyes sparkled with triumph and joy.

At last the Z wearing the gold-striped hood spoke, but he still did not budge an inch. "Hello, Paulin Broquet."

The detective snapped out of his nightmare, shook his head and muttered, "I'm not... I'm not Paulin Broquet."

A long, gloomy, harrowing silence followed this unexpected denial. The men around the detective stood like statues and the others behind the table were as still as the sphinx.

In a hoarse voice, from his dry, contracted throat, the detective tried to speak more loudly, "I tell you I'm not Paulin Broquet."

The same silence followed, the same indifference, the same immobility.

288

Broquet looked to the right and to the left, beckoning those closer to him as if they would understand better than the others behind the tables, the tribunal, farther away, who maybe did not hear him... But the guards had no reaction.

If the detective had not seen the hoods rising and falling a little with the breath, he would have believed that they really were made of stone or bronze, some inert, insensitive matter...

After a moment, as if the dramatic pause had served its purpose, satisfied with the terror instilled in the man, this prisoner, the gold-striped hood spoke again.

"Once again, Paulin Broquet, you can see that Zigomar is the strongest."

Broquet tried to deny again, "I'm not..."

But Zigomar, or the one in the role of Zigomar, cut him off, "Be quiet! You'll speak when Zigomar allows you to speak! Well, luck favors you. Luck, that god of the police... has done things for you already. It pulled you out of the death sentence pronounced by Zigomar. It saved you from the watery grave that no one before you had escaped."

Broquet mumbled, "But since I told you that I'm not..."

Zigomar went on without paying him any attention, "You got out of the Barbottiere alive. And you made sure to come here to tell us so we wouldn't waste our time looking for your corpse on the banks of the Seine. It's perfect."

Broquet tried to talk, "I've never been in the Barbottiere. I'm not..."

"Zigomar," the speaker raised his voice to drown out the detective, "Zigomar pays homage to your courage, your bravery... and your heroism on that night. And Zigomar expresses admiration once again today for this new effort."

"It's not me!"

"Except you must understand that luck alone can't favor you always. Zigomar, who is stronger than luck, will have revenge. Again you are in the hands of Zigomar... Once again nothing is left to chance..."

Broquet stuttered, "P-Please! Have mercy!"

Zigomar shouted, "Mercy! You ask for mercy! You, Paulin Broquet, you're asking Zigomar for mercy!" He laughed long and loudly. "Oh, truly a strange turn of events. This is really a surprise. Paulin Broquet asking for mercy."

"Since I'm not Paulin Broquet..."

"That's enough. Before going any further let me tell you that we are savoring one of our most beautiful victories here. We've been waiting for this moment for a long time. And like you we've been preparing our action. You, Paulin Broquet, are not the only one who knows how to lay a trap. The Broquet Brigade is not the only one who acts by both force and cunning. The Broquets are wonderful but the Zs are more so! This is proof!"

After a brief pause Zigomar went on, "So you got some agents watching us in our friend Clafous'... and the 'Enfants de l'Aveyron' where we thought we were safe is full of traps. When one of us takes a car to come here, the Broquets follow him. The lieutenants of Paulin Broquet dress up in army uniforms and tease the tender heart of our dear, sentimental and spacious Madame Melidon. And finally you prepare an attack and hope to repeat the performance of the Barbottiere at Zulma's. It was bold, I admit, but foolish of you and I'm surprised that you didn't remember that old proverb—Once bitten twice shy. Zigomar will never again be taken by surprise."

The speaker stopped as always after a sermon. Then he resumed.

"So, we know that Paulin Broquet has set a trap around the Melidon house and that he thinks we're caught in it... but we, too, have made preparations. We will escape and victory will belong to Zigomar! We let you watch our men climb calmly up the ladder. We let you pretend to ring the bell and use the key your Baiter was so clever to make for you. But you should know that a little modeling wax was stuck to Zulma's key and Zigomar knew exactly how Broquet would enter the house. And you should also know that tonight the watchman in the office is one of Zigomar's men... and as soon as Paulin Broquet entered the house, no matter how careful he was, he was already Zigomar's prisoner.

"You entered the house where Zigomar is master. You came all the way up to the third floor without suspecting a thing. You locked the door of the closet on the stairs out of precaution... A wise move... You had to do it... but Zigomar knew you would and had pulled out the bolt. So, the door didn't lock and stayed open. In case you opened it two Zs were waiting to do what they did anyway a few seconds later when you kept climbing up the stairs.

"And now here you are, tied to that chair, which will be a seat of torture for you because we're not just going to kill you tonight, we want to savor the vengeance and really enjoy capturing you!"

"Mercy! Have mercy!" Broquet cried out, tears rolling down his cheeks.

Zigomar stopped again, astonished. Like him, his acolytes stared agape at this man who sat there before them scared witless, trembling and acting like a coward in the face of danger and being spineless at the prospect of torture. They all remembered Broquet's bravery, his commendable attitude in the cave of the Barbottiere. They could remember him standing defiant, proud, his arms crossed and smiling while surrounded by the Zs who were screaming out for his death. At that time, which was as terrible as the present, Paulin Broquet proved himself to be admirable, heroic, wondrous...

And now he was a trembling coward, sweating in fear, panicking... a human wreck who was crying and begging for mercy.

But Zigomar could not be discouraged by the puzzling babble. He made a sign.

Two of the men standing behind Broquet came up closer. Together they turned a winch that was fitted to the back of the chair. Broquet howled in pain but one of the men who stood in front of him stuffed a balled up cloth into his mouth to muffle his cries.

The winch was an adaptation of the famous "Spanish Garotte" but instead of strangling him the collar pulled the ropes tied to his arms and shoulders. They pulled the limbs in opposite directions than was natural. As a result, the pain was extreme... and a little more pressure would inevitably break his arms in several places: wrists, forearms, upper arms and finally the shoulders.

The torture must have been dreadful. And it could last for a long time. Death would not come to deliver the victim until long hours had passed in indescribable suffering.

Paulin Broquet knew right away what kind of torture they were going to inflict on him. He felt lost.

15. The Garotte

Zigomar made another sign. The torturers turned the winch to loosen the ropes. Broquet took a deep breath.

"That's only the first round," Zigomar said calmly. "It ought to give you an idea of what's to come."

Broquet started to moan pitifully. "Mercy! Mercy! Kill me but don't make me suffer. I'm not Paulin Broquet."

Zigomar stared at him silently for a moment, then he said, "We'll hold off your suffering but you're going to talk."

"Talk?"

"Yes. You're going to answer my questions, tell me the truth, tell me everything I want to know."

"And you won't torture me?"

"No. Will you answer?"

"You want me to betray my chiefs?"

"Will you answer?"

"I can't. Kill me."

At a sign from Zigomar they gagged him again and turned the winch. Broquet could not scream so he tried to wriggle free. But his legs were tied like his arms and he could not move an inch.

They waited a few seconds before releasing the pressure like the first time. They took out the gag but all he could do was moan.

"Are you going to talk?" Zigomar asked.

Paulin Broquet was already in unbearable pain. He dropped his chin and muttered, "Mercy! Please, kill me right now."

"You don't want to talk?"

"Mercy!"

"So one more turn… this time it'll break your wrists."

"Please, please…"

"You'll talk?"

"Yes."

Zigomar asked, "Why are you saying you're not Paulin Broquet?"

"It's the truth… the truth…"

"We all recognize you here. We all know you."

"Yes, you should recognize me. It's necessary that you believe I'm Paulin Broquet."

"Why?"

"Because they still don't want to reveal that he's dead."

"Dead! They think he's dead?"

"But he is… he really is."

"The truth?"

"He was killed in the Barbottiere."

"Ah! How do you know that Broquet was killed in the Barbottiere?"

"First of all at Clafous', the night you executed him, the Zs said so... then after the explosion they searched and found two corpses."

"Two corpses? Who were they?"

"A policeman stabbed in the back."

"And the other?"

"Paulin Broquet."

"The other body wasn't the police chief who was with the officer?"

"No, it was Broquet."

"That's a lie."

"I'm telling the truth. How could I lie? I'm telling the truth..."

"Where did they find Broquet's body?"

"Near the big vault that collapsed, at a shaft opening. They figured that was where you threw him."

"Then?"

"But the shaft was filled up with water by the storm. Broquet drowned and floated to the surface. Since they didn't want to make it known that he was dead, they said it was a sewer worker, just like the policeman... They carried it away in secret so nobody would recognize it and cause a panic in the public if they found out Paulin Broquet was the victim of Zigomar."

Zigomar looked at his assessors, as if questioning them. As an answer they bowed their hoods. Apparently Broquet's story, told in this way, under these circumstances, where it was more than reckless to try to lie to his captors, sounded sincere to the criminals.

Zigomar asked, "But the Broquet Brigade didn't break up. The Broquets weren't disbanded."

"No."

"Who's leading them?"

"Gabriel."

Another silence. Another questioning look from Zigomar. Another nod from the hooded judges.

Obviously their spies had already given Zigomar this information. He knew perfectly well that since the Barbottiere affair all orders to the "Broquets" were coming from Gabriel... and that Gabriel had taken over from his dear departed boss.

Paulin Broquet's betrayal, therefore, at this time, only confirmed what they already knew.

Zigomar asked his prisoner, "Do you know about the theft of Baroness Van Cambre's necklace?"

"I've heard about it. The poet Anthime Soufret told a number of people about it, but no charges were ever filed... and they dropped the case."

"Who is James Twill?"

"I don't know."

"Be careful!" Zigomar said. "One twist of the ropes will make you talk."

"I don't know… I don't know…"

"Well, this James Twill is you!"

"No!"

"It was Paulin Broquet."

"No."

"You're lying again."

"Paulin Broquet died in the Barbottiere and he was not James Twill."

"We'll see about that."

He made a sign. The torturers stuck the gag in Broquet's mouth and they turned the winch. Broquet twisted and trembled in excruciating pain. A cold sweat ran down his forehead; his eyes were bloodshot. When the torturers finally took the gag out, his mouth drooled bloody foam.

"So," Zigomar asked, "do you insist on saying that it wasn't Paulin Broquet?"

Paulin Broquet answered, "Yes."

"Another turn to refresh your memory… Admit it, it was Paulin Broquet!"

"Pain won't make me lie."

"So, you don't know anything about this James Twill?"

"We figure he really is an American thief."

"What else?"

"He pulled off his job and left Paris."

"What makes you say that?"

"It seems that… but Gabriel hasn't confirmed it… it seems that the necklace was taken apart and the diamonds smuggled into England to be sold there."

"Is that true? Do we need another turn?"

"It's the truth."

Zigomar let Broquet catch his breath. The prisoner's chest was heaving. They could see the pain he was in.

And Zigomar could not imagine how any man in such suffering could be heroic enough to hide the truth.

After a moment the interrogation continued.

"Since you deny that you're Paulin Broquet, who are you?"

"A agent of the brigade."

"A broquet? A leader?"

"No, just a broquet."

What's you mission, your role in all this?"

"My role is tragic tonight because I'm supposed to play Paulin Broquet."

"What do you mean?"

"I look like him."

"Nobody looks exactly like another man… it's impossible."

Paulin Broquet shook his pale, aching head, "Sorry but as you see it's very possible. And this isn't the first time such a thing has happened."

"You think so?"

"I'm living proof."

Zigomar stared at his prisoner again but Broquet looked in bad shape, on the verge of passing out. His head drooped on his shoulder and his breathing was uneven.

"Oh, the pain, the pain."

"Why do they want you to play Paulin Broquet?" Zigomar asked.

"For the same reasons that they buried the news of his death... so as not to alarm the public and to make them believe that Broquet was still hunting the dangerous Zs."

"Really!"

"It's a concession to public opinion... and to avoid any complaints, demands and ultimatums from the police. And then it keeps the petty criminals from getting too reckless."

"Go on," Zigomar sneered.

Broquet did not answer right away. He breathed heavily as if talking was a painful effort for him that only increased his suffering.

Finally he spoke slowly, "Well, it's absolutely necessary to show a Paulin Broquet because we can't keep it secret forever. So, they chose me because of this resemblance. It's me you see out in public. And even before the affair at the Barbottiere, while the real Paulin Broquet was working somewhere else, I stayed in Paris, went out and played my role."

"And it worked?"

"Sure. Nobody ever suspected that Broquet had a double. Tonight is the first time..."

Zigomar told his torturers, "Search this man. Bring me whatever you find in his pockets."

While they searched him the bandit chief said, "If I find some proof that you're telling the truth... okay, I promise we'll stop torturing you. If you're lying, you will regret it when your bones start breaking."

They put what they had found on the table in front of Zigomar. There was a revolver, a knife, fake facial hair and some papers. Zigomar ignored everything but the papers.

"There's no name or address," he told Broquet.

"No, there never is. They're orders that only have our badge number... we all have one."

Zigomar read aloud, "Enter Zulma's. Look around. Listen at workshop. Come back and signal at the window. It's signed 'Gab'."

"Right, Gabriel. He's giving the orders, see, not Paulin Broquet. And these are mine... they're secret... I wasn't supposed to get caught so there's no back-up plan. That's the proof that everything I said is true."

Zigomar did not answer. He stopped moving again... and kept silent.

Paulin Broquet started moaning again. Then he broke the silence and whined, "I didn't lie. I told the truth. It's Gabriel who's giving the orders. He planned the whole thing for tonight. But he's not as smart as the boss and the plan failed... You found out all about it... and now I'm done for."

After moaning some more he added, "The proof that I'm not Paulin Broquet is that you caught me."

"We already caught him once before."

"Sure, but he's not the type of man to get caught twice. He wouldn't have been so stupid as to come alone into a house full of Zs... and try to sneak into the new Barbottiere... Me, I had to follow orders and this is the result... Broquet wouldn't have locked the door on the stairs without making sure it really locked. He wouldn't have continued up the stairs without making sure there was nobody behind the door... Me, I didn't think the lock might not work."

Zigomar and his assessors listened to Broquet without moving, without showing any reaction to what he said. Did they believe him or not? Were they playing with him? Or were they fooled... This was the agonizing problem whose solution was hidden behind the hoods.

Finally Zigomar spoke. "What's your mission? What were you supposed to do?"

"My orders are on the paper you read."

"Give me all the details."

"Gabriel and his men, the entire brigade, are surrounding the house. I'm just supposed to make sure that the meeting is taking place and then give the signal."

"What's the signal?"

"A loud whistle."

"You didn't have a whistle in your pockets."

"I can do it with my fingers."

"That's all?"

"That's all."

Then Zigomar made a sign. The torturers untied Broquet and stood him up.

Broquet started shaking again. "What are you going to do to me?" he groaned. "You promised not to torture me. You swore! Please, I told you every-thing..."

One of the torturers put the gag into his mouth to stop his whining, his moaning, his begging for mercy. Only in his eyes could they see the terror he felt.

Two others had brought in a heavy, wooden bench. They lay him on it and tied him tight, but they left his legs free. Broquet, therefore, could still move his legs like any man just lying on a bench.

It was refined cruelty because at the same time they put a noose around his neck, hanging down from the ceiling, and pulled the rope so that if he moved at all, if he tried to jump up he would be hanged and strangle to death.

Then they tied a pack of dynamite to his chest. There was a long fuse attached that ended at Zigomar's desk. One of the torturers placed a lit candle on the desk.

Zigomar spoke solemnly, "Whoever you are, agent of the famous brigade, simple broquet or chief, you do indeed bear a singularly close resemblance to Paulin Broquet. You may have his face but you do not have his soul.

"Zigomar takes pleasure in bringing justice to his enemies. When Zigomar had Paulin Broquet at the Barbottiere he congratulated his bravery and courage and mad daring. His heroic stance in the face of death made our triumph all the more beautiful. He was an enemy worthy of being vanquished by Zigomar.

"But you're pathetic... chicken-hearted, shaking like a starving jackal caught in a trap! You're dying of fear... and you can't do anything but cry and ask for mercy. Paulin Broquet would have defied his torturers and insulted the judges... and laughed harder at the torture itself. He proved himself a good soldier dying for this cause. You, however, betray your comrades, your chiefs, you failed in your duty... it's shameful. You're a gutless wimp. Zigomar kicks you away like a dog and instead of respect he pours scorn and mockery on you."

He took the fuse and lit it with the flame. Then he blew out the candle.

Broquet begged, "Mercy, please, have mercy!"

Zigomar said, "You have time to pray for your vile soul, if you have one, to the God of Traitors, because this fuse will take five minutes to burn down before the dynamite blows up your cowardly heart."

Suddenly the lamps hanging from the ceiling went out. Broquet heard pounding footsteps. He felt a cold wind coming from an open door or window. Then he understood that he was alone in the attic.

In the darkness now a little red light appeared on the floor. It was the fuse burning down, getting closer and closer, little by little, slowly, steadily... In less than five minutes it would reach its goal... inevitably.

16. The red dot

Paulin Broquet watch the burning fuse, the red dot, from his bench. But he wasted no time in idle thoughts. Two minutes had passed. He had three minutes left.

Watching the fire burn across the floor Broquet figured that the bandits did not measure the fuse correctly. Zigomar had said five minutes. It would explode a few seconds before that. Never had a man known more acutely the meaning of the phrase 'every second counts'.

The Zs had left his legs free in their ultimate cruelty, thinking that out of panic and fear he would try to move, to wriggle free... or to get away from the red dot that would follow him everywhere and finally blow him up. And anyway the bench would tip over and Broquet would hang himself with the noose. One way or another he was going to die this time.

But Paulin Broquet who had just seemed weak and spineless, who was crying and begging for mercy, was now acting very differently.

His legs were free... that was a big thing. He was careful not to make any quick movements, not to fall off the bench, not to hang himself in the noose.

Agile as he was, good at all sports, being tied to a bench was not such a terrible ordeal. It was simply a gymnastic exercise like he and his men had practiced.

First, he brought his knees up and tried to knock the dynamite off his belly but it was too tightly attached. He figured he was wasting his time. And he had barely two minutes left. So, he thought of trying a jackknife to jump up but if he failed he would hang himself and die. He gave up the idea. And during those few seconds the red dot kept creeping forward.

Broquet thought of one last move. While they were gagging him, he had clenched his teeth as tightly as he could and pushed his lips out. Now he opened his mouth. The gag was loose so he sucked it into his mouth. He could not talk but he could bite. Broquet had a good, solid jaw. The knot of the noose was not behind him but in front of his face. He reached up and caught the rope with his teeth. He did not hesitate. He clamped down with his jaws and overturned the bench. The red dot was almost on him.

Now he was on his knees and he just had to stand up, lifting the bench still tied to his back. Once on his feet he could let go of the noose, leave the rope hang down to his chest and look at the red dot.

Luckily it was still on the ground. Broquet lifted his foot and stamped on it. It went out. Now he could breath. There was no explosion and no hanging to be feared. But he was not saved yet because he was still a prisoner, tied to bench with his neck in a noose.

What he could worry about was Zigomar coming back after not hearing the explosion. But that should not happen for a while. Zigomar knew that fuses are unreliable and sometimes burned a lot more slowly than calculated. It took nothing to delay a fuse—a little humidity, a little fraying, an undetected flaw… Prudence required him to wait to judge if the fire not only stopped but went out. Otherwise, if they came back too soon, they would blow up with everything else. They had to wait as long as possible.

So, Paulin Broquet did not really fear Zigomar's return. But he was still stuck in the attic, bound to the bench with a noose around his neck that he could still not untie. He could look around, work his jaws, move his legs—that was all.

You are probably thinking that this was a lot for a man who should have been blown to smithereens by dynamite, if Zigomar's plan had worked out… and you might say he should be celebrating his fate since he was still alive. But all things considered, between being blasted to bits and being bound, gagged and unable to move, was one really much better than the other?

Nevertheless, a man like Paulin Broquet could not just focus on saving his life. For him this was not enough. It was only a start. He had everything else left to do: escape, slip through the hands of Zigomar again, get back to his men and get to safety.

A few minutes ago while he was rolling his eyes pretending to be scared, he had looked around. He had studied the strange photography workshop. To the right the slant of the ceiling told him that the roof was there… and therefore the side facing the street. A square, black flag was hanging from wires and sometimes it moved a little. It did not take a genius to figure out that there was a skylight behind it, an opening that gave access to the roof. But how high up was it? Could he reach it?

He was strung up by the neck like a goat on a tether and was just as restricted in his movements. Moreover, how could he navigate in the dark without bumping into a chair and giving himself away to the criminals who were certainly listening and would come running in?

He told himself, "I can't sit here forever like this. I have to do something."

First he turned in a circle and while doing so chewed on the gag. Since chewing was not enough he also rubbed his head against the bench, against the corner, not so much to cut the cloth as to slide it down. They had bound him quickly, figuring that he would stay put for five minutes, and so had tied it on his ears instead of above them. Thus he did not have to undo the knot but by pressing his ears against the bench could to push it down. It fell around his neck next to the noose.

While busy at this work, which ended up making his ears bleed, he stepped closer to the window… until he reached the end of his rope. Why did he do this? What was he hoping for? Did he think he could reach the window and open it? What then with his arms tied to the bench and the noose still around his neck?

Luckily he did manage to reach the window. He felt a breeze on his forehead and even brushed against the black flag that kept the light out of the attic. Broquet stretched out his neck as far as he could. The rope was just long enough.

As the drape was fluttering he could grab it in his teeth. He bit down and when he felt he had a good grip he pulled, without shaking it but hard. The flag was nailed to the wall. It pulled free and dropped to the floor.

Through the window Broquet could see the sky twinkling with stars as if smiling down on him. He felt the same joy as when he saw the hole in the sidewalk from the sewer. But just the same he knew his ordeal was not over and he was not free yet. He wasted no time.

The window was a kind of skylight formed of two panes of glass in an iron frame. Typical skylight in the attics of Paris. It let in a dim light from the gas lamps on the street. The street where his men were waiting for his signal. If only he could give it to them! But how?

The window was barely ajar, raised up on a couple of hinges. Not enough for sound to get through. He could yell and scream and nobody on the street would hear him.

He measured the distance with his foot to see if he could break the glass. But the window was on the edge of the roof and he could not reach far enough—his leg was a couple of inches too short. He stretched out, pulled the rope tight, risked strangling himself. He still could not reach it.

Everything he had done so far was rendered useless by a mere two inches. All the courage and willpower and energy he had spent for nothing.

But Paulin Broquet would not give up. He would never lose hope. He decided to give it one last shot, one final try, something crazy… his last card.

He knew that if he did not give the signal—even being gone for so long—his men would not move, would not come to save him, would not enter the house and risk spoiling the plan. It had been agreed upon, understood, ordered. There was nothing to hope for, therefore, on that score.

On the other hand, if the Zs did not hear the dynamite exploding they would come to find out why. Broquet knew he would be lost then. He had to try to save himself.

He imagined taking the noose between his teeth. Then he would jump forward, gain the extra inches and break the window. He could swing back into the attic hanging by his teeth. He had done plenty of physical exercises with his jaws: he had held onto a trapeze, played tug-of-war like a dog…

So, he bit down on the rope and tugged on it hard to make sure it held. He took a couple of steps backward and breathed in through his nose and…

Just when he was about to jump he heard a whistle echo through the night.

17. The masked stranger

Despite the late hour a big crowd was gathering on Avenue de Suffren and Avenue de La Motte-Piquet. Concerned neighbors, curious passers-by, stragglers from the seedy nightclubs, customers from the bars and restaurants, even a few soldiers had come running up.

A police line had been quickly set up and was keeping everyone on the opposite sidewalks, holding back the crowd so that the firemen could do their job. From across the street the admirable Parisian firemen could be seen sprinting around and examining the Melidon house, making sure that no fire would break out from some smoldering recess.

The tenants had woken up, jumped up, and now from the second floor they were all in the street wearing whatever they could throw on. Madame Zulma was barely conscious because of her asthma and her sensitive heart, which was supposed to avoid any shock. She was being given the necessary care at a neighbor's.

As for Monsieur Melidon, in his slippers and bathrobe, wearing a nightcap like General Bugeaud in the famous song, he was standing at his front door carrying his valiant sword from his days in charge of military beds. Like everyone he had woken up with a start. But the soul of a hero that lay dormant in his huge body believed that the enemy had come so he ran for his sword, ready to defend the land.

The cause of all this commotion that had stirred up this usually peaceful neighborhood and that threw the calm household into confusion was a violent explosion. An explosion that went off in the photography studio of Monsieur Grandel.

In the initial panic they had no idea what it was. The frenzy and terror made them think the worst. In the crowd there was talk about bombs, anarchists, Russian terrorists, an attack... Then the police came and the firemen climbed up into the attic, which calmed the wild imaginings and brought things back to reality.

In the end they found out that it was just an accident like often happens, unfortunately, with careless photographers. They said it was some magnesium that had caused the explosion, blowing a big hole in the roof and destroying pretty much everything in the attic. The fire had burned all the drapes and material that the photographer used to reflect or shut out the light. They soon found proof of the cause of the fire.

But one part of the roof had escaped the destruction. And there was one regrettable death in the accident. They said that Grandel was the victim of his own carelessness or bad luck. His body had been blown to bits and scattered all over the attic. The police and the firemen had to pick up the misshapen, unrecognizable remains and put them in a crate.

When their dreary harvest was over, while the firemen kept working on the roof and in the attic, the police brought down the crate full of flesh and bones, put it in a wagon and sped off to the Morgue, leaving behind them, after the initial fright and terror, a horror looming over the crowd of onlookers.

In this gloomy crowd were Paulin Broquet's men... and also Zigomar's. The funereal wagon passed by them all.

During the day the crowd got bigger, even more curious, more eager to know about and happier to taste a little of the horror.

So as the growing crowd watched the Melidon house anxiously and those in-the-know, who are always found in such cases ready to give gullible listeners gory details about the event that they really know nothing about, were telling stories as if they had been there when it happened, Gabriel and Baiter were back in the house in Neuilly at the bedside of their boss.

Paulin Broquet smiled at his lieutenants but he was pale and as hard as he tried he could not hide all the pain he felt. From time to time Simon would wipe his forehead with a vinegar-soaked towel.

Dr. Robert Montreil came to change the bandage on Broquet's left arm. He laid it gently along his side on the sheets, then went to the other side of the bed and pulled the covers off the right arm, which he was also going to bandage. Like the left arm the right looked skinned, peeled... The lieutenants could not hold back a cry of fright and disgust.

The muscular arm they usually admired, with all its nerves and tendons perfectly formed under clear, supple skin, was now nothing but a shapeless limb at the end of which was a limp, bluish hand.

Robert picked up the injured arm, felt it, studied it, examined every muscle, ran his expert fingers over it to find out if any bones were broken under the murdered flesh.

"Well, doc, anything broken?" Broquet asked.

"No, luckily."

"Bravo! So everything will be all right." He tried to smile at those around him who were suffering mentally as much as he was physically.

Robert had Gabriel take Broquet's hand and hold the arm out away from the bed. From a basin that Baiter had brought over he soaked up some antiseptic solution with absorbent cotton and trickled it carefully over the wound. Then with the help of Baiter, who knew quite a lot about medicine, he started bandaging the arm.

"It's despicable," he muttered. "It's unspeakable cruelty. These people are savages. They're the disgrace of society and deserve no mercy, no pity."

Gabriel and Baiter had tears in their eyes as they nodded in approval with the doctor.

When the bandage was done Robert told Broquet, "There you go, my friend, all wrapped up. May heaven heal you now."

"Thank you, doctor."

"For the moment there's nothing we can do wait. You'll need to be patient. You can take the medicine I sent out for and try to get as much sleep as possible. That's it."

When a member of the brigade whom Gabriel had sent to the pharmacy came back Robert gave some of the sedative to the detective. He waited along with the lieutenants for the drug to take effect, then he left, leaving one of the lieutenants with precise instructions.

All this happened, as we said, in the morning. A taxi had been sent to the hospital to fetch Robert. A man had come in and rattled off why he was there. It was one of Broquet's agents. He looked like an ordinary businessman and would not have been noticed if any spies were around.

Robert asked a colleague to cover his rounds and left right away. The taxi was a normal car but the driver was also a broquet and he knew how to throw off anyone who might be following them, which was always to be feared, all the while taking the shortest route to Neuilly. They had no problems.

Now that the bandage was on and Broquet was asleep Robert was listening to Gabriel give him a quick summary of the events of the night, telling him everything he knew about the drama.

After telling Robert, whom he knew he could trust, how the trap had been set to catch the Zigomars in their lair, Gabriel added, "The Melidon house is not too big. We should've been able to sneak in quickly but we couldn't do it knowing if it was worth the effort... if we could really catch this terrible Zigomar. The boss wanted to see for himself first. He was supposed to give us the signal by whistling... Only then were we authorized to intervene."

"It was still pretty reckless for him to go in alone."

"Obviously. But danger is intoxicating to Paulin Broquet... and neither the Barbottiere adventure nor this latest at the Melidons will cure him of it. Besides, this time the danger wasn't so great. The boss was just on a reconnaissance mission. We knew where he was. We were on alert and we could have run to help him at any time. The door of the house was unlocked, the stairs open... a hop, skip and a jump and we were there."

"Okay."

"We had waited long enough and were getting impatient... worried."

"I can imagine."

"We finally heard the whistle and rushed in. And we bumped into Broquet on the stairs. He stopped us and ordered, "Down, down! Get down! The attic's going to explode!"

"Oh my!"

"The explosion went off almost at the same time. No need to describe the chaos, the terror felt by the tenants and the neighbors. But it worked in our favor. We could do whatever we needed to in the commotion. So Broquet told me to go to the butcher and get some meat, bones and other stuff and bring it secretly into the attic. I would pick it all up later and pretend like they were human remains. Then I was to meet him in Neuilly. 'The Zs have to believe I'm blown to bits and the public has to think the photographer was killed by his magnesium.' And that, doctor, is the story. Only Broquet can tell you about what happened before."

"When he's feeling a little better he'll tell us."

"Oh, doctor," Gabriel said, "I forgot to tell you that when we saw Broquet he was being helped by a man in long, gray pants with a loose-fitting shirt like pajamas."

"One of yours?"

"Not at all. We didn't recognize him. See, he had a wolf face on."

"A masked man?"

"When he saw us coming he told the boss 'Goodbye, hero. Goodbye fabulous Paulin Broquet' and he dashed away. But Doctor, what was even weirder than the wolf mask was that this stranger, when he turned to flee, dropped the cap on his head... and a mane of hair fell down that in the glow of the light on the stairs shined like molten copper."

"It was a woman?"

"It was a woman."

18 The hero's tale

Paulin Broquet woke up late in the afternoon. He had slept all day long.

"Are you feeling better?" Robert asked him. The doctor had come back a little earlier in Broquet's taxi, which had come to get him at the Opera. When he stepped out of his office on Rue des Mathurins Robert always passed by there. So, he got into the car and was brought back.

To the doctor's question Broquet answered, "Yes, doc, I feel a lot better. Except for my arm everything's fine."

"Does it hurt a lot?"

"Nah. It just tickles kind of unpleasantly."

Robert took his patient's temperature and looked satisfied. He allowed him some food and said he wanted to leave the bandage on for a few more hours but he would come back in the evening to change it for the night. He arranged a time with one of Broquet's men to pick him up in the taxi and then left.

"My brother Raoul," he said, "who I'll tell about this troubling development, will certainly want to come and wish you well."

"Thanks, doc. I'm touched by the interest the Montreils are showing me."

"My brother will want to see you, so I'd appreciate it if I could bring him with me tonight."

"Gladly."

Broquet gave a few instructions to his agent to bring the two brothers back without being noticed.

"You've got to be especially wary around Rue Chalgrin. And watch if anybody leaves the building after the Montreils. Got it?"

"Got it, boss."

Robert was intrigued and asked the detective, "What do you suppose? That there's a spy in our building? A partner of the Zs? Someone who might betray us?"

"I suppose nothing, doctor. My method is to work only with known facts and not to move forward into the pitfalls of suppositions and hypotheses. But if there is one thing for certain it's that the night when you tried to break into Bejanet's safe was the very night they got the drop on you. It was your sword found near the wounded night watchman. You didn't bring it there and it didn't walk there by itself... so..."

Robert remembered the events that led up to setting off on their thieving expedition, the weird creaks in the hallway and also Raymonde's suspicions about their butler Marcelin whose presence in the rooms seemed particularly unusual to her. But like Paulin Broquet was saying, you should never act on just guesswork and in this case... he had only suspicions and suppositions with no proof at all. So, he kept silent.

He left the detective's villa and went back to Paris, Avenue de Clichy. After visiting his patient Dr. Robert went down Rue des Mathurins and back to the shared apartment. He was waiting for Raoul who had gone as usual to Ganneron Alley to spy on Riri and feed his infatuation with the blonde beauty.

When the lawyer showed up, the doctor told him, "Oh, Raoul, we have to get back to the house quickly. After dinner, when mother has gone to bed, we'll fix it to leave without being seen."

"But what if Raymonde sees us sneaking out?"

"We'll make up some excuse... if she questions us... which would be a change for her."

"Okay. Where are we going?"

"To Broquet's secret house in Neuilly."

"All right, but why? What's wrong?"

Robert told his brother what he knew about last night's adventure. "Broquet tried a real bold move, which I myself find a little reckless... against Zigomar."

"He won't let it go... he'll keep on it."

"I hope so, but once again Zigomar got the upper hand. Our heroic friend is badly wounded. But formal orders—not a word of this nocturnal visit in our house, not even in our rooms behind locked doors."

"I thought as much..."

"Yes, the walls have ears. As for us, officially we have no more business with Broquet. Like everyone else we think he's missing... or dead. Anyway, we know nothing about it."

"Got it."

Staying in bed was turning into a torture for Paulin Broquet. He was sitting up on a mountain of pillows that Baiter and Gabriel had piled up behind him. With a clever arrangement of cushions on both sides of the bed, they had formed armrests so that he could rest his wounded arms without feeling too much pain.

Broquet's fever had dropped and he had asked for food, which was, Dr. Robert had said, a good sign. Gabriel and Baiter tried to feed him like nannies do to babies.

Now the detective had sunken back into the pillows and was starting to digest peacefully, with one of his best cigars clenched between his teeth.

He was pleased to see Raoul come in with his brother. Broquet was the one who had first requested Robert's help and showed the way to get him here without being seen. He did not want to lose sight of the two brothers who were as involved as he was in solving the strange problem that put at risk the family honor of one and the professional honor of the other.

Smiling, therefore, and apologizing for not taking the cigar out of his mouth to greet them properly, Broquet still gave them a warm welcome. They both showed him the greatest sympathy.

Everyone sat down around the detective and lit their cigarettes and cigars. Simon played butler along with a partner, a kind of giant called Grimaut, a valuable agent in the brigade who had hands like hammers, a neck as thick as a bull, shoulders you could put a house on and a bulldog's jaw, but the kind, clear eyes of a Newfoundland dog.

Grimaut was not as intelligent as the old clown or as clever as Baiter or as ingenious as Gabriel, but he knew how to obey and carry out orders to the letter. Well, they never gave him any sensitive missions but when they needed a horse-cart or a catapult they called him. It was in his arms, like a baby, when the attic exploded, that his injured boss was carried down the stairs and out to safety. It was him who lifted up the patient in his huge arms to lay out the pillows and then laid him down gently.

It would have been foolish to try to enter the house. Grimaut would stop any unauthorized person and only had to pat the intruder on the head and the poor guy would be driven into the floor like a stake into sand or he would be crushed as if a giant stone had dropped on their skull.

Clafous, whose physical strength was legendary, was just a little boy next to Grimaut. But Grimaut never abused his strength. He was the picture of kindness, gentleness and as Broquet was fond of saying he treated the human race like farmer's wife gathering eggs.

But Grimaut needed someone to lead the way. That someone was Simon. They met in the circus. One was a clown and the other a strongman. When Simon joined Broquet's brigade, Grimaut naturally followed him. His colossal size was difficult to hide so Broquet had a tough time using him on clandestine missions. So, on the night of the expedition to Zulma's he did not join the "broquets" until late, when Simon had finished his surveillance of the Count de la Gueriniere, which the boss had assigned him, and figured he and his giant comrade should help out the brigade.

Paulin Broquet looked around at the people in the room and looked pleased to be surrounded by affectionate devotion and sincere sympathy.

Raoul said to him, "My brother told me about what happened. Let me tell you that I don't understand how you, as smart as you are, after escaping from the Barbottiere, would throw yourself into the lion's den once again."

"Had to," the detective still clenched the cigar in his teeth, "but it was different. I was only checking it out for my men to attack. I have to admit that Zigomar was smarter than me."

"He would have to be."

"Yes. The watchman downstairs was one of his men. And I didn't think of trying the door on the stairs to see if I really locked it. I was caught just like you and your brother at the notary's."

"With a bag and chloroform?"

"A bag without the anesthetic."

"So, it could really be…"

"Hold on! I was tied up by an expert. I know and can recognize a professional job when I see one. Then they brought me to sit before Zigomar. The black tables, the standing hoods, everything just like at the Barbottiere. Zigomar had his gold stripes and the flaming red Z... Bound and gagged... impossible to move, to call out, to give any signal to my men, I felt pretty lost, just like when you've lost all your courage, all your calm, all your will to fight to the end by any means possible."

"Are we talking about Paulin Broquet here?"

"I disguised myself without physically changing, just different enough to make someone hesitate while looking at me. I did it without fake beards or makeup, just combing my hair differently and changing my expression, the look in my eyes and my smile. It was me without being me. It was all I could count on to survive."

"A long shot."

"Very long indeed... but a shot nonetheless. I figured that since I was in front of a mock court, a stage, I ought to play a part. So, I tried to look and act as little as possible like the Paulin Broquet they knew, the Broquet they'd seen under pretty much the same circumstances. I played the role of a coward, a wimp, a crybaby."

The audience smiled when Broquet said this. "You!" they laughed. "Paulin Broquet a wimp... a crybaby! Who could believe that! Obviously it was nothing like you."

"I gave a great performance of a man in full panic, ready to do whatever it took to survive. Zigomar and his cronies were astonished. My attitude confused them. I realized this right away. They were expecting a replay of the Barbottiere. The scene was so different that they hesitated and finally changed their plans.

"I was crying, begging for mercy. I was a trembling wreck... afraid of dying... But Zigomar is no fool. He wanted to know if I was just playing, if I really was Broquet... or if I was just one of my agents pretending to be Broquet while the real one was working elsewhere. So, Zigomar tortured me."

"The bastard!"

"He gave a few turns to the *garotte* whose ropes—as you saw, doctor—bit into my flesh while twisting my limbs."

"It must have been horribly painful."

"Yes," Broquet answered curtly. "Yes, very painful. I felt my body being pulled apart and was mindful enough to know that one more turn would break my arms."

"And you kept playing dumb?"

"Yes, I kept being the false Broquet, swearing to it, proving it."

The listeners shuddered, "Oh, you're incredible. What you did was pure heroism."

"Hold on... Zigomar wanted to know if I had escaped the Barbottiere. On the rack I said no. Zigomar wanted to know if James Twill was Paulin Broquet.

On the rack still I said no. Could you doubt a man insisting on these things under the torture I endured? Zigomar ended up believing that he was not holding the real Paulin Broquet. So, by putting me on the rack again he made me betray myself. He asked me all kinds of information that I gave him willingly. He asked me about the signal to call my men. I gave it... because if he gave it my men would rush in and save me... and because tomorrow we'll change it."

"Oh, that's great, boss," Gabriel said.

"But Zigomar was still a little suspicious despite my confessions so he had me tied to a bench. They put a noose around my neck, hanging from the ceiling just the right length. If I moved I would hang myself. Plus he tied dynamite to my chest."

"The rats!"

"Dynamite with a fuse that was supposed to last five minutes."

"How awful to torment a man like that."

"Lastly they gagged me and after one last Zigomar speech his men, his executioners, all the Zs disappeared. They left me in total darkness, tied fast to a bench, at the end of a noose, watching a red dot creeping across the floor to blow me up."

Broquet said all this very calmly, smoking his cigar. His audience, on the contrary, was on the edge of their seats. He went on to tell them, like it was the simplest thing in the world, how he overturned the bench, stamped out the fuse and got over to the window.

"By then," he said, "five or six minutes must have passed, no more, since Zigomar had left me to my gruesome fate. Then I heard someone whistle the signal."

Gabriel and Baiter jumped in their seats. "What's that, boss? It wasn't you who whistled?"

"No, my friends."

"Who was it then?"

"Zigomar no doubt."

"What? Zigomar?"

"But of course."

"How could he?"

"Because I'd given him the secret when I betrayed Broquet under torture."

"Oh, right, boss."

"I wasn't just betraying Broquet but preparing the only way to save myself. In fact, I was thinking that Zigomar didn't tie the dynamite to my chest just to kill me alone."

"But..."

"One thrust of a sword could have done the job. More quickly and cleanly. But Zigomar knew, through my confession, that at the sound of the whistle the 'broquets' would invade the house and first run up to the attic. He was counting on you arriving right when the explosion would go off so there would be more than one victim."

"The villain," Dr. Robert muttered. "His brain is built for evil!"

"Yes but his plan would not have worked out as he hoped. Dynamite is a powerful explosive but it doesn't blow in the same way as powder, say, in volume... in area so to speak. It goes up and down but not so much outward... So, the worst that could have happened if you rushed into the attic would have been pieces of the roof falling on your heads. As for me, I would have been blown to bits."

There was a moment of awkward, painful silence. They had just suffered through those final minutes of agony that this brave, heroic man was recounting so calmly, with a smile on his lips.

19. The golden-red braid

The listeners felt so terrified during the story that they could not speak.

Finally, Broquet spoke to Gabriel, "Give me another cigar, this one's too hard to puff. It's hard enough to talk while smoking and this one's just making it harder."

Gabriel took the cigar from his mouth and chose another from the box. He cut the end and put it between Broquet's teeth before striking the wooden match (because, as you know, the detective never used wax matches).

He took a few puffs and said, "That's better."

Stuttering at first Gabriel said, "Excuse me, boss. We know it'll bore you to hear how much we and all your men admire your courage and your cleverness... but I'd like to talk a little bit more about this whole affair."

"Good, I'm listening."

"There's one thing that's still a little obscure."

"What's that?"

"You were tied to a bench. They left you like that out of cruelty, probably hoping you'd hang yourself."

"So what?"

"You were able to get to the window but still with the noose around your neck..."

Broquet looked straight at his lieutenant, "And you want to know how I got out of the noose, untied the bench and met you on the stairs?"

"If you don't mind telling us... because you didn't say anything about that, which must have been the most dramatic part of all."

Paulin Broquet spoke in a strange voice, very slowly, "It was weird indeed." He took a few seconds before deciding to speak. "Well, here's what happened... and my friends, it's no less mysterious to me than to you. I've been trying to analyze the incident... to understand it... I'm in the dark."

Broquet took a few puffs on his cigar before resuming.

"So, I was in front of the window but I couldn't reach it. I only needed a few inches of rope but there was nothing I could do. Then all of sudden I feel two hands on me. A deep but gentle voice, obviously trying to disguise itself, whispers: 'Paulin Broquet, don't be afraid. You don't know the person near you... you can't know... but he saw everything that happened here. He saw your heroic lie and he admires you deeply. He's helping you get to the freedom that you so bravely deserve and he wants to see you back with your friends. He doesn't want to see you fall victim to this hateful crime. Do everything I say... and let me guide you without worrying about any more traps. Do you trust me?'

"I said I trusted him. 'Thank you. I couldn't come earlier to save you because the Zs were still in the house. Now they've left. Zigomar himself was the last one out. He's the one who just whistled. He's waiting on Avenue de Suffren for the explosion that will signal his new triumph.'

"While talking the stranger had taken my noose off and with a knife was cutting the ropes around my arms. Then he removed the dynamite and placed it on the windowsill. After that he held the knife out to me and said, 'Take this weapon, if you doubt me, and at the first sign of danger, if you think I've betrayed you, you can stab me in the chest.'

"And he forced the knife into my hands. But I refused. I told him that I trusted him. In the light from the window I saw a young man dressed in loose-fitting gray suit with a big, cloth cap. He was masked.

"While he was whispering in my ear I could smell his breath. Behind the mask that only hid the top of his face I could see a nice-looking, well-defined mouth with teeth that shined like pearls in the light. I saw a strong, sharp chin but round below being pushed up by tight collar of the coat. This chin, the lips, the cheeks that were as smooth as silk and not trace of a moustache... but I couldn't tell if a razor had anything to do with it. In any case, this young man must have been very fine looking with those bright eyes sparkling behind the mask.

"When he spoke to me his breath was fresh but with a slight scent of Turkish tobacco. When he bent down to cut my ropes his body gave off a faint, exquisite scent... gentle but a little sharp and strong, the kind favored by the English.

"So, he untied me, threw the ropes onto the ground, then bent down again to pick up the fuse. He rifled through his coat pocket, took something out that he put on the end of the fuse, then he spit on it and I saw the red dot reappear in the darkness... off again on its slow, implacable course. 'Zigomar will be happy,' he said. 'He's going to get his explosion. But the dynamite explodes up and will make more noise than damage.'

"He grabbed my hand. 'Come with me. We've only got two minutes to get downstairs.' But my legs were so cramped from the ropes that I couldn't walk and I fell on my first step. The young man picked me up and carried me in his arms. He was remarkably strong because I'm pretty heavy. Anyway, he carried me like that down the stairs and put me down on the landing when you showed up. You know the rest."

Gabriel asked, "But you, boss, do you know the rest?"

"What do you mean?"

"Do you know what became of the young man with the beautiful eyes and pearly teeth, who smelled of Turkish tobacco and English perfume?"

Broquet had a big smile on his face but he said nothing.

"Well, boss, after putting you down, when that strange young man saved himself by running away... he dropped his cap."

"Aha."

"I picked it up. It smelled of that peculiar perfume."

"A nice souvenir," the detective laughed.

Gabriel added, "And when the cap fell down so did a bunch of long, golden red hair. It was a woman!"

Broquet said, "Oh, you saw… a woman!"

"Yes, boss."

"Well, my friends, yes, it was a woman. And that's what I don't understand. Who was she and what was she doing at Zigomar's? Why did she want to defeat the sinister crooks? Why save Paulin Broquet? A woman… A woman!"

But the detective, probably just to take their minds off these strange revelations, changed the subject. He turned to Simon, "And did you carry out your surveillance mission last night?"

"Yes, boss. As always I followed the Count de la Gueriniere… to the club, to the Lutetia, to Lucette Minois' and finally to his home."

"Good. So, while you were watching him yesterday, just like the night of Bejanet's robbery and Bilmat's too, like in Itonville, your Count was presiding over the Zigomar assembly. I recognized his voice. And he oversaw my torture!"

20. A cruel revelation

These various incidents that the two brothers were mixed up in as both doctor and friend, did not discourage them from the goal they had set. But the job was getting more and more complicated. They saw that it would be a lot harder for them to accomplish their mission of honest compensation than they first thought. Moreover, Monsieur Grillard had warned them of the difficulties awaiting them when he gave them his sage advice. But even this did not deter them.

With the support of Brunel, who was proving to be admirably devoted, and the information from Broquet, whom they consulted—always in secret—in all delicate matters, they were still hoping to reach their end.

Among the files that should have taken more time to deal with there was one that, for particular reasons that are easy to guess, they did wanted to treat first: The Menardier file.

Now, from this file, one of the oldest if not the oldest that Brunel had, almost nothing or just a few random pieces had survived. In one of the Montreil's first registers Brunel had found this entry under the name of Menardier to the amount of two million. But with no other comment.

"Get this two million," Raoul said after discussing it with his brother, "to Madame Menardier." Then he added sadly, "After what we know now from the other files, we can presume that this two million is not a deposit made by our father..."

"A debt collection," Robert said.

"I think so too," the chief accountant agreed. "If the amount had been deposited by Monsieur Montreil, we would've found the receipt. But there is no receipt..."

"Maybe," the lawyer said, "we're looking at the money given to our father by his friend Menardier. Maybe this is what the poor man's lawyer was calling the origin of the Montreil fortune, based on broken promises, theft and the death of an honest man."

"Monsieur," Brunel told Raoul, "don't speak like that about your father."

"Alas, the same words were spoken in open court... and printed. It feels to us, to my brother and me, that they're branded onto our chest. Come on, Monsieur Brunel, let's finish this painful task and get the two million to Madame Menardier. Look at the books. Try to find the amount of the sale of Menardier's properties, his factory... then we'll take them the fortune that rightfully belongs to them, which Menardier had trusted to our father."

"Okay, but it will take time because we can't make any mistakes. I need to find the other documents that are probably with Grillard or Bejanet."

"We're relying on your diligence and devotion. But we have to move delicately and act discreetly so that nothing leaks out before we're sure of everything."

There was indeed reason to fear that if rumors of the brothers' project got out a swarm of people would descend onto the Montreil bank claiming damages, thefts and extortion. It would be a horrible blackmail whose scandal the two brothers wanted to avoid at all costs.

They were hoping to make up for their father's misdeeds thoroughly, unconditionally, but Brunel wanted to protect against any kind of exploitation that would surely come about.

Above all, Robert and Raoul wanted nothing of their work to reach the ears of their mother or sister. Especially since they did not want them to suspect that these restitutions would spell their ruin.

"Us boys, you being a doctor and me a lawyer, will always manage."

"Sure, but Raymonde?"

"Ah, Raymonde. Hard question!"

"Can her marriage with Captain de Rennebois still go through? Should we tell her why she has no dowry and reveal to her what her father was really like?"

"No, no, never. Keep her in the dark about everything. Her mother too."

"What's the use anyway? It'd be pointless... Maybe after sacrificing everything to save our family's honor we'll have enough left over to afford her marriage."

"Let's hope so. You and I, we'll give whatever we've got after the bankruptcy."

"Naturally and moreover she can have our share of mother's wealth as well."

"That's right. Maybe we'll build a dowry as big as the captain is expecting or at least one that's acceptable..."

"Yes. In our poverty that she'll know nothing about we will have the satisfaction to know that we guaranteed her happiness and in this disaster at least one woman will come out the better for it."

As for Madame Montreil, she could never suspect anything and never hear about these sorrows.

Monsieur Brunel made sure that the profits of the bank, as far as they were honestly earned, were enough to support the lifestyle that the Montreil women were used to. But one day, as still happens at the bank, Raymonde thought she might surprise her brothers and went to Rue des Mathurins to ask them to go with her to do some shopping. The servant who was watching over the apartment said that the brothers would be back soon. Raymonde figured that she should wait.

Not being able to go if they came back too late, she postponed her shopping and decided to go back with them at dinnertime. She was happy to do so. Therefore, she went into their salon, which was also used as an office for them.

It was there, on a big table, that they had laid the newspapers and files that dealt with the different cases they knew their father was involved in. No one was allowed into the salon. But the servant did not believe the strict prohibition applied to the sister. He let Raymonde enter the salon.

Out of boredom the young lady grabbed one of the papers at random. Her eyes were automatically drawn to the column marked with a blue pencil. And she cried out... A cry of surprise, astonishment, worry and pain...

And as if bewitched by this article she read under her breath, seeming not to believe her eyes and needing to hear the words to lend faith.

In this article they talked about how Montreil had made his fortune, about questionable beginnings, about the case of Menardier and his death. They called this kind of work by the banker on Rue Le Peletier usury or worse... theft!

"Usury... Theft... my father, a thief," Raymonde muttered. "My father caused the death of Menardier and the suicide of other clients, the ruin of many families. My father... my father..."

And Raymonde, who loved and worshipped her father as much as her two brothers, after reading these revelations, felt the same dreadful sorrow, the same depression as Robert and Raoul. But being energetic and loyal, she did not listen to her grief and wanted to know, like her brothers, all about the great evil that was falling upon her out of this shameful memory of her once-venerated father.

After this newspaper she took another, then a third and she read, read feverishly... painfully, eager to read, to feel this hateful suffering flood her damaged soul. In each report a new aspect of her father's character was revealed and the infamy of his life appeared more and more clearly.

"If he wasn't my father," she said, "I would say this man was a criminal. But it's my father!"

She was so absorbed in reading that she did not hear the door of the salon open. Robert and Raoul came in. They saw Raymonde holding a newspaper, but hoping that she had not yet had time to find the article that registered their shame, they ran and snatched the paper out of her hands.

Together they cried, "Raymonde! Don't read that!"

"Too late," she sighed. "I've read... I know everything!" With her eyes full of tears she fell into her brothers' arms. "What shame! What shame!"

"Dear Raymonde, we were hoping you would never find out."

Raymonde pushed away, "Why? Why hide this from me? Am I not your sister and don't I have an equal part in the inheritance of our unfortunate father? I want it... I demand it... whatever the fortune, the glory... or the dishonor."

"Don't say that word, Raymonde."

"Oh, let's not be afraid of words. The deeds are there. And I thank chance for letting me know it... in your room. I could have learned it publically and been crushed by the atrocious news in front of everyone."

"Oh Raymonde, who would dare do such a thing to you, a young lady? You've got nothing to do with all this."

"I'm as involved as you, brothers. And when we see the respected men commit such infamies… we have to expect all kinds of dirty tricks and acts of vengeance from others."

"Listen to us, we'll explain everything."

"Excuse me. We already got a whiff of public opinion at our father's funeral. I haven't forgot. And I was trying to know why…"

"You too?"

"Oh, I was far from suspecting the real reason. And not knowing it would've gone on with my head held high, proud of my name, blind to the hateful looks and deaf to the scornful whispers… that they could say my clothes and jewelry, my car and all this luxury was paid for by theft, usury… death."

"Be quiet, Raymonde, be quiet! You've no right to say these things!"

"No, but I can't stop the people from saying them. And that's my greatest grief."

After a short pause to wipe away her tears she went on.

"And now that we know all this, what are we going to do to stop them talking? Because our name cannot be burdened with this infamy."

"What we're going to do?"

"Yes. Because you don't want it any more than I do, right? To keep this ill-begotten fortune… you can't…"

"Certainly not."

"What have you decided? To give it up?"

"Yes, to give it up."

"Great. How?"

"We're gathering the files of our father's clients and giving them back their money… with interest. For those who already paid we're giving back the exorbitant interest."

"So all the criminally acquired money will be reimbursed?"

"All of it. But we have to warn you, Raymonde, that we will be a little ruined."

"We shouldn't stop for that. We have to redeem our honor and the memory of our father. And if necessary sacrifice our last 100-franc bill for it."

"But you won't have a dowry."

"Too bad."

"You marriage will be destroyed."

"Why? If Fabien de Rennebois breaks it off because I have no dowry, it means he doesn't love his fiancée, just her money. Now, since I want a husband who loves me and whom I can love, I will deny him… but I don't think I have anything to worry about. Anyway, I'll tell Fabien myself."

"You'll still have some money from our mother. Raoul and I will give what we can."

"Not at all, not at all," Raymonde insisted. "I'll tell Fabien what it's about."

"But not about everything?"

"Sorry but I can't hide anything from my fiancé. And I don't want my husband to find out the truth one day and be embarrassed by his wife's family."

"Certainly, but..."

"If Fabien doesn't understand and leaves, it means that his heart is not equal to ours, that he's not worthy to be your brother. So, it won't be him leaving the daughter of a usurer but rather me saying goodbye, as is right, to a dowry chaser."

Raoul and Robert squeezed their sister's hands tenderly as she revealed her noble sentiments.

"Let's hope," Raoul said, "that your fiancé lives up to your hopes and is worthy of your... oh, your trust. Whatever happens we'll make sure you're happy."

An open, spontaneous nature like Raymonde's cannot wait for long in uncertainty when such a serious problem arises. Her life was depending on it. She wanted to know the outcome as soon as possible, even if it meant causing him horrible grief.

"But now," she told herself, "I have to face all the pains, all the humiliations, all kinds of dirty tricks because I'm poor!"

That evening, with authorization from her mother, she sent a breakfast invitation to Fabien de Rennebois for the next day. Raymonde was expecting to receive a telegram accepting it and expressing his joy. She experienced her first sorrow.

Maybe it was the cruelest sorrow, the most personal, that no one could share with her, coming from her love and affecting the very heart of her love.

The captain sent a telegram in response, of course, but the message said that he had a pressing, urgent duty and was sorry to have to turn down her gracious invitation. He hoped to come another day and present his excuses.

Raymonde turned pale on reading the message. It was a horrible blow for her, but no tears welled up in her eyes. With a sad smile she showed the telegram to her brothers and then answered her mother:

"It's irritating, really irritating. Fabien can't come. He's held up by an unexpected duty... totally unexpected. He'll probably come soon to apologize."

Robert and Raoul read the telegram and thought that the captain had heard something. The rumor that the Montreil sons were paying back the money stolen by their father might already have spread... It must have reached the ears of the captain sooner than any other interested party because it would mean, no doubt, the ruin of his future family.

Being alone with Raymonde they tried to comfort her.

But Raymonde snapped back, "Of course this telegram confirms our worst suspicions but until solid proof to the contrary I can't imagine that the man I love, who is still my fiancé, has such a vile soul. It's the first time, yes, that Fabien has answered me like this, but it could be pure coincidence. Besides, we have to believe what he says and wait for his explanation. If I'm wrong in giving him my affection, I will make amends by taking it away… and showering it even more upon you, my brothers, and upon our poor mother."

Raoul and Robert had to leave their sister to wait for her fiancé's justification. They went to the bank where Brunel met them with new files.

That afternoon, however, Captain de Rennebois showed up at the Montreil house. The captain was as affectionate as always to his future family. Raymonde watched him, studied him. She felt wonderfully happy because she saw the Fabien she knew, the fiancé she loved.

But did he really know nothing of the truth, of the new situation? And when he found out, would he be the same Fabien she was seeing now?

The captain explained to Madame Montreil the reason why he could not come to breakfast in the morning. "Oh, Madame," he laughed, "what a job defending your country. They imagined the enemy suddenly invading the forest of Fontainebleau. We took up arms to flush them out of the trees. It was, I admit, a nice little outing… but I was thinking of you and would rather have done my field duty another day. Alas, Madame, excuse me, but we did save the fatherland."

Madame Montreil accepted his explanation with a smile, then she gave some excuse and retired, leaving the engaged couple alone for a few moments.

Raymonde said that her brothers had asked her to meet them and she told the captain, "Let's surprise them!"

So, she dragged Fabien to her brothers' rooms. She brought him into the salon between the two bedrooms, then closed the door.

21. Between lovers

Fabien was a little surprised. He watched Raymonde, wondering what it all meant.

Raymonde turned to face him and asked him point blank, "What was the real reason you didn't come this morning?"

"The real reason?!" Fabien did not know what to say.

"Yes. I don't believe a word of what you told my mother. You can't lie very well. You were repeating what you memorized. So, if you didn't accept our invitation, if you didn't come, it was for something completely different than field duty."

Fabien smiled and said, "You guessed it, my dear Raymonde, there was another reason, but it's not important. Please, even though it's not completely true, accept it for the time being, at least for your mother's sake."

"Sorry for pressing you... Fabien... I want to know the real reason."

"It'll hurt me to tell you."

"Why?"

"Because even though I'm a soldier and ready to save our country, I still have scruples and a streak of modesty. I don't like playing the champion."

"I don't understand."

"My dear, I can see you're worried, troubled, anxious because of me, which makes me proud and sorry at the same time. So, I'll clear the matter up for you." He paused, then said, "Since you're determined to become the wife of a soldier, I'll appeal to you heart and when all danger has passed I'll prove to you how good a soldier I am."

"So far you've given me nothing but words. I want to get to the deeds."

"The deeds... we'll get there... but I beg you not to demand the reason... for this deed."

"Why?"

"Do you promise?"

"I promise."

"Good. Now here's the truth. This morning I wasn't on duty in the countryside or in the forest... or against an enemy. No, I went into a field with a friend and I stabbed him in the arm."

"You fought?" Raymonde gasped.

"In a duel. I telegraphed you the moment I got in the car with my swords. As much as I wanted to, I couldn't accept your invitation. I was hoping I wouldn't die... or kill my friend, but I couldn't think of coming to breakfast afterward. You don't know that a good duel, both civil and military, ends up with no result when it's with pistols and on the slab when swords are drawn. We soldiers have a saying: when the rabbits are on the skewer, it's the chickens who are cooked. It's an old French tradition."

"Were you hurt?"

"No. I'm good with swords. My adversary as well. We've known each other for a long time. We're equals, the same level... and we wanted to get it over quickly, it seems, with the blades out. I got him. Then we shook hands and had breakfast because you build up an appetite defending your honor. And that's the truth."

Raymonde was serious, grim when she asked, "Why did you duel with a friend?"

"My dear Raymonde," Fabien also turned more serious, "you promised you wouldn't ask."

"Indeed... but I didn't agree not to tell you."

"The official report says 'private matter'."

"Which means that they insulted someone very close to you... because it wasn't you who committed the offense."

"Certainly not!"

"And being my fiancé it couldn't be over some girl in the barracks."

"Oh, Raymonde!"

"Therefore, they offended your family, your father. But General de Rennebois had the most glorious career a soldier could hope for... and your mother, like mine, is a saint."

"It's true, Raymonde, if our hearts are the same it's because our mothers are the same."

"But our fathers?" Raymonde blurted out.

Fabien flinched. "Our fathers? What do you mean?"

The young lady stared hard into his eyes, interrogating them, trying to read in them. Fabien held her gaze, steady and sure.

Raymonde went on, "Your family is beyond all reproach, so if you fought this morning it's because they had went after mine."

The captain was surprised and showed it.

Raymonde said, "I knew it! Oh, you can tell me everything."

"Only because your father won't ever hear about it."

"What do you mean?"

"We were talking among friends about the fortunes of financiers. One of them said they could only be gotten through dishonesty. I reminded him that I was lucky enough to be your fiancée and I thought Monsieur Montreil was the most honorable man in the world."

"Oh!"

"My friend was obviously worked up and didn't want to back down before the others. He said Montreil was no better than the others, even worse. I begged him to take back what he said. He refused. It earned him my steel in his arm."

More grim than ever, Raymonde spoke slowly, "Your friend was right."

"Right?" Fabien shouted. "How so?"

"My father was not the man we all loved and respected."

"What do you mean?"

"The thirst for gold made him do certain things that my brothers and I are devastated about today."

"Look, Raymonde, I'm a soldier, I know nothing about business. I can imagine, sure, that sometimes there are risky speculations… thorny issues… But I'm sure that none of your father's actions were dishonorable."

"Sorry."

"Your father?"

"To acquire his great fortune he used means that were not only against honor but against the law."

"Oh."

"In short, my father was merciless in business. He speculated on the misfortunes of people. He lent money at usury rates…"

"Monsieur Montreil! What are you telling me?"

"He caused the ruin of many clients. He's accused of pushing them to death, to suicide."

"Ah, what are you saying? How do you know?"

"My brothers found out by going through the legal journals. The *Gazette des Tribunaux* talks all about it. My father stole a fortune from one of his friends, ruined him… drove him to his grave."

"That's dreadful!"

"There was a legal case for the poor man and a lot of others."

"Your father won, I suppose. They were false accusations…"

"My father won because he was rich and powerful. And extremely clever. He knew how to take precautions. He did win the cases because the law was followed to the letter. But morally he lost and every victim who advanced his finances, who fattened his safe, was one more loss for his honor. In short, our fortune is the result of the worst kind of usury."

"Dear Raymonde," the captain said, "I'm so sorry for you."

"And it's because my father was a horrible usurer that all of Paris scorned him on the day of his funeral."

"I remember that painful day… that agonizing puzzle for all of us…"

"There you go! I'm the daughter of a usurer!"

"You're not responsible, Raymonde… for the sins of your father."

"But I profited from them."

Captain de Rennebois looked at Raymonde as if he did not understand what she had said. After a moment he spoke, "You told me your brothers know about the situation. They'll do what their conscience demands to remove the stain, for you and for them, of this cursed inheritance."

"What do you mean, Fabien?"

"If the children can't be held responsible for their father's faults, they cannot, as you claimed, profit from them."

"And so?"

"So Robert and Raoul have to fix the misdeeds of the past as much as they're able."

"And give back the ill-begotten gains?"

"Absolutely."

Raymonde held out her hand. "Oh, Fabien, you're thinking the same thing as my brothers and I."

"Nothing else can be done."

"We're going to give back the money."

"Perfect."

"It'll be the ruin of us."

"It's a great misfortune, but it's necessary."

"We'll be poor."

"I'm not very rich but if this is necessary, make Robert and Raoul understand that all my assets are at their disposal. You can never pay too much for your honor."

Raymonde trembled with joy as she listened to the captain speaking frankly and clearly. She added, "But if I'm poor I can't be your wife."

"Why not?"

"I'd have no dowry."

Fabien jumped. "Raymonde, it's you I love! Your dowry and fortune is for you. Me, I ask for nothing but your love. If you're true and faithful, even if we're both poor since I'm giving what I have, if you're true in your love for me... I'll thank you forever for this happiness..."

Raymonde, who had made an extreme effort to stay calm, broke down in tears. "Fabien, dear Fabien, you make me so happy! I love you so much!"

"Raymonde, let's not ever talk again about the vile subject of money. I'll fix things with your brothers... and Captain de Rennebois' wife will be able to go anywhere with her head held high and no one will whisper the slightest accusation. Raymonde Montreil will have paid and made amends. Madame de Rennebois will be very happy as the wife of a poor captain who will love her forever."

"Oh, Fabien, no woman has ever had such proof of love. No woman will ever face life with so much calm, certainty and happiness as I do now. You have my heart! You are more than worthy of being a brother to my brothers. And I love you more than the world!"

The two young lovers shook hands very warmly.

At this moment, in Raoul's room, they could hear someone bumping into the furniture. Raymonde figured that Raoul had come back.

"Oh," she sounded overjoyed, "Raoul is here!"

She called her brother while hurrying over. But she stopped short, stunned, when she got to the open door, which a simple curtain was covering. In the room she saw neither Raoul nor Robert but the butler.

"You, Marcelin!" she cried out. "What are you doing here?"

"My job, mademoiselle," the butler answered.

"At this hour? It should already have been done."

"It is done. I came to deliver these letters that just arrived."

"Okay, go ahead." Raymonde closed the curtain and went back to Fabien. "That man was spying on us."

"Marcelin? Why? What for?"

"I don't know but I don't like the way he looks... his eyes are shifty. He disturbs me. And I think my brothers would do good to let him go. It's not the first time I've caught him spying on the house."

22. Painful secrets

Luckily, as Dr. Robert had observed, the torture had not broken Paulin Broquet's bones. Only the flesh was damaged, the muscles torn up. But Broquet's muscles were topnotch, as they say in sports, and it would only take some bandages, time and patience to get him back in shape. After two weeks he could use his hands and needed no help to smoke his cigarettes or cigars.

This time, however, Zigomar could not doubt the death of their terrible enemy. For him to pull through this new dilemma in which he had, let's admit it, stupidly thrown himself, it would take a real miracle.

The Zs could surely not have suspected the unforeseen arrival of the mysterious woman with flaming hair.

The explosion had taken place as expected and pretty much at the right time. They had seen them pulling out the pieces of flesh, the bloody remains, from the wreckage of the attic. They had to believe that this time the man who was or was not Paulin Broquet had been killed.

But at Clafous' no one talked about the incident. They were careful from now on.

Paulin Broquet apparently fell into the category of the dead who had to be killed twice. So, they had killed him twice. Now it was done for good... forever. Broquet was as dead as could be. And Zigomar could go about its business and get back to work on what the detective had been hindering.

As for Paulin Broquet, he had to suffer patiently and wait to get better.

Meanwhile, life went back to normal for our other friends.

Madame Laurent, who had taken a real liking to Riri, went to see her at work. They had agreed that they would never talk to anyone about what happened at Ville-d'Avray. They would never pronounce the name Andre Girardet or the name of the Montreil lawyer, neither to Marie the hunchback nor Madame Menardier nor even to Monsieur Laurent.

Monsieur Laurent, in fact, as we know, knew nothing about the visits that his wife paid to the sick man, so alone and so sad in his rich, elegant villa... that neighbored Aunt Melie.

And Riri saw that to mention the name to her mother would lead to explanations that she could not give. It was better to say nothing at all. Riri could not lie. She would have to tell the truth.

"And Mama," she told Madame Laurent, "will be alarmed. She'll start shaking every time I leave the house and worry until I get home. Mama doesn't need any more worries in her life. It would be a useless torture for her heart. She suffers enough already, poor Mama."

However, once in a while Riri and Laurent called the sick man at Ville-d'Avray. For Andre Girardet these conversations were a few minutes of joy. He felt less lonely, less abandoned to his tragic fate. Riri's voice livened him up like a charming birdsong, even when you cannot see the bird. And he was grateful to the young lady for this.

Through the telephone the crippled Andre Girardet, stuck in his chair, was connected to the world. It was kind of pitifully symbolic. And he, too, became enamored of the exquisite young lady. Madame Laurent became his sweet intermediary whom Riri could refuse nothing. Thus she had agreed to accept his help without offending her pride. And Riri could thus bring a little relief to her house and better care for her mother.

So that no awkward suspicions could arise, to cut short any wicked insinuations from M'ame Bochu when she came to have a glass of Curacao, Madame Laurent went with her to give the concierge all the back rent due and get receipts.

"As for the next apartment," Laurent told Riri, "if they want you to leave here, don't worry about it. The two of us will find something that both you and your mother will like."

Riri did not know how to thank her enough. "I'll never be able to repay you for everything."

But she could not refuse. Taking Andre Girardet's advice, Laurent first showed her that what they were doing would please her mother and be of great advantage to her. Now Riri was feeling more confident in life. She was feeling less alone, less isolated, more protected against all the traps and pitfalls, all the unforeseen dangers that Paris held in store for pretty young girls alone.

She had a friend in Ville-d'Avray and a protector in Paris... a big brother who would run to her help and protect her at the first sign of trouble. She guarded the letter that Girardet gave to her the night of the attack. She carried it with her at all times in a little, silk purse that he had made herself for her precious treasures.

In spite of this she still thought of that other letter, also kept safe and sound at home. The letter framed in grief... that said such tender, sweet things to her, so different from all the others she had received. The letter that told her, in short, pretty much what Andre Girardet had said aloud:

"You need someone by your side who will protect you, who will be your big brother... I ask nothing of you but the joy of being the one you can trust... the one who will free you from your troubles, from all danger so that you can finally smile at the future..."

And every time Riri called her poor friend in Ville-d'Avray, every time she touched her little purse with the letter, when she reread his words, every time, by some strange phenomenon she could not explain, Riri remembered the other letter that she treasured and she saw again the image of the young man in black with the kind face who dared not speak, who did not follow her down the alley, who never harassed her on her way to work, but who watched her from afar with such respectful tenderness.

And Riri told herself, "I would like Monsieur Girardet's friend, the one he said would be my defender, my big brother, to be like him."

As for the Count de la Gueriniere, after the affair in Ville-d'Avray he did not pursue her so much. Maybe the way he had been treated by the men who ran to Riri's aide, the wounds he was forced to bear on his face, all this kept him from showing himself too openly.

Riri barely saw him three or four times on the street... a glimpse... in the shadows. Or he was in a car as Riri passed by. She never spoke about these sightings to anyone. It would do no good. She wanted to believe that from now on the Count would stay calm, leave her alone, that she had nothing more to fear from him. And yet Riri was smart and told herself:

"I'm still surprised because a man like that, who has the audacity to attempt a crime like the trap I almost fell into, wouldn't stop so easily. His lover's pride was injured, his pretty boy face was slapped... too hard to accept defeat lying down."

Riri's common sense was not wrong. It was more than certain that the Count was preparing his revenge.

But Riri was no longer worried about it. She believed she could stand up to the wretch. She felt strong, armed, supported.

"Don't I have a defender now? I just have to call my big brother for help."

Poor Riri could not know how long it could take for this help to come. She could not imagine what a man like the Count de la Gueriniere was capable of... and what abominations his brain could cook up to get his revenge and conquer a girl!

Surely the defender that Andre Girardet had given to Rirette would come too late, but Pretty Riri had nobody else... and he did not even know about his mission. He would be called in case of danger... and let it be said without joking, there was a good chance he would come like the cavalry... too late.

But Riri had another defender whom she was completely ignorant of and who had never lost sight of her, who would arrive on time... or earlier. It was one of Broquet's men who, just like Simon the clown was watching the Count, was jealously watching over the young lady.

In spite of this surveillance, which he knew was done well by his men, Paulin Broquet was still worried. Aware of the treachery of his enemy, he knew that the Count would not stop there and accept defeat with no hope of revenge. There was no question about this.

Also aware of this man's cleverness, his imagination and ingenuity when it came to doing something bad, Broquet thought (and not without good reason) that the Count knew they were watching over the girl who had almost fallen victim to him. Therefore, he would not attack openly. He would find a new way to put her at his mercy, this time allowing nobody to come to her rescue.

Broquet anxiously wondered what new, infamous plot the villain was cooking up for Riri. But he was careful not to show anything when the lawyer or doctor talked about Riri and the panic they felt for her.

As Broquet was getting better, Robert and Raoul had told him in the course of one of their long conversations about the distressing discovery they had made concerning their father and Monsieur Menardier. While changing a bandage Robert spoke about the first cruel finding and at the same time talked about his brother's sorrow and the grief he himself felt for everything.

Broquet answered the doctor, "Trust in the future. You and your brother are on a path where only the honest follow. Pursue your goal without burdening your hearts with any more anxiety."

"But Raoul loves Riri."

"So much the better."

"How is that better? Do you think that what was possible before this awful discovery can still be so?"

"Why not?"

"Do you think Menardier's daughter could ever love the son of the man who ruined her father, who caused her unhappiness, who made her and her sister orphans?"

"Why not? Why not when the orphan is Riri? And when the one who loves her is Raoul?"

Robert looked puzzled as he muttered, "Why not when the orphan is Riri... And when the one who loves her is Raoul?" Then he cried out, "Yes, indeed, Riri... and Raoul... They both have such big hearts, such good and beautiful souls... Yes! Raoul and Riri. Maybe... Why not, indeed?"

The detective said, "Let it go, doctor, and you who perform miracles with your science, believe also that love can do things absolutely amazing. Anyway, if you want, I'll talk to your brother about it... one of these days."

"Oh, if you could comfort him..."

"Comfort him? Not at all. Encourage him, yes. And give him hope."

"What hope?"

"You'll see. Let me do it. I'll very gently get your brother to talk about his secret, which we all know about, and I'll give him some information about it that he doesn't know about yet and that will certainly cause him not only a great surprise but joy as well. It'll dissolve his sadness, get rid of his distress and bring some rays of hope to his aching soul."

A few days later Robert brought his brother with him to the detective's. The doctor checked the bandages, made sure the patient was healing, then excusing himself for an emergency he left his brother to chat with Broquet for a while.

Although Baiter had gained a well-earned reputation among the Broquets for his talent for making people talk, his boss was no slouch in this field and knew better than anyone how to open lips that were sealed by furrowed brows or suffering hearts. Besides, lovers want nothing more than sympathetic ears to hear about their obsessions. It seems that talking aloud about a beloved is to call them forth, to feel them near, to see them again up close.

Within minutes Raoul was glad to have a man like Paulin Broquet to confide his suffering. He told the detective the whole story, which he already knew and even better than the narrator. But without interrupting Broquet let Raoul spill out his sad tale.

"There it is," the lawyer concluded, "I've met a young lady with whom I feel I could share the rest of my life, whom I am fated to loved immensely. She's more beautiful than any other woman. If only you knew, my friend... She's blonde like you've never seen... like they don't make anymore... Her eyes are light blue, purple, as clear as the summer sky. And what a smile! How sweet she is! And so charming... The moral woman fits the physical woman, so to speak. The beauty of the soul is equal to the splendor of the body in this marvel, this unique creature... Love came to me through those wonderful eyes. It is love, they say, that hits us hardest but also that leaves the quickest. But this one has conquered my heart. It is anchored there. It's not the girl's beauty that struck me... it's the woman who is so beautiful... You see what I mean? It's not Rirette but Riri."

"Oh," Broquet remarked simply, "there's a lawyer's distinction if ever I heard one."

"No, listen. Seeing Riri... starting to love her... not a minute goes by I don't think of this: Riri's a worker, a seamstress, you could lure her in like a little Parisian sparrow with something shiny, for a fling... but the thought that I'm rich hasn't even crossed my mind... or that I could just make her my mistress... I've always thought of the possibility of marriage, of taking her as my wife."

"A working girl, a seamstress for your wife?"

"Yes because I know that her radiant beauty is the rare and precious gift of a chosen soul, an exquisite heart. I'm sure that this girl who shows such great affection for her mother would make me the happiest of men, if I were lucky enough to get her to love me..."

"She's poor. Her mother has no money."

"But she herself is such a treasure!"

"You're a millionaire."

"Hold on, my friend. Let me tell you something. You just said a word that calls in doubt all love... millionaire... money... that cursed money. I've thought a lot about all this. Before asking Riri to become my wife I want to be sure that she doesn't love me just for my money but for me. Plus, I've never let her know who I was... I talked to her and once I wrote to her, but she only knows me as Raoul... and knows nothing about my wealth."

"What did she do? How did she answer your letters?"

"She didn't."

"Oh."

"But what answer could she give? Should she? No…"

"How would you know what she thinks?"

"There are all kinds of ways."

"Well, have you seen anything to give you some hope?"

"Maybe I'm fooling myself… or flattering myself, but it seems to me, maybe it's just a personal feeling, that in the end it was all justified. I feel that since my letter I'm no longer a stranger to Riri. I've seen her from afar and she's spotted me several times. Our eyes met. I think she didn't look away… right away. She didn't smile at me, no, I can't say that… You know Riri, as pretty as she is, she always looks serious and sad… but I thought I could read in her eyes a kind of friendly sparkle, a ray of kindness. No more fear or fright or rejection like I saw when some unwelcome stranger approaches her… but rather the satisfaction of seeing someone who you like to see.

"Once again, my friend, I can assume my wishes are coming true. And yet… a few nights ago I became bewitched again on Avenue de Clichy because by chance the busy street pushed Riri right close to me. I brushed by her and almost bumped into her… and as I took off my hat to say I'm sorry… or to say hello… at the same time Riri looked straight into my eyes, certainly recognized me and without showing any surprise or irritation she gave me a smile, which I carried away with me jealously as if I'd found the most precious diamond in the world."

"In sum," Broquet said, "since you love Riri, it's to be expected that Riri is no longer… I don't want to say hostile but indifferent to you."

"Yes, that's it."

"Well, someone who's decent, loyal and honest like Rirette can't hide her feelings. A loving, uncompromising heart like hers doesn't do things halfway. Therefore, I say that Riri smiled at you because she likes you… and I imagine that for Rirette liking will turn into loving."

"Dear me!" Raoul sighed.

"Why 'Dear me' and this tragic sigh? I'm sure that this love is not an illusion, a hope, just a speculation on a future possibility. I say that love, which is completely sincere, absolute, definitive for Riri, I am sure this love exists, that it's alive and… lively and strong… and it…"

Raoul cut him off, "No, it is a tragedy."

"What are you talking about?" Broquet said. "I don't understand you."

"Why not?"

"You were depressed just because you didn't know if Riri could really love you. I'm telling you that she does… or that she's about to. And you moan and sigh and cry 'Dear me'."

"Oh, my friend, it's because I can see the reality behind it all."

"What do you mean?"

"I won't go to watch Riri anymore. At least I won't let her see me. I want her to forget about this Raoul who wrote to her, who she smiled at..."

"Why?"

"Because this Raoul is the son of the banker Montreil."

"So?"

"So between the son of Montreil and the daughter of Menardier there can exist nothing but hatred."

Paulin Broquet snapped back at the young lawyer, "My dear friend, when we're in love like you and we've got ideas like that in their head, do you know what we do?"

"Cry."

"Not a bad idea but there's something better. Change of scenery. We go to the countryside."

Raoul looked at the detective surprised, wondering if he was being serious or joking.

"You know what you should do?" the detective continued. "You should go tomorrow morning and ask to have lunch with your friend Andre Girardet... in Ville-d'Avray. If I'm not mistaken you haven't seen him in awhile."

"That's true."

"You know he's sad, alone, abandoned... and a visit from friends would do him a world of good."

"Yes, he's a good friend."

"You also know that Andre Girardet has loved and been heartbroken. So, go and talk to him about your problem. No one would understand you better."

"You're right!" Raoul almost screamed. "Yes, talking about your love problems with someone who has suffered so much would give a little relief to my aching heart. I'll go tomorrow."

"Even better because I believe he has something to confide in you as well. I think he called upon your services without telling you and he'd be glad to explain everything in person."

"Great! I'll say hello for you."

"No, no. I'm dead. I was blown up by Zigomar."

"Oh, right..."

"One more piece of advice: when you talk about your love don't mention Riri's name."

"Why?"

"Believe me, don't say her name or her mother's name. Take my advice. You'll find out why and you'll thank me."

"I'll do as you say then."

331

23. Love by telephone

Soon after Raoul bid farewell to the detective and the car took him to Rue des Mathurins. The next day he announced that he would not be having lunch at the house because he had to plead a case in Versailles. At 11 am he was driven to see his Andre Girardet. He had sent a message as was expected.

It was, in fact, as Broquet had said, a real joy for Girardet to see Raoul again. Andre Girardet was a few years older than the two brothers but they had met at the same school and become fast friends. Although the three of them had taken different career paths and thanks to the hazards of life they did not live near each other, still they never stopped keeping in touch and giving each other news.

Then Girardet left for the colonies. He had asked out of the blue, as a favor, to take part in an expedition that was so dangerous that the Ministry of War would not even assign an officer. Girardet came back on a stretcher. And since then he had not left his couch. The wounds he got in the rice paddies of Annam (old Vietnam) had turned the youth into an old man.

But even though Raoul and Robert suspected some tragic drama, they never tried to unveil the mystery of their friend's secret. Andre never talked about it.

Moreover, the brothers never met the kind and affectionate Madame Laurent, the only confidante for his past love and present tears.

"It's so nice of you to come see me," the sick young man told Raoul when he showed up at the door of the salon. "How can I ever thank you!" He held out his bony hands. "Oh, Raoul, my good friend, I'm so happy to see you."

The young lawyer gave him a friendly hug. Then he pulled an armchair close to the couch and sat down. "Don't thank me, Andre. I've come out of pure selfishness."

"It's all the same to me as along as you've come. My selfishness will settle for it without thinking of yours... unless you've got something to confide in me... to ask me to do something for you... or some sorrow that you want to unload on me..."

Raoul bowed his head, "That's it."

"I saw it when you came in. When you care about someone, see, whatever they do to hide it you can always guess their true feelings, their worries, and behind their smiles you see the tears they're holding back."

"Oh Andre, you're too understanding, and clairvoyant."

"No, I just care a lot about you. I know you well enough and I suffer too, living all shut away and left to myself I see better because I have no more horizon."

"I'm like you, Andre, imprisoned in grief. For a little while I glimpsed a new life. Like on a beautiful day I saw a blonde sunrise arising... then a thunder clap destroyed everything. I was thrown down, crushed by the storm. And I couldn't even look into the two blue spots of sky that were the eyes of my beloved."

"Oh," Girardet sympathized, "I'm really sorry for you. I didn't know how painful it was for you."

"There is one woman in the world..."

"A woman?"

"A young girl. She's just 20 years old. Everything heaven loves in woman, grace, beauty, charm, has been given to her as a masterpiece, an ideal link between this world and divinity."

"You loved her... you love her."

"I will always love her."

"Poor soul. She can't, mustn't... doesn't want to love you back..."

"Maybe she does love me..."

"So?"

"But I can't love her anymore."

"Why?"

"I'm the son of the banker Montreil."

"I don't understand."

"My dear friend, Robert and I were so convinced that our father was honest that we were the only ones who didn't know that in reality he was the banker Montreil."

Girardet waved his hand. "Enough, Raoul, stop. I don't need to hear it."

"So you know too. You knew... like everyone else. So I just have to tell you that the young lady I love is the daughter of one of my father's first and worst victims."

"Be quiet. Be quiet. I forbid you to talk about your father. It's vile slander."

"It's all laid out in the legal journals. Robert and I read them... and Raymonde too."

"Raymonde! Your sister Raymonde?"

"Yes."

"Oh, my poor friends! You don't deserve such suffering. But it isn't, it can't all be true. No, your father, like all men who succeed, had enemies. When a head rises above the crowd, it becomes a target for insults, for slander."

Raoul responded gently, "Thank you for defending my father, but we have proof of his actions, not only from the journals but in the bank."

"It doesn't matter! For me, for everyone who knows you, you and your brother and that charming Raymonde, the banker could not have undertaken such reprehensible speculations. But he was your father and he gave his children good hearts and beautiful souls. We shouldn't look at anything else."

"Thank you, Andre."

"As for the young lady, if she knows you she'll love you. And if she loves you nothing else will matter. Otherwise her heart is not worthy of yours and despite her beauty I encourage you to sacrifice your passion, which would then be only a fantasy, a desire for love... and you'll get over it."

Raoul sank back in the armchair. He listened but could find nothing to say.

Andre continued, "If she has a good heart, she'll understand that money does not make you happy, that a grievous past is no legacy for future children... and that love is stronger than bitterness, stronger than hate, stronger than everything."

Then slowly, almost in a whisper, he added, "To love! To love! What a sweet and wonderful thing! Love should complete a life, fill up your being. Without love no man's career, no matter how brilliant it is, can be complete. No woman has fulfilled her sacred mission if she has not loved. To love is more than just feeling your heart beat faster. It is taking possession and seeing your soul. Living without love is just breathing and moving around... it's not truly living! What joy, what happiness! Love is so powerful that it can keep people like me alive, those who want to die for it... it makes our suffering precious and in those who are already dead it leaves their soul radiant with just the memory of having loved."

After a short moment of silence, after drying his eyes, while the young lawyer wiped his own, he spoke a little more loudly. "There now, my good Raoul, no more tears. You didn't come here to cry with me. Come on, look up, buck up, have a little confidence. Nothing is as bad as you think. Go on, be loved! I'll take care of the rest. What can I do, being stuck on this couch of pain, to work for your happiness? It's my secret. You'll see, you'll see... Now, enough of this. We're going to eat. You'll have some fresh water... and some champagne, which I prefer. Then after lunch you'll give me the name and address of this marvel, this treasure, this angel... and I promise you that in no time at all you'll see that radiant blonde sunrise on your horizon once again."

Andre tried to laugh. Then he added, "Ok, I'll share a secret with you. I know your courage and your kindness I've got some work for you."

"Well done."

"Here it is. Oh, it's not that you're a specialist in young blondes with blue eyes who are masterpieces of charm and grace... Me, too, I have a model, a young lady who, now don't get upset, is surely the equal of yours. Unfortunately she can't be my sunrise. She's as beautiful as she is wise, as affectionate as she is beautiful, as loyal as she is blonde... and as poor as she is wise. She's alone in Paris and being an orphan she needs a defender. Since I am no longer a knight in shining armor, I've appointed you in my place."

"Thank you. You can be sure..."

"I know. So, this girl has your name and address in a little purse. At the first sign of danger she's to get in contact with you."

"I'll come running."

At that moment the telephone rang and interrupted the conversation. Girardet picked it up from the table on the side of the couch. He listened... and spoke:

"Oh, my dear girl, I'm so happy to hear from you. How are you?... Me, oh fine. This morning I'm not alone... One of my dearest friends dropped by. You see how happy I am... We're talking about very serious matters, the most serious in the world: Love... Yes... love... He's in love and is hurting... crying. Of course it's real love. Why? Because he's got all kinds of outlandish ideas... but of course it's always like that... He's kind, got a big heart, a good soul, and listen, he's handsome... Exactly... That's what I told him but he doesn't know if she'll love him enough... There was a tragedy... The girl he loves is very poor and he he's very rich... Naturally, to make her his wife... Yes, but now he's the one who's poor and she's becoming rich. He's afraid he won't be loved. What's that? I don't recognize your voice. Are there two of you on the phone?... She's there! Oh, but that's a dirty trick... Hold on..."

Andre Girardet held out the receiver so Raoul could hear.

"Here, listen to what my blonde sunrise thinks of all this... Listen. Hello? Hello... Yes, he became very poor and her rich... That's your advice... Well, if she deserves to be loved... She ought to love him twice as much now that he's poor... That's what I told him... If only his lover's heart were as big as yours... She's blonde like you, has blue eyes like yours, a smile and charm and grace just like you. But, really, does she have your heart? I hope so... because he deserves a lover like you, another Rirette, as beautiful and wonderful as my pretty Riri..."

Raoul jumped up and cried out, knocking the phone down in his shock. "Riri! Riri... but it's her!"

"Her?"

"Yes, she's the one I'm crazy in love with, that everything is keeping me from. The daughter of the poor man my father ruined, killed... It's Riri! Riri Menardier!"

Andre Girardet shuddered. But he did not get up. He pretended to laugh, "Aha. So, it'll work out even better than I thought... if you don't cut off our communication every time we talk. Pick up the phone and let's see if they're still there."

He rang.

"Hello? Hello... Left? Well, well... Riri was with Madame Laurent... They must have been furious with the operator."

He hung up and looked at Raoul. "So, you heard Riri herself answer..." He held out his hands and said, "Come on, Raoul, there's hope now. The blonde sunrise is there, the new day is coming. Yes, sing out your joy, go on, cry if you want! Shout it out! Go crazy! You can love, love love!"

24. The microbe hunter

Luck plays a role in love but it had nothing to do with the lovers' scene on the telephone. Paulin Broquet had arranged the whole thing.

He had got Baiter to follow Raoul and make sure that the day after seeing him he would keep his promise and go have lunch with Girardet. Baiter made sure Raoul was in the house before he went back to Paris to find Madame Laurent and tell her to find Riri and call Ville-d'Avray.

However, even though Baiter had got Laurent and Riri to call at the appointed time, he left them free to say whatever they wanted to Andre Girardet. No rules were set. It was, therefore, Riri's true feelings that Raoul heard over the phone.

Almost at the same time another event, without such dramatic consequences this time, happened to give a little relief to these worries.

Alice de Brialle told Raymonde that she was coming to Paris for a few days to visit her father and she wanted to go on a shopping spree in all the department stores, fashion designers and hat shops.

"Don't do anything without me," Irene de Valtours telegraphed, "I want to be in on the plundering of Paris. I also need to get dressed, do my hair and look presentable. Way up here in Brittany I'm turning wild."

Therefore, they waited for Irene de Valtours and two days later the three friends, Raymonde, Irene and Alice were on the march.

For an escort, to accompany them in their plundering of shops they had two faithful servant knights, completely devoted and slaves to their fantasies: Captain de Rennebois and Raoul; and two other knights who were also faithful but made up what the Captain called the active reserve: Captain de Cazeaumont and Dr. Robert.

In these operations there was even a fifth body: "The white sleeve!" Captain de Rennebois used a polite phrase.

"The enemy!" Alice said bluntly, "The enemy we must sniff out, engage, outwit and conquer."

The white sleeve, this enemy, was none other than the Count de Marnais.

"How did he know we were coming?" Alice asked her friends. "Because I was careful not to let him find out anything. But the day after we set up camp he came to ask about me, to offer to drive me wherever I wanted... I thanked him and let him know that I had no need of his services."

But the Count de Marnais apparently did not understand. Chance often threw him on the path of the friendly little caravan... over which his presence cast a chill. But what joy when they went all day without seeing him!

The Count de Marnais used the excuse of what he kept calling his happy future cousin. He acted even more affectionately because the Captain de

Cazeaumont had just escaped a sickness that was as terrible as it was mysterious. Of course nobody around the patient had known about the shot given by Rennebois or about the secret serum used by Robert to pull the dying man out of the grave.

The Count de Marnais asked his future cousin for some details. He also interrogated the private doctors and military medics in Orléans. The development of the sickness, its progress and final, unexpected healing, was most intriguing to all of them. But the although the Captain de Cazeaumont had been informed, he said nothing about it to his fiancée's cousin. Moreover he politely declined the room offered by de Marnais.

"I'm still sick," he said, "and I would be a very bothersome guest."

On the advice of his friends Raoul and Robert he went down to the Army Hall where he found his comrade Rennebois. When he could go with the little caravan on their skirmish it was only a short walk from the Army Hall to Rue des Mathurins where Raymonde's brothers lived and where everyone met in the evening to dine at the Montreil's, an invitation that was never extended to the Count de Marnais.

It was on Rue des Mathurins that they found Robert. Busy with the hospital and his house calls, the doctor was unreachable all day long. On the other hand, Irene de Valtours arrived early in the morning to pick up her friend Raymonde and she did not leave her side until late in the evening when the two captains, her bodyguards as they said, brought her back to her father's.

Irene de Valtours was younger than Raymonde and Alice and very pretty, a subtle and elegant beauty, blonde with purple eyes. She looked a little like Riri. But only Alice and Raymonde seemed to notice her beauty, to appreciate her grace and enjoy her charm. The men were busy with their own loves, so neither their hearts nor their eyes lingered on Irene.

Rennebois was devoted to Raymonde and Cazeaumont had eyes only for Alice. Raoul was utterly taken by Riri… and Robert's sorrow buried him in his work.

Since the arrival of Cazeaumont, moreover, Robert had resumed some research that was obsessing him. He was there for Irene, just like for Alice and Raymonde, but he was thinking too much about his research in organic chemistry, about his problems of the serum, to see how pretty Irene was, to see her golden blonde hair, her smile, the purple sparkles in her big eyes.

He was hunting microbes and for the moment he saw nothing but what he could find under his microscope. He did not even suspect that Irene had looked upon him with eyes full of more than just curiosity. He did not feel that in taking her arm to lead her into the dining room, her hand trembled. He did not notice that when he talked to her, she turned pale and when she had to answer, she blushed and fumbled with her words.

Since Robert had sacrificed his love of Riri for his brother, he closed off his heart to seducing women and his eyes looked at Irene's beauty without seeing it. Not being able to love Riri, Robert gave up all thoughts of love. Figuring that there was no beauty in the world for him, he chased after the most dangerous microbes and he put all his energy, all his heart into this scientific hunt.

One day Raymonde caught Irene sitting alone, trying to hide her tears in a corner of the salon where she thought no one could see her. Raymonde sat down beside her. She liked to play mommy to her younger friends and especially to Irene who she used to call her little girl at school. She pulled her neck gently toward her chest and kissed her forehead. This is the way you can make a woman or a child—they are often so similar!—open up their hearts and tell their secret pains.

"What's wrong, Irene?" she asked.

"Nothing. Just nothing, I promise,"

"So why this sorrow?"

"It's not sorrow?"

"Then what?"

"I just wanted to cry a little."

"As you like. You can hug me tighter. There, that's better. You'll be able to do what you like... however strange it seems... whatever it is I don't understand... because you've got no reason to cry, right?"

"No, no reason. I'm happy here."

"Oh, is that why you're crying?"

"Not for that... but because it's over..."

"What's over?"

"In a few days I'll be leaving. I'll be leaving you and Alice and everything that makes me happy... and I'll go back to my sad Brittany, into the dark, cold old manor where I die of boredom."

"My poor girl."

"I'm alone up there for days on end... for months, alone, alone! If you knew how gloomy it is! It's depressing... I've lost interest in everything. Riding horses to go where? To see what? Trees... bushes... Play music for whom? The gentlemen in the tapestries? Oh, I'm sorry, I'm old and hopeless..."

"But your father?"

"My father is buried deeper and deeper in dark thoughts. He's taken on the soul of the manor... dark... dark... shut in. He shuts himself in and talks to no one, sees no one, wants to entertain no one... My father loves me, of course, but silently, in his dark moods. He doesn't see that I'm 20 years old, that I want to live a little... like everyone else... and that I'm dying in that prison where he's shut me up with him... with his desolation. My father is scared of gossip. He runs away from the world and dives deeper into the worries that I know nothing about but whose painful burden I bear."

"Irene, but your life should be joyful and gay."

"And, dear Raymonde, you know that I love to laugh and sing and I'm always active. Up there I'm learning how to die.'

"No, my dear girl, no…"

"Yes! You're happy. You have a great sorrow, it's true, but you love… Alice also has her troubles, her grief, but by being in love her heart can comfort her. I have no more mother and I have to retreat into silence between those high walls and towers where nobody dares comes close…" More tenderly she added, "And yet you know, don't you Raymonde, that like you and Alice I, too, have a little heart that can love? You know I have a soul that would be happy to give itself…"

"Yes, and whoever you love will be happy."

"Certainly. I would love so much, so well, so totally… forever… like you and Alice. But here I am, I have to confess my heart and my soul: You're 20 years old, the age where the flower of love blooms for other girls but not for you, secluded, shut away, it's not for you… Your fate is loneliness and neglect. You see, Raymonde, it pains my heart and my soul and that's why I'm crying."

Raymonde leaned over Irene and kissed her gently. "My dear, I'm not questioning you… I won't ask you anything because maybe you yourself don't know what to answer and maybe you don't even know the secret you're keeping."

"I have no secret, Raymonde."

"That's what I said. Well, in spite of everything believe me, believe your little mother, there is no tower so high, no wall so thick that love cannot overcome. And Brittany is not too far to go to find a beauty in a magic castle. Believe me… you're 20 years old and your springtime is just starting. Give it time to plant the seeds of love, to take root. I promise that like Alice and I your heart will soon find a radiant flower."

Then, not giving Irene any other explanations she dragged her into her bedroom, washed her red eyes and told her, "Quickly now, they're waiting for use. Kiss me and smile. Be happy, behave nicely… just as if Dr. Robert were here…"

But, Dr. Robert was not there. He was not with his microbes either. He was at Paulin Broquet's and was talking seriously with the detective.

"In sum," he was saying, "in barely three years at the Brialle mansion, three horrible, mysterious deaths occurred."

"Madame de Brialle died first?"

"Yes. She was in good health, had no diseases… then all of a sudden she was bedridden, started vomiting violently, had a constant fever… and died in agony within three days. Almost right away her body started rotting."

"Around when did this happen?"

"A few days after the opening of hunting season."

"Who had been at the mansion?"

339

"Madame de Brialle celebrated the opening very festively. It was a family tradition. As always there were a lot of guests. One of them—and here is where it gets serious—was the Count de la Gueriniere."

"I could have guessed," Broquet said. "And then?"

"It was the Count de Marnais who got him invited."

"Okay, but after? The second death?"

"The son, a strong kid, brave and full of life. Struck down and died with symptoms just like his mother."

"Was the Count de la Gueriniere around?"

"No.

"And the Count de Marnais?"

"Yes."

"Okay. The third?"

"A little girl."

"Poisoned too? Tetanus?"

Robert raised his voice, "This time I was there when the girl died. But they called me too late. They didn't want me to perform an autopsy but I still got to examine the little corpse and I took some of the linen to run some tests… to find proof of what I suspected."

"What was the sickness?"

Robert answered solemnly, "Typhus… the plague!"

25. The strange horseman

In spite of his self-control Paulin Broquet could not help shuddering. He asked the doctor, "Did you say the plague?"

"Yes, typhus, the plague," Robert declared.

"Doctor, come on, are you sure about this?"

"Absolutely."

"What you're telling me is really surprising... really serious."

"I'm sure of it. Like you, when I made the discovery I was taken aback, dumbfounded. I couldn't bring myself to believe what I was seeing. First the little girl and then the captain."

"And Captain de Cazeaumont was the same?" Broquet asked.

"The same. He was plague-ridden. And he provided irrefutable proof of my findings because he was alive thanks to what I gave him—a very strong anti-plague serum that I got from Dr. Roux at the Pasteur Institute."

Broquet was silent for a moment, then he asked, "Isn't the plague mostly contagious?"

"Not like you'd think. It isn't contagious in the sense that it can be caught, but it propagates, it's transmittable... through water. But the worst ones to spread the horrible disease are birds, rats and mosquitoes."

Broquet had another question for the doctor, "Has anyone outside the Brialle family been infected? Have any other cases been reported in the area?"

"No."

"Therefore it's only in the Brialle mansion that..."

"Excuse me, my friend, but when Captain de Cazeaumont was put to bed he had not been to the Brialle mansion for several days."

"Aha!"

"It was when he got back from Paris where he was with the Marquis and his fiancée Alice... You know that our friends took a trip to Orléans to attend the funeral of my poor father."

"I know."

"But maybe you don't know that during those few days that Madame de Brialle and her daughter spent in Paris the Captain stayed with his future cousin, the Count de Marnais."

At these words Paulin Broquet threw up his hand, "Stop! Say nothing more."

Robert looked surprised.

"The murderer," Broquet went on, "I do mean murderer of Madame de Brialle, her son and the little girl, as well as the attempt on Cazeaumont's life... is the Count de Marnais."

The doctor nodded.

"The Count de Marnais," Broquet concluded, "the friend of the Count de la Gueriniere and partner of Zigomar!'

Broquet said this with a trembling voice, so full of pent-up energy that Robert as astonished.

In fact, Broquet still appeared very calm, in control and never let himself get carried away even during the most heated discussions. He did not even raise his voice. It follows, therefore, that what was happening here, what he felt while listening to the doctor, was having a very powerful effect on him.

After this outburst he kept silent for a moment. He took his time, as if he were trying to regain his self-control, get hold of himself. He rolled a cigarette very carefully and lit it slowly. Between the first puffs of smoke, very calmly, he asked Robert, "Do you know the Brialle family well?"

"Very well."

"The Marquis has a great fortune, doesn't he?"

"Yes. He gets a lot of money from his properties and other income from his wise investments in certain very prosperous and very diverse business affairs."

"Okay. How closely related is the Count de Manais?"

"He's the grandson of the Marquis' older sister."

"Does the Marquis have other relatives besides the sister close enough to stake a claim on the fortune?"

"I don't think so. A few distant cousins, some by marriage too but very old and for the most part very rich themselves."

"The Count de Marnais, therefore, without the marquis' children, would become the sole heir of the huge Brialle fortune. It explains everything. We've got it. There's no more doubt about it. We're dealing with murder."

"I understand but it's awful."

Broquet asked again, "Has the Count de Marnais tried by other means... to get the inheritance? Marriage for example?"

"Yes. He asked for his cousin Alice's hand."

"Who had the good sense to refuse him."

"He asked several times. Even being refused wouldn't stop him. He kept hoping he could bring her around... but she thinks he's a real louse."

"So, it was when she got engaged to Captain de Cazeaumont that the Count figured he had to give up all hope and he made his decision..."

"He had been a good sport about it. The first to congratulate his cousin and his future cousin."

"But right away he started his gruesome project to grab the inheritance that was slipping away from him. A very simple plan. Remain the sole survivor... of the whole family. Madame Brialle, her son and the little girl disappeared. The marquis, the poor man who's dying of grief, wasn't a problem. Alice, whose fiancé was about to disappear too, would be the only one left in the collapsing house and would eventually give in to the Count de Marnais... or else she would have to disappear in turn."

"The wretch! Luckily the captain was saved. Now he's vaccinated and safe from any new attack."

"Yes, but by saving him you condemned his fiancée."

Robert shuddered, "No! He wouldn't dare!"

"On the contrary. With Alice dead there's no one left but the Marquis. Then the Count de Marnais would be the sole inheritor and only have to wait for the Marquis to shake off this mortal coil, which won't be long, so he can grab his millions."

"You're right," the doctor said, "and the wretch is probably preparing a new attack as we speak."

"What makes you say that?"

"With the excuse of trying to shake the Marquis out of his depression, so that his cousin can have some distraction, the Count decided they should have a hunt like in the old days. He's organizing it, as the man of the house now, along with the captain, his future brother-in-law."

"Aha! During the hunt the house will be full of guests and the attack will come... Yes, most likely... There will have to be a lot of people, strangers, so that no one can recognize the murderer or even suspect a crime."

"Of course."

"But who is the appointed victim now?" the detective wondered. "And how will they fall? The Marquis, Alice and the Captain? A mysterious poison, the plague or a hunting accident? There's another problem for us. And I have to admit that this problem is the thorniest one for me."

"Me, I'm terrified. How can we warn them about the tragedy we foresee? What should we do?"

Broquet asked, "You're obviously invited to the hunt?"

"Yes, along with Raoul and my sister Raymonde. Alice de Brialle also invited her friend Irene de Vallours. Since she's coming from Brittany she'll pick up my sister when she passes through Paris."

"You'll be going to the Brialle's?"

"Not me. I have too many patients who need me."

"And your brother?"

"He hasn't decided. There are other, much prettier things than mine, that are keeping him busy."

"Yes, yes," Broquet smiled. "Well, Pretty Riri will wait... but Raoul has to accept the invitation. He has to be at the Brialle's."

"He'll be there. And if need be, you know that you can also count on the courage and energy of my sister Raymonde."

"We just might need her valuable help..."

Around three weeks after this meeting, the Brialle mansion was welcoming its guests, not as many as in past years. There were only a few old friends of the

Marquis, some chateau owners from the area, Raoul Montreil, Captain de Rennebois and his friend de Cazeaumont, then two or three friends of the Count de Marnais, Baron du Jard and the decorative Baron Dupont.

However, this year, since Raymonde and Raoul Montreil were guests, the Count de Marnais did not have the indiscretion to invite his close friend the Count de la Gueriniere.

Captain de Cazeaumont and Captain de Rennebois were accompanied by their orderly to take care of their horses. Cazeaumont's orderly was known to the mansion, a big guy who had been with him since he had entered the service. Rennebois' orderly was there for the first time. He was with the captain at Fontainebleau... Let's just say right off that he was none other than Baiter.

Among the extra people hired to serve the guests the Marquis de Brialle had brought in a butler who was assigned to Raoul and the captains. This butler was Gabriel.

For their part, Baron du Jard and the splendid Baron Dupont had brought no servant and made do with what was provided. To the great surprise of Gabriel and Baiter, they accepted the servants of the house who had no attachment to Zigomar.

Paulin Broquet was kept up-to-date on every point, including this one, and far from seeing the lack of evil plans he simply said, "We better keep our eyes peeled."

The lesson had been taught by Gabriel to Raoul, the captain and Raymonde. All three of them, without saying anything but with the help of Irene and Captain de Cazeaumont, were supposed to watch over Alice constantly. Always surrounded, Alice was not an easy target and by watching her they would be watching themselves because the Count de Marnais and his cronies would never dare to go after several people at the same time.

Moreover, by chance and as a precaution Robert had given his brother a case containing some vials of serum for different poisons. Captain de Rennebois, who had effectively and militarily given the shot to his comrade Cazeaumont, was in charge of applying them if need be.

"Because," Broquet had told the doctor, "there's nothing easier than giving a little evil prick, even with people watching."

"What do you mean?"

"There are no parrots in the mansion. Plague-ridden rats would already have killed everyone, so they don't exist. Mosquitoes don't live in the Beauce. But in the countryside we can offer a rose that's been soaked in poison... offer it so that it pricks whoever takes it..."

"Gloves would protect them."

"There are other kinds of thorns. In the country it's really easy to get pricked with poisoned thorns, even without meaning intentional harm. Just walking... or dancing... nothing easier than getting scratched by something tipped in poison. The last resort: dip a fingernail in the mortal substance and pretending to pick off a caterpillar or some other bug from the arm or neck of the victim, scratch them slightly and inject the agonizing death."

"Yes, that's all possible, but Alice can be warned, wear thick gloves and dress in clothes to protect her from scratches, even a veil... whatever your advice, we'll follow it to the letter."

Despite all these precautions Paulin Broquet did not feel good about the fate of his friends. Since the guests of the Marquis de Brialle were only supposed to stay for a few days, Broquet thought that the attack—and he had no doubts about the Count de Marnais' intentions—would take place promptly. Therefore, he too had to act swiftly to try not just to defend against it but even to stop it from happening.

But how? In the first place, he had to figure out what type of attack and how the assassin was planning to kill. Not an easy job. The detective had never taken on such a delicate mission. But we know that things like danger are problems that make Broquet even more determined.

For two days they went hunting without a single problem. After a day of walking and riding the guests had gone to their rooms following a well-deserved meal. The next day was shaping up to be just as busy.

After a final chat in the long hallway, the three friends, Raoul, Rennebois and Cazeaumont said goodnight and went to their rooms. Raoul had just gone to bed. He was about to turn off the light when a man suddenly appeared in front of him. He seemed to come out of the floor like some magic hero on stage popping up through a trapdoor. Before he had a chance to scream his mouth was covered with the man's hand.

"Be quiet! It's me!"

The man stepped into the light so that the lawyer could recognize him. Then he took his hand away from Raoul's mouth.

"How the devil did you...? Only Paulin Broquet could pull off such a trick. What are you doing here?"

"You'll see. Now that you know who's snuck in to disturb your sleep you can turn off the light so you don't look suspicious. We can talk just as easily in the dark."

"Okay. It's done." Raoul drowned the room in darkness. He knew that he had to obey the detective immediately and without questions, without even trying to understand why. Still, he asked, "Are you going to spend the night here?"

"Yes but your butler has fixed everything up. On the couch over there I've got a pillow and blanket, everything I need. Don't worry about anything. Now listen to me."

First Paulin Broquet went to the door. He put his ear to the lock and listened for a while. Satisfied that no one was outside he went back to Raoul's bed and spoke in a whisper.

"I've been here a short time. No one knows about it. The Marnais, Jard, Dupont, everyone thinks I was blown up at Zulma's."

"That's right."

"So nobody will bother me, but you have to help. Your future brother-in-law and Captain Cazeaumont, even your sister and especially everyone else here mustn't know not only that I am here but also that I am alive."

"Got it. You can count on me. What should I do?"

"For now, nothing suspicious has happened... or have you seen the Count de Marnais and his charming friends put into action any of their deadly designs."

"No."

"That doesn't mean they haven't tried anything, just that they haven't succeeded yet."

"They can't succeed... that's why you're here."

Paulin Broquet nodded, "Yes. Here's what you're going to do. First, tonight, sleep."

"Sleep?"

"Plain and simple. And don't worry about me. Tomorrow you'll go out as usual, go hunting and keep an eye on Alice, as we agreed."

"Okay."

"In the meantime, I'll go through the house here, examine it, investigate... we'll talk at night and I'll tell you what we'll have to do the next day. Now, good night."

"Good night then," Raoul reached out in the darkness and shook the detective's hand warmly.

During the first part of the night, Broquet stayed on guard, listening at the bedroom door. Only towards morning did he decide to lie down on the couch, curl up in the blanket and get some sleep—not the sleep of a cop with one eye open but of a hunter... like a rock.

Raoul slept straight through until the morning, until the horns blew the reveille in the park. When he opened his eyes, he remembered and looked for the detective on the couch. Broquet had disappeared. Raoul got dressed and went downstairs with the captains to join the other guests for breakfast.

Soon everyone was saddled up, the dogs were barking, the horses huffing and the horns saluting the rising sun. Among the whips, the captains' orders were carried out. Their chiefs authorized them to follow the hunt.

As the hunt was crossing a clearing and heading back into the woods, on the road cutting through the forest they ran into a young rider who looked very fit and was out for a ride, smoking a cigarette, letting his horse go wherever it wanted. The hunters did not know this man, a stranger in the area, but they admired his horse, a remarkable thoroughbred that looked endowed with marvelous qualities.

For Baiter, however, it was less the horse than the rider that caught his attention. Moreover, the young horseman had stopped to let the hunters pass. He sat at a distance watching the masters, the women, the hunters, whips and terrier men ride by.

Baiter was last. Since the young rider had stopped, he had not taken his eyes off him, wondering where he had seen those big, clear eyes and that mouth barely covered by a brown moustache and that seemed, despite the cigarette half hiding it, quite elegant. Suddenly their eyes crossed… for a moment they looked at each other, seemed surprised, even nervous. Then abruptly the young rider snapped his reins, turned around and galloped away. In the process a ray of sunlight shot through the branches and struck the rider's neck, reflecting a tawny stripe.

To the great surprise of the rest of the company Baiter spurred his horse, jumping off to the side and separating from the group as if the animal had suddenly gone mad, stung by a hornet or something. Then he sped off in the direction of the young horseman.

It was a wild ride. You could see the two horses racing, flying down the path in a fury. Baiter's horse, which belonged to Captain Rennebois, was strong but he was no match for the young rider who was quietly pushing his horse with ease, the result of great knowledge and experience… and admirable self-control.

After the race down the path, the young rider came out on a plain. As if playing in the fields he jumped his thoroughbred over hedges and fences and put some distance between him and baiter. Then he dove into some woods and disappeared under the branches. Baiter had to give up. He had lost.

Discouraged but thoughtful, with his horse covered in lather, he went back telling himself, "Maybe I made a mistake."

He came to the clearing where he had lost his prey to look for the trail going back. There he found the cigarette that the rider had been smoking and had dropped during the chase. Baiter picked it up, put it carefully in his pocket, then after rubbing down his horse with some grass he went back to join the hunt.

"What got hold of you?" Captain de Cazeaumont's brusher asked him.

"It wasn't me," he said loudly enough for everyone to hear, "but the horse. I don't know what happened, maybe he got jealous hearing you compliment that young man's horse. Well, probably he got the itch and wanted to show me what he's worth. Anyway, I ended up getting my friend to listen to reason and brought him back. That happens sometimes with him, all of a sudden wanting to race the others… I've almost broke my neck a number of times, stupid nag!"

But baiter quickly caught up to his butler Gabriel and told him what happened. "And this young man," he concluded, "who just happened to be where the hunt was going, was the one who had saved the boss from the explosion at Zulma's!"

"It's the young woman with copper hair."

347

25. The winged assassins

Paulin Broquet listened attentively to what Gabriel, acting as butler, had heard from Baiter. He looked at the cigarette and tore up the paper. "It's English tobacco, the kind that young woman who saved me was smoking. I recognized the opiate aroma on her breath." Then he concluded, "All this means that Zigomar is going to strike. We knew it anyway, but this doesn't tell us why this woman rescued me from the hands of the bandits... or why we're seeing her again today, riding around the Brialle mansion."

Nevertheless, Paulin Broquet did not lose any time searching for the key to the mysteries now. Without dawdling over this new and mysterious addition, he held fast to the goal that had brought him here.

With Gabriel he could sneak into the bedroom that had been given to Raymonde Montreil and into Irene de Valtours'. They were rooms usually occupied by Alice so that the three friends could stay together in comfort. The three rooms were all connected to a little salon where Alice and Raymonde saw their fiancés and Raoul, where the Count de Marnais sometimes came to ask if he could say hello to the girls.

After examining the rooms of Raymonde and Irene, Broquet lingered longer in Alice's. When he entered the girl's room he told Gabriel, "It smells of Russian leather."

"It does, boss."

"Why? It's not an odor that Alice is especially fond of."

"I don't know, but it's coming from that leather blotter on her desk over there. It was a gift of friendship from the count to his dear cousin."

"Did he give it to her a long time ago?"

"Just a few days ago."

"Aha!"

Broquet said nothing more. He made a tour of the room, searching, examining, investigating...

The room was elegant with white, Louis XVI furniture. Among the white furnishings a few objects caught Broquet's eye: A blue, silk lampshade in the shape of huge flowers and a nightlight that was also blue. In truth, these objects, even though they were not from the époque or even in the style of the rest of the furniture, just like the modern desk blotter would not have stuck out if they had not been blue.

"A little too blue, in fact," Gabriel answered Broquet's remark.

"But everything's like this on purpose," the detective observed.

"On purpose?"

"Exactly. They're obviously more presents from a very friendly cousin."

"Right, boss. The Count de Marnais says he got these things in a charity lottery. Since, as he says, they're decorations for a girl's room, he asked his cousin to accept them as a gift. Mademoiselle de Brialle could not refuse."

"Does she keep the light on while she's sleeping?"

"Yes, boss."

"With the blue silk shade?'

"Yes, boss. Apparently it turns the room blue, which is kind of nice."

Broquet smiled. "Good! Now I know what I want to know. I've got pretty much the whole picture."

Then he went to the door and examined it.

"Aha! There's some strips fitted in here, top and bottom... no drafts of air or anything else are getting through this door."

Then he studied the lock. It was just a bronze knob, carved like the hinges... no key, but a bronze, carved face as a cover over the lock.

"Also impossible for the wind or anything to pass through this lock."

Broquet rubbed his chin, which meant he was puzzled. He started examining the walls and the ceiling.

"Uhm," he furrowed his brow, "maybe I'm on the wrong trail. Could all this be here just to fool us, to make us search in one place while the attack's coming in another, in a different way... that we have can't even imagine?" He thought longer and added, "And yet!"

He grabbed the shade and examined it, carefully inspecting the folds of the big blue flower. He found nothing.

Then he went to the desk. He sat in the small chair but did not look through the drawers. Instead he pored over the grooves in the wood as if he were counting the grains of dust. He also examined the Russian leather ink blotter, the gift from her thoughtful cousin.

And suddenly he cried out, "That's it! I've got it! I knew I wasn't wrong and here's the proof."

"What is it boss? What'd you find?"

"Look here... here..." Broquet was pointing at a barely visible spot on the blotter.

"That?" Gabriel was surprised. "But that's a mosquito."

"Yes, a mosquito," the detective responded. "You said it, a mosquito! Look, it got its stinger stuck in the leather and couldn't get free. It died like it was caught in a trap... and it was."

Broquet took a sheet of paper and an envelope and after delicately lifting the mosquito out of the leather blotter he slipped it in. Gabriel was intrigued by the whole scene.

"Aren't you surprised that in this closed up room, especially at this time of year, there's a mosquito in here?"

"I guess so, boss."

"Well, this mosquito is what I've been looking for."

"The mosquito?"

"Yes, it's not your common culex, it's—I've study insects pretty seriously—it's an anopheles or a tiger mosquito, a female… it's the mosquito that carries the plague, that kills."

"Ach!" Gabriel shivered.

Broquet went on, "It's an undeniable fact that the Count de Marnais murdered his relatives by poisoning them, but how? How did he get the evil into their bodies? An injection? That's what we have to find out. So, this blotter and blue lampshade put me on the right track and now I'm sure… the Count de Marnais kills with mosquitoes."

The detective paused before continuing, "The anopheles and tiger mosquitoes don't sting in the dark. They hate daytime and are scared of red light, but blue light attracts them and drives them crazy. Moreover, they love the smell of leather. Russian leather especially gets them excited, like drunk, and they sting like mad."

"I get it, boss. That's why he gave his cousin these presents."

"Exactly," Broquet said. "Now we have to find out how the Count managed to keep the mosquitoes alive in the cold and get them into the bedroom because he's obviously made several attempts and here's one of them! I think that he didn't succeed because it's too cold in this room and the others dropped dead before fulfilling their deadly mission."

Paulin Broquet, remember, had spent most of the night spying on the hallway where the Count de Marnais' bedroom was. He had heard nothing suspicious. The Count apparently did not leave his room that night. So how did he get the mosquitoes into the girl's room?

Broquet wondered anxiously, "Maybe he did it on one of the previous nights before I came?"

"That's possible, boss."

"And he waited two or three days to see if it worked, if she'd start to get sick. Okay, in that case when he saw nothing happen he'd understand that his mosquitoes failed… and he'll try again under better conditions… he'll try again."

Then Broquet went back into Raoul's room where he was supposed to hide and where Gabriel would get him something to eat in secret.

When Gabriel came that evening with dinner he said, "Boss, the Count de Marnais just gave me a really weird order but you'll see what it means."

"What order?"

"Start a fire in all the rooms."

"Aha! And what's his reason?"

"To get rid of the humidity. It seems we need to dry out the house. The Count doesn't want anyone to catch a cold."

"Or the mosquitoes to freeze and miss another chance. Good, good, go ahead and start the fires… here… in the captain's room, for the young ladies, especially for Alice. The Count's right, we don't want anyone catching a cold… and especially not a fever!" Then he told him, "As for you, since it's more than likely that he will try again tonight, you wait in the hallway upstairs where the counts and barons have their rooms. You let them pass but when they come back, block the hallway."

"Got it, boss."

Broquet sent Gabriel away saying, "Tell Raoul Montreil to find any reasonable excuse to come to his room during dinner… before the others, just two minutes."

After dinner, while the guests were chatting over coffee, smoking and waiting for bedtime, Raoul excused himself to fetch some cigars from his suitcase.

Paulin Broquet told him, "Alice mustn't sleep in her own room tonight."

"Okay."

"Make sure that no one knows that your sister Raymonde will keep her in her room… guard her. And the nightlight should stay on in your sister's room as well as with Irene de Vallours. If they want to turn off their light they have to cover it with a red cloth, which should be easy to find, or even red paper, but it's important that it be red. Then close all the doors, shut off Alice's room… all this very discreetly, Raoul."

Everything was done as Broquet wanted. Alice knew that she had to obey without thinking. She pretended to go back to her room as usual, then snuck into Raymonde's. But someone took her place. This someone was Paulin Broquet who left the light with the blue shade turned on.

The mansion fell deadly silent.

During the day Paulin Broquet had visited the Count de Marnais' room and those of his friends. In Baron de Jard's and elegant Baron Dupont's he found nothing interesting after searching through their suitcases and bags. They had obviously taken precautions to bring no documents of loyalty, of their true allegiance, that all real villains always carry with them.

Nothing suspicious in the Count's room either. When Broquet entered, he smelled the bitter stench of methylated spirits but on the washstand a curling iron for a moustache lay on a hot plate. Nothing else stood out. Broquet was not happy. He sniffed around… and ended up at one of the Count's case that should have contained toiletries but was giving off this odor of methylated alcohol. This was no common wood alcohol but wine spirits that they use in laboratories.

A vial of this alcohol was lying near the hot plate. "Aha," the detective said, "the Count has a very sensitive sense of smell if he needs this alcohol to groom himself. This hot plate is put here on purpose. In the case must be the full bottle of this smelly stuff."

But the case was locked so that Broquet did not think he could open it without leaving a trace.

"Okay, okay! I'll leave it alone. We'll come back later."

Now in the middle of the night Paulin Broquet was in Alice's room, sitting in an armchair by the door, listening, waiting, still as a statue.

Gentle warmth had spread through the room heated by a fire made of vine shoots, lit on order of the Count during dinner, but which had dwindled down to embers buried under the ashes.

"Perfect temperature," the detective said. "It hasn't worked so far because it wasn't warm enough. But tonight is just right."

As he was whispering this, in the silence of the room, he heard a buzzing, then another, then more.

"Here they come!" Broquet remained stock-still. "I've been waiting for them and now they're here."

After floating around in the room, so to speak, searching for something, the buzzing came and surrounded him. Paulin Broquet had rolled up his sleeves leaving his forearms bare—forearms that were healed now but still bore the marks from being tied up at the new Barbottiere in Zulma's. He covered his face with his hands to protect his eyes and waited, offering his arms, his appetizing veins as bait for the mosquitoes, which were filling up the room now, carrying typhus, the plague, evil and death.

He let himself get stung over and over without moving, peeking through his fingers at the black dots that were drinking his blood and injecting him with dreadful poisons. This was an act of horrible heroism. But the detective needed irrefutable proof that would devastate the criminal. And he got it... with such courage and such stoicism! He was truly admirable!

When the mosquitoes were gorged with blood, as if drunk, one by one, they dropped off his arms. Their role was over or rather their mission was complete. In other countries they would have gone off and spread their diseases but here, despite the fire warming the room, the cold night still snuck in and got the better of them. The mosquitoes could not live in the lower temperature. They fell, well-fed, wings spread, their long legs sticking out.

Then Broquet very carefully gathered up the corpses of his winged assassins and placed them in a small metal box he had brought with him. Sitting back down he waited for hours watching the red dots on his arms get bigger as the wicked terror started doing its work.

26. *The precious case*

Later, when Paulin Broquet left Alice's room, slipping like a shadow into Raoul's room, the young lawyer was still asleep. In fact, everyone was sleeping. Except the detective and his faithful Gabriel.

Gabriel's mission was to watch the floor were the male guests were staying, just above where the young women had their rooms. Broquet's lieutenant, as ordered, was supposed to let the count (or whoever) pass by and go downstairs to accomplish his criminal act, but he was to grab him, tie him up and gag him on the way back before bringing him back to Raoul's room. But Gabriel saw no one leave the rooms occupied by the Count de Marnais and his friends. He thought the attack would not come tonight contrary to what Broquet said.

So, he was understandably surprised when his boss showed up in the hallway and said, "It's okay, I've got what I need."

"It's done?"

"Yes. Go and get some rest. You can tell me what you know tomorrow."

Broquet could see in Gabriel's eyes that no one had ventured into the hallway to release the mosquitoes into Alice's room. He imagined it was through the lock, despite the cover, that they had got in or through a crack in the door but since no one was on the stairs where Gabriel was lying in wait, his hypothesis fell flat.

Now Broquet had to find out how the deadly insects got into the room. "We'll see about all that tomorrow," he told himself.

He went into Raoul's room without waking him. He knew where Raoul kept the case with the serum given to him by his brother, Dr. Robert. He took one out, carefully filled a syringe and injected each arm.

Like the night before, he wrapped himself in a blanket, stretched out on the couch and slept soundly until Gabriel came as the butler bringing hot water to shave Raoul. Now that the rest of the house was waking up Paulin Broquet went into Raoul's bathroom where no one would normally enter and as usual hid himself in a closet behind a curtain.

While Raoul was getting ready he told him, "I think we've got our man."

"You did it?"

"I found the means so I've got the man."

"Bravo! Tell me all about it."

"Later. First listen to what we have to do today because the stakes are high now."

"Give me my orders, chief," Raoul smiled.

"First of all, for everyone else Alice slept in her room but had a hard night. She can talk a little about bug bites. Then during the day she'll say she's tired, that she can't go with the others, complain of a migraine, a bit of fever and she'll

353

stay behind. Naturally Raymonde and Irene will stay with her, then Captain Cazeaumont will seem very worried..."

"I got it!"

"Tomorrow Alice will stay in bed."

Alice de Brialle played her role marvelously, coached by Raymonde after she was given the script by Raoul. The Count took great pleasure in making fun of his dear cousin. When he came by in the morning to see how she was doing, she told him, "Not well... because of you!"

"What do you mean?" the Count looked surprised.

"You had the bright idea to heat up the rooms. I was suffocating all night long."

"Really... I was worried about the humidity."

"And we spent too much time around the dogs on a winter day. The pups gave me a present that I would rather have refused."

"What kind of present, dear cousin?"

"A flea."

"A flea?"

"Who can't stop biting me. I was covered in bites this morning. It's awful."

The Count de Marnais tried to joke, "Why didn't you call us, Alice, we all would've hunted the nasty little beast... sounded the horn in your room..."

"Sure, make fun, if you weren't so thick-skinned I'd wish the same thing happened to you."

Despite the bad night, however, it was shaping up to be a nice day. Alice looked listless, pale... exhausted. At noon she said she did not feel hungry and she did not eat. In the afternoon she did not feel good enough to go on the horse ride. She preferred to stay in the house. Even though she insisted they go without her, the plan was abandoned. Everyone remained in the mansion.

It was the last day that Baron du Jard and the elegant Baron Dupont were staying there. Pressing business demanded their attention.

"Is it you," Broquet asked Gabriel, "who's in charge of sending these gentlemen's bags?"

"Yes, boss."

"Good. Figure out how to get a hold of the Count's case I told you about."

"Got it, boss."

Gabriel slipped the Count's case into a big canvas bag. He brought it down with the help of Baiter who was giving him a hand in the courtyard. But with no one noticing this bag was not put on the cart with the others heading to the station but into the Marquis' car, hidden from view.

The two Barons said their farewells to the Marquis de Brialle and the other guests and were driven to the train by their friend, the Count de Marnais.

"They have a lot to talk about," Broquet watched them go from behind the shutters in Raoul's room. "It's perfect for us that they're gone."

When the Count de Marnais had left, Broquet went into his room and searched it with the help of his lieutenants. He had figured out that the Count's room was directly above Alice's.

"No doubt about it," Broquet said, "the Count didn't have to come into the hallway and risk being seen. So, he must have got them in through the floor."

Flat on his belly Broquet inspected the wood meticulously. Alice's ceiling was white with a gray-blue edging and moldings in the corner. Common sense said that the Count would use one of the moldings to get through the ceiling. Broquet thought that because of the heat needed for the mosquitoes, the hole would be near the fireplace. He went there first.

As expected it did not take long for him to find what he was looking for. One of the strips of oak was loose. He wriggled it up and saw the plaster. A tiny hole no bigger than a pinky finger was dug into it, right through the molding beneath and hidden in the shadows of the fabricated leaves.

"Now," the detective said, "we have everything we need. I'm going back to Paris. Dr. Robert will look at the mosquitoes I'm bringing and if we can find more proof, Gabriel, when you get the telegram you'll do whatever it takes to bring the Count back to Paris where Monsieur Urbain will have a few questions to ask him in the presence of the Chief of Police."

Then he rubbed his hands together, "Let's go! We're getting our revenge for that night at Zulma's."

All this happened very quickly and quietly so that no one in the house except Raoul knew about it.

Paulin Broquet told his lieutenants, "Now I'll leave you here. I have to go back. Even with the serum I feel a fever coming on and I can't get sick in this house."

As planned, Raoul made an excuse to do some shopping in Orléans. He got into a car with only his butler Gabriel. Broquet snuck in under the tarp with the suitcase. In Orléans, stored away safely, one of the detective's cars was waiting for him. During the whole trip Broquet stayed hidden in the back in case Zigomar's spies were on the lookout.

The Marquis de Brialle's car was a big family automobile for the country, able to carry many people but not go very fast. As it arrived bravely into the suburbs of Orléans, honking from behind called it to pull over and let someone pass. Raoul behind the wheel drifted to the right.

In no time at all a sports car sped by. The driver was a young man and in the bucket seat next to him was a mechanic. Both of them were wearing goggles and fur-lined coats. As he passed Raoul's car the young man automatically turned his head. He smiled like all proud drivers when they pass an old lemon, then he disappeared in a cloud of dust. It was brief, less than a second, like a flash, but Gabriel sitting stiffly in his gray suit and cap, next to Raoul, felt his whole body shiver. He was about to turn around and talk to his boss when the latter whispered from the back.

"Don't move. I saw."

"Him... Her!"

"Yes."

When he heard the honking Paulin Broquet had instinctively looked out the window and like Gabriel had seen not only the dazzling smile of the young driver but peeking out from the car, blowing in the wind over the fur collar, a long braid, fluttering like a flame, a long braid of golden red hair.

In the stables of the house that the Marquis de Brialle had in Orléans a car was waiting for Paulin Broquet guarded by two men. They transferred the precious suitcase of the Count de Marnais and Broquet transformed into a nice old widow. He sat in the car with his face hidden behind the veil hanging from an old hat. A nice old widow afraid of too much breeze but with a good revolver ready to shoot if attacked on the highway. Next to him was the Count's luggage that nothing in the world could take from him now. Presently the widow's car left the house.

As it drove down the main street to join the highway going to Paris, Broquet, even though wrapped up against the cold, could see the young man's (or rather woman's) sports car parked in front of a café and a few feet farther on, heading for the café, were two men. One of them was talking and the other listening intently. Completely absorbed in their conversation they did not turn to look at the widow's car that was skirting along the sidewalk they were on. But the old widow had time to see the two men and recognize them.

One of them was the Count de Marnais.

The other was the Count de la Gueriniere.

27. The Count de Marnais is worried

When he got back to the Brialle mansion the Count de Marnais quickly asked for news of his cousin's health. "Alice," they told him, "is not doing well. If it continues tomorrow, they'll send for the doctor."

Going up to his room to get dressed for dinner the Count trembled in horror when he saw that his precious case had vanished. He rang for the butler immediately. Gabriel came running.

"I'm missing a case!" the Count said.

Gabriel looked astonished, "The Monsieur is missing a case! It's not possible... I can't see how..."

"The case that was right here... Didn't you see it... lying here closed?"

"Indeed... It's missing?"

"It's gone!"

"Well, that's very odd."

"You're the one who took down those gentlemen's suitcases?"

"Yes. But I got help from the other servants." Then Gabriel raised his voice, "Oh, I see! I see how the mistake was made. One of them saw the monsieur's case closed up and thought it should get packed up. That must be it."

"How many suitcases did you bring down?"

"Two big ones and three smaller ones like yours... plus two other bags."

"Three small ones you say?"

"Yes, monsieur, I'm sure of it."

The Count de Marnais breathed deeply. "So that's it. My case is en route to Paris. It's packed up with the others. Those gentlemen each had one like mine. Okay, thank you."

Now the Count de Marnais knew that his case was in good hands and out of danger. Tomorrow he would certainly receive a telegram from his friends or a note to reassure him. And he would not be worried; he would save his anxious looks for his cousin whom he would take special care of...

Informed by telegram, Dr. Robert was at the villa in Neuilly when the detective's car entered with the usual precautions. Broquet brought the case into his office and stripped off the old widow's clothes. Without further ado he examined the locks.

"Oho, not easy to open. The Count is a cautious man."

But what is hard for others is a child's play for Broquet.

He got a little case out of a drawer, chose a few thin, steel strips in different shapes and wrapped them together with a screw ring, which he tightened hard. It formed a kind of misshapen key that he put into the lock. He wriggled it and forced it and finally took it out. The strips were lined up in the shape of a special-toothed security key. Broquet studied it, replaced a few strips and got new transformations.

"That's better," he said as he screwed the ring tightly. Then he gave it one complete turn, heard the click and the lock flipped opened automatically.

"As easy as that," the detective said.

The second lock was opened just as easily and the trunk revealed its precious secret. Paulin Broquet let the top fall back. In the upper compartment of the trunk were clothes and personal effects like any good trunk. But under these Broquet found a small, nickel pan that he had never before seen in gentleman's luggage.

"Aha!" he said. "Now it begins. See, Doctor, the bottom of this kitchen utensil shows traces of bluish black meaning it was recently heated. Now, since the Count de Marnais has no need to heat water to shave or make tea at the Brialle mansion, the water he boiled in this was used for something else. And I think we're going to find the answer right away. Let's keep looking."

Under this compartment they found hatboxes. Inside them were indeed hats: a top hat, a straw hat, a felt hat... and then, rolled up, folded, one those really light, really flimsy soft hats that are generally called "frivolous". Broquet lifted it carefully. He unrolled it and found a leather case... a portable doctor's pouch.

"This is it," he said. "Inside this is the secret of the terrible mystery."

He pressed a button and it flipped open. It contained three glass vials sealed with cotton plugs that held gauze under a rubber ring.

"These are test tubes," Dr. Robert stated. "They come from a laboratory."

"Tubes for heating up cultures, right? Otherwise known as hotels for microbes."

"That's it."

"Look, Doctor. These must be sleeping mosquitoes inside."

The doctor took the tubes. He went to the window to get a better look when he cried out in terror, "Yes, mosquitoes, but not your common European culex. These are the dangerous anopheles, the dreadful aedes. They're relentless carriers of malaria, yellow fever and the plague!"

"Exactly. Well, doc, it's with these insects injected with poison, safer than stabbing, that the Count committed his murders."

"It's awful!"

Broquet went on, "You weren't wrong in your research, doctor. You correctly identified the terrible sickness that took the life of Alice's young sister. But legally the police were powerless and the murderer got away. His medical crime, if I can call it this, saved him because there was no way to get proof."

"Indeed."

"This is the proof I need, the proof I've been looking for, that I myself am witness to... that's irrefutable. Now we have not only the instruments of the crime, so to speak, but also a victim who can testify."

"A victim? Alice de Brialle?"

"No, doctor, me!"

"You?"

"Yes." Briefly, the detective told Robert what happened at the Brialle mansion. "The night I knew that the murder, which is the right word, would take place, I sat in for the victim and I was the one attacked."

"You could've been killed!"

"The young lady would've have been for sure."

"You're a good man."

"I was doing my job." Holding out the small metal box to the doctor he said, "Here are the aedes that were suppose to kill Alice. I got them in her room... on my body. Now, doctor, stab me in arm... and take some blood."

"Why?"

"Because I was poisoned. Because I've got the plague in me. You're going to search and find it... and sign an official statement with your findings."

"So, you didn't take the serum?"

"Sure, but a long time after I was stung... to give the microbes time to do their work. I had to bring you proof."

Dr. Robert immediately took a blood sample, drawn near the big bumps on his arm, the cysts that were already swollen.

"Now, doctor," Broquet said, "dose me with quinine because I'm feeling a fever coming on. I can't get sick right now. If I'm strong enough, I'll go back there."

During the day Paulin Broquet, still incognito, went to talk with the chief of police and investigating judge Urbain. The crime was clearly established. They would give the brave detective an arrest warrant for the Count de Marnais, leaving him to do as he wished to nab the criminal without causing any harm to the poor Marquis de Brialle who had too much grief and pain in his family at the moment to be burdened with shame to boot.

In the Brialle mansion the Count de Marnais was looking less happy, less cheerful than usual. Since his two friends' departure he felt overwhelmed by so much worry for his acting skills to hide.

He had sent several messages to Paris and received as many back, which only seemed to increase his anxiety. Baron du Jard and the splendid Baron Dupont had answered that they did not have his case whose extraordinary disappearance was causing all this anguish. Despite all the searches on the railroad they found no trace of the case. The affair was becoming very serious for the Count de Marnais. Nevertheless, he pretended it was not important.

However, losing all patience, he announced the next day that he had urgent business in Paris where, he said, he would only stay two days, three at most... and he thanked Captain de Cazeaumont, Alice's future husband, the future master of the house, to stand in for him with the guests during his absence. He told the butler to come help with his suitcase because he was taking only one for this short trip.

Therefore, Gabriel went up to the room with the Count and on his orders put some toiletries in the suitcase. The Count closed it, grabbed his coat and told the butler, "Let's go downstairs." He went first.

Just when he was putting his hand on the doorknob to open it, the door swung open and a man appeared. At the sight of this man the Count de Marnais fell backwards, crying out, "Paulin Broquet!"

28. Getting proof

Before the Count de Marnais could recover from his terror, Broquet jumped on him, knocked him down and got him in a hold that was impossible to escape. Then he slapped the handcuffs on while Gabriel tied his legs. It was all done in the blink of an eye.

Paulin Broquet lifted up the crippled Count and threw him into an arm-chair, dead weight. The Count figured out right away what was going on. He felt lost. But pulling himself together he tried to look strong, to face the danger, to defend himself.

"What is this nonsense?"

"It's not nonsense," Broquet responded.

"If this is some kind of joke, it's not very funny."

"This isn't a joke either. The hour of justice has struck for you!"

"Ah, Monsieur, this is going too far! I won't let you... Even if you're just a common policeman, I take your actions as a serious insult and I demand satisfaction! I will make you pay for this!"

Without paying any attention to the Count's tirade, Paulin Broquet made a sign to Gabriel who went to the door and opened it. He stepped aside, saying, "You may enter, messieurs."

The Count de Marnais was alarmed to see the Marquis de Brialle, Captain de Rennebois, Captain de Cazeaumont, Robert and Raoul Montreil enter the room.

"Oh, my friends, my dear uncle," the Count cried out, "I'm so glad you're here! I hope you're going to tell this policeman that this prank has gone too far!"

Broquet showed the Marquis de Brialle a paper. "I'm sorry, monsieur, for carrying out this operation in your honorable house."

"I highly protest this," the Count de Marnais said. "Uncle, I'm family. I'm your guest. You have to let me go... and throw this man out the door like he deserves."

"I have an arrest warrant signed by the prosecutor's office in Paris and Orléans for the Count de Marnais, accused of murder."

The old marquis spoke to Broquet, "Do your duty, monsieur, even in my house. I will in no way obstruct the wheels of justice."

Broquet said solemnly, "Count de Marnais, in the name of the law I arrest you!"

"You're crazy! Uncle, come on, tell him..."

The marquis approached the prisoner and said, "You wretch, be quiet!"

"I protest! I appeal to the law!"

"Murderer!"

"Me, a murderer?! Oh, uncle, grief and sorrow have clouded your judgment."

"For you, vile and wicked man, I had nothing but kindness and to steal my money, to wrest the inheritance from my children, you killed my wife, you killed my son and you killed my poor little daughter."

"It's not true! It's a lie!" the Count shouted.

Paulin Broquet cut in, "No shouting. There's no need to trouble the young ladies who might hear you. They're laughing right now, thinking you've left because Mademoiselle de Brialle has never felt better than since you believed you killed her."

"You're crazy. I've never..."

Broquet turned to his lieutenant, "Gabriel, show these gentlemen the hole in the floor where the Count de Marnais let loose the mosquitoes."

On hearing these words the Count de Marnais turned white. But he tried to laugh. "Mosquitoes? Mosquitoes! Oho, Paulin Broquet is about to tell you one of his wild adventures. A hole in the floor? Of course it was made by mice. If you listen to him, he'll make you think that mice are mosquitoes."

"This hole," Broquet explained, "leads straight into Alice's bedroom. It's hidden in one of the rosettes in the ceiling near the fireplace."

The Count de Marnais barked out, "To make it easier for Santa Claus... the detective will come up with some extraordinary deductions."

Broquet went on calmly, "In fact, mosquitoes needed heat to survive and accomplish their sinister mission. That's why the Count de Marnais thought the rooms were humid the other night, the night of the crime, and had fires lit everywhere."

"What you're saying is ridiculous."

"The mosquitoes came through the ceiling, attracted by the warmth. They could fly around and land on the intended victim at will."

They sat the Marquis down in an armchair. Around him, also sitting in chairs brought over by Gabriel, were the two captains and the two brothers. Thus was formed a kind of tribunal before which the wretched Count de Marnais stood.

Serious and very calm, Paulin Broquet continued, addressing the Count who was trembling with rage and hate. "I have the authority to bring you to the Orléans prison without further explanation. But out of respect for the name of the Marquis de Brialle, for his family, I will keep you here until nightfall. Moreover, I intend to prove your heinous crime to these gentlemen. I'll let you deny me if you can... Raoul Montreil, being a lawyer, can help you in your defense. But I warn you that I won't allow any more insults or swearing, so don't make me gag you until we leave."

With this Broquet turned to the Marquis, "Dr. Robert will explain to you later how he came to suspect the truth about this evil plan that caused so much grief to your family. He proved it scientifically whereas I used my instincts to flush out the criminal. We worked together to find the truth, real proof, for justice to prevail.

"Messieurs, without a shadow of a doubt the crime was premeditated and the multiple attempts are obvious. The motive is profit. Even though the Count comes from a noble and illustrious family, he's broke. He thinks work is unworthy of a man with a title. He was looking for an easy way to satisfy his expensive habits, even dishonorable acts that should have been unthinkable to him.

"Did he himself come up with the idea of getting hold of his uncle's fortune through a crime like this? Let's say that he was impelled by necessity, that he was just a tool in the hands of a close friend, a man whom he had introduced here and who must have helped him in the previous crimes and given him the weapons for this last one."

"You have no right to insult my friends," the Count spoke up, "and to accuse them like this." Recklessly carried away by his anger, the prisoner added, "The Count de la Gueriniere is beyond your reach."

Broquet watched him calmly. "I didn't name anyone. It's the defendant who identified his accomplice."

"You didn't name him," the Count tried to cover his slip of the tongue, "but the reference was obvious. We know your feelings about this perfect gentleman whom you've being trying to turn into a criminal at all costs... Why, just recently..."

"No need to talk about that here," the detective cut him off. "In that matter the Count de la Gueriniere was found innocent, true, but he still shows up at every crime, every evil exploit committed by Zigomar. Now, the Count de Marnais is fully aware of all this. In spite of everything he can still call himself a friend, a character witness, a close ally of the Count de la Gueriniere, who is none other than Zigomar!"

"He's not Zigomar! It's not true, no, no!"

"Doesn't matter. We're not here today to deal with that. I'm telling you, messieurs, that the Count de Marnais, either alone or with a partner, is trying to rob you and he committed the worst, the most cowardly crimes imaginable."

"You're lying."

"He cast this house into mourning three times. Then he tried to kill Captain de Cazeaumont because he would marry Alice and foil his plans, thereby destroying all the progress he had made by his previous crimes. But the Captain was snatched from the hands of death by Dr. Robert with the timely help of Captain de Rennebois."

"You?" Cazeaumont said. "So it was you who gave me the life-saving injection!"

The two officers shook hands warmly.

"Yes, but he's the one you should be thanking," Rennebois pointed to Paulin Broquet. "He's the one who saved you... who is saving all of us."

The detective raised his hand to ask for silence before continuing.

"Since the fiancé survived the attack, Alice needed to die. The Count de Marnais had hoped to marry his cousin and get a fortune in the dowry. But Alice denied him, so her death was decided. By adding this death to the three previous ones, the Count de Marnais was destroying any hope of marriage so the precious dowry would stay put and he would become the sole heir of the Marquis de Brialle."

"Oh the wretch! The villain!" the old marquis spat out.

Broquet went on, "This time the attack was prepared more carefully than ever. The Count had become a master in the art. The mosquitoes that he wanted to use love the color blue. The Count offered his cousin blue lampshades that he had custom made but which he pretended he won at a charity. The mosquitoes, therefore, were going to be attracted by the shades or by the night-light. Moreover, mosquitoes love the smell of leather. Russian leather makes them especially excited. The Count didn't forget to offer his cousin a magnificent desk blotter made of Russian leather that would decorate Alice's room."

The Count de Marnais, who had listened without interrupting so far, suddenly blurted out, "If this matter weren't so important, so serious, we would all be laughing at this schoolboy nonsense."

Without even looking at the prisoner, Broquet continued, "I don't need to tell you, messieurs, that everything I'm saying has been scientifically proven, studied long and hard by different specialists. Dr. Toussaint Bintal recently published some articles on this subject that cause quite a splash in the medical world as well as in the general public. Well, Dr. Robert Montreil will give you all the scientific explanations.

"As for me, because of the unique nature of the crime and because of the family of the guilty party, I proceeded carefully by relying on Dr. Robert's infallible knowledge. And today I can be absolutely certain of making no mistake by arresting this murderer!"

29. The final torment

Paulin Broquet resumed, "I hid in this house and followed the Count de Marnais. I saw that his first attack failed because the cold paralyzed his unknowing but dreadful accomplices."

"Madness! Absurdity!" the Count spluttered.

"The Count de Marnais was keeping some mosquitoes in test tubes. Sleeping mosquitoes sent to him from countries where yellow fever is constantly raging."

"Disgusting," Raoul and the angry captains murmured.

Broquet went on, "Here's how he got these death-dealers. Partners of Zigomar went to South America where there's lots of yellow fever and hunted the murderous mosquitoes on shores of lakes and ponds. They chose young, strong subjects and had them feed for a long time on infected blood. Then the mosquitoes were not sent to France but brought over, cared for during the trip like precious cargo, like exotic animals. The plague takes 15 to 20 days in the insects' digestive tube to become powerful enough to kill when dropped into the blood of a stung victim.

"15 to 20 days, that's the time it took to arrive in Europe from the infected countries. During this period the future assassins were completely harmless. During the trip on board the ship the Zigomar ally was out of danger and could secretly, meticulously take care of his dear pupils in his private cabin. He kept the mosquitoes in a kind of bowl with a little bit of water, covered with gauze and tucked into a traveling bag for extra protection.

"In the evening the Z man slipped his hand under the gauze. Thus they were fed, staying strong and healthy, ready to fulfill the terrible mission prepared by an invisible master... the chief of the Zs! But closer to Europe the temperature dropped quickly. The mosquitoes went numb. This was serious because the microbes in their digestive tubes were mature. A sting would inevitably cause the death of their victim now. The Z man carefully picked up his groggy pupils and put them in test tubes, remembering to inject himself with the anti-plague serum given to him by Dr. Roux. He could disembark calmly and give Zigomar this frightful weapon sleeping in glass tubes like a poisoned sword in its scabbard."

"None of this is true!" the Count de Marnais shouted.

Broquet demanded silence. "The man entrusted with this mosquito mission was Zigomar's most valuable partner. It was Tom Tweak!"

They listened to the detective in fear and anguish.

Broquet continued, "These mosquitoes, like all insects, can live for a while in a state of slumber. They come back to life when heat wakes them up. For this the Count put a pan with water on a little cook stove so the steam would heat up the test tubes. The mosquitoes woke up and were hungry after their long fast. The Count only had to dump them through the hole in Alice's ceiling so they could finish their nasty work."

"That's ridiculous!" the Count was slumping in the chair.

"How it was done for the three previous crimes doesn't matter. Let's stay with this last attempt. On the evening when the Count ordered the fires lit, Alice went to sleep with Raymonde who was in on our secret. Me, I took her place in her room. The blotter smelled strongly of leather, the blue light was on and the room was heating up. All this for the benefit of the mosquitoes. I heard them buzzing in the room. I rolled up my sleeves and offered them my arms. They accepted with great pleasure."

Broquet rolled up his sleeves and showed all the mosquito bites on his arms.

"There's the proof. The mosquitoes must have found me tasty because they drank so much they got drunk and as a thank you for the feast they left behind all kinds of diseases in my veins. I picked up some of these mosquitoes with all the respect due to members of the fairer sex because only the females sting and drink blood. Only the females carry death. These insects were valuable to Dr. Robert. He was able to compare them to the ones found in the test tubes kept in the case that disappeared so mysteriously."

For some time now the Count had lost his arrogance. The more the detective piled up the proof of his heinous crime, the more lost he felt. And his head drooped. All his energy, all thought of denial or defense was snuffed out. He was devastated.

To avoid any last defiance Paulin Broquet turned to him and said, "The case you were so worried about was not taken by Baron du Jard or Baron Dupont by mistake... It was me. At this moment it is in police custody as a piece of evidence."

The Count de Marnais had nothing to say.

"There you go," Broquet concluded, "everything needed to prove the guilt of the Count de Marnais. I wanted to show this to the Marquis de Brialle to excuse myself for having worked in secret in his home, especially against a man who is, unfortunately, a relative."

"No, no," the old Marquis protested, "this individual is not a member of my family. I deny him! Let justice follow its course... and punish this murderer!"

On hearing this the Count de Marnais jumped in his chair. "My uncle, you don't see... you don't understand that this is all wrong, it's fiction, absolutely impossible... I can't have committed these crimes!"

The Marquis stood up. "Be quiet, wretch! Murderer! Curse on you!"

A voice near the door spoke, "No, my father, don't curse him. Let justice follow its course. But you, don't curse the poor man... don't curse."

The Count de Marnais sat up straight. "Alice!" he cried. "Alice, oh, I'm sorry!" As if desolated, in tears, he fell to his knees.

On seeing the villain collapse Paulin Broquet walked over to him and loosened the handcuffs that were hindering his movements. The Count could then wipe his eyes.

"Alice," he blubbered, "dear Alice, yes, I'm guilty... yes, I killed. But it wasn't for your father's fortune... It was to have you. I loved you... I was crazy in love with you."

"Wretch!" Alice murmured.

"You refused me. I couldn't stand the idea of you being another man's wife. I wanted to snatch you from your fiancé, hoping to win you over some day. Then, because you hated me more and more, I wanted to take revenge... and I wanted to kill you. I was a wretch, I loved you, I was mad! Take pity on me!"

Alice responded, "Pity? I can't have any for you. But perhaps my father and I could forgive you."

"Forgive me?"

"If you can make amends. You're not the only guilty party."

"No!"

"You were dragged into this. You obeyed that man I refuse to name... Well, help the work of justice, make it easier for the men trying to prevent further crimes."

"Yes, I will talk... later... I will talk, but promise me your forgiveness. Alice, swear it."

"Atone first. Show that as low as you fell, you still have the heart of a gentleman. Every fault has a price. Everyone lost can be redeemed. Pay the price and be the Count de Marnais one last time. Then my father and I will forgive you."

She stared at her beaten cousin for an instant. Then she turned to leave and placed her hand on a small table next to the Count. On this table she left her handkerchief. And in the handkerchief was a pistol.

"Come, father," she took the old man's arm, "come. There's nothing for us to do here until we hear more."

She led the Marquis out. The captains and the Montreil brothers, deeply impressed by this dramatic scene, followed in silence.

The Count crawled on his knees to the door, weeping. "Alice... dear Alice, pity... I'm sorry, so sorry!"

Paulin Broquet dragged the Count into the bedroom, lifted him up and sat him in the armchair where he slumped again, broke down and cried. It was not the right time for an interrogation. Besides, that was for the judge in Orléans to do first and then for Monsieur Urbain who was waiting for them in Paris.

Special measures were taken from then on in order to organize the transport of the criminal to Orléans without arousing the curiosity of the servants, which would embarrass the masters. Broquet figured that the Count was too dejected and too cowardly to try to escape so he left with Gabriel. The bedroom was on the third floor of the mansion and the floors were very high. No fear of escape was conceivable. Nevertheless, Paulin Broquet locked the door behind him and left one of his men in the hallway.

Broquet sees everything and certainly did not miss Alice leaving her handkerchief within reach of her cousin. Maybe a pistol shot was the best conclusion to this adventure, which would redeem some of the villain's past and avoid the shame for this afflicted family that did not deserve these misfortunes. As for himself, his honor as a detective would stay intact—he had arrested the guilty party... and it little mattered whether he were tried by a jury or carried out justice himself. Without a shadow of a doubt Broquet leaving with Gabriel was giving the Count de Marnais one last chance to earn the forgiveness of his family.

However, more than an hour passed, long and forlorn, without any gunshot breaking the silence of the grieving house.

Dr. Robert was being helped by Raoul and Captain de Rennebois to take care of the Marquis who had fainted amidst so many emotions. In the salon reserved for the young girls, Irene de Valtours and Raymonde, along with Captain de Cazeaumont, were comforting Alice as she prayed and wept. They felt death looming over the mansion and each of them waited with heavy heart for the signal of redemption, of justice, for deliverance in the sound of a gunshot.

Half an hour more ticked off in this trance, in this silence. The car that was supposed to take the Count de Marnais was waiting. Night fell. It was time to go to prison.

Broquet muttered, "The coward." He went back to the Count's room to bring him to the judges since he did not have the courage to do away with himself. "Nothing?" he asked the guard at the door.

"No, boss. He was pacing, crying, mumbling... That's all."

Broquet opened the door. It stuck when he pushed. He pushed harder, opened it and entered the room. It looked empty. But on the floor, in the light of the lamps that Gabriel was bringing in, Broquet saw the Count's body lying in a pool of blood with his throat slashed. On the mirror over the fireplace, traced in blood, shimmered a big Z, the mark of Zigomar.

30. Riri the thief

The next day the local papers and those in Paris announced the news that the Count de Marnais, the elegant gentleman so well known in Parisian social circles, died in an accident. Paulin Broquet was in charge of telling the chief of police in Orléans what to say and of editing the doctored report that they showed the public while the real report was kept absolutely secret.

The day after this tragedy a hearse came to pick up the body and bring it back to Paris where it would be buried in a family plot.

The marquis de Brialle and his daughter Alice forgave the murderer as promised but did not want to lay his remains in the same cemetery and the same tomb as his victims.

The Count de la Gueriniere, Baron Dupont, Baron du Jard, the bankers Van Cambre and Guttlach and friends from their club and the armory accompanied the Count to his final resting place. And that was the end of the wretched man.

The mysterious, dramatic death was a hard blow to the Marquis' guests. Broquet gave them an explanation:

"The Count de Marnais was probably out to get help for a new crime. Having lost his partners Baron du Jard and the elegant Baron Dupont, he had to bring in the famous Zigomar. Now, Zigomar is a most clever man, bold and dangerous. He was obviously hiding in the Count's room, waiting. Maybe I came at the right time to foil his plans, to ruin his criminal conspiracy. Then everything changed completely. The Count was confronted, arrested, and he broke down before the Marquis and his cousin, had a moment of weakness, of remorse... because I don't think he was faking it at that moment.

"It proves that there was still a little loyalty, a little honor left in his heart. But Zigomar could not allow that. To be a real Z every weakness and all remorse must go. The Count was promising to talk. He signed his own death sentence. The law of Zs is explicit, uncompromising... and unforgiving. Cowards, weaklings and traitors are executed without mercy! Zigomar was here. He witnessed the scene. He heard everything. He made his accomplice pay for his cowardice and remorse and by cutting his throat he kept him from talking.

"The mark of Z signed in blood on the mirror was to show off his power... and to show all the other Zs that the invisible master had punished the traitor according to their law."

Dr. Robert also gave some scientific details about how the terrible mosquitoes had spread death. He explained about the microbes growing in the digestive tubes of the mosquitoes and how the insects transmitted them by stinging a human.

They listened, fascinated and frightened at the same time. More than anyone else Irene de Valtours was on the edge of her seat, not only paying attention but also looking very attractive. She was devouring the doctor with her eyes and unaware of Alice and Raymonde watching her out of the corner of an eye, smiling to themselves as they saw the secret of the naïve and beautiful girl. A secret, Raymonde had said, that she herself might not know about.

As for Robert, he was concentrated on the terrible microbes, the plague germs, showing how they jumped on the blood cells and reproduced in the human organism causing mayhem and chaos that in three days would bring on a horrible death. And he did not see the blue eyes of Irene staring at him, following his every move as if enchanted.

But Raoul could guess the little secret. He was watching his sister's friend and thinking of the greatest compliment he could give: "If there were a woman as pretty as Riri, it would be Irene de Valtours."

When he was alone with his brother, off to the side, he joked with good humor, "Illustrious doctor, you have the prettiest listener in the world here."

Robert did not know who his brother was referring to.

"Now that you know," Raoul went on, "all the secrets of winged insects carrying evil in the stingers, your next job is to discover the joy of a man in the blue eyes and heavenly smile of a wingless angel, a blonde woman."

Alas! Dr. Robert could still not understand. And Raoul could not know how much pain he was causing his brother even while trying to make him happy.

An angel's smile and a blonde's blue eyes, for Robert, meant only Riri. Robert's heart had still not recovered from Riri tearing it out. It was because it did not want to see any blue eyes or charming smiles that Robert was so concentrated on his microbes and their transformations. Robert could still not see that there was another world outside of Riri and that it was his delightful listener, Irene de Valtours.

When the doctor returned to Paris with Paulin Broquet, Irene, just like the last time, fell into a long bout of sadness. Raymonde played mother and stroked her hair, "Come now, Irene, don't cry. Let the doctor's heart grow and evolve. Soon he'll see the microbe that's in you and that will grow infinitely big. It's a microbe that causes that wonderful, blessed fever we call love."

"What!" Irene was taken aback. "So, you know that I love your brother Robert?"

"Naturally."

"But does he?"

"He will... and he will love you back."

A few days later Raymonde and Irene also went back to Paris with Raoul and Captain de Rennebois whose leave was finished. Once again the Brialle mansion fell silent. The love between Alice and Captain de Cazeaumont should have made it seem less empty to the old marquis, however, after so much mourning. Irene spent two days with her little mother Raymonde, then her father came to get her and bring her back to her sad and distant home in Brittany.

Life went back to normal.

The day after he returned, Raoul ran up to Ville-D'Avray to see his friend Girardet. He should have told him everything that happened with the Brialles but all he did was ask for news of Riri. Everything was fine. Madame Laurent and Riri called every day now.

"And the Count de la Gueriniere?" Raoul asked.

"He leaves us alone," André Girardet said. "Riri doesn't see him on the street anymore. We don't hear anything about him. It's good."

Riri had regained her self-confidence and was finally starting to enjoy a calm life without worrying about the future. Well, one afternoon Perkins the dressmaker, her boss, called her into his office. She told herself that if it were to give her another job like in Ville-d'Avray she would refuse. No excuse, no threat would compel her to accept a suspicious mission.

Monsieur Perkins was in his office with a legal representative, Monsieur Portet, who ran the warehouse workers and was head of supplies.

"Mademoiselle," Perkins said to Riri, "for a while now Monsieur Portet has informed me about the misappropriation of tissue, silk and lace from the factory."

Riri jumped and cried out, "You suspect me? You think I'm guilty... me, a thief?" She was trembling and repeating, "You think I'm a thief?"

But Perkins tried to calm her down. He answered gently, "No, no. Like all the workers we're just asking you some questions."

"Sure, I'll answer."

"Have you ever taken anything out of the factory?"

"Yes, monsieur. Some bits of tissue, just scraps that were thrown away, that were useless... but always with the permission of the supervisor."

"Okay, okay. And recently didn't you take home some remnants of English lace?"

"No, monsieur! No, that would be stealing... and you know I could never..."

"I'll ask again: Did you not, even by mistake, take away some lace?"

"No, monsieur, no!"

"You're sure."

"I swear!"

"Okay, mademoiselle." Perkins spoke solemnly, "I regret to inform you that I have a report here saying that someone saw you taking place."

"Me? They saw me taking this lace? It's a lie! A lie!"

"I hope so, for your sake. Nevertheless, your word is not enough. I need proof."

"And how am I supposed to prove my innocence, messieurs? How can I prove that I'm incapable of stealing anything?"

"Very simply. Monsieur Portet will go home with you."

"To my home?"

"With a police officer."

Rirette was panicking, "Oh no, monsieur! No, don't come to my home! Oh, not the police, please! I'm begging you!"

"Believe me, mademoiselle, I'm very sorry. But I need, for you as much as for me, to confirm my belief and find some proof, I hope, of your innocence. It's the only way…"

Rirette begged, threw herself at his knees. "Oh, monsieur, believe me! I swear that I'm innocent. I didn't steal anything. But please don't come to my house! No, not that. Have mercy! If you knew… my mother is sick… almost dying. When she learns that you're coming because of me to search the house, when she learns that I'm being accused of theft… Oh, monsieur, it'll kill her! She'll die! Please, I'm begging you!"

Perkins spoke to Riri gently. "My child, I know it's cruel but it's necessary for your honor… to keep you house safe… If, as I hope, you prove your innocence, I'll be the first to announce it. So, let it happen. These gentlemen will act with discretion. Just follow them."

Riri gave up trying to stop what was inevitable. More dead than alive, in tears, she got in the car with Monsieur Portet and the police officer.

"Oh, messieurs," she told them, "I beg you, don't let my mother know anything or suspect anything. Be kind, please."

At Ganneron Alley the appearance of Riri with two men at this hour did not go unnoticed. All the neighborhood gossips got together to talk about what they knew nothing about. And the comments were made, conjectures born… and the nastiest, most malicious opinions took flight. It was so nice, so easy to pounce upon this pretty girl who was so unhappy, poor, defenseless and alone. The good women had themselves a time.

Riri brought Portet and the police officer up to her poor rooms, then she went to comfort her mother who was surprised to see her come back so early and with two men…

"I think," the police officer whispered to Portet, "that we're wasting our time. This girl looks innocent to me."

"Don't be fooled by appearances," Portet shot back. First he showed the officer the scraps of fabric Riri had taken and how she and her sister used their skill and imagination to decorate their poor room. "There you go," he said, "already some pieces I recognize that come from the workshop."

With Marie the hunchback looking on, the two of them started their search. Portet did so furiously, the police officer without enthusiasm. They searched the bedroom and when Riri came back they found the lace and silk hidden under the mattress. The theft was now undeniable, unquestionable, obvious!

Riri saw the lace and silk and was speechless… She did not understand.

Marie the hunchback was as bewildered as her sister. "It's me," she said. "I made the bed after my sister left this morning. But I can assure you that nothing was there… and it wasn't me who put those there."

"Fine! Just fine!" Portet cut in. "What we see is enough. Your explanations are of no use."

Riri looked stunned. Her brain had just received such a hard blow that it left her dazed. At Ville-d'Avray, in the face of danger, before an enemy, she proved to be brave and could defend herself courageously. Here, faced with this discovery, before this infamy, this treachery that she knew not the how or who or why, she had no strength to resist. She could not even feel angry. She was devastated, a body without a soul.

She looked at the messy bed, the lace and silk, and seemed to see nothing, as if bewitched. Like a little bird under the powerful gaze of a snake about to devour it.

The police officer did not want to prolong the tragic scene. He took her gently by the arm. "Come, my child, come with me."

Automatically, without the least resistance, Riri followed him. She did not even think of saying goodbye to her mother. She did not even glance at her frightened sister.

She floated down the stairs, went into the street, crossed the line of gossipers without seeing them, without hearing their insults. Being supported, almost carried by the considerate officer, she let him put her back in the car.

All the way to the station she sat mute, staring straight ahead, her mouth half-open, shut off from the world, until they put her in a cell. Then, all of a sudden, she snapped out of it and understood. She threw herself at the cell door closing behind her and shouted, "Mama!"

And she passed out, fell to the ground, as if she were dead.

31. Laurent in prison

That evening Baiter told Broquet that Riri had been arrested for theft.

"Another blow from the Count de la Gueriniere," the detective said. "That girl is no thief. Why is the scoundrel after her? He's obviously trying to put her in trouble, to crush her... so he can come to save her in her hour of need." Then he smiled, "He'll be too late. Just like with the necklace."

But Simon had entered and announced other, even more worrisome news: "Monsieur Laurent has been arrested."

"Laurent?!"

"Yes, for stealing."

"Him too? Tell me what happened."

"Bilmat filed charges."

"The mayor of Itonville, his father in-law?"

"That's right, boss."

"Okay, I can imagine... I see. It's clear as day. Zigomar has shown up again."

It was indeed Monsieur Bilmat who reported the theft against his son in-law. Two days earlier Bilmat was surprised by a visit from two people from Paris. One of them presented himself as a representative of a Parisian bank; the other came as a bailiff to take a statement.

The banker told the mayor, "Forgive me, your honor, for asking these questions, but it's a matter of honor of someone close to you... and of you yourself."

"My honor? What do you mean? Tell me!"

"Monsieur Laurent is your son in-law?"

"Unfortunately yes."

"Well, are you aware that today he is absolutely ruined?"

"Ruined? I thought he was only in a little trouble... but ruined?"

"He's using his last resources."

"Oh!"

"Yesterday, in fact, he was supposed to pay 10,000 francs."

"And he didn't pay?"

"He did pay."

"So?"

"Well, we knew that a few days before he didn't have a sous to his name."

"He found a loan..."

"Here? From you?"

"Me, no. I didn't give him a thing and I never will."

"Right. In Paris Monsieur Laurent is totally out of options. He came to see you. We thought you gave in, that you let him pass off your signature..."

The mayor jumped, "My signature! What's this got to do with my signature? Why is my signature mixed up in all this?"

"Because it endorses a loan to Laurent, your son in-law, for this money."

This time Bilmat slammed his fist on the table, shouting, "It's false! It's a fake! Listen up, my son in-law is a wretch! He's a forger!"

"Well, the money that's been lent out, you don't plan to pay it back despite your signature?"

"Never! Never!"

"Oh, but it must be, you know."

"Never I tell you! I'm going to file charges against Laurent! Oh, the crook!"

The bank representative let Bilmat's fit of anger pass before saying, "I'm telling you this, monsieur, to help you out, on behalf of the bank who holds the papers bearing your name… also to warn you for the sake of your honor. But it could be that Laurent has now found enough money to pay the other debts that will soon be due."

"Where's he going to find money if he's got no options in Paris?"

"But we know he has. He's declared it… that he could pay after coming back from Laigle here."

Bilmat suddenly swore, then he stared at the two men. "Hold on! Just wait a minute!" He left his office and went up to his bedroom. An idea had flashed through his mind that was almost unthinkable. He remembered that his son in-law had stayed the night and was in the house after he, Bilmat, had left. During this time Laurent was alone in his bedroom, right next to his own where he kept his money in a safe. He had not opened the safe since that day to check…

Now, tortured by a terrible thought, he was trembling as he opened it. The banker and bailiff downstairs heard him howling in rage, cursing his son in-law to high heaven.

"Robbed!" he shouted when he got back into his office. "He robbed me! Laurent is a robber! A forger and a thief!"

Bilmat looked like a raging madman.

"Robbed! Robbed!" he kept repeating. "He stole my money! The thief… the crook…" His anger pushed him to say, "He's Zigomar! I'm telling you, he's Zigomar!" And with fury he cried out, "He's a murderer!"

With that he stopped. Then once again he was struck by a hideous thought. "But, look, wasn't Laurent mixed up in that Montreil affair? Wasn't he suspected of murdering the banker?"

The two men nodded without saying a word.

The mayor could not hold back, "That's it! Of course! Laurent went to the banker to get his papers back… or to rob the safe. He killed him! He only robbed me but if I were here to stop him he would have murdered me too!"

The two men said goodbye, excusing themselves for any trouble they might have caused. But they had barely gone when Monsieur Bilmat, who was pacing his room like an angry lion in a cage, went back up to his room. He took one last look at the safe, then quickly packed a suitcase.

After checking a timetable he cried out, "I have just enough time to get to Paris before the courts close!"

He called for his coach and got taken to Laigle where he caught the train. He placed the formal complaint against his son in-law into the hands of the public prosecutor.

Early the next morning, Monsieur Laurent watched the authorities invade his office and present the warrant for his arrest. Outraged, he tried to defend himself, to protest, but Bilmat's complaint was formal. The officials seized the papers in Laurent's safe, including the ones bearing Bilmat's signature.

Now, Monsieur Bilmat had also filed against his son in-law for forgery and fraud. Moreover, these papers, according to the accountant's declaration at the Montreil bank who checked the litigation of the deceased banker and had been summoned earlier, these papers were missing from Montreil's and very likely had disappeared when he was murdered.

In a way, this established his guilt, declaring Laurent the murderer of Monsieur Montreil. The matter, therefore, took on enormous proportions.

Laurent, however, continued to defend himself courageously. He recognized the forgeries, of course: he admitted his guilt wholeheartedly. But he also admitted that he had no idea how the papers, which he knew better than anyone were locked away in the bank safe, could have found their way into his.

"Someone must have planted them there," he declared. "Someone took them from Montreil's and hid them here in my safe. But it wasn't me, I swear! It's not me!"

Such a defense could not be accepted by anyone. It was impossible... inacceptable. The investigating judge asked poor Laurent, "You were able to pay 10,000 francs while only a few days before you didn't have a sous. Where did you find the money? In Laigle?"

"Yes, in Laigle."

"But not from your father in-law?"

"No! Monsieur Bilmat mercilessly refused to help me in any way."

"So?"

"My wife came up with the money."

"Who gave it to her?"

"Her aunt... Aunt Melie."

After the authorities finished searching the office and sealing it up, they went to Laurent's home on Boulevard de Sébastopol. Bilmat was there. He had just told his daughter what was happening and said that he was taking her with him, that she had to get a divorce, that he would find her a new life, a new home, a new happiness.

But quite unexpectedly he found his daughter fiercely opposed to him. She defended Laurent and told her father that no matter what happened she would not separate from her husband.

"I can't judge you and your actions," she told her father, "during this regrettable affair. My husband and I wronged you, but you went far beyond any justifiable revenge. Your bitterness crushed and dishonored a poor man. One act of kindness could've saved us. You didn't understand it or want it, I'm sorry to say. But you will see that I remain faithful to the man I have devoted my life to and the worse his situation is the stronger will be my attachment."

It was at this moment that the authorities arrived. Madame Laurent ran into her husband's arms.

"Courage," she told him, "courage. You'll get through all this trouble. Just a little courage."

"My dear wife! What a tragedy!"

"You can count on me! On my loyalty, my devotion and my everlasting love!"

The investigating judge spoke to the young woman, "Madame, would you allow me to ask you a question?"

"Ask away, your honor."

"It was thanks to your help that Monsieur Laurent was able to pay his 10,000 franc debt?"

"Yes, your honor."

"Where did you get the money to give to your husband?"

Madame Laurent trembled a little as she answered, "But you honor, what does it matter where I got the money? I'm the one who gave it my husband and that's enough to prove that he didn't steal anything from my father."

"I'm sorry but I must insist. This point is, in fact, crucial in your husband's accusation and his defense. Did you go to Laigle to get the money?"

"Yes, your honor."

"And did you find it in Laigle?"

"Yes... in Laigle," she hesitated.

"But not from your father?"

"No, not my father."

"Tell us who gave you the money?"

Madame Laurent saw the risk she was running. And she was trembling. "Oh my, my, dear God!" she stammered.

But Monsieur Laurent came to her side, "It's okay, Octavie, just tell them. You can tell the truth in front of your father... You have to tell the authorities..."

But she continued to hesitate, unable to make up her mind whether to talk or not.

Finally Monsieur Laurent spoke for her. "Faced with her father's refusal my wife went to beg from one of her relatives, an aunt, Aunt Melie."

"And she gave the money?"

"Yes, your honor. It was Aunt Melie."

Monsieur Bilmat stepped forward and shouted, "That's not true! It's a lie!" Everyone looked at him. "It's a lie, Octavie, my daughter, did go to Laigle to see her Aunt Melie. But I saw her the next day and she told me she didn't give a thing to my daughter."

Monsieur Laurent was startled. He grabbed his wife's hand. "Speak up! Tell the truth! Tell them! Tell us! Tell me where you got the money. Who gave it to you?"

Octavie stayed silent.

"It's me asking, not the judge, not your father, but me, your husband. Speak!"

"Don't ask me. I swear that you can take the money without fear... without shame..."

"That's no answer! I want to know! Tell me who gave you the money."

"I can't. But I can tell you, I swear that..."

Laurent exploded in anger, "Damn it! You can't say? If you don't give me the name, it's admitting your guilt! You have a lover! Your Aunt Melie... is a lover. But speak. Admit it! What's one more shame to me now? Admit it! Your lover gave you the money!"

Laurent was furiously shaking his wife's wrists, bruising them. She fell to the ground and he dragged her over the floor. They grabbed him, tried to pull her free. They had to fight with him.

"Leave me alone!" he screamed. "Let me kill her, the wench! Kill her..."

The officers had to slap handcuffs on him. He was threatening Bilmat and cursing his poor, devastated wife, promising the worst vengeance when he got out of prison. It took all the people there plus the neighbors, who had come over at the noise, to wrestle Laurent into a car to take him to the holding cells.

At the holding cells, almost at the same time but in a completely different manner, Pretty Riri was arriving. And the two unfortunate, devastated victims of fate who did not know each other, so far apart were they on the social ladder, were now neighbors in prison. A mysterious bond connected them. A bond of gentleness, affection and devotion... and watching over their misfortune was the precious, admirable soul of Andre Girardet. For one he was an older brother; for the other he was the good Aunt Melie.

32. Cursed and blessed

Riri had an awful night. A heavy sleep, more exhausting than staying awake all night, kept her in a lethargic state infused with hideous nightmares and dreadful fear. In the morning, however, she pulled herself together. Her brave soul got the upper hand and although she cried when she thought of her mother and sister and the horrible night they must have spent in their miserable lodgings, now at least she was regaining her strength, her mind and getting ready to defend herself.

She got information from the nurses and guards. Learning that she had to be accompanied by a lawyer during the interrogation made her feel better. She asked for paper and wrote a telegram to Monsieur Raoul Montreil, attorney, referred by Andre Girardet.

Soon after her arrival Riri was taken to a special infirmary until they signed the order of transport of Saint Lazare prison. Her telegram had not been out long when they announced a visitor.

Riri could never have imagined that her message had been received and Montreil had come running. She was thinking, therefore, that they had probably realized she was innocent at the workshop and sent someone to fetch her. At the same time she was afraid it might be a neighbor coming to tell her something awful happened in her apartment that night. She could not bring herself to believe that the people who were taking care of her, Madame Laurent and Andre Girardet, had heard of her unjust arrest and sent someone to help her in this new ordeal, maybe to save her.

While all these thoughts were rolling around in her mind, they introduced the visitor.

Riri was outraged, thrown into a panic and right away screamed, "You! You here!"

It was the Count de la Gueriniere.

They had brought Riri into one of the rooms where the lawyers talk with their clients. It was furnished with a table, a bench and an old, straw chair. Riri was sitting at the table but when she saw the Count she jumped up and stood in a defensive position.

The Count entered looking as gentle and kind as possible. "Mademoiselle," he said from the doorway, "I heard about your awful misfortune but I cannot believe you are guilty. I come to offer my help, to beg you to let me aid you in proving your innocence."

Riri just let him talk.

"You're alone in the world," he went on, "without money, without support, without a defender. You're a victim and wicked fate inevitably preys on the weak ones like you."

"No, monsieur," Riri replied, "fate is heavy on me at the moment, perhaps, but I have my rights... and I have an powerful protector... justice itself."

"Of course, but it will take time, a very long time and you can't stay here far from people dying of worry outside."

"My sister and my poor mother."

"Yes. So, I took it upon myself to come here as a friend, a defender. I'm rich and I'm powerful. I have the means to give you your freedom, I come to ask you to let me do this for you, to do this favor for you..."

"I refuse. They brought me here and accused me of stealing. This theft will be proven to part of some wicked plot. I intend to leave here only when justice will recognize the mistake... when my innocence and loyalty will be known to all. I intend to leave not by some favor but by my right... and only to the applause of all good honest folk, sure that my place here will be taken by those who set this wicked trap for me."

"But in the meantime, mademoiselle, your mother and sister..."

Riri held up her hand to stop him, "I'm ready for all sorrows."

The Count took a tone of deep sympathy, sentimental commiseration, "Mademoiselle, I have already obtained your pardon. Let me get it by giving me your hand."

"It's no use, monsieur."

"I wronged you. I'm guilty and I'd like to make up for it. I acted badly toward you... but my excuse is the great love, the boundless passion I feel for you and that drove me crazy! My heart deranged my mind and made me do something I regret. That act, oh, I see how cowardly and wretched it was. I want to atone for it. I want you to forget it. I want you to know how sincere my love is. I want you, Riri, my beloved, to respect me! I want to hope that one day you will give me your hand... like to your best, closest friend, to your devoted spouse... who is begging right now for your forgiveness."

Riri replied coldly, "I have no respect for you... and..."

"Ah, you hate me!"

"No, I don't hate you. But I do feel the greatest contempt."

The Count took a step forward, "Don't say that!"

"Please, go away."

"Don't say that, Riri! You're tearing my heart apart!"

Riri spoke haughtily, proudly, "Enough, monsieur! I've heard enough, more than enough... Now go away!"

"Please. Not until you have given me that one word of hope..."

"No! I think you're the vilest, most cowardly, most wicked man! Enough! Go!"

The Count came forward again. He was crying... Riri backed away until her back was against the wall.

The Count opened his arms to take her, "One word, Riri. One single word of pardon... of pity... in the name of what you hold most dear... one word of forgiveness."

"Get back! Leave me alone! Your being here disgusts me. Go away... or I'll call the guard to take you away."

"Riri, my love, please..."

"No!"

"Riri..."

The Count was slowly getting closer, just about to grab Riri when a hand crashed down on his shoulder.

"Come now, monsieur," a voice boomed, "don't you understand? It sounds pretty clear. You disgust her. Now go away."

The Count spun around and stammered, "Raoul Montreil."

Riri escaped and ran to Raoul, "You! Oh, you, you!" she shouted with joy." She hugged him closely. "Oh, defend me! Save me! Take me away from this horrible man!"

"Come on," Raoul said, "how many times do you have to be told to leave?"

"But monsieur..." the Count babbled.

"There's the door. Push it open and leave."

"What right have you..."

"Mademoiselle Menardier has done me the honor of choosing me as her defender. Go! Get out! Without another word. The sight of you is unbearable to us. Go!"

The Count was trembling with rage now, "It's not going to happen like this!"

Raoul was fed up, "Oh, enough! Guard! Come and take this person away!"

The Count jumped at Raoul. The lawyer raised his hand to slap him but the Count blocked it in mid-air.

Now standing face to face, the Count whispered through gritted teeth, "I will kill you."

"Like my father?" Raoul said.

The reply worked like magic. The Count suddenly dropped Raoul's hand and backed away. The guards came rushing in and pinned his arms as they dragged him away.

Raoul held Riri's hand, "Don't be afraid of that wicked man. He can't hurt you now."

"Oh, thank you, monsieur. You're brave, you're good, thank you. But he can hurt you... if you knew what kind of man he is!"

"Don't worry, he just might have finished hurting anyone." Then he added, "But I'm taking you away."

"Taking me away?"

"You are temporarily free while I work hard to prove your innocence."

"You don't think I'm guilty, do you?"

"You, a thief?! Oh, you'd have to have a corrupt mind like those people to imagine that justice can be so blind and that a young woman like you can be found guilty on such flimsy, superficial evidence."

Soon afterward Riri was sitting in a car next to Raoul, her defender. He was preparing her for the awful news awaiting her at home.

Her mother had been alarmed by the men coming to the apartment in the afternoon with Rirette. They had to tell her. They could not hide what was happening.

Marie the hunchback was too burdened with grief to be able to keep the painful secret. Her distress and her tears betrayed her. So, it became unbearable in that poor home and the tragedy that unfolded in that little room is beyond words.

"My daughter a suspect! Riri a thief!" the sick woman cried. "No, it's not true! It's not true!"

It was such a hard blow that she passed out. Marie could not wake her up. She was growing desperate from her useless efforts when Dr. Robert luckily showed up.

"Oh, doctor! Come in, come in… Mama's dying!"

It did not take long for the doctor to see that Marie was not mistaken. Madame Menardier was worn out by so much misery and sorrow and would soon be seeking rest… the eternal rest.

"But," Robert asked, "your mother was getting better lately. How did this happen? What caused this sudden attack?"

The hunchback told him quickly about the dreadful event.

"What?!" the doctor cried out. "Riri… your sister arrested, accused of stealing… but that's crazy! It's shameful! It's impossible! Please, tell me that my brother is her lawyer. He'll take her case… Buck up, it will be all right. You're going to get your sister back. Now come and help me take care of your mother."

But Marie was sobbing, weeping, trying in vain to be of some use to the doctor.

Robert needed medicine that he did not have and honestly he could not send Marie to fetch them. He had decided to go himself to the pharmacy when someone knocked at the door.

"Ah!" Marie the hunchback was trembling. "Who now? What new evil is coming to our home?"

However, encouraged by Robert she went to open the door.

Two men dressed in work clothes stood in the doorway. "We've come from your friend Fernand who will be here soon… after work… to help you out."

"Yes, yes, come in, friends," Robert piped up. "Come in, you can be a big help."

They entered slowly, making as little noise as possible with their big work boots, holding their hat and cap in their hands.

The taller of the two went up to Robert. "If you need something, my friend Le Degourdi can go get it."

Robert said, "Thank you. Your friend can hop out and do two important things for me."

"Whatever you need," Le Degourdi said. "Just tell me."

Robert jotted a few lines on a piece of paper. "This to the telegraph and this other at the pharmacy. Come back quickly... And this note to my brother." He gave him a coin and went back to his patient to wait for the worker to return.

Le Degourdi was fast. He had the medicine sent back and went to take care of the telegram and the note for Monsieur Montreil, attorney. The telegram was for Gabriel, Paulin Broquet's lieutenant.

"Okay," Le Degourdi said, "let's deal with the lawyer first."

He put the telegram in his pocket and got driven to the Montreil house. Raoul was not home yet so he went to the apartment on Rue des Mathurins. He did not find Raoul there either but knowing that the lawyer spent every evening there he left Robert's note and then went by the Court of Justice where he might run into Raoul Montreil.

Le Degourdi did, in fact, meet Raoul who was, you can imagine, struck hard by the news. Right away he went to get Riri's temporary release. But it was too late in the day. Moreover, Riri had just been taken sick to the infirmary and the doctor on duty would not authorize her *exeat* tonight. They had to wait until morning.

Therefore, Raoul went back with the worker to the Menardier home. He got there when soon after the sick woman had woken up. She was holding Marie the hunchback in her frail arms, weakly... and caressing her. Marie was leaning on her mother's chest sobbing.

In the room there were also Fernand, his wife and the sculptor Paul Germault, who had been told.

Slowly, with obvious pain, the sick woman spoke, "Dr. Robert, I owe my last days of rest, of well-being, to you. You're the one who showed me that everything is not dark and evil on earth. It's your heart, your generosity that lightened my suffering. I owe you a debt of gratitude that I will never be able to repay except from on high."

"Madame," Robert said, "please, don't lose hope."

"No, doctor, your science could stretch out my misery for a few days, but this last malice of man is too much to bear." She wept. "My daughter, my Riri, my pretty Rirette, in prison like a criminal! In prison! I'll never see her again!"

Robert told her, "Excuse me, madame, you will have the joy of seeing your daughter again and hugging her because she will be here soon, maybe any minute now."

"How's that?"

"My brother Raoul is a lawyer. I just sent him a telegram. He'll take up your daughter's defense, do what needs to be done, and you will see Riri."

Just then the lawyer and the worker showed up.

"Here's my brother!" Dr. Robert cried out. "Well? Where's Riri?"

Raoul saw that he had to lie. "Free. It was a case of mistaken identity. She's innocent. She'll be here any moment. One last formality to take care of… and she'll be here."

The sick woman held out her hands, "Oh, thank you, monsieur! Thank you both. You are giving me my final joy."

Madame Menardier, however, looked weaker every minute. Despite Robert's care life was quitting this weary body. The soul was longing to be free of the prison where it had suffered so much. She passed out again and Robert had a hard time bringing her around.

Weakly, in a whisper, she asked, "Is Riri here?"

"Not yet, mother, but she won't be long."

"Oh, I'll never see her again… I'll never see her…"

"Mama! Mama!"

The dying woman said, "Are you there, doctor? And you monsieur lawyer?"

"Yes, madame, we're right here."

"Good. I don't want to leave with this secret in my heart. Dr. Robert, listen… Monsieur lawyer… You do what you have to… for my children… for my orphans…"

She paused before continuing.

"My husband was a man of honor, a hard worker… loyal… he amassed a fortune and owned a big factory with one of his childhood friends as a partner. He put all his trust in this man, gave him his signature and deposited money in his bank. But this man was a thief, a criminal and my husband was ruined. He wanted to save a little for his family so he went back to this old friend and, messieurs, that night they brought my husband's body back to me… shot to death. What had happened? Did he commit suicide? Did his friend kill him? Either way I was a widow and my poor children destined to poverty."

The sick woman was wearing herself out by talking. Her voice became softer and softer. Robert and Raoul were leaning over her bed, closer and closer.

"Madame," they said, "reparations will be made. The money will come back. Your children…" They could not finish. As if the earth opened up beneath them they collapsed. They fell on their knees with their heads against the dying woman's bed.

"It was the banker Montreil!" Madame Menardier said. "Montreil the usurer! Montreil whose name means theft, infamy, death! Curses on the banker Montreil!"

It was the last glimmer of life from the dying woman. She sank into her pillows. And even more weakly, her voice coming from a distance:

"But you… I bless you. Robert, Raoul… I bless you… I entrust my children to you, to your generous hearts, your noble souls. I entrust my poor Marie and my pretty Rirette… Riri… to you, thank you, Robert and Raoul… Blessings for you."

She tried to raised her hands, but he could only, barely lay them on the bowed heads of the kneeling, sobbing brothers.

"Robert… Raoul… Marie… Riri… my children, I bless you…"

She died quietly. And a trustful, kind smile finally crossed her face.

The worker who had come earlier with his comrade stepped up to the bed.

"Rest in peace, madame," he said solemnly. "The orphans, your children, are not alone in this cruel world."

He closed the dead woman's eyes and lightly touched the brothers' shoulders.

"Come, messieurs, come away."

The two young men struggled to their feet and followed the worker into the next room where the door was closed quietly.

"Messieurs, get a hold of yourselves. Your grief is going to betray you."

"Ah, my friend, if only you knew!"

"I know, monsieur Raoul Montreil. And Dr. Montreil."

The two brothers were surprised. "What? How do you know?"

"Well, I'm the only one here, don't worry. No one heard you addressed by name. The poor woman was speaking too low. Only you could hear her."

"What about Marie?"

"She fainted a while ago. She didn't hear anything. She knows nothing. So, you sons of the Banker Montreil are the only ones who know the secret that the poor woman was keeping."

"We also know our duty." Raoul asked, "But who are you? Why are you here?"

"I came without intending to witness this tragic scene. I'm here to right a wrong, to save an innocent girl and to root out the clever man who's guilty… to fight Zigomar!" Then the worker told the brothers, "On your honor, don't betray me."

He took off his wig and showed himself.

"Paulin Broquet!" they gasped together.

He shook their hands cordially.

"Now, gentlemen, we each have our jobs to do, working toward the same goal, so let's wish each other luck and courage. The hour of justice is at hand. Let's go!"

Zigomar

20^c LE VOLUME

par LÉON SAZIE

BOOK THREE: TIME FOR JUSTICE

1. The poet is discreet

The pioneer poet Anthime Soufret was unquestionably and, as he himself asserted, an extraordinary, original genius in poetry.

He only felt really at home when he was wandering in the upper regions of the ether, when he was soaring like an eagle... but in the boring, down-to-earth life of a simple mortal, he was naïve and astoundingly innocent. Just as few people (among the gifted) managed to understand his complicated poetry, so he (this genius creature) understood nothing about the simplest matters of everyday life. And he was completely lost, like a plucked chicken, when a situation he was involved in took a dramatic turn.

Now, two or three weeks after the theft of the necklace, he could not, because of his special, extra-sensitive, extra-delicate nature, he could not get over the violence he had felt in the elegant but evil apartment of his fervent admirer and faithful friend, the unfortunate Count de Marnais.

The sudden death of the Count de Marnais was called an accident. At another time it might have an effect on him even though in reality nothing in the world was more important than himself whose every movement, every word—he believed—was of interest to the entire universe.

But since his adventure in the bachelor's apartment he bore a grudge against the Count de Marnais. His friend's death left him cold and he could not, even for a second, waste any thought on it... and especially not a word of verse.

Thus he, the poet, got his revenge for that evening at the Count's when he was caught between two thieves: the American James Twill and the other gentleman. Just the thought of it gave Anthime Soufret goose bumps (despite being an eagle). Later, still outraged, for the umpteenth time, just between friends, he told the story of that tragic night to one of his sincere admirers. He was a fervent disciple with a big felt hat, a mess of long hair, a pointy beard that drooped over his broad black scarf that served as a tie and replaced a vest, maybe even a shirt as well, a true poet himself from the school of Anthime Soufret. This disciple, when he was not feeding of the wonderful verses off the pioneer, when he was not drifting in the majestic radiance of the sun that was Anthime Soufret, this disciple was known by the name of Baiter.

A few days later the pioneer agreed to grant his disciple a favor: he would take him out to dinner. So, they went to the Café des Artistes on Rue Lepic, which they usually call La Bonbonniere in the world of art and letters. Between the healthy soup, the veal escalope, the homemade pie and apple jam that he wolfed down, he told again, mostly for the sake of the nearby diners, the adventure to his disciple who knew it only too well but still, out of respect, pretended to be as outraged and as astounded as all the previous times.

At a nearby table a customer had sat down almost at the same time as them. He was, it was thought, a painter. He had white hair and a long white beard. Like everyone he was listening to their conversation without saying a word.

"No matter what," the pioneer was saying, "whatever they do, the thieves and pickpockets, American or otherwise, even the famous Zigomar himself, will be cheated themselves if they attack us again."

"How's that?" Baiter asked.

"Because the Baroness has taken precautions."

"By doing what?"

"She put her jewelry in her husband's safe. And this safe in his office is a monument, an impregnable fortress that no one can break into."

"Good safeguard indeed. But unfortunately a little late, like all good safeguards... because that river... of diamonds... is flowing far away... if it's still flowing at all."

"Wrong, my friend," the poet said. "The river came back."

"What?!" Baiter was startled.

"Didn't I tell you?"

"No."

"Well, it's the strangest thing. Go figure that two or three days ago the Baroness was called secretly to the police station."

"For the theft?"

"No, for the recuperation. The chief told her, 'Madame, nothing of this will leave the station, nothing will be made public. Rest assured! We know that they robbed you of your rings, expensive jewelry and a diamond necklace you were wearing that night at the Guttlach party'."

"How did the police know all this?" Baiter asked. "That's impossible."

"Bah! That's what they're there for. I'll continue. The chief said, 'We also know under what circumstances the crime was committed, despite the efforts of Anthime Soufret'..."

"So, he knew everything?"

"That's his job. Why are you so surprised? I'll go on. He said, 'Now, one of my agents was lucky enough to get his hands on a cat burglar... an American called James Twill."

"Your thief?"

"Our thief, exactly. Stop interrupting!"

"Sorry, it won't happen again."

"Good, I'll continue. The American James Twill, who is part of the Zigomar gang..."

Even though he promised not to interrupt the pioneer, the faithful disciple, when he heard the name Zigomar, could not help crying out, "No! Zigomar?" And as if it was something both frightful and fantastic, he added, "You were robbed by Zigomar?"

Modest as always, the poet nodded and his long hair swept over the table. "Exactly! By Zigomar!"

To affect Anthime Soufret like this nothing less would do! It took the most famous, the most terrible, the most dangerous criminal in all of Europe... of America... of the universe... it took Zigomar!

The name pronounced aloud made every table at the Bonbonniere start talking, commenting, calling up memories and telling stories of new exploits. Everyone had something to say about Zigomar.

Only a Scottish cartoonist, whose face was hidden beneath his bushy hair and thick black beard, only his eyes shining like a Venetian mask in all that hair, denied Zigomar. Being a humorist he had an accent from Toulouse. And he never shared the public opinion, professing only his own infallible judgment.

"Zigomar," he spoke calmly, almost chanting, "what a story! I've never seen him, so he doesn't exist!"

Next to him a writer who was bald with a hint of a moustache jumped in his seat. He knew Paulin Broquet. He had been to the Barbottiere, interviewed Zulma and he had seen Zigomar! Yes, Zigomar, the invisible master—he had seen him!

The two friends were arguing about Zigomar when Anthime Soufret interrupted. To demand silence the pioneer raised his hand, the hand that plucked the golden lyre but that was not often washed and whose uncut nails were rimmed with black as if for mourning.

He said, "So, the police chief added: 'This American James Twill of the Zigomar gang was arrested by one of my officers. They searched his rooms and found many beautiful pieces of jewelry among which was one superb river of diamonds.' After careful questioning the acolyte ended up confessing that he had stolen the necklace from the Baroness Van Cambre. He told them where and how."

"So the Baroness got her diamonds back?"

"Yes. In return she left a little donation to the Emergency Fund. And to thank the officer who got her jewels back, to send him a little something, she asked for his name... It was the famous detective Paulin Broquet."

"Paulin Broquet!" Baiter said. "Oh, of course, I've heard of him. They say he's very clever."

Casually, as if it were nothing, the poet who recognized nobody's superiority except his own, responded, "So it seems. But we don't need his cleverness anymore. Now the diamonds are safe and secure, beyond the reach of thieves... even the famous Zigomar can't crack the Baron's safe."

"Let's hope so."

"It's sure. Moreover, for more peace of mind, I told the Baroness that I myself would never more go outside with her, with or without her jewelry."

"That's wise."

"You see, don't you? In these dangerous rendezvous I can't risk compromising my quality as a poet, my elevated character as a pioneer... the dignity of the great mission given to me in this world."

Baiter said he understood perfectly well and he agreed wholeheartedly with the poet's wise and prudent decision. Without blinking he said, "A poet like you can't run the risks of a simple mortal."

"No!" Soufret approved.

"But," Baiter hinted, "that means you have to stop your poetry and musical evenings with the Baroness."

The poet shook his head, making his hair swish like a flyswatter across his forehead filled with so many wonderful thoughts.

"Not at all, no," he said. And as if he were the embodiment of discretion, confidentially, he raised his voice. "On the contrary. The evenings will take place at the Baroness' house from now."

"At her house?"

"Yes. It's much safer there. And much less bothersome for me." Still with the same discretion he declared, "I can even tell you, my dear friend, that on Thursday next I will have with the Baroness... an evening... and after dinner a new piece of music that the Baroness composed for my verses."

"Next Thursday?" his faithful disciple said casually.

"Yes."

On hearing this painter with the white beard automatically turned to the poet and his disciple. His strange eyes stared at them, seeming very interested in everything that was said.

"Why next Thursday?" Baiter asked. "Is it a weekly event or just this once?"

"It's a date chosen by circumstance," Soufret answered. "In fact, the Baron has a big dinner that night with his stockholders and there's some party or something that the servants asked to go to. The Baroness gave them the night off, keeping only the cook and the butler to serve us." Then, admirably oblivious, he added, "Thus we'll have the whole house to ourselves, completely deserted, silent, calm... We'll be able to enjoy my poetry without anyone or anything bothering us... and listen to the music, too, of course. Oh, it's going to be a wonderful evening!"

To savor the charm of next Thursday evening a little early, he willingly accepted the glass of beer that Baiter offered him in a café in Place Blanche. Baiter lit his pipe and did not listen to the pioneer poet talking about his genius. But there came a moment when the buzz of pompous, empty words started to tire him. It was also time for him to meet his boss. He paid for the drinks and dragged the poet out.

Anthime Soufret had talked well and drunk well. His legs were having trouble supporting his glory. He walked as crooked as his verses. Baiter held his arm to cross Place Blanche, then led him up Rue Lepic. He left him by the house where the poet had his room, where he believed he towered over Paris, where he could look out the attic window and see the City of Lights stretch out as if on bended knees before him.

Presently Baiter was at Broquet's, where he was giving his report. What mainly interested Paulin Broquet was the date the poet had made with the baroness next week.

"All right," the detective said, "it's clear as day now that if there's not already something in the works for Zigomar, then he certainly won't miss his chance next Thursday."

Baiter said, "So, Soufret's being trailed by the Zs…"

"Maybe it's for his golden verses," Broquet laughed.

"More likely for some information about the Baroness that he can't just ask the Baron."

"Most likely."

"You know, boss, at the restaurant there was an old painter with a big white beard who tried not to show it but was listening hard to everything the poet said about his ethereal trysts with the Baroness."

"And the painter was Baron Dupont, right?"

"You got it."

"All right."

Paulin Broquet kept silent. He lit another cigarette before speaking again.

"So, the job's set for next Thursday evening. Perfect! We'll see about that…"

2. The beautiful stranger

The dance was in full swing at Clafous'. The waltz fans were having the time of their lives. The dance hall at the Enfants de l'Aveyron rang out with shouts of joy and the perky giggles of young women that sang along with the bare-bones orchestra.

Around a table near the back in a dark corner three men sat in front of their glasses of the famous old Aveyron wine. They were watching the dancers and the people who came to see the dance.

One of these men was rather old. He wore a dirty, misshapen, gray hat and had a bushy, white beard. His shining nose drooped almost all the down to the stubby, blackened pipe stuck in the corner of his mouth. He looked like an old worker who had had done all kinds of work but whose week usually had more than one weekend in it.

The other man, however, was elegant and well dressed in perfectly bad taste, very fashionable for certain types of people who came to Clafous'. He wore a dark suit, white socks in polished shoes, a shirt with colored stripes and a very high collar surrounded by a bright pink tie with a diamond pin. He also had big rings on his fingers. A handsome young man with bright blue eyes, a thin black moustache tracing a mouth with sharp teeth, a jutting chin and a generally tough, cruel look. He was typical of those gentlemen who, thanks to their masculine, brutal beauty and their hard fists, find easy living off the charm of hatless or gussied-up women who wait on corners or walk the streets or frequent the music halls and night clubs.

As for the third, with his bearded face and a gray hat lowered over his eyes he was dressed as a worker. Smoking a wooden pipe he watched the room, listened to his friends but spoke little, saying only one word or just nodding and shaking his head as a comment.

Several times the three men answered the greetings of people passing by their table. But generally they looked too absorbed in the words of the old man. The younger man was furrowing his brow and flicking the ashes of his cigarette with a sharp, violent movement.

"My boy," the white beard said, "I believe we're being a little slack... we're slowing down."

"Why do you say that, uncle?"

"We start a job that takes a lot of time, playing for big stakes but getting little out of it."

"I don't agree with you."

"It's been a while since our men have got anything."

"Because they don't work."

"They're grumbling."

"Let em grumble. They'll be singing a different tune when we make a big payout."

"Sure, but when?"

"Soon." The nephew was getting impatient. "Our men know that we can't make a payout every week. They're not wageworkers. They're partners suffering the fluctuations of the business. So what do they have to complain about?"

"They think we're failing too often."

"Yeah? They say that?"

"Not in those words but they're thinking it aloud."

"The louts! They're useless for anything but robbing rich villas, working in the suburbs or in the maid's room... Fools! Creeps! They're happy to share 40 sous, to get away with half a dozen teaspoons or a tin clock!"

"They only understand immediate profit."

"Our operations are for the long-term, sure, but they'll be rolling in it."

"They haven't been happy."

"That's not our fault, but everything will be all right. We're here tonight to give orders, to prepare everything."

"For Thursday?"

"Right. We have to get our revenge... for the necklace." Laughing, he added, "I think there'll be a big payoff this time."

They uncle waggled his white beard, "Yes, I think so too. Now, my boy, let me tell you something because we can talk here in peace... You're jeopardizing yourself and wasting time by taking useless risks chasing after your Riri."

The nephew jumped. "Uncle, I know where you're going but we've already talked about it."

"Riri almost cost us dearly a few times. For no good reason in my opinion. Look, she's pretty, I get it, but there are others just as pretty... and who are a lot easier to get."

"They're not Riri."

"So you're really in love?"

"Maybe."

Uncle grabbed nephew's arm and shook it. "But, boy, you can't fall in love!"

"No!" the gray hat barked out now.

"Yes. When love is not only a heart full of joy but also a pocket full of cash. Riri is gorgeous, one of a kind..."

"What good's that do?"

"And Riri is also about to come into millions, you know this as well as I do."

"Sure, but..."

"We found it out in the Montreil's papers about the Menardier family. It's for this as much as for her exquisite charms that I'm chasing Riri. I tried to compromise her, to trick her into becoming my wife. It's only by becoming her husband that I can start the process of getting back the millions stolen by the good old banker Montreil."

"Okay."

"My plan backfired. I came up with stealing that lace and arresting her. I was hoping that she would panic and fall into my arms when I came to free her."

"Raoul got there," gray hat said. "Complete failure."

"And today," uncle continued, "the Montreil sons, the naïve boys, are giving back the money earned by their charitable father. Riri is going to come into a fortune… and our latest information says that Riri loves Raoul. So, why do you want to keep chasing her?"

The nephew slammed his fist on the table and gritted his teeth. With his eyes full of hatred he snarled, "Because I love Riri! There!"

"You're crazy," gray hat said. "Yes, completely whacko!"

"Maybe, but I love her. I want her. You hear me, I want her! And when I want something, nothing can stand in my way. Yes, I want her and I'll have her. Whether as my wife or my mistress I'll have her. I want revenge for my first failure at the villa. I also want revenge on Raoul. I have to make him pay for slapping me in front of Riri. You get it, I want revenge on Raoul and Riri and I can't except like this… by taking Riri!"

The old uncle shook his head. "You'd do better to leave everything alone and start concentrating on our next operation that mustn't fail."

"Oh, that I can do."

"One last piece of advice: since you're so in love, you might as well throw yourself in the river…" It was obviously a play on words. It brought a smile to the face of the nephew.

But almost at the same time this smile, just crossing his face, was replaced by a scowl. "Look! Over there!"

The nephew nodded toward a couple on the dance floor. Gray hat had also seen them. A shiver ran down his spine and despite himself a curse in English escaped his lips. The three men watched on anxiously.

A young man, well built, with the face of a brute, whom they called the "Terror of Ornano" and a tall, shapely woman with dark eyes and red lips that parted slightly into a smile revealing the teeth of a young wolf. She was radiantly beautiful with dazzling fair skin under the braids of thick black hair.

Men stepped aside as the woman advanced and started to waltz. Murmurs of admiration, humming desires and eyes staring madly as she danced.

It was an indescribable moment when the passionate frenzy broke loose from all these strong young men living for love and the need for crime, which hand in hand with this brutal love.

Everyone stretched their necks trying to get a whiff of the inebriating perfume that exhaled from the twirling beauty who showed up for the first time tonight. Their hands automatically clenched the revolvers in their pockets or caressed the silent but deadly switchblades.

There certainly would have been a fierce battle for this woman right away, blood spilled for the conquest... but she was in the arms of the "Terror of Ornano"... and even the most heated of them held back.

"Look!" the nephew said again.

"I see," gray hat said.

"Me too," the uncle looked not only surprised but angry and worried as well.

Then the three men stood up. They took up posts among the crowd where the two dancers were sure to leave when they were finished. But at the same as the three of them, two men, two peaceful workers who were sitting at a nearby table also stood up.

One of them asked, "You're sure now?"

"Yes, boss," the other answered. "No doubt about it. That's Baron Dupont."

"And the other?"

"I don't know him."

"That's my dear colleague Tom Tweak."

"The American detective!"

"None other. But the third... Oh, I think it's him but he's got a really good disguise so I'm not sure."

The two men were (you've already guessed) the detective Paulin Broquet and Baiter who still came to Clafous' for information, trying to find out if, as they suspected, as they were led to believe at the Bonbonniere by the pioneer poet's indiscretions, something really was being prepared for next Thursday.

The dance ended and the dark-haired waltzer along with the "Terror of Ornano" left the floor. They crossed through a row of panting, trembling men ready to pounce. The Terror had slipped his arm around the neck of the woman and his big hand engulfed her left shoulder. He held her tightly against him to show everyone that she was his, no question about it... and before touching her the toughest of the fighters and the king of the pimps would have to go through him. No need to say that no one moved a finger.

But the Terror of Ornano and his new girl passed right through Clafous' establishment. They had come, apparently, only for one dance. It was obviously a big enough success for them.

So, they left the Enfants de l'Aveyron like a royal couple between two rows of admirers and courtiers. Then, still holding each other, they slowly turned onto Boulevard de la Chapelle.

At this time of night the boulevard was dark and deserted. On the sidewalks where the seedy cabarets cast their pale lights, under the huge arches of the Metro forming dark and dangerous shelters, a few pedestrians were scurrying by. Gusts of wind whirled and hurled through the shrill whistles or rumbling growls of the locomotives lumbering back into the Gare du Nord.

The beautiful stranger with velvety eyes and her formidable companion walked side by side, hugging intimately at the slightest sound on this grim street. The Terror of Ornano knew his strength and believed he was safe in this regard, his realm. He bragged about his conquests of love all the while squeezing her more tightly and kissing her dark hair that was held back by a black velvet ribbon.

But the Terror was suddenly interrupted in his wooing. Three or four men jumped on them, tearing him away from his gorgeous dancer. Two of them tried to drag her away. But it only took a few seconds for the Terror to snap out of his surprise. He shook off his enemies like a wild boar freeing himself from the dogs biting his ears. He got hold of them but in the process slipped on the curb and fell to the ground. The battle went on just as fierce in the gutter.

For her part, the young woman fought valiantly against her would-be kidnappers. She swung around and grabbed an arm, bent it back and threw the attacker to the ground as he screamed in pain with a broken arm. Right away she jumped on the second assailant and grabbed his throat, trying to get him in a chokehold. But the man knew jiu-jitsu. He knew how to parry her attack. She fell back but only to prepare another offensive.

Now the other two men left the Terror on the ground and came up on either side of her, ready to grab her if she tried anything. The young woman stopped in her tracks, but showed no fear. She took a few steps back, not to run away but only to widen the field... and all of a sudden she threw out her right hand.

The three men backed away, screaming in pain and covering their eyes that were being burnt by some corrosive liquid. The free woman ran up the boulevard. As she passed through a circle of light from the streetlamp, from under the dark hair that had been mussed up in the battle, a golden stream of reddish hair escaped.

"Her!" someone shouted. "Boss, I'm sure of it!"

"Go!" a second voice said.

And Baiter, watching the scene with Paulin Broquet from the shadows of a Metro pillar, ran after the mysterious dancer. She had crossed an empty lot where a car was waiting for her on the other side with its engine running. The woman opened the door and jumped in.

"Let's go!"

As she turned to close the door, right next to her on the backseat, Baiter dove into the car. But he screamed immediately and covered his eyes, blinded like the other enemies by some acid spray.

The woman grabbed his wrists and tried to wrestle him out of the still open door as the car sped away. In the glare of headlights, however, she saw Baiter's face.

"Oh!" she uttered with surprise. "You! Why? What a pity! You, a 'broquet'!"

Then she closed the door and looked at Baiter again.

"Don't worry. What you're feeling right now, what's blinding you is not dangerous. It's just strong perfume mixed with alcohol… Wait a second, let me throw some water on your face and in a few seconds the burning will stop."

She opened a drawer in the car, which looked customized like Broquet's, grabbed a thin sponge, a small carafe of water and washed out Baiter's eyes. The pain disappeared. Baiter was able to open his eyes.

"Feel better?"

"Pretty much."

"Phew. I hope your wonderful boss Paulin Broquet forgives me for what I'm about to do to his brave lieutenant."

These words were barely out of her mouth when she threw a hood over his head. Inside this hood was full of cotton and, just like with Zigomar, a tube of chloroform. Baiter tried to fight back but the redhead held him fast and in no time at all he lost consciousness.

3. The Terror of Ornano

Paulin Broquet and Baiter were not witnesses to the street fight by pure chance. When the Terror of Ornano had left the dance with the stunning beauty they had seen the others follow them. The others were Tom Tweak, the fashionable Baron Dupont and the mysterious nephew who signaled to a few customers in the Enfants d'Aveyron.

This small group trailed behind the couple, who suspected nothing, and attacked without warning. Apparently they wanted to grab the woman for Zigomar. But the stranger with the black wig managed (as we've seen) to escape her enemies. So, after missing their chance they just left the Terror of Ornano in the gutter. The half-blind leading the blind, they vanished into the dark streets.

The Terror stood up and looked around for his enemies. He was furious, cursing up a storm, shouting threats, waving his huge arms and shaking his iron fists when all of a sudden his hands were caught in mid-air by steel cuffs... he was arrested, silenced and immobilized. Totally stunned by this new fiasco that was more surprising than the first, the Terror felt himself lifted up and thrown into a car that came screaming up to the curb.

Baiter woke up the next morning in the Saint Jacques police station. He had been found sleeping soundly on a bench on Boulevard Saint Michel and brought back by two policemen who led him slowly through the streets. After a long nap that nothing could bring him out of he had a lot of trouble getting himself recognized by the chief who could not understand how a lieutenant of Paulin Broquet ended up in such a situation and even more astonishing that he could not explain it himself. The comic side of this curious adventure did not escape the special agent who had unconsciously broken the law and spent the night in jail...

The Terror of Ornano, on the other hand, was brought to jail by Paulin Broquet. The next day they brought him into to see the chief. The Terror raised hell, yelling for his lawyer. Two guards were there to hold him fast but they let him scream at will. When he got tired of yelling Baumier and Broquet finally came into the room.

The Terror wanted to start protesting again but the Chief of Police cut him off, "Be quiet! Don't yell. We don't want to keep you."

"First of all, I didn't do anything," the Terror shouted. "They attacked me. I just fought back myself. It was legal self-defense."

Broquet spoke up, "I said as much to Monsieur Baumier. It's me who arrested you."

"You? Paulin Broquet? Good Lord, I knew it. Only Paulin Broquet could do that to someone like me." He paused for a second then said, "So you saw, right? You know I didn't do anything."

"That's right."

"You're not keeping me?"

"No."

The Chief said, "I already told you that."

"Sure, sure, you told me… but with all due respect, I'd like Paulin Broquet to tell me so."

"Oho!" Baumier raised his voice, "So you don't believe me?"

"Course I do… only… with Broquet it's more sure."

Such was the power that Paulin Broquet wielded among the worst criminals, the most dangerous men like this one. Everyone feared the detective, they trembled at the mention of his name, but everyone also knew him to be strong, brave and honest and they admired him for it. They knew he was just and loyal and even though they were enemies they recognized his power and knew that he might always fight but he would never betray.

Like all his peers the Terror preferred Broquet's word to the Chief's assurance. And the Chief knew it but took no offense.

"So, Monsieur Broquet, tell it to the Terror."

Broquet said, "You're free. You can go in a minute. You just have to give us a little information."

"About my partners, never! Look, Broquet, don't even ask me."

"Not about your partners. Here, I'll take off the handcuffs before asking. You'll see."

"Okay, Broquet. I see I can answer without any tricks."

"To assure you even more," the Chief said, "I'll let Broquet ask the questions."

"Right, I'd prefer that, if you don't mind."

So Paulin Broquet started questioning the Terror of Ornano.

"The woman you were dancing with last night at Clafous'… she's new, not from your neighborhood. Who is she?"

Faced with questions that in no way affected his honor as a man of the streets, the Terror took no time to answer, "To tell you truth, Broquet, I don't really know much myself. Who is she? No idea. Where'd she come from? She didn't want to tell me. She said 'I'm here. Isn't that enough? You don't need to know where I come from or how I got here.'"

"How'd you meet her?"

"One night as I was going into Clafous' she stepped in front of me and said 'You're the Terror of Ornano, aren't you? Good, I have to talk to you.' I said we should go in but she said 'No, not here, not today.' She dragged me into another bar where we talked. I watched her. I didn't know her, never even seen a woman as beautiful as her."

"Her name?"

"Call me what you want is what she told me."

"Is she your mistress?"

"No. No, she's not my mistress."

"Oh!"

"That surprise you? Me too... but I'm telling the truth. It's the first time a woman's been with me for more than hour without me staking my claim as boss in this neighborhood... but she..."

"She's not from the neighborhood."

"No. Besides, you can imagine, she's not like the others. Is she from high society? I've seen them too. Plenty. Big names, important names. Now being snobs is in their blood, their main vice I think and they get bored with their husbands and lovers so they come looking for men down here, in the underbelly. And the tough guys treat them hard, hurt them and make them scared... give em a taste of crime. These pretty dames, all perfumed and anemic, need the stench of dives and the traces of blood on the hands of murderers who they want to be their lovers... You know how it is from the feathered crowd that ends up in court. It's the same for the rich. When a woman's committed a crime, they all fall madly in love."

"We can skip all that. What about her?"

"Not like the others. No fuss and bother, no swooning, no trembling. She's got nerve, a strong will... all calm. Look, when I tried to get too close to her, to show her like the others what I'm the boss, maybe giving her a little slap like you have to do sometimes, she caught my wrist, held fast, twisted my arm back with her little hand and forced me down to my knees. Me, the Terror or Ornano kneeling before a woman!"

"And then?"

"She just said 'I give the orders. You have to obey me. I do as I want, when I want. I need a strong man. You're the strongest so I chose you for what I need. If you want to obey me, shake hands and we've got a deal. If not, goodbye and good riddance.' She was even more beautiful... I had to obey."

"What did she want?"

"Oh, a fantasy. Go into the Enfants d'Aveyron and dance. But she didn't want to go alone and be bothered by other men. She thought that with me on her arm they'd leave her alone."

"Which is what happened."

"Right. She also wanted to see members of the Z gang."

"Oh?" Broquet was really intrigued now. "Why?"

"She didn't say. She asked me if I was a Z. I said no. You know it's true. I'm my own master. I don't need a gang, to work for someone else, right? I'm the Terror or Ornano. Right, I live like all 'Terrors' but I'm honest. I'm not into blood, you know that, Broquet."

"Yes. Go on."

"So I said I wasn't a Z but I had friends who were. And I'd show her them. She asked if I knew Zigomar."

"Ah, Zigomar... why Zigomar? Did she want to meet him?"

"Seems so. Except I told her that nobody knows Zigomar, they obey him without knowing him. He's the invisible master, with all the power and fear… but nobody knows who he is."

"She was satisfied with your response."

"She had to be. Except she kept asking where the Zs met after Clafous'."

"What'd you say?"

"I said the Zs used to be at the Barbottiere but they blew it up to kill Paulin Broquet. And she shouted at me 'They tried to kill Paulin Broquet at the Barbottiere?' Sure, I said, but Broquet's all alone stronger than all the Zs put together."

"You flatter me."

"No, everybody knows it."

"Let's get back to your pretty companion."

"After the Barbottiere, I said, Zigomar and his men met at Madame Zulma's but they blew that up too, once again trying to kill Paulin Broquet."

"I have a hard life."

"That's what she said… laughing. But I told her that Zigomar had tortured a poor devil who looked like Broquet and they blew him up with dynamite thinking he was the real Paulin Broquet. As for Broquet himself, he was strolling around somewhere else that night. Proof is that here you are and the other guy is dead and buried. Oh, that one made her laugh. Really cracked her up. Then she asked me if I'd heard about a new job. I said I wasn't sure but the Zs would be at Clafous' as usual to get their orders, to know when to meet at the new Barbottiere…"

"And where is the third Barbottiere?"

"That I can't say. Nobody knows yet. They talk about the Caveau de la Baleine on Rue Jonas… barrière d'Italie. But it's not for sure. She told me 'Forget about it. Let's dance.' I took her to Clafous' and it was great. All the boys were ready to kill for this woman. Oh, if she wasn't with me, even in the Enfants, they would've brought out their knives for her." Then turning angry the Terror continued, "And I was a complete idiot. I should've kept an eye out when we left. They were too hot… so the cowards, it took a bunch of them, jumped me. They took her away! But I would've got her back, for sure, but you got me… and here I am." He concluded, "Now I've lost honor…"

"Why?"

"Because I didn't protect the woman with me. And I'll have to get revenge. There will be a lot of fighting, but you're my witness, Broquet… I didn't start it. And I'll be justified… even if I have to kill someone."

"Okay, okay," the detective said, "Everything will work out. First of all, listen up and calm down: they didn't take your woman."

"They didn't take her?"

"No, because she defended herself. She took down three men."

"Three! Sweet! I'm telling you, she's as strong as a Terror... if he were a woman."

"And she got away alone in a car. And I believe, my friend, that you won't see her again. Neither you nor the others."

"How's that?"

"She saw what she wanted to see. She saw Clafous' dance and the Z gang. Her curiosity is satisfied. Now she'll go trying to satisfy her thirst for adventure and use those extraordinary powers in her little hands."

As the Terror of Ornano was staring dumbfounded at him, Broquet patted him kindly on the shoulder.

"Now you can go. You're free. But believe me, don't try to pick a fight with your old friends. They've got nothing to do with all this. It's all about Zigomar."

"Zigomar?"

"Yes. Now, since Zigomar is untouchable, you'll be wasting your time trying to fight him. But you're free to do what you want with his gang."

"You'd like that, wouldn't you, Broquet?"

"I reserve my opinion."

"Okay, but the woman, what's become of her?"

"Go and find her," Broquet laughed. "Look for her. We're always looking for the woman."

Soon afterward he got the Terror of Ornano released by the police. He told the Chief, "This guy is a marvel of brute force, but not an ounce of brains. Zigomar always refused to use him because he's afraid of his stupidity. They can't trust him. Without even realizing, he'll tell you everything he knows."

"I saw that."

"We got everything we needed from him. Now he'll go off and start looking for the mysterious beauty with golden red hair."

4. A charming evening

Just as the wonderful pioneer had unwittingly told his disciple Baiter, on the following Thursday Baroness Van Cambre gave the night off to all the staff, keeping only the cook and the butler to serve her dinner. And the Baron went off to dine with the stockholders.

Paulin Broquet, in fact, knew where the stockholder dinner was being held. Among the waiters there was the clown Simon with a mission to make sure that the Count de la Gueriniere came and stayed.

The dinner was basically like most stockholder dinners: a wild night with friends of the same social circle and some pretty women. It was a "charming soirée" as the poets say.

The men were dressed to the hilt and the women made up deliciously. Baron Van Cambre was between two singers bound for the Opera and the Opera-Comique who were looking in finance and politics for some "strings to pull". The very pretty singers were giggling at every word the very rich baron was saying to them.

Nearby the financier Guttlach was very taken with a little dancer to whom he whispered (in his typical accent) things that he thought were extremely witty and made the dancer snort with laughter. He was smitten. They had guaranteed him that the little dancer was not yet 17 years old. She was very cute and let him believe it. But it was more likely that this thin, bony, even scrawny little thing with a baby's haircut had passed 17 a good seven or eight years ago. But we are happy with illusions. Guttlach only like little girls and was quick (philosophically) to love only those who looked like such.

As for the Count de la Gueriniere, he was, as always, amusing, cheerful, world-wise and witty. He told the beaming financier, "Watch out, old friend, you'll be eaten by rats. Rats with their baby teeth bite harder..."

Lucette Minois had been at dinner but left to get on stage on time. She was supposed to come back to meet the Count after the show.

And the party went on merrily. It looked like it would not finish until the wee hours of the morning.

In the meantime, in Baron Van Cambre's house, the imposing and tender Baroness was dining very poetically with the pioneer Anthime Soufret. With dinner finished coffee was served in the little salon. The Baroness' jeweled fingers dropped sugar into the poet's cup. Then she started on the piano for him to digest the nice meal with music.

She was an excellent musician as it happened and cradled him in waves of harmony. "I composed this," she cooed, "thinking of you, my poet."

Soufret made a patronizing gesture with his hand, then sat back to digest his meal after the baroness had his empty cup taken away. The scrawny pioneer whose normal meal consisted of liver pâté, for whom veal escalope with spinach was a feast and who on really festive occasions might treat himself to a Bercy steak, this scrawny pioneer at the moment, with his eyes half-closed, had sunk blissfully down into the soft armchair. With his hands folded over his belly—his belly full of so many good things this evening—he was dozing off peacefully... in music.

He let the stupor from the fine wine carry his mind away to a blue country where poets like himself were appreciated for their true value. A heaven in which the odalisques, those Turkish concubines, both lithesome and ample at the same time, were flitting about amongst the incense and flowers with an ideal smile, offering the poets like him, on golden trays, the best foie gras and truffles, pouring frothy ambrosia into their gem-studded goblets!

All of a sudden it felt like a disaster struck the land. It was like some terrifying earthquake that threw him down... down...

He, the poet, felt pushed and shoved, tossed around horribly, then he felt a shock and his whole, skinny body, the tight, bony envelope of his immense and magnificent soul twisted into hideous pain.

Yanked out of his voluptuous lethargy so suddenly, he woke up scared and alarmed. He wanted to scream but all he could do was moan. He tried to move but it was impossible. However, he managed to open his eyes and become frightfully certain that what he thought was a nightmare was in fact very, very real.

The pioneer poet saw himself tied up, gagged and lying on the floor. Near him the Baroness had fainted, also bound and gagged.

Anthime Soufret told himself, "For sure with the Baroness I can never have a peaceful night out."

His terror became unspeakably worse because the men who had just attacked them were prudent enough to turn off the lights and plunge the salon into deepest darkness. He did not like the dark. He was scared at night... especially in a situation like this.

Squirming around he tried to wriggle free but all he did was knock over a table with a vase of flowers. The flowers fell on top of him. Of course the poet should have found it natural to be covered in fragrant petals but with the flowers came the vase and he got a little shower.

Dazed now and fearing another bath, cautiously Soufret made the wise decision to stop moving. He remained still, soaking in his little puddle like a duck. A duck? Him? No, a swan!

How long did he stay like that? Longer than he wanted. In the end, from upstairs where the private rooms were, he heard shuffling feet, furniture moving, objects breaking and doors slamming. Then loud, high whistling, shouts and finally gunshots. This was not helping Soufret's morale.

Confident that they had all the time in the world and they would not be disturbed, the thieves were breaking into the Baron's safe. Exactly two days before the Baron had bought some very expensive bearer securities and made some other valuable transactions. The money he kept temporarily at home was supposed to be spent on a speculation that he had talked to his friend Guttlach about in front of their mutual friend the Count de la Gueriniere.

Besides the usual cash in the safe—the hundred and some odd thousand francs always kept in reserve—there was now more than two million worth of various securities. And that was not counting the diamonds that his wife gave him, which were not only gorgeous but also priceless.

And here with all this treasure, precisely on the evening when the Baron was having dinner with the gallant Gueriniere and Guttlach, the Baroness happened to give the night off to her servants who went to a party with other domestics.

When the Baron was leaving for his stockholders dinner he gallantly expressed some concern over leaving his wife alone. The Baroness reassured him, "I'll ask Monsieur Soufret to come over. We'll make music and poetry... until you get back... or the servants..."

Completely at ease, free of worry, the Baron went to dinner with the board members and others as we know.

Therefore, the thieves entered the house and started their operation as calm as could be.

Paulin Broquet, meanwhile, was almost certain that the Baron's house was to be robbed this night. He was not mistaken.

Baiter had got the poet talking and knew that the diamonds were in the Baron's safe on the second floor. He also knew that the servants were away and the house was more or less deserted.

"The job is all ready," the detective thought.

With his usual caution and remarkable skill he prepared the trap for the Zs. He laid out the net that Zigomar and his gang would fall into.

Simon the clown who was serving at the dinner sent several messages confirming that the Count de la Gueriniere was staying with his friends Guttlach and Baron Van Cambre.

Broquet told Baiter and Gabriel, "Remember that every time the Zs strike, Gueriniere is parading around at some party."

"That's right, boss."

"So, tonight, as usual, the Count de la Gueriniere is at the stockholders dinner... while the Count de la Gueriniere is committing his robbery." A fact that had been proven several times to be true.

The Count de la Gueriniere went to the festive dinner alone. Meaning that his other close friends, besides Guttlach and Van Cambre, were not with him. In fact, the dashing Baron Dupont who should have been there had sent a last-minute telegram excusing himself, saying that he was sick. Baron du Jard had been out of Paris for two days. As for the Count de Marnais, we know how tragically Zigomar had eliminated the poor guest from the banquet of life.

But for Broquet the sudden sickness of Baron Dupont and the absence of du Jard simply meant that these two intimate friends of Gueriniere had gone to lend their invaluable help to Zigomar.

Therefore, Paulin Broquet had set up his men around the neighborhood of the Baron's house. The order was to let everyone pass but to follow anyone leaving the net and a little farther on arrest them, put them in a car and drive them to a secure location. But they did not have to follow these orders because no one suspicious tried to leave the neighborhood.

Broquet hid near the house for many long hours, patiently waiting, spying, ready to act but nothing out of the ordinary happened. No one walked by or entered the house.

"Are we wasting our time? Have we been hoodwinked by Zigomar?"

Gabriel and Baiter did not know how to respond.

"We've been here a long time for nothing. But it's the exact time when something should be happening. Nothing's moved. The Zs are cautious men, sure, and smart... but they didn't even try to avoid the net... I can't understand it. There's two possibilities: either the robbery is already done or for some unknown reason they called it off."

"I don't think so, boss," Baiter said. "The job was all ready and the circumstances are too perfect for nothing to happen tonight."

"So let's keep waiting."

It was the arrival of a stranger that gave the detectives hope again. The passer-by, however, looked completely ordinary, not suspicious at all. He was a young man, well dressed, who looked like he was coming back from a club or the theater and just walking home on this beautiful night. When he reached the Van Cambre house, the stroller suddenly stopped. He looked both ways, listened carefully, watched the street... then he sneezed loudly three or four times in a row.

"Oho!" Broquet said, "There's a guy that really needs to make sure nobody sees him when he sneezes."

After sneezing the man crossed the street and waited... not long. Two minutes later an upper window in the Baron's house opened quietly and a white handkerchief waved out of it.

"Nice," Broquet said. "They're telling the guy he should use a handkerchief when he sneezes. Nothing beats it." Then he added, "They're also telling us that the job's on tonight, that they're already inside working. Perfect. But when and how did they get into the house?"

He had no time to figure it out now. He told Gabriel, "Let's go!"

"Okay, boss."

"Our men are ready?"

"Everyone's at their post."

Silently they left their hiding place and after they, too, made sure that no one on the street could see them and the sneezer had gone around the corner, they headed for the Van Cambre house.

The sneezer was obviously the lookout who was supposed to watch the street and probably come at an appointed time to check in. With their mutual signals they were telling each other that all was well and there was nothing to fear.

Paulin Broquet knew that to get into the house tonight they could ring the bell and go in through the front door. Logical, of course. But that was certainly not his intention. He did not think about the big garage doors either. Not even the smaller door in them for people to go through.

A few days ago he had got hold of a key to a small service door. Tonight it would certainly not be bolted from the inside since the servants had to come back. When he had come by earlier he unlocked it so he only had to turn the key once to open the door. It went smoothly.

Broquet opened the door quietly. But he did not jump into the house right away. Someone might be behind the door. One of the thieves on guard... then he would be grabbed and tied up before he knew what was happening.

Instead of walking right in Broquet bent over, almost crawling in on knees. Like that he figured he would surprise anyone on guard. He would take advantage of it and before getting knifed in the back—the only danger he could fear now—he would grab the sentinel around the legs and throw him to the floor.

But to his great surprise no one was behind the door. So, he stood up and waved in Gabriel. After Gabriel and Baiter were inside a few more men came in while others waited outside, watching that no one leave the house and ready to help their boss if needed. The operation was prepared for all contingencies as usual.

With his lieutenants and men wearing shoes whose soles were powdered with resin so they would not slip on the waxed floors, he went down a hallway that led to the servants' kitchen. The door to the kitchen was closed but light could be seen around the edges. This was a serious obstacle.

Broquet listened with his ear against the lock. He heard snoring. Then he opened the door slowly... very slowly.

He saw the table still full of plates and bottles and in their chairs around it, leaning on it or with their heads thrown back were the butler, the chef and his assistant. As he snuck in Broquet caught a brief whiff of opium. He knew what must have happened here. A fourth chair left empty proved it.

A friend had come over and eaten with them. This friend offered them cigarettes or cigars that put them into a deep sleep that the thieves took advantage of... and also Paulin Broquet.

Without another thought of the sleepers Broquet and his men went into the house. It was completely silent. The piano, whose notes could be heard outside, had suddenly gone mute in the middle of a melody.

Broquet remembered Francesca da Rimini and her lover Paolo with that precious book one night suddenly stopped reading ... He remembered Juliette who could not finish her sentence in front of Romeo... But were these charming images really the same as the imposing Baroness Van Cambre and her gaunt pioneer Anthime Soufret? Besides, it was not yet time for a poetic tryst.

5. With a blowtorch

Hearing no snoring nor sighing in the dark salon Paulin Broquet, a cautious man even though curious by profession, did not investigate further. He took the long hallway that led to the stairway up to the bedrooms. He wanted to get upstairs as quickly as possible to where the handkerchief waved at the man with a cold.

His men were positioned for attack. They stood by the doors along the hallway and on the landing. All of them had a pair of handcuffs, a thin but strong cord, a rubber truncheon and a revolver. They met nobody in the hallway or on the stairs.

Obviously the thieves thought they were so well prepared that they had nothing to fear. They made the mistake of not guarding themselves enough and relying too heavily on their men outside. They were working now, therefore, without a worry in the world. And even though they had put on their red or black Zigomar hoods to commit the robbery, they had now thrown them back because of the heat.

Broquet stepped forward. He heard a sound coming from a room that he knew was the Baron's room where the famous safe was. That was where the thieves were. And the sound... a kind of whistling noise. Broquet guessed what it was.

The thieves were opening the safe with a blowtorch. It was a new way of breaking in that no steel plate could resist. With the oxygenated flame biting through the steel the blowtorch could open any safe easily.

However, this infallible method had one big drawback that was the last safeguard for those still putting their faith in the cumbersome furniture: the robbers were robbed themselves using this method. Meaning the heat from the blowtorch was so strong that inside the safe everything was burned. If there were papers, nothing was left but ashes. Everything was melted... gold lost its value and jewelry was destroyed.

But the thieves at Baron Van Cambre's house knew this and did not want to jeopardize the fruit of so much preparation, trouble and skill. Since they had time on their side and were sure they would not be disturbed, they knew that they would manage in time and get what they wanted. They were so confident in their success that they had turned on the lights in the room. They figured they would get the necklace, jewelry, cash and other goods completely intact.

So, having stripped the Baron's bed they put the mattress in front of the safe, they started to work on the big, iron hooks on its side. They pulled it down on the mattress to cushion the fall. First they checked if the back of the safe was as solid as the front so they could not quickly get through using the usual crowbar and other traditional instruments. Then they decided to use the modern blowtorch method. But knowing its flaws they also knew how to fix it so that nothing would be lost.

They flipped the safe over again so the bottom was up. This was the best way. First of all the objects in the safe would fall down and the iron shelves would fall on top of them, protecting them from the extreme heat. Moreover, the bottom of safes, which normally could not be accessed from the floor, was generally less solidly built than the other walls. Furthermore, the heat from the blowtorch would not reach all the way down and so do less damage. Thus, the money and valuables, the jewelry and diamonds would come out unharmed by this clever maneuver.

The operation seemed to be going perfectly. The thieves were already congratulating themselves for reaching their goal when all of a sudden the door swung open.

"Nobody move!" Broquet shouted.

There were six men in the room. All of them immediately covered their faces with their hoods. But Paulin Broquet had time to see their faces, which were fully lit up when he entered.

A man with a white beard was watching the gas cylinder. It was Baron Dupont.

The man wielding the blowtorch, actually breaking into the safe was recognized by Broquet, Gabriel and Baiter as the Count de la Gueriniere. And he was wearing the red hood with a big golden Z!

"Aha!" the Count said. "It's Paulin Broquet"

For this particular operation Broquet had worn no disguise. He wanted to be himself from now on.

When he shouted "Don't move!" Broquet rushed into the room with his men. He leapt at the Count, at the hood with the golden Z, at Zigomar!

From the doorway to the safe was a good 20 feet. A big desk in the middle of the room was a kind of obstacle so that Broquet had to go around it to get to the thieves.

These criminals, as we know, were remarkable men who were equal to Broquet's men in boldness, self-control, discipline and training. They showed no fear. The surprise caused no panic among them. In all evidence they were fully prepared for an eventuality like this. Everyone knew what they had to do to save everyone else. Everyone had their assigned role, their specific orders to work quickly and escape in good order if need be.

First of all, one of them swung a pillow at the ceiling and broke all the light bulbs. It turned dark but almost right away the blazing blowtorch filled the big room with its red glow as if they were suddenly transported into a furnace.

The Count knocked the tip off the blowtorch and a wide flame, a kind of fan of fire shot out. He pointed the flame at Broquet and his men. But he did not keep the blowtorch. He put it on the safe with another tool on top of it to hold it in place, thereby forming a kind of wall of fire.

While the blowtorch was spitting its fire at the detectives the Zs escaped by running toward the backroom, insulting them and laughing, confident in their plan.

The flaming jet surely surprised Paulin Broquet, but it did not stop him. He went straight at the fire with his hat in front of his face to protect his eyes. To all eyes an ordinary hat, in fact it was made of leather and therefore fireproof, to some extent. He got his hands burned a little but he quickly managed to find the valve to turn it off. Then he whistled loudly for his men to guard the house and he led his two lieutenants after the thieves.

The bandits thought they had dealt with Broquet. They figured they would escape easily but the special whistle they heard told them otherwise. One of them, posted as a lookout in the little salon downstairs with the Baroness and pioneer, ran out when he heard the noise. He saw Broquet's men position themselves around the house, preparing for an attack and immediately warned his comrades.

The Count and his partners already realized that the house was full of police. Since they had to get outside they would have to fight it out. So, they went into the hallway leading to the stairs. But Broquet's men were there to keep them from escaping. Guns started talking.

This happened in semi-darkness because one light in the ceiling was always lit in the hallway. In the dim glow they could only see the silhouettes but not the faces of others. Shouting and swearing was the only way to recognize each other because with the first shot Broquet's men ran forward and got too close for the enemies to risk shooting their own. On the other hand, Broquet's men had orders to use weapons only as a last resort. They braved the gunfire without answering back. They wanted to capture the Zs alive.

Now there was a terrible fight. The thieves brought out their knives and swords while the detectives had their billy clubs. Broquet had given specific orders not to kill but to capture them and make sure they could not escape. The detectives, therefore, tried to disarm the enemies by hitting their hands and arms with the rubber truncheons. It was hand-to-hand combat, one-on-one, with cries of rage and fury, screams and howls of pain...

A few minutes of chaos, anger, agony and horror passed in the hallway. Then the chase began through the rooms and hallways, down the stairs... After a while the detectives came back alone. They criminals had escaped, given up the fight and ran away.

But Paulin Broquet was not there. Gabriel, Baiter and the others yelled out for him, fearing another tragedy for Broquet.

"Boss, where are you?"

A happy voice answered, "Over here! Look, I've got him!"

"Who?"

"Zigomar! Here, take a look."

And happy as could be but still shaking he dragged a tied man into the hallway. He was tied up, his hood ripped off, his clothes in tatters—he was in a pitiful state.

The detectives leaned over the unconscious prisoner on whose chest could still be seen, half torn off, a golden Z. All together they shouted out, "The Count de la Gueriniere! Zigomar!"

Broquet did not want his man to escape this time. They had to nab him at any cost. So, just like with the blowtorch he dove straight into the bullets and blades and did not slow down, did not stop fighting his way through the bodies. Was he wounded? He did not care. He got his man!

Zigomar was caught this time.

"And the others?" Broquet asked his men. "What did you do with the others?"

"Got away. Except for one prisoner."

"The Baron? Where's the Baron?"

"Got away."

"No! No!" Broquet said. "No one can get away... We'll get them. Search everywhere. We've got to get them. They can't get out of the house."

He dragged the Count roughly in Van Cambre's bedroom and threw him like a dead weight onto the desk, making sure he was securely bound. Just then the frightful cries of a woman came echoing up from downstairs.

"They're killing the Baroness!" Broquet yelled. "We've got to help her!"

His lieutenants ran out. He called one of his men, a kind of giant whom we have seen, and said, "Grimaud! Watch this man for me, watch him well. He's Zigomar."

"Got it, boss."

Trusting his giant to guard the prisoner, Broquet ran into the hallway and told his men there, "Don't let anybody by. We'll get them all. My friends, today is a good day. It's victory! Just one last job to do."

And he rushed downstairs toward the little salon where a woman's screams were ringing out again. They turned on the lights and found that the Baroness had managed to roll down the hastily tied gag. And they found her on the floor, near the poet who had fainted in fear. She was writhing around in a nervous fit. This was the funny part of the whole drama.

"Take care of these two puppets," Broquet told one of his men. "We're going after the Zs. No one can escape."

With Gabriel, Baiter and the other men, he searched the whole house for the thieves whose sudden escape, so admirably carried out, had caused him such a surprise. Broquet could not admit that the Zs had snuck outside and got away so easily. There were maybe a dozen of them and except for the two prisoners the others had vanished as if by magic. He wanted to how and where they had fled.

A few drops of blood gave him the answer. Like the little white stones used by Hop-o-My-Thumb to mark his path home, the red droplets led him to the attic and the servants' quarters. In one room in the corner of the house, the bloody trail stopped at an attic window. From this window a solid plank of wood had been laid out to form a narrow bridge to the roof next door. The window open in the other attic left no doubt to the prompt and mysterious escape. It was the same way, prepared long in advance, that they had got into the house, which explained why the detectives waited such a long time in the street without seeing anyone.

This was how the Zs had just got away. Zigomar, once again, had slipped between his fingers of Paulin Broquet, who smiled when he saw it.

"Well done. Well thought out. I didn't think of this. When we were waiting in the street they were getting in right over our heads. Very clever. Well played, Zigomar!"

Just in case a few Zs did not have time or were too injured to follow the others, he pushed the board and watched it fall into the yard. Then he closed the window and went downstairs.

"They got away," he told Gabriel, "but we still didn't lose the match because we got the one we wanted most."

"Zigomar!"

"Yes, Zigomar. Now I think we've unmasked the famous bandit: the Count de la Gueriniere! We caught him red-handed. He can't deny it or find an alibi. We've got him, my friends. We finally captured the elusive Zigomar." Then he added, "At the same time we've got the solution to the thorny problem of the strange doubling of this character. When we're dealing with Zigomar, whom we always saw as the Count, another Count shows up somewhere else, far from where we were facing Zigomar."

"That's right, boss."

"Zigomar gets away and the Count de la Gueriniere laughs at us."

"But today we got him, boss, we caught Zigomar."

"I think so. But we still have to prove that this Zigomar, whom I think I hurt pretty badly, who's lying up there unconscious, with no hope of escape, being watched by Grimaud, who is stronger than any prison door... that he's really the Count de la Gueriniere."

"But there's no doubt about it, boss. We saw him and recognized him."

"Come on, let's try to prove it for good."

He went back up to Baron Van Cambre's room where the giant was guarding the prisoner. But on opening the door the strong stench of burnt flesh struck the detective and his men. Everyone turned on their flashlights and at the same time switched on the lights in the hallway.

When they went in Broquet and his men, who had seen many gruesome sights in their time, all cried out in horror. Grimaud was lying on the ground, face down. A sword was sticking up between his shoulder blades. The guard of the sword was in the shape of a Z.

The Count de la Gueriniere was still on the table but he was free, all the ropes were loose and hanging down, allowing him to escape. But he did not escape. A powerful blow, a blow from a heavy club had cracked his skull open. Moreover, to make him unrecognizable someone had taken the blowtorch and burned off his face. The silk hood had not gone up in flames but just melted into a black mass covering his face and part of his chest.

For a few seconds Paulin Broquet stood still, stone-faced before his hideously disfigured corpse. He seemed to be looking for some clue in the blackened scab, some recognizable trait in the bloody blisters that would prove who this creature was.

On sizzling the face the blowtorch was swung quickly from right to left and brought lower than the head. It had burned the neck. There was no collar and the top of the jacket was still smoking. The red, silk hood, all mangled from the flame, still carried the golden Z that had miraculously escaped the fiery jet. This Z confirmed that the corpse was the man whom Broquet had fought and conquered... the corpse of the man whom he and his men had recognized as the Count de la Gueriniere. The golden Z was all that was left of Zigomar!

Paulin Broquet told his lieutenants, who were still frozen in horror, "Give me some light."

Baiter and Gabriel swallowed their disgust and brought over their flashlights. Broquet told them where to point them. "Like that," and he told them to keep still. Then he leaned over the corpse.

Very carefully, very meticulously, one by one he removed the shreds of the burnt hood, trying to find some trace of a face under the crumbling soot. Sometimes he took off a piece of half-cooked skin with the hood. It was macabre. Broquet, however, continued his sickening work without pause, without faltering and with great skill, with the surprisingly delicate fingers of an expert surgeon.

But as calm and self-controlled as he was he could not help shuddering in horror and disgust when he finished his gruesome job. The head was so burnt, so ruined by the blowtorch that it was impossible to see any distinguishing marks. The hair, eyebrows and moustache were gone; the boiled eyes were popping out of their sockets; and the swollen lips were half-open in the form of a sneering, insidious grin.

Broquet laid the remains of the hood back over the frightful head. This time the big golden Z was over the face as if to certify once and for all that the corpse was really Zigomar.

Broquet turned to his lieutenants, "Death that keeps its secrets so well can sometimes tell great lies."

Just then hurried footsteps and shouting came from the hallway. Broquet turned to see what was happening, but saw what he was not expecting.

In front of him on the pearly gray wall, just like in the Brialle mansion, traced in blood he saw a big Z, menacing, gigantic, an insult and a new challenge... Again the sinister sign of Zigomar.

At the same time in the doorway of the room appeared a panicking Baron Van Cambre. Just behind him, clean and fresh, dressed to the nine, with a flower in his buttonhole, stood the Count de la Gueriniere.

6. The marked man

It was a Parisian event even more emotional than the robbery of Baron Van Cambre's house. It had everything: romantic adventures, brawls and courage and ingenuity but also cunning and villainy.

The binding of Anthime Soufret the poet and the majestic Baroness was the subject, we can imagine, of many clever comments but only among the high society. The public saw a drama... tragedy... and crime.

Although the Z gang's audacity was astonishing, the bravery of Broquet's Brigade was admirable beyond compare. Broquet had saved the baron's safe, at least what was inside: several millions; and he had caught one of the robbers alive along with the disfigured corpse.

What added to the horror and to the mystery of this capture was the violence with which the partners in crime treated their accomplice. When Broquet had tied him up he was alive, badly hurt and unconscious from the fight but still alive. Then they found him with his head bashed in, his face burned off, murdered and mutilated. Broquet understood the reason. Circumstances demanded it. It was an awful decision but necessary, made on the spot and carried out without hesitation by the Zs because Broquet and his men had recognized the Count de la Gueriniere this time. And that could not be... Zigomar could not be recognized... could not be identified... Zigomar had to be the invisible master... uncatchable!

Now here is what is the most surprising: when Baron Van Cambre was told of the drama at his house he left his charming soiree right away and came running with his friends. One of the first to enter the scene of the crime was the Count de la Gueriniere who had been the life of the party, witty and giddy and wild. Simon the clown was serving him at the dinner and not lost sight of him for one minute the entire night.

One question was more important than all the other painful, harrowing mysteries: Why did the Zs decide to kill and disfigure their partner? The answer was simple. But so that this question not be raised in public, Broquet ordered his brigade to keep quiet about it. It was vital that they not know, that nobody even suspect anything. It was necessary that everyone think the burning was not intentional, not criminal, but the result of a tragic accident.

In the official report they declared that the man, whom they did not know, had simply been killed during the fight. It seemed acceptable to pretend that a tragic accident befell him with the blowtorch. The investigation, therefore, took its normal course. The dead man had to be identified but it would not be easy.

The wounded thief was brought to the prison infirmary and they had to wait for him to recover before questioning him. Luckily Grimaud was not seriously wounded from the sword and would be on his feet soon. The blade was stopped by a rib. The giant's bones were a match for the best steel. The sword hit no vital organs but the injury was still very painful and caused the big guy to pass out. When he woke up Broquet was at his bedside ready to ask questions.

Grimaud answered the best he could. "Here's what happened, boss. After you told me to guard the prisoner you went to help downstairs and there was no one left in the baron's room or the rooms next door. No more Zs, I mean. We searched everywhere after the fight."

"I, too, thought they'd all taken off."

"But look, boss, all a sudden four or five Zs came out of nowhere, without a sound, and they jumped me. They tried to throw me on the ground."

"You fought back."

"At first I was caught off guard. I fell back on the table but then I started fighting."

"I can imagine. And then?"

"I was like a wild boar trying to shake off a pack of dogs. And they were strong and stubborn, damn Zs, but I had my orders so I hit hard and got free."

"I see that. And after?"

"After? Well, the Zs were cutting the ropes around Zigomar. They were going to take him away so I jumped on them."

"Good."

"I wanted to get hold of him but they stabbed me in the back. I thought they'd done me in but before dying I didn't want to let him go... or at least not let them take him alive. I swung hard and hit him on top of his head and, whoop, blood came spurting out of his nose and mouth..."

"You didn't miss."

"No, boss. The others let him go and I grabbed him. I managed to get him back on the table like before and then... well, boss, I did my duty but I couldn't hold out any longer with the sword in my back. I passed out. That's it, boss, everything I know."

Grimaud said all this simply, naïvely, not seeing the great feat he had accomplished, just carrying out his orders. Broquet squeezed warmly his hand and thanked him.

"It's nothing, boss," Grimaud was a little emotional now. "Nothing at all. We'd all do the same for you." Not knowing what else to say he turned to his comrade, "Isn't that right, Simon. You'd do the same for Broquet."

All in all the whole matter fascinated Broquet. The merciless duel between him and Zigomar, between justice and crime and he felt the public anxiously watching this combat and waiting for the final outcome.

They knew that Paulin Broquet had faced off with Zigomar but they also wanted to know if he had caught the chief or wounded him, if the burnt face was the famous Zigomar or not. And they asked Broquet. They were waiting impatiently for his answer.

Obviously, he, too, wanted to know more than anyone. In truth, Broquet first thought that the Count de la Gueriniere was like any other adventurer showing up under an assumed name. Since the affair on Rue Le Peletier, since the Count was mixed up in the murder of Montreil, Broquet had done some serious investigating into this strange character. He had learned for certain that the Count de la Gueriniere was authentic, with a proven genealogy. They could follow him step by step, so to speak, through the life of high society.

Broquet found out, however, that the Count's father was not rich but lived a simple, hard life off the unstable income from some dismal land that he worked himself. All told, a good and worthy man whose existence was far from happy.

His son was forced to quit the military and ended up in Paris leading the life of an idle aristocrat, without a cent, looking for adventure and waiting for a wealthy marriage. He lived a rather wretched, questionable life, got mixed up in some suspicious speculations, rented his name out to some shady businessmen who loved to have a title to show rich suckers who still believed in such things. The most reliable income for this real nobleman, while waiting for the smile of a young lover who would become his countess, was the help from a lady love whom he visited every night. We won't talk about the other ladies whom he never refused...

During his career as a worldly Bohemian, he was caught up in a few dubious affairs. The police always found his name when they closed a club patronized by old, bejeweled ladies. They told tales of his fraud and cheating. All this, he said, was traditional for nobles. He paid no attention to it. Moreover, being skillful with weapons he was always ready to defend his honor (long since departed) in a duel.

Then one day everything changed. The Count left his furnished room at Madame Agathe's, Rue d'Amsterdam where he had stayed for quite a while. Madame Agathe rented furnished rooms and salons for romantic trysts. She had cared for him like a mother, lodged him, fed him in the morning and never asked him to pay. She was heart-broken when he said he got an unexpected inheritance and picked up and left. She felt like she had become a widow and lost a son at the same time! She was inconsolable. The Count, however, like a perfect gentleman, had paid his bill in full before leaving.

He went to live in a delightful little house. Soon afterward Madame Agathe (the poor woman) learned that he had become the lover of Lucette Minois, the charming young star of the Lutetia.

Here Paulin Broquet remembered the first time he dealt with the Count. He had just filed a complaint against an unknown thief who had got away with a magnificent necklace of Lucette Minois.

But the result of all this was the unquestionable authenticity of the Count and if he really was Zigomar then he was an incredible man.

"This Zigomar," Broquet declared, "is one of the most extraordinary criminals we've ever seen."

But privately Broquet thought that despite all his strength and skill and marvelous ingenuity the Count could not be in two different places at the same time. He could not be laughing and drinking with pretty girls in one place and in another be Zigomar the merciless killer! Logically in the modern world, far from fiction and fantasy, this was impossible.

Were there two Counts or two Zigomars?

Was there a Zigomar disguising himself as the Count de la Gueriniere?

That was what Broquet wanted to find out at any cost. The tide was about to turn in his favor.

We know that at the station the day after Riri's arrest the Count had the gall to offer to help the young lady. And we know how the chivalrous Raymond Montreil stepped in and chased him away. After such an offense Raoul was expecting to be challenged to duel... Nothing of the sort happened.

Now, Raoul and his brother Raymond would have been glad to see the Count at the tip of their sword to avenge their father, whom they firmly believed was murdered by this man. They were both looking for an excuse to get the Count on the field of honor; and with justice on their side they felt confident that one of them would make the wretch pay for his crimes. They truly believed that one of them, just like Raymonde hoped, would kill the villain.

But after the incident in the police station the Count de la Gueriniere seemed to avoid the brothers, who had no news of him for days afterward. This worried them. Raoul was determined to find the Count and offend him again.

By one of those strange coincidences of Parisian life, one of those chance encounters on the sidewalks of the city where everywhere seems to be a stage, coming out of a department store after doing some shopping, Raymonde and her brother Raoul ran into Madame Laurent and Riri just when the Count de la Gueriniere appeared out of nowhere in front of Riri, a little way off from Madame Laurent with the crowd between them. Thinking she was alone the Count did not think twice, peculiarly considering his usual caution, and tried to stop her, to talk to her, to pull her out of the crowd, to grab her hand...

Riri was scared, pale, trembling, trying to get rid of the intruder when Raoul showed up and delivered her. Sharp words were spoken between him and the Count. Since there were people around who knew both of them and were watching the scene, the Count did not want to take Raoul's insults without giving a harsh response. He sacrificed his usual reserve for his pride and vanity in public.

"Monsieur," the young lawyer said to him, "you have insulted this young lady once again. I am her lawyer, her defender... And today I will defend her like I did in court and I tell you that you are cad."

"Monsieur..."

"The offense you have committed I take personally. It's me you will deal with. Tomorrow my witnesses will find you."

By evening all of Paris knew about the altercation. A duel was inevitable. The next day, therefore, Raoul's witnesses went to see the Count de la Gueriniere. They were a friend from the office and a friend of Captain de Rennebois, both good swordsmen and experienced in such matters.

The Count had them meet two of his friends: Baron du Jard and the elegant Baron Dupont. In answer to the lawyer's witnesses these gentlemen said that the Count absolutely refused any encounter with Raoul or Robert Montreil. When the others insisted, the exquisite Baron Dupont spoke solemnly:

"Our client has 20 or more duels to his credit, all of them successful. His bravery is not at stake. He refuses to fight with Raoul Montreil. He has the right. His strength in arms and his past allows him to decline the meeting. If the Count offended Mademoiselle Menardier, it was unintentional and he is ready to apologize publically if she so desires."

Raoul's witnesses pressed on.

"Messieurs," Baron Dupont told them again, "there's another reason that justifies his refusal. You should keep in mind that through a series of unfortunate events the Count's name was embroiled in the affair of the banker Montreil. Propriety forbids the Count to risk killing the sons after he had to prove his innocence in the murder of the father."

Raoul's witnesses were forced to leave. But Raoul fell into a rage when they told him, the news. He wanted to blow his brains out. They had a hard time calming him down.

Captain de Rennebois came up with the idea of taking his future brother-in-law's place. At the time of the altercation between Raoul and the Count his fiancée Raymonde was present. Rules of dueling allowed him to substitute for a future relative to demand satisfaction.

This time everything happened quickly. Two days later, on a path in the garden of Andre Girardier's villa, the Count de la Gueriniere crossed swords with Captain de Rennebois. It was a heated battle.

Leading up to the duel the Count had told his friends, "This time I will show no mercy. They started this. They want to kill me and they pushed me to the edge. I'm not going to go easy on the Captain. He wields a sword like a soldier, meaning really poorly... Too bad for him! I'm going to drive my blade straight through him."

The Count was wrong. Even though a soldier the Captain was a good swordsman. The fight was long and hard but neither of them got the upper hand.

The duel had been kept secret so no one was there. However, Paulin Broquet and Gabriel were hiding behind some bushes disguised as a butler and footman, watching very closely the twists and turns of the combat.

In the eyes of Broquet this was of utmost importance, not only for the outcome of the duel, which he was hoping would be favorable to his friends, but also because he could study the Count even better than during the duel with the journalist Marc Colla.

The detective, let's remember, during the investigation of the Montreil murder, had declared that the murderer was left-handed. Since then he had tried to find out about the Count every time he saw him... was he left- or right-handed? So far he could not say and he wanted to know for sure.

During the duel with Marc Collas the Count used his right hand but the gentleman burglar who stole the Baroness' necklace shot his gun with his left! He could not explain this.

Today the adversary on the field was again using his right hand. And yet Paulin Broquet noticed that once or twice after a brief rest following a hard skirmish he came back holding the sword in his left hand. When he positioned himself en garde he switched it over to his right. Nothing, therefore, was cleared up.

"Oh, I know!" Broquet said, "Now I know!"

Before the duel Broquet had gone over to help the Count, to take off his coat and prepare himself. He was the butler lent by Andre Girardier. When the Count left with his witnesses Broquet stayed behind to straighten up. Alone in the room he snuck a small, glass vial into the Count's coat pocket. The vial contained a colorless liquid. Then he hurried to watch the duel.

The Captain looked a little more sluggish, more out-of-shape than his opponent. Like Marc Collas he lost his self-control faced with this marvelous duelist. He got carried away, got sloppy and made the mistake of trying to finish the fight with a burst of violence. He forgot the principle of the old masters: "The sword is a woman and is to be handled like a flower. She will betray you if you abuse her."

His game was falling apart and punishment was coming.

When another, more furious attack came, the Count's sword stabbed deep into his adversary's forearm, making it impossible for him to continue. In truth the Count was hoping for worse but he was still happy to have come out without being harmed.

They carried the Captain away. Robert and the other doctor took care of him. They forced him to lie down on the couch in Girardier's salon.

Meanwhile Broquet helped the Count get dressed. Despite all the control this hardened man had over himself, he could not hide being disturbed or keep his limbs from shaking. It was because he felt very awkward here in this garden, in this villa. But he could not refuse to duel in this place.

He hurried now, just like the sumptuous Baron Dupont and also Baron du Jard, to get out of the house as soon as possible. Being here brought back bad memories. The villa was too close for their comfort to where Riri had been stolen from them by their relentless enemies. They did not much like to revisit places where they had failed a job just like they loathed facing people they felt were stronger than them.

The Count's desire to leave was so great that he paid little attention to the butler put at his service. He suspected nothing and was not wary in the least. So,

Broquet helped the Count put on his vest and coat. Then, pretending to smooth out a wrinkle, to give a little brushing, he pressed the side of the coat. With this pressure the detective broke the small vial. He kept his hand over it while he brushed all around it very carefully.

When the Count left the villa soon afterward with his friends Paulin Broquet watched them go, telling himself, "Yes, you can leave now, Count! Whoever you are, I've marked you. I'll be able to recognize you. I will know who you are."

The vial contained a corrosive liquid that caused no pain but left a mark on the skin that nothing could remove. A liquid tattoo that no chemical, no reagent could erase. Time alone could wipe it out, maybe even two or three years. So, the Count de la Gueriniere was a marked man for a long time.

And Paulin Broquet knew now that he could recognize his man.

7. A little brandy

A duel is like good luck. It rarely comes alone.

With the Count de la Gueriniere, whose reputation as a duelist needed to be constantly upheld, it had to be so. Soon he was involved in another affair, but one that seemed to have nothing to do with the Montreil family, Riri or anybody else in that group.

The adorable Lucette Minois was the cause of it. She was the star of the Lutetia and the number of her admirers was in the thousands. You could say that every man who heard her fell in love with her. But there were just as many lost sighs, they say, without being able to prove anything because in this even less than anything else one must swear to nothing.

Nevertheless, the theater world gave her one official lover and only talked of more when it wanted to slander or because it seemed impossible to well-meaning folk that such a beautiful woman was reserved for the pleasure of only one man.

It must be said, to be honest, that Lucette Minois found her advantage, as they say in the wings, in the Count's love. Her lover was very generous. As a result, the admirer who wanted to see the exquisite diva smile not only had to show the highest discretion but also had to pay such a high price for it that it was out of reach for most people. It cost plenty and they had to keep the conquest secret. Now, some lovers are not up to it because they want everybody to know. Others fear the cold steel of the Count's sword.

However, for a little while you could see in a box; always the same, a spectator who apparently thought the show was extraordinary because he was there every night. Naturally, on the stage the actors did not think for one second that this guy came only for the show, as wonderful as it might be. No, they knew he was there for one of the crew but who?

This man, still young, very elegant, rather handsome, had a blonde beard and very carefully combed hair, a good-sized belly like all *bon vivants*, a look of self-satisfaction, but cheerful and easy going like a country gentleman come to Paris for a good time. They said he was very rich.

On stage they competed in grace and teasing winks to help him decide. A few of the little minds under the blonde or brunette wigs were already imaging pretty little dreams.

They ended up finding out his name: Mathieu, co-owner of a big sugar factory up north. In the wings where they were all waiting they called him the Beet!

They said he was a millionaire, but the Beet was saying nothing. He came to the show, listened, laughed, applauded with the tips of his fingers as one should, smoked his cigar, then left. He climbed into a superb car and nobody saw him again until the next night.

Nobody saw him outside the theater except Lucette Minois who ran into him a few times sitting, always alone, in a famous café at a table next to hers. Lucette was always with the Count and did not think any more about it. She did not even talk about the theater.

But she ran into this Beet again on the street. She would not be a woman if she did not understand. So, the Beet was coming to see her!

It flattered her, amused her and (let's admit) the fact that he was a millionaire was not without interest to her.

Being as discreet as her admirer Lucette Minois was careful not to say anything to her pretty comrades. She let them keep wondering who Mathieu was coming to see every night. She laughed at their little dramas trying to figure it out and she listened to all kinds of comments, hypotheses and the weirdest concoctions one could imagine.

Lucette was too shrewd to reveal her secret to the other girls and especially made sure that the Count suspected nothing. She was waiting for Mathieu to confess something to her, then she would see. Besides; she loved her lover. Yes, she loved him enough not to cheat on him unless it was really worth it.

For his part the Count de la Gueriniere seemed to truly love the star and was extremely jealous. Now, seeing that he was touchy, violent and always ready to fight anyone, Lucette, the clever girl, would never risk a compromising position between her and the other. In this case (by no means unprecedented) she continued her policy of expectation and her diplomatic waiting, which worked like a charm.

As for Mathieu, with his meek and mild ways, he also waited calmly for chance, backed up by great caution, to guide his amorous desires with no risk to himself or Lucette. But he was dealing with two sides, one very supple and graceful but the other strong and cunning. However careful he was to keep his feelings secret; the Count de la Gueriniere found out. But the Count did not let Lucette know she was being spied on and the Beet was completely ignorant.

The Count had fun playing the lover about to be betrayed. He watched the approaches and the weak defense, told himself he would jump in at the right time and show them, first Lucette and then the Beet, that you don't play with the Count de la Gueriniere. One more lesson for others to learn.

While this was happening in the world of the Lutetia—and this only interests us because the Count de la Gueriniere was directly involved—Paulin Broquet along with Robert and Raoul kept working on paying back the money to repair the memory of the banker Montreil. Several families who had cursed the Montreil name were already blessing Robert, Raoul and Raymonde just like the poor mother of hunchbacked Marie and pretty Riri had done on her deathbed.

Broquet was also looking for an answer to the mysterious file. He was sure that Bejanet; the longtime friend of Montreil, knew all about it from the start but he also knew that the notary would never reveal a professional secret even to serve justice. Therefore, Broquet could not count on his support and had to proceed as if he expected nothing even though he was working against him.

He gave Baiter a mission to find out what post office Bejanet used to send and receive his mail. Broquet was afraid it might be the big, main post office but Baiter told him that he actually used the one at La Bourse. Broquet looked satisfied.

From high up, without telling them why, he got the court to take the records from the months surrounding the banker's death. They were then submitted to Broquet who studied everything related to his case.

He found out that around May 17 Bejanet sent a registered letter to someone recorded simply as "Vardier. Ménilmontant." Broquet had the feeling he was on the right track. This was probably exactly what he was looking for.

He called Baiter when he got back home. "You're smart and sly... resourceful."

"I do what I can, boss."

"Okay, let's see exactly what you can do."

"Ask away."

"You know Ménilmontant?"

"Ménilmucky? Sure, boss."

"Okay, you're going there to flush out a Verdier."

"Man or woman?"

"Don't know. That's why I'm sending you."

"Okay, boss, okay. I'll see what I can do."

"Great. And not in too much of a hurry but try to find out right away."

Baiter asked nothing else. He set off immediately. His boss did not have to worry about him. He would find all the Verdiers in Ménilmontant. Only a man like Baiter would accept such a tough mission. Finding a Verdier, man or woman, among all the people in Ménilmontant—a needle in a haystack. But Broquet never gave his men a mission they could not complete, however hard it might seem. Before sending them off he prepared the way.

For Verdier it was no different. Of course he sent Baiter to look for a Verdier but he did not send him completely blind. He had given him a clue to follow.

"He was sent a letter from the post office at La Bourse around May 15. Got it?"

"Got it, boss."

"Great. You can go to the post offices there and check the records. They've been told to cooperate with you."

"Okay, boss."

"You find this Verdier. Check the mailman who delivered the letter and you'll know who he is or at least where he lives."

"That simple."

"Naturally. Under such conditions. I did all the work for you. But when you flush out our bird, just study him and then get back to me."

It was, indeed, pretty simple. Two days later Baiter could report to Broquet.

"Boss, it's done. I found the nest and the little bird who lives there."

"Speak up. Keep it short and simple."

"First of all, boss, this Verdier is a woman."

"I suspected as much. Older?"

"In her 50s."

"What else?"

"She doesn't do anything. She lives off her rental properties. She never leaves her little nest where she's been living for a long time."

"She sick? An infirm?"

"Right, boss. Old and tired."

"Relatives?"

"Just a grown son and a brother... who rarely come to see her."

"Their names?"

"Hold on, boss. An old maid does the housework. It's hard or better to say nearly impossible to get into the Verdier house. She doesn't let anybody in and almost never sees her neighbors. They say she's a maniac, a miser who's afraid they're all out to steal her money or kill her. She's locked herself in and put big locks on all the doors and windows."

"Is that all? No bear traps in the hallways?"

"Maybe. The old maid's got a snuff habit. I know because she came and bought her tobacco while I was picking out some cigars. We chatted a little and even... I lead her on a little by buying some snuff and forced her, without too much resistance on her part, to accept a glass of brandy."

"I should've guessed. And then?"

"Brandy is the good woman's weakness... brandy and snuff, her comfort in this wicked world."

"So, she's seen hard times?"

"Apparently. And the lady, that Madame Verdier, is another who hasn't been happy and doesn't deserve her troubles. Julie sighed—her name's Julie—when she told me this."

"Baiter, you compromised your mission with this woman."

"She's 60 years old. Look, after two or three meetings, trading snuff and brandy, on one of her good days Julie told me Verdier's been a widow for a long time."

"A widow?"

"That's what she said. She stayed a widow very young with her son... who caused her all kinds of trouble. And her brother's pretty worthless. When they come to see her she gets ill every time because she gets pains and those two worry her sick so her pains get worse. She's a poor woman in bad shape."

"Go on."

"Julie says that if Madame Verdier listened to her she would kick out her son and brother for good, far away so that she and the widow could end their old days in peace. But Madame Verdier is scared of her brother who will get revenge because he always comes to see right before the rents are due and he's there when they get in."

"What? She doesn't go collect them?"

"They come in the mail."

"Okay, okay, now we're getting somewhere."

"Hold on, boss. The brother makes his sister sign when the mailman comes. He takes the money pretending to invest it and gives her just enough to live on. Isn't that awful... fiendish... depressing..."

"And then?"

"Julie wanted Madame to leave but she won't because a fortune teller who reads tea leaves and tarot cards told her that her son and brother would do her harm."

Broquet stopped his lieutenant, "That's enough. Baiter, my friend, you're going to tell Julie, between brandys, that tea leaves can be wrong and the future is maybe better, that you should listen to only one fortune teller, got it? You're going to convince Julie to get Verdier to see a palm reader whom you know, who reads palms really well and says the most astonishing things, but always true. It's vital, understand."

"Sure, boss. Tomorrow I think we can find a palm reader."

"But in secret. Nobody can know. It has to stay secret. In three days it's Friday, the best day to look into the future."

"No problem, boss."

Baiter was such an expert at snuff and brandy that on Friday evening, as agreed by him and Julie, the palm reader was eagerly expected by Madame Verdier. The pythoness would tell her the truth and reveal the future to the poor woman whose life was one, long, desperate martyrdom.

But that evening, even though it was a Friday, the palm reader, Madame Roulet, could not come by. Baiter apologized to Julie and between two pinches of snuff and three glasses of brandy he told her that Madame Roulet had a prior engagement with a very important person, so they would have to wait until next week.

Madame Verdier, therefore, was forced to restrain her impatience and anxiety about the future and wait for Madame Roulet, the marvelous, popular, prized palm reader, to have an evening free.

Verdier told Julie, "I'm so anxious that she won't predict a future as miserable as my past."

8. *The severed head*

When the palm reading séance had been put off, the reason given by Baiter was acceptable but not exactly the truth. The real reason was completely different.

You can imagine that Paulin Broquet and his lieutenants wanted to be present at the séance but he had not organized or prepared it. He did not plan for Roulet to undo the messy future from the past read in the thin, cracked, fading lines of the sick old woman's hand. His plan was otherwise. He wanted to talk to Verdier through Roulet and in the occult atmosphere unveil the secret that she would not talk about in any other situation.

But then the day after Baiter had made the appointment something so sensational, so important happened that Broquet was driven in a completely different direction, but just as dramatic, poignant and mysterious as his hunt for the Zs and their chief Zigomar.

On one of those desolate empty lots that are scattered all over between La Villette and Buttes-Chaumont a man on his way to work in the morning had found a big package wrapped in newspapers. Out of curiosity he unwrapped it and fell back screaming in horror. The papers were holding the severed head of a woman! Her ears were missing, her nose sliced up and her lips torn off.

When the man screamed, the neighbors came running, then a crowd of curiosity seekers gathered and finally the police arrived.

Right away, in a burst of feverish energy, the police began their investigation, then the investigating judges came to help them. They searched everywhere hoping to find a clue to lead them into the puzzling crime but they found nothing.

Paris, however, was nervously demanding some information about the gruesome enigma. After two days of vain and exhausting inquiry, after sending out his best sleuths, Monsieur Baumier finally said that they had to get Paulin Broquet to help them with his knowledge, cleverness and daring. The police chief had given Broquet a few days off after the Van Cambre affair on that charming evening. These few days were spent as Broquet saw fit: chasing after Zigomar and helping the Montreil brothers in their retribution work.

Now Broquet was with the Montreils in their rooms on Rue des Mathurins. It was around 6 pm. Robert and Raoul were showing the detective some new documents when the phone rang. Raoul was closest so he picked up the receiver.

"Hello? Yes, that's right. And who's speaking? Doesn't matter? Of course it does. I want to know who I'm talking to... you'll tell me later... not a chance, I want to know right now! You're a cook! Where? For whom? Again doesn't matter... but... You want to know if there's someone in my office who's sitting at the table?" Raoul yelled in anger now, "Your joke is not funny and I hope you give me your name so I can…"

But Raoul did not finish. Paulin Broquet stood up and came over with a smile on his face. "Excuse me, but I think it's for me. Hand me the phone. Thanks."

Broquet spoke into the mouthpiece, "Hello. Yes. If I'm hungry? A little. I was invited somewhere else but if it's necessary I'll eat with you. Yes, yes, I'll hurry… the meal is served, good. I'm on my way."

Setting down the phone he explained to the very curious brothers, "What I was afraid of. Baumier is asking me to cut short my vacation and take over the severed head affair."

"The head found yesterday on that empty lot?"

"Yes. I was hoping they wouldn't need me and I'd be left alone for a few days but, well, we never get what we want in this old world. I have to go sit at the table, dinner is served."

Seeing the brothers confused by this he had to explain.

"Nothing is less reliable than a phone call. You should never use it to tell a secret. Besides the girls snooping around when it concerns them, there's always another ear listening in. So we use everyday language like you heard. Some of us are cooks or chauffeurs, some are carpenters or businessmen or whatever. Since we know who's speaking we understand each other and our secret is safe… to some extent at least."

In kind of a bad mood now because his plans were cancelled Broquet left the Montreils and took a car to the police station. Baumier was waiting for him.

"You're finally here. This'll work. The head, my dear Broquet, this head we found is starting to make me lose my own."

"Well, at least we'd recognize yours anywhere."

"I hope so." Then the Chief told him, "We don't know what else to do. We've searched everywhere, under every rock, checked out all the furnished rooms, questioned all the streetwalkers and found nothing, no missing girl, not a single clue…"

Broquet listened to the Chief, who looked nervous, waving his hands around or banging on his desk, while he just calmly rolled a cigarette.

"So the newspapers are all over us. They're calling us incompetent, bringing up all the unsolved crimes and mysteries we never unraveled. It's a living hell!"

"Sure, sure," Broquet responded calmly.

"They're messing with me, saying it's not murder but a simple suicide."

"To be expected."

"And they're challenging me to arrest the murderer. Oh, nothing too hard, just find the rest of the body… They're making up songs about the headless woman walking around who nobody sees."

429

"That's original." Then Broquet asked, "So, Chief, what do you expect from me?"

"What do you mean what do I expect?" The Chief was yelling. "I expect you'll solve the mystery!"

"That I'll find the body?"

"And the murderer."

"Is that all?"

"Yes..."

"Good, it's enough."

"You're the only one, Broquet."

"Who, me? Why not get some help from my clever colleague Tom Tweak?"

"Tom Tweak? You think he could..." The Chief yelled even louder, "Broquet, stop joking around!"

"I'm absolutely serious."

"Okay, but please, for today, leave Tom Tweak out of it. Forget about your pretty redhead, Zigomar and the rest of the Zs. Think only about this case, about this head."

Paulin Broquet tapped the ashes from his cigarette into the ashtray on the Chief's desk and spoke with admirable calm, "Okay, let's go see this head. Where is it?"

"In the morgue."

"Lead the way."

From the Quai des Orfévres to the gloomy morgue behind the majestic Notre Dame was not a long way. The chief and the detective went on foot. On leaving the station Broquet had told his lieutenants to meet him there but to take different routes in case anyone was spying on them.

Near Quai aux Fleurs Broquet, who missed nothing, noticed one particular peddler hawking his wares on the sidewalk. When he passed by their eyes met... and Broquet remembered seeing those eyes before, but where? And when? At the moment he could not get a fix on it. But he wanted to see the man again.

He could not just walk by again without looking suspicious so he stopped, pulled a cigarette out of his case and tried to light it but in the windy outdoors the matches kept blowing out. He cursed the matches and their makers, turning around trying to protect the flame in his cupped hands. He ended up with his back to the wind and his eyes focused less on the cigarette and more on the intriguing peddler who was selling a newspaper to a customer who was carrying a big briefcase like a lawyer or clerk on his way to court.

Well, Paulin Broquet knew everyone who made a career in halls of justice but he did not recognize this man. However, he did have a memory of him: this man was on Boulevard du Palais when he crossed it with the chief. So, this man was on guard duty. He had followed them all the way here and now he was right behind them, pretending to buy a newspaper and talking to the peddler who looked worried.

"Good," Broquet thought to himself, "they're tracking me."

With his cigarette lit he caught up to the chief who had got ahead of him a little during the whole show. But he had time to see the man with the briefcase walk away with his paper and the peddler moving in the same direction that he and the chief were taking.

Glancing back a few times he could see that the peddler was following them and he was sure that he would wait outside the morgue for them.

Broquet and the Chief, soon joined by Gabriel and Baiter, went down into the waiting mortuary, which also served as the amphitheater, where there was the big marble table and the freezers.

The crowd in front of the morgue was huge. They had to cordon off the entrance. In past days the mysterious head would have been exhibited in a big window that the crowd could file by slowly. Nowadays this macabre show was finished.

The poor souls who were washed up by life's dark waves behind the gruesome windows are no longer a hobby for the idle, one of those grisly curiosities of the capital for foreigners touring the Morgue after visiting Notre Dame. The revolting, morbid spectacle was abolished for good reason—there had never been any great results from the practice. To be allowed to see an unidentified body today you have to prove it is more than simple curiosity, that it really concerns a missing relative or friend. It is more moral, just and respectful.

At the time we are dealing with the exposition was still public. The news that you could see the severed head brought a crowd to the Morgue that was hungry for horror. But there was a racket, fights broke out, and the head was finally taken out of the window and put on ice.

When the Chief and Broquet arrived in the amphitheater, the Morgue employees had everything prepared for the head to be presented to the detectives right away. A young man was waiting there to break the ice around the clasp on the front of the locker. He rolled a kind of thin, iron shelf in front of a long, black hole where a corpse could be stretched out. From this hole he pulled out a metal plate covered in frost. On the plate that slid over the metal sat the severed head.

The rolling shelf creaked eerily as he pushed it over to the marble table. Then he put the plate and the frightful head on the table and stepped away.

The police approached the table and leaned over the head. At first sight Broquet and his two lieutenants reacted with fright: they shuddered. The three of them looked at one another nervously and said, "Her! The redhead!"

9. The dead hair

Like always after a serious confrontation with Paulin Broquet the Zs and their chief Zigomar stayed quiet for a little while, scattered around, off licking their wounds, vanished.

Except at Clafous' there were a few members who came by, obviously from the lower ranks, waiting for new orders or some information.

Their superiors, who knew, kept their meetings absolutely secret. After the Barbottiere blew up and after the adventure in Zulma's peaceful house, Zigomar had found a new lair. The Whale's Cellar on Rue Jonas had been named by the Terror of Ornano. Broquet had not had time to check it out but he was going to visit it soon. For, Broquet knew that Zigomar would be planning a spectacular revenge.

Paulin Broquet did not want to waste time on useless steps. He was waiting for Zigomar to prepare his attack so he did not have to fight in uncertainty.

We know how Broquet did not follow the somewhat outdated police methods. He did not chase after probabilities or deductions based on possibly false premises however logical they might appear. He only moved on facts, when the enemy was discovered. As a result, although he seemed to lose a little time at the start, he did not have change direction later and therefore could work much faster. This method, a little bit special, fit his character and worked for him. He liked it.

At this moment he knew that Zigomar was inevitably going to get revenge for the failure he suffered. Broquet was waiting for it, watching for it, ready for it, constantly on guard, with an immediate answer at hand.

His men likewise had been trained by and were proud of their boss, ready to do anything for him, with him, no matter how dangerous. Also knowing that the Zs wanted revenge they became bodyguards and watched over him, loving and admiring him more than any monarch could have bragged about.

Broquet was also convinced that the Zs knew all this and had seen that he was untouchable. He figured that in his hatred, in his rage Zigomar would take his anger out on the redheaded woman.

Broquet had said to his men, "Who is this woman? Where does she come from? Where is she going? What does she want? Why did she enter the game? What's pushing her to side with Broquet and at the same time drawing her to Zigomar? We can't even guess. We found her in our way, me first, I can say, having the pleasure of meeting her , then you, Baiter, at the Brialle mansion, in Orleans in the car after the Count de Marnais was murdered... afterward we saw her in Clafous' trying to meet Zs and get closer to Zigomar. Why? No way to know. A mystery surrounds this redhead that is absolutely impenetrable for us right now."

"That's right, boss," Baiter said. "As you told me I searched all over Paris for her, trying to find out where she lives, where she eats, all that. I haven't got a clue."

"But she's got cars and horses, people work for her."

"Yes, boss, but there's no way of finding them. If the redhead wasn't so beautiful, so young and charming, full of grace, I'd say she was a witch living in a magic castle and whenever she needs she waves her magic wand and makes her cars and horses disappear."

"And lays you gently down on a bench!"

"Sleeping, just like in a fairy tale. She's a fairy, boss. A redheaded fairy."

Broquet smiled, "But she freed Paulin Broquet who was about to die in Zulma's attic. Thanks to her Broquet was saved and could stop the Count de Marnais from his deadly work with the murderous mosquitoes and foil the plots of Tom Tweak and his friend Zigomar."

"That's right, boss."

"Thanks to the redhead Broquet is still alive and stopped Van Cambre's safe from being robbed."

"And the Zs were hit hard."

"They'll never forgive me. Zigomar needs to save his reputation and show his power and his inability to do it against me or any of you is why he took his anger out on the redhead."

"Boss, you're right," Gabriel said, "and now we have proof. The redhead knew the danger she was in because she got the Terror of Ornano to escort her. The Zs confirmed it when they tried to grab her that night at Clafous'. It certainly wasn't for her radiant beauty but in order to punish her for saving you. Since then Zigomar's been planning his vengeance."

Even though Broquet was sure that the redhead was condemned by Zigomar's barbaric sense of justice, still he and his men were terribly affected when they saw her severed head on the table in the morgue.

All three of them gasped together, "The redhead!"

She had so much hair that however careful she was to hide it under a hat or wig there was always a braid slipping out to betray her in the light. Here the head had a lot of hair but cut so that it would only fall to the shoulders. It was flat and pasted to the skull by the ice. It was as sad as the smile on her slashed lips that were parted to show her shining teeth.

It was a cruel, shameful picture and particularly gruesome but formed less of fright and disgust than of pity and regret.

The woman was young and certainly beautiful. She was dead, murdered, obviously. Great beauty in a woman brings mad love and attracts anger like a knife in the hands of the lover. A kiss is brother to a stabbing.

But why mutilate this woman's head and commit such a hideous defilement?

The only possible reason for the sacrilege was the need to make her unrecognizable.

But Broquet whispered to his lieutenants, who were probably thinking the same the thing, "It's pointless since no one knows who she is."

"That's right, boss. Why make the mystery of the redhead even more mysterious?"

"So there's another reason..."

Broquet let his heart talk for a few minutes of anguish and poured out his pity around the marble table as if before a coffin. Then he got a hold himself. The detective was back... the agent of justice.

Now the head would be nothing but a sinister piece of the puzzle to solve. He leaned over the table, took the severed head in his hands and examined it long and carefully. He tried to open the eyelids to see the color of the eyes, but they were frozen shut. They wanted to keep their secret, not to reveal if they were concealing amethysts or black diamonds, not to show what treasures lay behind their sorrowful veil.

So, Broquet duly left the eyelids closed. But he took a lock of hair that had stuck to the ice. He warmed it in his hands and examined it when it was thawed.

Gabriel, Baiter and the Chief watched him without moving, without speaking, just waiting. Broquet took a magnifying glass and put the hair under it. Then he looked up and turned to the others watching him.

"You know, Chief, that I made a comprehensive study of hair. I'm sure that hair can be a valuable help for anthropometric files."

"Really... that's very subtle..."

"Just like no hands or ears or palm lines are the same between two individuals, so no two hairs are identical. Why should hair be more subtle than a palm line?"

"I'm listening."

"The first problem is that the subject might be bald."

"Indeed."

"But he could also lose his hands. What would happen to the anthropometry then? Listen, hair, as everyone knows, can identify race. Negro hair is different from Dutch hair, for example. Japanese hair can be distinguished from a Parisian."

"No doubt."

"Therefore, if it is possible to classify hair by race, we can also divide them into more distinct categories, like an herbalist. And look at all the varieties, all the families! Black, brown, chestnut, blonde, wavy, straight, stiff, soft, thin, thick, coarse and so many others."

"It's a whole system you're starting."

"It's a neglect we should be rectified."

"But what do you do with the bald?"

"I was expecting that. There are many causes of baldness that are part of an individual's general health so they should already be registered. But baldness is never so absolute that we can't find some hair on then neck, for example, that can be used."

"I bow to you."

"Here, Chief, my knowledge of hair has allowed me to make a few observations whose importance will become immediately apparent."

"Let's hear them."

"The victim was a blonde. What you think you see is a post mortem lie."

The Chief was startled, "A lie after she died?"

"Exactly. The ash blonde hair was well cared for and very beautiful while she was alive but was washed in peroxide after death."

"What makes you say that?"

"I can prove it, it's easy. The dye or rather the discoloration did not give the results the same results as on warm, living hair whose natural liquids helps the dye. You can see here... take the magnifying glass... look, it's not regularly colored. The red dye from the peroxide didn't penetrate everywhere. The top of the hair is red but down below it's ash blonde."

"It's true."

"In certain countries, Italy for example, when a young woman dies their superstitions make them color the hair golden blonde. Apparently it's easier to get into paradise like that. The Creator prefers blondes. He made Eve blonde. Brunettes came after the apple when the devil got mixed up in it. Angels and saints are all blondes. In short, they dye the hair of the dead to make them more pleasing to God. I've had the opportunity to see that dyed, dead hair and they look exactly like this."

Broquet paused before concluding, "Therefore, Chief, we have to admit that the people who tossed this head—so that it could be easily found just by walking by—were counting not only on the disfiguration of the face but also the dyed hair to throw us off track."

"That's very possible."

"I'll go so far as to say that they were counting on the dyed hair especially and the mutilation was an afterthought."

The Chief listened to Broquet with great attention, much surprise and a growing anxiety. He was expecting the detective to reveal some ingenious clue to unravel the disturbing mystery but he did not.

Broquet said, "That's enough of my applied police science. For the moment I have nothing to add."

"That's too bad."

"I'll ask you now to leave me here alone. I'll tell you what I find. What I'm finding now, which I have a bad feeling about already, needs to be confirmed... surgically, by a doctor."

"The coroners are on their way."

"They'll make their report, good, but I need something else. I'd like to have Dr. Robert Montreil here. I'm used to working with him and he's a great partner."

"Do as you want," the Chief responded. "You have carte blanche. See you later in my office."

"Thanks, Chief."

When Baumier had left Broquet told Baiter, "There's a fake peddler by the entrance to the Morgue.

"I spotted him too."

"He's a Z, I recognized him. He was at Clafous'."

"Yes, boss, the man with the briefcase too."

"So, you saw everything."

"Yes, boss."

"Good. You get someone on him... start a fight... get him arrested... Let's get this guy."

"Understood."

"And you, Gabriel, take the car to fetch Dr. Montreil and bring him back here right away."

"I will have to tell him the bad news—another horrible attack by Zigomar."

"That's right. Now let's get going..."

10. The lying dead

Alone now, Paulin Broquet picked up the woman's head and examined it again. After a long while he mumbled, "Yes, that's it... I was right... I can't be mistaken... It's obvious but I'd still like to get a second opinion from Robert."

Then laying the head down on the table he said, "Poor woman, I feel really sorry. They wanted to make you play a role in their infamy but you couldn't lie. And soon, I hope, your head will join the body it was separated from and you can rest in peace, undisturbed, for eternity."

He walked around a little in front of the rows of seats, rolled a cigarette and started to smoke. Soon afterward Baiter came into the amphitheater.

"Boss," he said, "couldn't catch the peddler. He took off."

"I thought he might. Anyway, it doesn't' matter. Whoever is spying on us knows what they want to know."

"Meaning that Paulin Broquet is on the case of the severed head and he came to the Morgue to see it."

"Exactly what they wanted to achieve."

"So now what?"

"So now we have to find out why they wanted us on this case."

Broquet lit another cigarette and sat down, smoking slowly, silently, motionless, just watching the swirling smoke. He was, you might say, playing the cat.

Baiter knew that at times like this he had to leave his boss alone, go sit somewhere else, light a cigarette himself and keep a close eye on his boss.

Footsteps and muffled voices pulled the detectives out of their reveries and stillness. In the doorway at the top of the stairs Dr. Robert Montreil stood next to Gabriel. Broquet ran up to them.

"Ah, doctor, I'm sorry for kidnapping you like this but I need your precious help with a matter."

"I'm all yours, my friend."

"Gabriel filled you in... good... So, here's what I'd like from your impeccable knowledge." He led the doctor to the marble table with the severed head. "I'd like you to tell me whether I'm mistaken and gone off into fantasy... or I'm right and headed in the good direction."

"I'm listening."

"Here is the head of a woman, cut off and horribly mutilated... and as Gabriel told you it was found on an empty lot around Buttes-Chaumont."

"Okay."

"I examined it carefully and figure the poor thing's between 22 and 25 years old."

Robert lifted the head, looked at the teeth and said, "Yes, 25 at most."

"Then I say that she wasn't murdered, that there was no crime, just a profanation."

"What do you mean?"

"Listen, all of you, because this is of utmost importance to us. I say that this head was cut off after she was dead, at least one or two days."

While the detective was talking the doctor studied the gruesome remains.

"That's very possible," he answered Broquet.

The detective continued, "I say that this poor girl was mutilated after she had died because I'm sure that she died of natural causes, tragic perhaps but normal. I see no traces of an unnatural death."

Broquet pointed to the wounds.

"See the indentation on the nose and the sliced lips... they clearly show that they were post mortem. The blood was already stopped, frozen... see, doctor, at the tip of the wound, the veins cut by a sharp knife are still full of coagulated blood that didn't bleed out."

"That's right, absolutely right. Yes, she died before and the wounds are more recent."

"Good! Thank you, doctor. So, I'm on the right track."

"I believe so."

"Great. We can proceed with confidence." Turning to his lieutenants he said, "So let's go find out why Zigomar..."

"What?! Zigomar?" Robert cried out. "You think Zigomar did this?"

"Yes, we're sure of it. We're going to find out why he wanted to make us believe that this frightful head belonged to the beautiful, mysterious redhead."

"The redhead?!"

Baiter and Gabriel both reacted strongly, "What! You don't think this is the redhead?"

"I'm sure it's not," the detective declared confidently.

"But, boss," Gabriel said, "just now we recognized her, as far as possible in this awful condition, but we identified the gorgeous redhead."

"Right, boss," Baiter agreed. "And all three of us were affected, really bothered by it."

Broquet answered, "Yes, yes, my friends, that's true. At first sight, like you, I believed this severed head was our redhead. I, too, was shocked and like you I was fooled. The hair, the dyed hair and the pretty features underneath the wounds fooled me. But the spell was broken after a careful examination... when anguish was replaced by analysis."

After a pause the detective continued, "This head, my boys, was prepared, made up on purpose for us. They cut the nose so we wouldn't recognize her profile. The lips were sliced to deform her mouth that had smiled so radiantly at us."

Baiter and Gabriel listened anxiously to their boss. Broquet held the head while talking and shoed his lieutenants everything he had noticed.

"Doctor, you didn't know the redhead but your knowledge and experience will corroborate my deductions, I hope. Look here and tell me if I'm wrong. The redhead is gorgeous, strong, brave and healthy. Her cheeks are full, her chin firm and round with a little dimple…"

"That's right, boss."

"Baiter, you saw her better than anyone, tell us what you saw, what you remember."

"As you said, boss, her face was round, charming, pretty, a real woman. Even disguised as a man at Zulma's, even the young horse rider in the forest at the Brialle mansion, even as a chauffeur in Orleans there was no mistaking her. Her chin was so exquisitely feminine."

"Well, look here… small, pointy and bony with no dimple…"

"Big difference!"

"Look at her hollow cheeks with these protruding bones…"

"Yes, boss."

"It looks like the face of a victim of consumption, don't you think, doctor?"

"Absolutely."

"Right, where as the redhead was in good health, in the bloom of life. This woman here must have been pretty, sure, but she was thin, delicate, frail and sick. The other is tree growing in full sunlight… this one here was a sickly flower in a hothouse, withering away slowly."

"You're right, my friend," Robert concurred.

Broquet respectfully laid the head on the marble table and told his lieutenants, "Now let's go. Let's get out of this dreary building where we have nothing else to do and get back to the land of the living where we have a lot of work ahead of us. We have to find the body of this poor girl."

11. Shotgun with tips

When Paulin Broquet said "We have to", his men understood the meaning. They had to... at any cost... get results, reach their goal. Until now, in every one of their many and different cases, they had come out victorious. But they had never faced such a tough and complicated affair such as this. They had to, yes, but how to do what they had to do?

How were they going to fulfill their boss' desire? And as quickly as possible.

"We have to," Broquet had said again, "absolutely solve the case of the severed head before dealing with Madame Verdier."

Baiter had to visit his faithful friend Julie several times to get her—between two hugs and three glasses of brandy—to agree to make Madame Verdier wait. Soon Madame Roulet the fortuneteller would come and read her palm but for the moment she was preoccupied. There was no harm in waiting... and Madame Roulet would reveal the future in detail. Just a few more days...

In the meantime Broquet threw himself into the new case. He wanted to solve it quickly. The public, whose interest in the gruesome discovery was growing, wanted news. The papers were starting to criticize the police for taking so long to clear up the mystery. The general anxiety was getting so strong that even Broquet, who had friends and admirers in the press, was starting to fall from grace in the reports.

But wasn't it crazy to expect to find a body hidden somewhere in the vast city of Paris? There were plenty of examples, unfortunately, of vain searches for other butchered bodies. Experience said that if the body was not found after a few hours then all hope should be abandoned.

But Paulin Broquet never worried about precedents and paid no attention to examples. In his opinion every case was different. He always acted as if it were the first time such a case presented itself. It was a way not to make the same mistakes as his predecessors and not to get stuck in a rut.

First of all he sent Baiter and Gabriel to the hospitals to make an inventory, so to speak, of the bodies for dissection.

Then he sought out information about the deceased all over Paris. In the city halls, in the burial permits, he pulled out those that seemed to fit the probable date, age and cause of death of the severed head. Baiter went to visit the grieving relatives. It was delicate work and took great sensitivity, his special tact to investigate. But nothing fruitful came of it. All the young women who had died at the time were buried according to custom. No incident was reported to catch their attention.

Broquet ended up saying, "We would have to visit all the graves and that would be very hard and long, if not impossible. Maybe a good idea but very impractical."

Therefore, they had to look elsewhere. Broquet was thinking that since the Zs were responsible, which he was absolutely sure of, then it was among the Zs that they ought to look. So, he slipped some men into Clafous' to catch any rumors. He himself did not go.

He knew that besides the Enfants de l'Aveyron some bigger Zs sometimes met in a café around Place Blanche. It was there that Baiter had had drinks with Anthime Soufret one evening—Café Galant, named after the owner, a huge but quiet establishment that clashed with the gaudy places around it in Montmartre.

Meeting in different groups, separate but familiar, friends had gathered there for a long time, faithful customers. Everyone had their habits, their usuals, and many their own pipe kept in a cabinet.

The regulars came to sit around the marble tables to smoke and play dominoes. Artists who had had their hour of fame, the younger ones still on their way, salesmen, clerks, lawyers, writers, sculptors and men of independent means. There was a circle formed around a songwriter; another for fanatics of bridge. In the back some young men were talking horses and racing while the doctors took a break from their consultations by breaking the balls on the pool table.

This little world, without mixing with one another, coexisted peacefully and at midnight went back home, leaving the place to another kind of clientele coming from the theaters and off the streets.

Serving everyone, knowing their tastes, an expert waiter with sharp eyes, always in a good mood, never stopped except to look at the racing form and make his predictions for the next day. The friendly, helpful server was known to everyone in and around the café by the distinctive name of Shotgun.

He was crazy about racing and even though he had never set foot in a racecourse he pretended he knew all about horses and was privy to all the secrets of the turf. He willingly gave out tips that the customers, sportsmen and jockey club members slipped him in the morning. And when his horse won; Shotgun celebrated…

Good ole Shotgun. Besides his love of horses, which he never saw run, he had another passion: the police blotter… and a deep admiration for the heroic Paulin Broquet, whom he had never met. But by sheer luck, which proved to be extremely glorious, good ole Shotgun was a neighbor of Broquet and just like being an amateur of horses he thought he had the best tips, so living near Broquet he pretended to know everything about local crimes.

Among the customers who were part of no group Shotgun knew two or three well dressed young men who asked him for tips about the horses and his opinion on the sensational crimes of the moment. One of them who was apparently a salesman bet on the same horses as him, ran the same risks and sometimes even matched his bets. His name was Amblard and had become a friend.

When Shotgun was not working they met and talked. They even had lunch together. When their friendship was growing, after a few good tips had turned out well, Shotgun invited Amblard to his home to taste a meal prepared by Mrs. Shotgun.

This Amblard, still a young man and always well dressed, was sometimes joined at the Café Galant by a white bearded man and others of various age, but all of them either businessmen or salesmen who had their aperitifs in the evening or after dinner.

One of them came more often. He lived in the neighborhood and was called Gaston Soclet. They said he was an insurance agent. He was between 30 and 35, very quiet, friendly, an excellent customer to serve, who like his friend with the white beard took a keen interest in the horses by betting heavily.

Shotgun took great pleasure in serving his customers, his friend Amblard and the others. Despite his friendly demeanor, however, he was less attentive to anyone who was less interesting to him.

That customer with the long hair under a felt hat, a velvet suit and wide tie, sometimes came to meet an individual whom Shotgun did not like very much. It was the pioneer poet, the wonderful Anthime Soufret. Sometimes one or two other men, artists no doubt, joined this customer (whom it is not hard for us to recognize Baiter). And these customers never talked about horses or headlines, of the sensational crimes and seemed not even to know Shotgun's famous neighbor of whom he was so proud (these two were obviously Gabriel and Paulin Broquet).

Now, one or two days after Paulin Broquet was given the case of the severed head, disciple of the pioneer poet came with his two friends, bohemian like him, and sat at one of Shotgun's tables.

"Has Monsieur Soufret been in tonight?" Shotgun asked. "Or will he be coming?"

"He didn't tell me. It's been a while since we've seen him here."

"Okay, we'll wait."

Baiter ordered drinks that are ironically called aperitifs whose essence is to cut the appetite. Shotgun served him and his companion, Paulin Broquet dressed as a typical Montmartre artist, then went to chat with his friend Amblard who was sitting across from them at a table with Gaston Soclet.

Amblard and Soclet were sitting in the middle of the café. Behind them was nothing but the coat and hat racks. In front of them, behind a row of tables, was a wall painted with a fresco depicting chubby cherubs frolicking among roses as big as them and between the painted panels stood tall mirrors in which the whole café, particularly the front door, was reflected. As a result, without moving an inch, just by looking up, they could see everyone coming and going and pretty much everything happening in the café.

As we said, Broquet and Baiter were sitting across from, but placed differently. Baiter was in the fake leather bench against the wall, under one of the big mirrors; Broquet sat in a chair facing him. Baiter, therefore, could see Amblard and Soclet directly while Broquet could look in the mirror and see not only them but also everything they saw.

Broquet and Baiter were wearing big, felt hats like artists do, hiding their faces and keeping Amblard and Soclet from studying them and also from seeing part of the mirror. But this did not seem to bother them much. Maybe there was nothing to look for today because they did not even glance at the mirror.

Broquet and Baiter had an explanation for this. The tip-giver Shotgun gave it to them. The waiter was talking to Soclet, who was dressed in black like someone in mourning, trying to show some compassion.

"Come now, monsieur Soclet, don't beat yourself up. It's cruel, I won't deny it... a young woman, so charming... gotta say your girl was really nice and really pretty. The few times she came here asking for you, she talked to me and was always kind. I'd go to the funeral but, you know, work and all, I can't. Was it her lungs that did it?"

"Yes."

"Consumption. Horrible. Doesn't respect nothing. Hits the best of them. A beautiful young woman with everything you could ask for... taken away like that. It's like a horse when it's short-winded, gotta be a thoroughbred, they don't go far."

A bell ringing told Shotgun he was wanted elsewhere. He escaped with a "There you go!" and left Soclet looking puzzled by the strange comparison and odd expression of condolence. Amblard was rationalizing, even scolding his friend who kept wiping his eyes. All of this was witnessed by Broquet and Baiter.

"A pretty young woman recently died of consumption... and a friend of this Amblard who looks disturbed by it... oh, oh..."

But in Broquet's stock of information there was no Madame Soclet. Perhaps Soclet was not their real name or maybe she was his mistress with her own name.

"We'll have to see," Broquet said, "Shotgun will give us a tip."

15 minutes later Amblard and the grieving Soclet left. Shotgun ran up to say goodbye. Very friendly, intimately, Amblard shook his hand and said, "So it's set... one day this week?"

"Yes, on my day off, Thursday."

"Okay, but nothing fancy, regular food... I prefer it."

"No worries, my wife is Madame Shotgun but she won't kill you."

Smiling at his little joke he ran back into the café. Broquet and Baiter had overheard them and were intrigued.

The detective said, "Shotgun has got to give us a tip." Soon after, since the pioneer poet had decided not to show up, the two pseudo-artists left.

443

Around two in the morning, after a full day of good tips for himself and a few winning ponies, Shotgun went home exhausted, almost sleeping on the way. He lived in a small apartment in the same building where Broquet had a place. Shotgun was two floors higher.

As he was climbing the dark staircase he was suddenly grabbed from behind, tied up and gagged and taken away. Half-asleep, he thought it was some bad dream and he was becoming the hero of one of those local crime stories he loved to read about.

What did they want? His tips from the café? Or tips on the horses?

He did not have time to ask questions. He was thrown onto chair, still in total darkness. They freed his hands, untied the gag and the room was suddenly flooded with light. Before him stood three men. He recognized one of them right away. Trembling with surprise and excitement he jumped up and shouted, "Paulin Broquet!"

12. Rest in peace

Shotgun could not believe it. He looked all around in astonishment. After the nightmare this was a magical dream.

He looked as if he were in the presence of a miraculous vision, Paulin Broquet, his hero, his great man...

He was in the presence of Paulin Broquet, in his apartment, him, Shotgun! He could never have hoped for such happiness. Sincerely, naïvely, he was enjoying every second of this unexpected, fantastic adventure without wondering why it was happening.

Broquet did not leave him hanging in suspense for long. "Shotgun," he said abruptly, "you're a good man, even though you gamble too much... on the sly. You're honest even though you give out tips that are not always reliable. I've known you for a long time and I appreciate it even though you wait on me and my friends with less attention than Monsieur Amblard and his friend Soclet."

Shotgun wanted to answer, to say something, but he was speechless, not a word came out of his moustache because he was stupefied. What?! He was waiting on Paulin Broquet without knowing it, without suspecting a thing... and no better than the other customers!

Broquet asked him, "Look, my boy, don't worry, I'm not upset and we're going to become great friends."

"Oh, Monsieur Broquet... Monsieur..." he babbled, "Monsieur Broquet, uh..."

"Just wait, you just have to give me simple answers."

"Okay."

"Look, you knew Gaston Soclet's woman."

"Yes, monsieur."

"She died recently?"

"Yes, monsieur, around six days ago... consumption.

"Right. So, what was she like?"

"Kind of tall, very thin, but pretty, had a charming smile and big, blue eyes... with rings around the, poor woman, and rosy cheeks but hollow, you know, like consumptives..."

"Sure. Blonde?"

"Ash blonde."

"Was she Madame Soclet?"

"No, her name was Carmen d'Amata."

"Carmen d'Amata?"

"She was a singer once, big in the music halls. She was even at the Lutetia last year."

"The Lutetia?"

"Sure, but this year she couldn't sing. She was too sick, then she died. Oh, it was a beautiful funeral, flowers, singers, even some society folk."

"Society folk?"

"Her lover, Gaston Soclet, a nice guy and he loved her, went all out for her... knew some friends of her comrades. See, Carmen d'Amata was close to Lucette Minois and monsieur Soclet was friends with her lover, another sportsman, I think you know... the Count de la Gueriniere."

"Oh, we know him very well, yes. It's a good thing the poor girl had a ceremony worthy of her youth and beauty. So, Soclet loved her a lot, eh?"

"He thought he'd go mad when she died, especially the night of the wake when they sealed the coffin. Amblard was there, then Lucette Minois and her lover. It was hard for him to recover, poor Soclet, and he was half-dead at the burial the next day."

"Where was she buried?"

"In a temporary plot in Montmartre cemetery."

"That's great, thanks."

Broquet kept silent a moment and fixed his gray eyes on Shotgun. Then he suddenly raised his voice.

"So now are you going to change into a hand cannon?"

Shotgun stared wide-eyed, not understanding. "A hand cannon?"

"A blunderbuss?"

"Uh..."

"Sure, instead of being the good, honest Shotgun, you're going to become a blunderbuss, a pistol, a bandit's weapon."

Shotgun jumped and cried out in alarm, "What do you mean?"

"It's not enough to be Paulin Broquet's neighbor. For your glory you have to become a Z."

"A Z?"

"A member of the Zigomar gang."

Shotgun's teeth started chattering, "Me, a Zigomar? Oh, Monsieur Broquet, do you think... me, a Zigomar!"

Broquet waved his hand to calm the good man's indignation and asked him, "Have you introduced your friend, your betting partner Amblard to Madame Shotgun yet? Have you brought him home yet? Upstairs here?"

"Yes. Was that wrong?"

"What did he do that one time in your apartment?"

"He talked with us, with me and my wife. He thought our place was quaint... he looked out the window..."

"The one over mine?"

"Yes."

"And naturally you said I was your neighbor..."

Shotgun answered with a nod only.

"Always this obsession to give tips! So, Thursday you're having Amblard over?"

"Yes, a kind of picnic. He likes that. He only accepted my invitation to dinner if he could bring the wine... the champagne and cigars."

"I thought so." Then Broquet concluded, "That's fine. Listen up, if you want to stay my friend, you have to obey me."

"Body and soul."

"Okay, I get it," the detective went on, "Zalavi, Zalamor, as your friends say. Now listen, pretend nothing happened, like you don't know a thing. Don't say a word about any of this to your wife. Prepare a nice meal and don't be surprised at anything... don't be scared. Your dinner won't be wasted, you'll still have your champagne... but probably your guest won't be your friend Amblard."

"Why not?"

"Because your friend Amblard is Zigomar!"

Shotgun froze. He was too shocked to be scared and he could not say a word.

The detective went on, "You understand that in the hands of these criminals you, good ole Shotgun, who has great tips but can't see past the tip of your own nose, you are just an unconscious tool. They made you part of their long-planned scheme. They're conning you, using you to get at me again."

Shotgun protested, "No, Monsieur Broquet, I would never let that happen. I would never do anything to help them hurt you."

"Yes, I know, thank you. So, do as I say and don't worry about the rest, that's my problem. Go home now or else Madame Shotgun will get worried and start thinking you, too, have fallen victim to Zigomar."

Broquet shook his hand and Baiter led him away. The stairway was dark but Baiter did not want to turn on the light. Shotgun could climb up to his apartment alone in the dark but when they got onto the landing Baiter heard a noise. He stopped and listened carefully. Someone was rushing down the stairs trying to be as quiet as possible. Baiter brought out his flashlight and shined it on the stairs. He had just enough time to see a man's hand on the rail one floor below.

"Go home and say nothing!" he ordered before jumping on the rail and sliding down like a crazy child. It was the only way he could hope to catch the man scrambling down ahead of him.

Baiter slid fast, burning his a little from the speed, but all of a sudden he stopped. The smooth railing had abruptly turned rough and his pants stuck to it like glue. The other man must have sprinkled it with some kind of resin to prevent this.

So Baiter hopped off the railing and started running down the stairs. He did not catch up and when he jumped down the last few steps the front door was already closed behind his quarry. Baiter figured it would be useless to wake the concierge or go outside. The man would have already disappeared and there was no way to catch up or even see him on the street.

He went back upstairs to tell Broquet. The detective did not look overly surprised.

"We have to expect all kinds of reckless maneuvers now. It's war! An endless, merciless battle! But the end is coming. Victory will belong to one of us. It's logical that crime gets impatient and strikes hard but we have to trust the hour of justice."

He concluded, "In any case, the Z who was on the stairs, even if he saw us bring Shotgun into the apartment, he was sure he wasn't our ally before and he doesn't know what happened in here. But it's likely that if Zigomar was planning to do what it looks like he was doing—strike on Thursday—with the unintentional help of that innocent man, he'll cancel it. So now we can deal with the severed head with no more worries. Goodbye, my friends. Go get some rest because tomorrow's going to be a busy day."

In the morning, before heading to Quai des Orfevres, Paulin Broquet went out to get a picture of the poor, decapitated singer now that he knew her name. It was easy. He just went to the shops selling postcards of the pretty Parisian stars. But in these well lit, well posed portraits it was impossible to recognize not the living person who was really quite charming but the awful, gruesome thing that was the mutilated head of the young woman.

Nevertheless, Broquet was able to learn that Carmen d'Amata had gray eyes, a delightful smile and teeth that could rival Lucette Minois and the mysterious redhead. He also knew that her very long hair was ash blonde. He therefore had proof to support his theory that the hair was dyed after death. It was also support to show that Shotgun gave them a good tip.

All that was left was to see if Carmen d'Amata's coffin contained a headless corpse.

13. The Terror of Ornano tells all

When Paulin Broquet got to the police station Baiter had been waiting for a long time. He said, "I've got a big surprise for you."

"Tell me."

"I put it in your office under guard... the Terror of Ornano."

"Ah! What's he want?"

"To talk to you and only you, who he trusts. To reveal some horrible things... to tell all.

"Good."

"The Terror of Ornano looks crushed. He's tired, devastated... and angry... and looks like he's about to cry..."

"So let's go see him."

Presently Broquet entered his office. The Terror sat on a chair with his arms crossed, chin resting on his huge chest, silent, glum, motionless. When Broquet entered he stood up and shook his hand with a mixture of gratitude and pity, with affection and entreaty.

Broquet squeezed the bandit's hand with force, "So, my boy, you wanted to see me. You have something to ask me... or to tell me?"

"Yes, Monsieur Broquet, I'm going to tell you something... because you're a man who knows and understands life. You know that just because someone's the Terror, it doesn't mean he's a brute... arms of steel and iron fists don't rule out a tender heart! You understand that a Terror can live with women but never hurts them too much... maybe slap them around a little but they like it, shows them who's boss... and you can even male a few sacrifices for them... and then one fine day it happens that the Terror, who thought he was being clever, well, he gets nicked..."

"Nicked?"

"Yeah, he falls in love, okay."

"So, my boy, you're in love!"

"I can tell you, Monsieur Broquet, because you won't laugh at a poor jerk like me, big and strong, stronger than an bull but suffering like a baby! You know that love is a kind of sickness, worse than a fever, burns you up inside, stuffs up your head and cuts down the biggest of 'em."

"Sure does."

"Well, that's me. I've been hit, me, the Terror of Ornano... I'm in love. And look, I'm crying over it."

It was a most unexpected sight and quite touching to see this giant of a man get so emotional, lose control and start sobbing.

Broquet took pity on him, put his hand on his shoulder and said softly, "Go on and cry. There's nothing else to do when you're in love."

After a while, when the Terror had stifled his tears and could talk, Broquet said, "Now, tell me who you're in love with."

"You know very well who."

"Yell me."

"That woman who went to the dance with me. The one who wanted to get close to the Zs and find out who Zigomar was."

"Ah, yes, indeed, I remember we talked about her. She seemed very pretty."

The Terror of Ornano raised his voice, "Pretty! Oh, Monsieur Broquet, the prettiest girl in the world! Eyes so big they wrapped all around you, bright and sparkling and so gentle that they could hold you like in an iron chain but caress you at the same time, eyes so deep that you couldn't tell if they were dark blue or totally black. And that smile that made you want to die with every word she spoke... her body and arms and neck... hands so small they couldn't wrap around one on my fists but they could force me to my knees. Oh, what a woman!"

Paulin Broquet let the giant express his love but finally wanted to know what there was to tell him. "Okay, yes, a wonderful woman you're in love with. And they stole her away from you, kidnapped her? You want to know if I know where she is, if I can find her and bring her back to you?"

The giant shook his head sadly, "No, I just wanted to tell you that they killed her."

"Killed her!"

"Murdered. See, she was too beautiful. That night at Clafous they all went mad for her, attacked me to take her but she escaped that night. That was her death. They got her back and when she wouldn't give up... or give in, they killed her." Raising his fists he howled like a wounded animal, "Cowards! Wretches! Bastards!"

Then he told Broquet, "We have to get revenge... for her... and that's why I'm here. I'm going to tell you everything."

Broquet saw the confession coming and to make it easier and quicker he asked questions. "Okay, we're going to avenge her, the woman you loved, let's see, you said they killed her... are you sure?"

"Absolutely."

"How do you know? Who told you?"

"Look, Monsieur Broquet, you know that Clafous and at the Barbottiere I know everyone like in all the bars along La Chapelle, Rochechouart and Clichy."

"Go on."

"Of course these acquaintances are kind of a mix of everything, you can imagine, so naturally I know some Zs, as you know."

"Sure. So, you have some business with Zigomar?"

"Zigomar needs men like me and wanted to hire me but I always refused. You know, I'm the Terror, an honest man in my way, and I don't want to be a Z."

"I see the rest now," Broquet said. "The Zs get two birds with one stone. They get revenge on you and the pretty woman because you didn't want to give either to Zigomar."

"That's it!" the Terror shouted. "You guessed it!"

"But who told you all this?"

"One of my friends, the Quiche. He's a good guy. What he does is none of my business but we've always been pals. I knew he was a Z but he wanted to get out. Seems things are going so well in the gang... now that Paulin Broquet is getting mixed up in their affairs. They're getting more busts than bucks, so they're quitting Zigomar. See, he'd promised a big score and after the Van Cambre job there'd be millions to share. No job had ever been so carefully set up by Zigomar, that's for sure! Money was gonna come rolling in, but then Broquet happened and hit them hard, a total loss, injuries, dead and not a cent. The Zs don't trust the invisible master anymore. It's more the booty they find is invisible and they're breaking up... they're scared of Paulin Broquet."

"But what's the woman got to do with all this?"

"They accused her of helping you mess up their jobs. She was judged and sentenced."

"They killed her?"

"Yes, Monsieur Broquet. They killed her. And for the Zs to know that Zigomar took action against the traitor, for Broquet to know about the fate of this woman who betrayed Zigomar, they cut off her head and threw it on the empty lot in Buttes-Chaumont."

"I know all that. We found the head. I saw it in the Morgue. But tell me, do you know where and how they killed her?"

"Yes. I even know where they buried the body."

"Okay, where is it?"

"I'll tell you. I came here to tell you everything, except before I do you have to promise me something."

"Go on."

"Well, I only want my revenge for the woman I loved, but Quiche needs money. He's getting nothing from Zigomar anymore and thinks it's funny to ask Paulin Broquet but... Seems there's a reward being offered for the body. Quiche says that if you give it to him he'll take you to the house on Quai de la Loire where they buried the headless body in the basement."

Broquet answered, "Done. Your friend Quiche will get the reward when I see the body."

"You have to trust him when he takes you down into the basement."

"Of course, don't worry, I'll go without taking precautions."

"Plus I'll be there, if you want."

"Thanks, I accept. To get this done fast here's what we do: you fetch Quiche and tell him to wait for me on Quai de la Loire between 1 and 2 a.m."

"Tonight?"

"Yes. If it's possible we can go down right away, otherwise tonight… I'll have the money on me. Thanks to you Quiche can trust me. Okay, let's go… See you tonight."

"I think that should work."

"I'm sure it will. You'll see your beloved again and I promise you that you will get your revenge."

"Thank you, Monsieur Broquet, thank you. You can count on the Terror of Ornano, he'll give his life for you."

"Right," Broquet laughed. "Zalavi, Zalamor!"

He got Baiter to take the Terror down one of the countless corridors in the station and let him out at Place de Harlay. His pal Quiche was waiting for him.

In his office Broquet lit a cigarette and told his lieutenants, "My boys, let's prepare an expedition for tonight. We have a head but Zigomar is so great now that he's going to prove that this poor head has two bodies—one lying in Carmen d'Amata's coffin in the Montmartre cemetery and another, maybe, in a basement on Quai de la Loire. I can't wait to see it."

14. The second grave

As evening fell, before the doors closed a young man, elegantly dressed, entered the Montmartre cemetery carrying a bouquet of flowers and went to cry over a grave until the guards made their rounds and asked him to leave.

It was Gaston Soclet whose bitter grief brought the only homage that death allows: flowers and tears.

He watered the grave with his sadness, then drying his eyes he left the cemetery after looking down Avenue Rachel. He hurried as if he was afraid of being caught there in his sorrow. He took a few steps down Boulevard de Clichy and when he figured that every trace of tears had disappeared from his face he entered the Café Galant where his friend Amblard was waiting for him.

Soclet's movements were all being watched by Baiter nowadays and he in turn told Broquet everything.

"Good," Broquet said, "at least the poor guy is sincere, like the Terror. He loves, has a heart... we can work with that."

Broquet had got information about Gaston Soclet. Depending on how you look at it, it was either good or, according to ordinary morality, detestable.

Detestable because Soclet needed money badly and he did all kinds of things to get it: questionable speculations, betting on horses, playing cards and, Broquet could add, joining the Z gang.

But the money was for his mistress, Carmen d'Amata, who needed a lot. For her Soclet, being deeply in love, was ready to do anything and to risk everything. For her he fell prey to Zigomar. But Soclet's great love for his mistress was stronger than his need for Zigomar and he could not accept them mutilating her so grotesquely. This was beyond the pale...

Therefore, it must be said here that they might be on a wild goose chase, that Shotgun's tips might sound great but be putting them on a false track. There was the possibility that Carmen d'Amata was resting perfectly whole in her coffin and not mutilated.

"It was good for his men," Broquet said, "it was good the poor lover passed out and during those few hours he slept after putting his beloved in the coffin... Zigomar knows how to make people sleep so can take advantage of the time to do his horrible work."

"That's possible."

"Unless it's not Carmen's head. In which case the Terror and his pal Quiche might be telling the truth."

But we know that Broquet is not the kind of man to rest on his laurels and he does not like to waste time mulling over probabilities and hypotheses only to find no sure result, no practical and real solution.

"The best way to know," he said, "is to go and see her."

And this is what he did.

Provided with a special authorization Broquet sent some of his men to set up a watch around the cemetery where Carmen d'Amata's remains were resting. When night fell they started loosening the stone bring out the coffin.

The silence of cemeteries is always impressive. At night the imagination really runs wild through alleys of mystery. But this religious silence does not exist in the Montmartre cemetery. The dead must sleep badly there. Montmartre is so noisy that its lively sounds do not stop at the entrance to the fields of eternal rest. It makes a weird contrast. The impression that one gets in this cemetery located in the heart of the city is very special—if not more nerve-racking at least more typical, more poignant.

To be among the dead and hear the living.

The sounds of the huge city wash up there from the tramways, car horns, clopping horses and sometimes shouting from a party or the echo of a young lady's song gets lost in the branches where birds sing during the day.

When dark night came into the cemetery Paulin Broquet and his men were doing their dismal duty, lit only by a single lantern with blue glass that cast its rays on the spot they were working on. From a distance, from the neighboring houses that looked out on the cemetery, nobody could see a thing or suspect the macabre mission being carried out there.

Besides, it was plenty of light for the workers to finish their job.

When Broquet arrived around midnight the coffin was out of the grave and they were unscrewing the lid. Once the screws were out, with Gabriel leading the crew, the men stepped aside respectfully, leaving their boss to open the coffin as he had asked.

Broquet carried out this final operation piously. He pushed off the oak lid...

The corpse looked long and slender in its white shroud, a flower branch between its folded hands. There was a pillow with dainty lace... and on this pillow was a head! Under the thin shroud was the outline of a nose, a forehead, a chin...

Broquet, Gabriel and Baiter leaned over anxiously. The detective lifted the lamp to see better. Yes, in the coffin, on the pillow, there was a head. There was a head with the body of Carmen d'Amata.

But Broquet was never satisfied with appearances. He watched out for illusions created at first sight, as we saw at the Morgue. And just like he wanted to be certain that the severed head on the marble table was not the redhead, so here he wanted to make sure that this head really did belong to Carmen.

Gently, as if afraid to wake the dead in her eternal sleep, he pulled back the shroud.

"Hold this for me," he handed Baiter the lantern.

He put both hands inside the coffin and pulled out a plaster head that was cleverly attached to the decapitated corpse. The profanation was obvious. Zigomar had struck here.

Carrying away this piece of evidence they closed up the grave, but the coffin went into a special paddy wagon headed for the Morgue where Carmen's remains would be preserved for any future needs.

"Now, my friends," Broquet told his lieutenants, "let's go see our friend the Terror and his pal Quiche. Let's go see that curious body they want to show us in the basement on Quai de la Loire." Smiling, he added, "The body separated from a head that doesn't belong to it!"

Since his adventure in Zulma's attic where his recklessness, let's say, his unspeakable carelessness had almost cost him his life, Paulin Broquet no longer relied solely on his strength and courage and uncommon skills. With enemies like Zigomar you could not make any mistakes or leave anything to chance. Especially since this time more than ever, after being beaten by Broquet several times, Zigomar wanted a sensational revenge.

This rather extreme way to bait him, we might say, to lure him into chasing illusions by the misleading severed head, made one think that the affair was very serious, that the trap they were setting for the detective had been very carefully prepared.

This was one of the great battles between justice and its precious ally, Paulin Broquet, versus the kind of crime, the invisible master, the terrible Zigomar!

In the afternoon, in different disguises, Broquet had scoped out the area where the game was going to be played out and placed some well-trained, very disciplined men who knew their job and followed orders. By midnight everyone was ready for anything.

On the way Broquet met them in small groups or alone, making sure they were all constantly in touch, in sight and ready to come running at the first signal to help him out. They looked like men who lived by night, badly dressed and disheveled, with dirty boots and old caps pulled down to cover their shifty eyes. Vagabonds everywhere, mostly lazy and licentious, who are homeless and are always looking for a trouble, wandering the streets or lurking in shadows, hands buried in their pockets fondling their knives. Flowers of vice, seeds of prison, fruit of the guillotine…

To recognize his men in disguise Broquet had made a signal like the Zs. But whereas the Zs had a symbolic sign to know each other all the time, Broquet changed his for every expedition. Thus there was no possibility of betrayal or surprise.

Tonight the sign was very simple and rather crude but very appropriate for the characters they were playing. They would tap their right foot twice, scrape their shoe on the ground as if something was stuck to it, then tap one more time and move on. Only one in the group had to do this. When two groups met they made the sign as discreetly as possible.

If, however, they happened to meet partners of the invisible master, they made the sing of the Z. And if anyone said "Zalavi", they could not answer "Zalamor" like before because Zigomar had also changed the password. Luckily Baiter had overheard it one day and knew they would have to answer back "Zalavi", then the two groups would say together "Ramogiz" (the name of the famous tribe of gypsies that Zigomar claimed to be chief). Finally they made the sign of Z with their hands.

For, the Zs in the neighborhood were just as numerous as the Broquets. They knew that this job was well prepared and would surely succeed, restoring his former glory. The stakes were high and Zigomar was betting everything on tonight. Hopefully, they thought, he would triumph. Tomorrow Paris would be scared, totally crushed to see the famous bloody Z traced with the blood of Paulin Broquet.

Of course Broquet pretended not to notice anything unusual. His men were hidden just like the Zs. He was not supposed to see anything. He walked casually, not suspecting a thing, not even imaging that Zigomar was involved in the matter—to all appearances not even a real police matter.

Paulin Broquet who had been taken by Zigomar, had fallen into his enemy hands and had played a role in Zulma's attic well enough to throw doubt in the Z tribunal, this time had to play his role even better.

He wore no disguise, just like Gabriel and Baiter who were beside him. All three wore their usual suits. Broquet had a jacket but had put on a gray overcoat that was more noticeable. He wore a bowler hat and like always he was smoking.

Very conspicuously, therefore, Paulin Broquet rode down Quai de la Loire in a carriage with his two lieutenants. This quay running alongside the Saint Martin canal is one of the most picturesque and very busy. It is constantly full of different merchants who are continually loading and unloading the huge barges on the canal. Above all there are building stones; bricks, iron beams, bags of plaster and cement. There are also piles of animal hides headed for the vast warehouses of leather that are centered in the neighboring district.

During the day the quay are full of people, sailors, dockworkers and transporters. It is chaos of men, workers, goods, carts and horses. Everything is moved and moving, pushed and pulled, lifted and dropped among shouts and swearing, a frightful din and air thick air thick with dust, but at night, by some miraculous contrast, there is absolute calm and silence, a veritable desert.

The workers and carts and trucks have all disappeared as if by magic. The metal cranes have stopped creaking. There is no more whistling or smoke. Tarps lay heavily over the sacks of plaster and cement. No one is left but the customs officials who doze wearily in their gatehouses.

Therefore, on this dark, deserted, ill-lit quay, Broquet was waiting, looking for the men he was supposed to meet. In truth, knowing that Zigomar had prepared an attack, knowing perfectly well that the story of the corpse was just an excuse to lure them here—a great place for an ambush—he was fully aware of the danger he was in. But he remained absolutely calm, being careful to stay in the middle of the quay, between the sidewalk next to the houses and the hangars and quay itself, so to speak, that were full of stuff that the Zs could easily be hiding behind. At this distance, unless they shot at him or threw a bomb, the Zs could not surprise him.

At last the Terror of Ornano showed up, stepping out of a dark alley behind two tall piles of material.

15. The hangar

The Terror lumbered forward, swaying from one giant foot to the other, swinging his massive shoulders. "Good evening, Monsieur Broquet. My friend Quiche and I are here. Everything's fine for tonight, if you want…"

"Fine. Call Quiche over here. We need to talk a little before we get started."

"Come with me an we'll meet him."

"No, my boy, until an agreement's been reached between all of us, I'm not moving another inch."

"You're right. I'll go get him."

Broquet grabbed the Terror, "You I know. You're a good guy, not given to betraying people, but you can't answer for your friend. You don't know if he's playing you without you knowing. If he's got something against me…"

The Terror was offended, "No, no, that's not possible! I would've seen it right off. So, what, he thinks I'm an idiot? Thinks he can use me against Paulin Broquet… nothing doing! You know the Terror of Ornano keeps his promises. I'm with you. I'm all yours as long as you want me! If Quiche or anyone else, even Zigomar, tonight here, tries anything against you, well, fine, see these mitts, they'll strangle every one of them like farm chickens. I give you my word that Quiche will play fair… that we can go over with no fear of him."

"I'd like to believe you but… it'd be better if he came over here. Go get him. And make sure not to tell him anything we said."

"Of course! Look, I won't go get him, I'll call him over." The Terror whistled and almost immediately was answered in kind just a few feet away.

A man stepped out of the shadows and came slowly toward them. Quiche had on a cap pulled down to his ears. He wore a long blue coat like they wear around the slaughterhouses of La Villette. At a glance Broquet could see that the coat was covering, hiding other clothes. It made an easy disguise, a kind of Zigomar cape without the hood.

This did not make Broquet feel good at him. In fact, after the blow was struck, there was nothing easier than to throw off the hat and coat, step out wearing a new suit and walk off among the hiding broquets completely unrecognizable.

But Paulin Broquet kept his feelings to himself. He did not want to make Quiche suspect that he had been found out, that he had been "burned" as the police say. Knowing how to talk to people like Quiche was pretending to be, he got straight to the point.

"So, you know where the headless body is?"

"Yes, Monsieur Broquet," Quiche answered. "I know where the basement is where they put it."

Broquet noticed that Quiche did not try to disguise his voice. Therefore, this man believed he was not known to the detective unless he was so smug he thought there was no need, figuring that the enemy could not escape now.

"That's what your pal the Terror told me. He also said that you'll want the reward when you show me the body."

"That's right."

"I have the money on me. Plus, I haven't tried to figure out how you know all this... or what part you play in the whole thing. Once I see the body you'll get your money and... goodbye, nice knowing you."

"Got it. Follow me, it's not far."

While talking Broquet was scrutinizing the man's face. This time he was sure that he was not dealing with the Count de la Gueriniere but rather one of his lieutenants. Still, he wanted to know who this man was. But despite his piercing eyes, like a cat, that could almost see in the dark, he could not recognize the guy. Quiche hid himself well, what with his lowered cap, this upturned collar and keeping to the shadows he managed to remain obscure.

Broquet pulled hard on his cigarette, casually, trying to get more light to reflect off the guy's face. But it did not work. The two men were playing cat and mouse now, a match of wits. But Broquet had warned his men and they helped him cleverly. Baiter suddenly lit his cigarette and this time Quiche could not avoid the light.

As brief as the flame was, as quickly as Quiche turned away his face, it was still enough for Paulin Broquet. In those eyes, surprised and furious, he recognized one of the Zs who had the same look of anxiety and spite when Broquet had caught him with the others working on Baron Van Cambre's safe.

So, it really was one of Zigomar's more important lieutenants he was dealing with. But Broquet showed no sign of knowing.

"It's all agreed then," he said calmly. "It'll go just like we said with your friend the Terror?"

"Just like that."

"And you want your reward?"

"That's all. Don't worry. The Terror vouches for me. We've known each other a long time and he can assure you I wouldn't try anything against you... like Zigomar."

The Terror confirmed, "That's what I told him."

"And you understand that I'm deeply involved. Right now I'm betraying a man who knows how to get revenge. Therefore, I need to be careful and I'll need your help, for later, if he finds out... but hey, I need money right now, so..."

"Sure, fine, let's go. Show it to me."

Silently the small group started walking. Baiter was to the right of Quiche to grab his arm at the least sign of foul play or if he pulled out a weapon. Behind them came Broquet between his faithful Gabriel and the colossal, gullible brute, the Terror of Ornano.

The Zs had made a good choice of a man who could put them in touch with Paulin Broquet to drag him into this trap in which they were putting all their hopes.

"It's not far," Quiche said. "It's in that hangar over there."

"I thought it was in a basement?"

"Exactly. There's one there that nobody ever uses. That's why they chose it."

"Okay, let's go. We're following you."

Said hangar looked completely ordinary, like all the others you see in the docks used as warehouses or storerooms for cargo to load and unload, waiting for their delivery to other destinations.

During the few minutes it took to get to the hangar Quiche walked calmly next to Baiter without saying a word, making no suspicious movements; just keeping his eyes on the ground.

Then he said, "Got to go around the hangar because we might be seen going in the front."

"There's no guard?" Broquet asked.

"Sure, but I know him. We eat together and get drunk. So it's like going over to his place. Like the night we brought the body the guard was drunk and he knows nothing about the package he's guarding."

"That's good."

Quiche led Broquet and the rest followed them down a kind of dark, slippery alley full of mud and trash between two hangars. Abruptly he turned a corner and the back of the hangar appeared in a kind of small courtyard cluttered with wheelbarrows, ladders, pieces of wood and various objects that were hard to identify in the dark. Broquet, however, could see that everything was piled up, stuffed in tightly, apparently for a long time, so that there was not enough space for a person hide among the junk.

"So," he thought, "the danger's not here but inside the hangar."

Quiche did not need a key to open the door. He only had to push the latch and it opened. Right away Baiter stuck himself (so to speak) to Quiche as he entered. Like this he could grab him if he tried to escape or jump aside. If a trap had seen set he would drag the guy into it along with the prey they were hoping to catch.

Quiche understood what Baiter was doing. "You don't have to worry. I told you, there's nothing to fear."

Baiter simply said, "Go on, pay no attention to me, it's my habit."

After them came the Terror, then Broquet and lastly Gabriel into the hangar that in the dark looked huge. Only one lantern with grills hanging from a beam cast its feeble yellow glow into the space, making the rest seem darker still.

"Not exactly bright as day in here," Gabriel remarked.

"Just enough," Broquet said. "Enough for us to do what we came to do. Let's not waste time."

"Right," the Terror mumbled, "let's hurry and find the body of the poor girl... quick."

So far, while they were walking or talking about the situation, arguing the finer points of this peculiar enterprise, the Terror was calm and quiet. But now that they were nearing their goal, about to see the body of the woman he mourned, the poor devil was trembling, getting carried away by his emotions, his grief and his lost love.

Broquet's piercing eyes examined the place, trying to see beyond the pale light into the shadows. He could see that the hangar was a huge space full of sacks piled on top of one another and barrels stacked in pyramids. Sacks and barrels full of cement. Between them were narrow aisles left to move them in and out.

Broquet examined the layout. It looked normal, just like any other warehouse. The merchandise was stacked against the walls with all the little aisles leading to one wide central passageway. So, by going down the middle of the hangar they could check between the sacks and barrels to make sure no one was hiding.

He wondered where and how the Zs—if they really had set up an ambush—would come rushing in to attack them. He thought that if the Zs were not hiding inside the hangar—but really he could not figure out where—then they must be in the basement.

Broquet told himself, "In a basement again! But Zigomar ought to know that it never works out for him when he uses a basement. Unless he's really gutsy and set up the basement here to get revenge for the one at the Barbottiere."

He smiled to himself, "Zigomar must really think I'm stupid and naïve. We'll see."

Then one last thought came to mind, "Zigomar thinks he's won, that it's a done deal and Quiche just has to go through the motions... but why have all those Zs outside hiding in the shadows on the quay, surrounding the hangar? Obviously as a precaution. The Zs were still uncertain. Maybe in case a fight broke out with the detective's partners..."

During these reflections Broquet wasted no time. He took the lantern off its hook and grinned at Quiche, "Doesn't bother you if I take a look around, get my bearings here?"

"If you want," Quiche responded. "I don't care. Look around, search everything, all you'll find is cement."

As calm as could be Quiche leaned against the wooden beam where the lantern had been hanging. Baiter leaned against the same beam. Gabriel sat down nearby on a bag of cement next to the Terror, who was crying quietly with his face buried in his enormous hands.

Paulin Broquet first walked around the nearest corner that was walled off but with a window, forming a little room. The door was closed but he could read the word "Office" on it. In fact it was a room for the accountant and cashier during the day. At night a cot had been unfolded for the guard to rest between rounds.

Broquet lifted the lantern, trying to see through the dusty window if anything suspicious lay in wait. He saw a table, a desk and the cot between the two. On the cot was the guard. It was very hard to see him through the dirt and grime on the window, which made him want a closer examination. He only had to push the unlocked door to enter the room.

Quiche watched him casually. "He's wasting his time."

Broquet went to the cot and held out the weak light. Just like Quiche had said the guard seemed to be dead drunk. He was lying but rather collapsed on the cot. He arms hung down and one leg was touching the floor. Like a drunkard stumbled in by habit and overcome by sleep in front of his bed. He slept soundly, deeply.

Broquet had studied the countless ways a man could sleep and knew very well how drunken men dozed, so he watched this one carefully. He slept but he did not snore! This was surprising. Drunks usually snore in their sleep. They feel such animal pleasure that they breathe their contentment from their mouths. The animal gets the better of the man. A man sleeping off his wine, burning off his alcohol, needs a lot of air to breath. He cannot get enough to fill up his lungs through his nose and his overheated bronchial tubes need cool air. That's when the mouth opens to gulp in fresh air. And the sleeper who breathes through his mouth snores... that's a fact. There is also the bad position of the sleeper that obstructs breathing...

Now, this guy should have been snoring but wasn't. Why?

Moreover, Broquet knew that nothing was harder to imitate than sleep, no sound trickier to fake than snoring. Someone pretending to sleep and snore fools no one. It's the same for forced laughter versus real laughter. Everyone can the difference between the two.

Therefore, Broquet knew that the night watchman, drunk as he was and lying like he was fast asleep, should be snoring... so he concluded that he was not sleeping. He must have known it was impossible to fool a trained ear like Broquet's and taken the only option open to him—don't snore. But his silence was just as telling.

Broquet stepped back from the sleeper. He put the lantern on the desk so that it shined on the man's face, then figuring that Quiche was watching him he went to search the office, looking in the corners and under the furniture. He ended up on the other side of the cot.

Facing the sleeper now, able to see his face, even though half-hidden by his arm, Broquet recognized him. "Aha," he said, "I know why he's not snoring.

It's because great sorrow is silent. The guard will never get over the loss of Carmen d'Amata. The dead drunk watchman is Gaston Soclet."

Broquet studied him carefully to make sure that he was not pretending. He was indeed sleeping deeply. His breathing was weak and irregular, almost like he was sobbing. Furthermore, from behind his closed eyes, tears were starting to drip slowly down his face.

"The poor guy's dreaming of her."

The detective understood that this lover had become too softened by sorrow, his heart too broken to be of any use to Zigomar. They obviously wanted to get rid of him, a hopeless stooge, a burden, maybe a danger now. So, Zigomar put him into a deep sleep and brought him here to be another casualty in the coming battle with Paulin Broquet.

And the inconsolable lover knew nothing, not where he was or what fate, what death awaited him as he dreamed of love and wept over his departed sweetheart.

16. The vampire's grave

Having found nothing in the office, which meant nothing, Paulin Broquet went back into the hangar.

As he passed by his lieutenants and Quiche he said, "The guard's sleeping like a log."

Holding his lantern the made an inspection of the hangar. He walked to the end of the central aisle, all the way to the big doors that opened onto the dock where they loaded and unloaded all the sacks and barrels. They were wide double doors with an iron bar holding them closed along with a huge padlock. Broquet examined it carefully.

"Okay," he told himself, "It's shut tight... maybe too tight. I have to look reassured. It's perfect. Pretend I'm satisfied now, nothing suspicious, nothing to fear."

He went back, lifting the lantern here and there to peak behind the piles. He saw a few sacks were flatter than the others as if some cement had leaked out. They must have been split open and put back in such a way to keep more cement from spilling out.

He also noticed that when he rapped on a few barrels the covers were not nailed down but only laid on top, which was a big mistake.

Broquet picked up a pinch of cement and rolled it between his fingers to check the grain and the quality. He wet it with some saliva.

"Oh, it's quick-drying cement for hydraulic work. They've cut it with something. A few seconds in water and it should harden, as solid as stone."

Then he looked at the floor. It was mostly hard earth, a dirt floor. But closer to the office they had started putting floorboards. Exactly where the loose barrels stood. Broquet pressed down on the boards and he felt them move a little. "Hmm, that's strange. A floor meant to support this heavy weight should be stronger than this."

As he was walking around the floorboards, measuring them, examining them, Quiche yelled out, "That's how we get down to the basement. They're movable. To your right is the door."

"Ah yes, yes, so it is. I was wondering about. Exactly what I was looking for." But he was thinking, "The floor's been rigged. That's where the danger lies."

To warn his lieutenants about his discovery he gave the signal with his foot. He tapped twice, scraped the floor and one more tap.

Then he said calmly, "Let's go down."

Quiche pushed off the pillar and came over to the floorboards, followed by Baiter. The Terror dried his eyes, stood up and came over with Gabriel.

"Oh," the Terror said, "Monsieur Broquet, now that we're about to see the girl's body, I feel like something inside me just broke. It's stupid but I've lost my strength… my courage… my heart's torn up…"

"All right, fine," Quiche said, "you can sing about your love later. We're wasting time. Lift up the trapdoor."

The Terror of Ornano bent over and grabbed an iron ring and pulled it. The trapdoor opened—it was only 3 or 4 feet square. As it dropped down onto the floor a gust of cold, humid air burst out of the black hole. It smelled musty, like basement.

Broquet swung the lantern over the darkness, "Ah, there's the ladder. Let's go."

Baiter pushed Quiche forward, "You first."

Quiche climbed onto the ladder without hesitating. Baiter was right behind him.

"Look out!" Broquet said. "Light!"

Baiter immediately turned on his flashlight and shined it into the basement. Although it was quick and unexpected Quiche showed no signs of surprise. Baiter's light, like all flashlights, was not very bright but it was enough to see the whole basement, which was really more like a cellar. There was not much in it: some old broken barrels, torn sacks, tools, wheelbarrows turned to scrap iron. It was a junk closet.

The walls seeped water. A big pipe rose up in one corner. In the dim light Broquet could see a metal cable running up along the pipe. It sparkled, so it was new, recently installed, not long enough to rust. They had forgotten to hide it, to paint it, to cover it up. Maybe they were thinking that if could not be seen at night or that there was just no reason to hide it.

But the cable seemed out of place to Broquet. He wondered what it was for. He swore that the first thing he would do down there would be to see where it led. And so he went down after Baiter. Then came the Terror and lastly Gabriel.

The ladder they used just a simple, rickety, old ladder. It was slowly falling apart in the humidity. Indeed it was a miracle that it could still support the weight of a giant like the Terror for the ten feet or so it took to descend.

Now Broquet, his lieutenants and Quiche were in the cellar. On a sign from his boss Baiter turned off his flashlight leaving them to the dim light of the lamp. The floor was greasy, uneven and covered with mud and puddles of water.

Broquet looked all around trying to find the trap he suspected but he still could not see it. He went over to the pipe but there was a big pile of stuff in front of it and he could not see where the cable ended up.

Suddenly the Terror moaned, "The cowards! This is where they hid her!" He turned to Quiche, "Well? Where'd they put her?"

Broquet had noticed that there was no sign of the floor being disturbed, no trace of digging. Terror's question, therefore, was more than appropriate.

"Where'd they put her?" he asked again.

"I don't know. I know they put her here in this basement but where and how they hid her I don't know... We'll have to search."

"Let's begin in this corner," Broquet pointed toward the pipe with the mysterious cable.

Quiche made no objection and started picking up some objects to move them up to the hangar. All of a sudden a foot stamped twice on the floorboards, which made the Terror jump. Then a shoe scraped the floor before stamping a third time. The signal!

"What's that?" the Terror asked.

"Don't move," Gabriel barked.

But before the third knock was heard Broquet had already jumped on Quiche. In the blink of an eye he was on top on him on the pile of junk and before he could scream out he had stuffed a handkerchief in his mouth.

With Baiter's help they took off Quiche's coat and cap. Broquet took his own overcoat, the light colored one that could be easily seen, and his hat and put them on him. With a blade in his hand he dragged the disguised man over to the ladder.

One word," Broquet whispered in his ear, "one false move and I kill you."

Through the opening up above they heard a voice. Boss, are you there?"

"Yes," the detective answered. "What's going on?"

"Come up here quick! It's a trap! The Zs are here! Come up!"

"I'm coming."

Quiche tried to fight, to pull the gag out of his mouth but Broquet had him by the wrists and twisted so hard that he almost broke them. The scoundrel choked, knew he was beaten, could not defend himself or cry out and figured that his only hope was in flight.

Therefore, he scrambled up the ladder. He had barely reached the trapdoor when he was grabbed and lifted up. His head was smashed in with a club and his chest stabbed repeated with a sword.

At the same time shouts of joy, laughter and insults boomed out. The Zs were singing their triumph. They had finally killed Paulin Broquet!"

"We did it! The smartest of the smart! They sly old fox you got to kill over and over! We got him!"

They threw the corpse around, kicked it over the floor all the while chanting their lurid cheers. For a while, like savages, in their joy they even danced around the lifeless body. Quiche had fallen face down on the floor. The head wound had killed him straightaway and covered his face with blood and pieces of his brain. Dust and cement stuck to it and made a gruesome mask that rendered him unrecognizable.

The Zs really could believe—never suspecting the change of clothes in the basement—that they had really been victorious this time, that the corpse they were playing with was truly their terrible enemy, so feared, so formidable, so hated…

"Long live Zigomar!" they yelled. "Zigomar the victor! Zigomar the master! Long live Zigomar!"

They howled and hollered, raised their arms and shook their clubs and swords, still dripping with blood.

"Zalavi! Zalamor!"

The ones wearing black hoods formed a circle around the four or five chiefs in red hoods. In the very middle stood Zigomar who bore the gold embroidered Z on his red silk hood. The black hoods also carried lanterns, probably found in the hangar; the red hoods held small flashlights. All of them were voicing their enthusiasm, rendering homage, showing their respect, shining their lights on the golden Z.

And this eerie scene was terrifying!

Paulin Broquet looked on because after killing their partner who they thought was him he had sneaked out of the basement without them knowing. During the hullabaloo they had forgotten about Quiche. He who was now the new Quiche was able to slip away. They must have figured that Quiche had put on his hood like the rest of them, that he was with the Zs and after fulfilling his mission was taking part in the celebration.

Meanwhile, Broquet took advantage of this and got away, hid behind a pile of cement sacks. He watched the dramatic scene and waited for the right moment to start his own attack. Attacking these men right now, a lot of men, burning with passion, proud of their victory, would mean a certain defeat and an inevitable death. It would also be sacrificing the lives of his two lieutenants who would come up to defend him. It would be a really bad decision. So, Broquet stayed put, hiding in the shadows. It was a matter of minutes, seconds even.

With gun in hand he waited for the moment, any time now, when he could plant a bullet between the two eyeholes of the red hood, which was not, like at the Barbottiere, a dressed up mannequin. He, the man of justice, against the golden Z, the king of crime…

But one of the huge pillars holding up the roof was in his way. Broquet could not shoot. The Zs had no idea they were being spied on and were only concerned with expressing their joy. It made the scene almost unreal and particularly dramatic.

"My friends," Zigomar said after commanding silence, "with a man like this whom we have just vanquished, we can never take to many precautions, as you know. We believed we had killed him twice already, this marvelous adversary, the only one to escape us, by some miracle. But here he is because Zigomar laughs at miracles and always gets his enemies. Here he is on the ground at our feet. To make sure that he won't come back this time let's put him in a grave he can never escape… a grave that will embrace him like a vampire, swallow him; absorb him and keep him forever."

467

"Hurray! Long live Zigomar!"

"My friends, Zigomar has prepared the cement. It's quick drying, instantly with water. The water will flow into the cellar like a tank. The cement will mix with it and anyone searching here will be working in vain. The corpse of Paulin Broquet will a tomb for eternity."

"Hurray!"

"And as burial companions we'll give him his two lieutenants. They'll be buried alive in the vampire's grave, wrapped forever in cement that will take only minutes to harden into a stone coffin that no pick will be able to open."

Zigomar waved his hand. "Pour the water."

A black hood went to the back of the hangar and pulled a metal ring.

Broquet could tell that it was attached to the cable that had intrigued so much. He heard the sound of rushing water and knew that the device was rigged to open the pipe in the corner of the basement.

At the same time the other black hoods emptied sacks and poured barrels of cement over the floorboards. It kicked up a thick cloud of dust. The cloud rose up between Broquet and the gang of Zs who were stepping away. It also hid Baiter as he escaped and ran to his boss. Broquet saw him coming out of the trapdoor. He jumped out to lead him back to his hiding place.

"Go outside," he said, "and give the signal! Get everyone in here double quick!"

"But, boss, you're not going to stay here..."

"Go! Give the signal!"

"You alone... against all of them?"

"Hurry!"

Baiter obeyed. With his incredible agility, which we know now, he snaked around the barrels and along the piles of cement. He was almost at the door when two black hoods came out of the office where the guard slept. These two were carrying out poor Gaston Soclet who was crying in his sleep, the deep sleep that was not deep enough to bury his grief.

Baiter tapped twice with his foot in the shadows to let them pass. The two men went to throw the body, already like a corpse, into the group of red hoods.

"My friends," the golden Z spoke again, "here's a companion who we trusted but now, because a woman he loved is dead, wants to leave us, abandon us! He has a soft heart, cries all day long over a woman and his heart has melted in his tears. This man will be leaving us tonight. A man like this, a victim of love, dominated by a woman, giving in to grief... he is not worthy of being a Z, of being with Zigomar! You know it! Zigomar wants you to be with him zalavi, zalamor!"

"Yes, yes! Zalavi! Zalamor!"

"Well, he who is no longer with Zigomar is going to join those who are against Zigomar."

"Death!" the Zs howled. "Death to the traitor!"

Zigomar held out his hand, "Do it!"

The black hoods dragged Soclet, still fast asleep and probably dreaming his sad dream, maybe weeping over his Carmen at this moment... they dragged him to the edge of the trapdoor and threw him on a pile of cement.

With iron bars the other Zs pounded on the floorboards. Broquet finally understood why he found them loose. He was not mistaken when he figured they were rigged for a reason. In fact, the iron bars were pounding on a support beam and the floor was starting to give way over the basement where water was slowly flowing over the cement.

Broquet thought of his lieutenant Gabriel who was still down there. But Gabriel knew what he had to do. He would escape like Baiter had when the time was right.

All of a sudden the floor stopped slanting down as if something had got in its way, holding it up.

"Work the other side!" Zigomar ordered.

The black hoods went to pound on the other side of the floorboards. A barrel of cement tipped over and rolled into the open hole where it broke the ladder in its fall.

Broquet shuddered at the sight. Gabriel's escape was just cut off. The detective immediately untied the rope around his waist to throw it down for his lieutenant, but right then the iron bars, which were creating a thick cloud of dust, made the floor lean even more, spilling the sacks and barrels and the body of Soclet into the basement.

The Zs shouted in triumph again. They leaned over the gaping hole as others dragged over the body of the one they thought was Paulin Broquet to throw him into the vampire's grave, as Zigomar had called it. But at that moment the booming, furious, menacing voice of the Terror of Ornano echoed through the hangar.

"Zigomar! You coward, you wretch! You are no master! Tonight the winner is once again Paulin Broquet!"

There was a moment of silent astonishment among the Zs. They froze on the edge of the tomb.

"What? The Terror's still down there? The idiot didn't come out behind Quiche?"

"Me?" the giant shouted, "I don't care if I die here. I even glad... But I'll have my revenge for the woman you murdered... Long live Paulin Broquet!"

These final words were met with a fit of laughter. The Zs were doubled-over... but they stopped laughing in a flash.

From the cellar, as if launched by a catapult, a man sprang out. All the Zs recognized him.

"Gabriel!" they yelled.

Gabriel landed a few feet away from the Zs. The black hoods jumped on him right away to throw him back.

469

"Death to Gabriel!" they shouted. "Just like Broquet... Death to them!"

Two of the hoods cried out in pain, staggered and fell into the basement. A third almost collapsed to the ground before tumbling into the dark hole. The others got scared and shocked and instinctively backed off.

The red hoods shined their flashlights on the spot where the unexpected disturbance was taking place. In this circle of light an unimaginable apparition emerged. The lit figure, eyes on fire, standing tall, looked huge with two Zs lying at his feet. The detective appeared as if sprung from the ground in front of the black hole, like a vengeful god come to punish the guilty at the hour of justice, the moment of apotheosis!

Screams like nothing heard before, indescribable screams of terror, surprise, fear and dread came out of all the Zs who were just a minute ago shouting with joy and celebrating their victory.

"Paulin Broquet!"

It was magnificent.

Broquet helped Gabriel stand up. "Buck up, old boy."

Then he charged alone into the group crying, "Just you and me, Zigomar!"

17. The duel of flashlights

Paulin Broquet charged, making a hole in through the red and black hoods. He was trying to reach the only red with a golden Z, trying to get at Zigomar. To get him during the confusion, to grab him and tie him up.

Unlike the battle at Van Cambre's house this time he would not let him escape. He would guard him personally and never leave his side until he saw the prison doors shut.

But of all the Zs only Zigomar had not panicked. When he recognized his implacable enemy he understood the situation, saw the danger, but also the means of defense.

Of course, like everyone he was really surprised to see Broquet show up when he thought he was dead. He, Zigomar, had planted the sword in the detective's back. He had killed his enemy like a matador, lured him into this corner of the arena, trapped him, readied him for the swords. Everything had worked perfectly. Zigomar rightfully thought he had won. He had killed him on the spot, stabbed between the shoulder blades straight through the heart... it was a beautiful blow, fit for a king on a royal feast day. And the victim had fallen like a bull.

But the man killed so magnificently by the master, the king of Zs, always the victor, the man whom Zigomar had killed was not the one was supposed to fall under his sword. It was his assistant, a banderillero, waving a cape, stunning the beast, bringing it forward for the death blow; he was a Z, one of the best, the bravest, the cleverest of all, who was called Quiche in the crime world, he whom he trusted the most, his friend. Zigomar understood this immediately.

His trap was marvelous, of course, and masterfully planned. It worked until the very last moment. But Zigomar was dealing with Paulin Broquet. Even though the detective pretended to fall into the trap, it was only to fool his enemy so he could fight on his own terms.

On both sides it was an admirable, ingenious, courageous fight.

Zigomar, however, after the initial surprise had worn off, knew that Broquet had escaped his trap and gone on the offensive. He was ready to fight and spoil their victory. His own triumph would be ever the sweeter.

As always Zigomar had planned his escape at the same time as the attack, which is not only prudent but the best tactics since victory often belongs to the one who thought of his retreat.

"Just you and me, Zigomar," Broquet had shouted as he pushed his way through the hoods to get to him.

"Come on then, Broquet," Zigomar had yelled in answer, but he jumped back, separating himself from the men being beaten away by the detective's fists.

He got some distance and light as a cat jumped on a pile of cement bags. Climbing to the top he blew on a metal whistle with a special, shrill tone that carried far. From outside another answered this signal.

The red and black hoods, however, had finally got hold of themselves after these brief minutes. The signal snapped them out of their stupor and they saw that there were only two broquets. Two against all of them, ten times more... and the other Zs were on their way. Hope filled their hearts again and they could smell certain victory.

Once again they cried out, "Long live Zigomar!"

They rushed at Gabriel with their rallying cry, "Zalavi! Zalamor!"

Paulin Broquet was trying to reach his enemy. He leaped onto a barrel in front of the pile of sacks and then scrambled up the pyramid across from him. But just as he reached the top Zigomar's gun fired and Broquet felt the bullets bite into the barrels at his feet.

Broquet saw only the flash from the pistol because it was almost pitch back and despite his keen eyes he could not see his adversary. But the flashes were like lighted targets in the night, quickly come and gone but enough for a sharp-shooter like Broquet to hit the bull's eye. But his shot was answered only with a burst of laughter. Then Zigomar fired again. And Broquet shot back... without effect. More laughter and another shot. This time Broquet did not react. He did not fire back because he wanted to know why his shots missed.

It was too brief a light for him to see well, but he realized that Zigomar was on the other side of the pile, sticking his hand between two sacks and shoot-ing from a safe hiding place. This was not enough for the detective who wanted to see better. He took out his flashlight and shined it at the target but he took care to lay the flashlight on the top barrel and crouch down behind it. He ducked when a bullet came whistling by.

"A few inches closer and I'd be a goner," the detective thought.

But he saw his enemy now. And his enemy could not see him. But Zigomar would not stay put there. He, like all the Zs, was as well if not better equipped than the broquets. He turned on his flashlight and stuck it in the sack he was hiding behind. And now he could his enemy too.

The two men sat still in this stand off for a few minutes, both holding fast with their incredible agility and balance. It was impossible for either of them to move without being seen, without getting a bullet in whatever part of their body showed. Because Zigomar was as good a shot as Broquet and the top of his pile was only 20 feet from the top of the barrels. It was clear now that whoever gave in, out of fatigue or slipping or whatever, would get a bullet from the other.

But Broquet did not want to kill Zigomar. Nor did he want to be killed by him, of course, especially when victory was so close.

In fact, although the Zs had answered Zigomar's signal, his whistle, they certainly did not seem in a hurry to help their chief in danger. When Broquet realized this he also guessed the reason. The shouts coming closer confirmed his hunch.

Baiter had gathered the broquets and they were surrounding the hangar, keeping the Zs from helping their partners. There was screaming and yelling and gunshots all around the hangar.

Apparently this happened often enough in this area deserted at night that the people living nearby the docks paid little attention. Nobody lifted a finger. They preferred, as the saying goes, to let the people work out their own problems.

Over all the racket Broquet could hear his men, recognized their voices, particularly that of his faithful Baiter.

"We're here, boss!" he was hollering in case they were fighting inside as well.

And now Broquet felt like the master of the hour, master of the minute, master of the situation. He only had to wait. Zigomar would try to escape... and he would show himself. Broquet would shoot but only to wound him, to stop him. He wanted to take him alive.

All of a sudden the big door of the hangar was struck by blows from an axe.

"We're coming, boss!" voices yelled.

The broquets were entering which meant the Zs had fled.

Almost at the same time a few broquets holding flashlights came through the small door from the alley. "Boss, we're here!" they shouted. "Long live Paulin Broquet!"

Now Zigomar saw they danger he was in. He whistled again and with surprising swiftness the red and black hoods vanished.

During the few minutes that all this took—quicker in reality than in writing—Gabriel had the chance to grab one of the iron bars that the Zs had used to drum on the movable floor. He fought off the Z gang, swung with all his might, whacked everything around him, in short did really fine work.

The Zs who were running around, bumping into each other and keeping to the shadows, did not dare use their pistols. They had learned their lesson at Van Cambre's house where they had shot one another. Here was even a greater risk of hitting a comrade if they fired a shot. And not knowing where their chief, the invisible master, was kidding, they feared shooting him.

Before them stood only one man, a maniac... a tremendous fighter, okay, but in no time they would get the better of him. They blocked his blows and tried to grab him as he swung wildly and fiercely.

Zigomar must have given orders to this effect. As Broquet found out later he wanted one of the lieutenants as a hostage to question him and then trade him back for the Zs being held prisoner by Broquet.

While the Zs were trying to capture Gabriel alive, therefore, but could not get close without getting hit by the iron bar, the whistle echoed through the hangar, the signal for new orders, the command to retreat. And this order, it must be said, was carried out eagerly.

However, on top of his cement sacks Zigomar could see the gravity of the situation better than anyone. His men had to abandon the battlefield in defeat after celebrating a victory. He, the king of crime, a formidable fighter, magnificent in his rage, even faced with threatening danger and imminent capture, he did not want to admit defeat.

He had sent his men to safety! He, the chief, wanted to be the last to go. He would hold out until the last second like the captain of a sinking ship before the sea carried the wreckage away.

He threw off his hood, revealing his face, and moved into the light.

"I see you!" the detective cried out. "I see you perfectly, Count de la Gueriniere! I know you now, Zigomar!"

"Show yourself too!" the bandit yelled back. "If you're brave, stand up!"

Paulin Broquet climbed onto the top barrel and stood there calmly without saying a word. He took his flashlight, raised his arms and shined the light down on himself. It showed admirable courage but also reckless folly. It was typical Broquet!

Zigomar did the same. Full of rage and fury, as soon as he was standing up he pointed his gun at his enemy.

Broquet laughed, "Clumsy!" he barked as the bullet hit the barrel. "Too low!"

He had counted. That made five shots that Zigomar had taken and since the guns these criminals usually used only held five in the chamber Zigomar was empty.

Broquet took aim at Zigomar, "Give up or I'll put you down! Give up now!"

"Never!" the bandit howled.

Broquet had Zigomar in his sights and could have fired but he just held him there. "Hey ho!" he called to his men, "Over here! Get him!"

His men came running. Gabriel was already climbing the pile. Baiter answered, "We're coming! Hold him there, we're coming!"

The last of the red hoods saw the danger their chief was in and ran back to the foot of the pile. The battle was going to start all over again. One of the hoods climbed up to Zigomar and said, "Come on! Let's go!"

When Zigomar wanted to stay and face his enemy who was still threatening him with his gun, the red hood grabbed him in his arms and lifted him up. Almost at the same time a gunshot rang out. One of the red hoods had seen Broquet on his pyramid, cutting a sharp figure in the dark hangar, and fired at him.

Broquet staggered and fell over. He rolled from barrel to barrel while Zigomar, as the ultimate insult, being dragged away by his man, yelled out, "Another time, Paulin Broquet!"

18. The duel continues

The fight was not confined to the hangar. It spilled onto the dock, which was an excellent battlefield being deserted and run-down. The broquets chased down the Zs and caught up to them one by one or in groups, engaging in new battles that promised no sure outcomes.

Zigomar had not chosen this hangar at random—it was his home territory. He was setting this up for a long time. Everything, cement, barrels, sacks, belonged to him. The hangar had precious resources and the Zs used every one of them.

Zigomar was very cautious—only once had he been defeated at Van Cambre's—and prepared for every contingency, including a possible retreat. So when the broquets showed up, the Zs seemed to just disappear. They found only the wounded.

The others Zs, including Zigomar himself, unwillingly, vanished through a secret door that led onto the dock. On their way out they took off their hoods and dropped them in the dark.

Now that all the detective's men were in the hangar the Zs were logically counting on sneaking outside and beyond any stray broquets left on guard. They could split up on the huge, deserted dock and get lost in the little, winding alleys.

But as we saw the fight was still going on outside, against all their expectations. Because even though Zigomar had an escape plan, Paulin Broquet also had a plan for a total and decisive victory.

All the broquets did not rush into the hangar but like hunters on the prowl some stayed on the dock and next to the alleys, waiting for their prey—the jailbirds, so to speak.

Broquet himself was still in the fight. By some miraculous luck he was not crushed by the barrels of cement tumbling down the pyramid. And it was the pyramid collapsing at the very moment when the red hood fired his gun that saved him being shot. Being agile and athletic Broquet knew how to fall without hurting himself and he landed on his feet, ready to chase his enemy when he saw one of the Zs limping through the open door and into the dark hallway. Broquet sprang over, grabbed him by the neck and threw him to the ground. He jumped over the body and ran down the escape route.

As usual Broquet was heading recklessly into danger. If the Zs running down the narrow hallway turned around and recognized him, he would be right in their line of fire with nowhere to hide.

But the Zs were thinking only of escape. They were in a lost battle where they no longer about revenge or victory; everyone was thinking only of himself, of saving his own skin, of escaping, of fleeing. It was a rout!

Maybe also the Zs in front of him, who were not even thinking of turning around, thought he was another companion trying to reach safety. He, too, did not waste time by turning around to see if anyone was after him. He kept running as fast as he could in the narrow passage with a slippery floor.

Broquet faced the same problems as the Zs trying to escape over the difficult ground. For a few minutes it was a grueling, exhausting race. Then came the fresh air and right after his prey Paulin Broquet stepped onto the dock. Thanks to his keen sight he could recognize the man he was chasing.

"Zigomar!" he shouted. And with a second wind, a new-found strength he bounded after his enemy.

But Zigomar had a head start and was already running full speed. He heard the detective's shout, however, and turned his head. "Bah! It's Broquet!" He stopped, turned, raised his arm… and fired.

Broquet had counted five shots before and believed his enemy was out of bullets. But the Zs also knew their chief had emptied his gun. The red hood who had pulled him out of danger, out of Broquet's hands, so to speak, was smart enough to give him another gun whose chamber was full.

The duel begun in the hangar could start over again here in a setting that was just as picturesque and perhaps even more dangerous because the two adversaries, in their hatred, apparently, were going to run at each other shooting at point blank range.

Here, moreover, Zigomar had one important advantage over the detective. Zigomar held a fully loaded gun while Broquet had already spent more than half his ammunition. But we know that this detail (for him it was only a detail) was too minor to cause him any worry.

Broquet saw Zigomar aiming at him but he kept on coming. At the precise moment when the criminal fired he jumped to the side. The bullet would have killed but as it was it only put a hole in his coat.

"That's better than last time!" Broquet shouted.

He jumped again because Zigomar was firing a second shot.

"All right, that's enough!" the detective yelled. "You're going to end up hitting me!"

He fired back and Zigomar also leaped away. But Zigomar dropped to the ground. Broquet never missed his target.

He could have easily killed Zigomar but he wanted to take him alive. It was enough just to put a bullet in his thigh. Then he ran toward him as he was struggling to his feet.

Zigomar whistled loudly, shrilly, and emptied his gun at his enemy, as fast as the barrel would turn. Shooting wildly as he staggered, not a single bullet hit its target. When Broquet was standing a few feet away Zigomar had his sword in hand. Broquet knew how to handle himself against a sword: a quick kick to the wrist parried the blow and he threw his enemy to the ground, trying to get the handcuffs on him.

Even though Zigomar was wounded he was still a formidable, dangerous adversary. We know that he was exceptionally strong and just like Broquet he knew all the secrets of European fighting—French kickboxing and English boxing—and also the Japanese, which was a rare skill at that time. He started a terrible battle with the detective, harder on the ground where the defender had a considerable advantage.

Broquet had to first beware of the sword and revolver that Zigomar was wielding now like a billy club, a sap or brass knuckles.

And the duel went on in full fury. It was a merciless, pitiless duel. Two wild beasts blinded by rage looked no less fierce than these two implacable enemies.

Zigomar was trying to hold out as long as possible. Of course he understood that in this situation Broquet would end up getting the better of him; he would win. Not only was his wound hurting him but also he was losing blood and feeling weak.

Still, he had time and strength enough to whistle, to warn his companions. He was hoping that the signal would bring them to his defense. On the ground, injured, beaten, he was still hoping to get his revenge and turn this defeat into a triumph!

During the few minutes of fierce fighting where the two men, now in rags, both wounded, covered in blood because after the guns and swords were thrown off, after the punches, they bit each other; you could hear nothing but moaning and groaning from their muscular chests, just those tragic 'Ughs' with every effort.

This time Paulin Broquet was on top of his adversary, eyes wide with the fury of combat, and he could clearly see his man. If it was anyone else, a simple Z, he would not have risked his life like this, not wasted his time trying to take him alive... Yes, it really was the Count de la Gueriniere that he was fighting. It really was Zigomar!

Oh, it would be hard to capture him and painful, but he would do it! He would not let him get away even if it meant his death.

Moreover, even though he had not given his own signal, he figured that his faithful lieutenants would come to help, that his broquets would come searching for him, that they would get here in time... If the Zs came to help their master, they would run into the broquets.

In any case, Zigomar would be caught.

The detective fought valiantly. He was counting on the final victory of justice!

19. A sergeant in the know!

Heavy footsteps pounded on the pavement as people came running over.

Paulin Broquet saw them and shouted, "Over here! Over here!"

They were policemen who had heard the gunshots. But they did not know where to go on the huge dock amidst the mountains of materials. They were drifting around, running to and fro, full of good intentions, doing their duty but lost. With Broquets shout they headed for him.

Zigomar also saw them and shouted out, "Help me, friends, help me!"

The officers answered, "There they are!" In no time they were on top of the two brawlers.

"Help me tie him up," Broquet said.

"Help me!" Zigomar ordered. "Don't let him escape!"

Then in this tragic scene something happened that was really funny, absolutely absurd given the circumstances. It happened fast, hurriedly, like the last scene in the second act of a vaudeville farce where the actors get carried away by the outrageous action as if drunk on the dizzying nonsense.

Once again the police farce had to be played out.

But we have to admit that in this case it was very hard for the fine officers to form good and sure judgments. First of all they were leaning over the fighters who looked like one tangled mass. As usual, following their tactical regulations, they started by trying to separate the two men, wanting to hear both of them.

"Let 'em explain it to the chief," the sergeant said, for there was a sergeant present.

The officers got a good grip on them but it was no easy task separating the combatants, especially since Broquet did not want to let go of the Count. He hung on to him like a dog on a wild boar and every time they pulled him off he ripped a piece of clothing.

"He's rabid," the sergeant observed.

Then he got in front of him and tried to get control, to protect the other... the Count de la Gueriniere... against the attacks... and got helped by the other officers.

"Come on, stop yer bellyaching!" the police told their captive.

And Paulin Broquet found two new adversaries in front of him... two police officers... two representatives of the law. For, the Count was freed and trying to stay out of the fight and keep his distance under the protection of the police!

"This guy attacked me," he was saying. "He shot me. Good thing you came when you did, friends, but watch out—he's crazy!"

Broquet was in rags, bloody, appalling, looking exactly the picture that the Count was painting.

Struggling against the police, pushing them away, trying to break free, he barked, "In the name of the law help me!"

It sounded comical to the officers to hear this man invoking the law.

"This guy's a criminal," Broquet yelled. "He's Zigomar!"

With this name the police could not hold back their laughter.

"Right, pal," the' sergeant said, "right, it's Zigomar. But calm down... or you're gonna think I'm Zigomar."

"I'm Paulin Broquet!" the detective said.

"Well, that's nice. Now you're Paulin Broquet. We got Zigomar the king of thieves and Paulin Broquet the king of detectives. That's just fine."

"I am Paulin Broquet."

"Enough!" the sergeant was talking seriously now. "Don't joke with that name, hear me! Paulin Broquet is the boss of all of us... he's sacred! I know him, I do... and I'm gonna be" taken in by the likes of you!"

The detective did not know how to make this man see reason. "Okay," he said, "hold onto this criminal and hold on to me too. Let's all go to the station. I'll show you proof... but in the name of the law, on your honor as a good man, as a servant of justice, don't let Zigomar escape!"

At this moment, once again, noises rang out and other people came running. A little hope flashed in Broquet's mind... maybe they were his men. But they were more policemen and a customs officer carrying a lantern.

"Ah, now you're going to recognize me," Broquet said. "Over here, quick!"

While waiting, just for a second, he had time to stick two fingers in his mouth and whistle a signal to his men.

"You see!" the Count told the officer, "see, he's calling his accomplices!"

The newcomers surrounded the Count who looked like he was about to pass out. They held him up. The customs officer stepped up to the sergeant holding Broquet.

"What's going on?"

Broquet told him, "Lift up your lantern to my face. Sergeant, look at me since you know Paulin Broquet. You'll recognize me."

The customs officer lifted the lantern and shined it on the detective. Immediately he cried out, "It's Paulin Broquet! I know you! And we finally got him!" Turning to the sergeant he said, "That guy's a looter on these docks. He's the worst thief in the area and the Zigomar of smugglers!"

The evidence was conclusive. The cops needed nothing more. And Broquet understood.

The sergeant and his partners were real police but the newcomers and the customs officer were members of the Z gang.

Broquet figured that any attempt at explanation, to shed any light on the situation would be useless. He whistled again and tried to fight back, to grab the Count who was being taken away by the newcomers.

He started by punching the customs officer who fell on the ground with the lantern. Then he tripped the sergeant who swore as he went down. The officer who came to help his superior got a head butt in the belly. It was like getting hit by a bull... he went rolling on the ground but managed to drag Broquet with him.

The detective got up without being hurt but he had lost precious time, which the false agents used to save themselves and the Count de la Gueriniere. They were helping him limp away.

The Count knew the heroic price of a few seconds. He called on all his energy, all his strength, all his willpower! Knowing that it was a matter of life and death, of his freedom, of his past and future as Zigomar, sneering at the awful pain he was feeling, he ran, ran towards the bridge where a car was waiting for him on the other side of the canal.

As the Count and his men were reaching the bridge Paulin Broquet was running as fast as he could to catch up to the group. He even more energy into this chase than he did in shaking off the policeman trying to hold him back. In answer to his last whistle he heard the signal from his men telling him they were coming to help.

The Zs carrying Zigomar away also heard the signal. They ran even faster, counting on having time to cross the bridge and reach the car whose headlights they could see on the other bank and whose engine they could hear rumbling. In their feverish haste to reach freedom, ever so close to them, they forgot about the detective whom they had seen fall but get up again right away and who was now gaining ground, catching up and finally right on top of them...

Paulin Broquet, therefore, managed to fall on them. Caught by surprise they did not have time to pull out their weapons, guns, clubs, whatever, to defend themselves. Broquet himself had lost all his weapons during the earlier fight but he still had his fists, which were as strong as the best clubs.

With a chop to the neck of the Z to the right Broquet dropped him to the ground unconscious. To his left he kicked the guy in the belly and sent him rolling away gasping for breath. This happened in a split second and with expert combat skill.

Broquet shouted for joy... once again he was alone against his enemy. The duel between him and the Count, which was so often interrupted, started up again. But this time it was the final round, the decisive moment, winner take all. And the winner had to be on the side of justice.

The crook was cornered and in no state to defend himself. The detective wrestled him to the ground easily. The Count de la Gueriniere, the trained fighter, the skilled duelist, was beaten.

Zigomar, the invisible master, who always claimed victory... Zigomar was vanquished!

20. In the water

Paulin Broquet only had to put his prisoner in cuffs, hold him steady, control the last ditch efforts to struggle against him... and suffer the insults. He only had to keep him down until his men arrived, which should not take long. He heard them shouting; he heard their footsteps coming closer.

Broquet had fallen with Zigomar at the foot of one of the lampposts lighting the bridge. Sitting on top of his enemy he could put all his weight on his chest and watch him.

He said, "Yes, indeed, it's you, the Count de la Gueriniere or whoever, but it's you, Zigomar. I need to see you better, to see who you really are. I marked the Count when he was fighting with Captain Rennebois... I marked you. There's an indelible stain on your chest that nothing can erase. I want to see it because it will prove to me that you really are the Count de la Gueriniere... the Count de la Gueriniere really is Zigomar."

He got up a little, keeping his left hand on the Count's throat and putting his knee on his belly. Then with his right hand he tried to rip off the torn vest and shirt. But the Count started struggling desperately. Seeing that he was not going to manage so easily Broquet sat himself back down.

Holding him crushed under his weight he took his hand off the Count's throat and slid it behind this head, down by the nape at the junction of the spine. Then he put the fingers of his right hand into a precise spot in the belly. He applied a quick pressure with both hands at the same time. The Count stopped groaning and stopped struggling, his arms relaxed, his head rolled to the side and his legs stretched out on the ground. He was passed out, as still as a corpse.

This was one of the three secret jiu-jitsu moves that Broquet used to immobilize his enemy. It was a move that was sworn never to be used except when absolutely necessary because when used by an expert it caused fainting but if misapplied it was fatal.

Seeing Zigomar lying motionless Broquet listened to his chest and said, "Good." He ripped off the shirt, then the silk undershirt and laid bare the Count's chest. And he shouted for joy.

"The mark! There it is! The yellow stain I put on you!"

But at that moment Paulin Broquet was yanked off his prisoner and sent rolling on the ground. He was all wrapped up in his discovery, in the mark that would give him the long-sought solution to the agonizing problem. He was looking only at the stained chest and had forgotten about everything else, no doubt believing that his men were coming to help him.

He was surprised by the sudden attack but he jumped quickly to his feet and was back at the Count's body. In front of him protecting the prisoner stood the sergeant.

481

The sergeant was furious and wanted revenge for what this man had done, this man who had thrown him, a police sergeant, to the ground and who must surely be a dangerous criminal whose capture was absolutely necessary.

Before this man, therefore, whom he had taken for a bandit at first sight and whom he saw even more fiendish with his panting victim, the sergeant had followed the rules and unsheathed his sword. He was hoping that the threat of arms would tame the wild beast.

Paulin Broquet figured that the sergeant was probably not working for Zigomar but he knew that he would not listen to reason. This was no time for talking anyway. It was time for action, quick and decisive. The Broquets were farther than he thought and on the other the side of the bridge the Zs were probably rushing back.

Of course Broquet did not want to start fighting again with his prisoner. He knew that human strength had its limits, even among hardened masters like himself. He also knew that the Zs, now, would not hesitate to stab him, shoot him or beat him to death if necessary.

The Count was passed out and could not escape. Therefore, he could face off against this new, very inconvenient enemy. He had to get rid of this good sergeant who was playing his game of cops and robbers so well. So it was with the sergeant now that he started fighting.

Dodging the sword thrust was easy enough. Then he went on the offensive. He started by disarming him, then he tried to grab him around the waist to take him down. But the sergeant was heavy and he knew how to fight. Moreover, he had the rage on his side and wanted to get this man, to do his duty, which was to arrest criminals, dangerous people like this miscreant here. So, he fought with Paulin Broquet.

Every time they were face-to-face Broquet said, "I told you I'm Paulin Broquet. The other guy is Zigomar."

Becoming more and more furious the sergeant only answered by swearing at him... and fighting more fiercely.

Wrestling together the two men finally tripped on the curb and fell to the ground, rolling over to the iron railing on the bridge. In their fall they let each other go. Broquet, being lighter, was the first to get up. He jumped over to his adversary and said, "Come on, let's get this over with."

As the sergeant was struggling to his feet he reached out for him but Broquet grabbed his wrists, swung around and pinned the sergeant on his back like sack of dead weight. Then he leaned over the railing and tossed his package into the canal.

When Broquet turned around he saw Baiter and Gabriel. "Zigomar! Zigomar is over there!"

He ran to where the Count was left as good as dead. And he screamed in rage... Zigomar was gone!

But on the ground, in the pale gaslight, a big Z was written in blood.

From the other side of the bridge they could hear shouting: "Zalavi! Zalamor!" and the sound of a car speeding off at full speed.

Paulin Broquet started to laugh. Then he leaned over the railing. "Okay, let's go. I've got to save this damn sergeant from drowning."

And he dove into the canal.

21. The good death!

Ambulances and paddy wagons escorted by the police at Broquet's request carried the injured Broquets and Zs to the hospital or jail.

The detective's men, the winners in the end, kept watch over the hangar, aided by a few policemen. The victory had been magnificent. Broquet had broken up the Zigomar's gang. He could be satisfied with a good night's work.

He had changed, put on a dry suit that was in his car parked in front of the hangar now. Gabriel, Baiter and Dr. Robert Montreil, who had been summoned, took care of Broquet when he got out of the canal.

He was laughing, "The bath felt really good. A nice cold shower is always refreshing."

Dr. Robert also had to take care of the sergeant whom Broquet had fished out of the water because the poor devil did not know how to swim. When he came around, an ambulance took him away before he had the time or presence of mind to know what was happening.

Broquet had spent an excess of energy and willpower. Anyone else, after running around, fighting and diving into the water, would have been exhausted, drained, dead on his feet as they say. But not him. Once dried and changed he got some bread and cheese from his car and had a snack. He swallowed some coffee that Baiter brought him, then he lit a cigarette. He was back, alert and cheerful, after this short break.

Now the tragic hangar was lit up with big lamps. Broquet's men, under Baiter's leadership, were searching for Zs who were wounded or hiding. They wanted to make sure that there were no traps left lurking in the corners.

In the meantime Broquet went down into the basement on a new ladder. Still smoking a cigarette he questioned his lieutenant Gabriel.

"Sure," he said, "everything went as planned. Quiche played his Zigomar game and thanks to the poor Terror of Ornano, pretending to show us the headless body of the redhead Zigomar lured us into this basement. We were supposed to die here, buried in cement. We should be lying in this vampire grave. I have to admit it was a new level of crime, a real Zigomatic innovation."

"It didn't quite work out."

"No. If Zigomar were more astute, more psychological, he would have understood that Paulin Broquet had listened too eagerly to the Terror's story and trusted too easily the Quiche's betrayal. He should have figured that Paulin Broquet was already burned, or rather frozen, in a basement and would be suspicious of anything happening underground, afraid of any cellar, just like he would question any attic in memory of Zulma's... once bitten twice shy."

"Naturally, boss, but Zigomar thought his scheme of the severed of head was so great… he thought that Paulin Broquet would jump head first into the affair that was right up his alley."

"Yes, exactly. Zigomar figured being bugged by the sarcastic press, all the jokes about the missing body of the headless girl, Broquet's pride would be hurt and he'd defend his reputation. He'd want another feather in his cap and so fall into the trap. A trap, I gotta say, that was well laid out."

"Right, boss, but you played the sucker so well that Zigomar was caught in his own trap and you came out on top."

"No," the detective said. "It's not over yet." He lit another cigarette and asked Gabriel, "How come you left me alone for so long?"

"Boss, we didn't leave you at all. It's you who left us."

"What do you mean?"

"Look, we were watching you the whole time on the barrels and we were surrounding Zigomar when all of a sudden your barrels collapsed."

"I came rolling down with them. I still don't know how I wasn't crushed by them."

"The crashed messed us up. We went searching for you, but we couldn't find you. We figured you were either buried under them or you'd rolled into the basement. I have to admit we got a little panicky. One of us jumped into the basement to look for you."

"He didn't find me, so?"

"Your inexplicable disappearance worried us even more. I can't tell you what we were thinking, fearing… we looked everywhere, ran all over the hangar calling out for you. It made us crazy."

"Okay, my friend," Broquet squeezed the hands of his lieutenant. "Go on."

"So when we heard your whistle, your signal, we could breathe again because you were still alive… and we ran to help you." Then Gabriel asked, "Where'd you go that whole time? What happened to you?"

"I was lucky enough to roll with the barrels right by the Zs' secret escape route."

"I knew it! Of course, since it'd be reckless and dangerous to follow them alone, you went ahead, risking another trap, tempting death…"

"Forget about it," Broquet said. "So, when you heard my signal?"

"We rushed out and after running around the dock a little we finally saw you on the bridge and went over."

"Too late."

"Too late? How's that?"

"I had Zigomar."

"You'd caught Zigomar?"

"There was no doubt about it this time. It was really Zigomar, the Count de la Gueriniere. I saw the mark on his chest."

"And he got away?"

"No, the police saved him."

"The police? What the…"

"Yes, a brave sergeant who apparently knew Paulin Broquet took me for a criminal… for Zigomar!"

"No."

"Yes. I tell you the whole story later." Then he told his faithful lieutenant, "But tell me what happened in the basement after I left."

"Oh, boss, just like you guessed Zigomar lured us into the hangar to drown us in the basement and kill you. It was to fool him that you pretended to fall into his trap and you wore that gray coat on purpose… to be easily recognized."

"That's right."

"Baiter and I were impressed ho you got Quiche to put on your coat at the Zs signal and climb the ladder instead of you, thereby getting stabbed instead of you. That was brilliant."

"But the Terror?"

"Oh, the poor devil. He was watching the whole thing without a clue. He couldn't admit that his friend Quiche was a traitor. He didn't want to believe that the Zs had used his grief, his tragic love for the redhead and made him, the Terror of Ornano, break his word to you. He was furious and wanted to go up to kill everyone, to pulverize the Zs and tear Zigomar to pieces."

"Poor devil."

"I had a hard time holding him back. If the ladder had broken he would've got up there and done something crazy."

"So what happened after the ladder broke?"

"The Zs turned on the water and started opening the trapdoor that held the cement."

"Right, the quick-drying cement that was supposed to hold us, swallow us up. It was a good setup: the more we struggled against the cement, trying to get free, the more we mix it up and help Zigomar's heinous plan. He was obvious that we would end up exhausted from the effort and buried alive in that grisly grave."

"Yes, boss, but the Terror told me, 'You gotta get outta here! Don't stay! It's death!' So, pulled over some big barrels and piled them up in place of the ladder. He helped me climb out to safety. He was a hero! When the floor with all the cement started falling he steadied the pile for me with his huge hands… 'Save yourself!' he shouted. I was trying to get him to come with me but he cried out, 'You tell Broquet that the Terror of Ornano is no traitor'." Then he literally threw me up and out of the basement."

"I saw that."

"Yes, boss, but to be able to do it he had to let go of the stuff and as the floor dropped with all the cement, so did the Terror with all the barrels."

"Well, let's go see."

Men from the brigade had found another ladder. They were armed with lanterns and flashlights. Broquet and Gabriel could go down into their intended grave. The water did not have time to reach all the cement. Zigomar's plan had failed. But they saw the pitiful state of the Zs whom Broquet had tossed down while defending Gabriel. One of them was dead, another groaning...

They also saw poor Gaston Soclet in his tragic sleep.

Lastly, under a layer of cement, they found the body of the Terror of Ornano. He had fallen on his back and was lying with his arms spread out. His chest was crushed under the weight of all the barrels. In his chest his heart so full of frustrated, tough, naïve and profound love, so much love for the mysterious redhead, was also crushed.

22. The heart departs, the soul soars off

When Paulin Broquet, after that busy night, got back home in the morning, he found the old clown Simon rolled up in a blanket and sleeping on the floor of his office. He had been waiting as ordered.

"So," Broquet asked, "your friend the Count de la Gueriniere?"

"Well, boss, like always we spent the night maybe not together but still side by side."

"Ah… at the Lutetia?"

"Yes, boss. Lucette Minois was more charming than ever."

"I won't ask for details about your love for Lucette."

"But boss I've never talked about that."

"Talk to me about your Gueriniere."

"He was in his box with his friends."

"Baron Dupont?"

"No, not last night. Dupont dined at the club, showed up briefly at the theater and then disappeared."

"Good! And your Gueriniere stayed there?"

"Yes, boss."

"After the show what did he do?"

"He went to eat with Lucette Minois, a few other performers and the regulars."

"Aha! You're sure of that?"

"Absolutely."

"You followed the Count all the way home?"

"And I watched his place for a pretty long time. François came to replace me for the rest of the night. He'll report in around noon."

"Good." Then he almost shouted, "I wonder, Simon, during this surveillance mission, if you weren't hooked by Lucette Minois."

The clown was startled. His pug nose twitched and his mouth formed a perfect circle. He was so surprised to hear this observation that he had nothing to say.

"You're sure you kept an eye on the Count the whole time?"

"Yes, yes," Simon affirmed. He held up his hand to swear to it.

"Perfect. But while you were watching… mostly Lucette Minois, at the same time I was on the docks doing to the Count what you want to do to Lucette. I had in my arms, squeezing him tightly…"

"The Count?"

"Yes. No mistaking him because I bared his chest even more than Lucette on stage. And I saw his beauty mark, bigger than the one you adore on Lucette's shoulder, the size of my hand that I put on his chest myself."

This time the clown Simon did not just open his mouth and wrinkle his nose, he rolled his bulging eyes. He coughed out, "But boss, I'm sure about my Count."

"Me too."

"So, that means there's two counts."

"Two... and one who was caught at Van Cambre's makes three."

"Three!"

"Got to admit that's a lot of Guerinieres."

"Well, I don't get it."

"Don't try to unravel the mystery. Go get some sleep."

The clown walked away bewildered.

Broquet called after hi, "By the way, what about your rival?"

"What rival?"

"The other admirer of Lucette Minois."

"Who?"

"I know there are many but I mean the guy with the factory up north, the sugar maker."

"The Beet?"

"Right. What happened to him?"

"Dunno, boss. Haven't seen him around for days."

"Okay. From now on you'll be watching him too."

"Yes, boss."

Simon went to get some sleep even more puzzled than before.

Paulin Broquet went to his bathroom and took a shower. Then he went to bed to get a few hours of much needed sleep after such a busy, exhausting night.

A few hours later, as he was sitting down to eat, his butler handed him a visiting card from someone who wanted to see him right away on very important business. It was the head clerk from the notary Bejanet and, in truth, it was very surprising to Broquet. He let him in immediately.

What could Bejanet's clerk want with him? Was it about the death of the banker Montreil?

As usual Broquet wasted no time. He came straight out with his questions about this strange visit.

The clerk answered, "Monsieur Bejanet sent me here on a most unexpected and curious matter, something we don't often see in the notary office but that isn't completely foreign to the nature of our business."

"I'm listening."

"Well, he's just received authorization... with the funds to back it... to purchase a burial plot in perpetuity at a cemetery of his choosing."

"Okay... so?"

"In this order they request Monsieur Bejanet to consult you before making his choice."

"Me?"

489

"Exactly, Monsieur Paulin Broquet."

"Why?"

"Because it's from you or rather through you that we will take possession... of the body of the person to be buried in the grave."

Broquet was really intrigued now.

The clerk went on solemnly, "So, Monsieur Broquet, do you know where the body is?"

"A woman?"

"No, a man."

"Do you have a name?"

"We don't. They didn't give us one."

"So, how could I..."

"But there was a nickname given that might help identify the body."

"A nickname?"

"The Terror of Ornano."

Broquet could not help shivering. "Indeed, that's enough to know who it is."

"Monsieur Bejanet was hoping so. The aforementioned Terror of Ornano died, apparently, last night. The authorization didn't tell us how but it doesn't matter as long as the death is legally recorded. Monsieur Bejanet will ask you to identify the body and give us the death certificate. You can then name the cemetery where he should be buried and the date for recuperating the body so that the usual prayers and process for the burial of the said Terror might proceed as usual."

Broquet asked, "Could you tell me the name of the person who gave this authorization?"

"There is nothing legally against it. Professional secrecy doesn't apply here... but it's not possible."

"Why?"

"The authorization was handed over to us with the funds by the bailiff Grillard. Now Grillard felt unable to refuse such a special mission even though the person behind it desired to remain anonymous. It's all done according to the law and even has precedents..."

Broquet interrupted, "Go and tell Bejanet that like him I will do everything I can to carry out the request."

The clerk bowed, then added, "But I must warn you that there are no funds attributed to your part in this."

"Yes," the detective said, "yes, there wouldn't be."

"You won't refuse because of this?"

"On the contrary."

The clerk looked alarmed at this man who would work for no money. It seemed incredible to him, unimaginable! It overturned all his notions of the legal system, of the legal profession, of the law... because the foundation of the law was money.

On the stairs, as he was leaving, he snapped out of his bewilderment and mumbled, "This man did well to enter the police force because he'd make a really bad notary."

A few days later Paulin Broquet had done all that was necessary to prepare the burial of the Terror of Ornano. In the carriage was the clerk fulfilling the duty his firm had assigned him... and to get the final signatures at the cemetery. But on foot, behind the coffin holding the mutilated corpse of the Terror, behind the poor devil who had redeemed himself in a brave death to save the life of one of Broquet's men, behind this loyal, loving criminal, walked the detective and his two lieutenants.

Three wreaths lay on the coffin. One was offered by Broquet and another by his lieutenants and the men who were at the hangar. The third was made of simple wild flowers. It was huge and superb. A wide, silk ribbon, copper-colored with moiré patterns, enwrapped it. The ribbon floated in the wind looking like a long, red braid of hair... from the redhead that the Terror loved so much... poor boy.

23. No drinks for Martinet

In the meantime, Paulin Broquet went to the police infirmary several times to visit the two Zs who were captured in the hangar.

One of them was seriously injured. In everyday life this man was a naturalist. He was involved in the conservation of birds and above all in the preparation of anatomical parts for schools and laboratories. His name was Martinet. They said he was a former medical student who had made a living during his studies by preparing the "stiffs" that his dear comrades sent him. Deep down he was a good man, skillful in his art, who could have become a surgeon because he was also very intelligent but two stronger qualities ruled him: laziness and drunkenness.

Doing nothing and drinking, there lay his happiness. Doing the least possible while earning a lot of money and drinking as much as possible were his rules of life. To have enough to drink he was willing to do anything within his capacity that did not compromise his conscience... because he was an honest man. Lazy and drunk but honest.

A man like this was easy prey for Zigomar who knew how to recruit people he needed in all fields, all jobs, all levels of society. Zigomar knew how to manipulate men by their vices. He gave enough to Martinet to satisfy his and the man belonged to him.

For his part Paulin Broquet was as clever a psychologist as his adversary. Today he had Martinet in his hands and he knew he could control him by controlling the access to his vice. Figuring that Martinet could give him some valuable information he asked the doctor to deprive the patient of all alcohol, even wine! After two days on this diet Martinet was ready to bare his soul for any drink that was not water, tea or milk.

When Broquet showed up as his savior with a glass of Bordeaux for the patient he gained his trust. When he promised cognac the naturalist in turn promised to reveal all his secrets. Anyway, these secrets were neither big nor important.

Zigomar was careful not to confide in this kind of person who might compromise him and cause problems later on. Moreover, this was the first time this guy had actually taken part in an expedition and he did not even know what it was all about or what he was supposed to do or why he had to wear a black hood. He even thought that the whole thing was just joke, a night of fun, a little drunken revelry. He had followed them there but he was just looking for where they were hiding the bar. Still, he was sure that Zigomar wanted (without actually telling him) to use his surgical skills for some nefarious work.

Paulin Broquet, therefore, ended up getting the drunk to talk about some of his life adventures, which Martinet had no idea were being orchestrated by

Zigomar. The detective had already guessed, knew almost for sure that Carmen's head was cut off by this Martinet. He just wanted to know how it was done. And with a shots of cognac, Broquet got Martinet to narrate the tale of the gruesome operation.

The bed Martinet lay in was in a corner at the back of the infirmary. Broquet arranged this to make it easier for him to talk without the other patients, the two or three Zs among them, overhearing. Naturally Broquet did not come as a detective but was introduced instead as a doctor, again to loosen Martinet's tongue.

The macabre scene unfolded at Carmen's place, as Broquet had imagined. "They brought me," Martinet said, "into a house where there was this dead girl. Dead for two days... of consumption. I could tell at first sight."

Broquet remembered his prognosis examining the head of the marble table in the Morgue. Martinet, just like Dr. Robert, corroborated his deductions.

"A legal death," Martinet went on, "so a regular burial... to take place the next morning."

"Then they had already put her in the coffin?"

"Just had to screw the top on."

"Who was there for the wake?"

"Only two people. A young guy, well dressed..."

"The husband?"

"Or the lover, who knows. But he didn't look too upset. And there was this guy's uncle."

"His uncle?"

"Another gentleman, even more elegant... with a wonderful, white beard."

Broquet knew they were talking about the Count and his uncle Baron Dupont.

Martinet slurred on, "What these gentlemen were expecting was really weird. They asked me to cut off her head."

"For what reason?"

"To make a mold. They wanted to remember her face, exactly how beautiful she'd been."

"And then?"

"I told them they could just as easily make a mold without removing her head. They said they couldn't... I offered to do it myself on the spot but they were refused. They had an artist already picked out. They would pay me just to take off her head. It was a friend of mine who got me the work and he'd warned me. I had to do it so as not to disappoint him. Besides, I was well paid. And it wasn't really a crime even though it was almost impossible to get legal authorization for an operation like this. In short, I did the job. I'm good so it only took about 20 minutes and the head was cut clean off."

"And then?"

"Then they drove me back home and that was that."

Broquet asked Martinet, "Do you know the name of the young lady?"

"Can't say that I do."

"If we showed you the head you could recognize it?"

"Absolutely."

"And if we showed you one of the people who were there, the nephew or uncle, you'd recognize them?"

"I think that'd be easy."

"Very well."

Broquet was going to ask a few more questions of Martinet but some doctors and nurses making their rounds interrupted him.

"See you tomorrow," Martinet said.

"Til tomorrow. Say, would you like more cognac."

"Of course."

"I'll bring some."

The drunkard sunk back into his bed. He would wait patiently until the next day that would bring him more drinks.

But early in the morning, when the nurses went to prepare their patients for the doctors' visit, they found Martinet dead in his bed. He had been strangled by a rope that was tied to the headboard.

Zigomar was there and once again he had punished a traitor.

Paulin Broquet did not follow up on this new case. There was nothing sensational about it. The Zs in the infirmary had done plenty wrong to earn the rigors of the law. More importantly, there was another hero in this adventure that deserved his attention: Gaston Soclet.

The poor lover of Carmen d'Amata had miraculously escaped the grisly death destined for him by his friend Amblard alias Zigomar. When he fell in the basement he was lucky enough to drop onto the pile of wheelbarrows and wooden crates built by the Terror when he tried to hold up the collapsing planks and keep Gabriel from being knocked out by the falling debris or drowned in cement.

Soclet was carried away from the hangar still plunged in deep sleep. He woke up late in the afternoon in a police cell where Broquet had set up a cot. It took him a long time to come around and realize what had happened. When he saw himself arrested and in jail he did not react in anger or despair. He lay in his bed and wept again for the woman he had lost who, it seemed, had taken with her his peace of mind and his reason to live.

Broquet came to see him in the evening. The meeting between the two men was very touching.

"Ah!" Soclet groaned, "I know you, Monsieur Broquet. I'm one of your enemies. I fought against you. I don't know how it happened but now you've got me. It was a good fight. I'll obviously go to court... just as well... I won't say a word. If you can send me to the scaffold, oh, as soon as possible, I'll thank you."

Broquet let the tragic lover exhale his grief and then spoke gently to him, "There's no question of the death sentence here. You fought me, yes, I know, but I also know something else."

"What do you know? That I'm a thief, a forger, an accomplice of Zigomar... one of the head Zs... that I committed crimes for the invisible master... Yes, it's all true, I don't deny it."

"I know something else."

"What?"

"Why you were in his power."

"I don't understand."

"I know that Gaston Soclet..."

"That's me."

"Yes, that Gaston Soclet was a good kid who made an honest living until the day he met Carmen d'Amata."

The name struck Soclet like lightening and he moaned, "Carmen, Carmen, Carmen..."

"I know that you did all that to fulfill her needs and your excuse, if you can call it that, is not in your passionate nature but in the strength of your love for this woman."

"I loved her, yes. I loved her so much that to satisfy her fantasies I was ready to do anything. Crime was not something horrible, it was a duty. I was ready to sacrifice my honor and even my life."

"I know."

"And now that she's gone, my life means nothing."

"I know. I also know that you went secretly every night to weep over Carmen's grave."

"How do you know that?"

"And I know something you don't know."

"What?"

"That you wept over an empty grave."

Soclet looked shocked.

"Yes," the detective went on, "you wept over an empty grave because Carmen was not in the coffin under the ground you watered with your tears."

Soclet could find nothing to say.

"Carmen d'Amata," Broquet continued, "was like you an unconscious tool in the hands of the criminal you made your friend."

"Amblard?"

"Zigomar!"

"How could Carmen have been..."

"Oh, the poor thing should never have been disturbed but Zigomar needed a blonde girl, just the head, the pretty blonde head that you loved and who loved you. He didn't flinch before the sacrilege when he pulled Carmen from her coffin to use for his heinous designs."

"Ah, Monsieur Broquet," Soclet wailed, "speak more clearly. I don't understand. I'm afraid to understand."

"Look, the severed head we found on the empty lot around Buttes-Chaumont was Carmen."

"You're lying."

"No."

"You're lying or else you're crazy."

"No, I'm telling the truth."

"You hate Zigomar so much that..."

Broquet grabbed Soclet's wrist. He looked him straight in the eye and rattled off, "I don't hate Zigomar. I fight him because he is the enemy of society, he's a villain, the most formidable, clever, merciless criminal on the planet. I'm his enemy because I serve the law. I will never stop fighting him, never surrender, but I will also never do anything dishonest."

"But why talk about Carmen, why tell me Zigomar used her, why lie to me in my grief?"

"Because it's the truth and as unlikely as it sounds I can give you irrefutable proof."

"You're going to show me her empty coffin?"

"Better. I'll show you Carmen herself."

Soclet cried out, "Carmen? Alive?"

Broquet did not answer. He said, "Listen to me. If I show you what Zigomar did to Carmen, how he used her for his nefarious schemes, how he thanked you by treating the corpse of your lover like he did... will you agree to give me all the information I ask of you?"

Soclet responded, "I'm not a traitor. I'd like nothing better than to bite off my tongue. I'll never give up a friend."

"If I can prove that Zigomar wanted to kill you."

"Doesn't matter."

"That Zigomar gave you up to me."

"Still doesn't matter."

"That he profaned your lover's corpse."

"Well, that, yes. If Amblard... if Zigomar did that, if he touched one hair on beloved's head, he will be the most wretched, vilest creature on earth. If he mutilated my girl, I'll give him to you. I'll tell you everything I know. And I was one of his lieutenants so I know pretty much all his secrets. I'll tell you whatever it takes to capture him and get revenge for my dearly departed... to punish him for his unforgivable infamy."

Broquet let go of him. "Good. Now be strong, be brave and prepare yourself for the worst proof you can imagine."

Soon they left the station in a car and went to the Morgue. Gabriel and Dr. Robert were brought in to accompany them. Baiter and a few men organized surveillance around the car. Judge Urbain and Chief Baumier were already waiting at the Morgue for the chilling confrontation.

On the big, marble table lay the body of Carmen d'Amata. They had taken her off ice and covered her completely with a sheet, looking as if she were carved out of the marble itself.

In a corner of the room, standing on end, leaning against the wall, was the coffin padded with white satin.

Paulin Broquet led Gaston Soclet up to the coffin, the first step on this painful calvary. "Do you recognize this?" he asked.

All coffins look alike but the white satin where the pretty girl was going to sleep forevermore, the lace with which the lover had decorated this final resting place, these were unique.

He reached out and touched it, trembling with emotion, respect, love and terror. "Yes, I recognize it."

"Okay, come here," Broquet pulled him way. "Be strong now." He brought him to the marble table and spoke softly, "Here's the body of Carmen d'Amata."

Slowly, gently he lifted the shroud. He uncovered the shoes, then the silver-sequined dress under the dainty lace. Little by little as the shroud was lifted Soclet leaned closer and closer over his dead lover, recognizing the clothes.

"Yes," he sputtered, "those are her shoes... her stockings... finest silk in the world... but not as fine or soft as her skin... my Carmen. Often... sometimes she only put on one and covering my eyes she asked me which leg was stockinged. I always lost... my darling..."

Dr. Robert stood beside him ready to help if his emotions overcame him, but it was only sorrow talking, the sorrow of remembering all the details of love.

Broquet kept raising the shroud. The hands appeared, holding flowers. The flowers, from the humid grave and then in the icy cold, were preserved as pretty and fresh as the day they were cut.

"Oh, her hands... her rings... bracelets... her soft hands, so tender, they touched like a kiss... I held them in my own to warm them when they were cold, to kiss them... they were the cradle of my heart... the lovely hands of my beloved..."

He tried to hold them, to lift them to his lips and kiss them, but the hands and wrists, the arms entire were frozen stiff and would not move. He leaned over to kiss them but straightened up right away. "They're so cold! Frozen! Colder than the day she left me for good. Oh, it's like my poor Carmen's died twice now!"

Broquet turned to him, "And it's now that I need you to be strong... and smart. Look! Look what Zigomar did to the girl you loved."

Slowly he pulled away the last of the shroud, uncovering the breast... the shoulders... then nothing.

Gaston Soclet was watching the detective's movements while sobbing and muttering about his dead lover. Now he fell silent, shocked. He could not comprehend.

Then suddenly he called out, "Carmen! Carmen!" As if she had suddenly just disappeared in front of his eyes. Louder and louder he shouted, "Carmen! Carmen!" And finally he blabbered, "Oh Carmen, come on, why are you hiding?"

He leaned over and when he saw the severed neck he jumped back. "The head! The head!"

Broquet yanked away the shroud and uncovered the head.

Soclet stared at it. "That's Carmen... my Carmen... so pretty, blonde, sweet, so lovely... That's what Zigomar did to my Carmen! That's my Carmen!"

He looked at everyone around him for a moment and then broke out laughing. "That's Carmen! My Carmen! Ha ha ha!"

Soclet had gone mad.

24. *What is read in the hand*

They led away the poor guy who was overwhelmed by love's sorrow and had lost his mind. Instead of bringing him back to prison Dr. Robert sent him straight to the insane asylum.

Paulin Broquet was upset by this unexpected result of the confrontation. He blamed himself, accused himself of cruelty.

"No," Robert told him, "there was no cruelty or inhumanity on your part. Identifying the body was necessary, as you know."

"I thought so."

"You took all the precautions that human kindness demands. Therefore, your conscious should be free of all worry. You couldn't know, nobody could know how he would react."

"That's true. It was the first time that I've seen it happen, but still I wonder if I went too far, beyond what was strictly needed for the job."

Dr. Robert responded, "Don't feel bad. As long as your common sense and experience are guiding you, you will be acting fairly and honestly... and I'll add humanely."

"I was counting a lot on the revelations that Soclet's anger and indignation and thirst for vengeance would compel him to give us. And this is the tragic result."

"Look, if the poor guy had gone to court what would he have got?"

"Hard labor for life most likely."

"So, a life of torture and suffering, a long martyrdom."

"Right."

"In your opinion, was this guy less guilty than he seemed to be?"

"Definitely. I consider him to be a victim of Zigomar and a slave to his love for Carmen. It was for love that he committed all those crimes."

"He loved a lot so he was forgiven a lot. And divine justice took pity on the sinner. It did not acquit him or punish him, it annihilated him. Gaston Soclet who committed his crimes for love is, by love, delivered unto the true life just as if the guillotine had dropped its blade on him. He sees and breathes and thinks about his Carmen but even though his heart still beats, his soul is dead."

Nevertheless Broquet let a few days pass after this incident. Then he told his lieutenants, "My boys, let's not fall asleep. We have to keep moving forward. I really need clear up a few things and I'm counting a lot on this Madame Verdier. So Baiter, you go get some more snuff with your girlfriend and have a few drinks. Yell her that Madame Rollet the fortune teller will come see her the day after tomorrow."

"Got it, boss."

"I'll deal with Rollet. I'll tell her what questions to ask and take care of everything."

Two days later, therefore, around 9 pm, Madame Rollet showed up at the Verdier home where they were waiting impatiently for the visit of this woman and her dark revelations or perhaps her words of hope.

The chiromancer, Madame Rollet, was an old woman, still strong but stooped over. She was dressed in a skirt that went out of style 30 years before and a Basque jacket over a brushed cotton corset. A tilted hat sat on a tight bun of thin, gray hair that curled at its frizzy ends. She wore tortoise-shell glasses and on her neck, to hold in place her fluted collar, a big medallion containing the portrait (bust and profile) of a military officer with his decoration and sword and impressive moustache. It was the portrait of Monsieur Roulet, administrative captain, died serving his country at his desk and leaving Madame Roulet a widow too young and, as they say, inconsolable. Her hands were in mittens holding a small, leather pouch with a metal clasp that protected her diving instruments, the tarot cards.

Recommended to Julie by her brandy man, Madame Roulet was very warmly welcomed. Julie introduced her to Madame Verdier who was on pins and needles, sitting in a big armchair and trying to move as little as possible because the slightest movement caused her great pain.

Madame Roulet took the seat that Julie offered her across from her poor mistress. In the light glowing from the green lampshade Madame Roulet studied Madame Verdier very carefully.

"Oh, Madame," the sick woman said, "you see a poor old invalid whom life has not smiled upon…"

But Roulet interrupted, "Madame, say nothing. I will do the talking. Anything you can say to me, I will see. And I will see what only I can tell you."

Madame Verdier was thin and wrinkled, much older than her actual age. She bore the marks of suffering, both physical and emotional. She was a creature of pain, a victim of life. However, her eyes were still good and emanated tenderness, weakness and fear. She felt immediately reassured and happy to find someone interested in her in this state of misery, someone to talk about the future and hope, even if it was all lies!

She reached out her wrinkled, bony left hand to the fortune-teller who wanted to read her palm before spreading the cards. Madame Roulet took it and examined it under the lamplight, then she spoke.

"Ah, Madame, here is a hand that shows a lot less head than heart. You have always been dependent on those around you. You have loved a lot… and constantly suffered. Your heart has made your life unhappy…"

"So true," Madame Verdier murmured.

Still bent over the skeletal hand Roulet went on, "You once had… affection for someone… very deep and sincere on your side but much less… or none at all from the other."

"Ah!"

"You were in love but he didn't love you. You were young, pretty and... that was all he saw in you. The love you showed, your sincerity, your devotion... was not answered by the one you wanted to spent your life with... he was just selfish, self-seeking, a social climber who used people, broke whatever got in the way of his goal... a very intelligent man but without an ounce of heart..."

Madame Verdier shivered at the sound of these words.

"You had a child."

"Yes."

"I see a boy."

"That's right."

"Don't tell me, I'm reading... I'm reading... there, in this line. A boy who... that's weird, it looks like he has more of his father than his mother."

"Alas," the sick lady mumbled.

"Say nothing! I see everything! The boy is like his father, ambitious, selfish, loves money, the high life... and he's ready to do anything to get it."

"Yes."

"Madame, if I weren't afraid of hurting you I would tell you that he could go so far as to commit crimes."

The old lady said nothing but she choked back a sob.

From that point on she belonged to the fortune-teller who was so unexpectedly reading her wrinkled palm where her life of suffering had apparently left its grievous marks. Since the diviner was reading so many things in her hand, since she saw all her past, since nothing escaped her, Madame Verdier did not try to hide anything. She was also happy to meet a woman who could, by knowing her so well, understand her. She felt like she had an old friend. The time for confession was coming soon.

Madame Roulet continued to get to the heart of the matter, "Oh, Madame, I see a sudden break, an abrupt change in the situation... like a divorce... this line here cut by another... a separation 30 years ago... or 35."

"Exactly."

"But... if I won't upset you I'd say this break, despite the son you had, was not of a legitimate union... you weren't married."

Madame Verdier trembled, "You must be the devil to be able to read all that!"

"No, Madame, but everyone's life is written in their hand like in a book. You just have to know how to read it." She paused, and then, "Do you want me to continue? Good. Wait, I see Mercury here, the god of money. This cross at the juncture with the head line shows that the man who abandoned you did it for money... a businessman, a financier, a banker..."

Madame Verdier shivered again. "Yes, yes, that's right. Oh, you can read the past but can you also see the future?"

"Maybe. Let me see."

501

The old lady wiped her sweating palm and held it out again for the chiromancer.

"You are unhappy now but the future will change everything."

"You think so?"

"Have I been wrong yet?"

"No."

"So I'll continue. You are under the control of two people... two men who have enslaved you your whole life. They're threatening you but you will escape them."

"Really? How?"

"Don't ask what I can't see. I just know—and you can be sure of it—that you're going to be freed and finally have some peace and tranquility... and well being."

"Oh, if that were true!"

"It's written here very clearly. It will happen."

"You make me so happy! You make me feel good! Yes, it has to happen since you say so, since everything you say about the past is true." And the confession comes out. "I feel like we're old friends. You know my sorrowful past and I feel confident talking to you. You saw I was young and pretty... I was 20 years old when I met the man who would father my son... I was on the stage, a singer, and I can say that I had some success. My brother was also in the theater. He sang baritone. We were born into it, the children of artists. My brother introduced me to a young banker he knew... who was responsible for everything that followed."

"I see that."

"No need to tell you that after throwing me into the banker's arms he made a terrible scene, crying insult, betrayal, dishonor... then for the price of his silence he got a nice pile of money. On stage I was called Rosine Verdier. My lover seemed to really love me at first or at least I believe everything he said and did. He gave me lots of gifts, money that my brother invested and that I never saw again..."

"I understand."

"For a year I lived happily with my lover. Then when I was about to bring my son into the world, two months before the birth, my lover stopped coming to see me. He stayed away for days on end. Finally I got a letter with a big check along with his regrets and farewell."

"It almost always happens like that."

"My lover had just got married."

"You never saw him again?"

"No."

"He never even got in touch?"

"No. I mean, my brother learned of the marriage and wasn't satisfied with just a check. Using the child as an excuse, threatening a scandal, he went over and over to get more money. The banker was scared and his only peace of mind came after he paid."

"That's called blackmail."

"Then I don't know what happened between the two but my brother stopped going to the bank. He made me write. Me, I'd cut all ties with that man. I had my sadness and my son and I was trying to start life over again. My brother forced me to write. I had to ask for money, lots of money, I don't know how many times. And the banker always answered two days later. I never saw a cent. My brother was always here to collect it and leave just enough to get by."

"How nice of him."

"My sadness and the shame eventually made me sick. My brother finally locked me up here. He was afraid I'd write to the banker and tell him the truth. I'm a prisoner being guarded by my own son."

"By your son?"

"My brother raised him. I was too sick to take care of a child. My brother raised him in his way and they are the same, not very pleasant, two peas in a pod…"

"That's awful! I'm really sorry for you, Madame."

"What do they do? How do they live? I have no idea. I've been shut up here for years on end without being able to leave. I know nothing about the outside world. I'm constantly worried that I'll find out my son is a criminal, that he's been arrested and… oh, Madame, it's killing me slowly."

"In that case, my dear lady, you must have been terribly hurt, maybe stricken with terror a few months ago."

"Why?"

"Because the banker Montreil was murdered."

Despite her pain the old lady was suddenly on her feet, which had not supported her body in a long time. She cried out, "Montreil the banker! He was my lover! He is the father of my son! Murdered? Murdered!" Her hands and voice were both trembling. "They killed him!"

At that very moment the door opened. A man jumped into the room.

"Him! My brother!" the old lady screamed in fright.

The man seized the sick woman by the neck. "You talk too much!"

"Baron Dupont!" the fortune-teller yelled as she got up to fetch the nurse.

"And you, Paulin Broquet," said a voice behind the pseudo-diviner, "you heard too much."

"Zigomar," Broquet said. Zigomar!"

But as he turned around a club came crashing down on his head. Bleeding out of his nose and mouth he lost consciousness and fell to the floor next to the body of the old lady who had dropped dead at the unexpected sight of her brother and son.

25. When we love

We need a moment to get away from this tragic house and travel back a few days to catch up with other characters.

They were not able to hide the preparations for the duel between Raoul and the Count from Raymonde, who had witnessed the altercation in front of the shop. Nor were they able to hide the Count's refusal to meet the son of Montreil the banker. Inevitably she learned of Captain Rennebois' substitution for Raoul. Knowing this Raymonde took her fiancé aside and spoke point blank.

"So, it's you, Fabien, who's going to fight instead of my brothers... don't try to deny it! Anyway, it has to be."

"What? It has to be? What do you mean?"

"I once believed, right after my father's death, that my brothers would have to bring justice to this wretch. He's constantly avoiding them so it's you, who will be their brother when you become my wife, you have to right the wrong. I hope you will avenge us."

The Captain was astonished at his fiancée's composure.

"Why?" Raymonde said. "Am I not going to be your wife? A soldier's wife? I have to be as strong as you. Since you're going to fight, all I can say is good luck!"

But on the morning of the duel, gripping the telephone—not at home but at her brothers' place on Rue des Mathurins—she listened anxiously to Andre Girardet giving her details of the combat. And her heart was beating false and hard.

She knew that the Count was an adversary who had never been defeated and the Captain was risking his life, but still, every skirmish, every comment on her fiancé's bravery made her tremble with joy, pride and hope.

"The wretch will finally be beaten;" she said. She was counting on the Captain's victory.

When Andre Girardet announced the end of the duel, with Fabien lightly wounded, she screamed in anger. Then her finance's mind rose up and she got worried about how minor the wound really was.

At that moment someone came in, sent by Raoul. "I came to get you, Mademoiselle. Don't worry, my name's Baiter, one of the Broquet Brigade. Here's what happened: after an admirable fight and some questionable luck, the Captain made a mistake and got stabbed in the arm."

"Is it serious?"

"No. But Robert and Raoul asked me to bring you to the villa to congratulate the wounded, which will be warmly appreciated."

Broquet's car was waiting downstairs.

Raymonde arrived soon and met Madame Laurent who was not aware of the duel but had come to visit her sick friend Girardet with Riri and her sister Marie. After the death of their mother the two young ladies had been staying with Laurent in a room that they decorated tastefully.

Raoul was taking care of the Menardier legal affairs and had told them a few days earlier (with quite an emotional reaction) that the two sisters' fate was very different from they believed.

"Your father's case has been reexamined. It came up for appeal... and it won. Unfortunately, the bank where Monsieur Menardier's funds were found couldn't find your mother's address since she cut all ties with the world after your father's death and therefore couldn't claim her rights. Your fortune is restored and now you have millions deposited for you in our bank."

The young ladies thought they were dreaming. But since Raoul was telling them this, it must be true. And the asked Madame Laurent, along with Raoul, to help them because they had no idea what to do with all the money.

First of all, knowing about the Laurent's troubles and why Monsieur Laurent was in prison, they told Raoul, his lawyer, to take everything needed to pay off the creditors of this family that had been so kind to them. Raoul agreed with this generous idea.

Madame Laurent hugged the girls tenderly, "Thank you, my dears, but Raoul was just shown me the results of some of my husband's operations, some rather bold speculations that had crashed at first but are now doing quite well. We've got our money back and more! My husband is saved and I hope to see him soon."

"Monsieur Raoul is our life-saver," Riri smiled.

"He deserves to be happy," Marie the hunchback said.

"Yes," Riri lowered her eyes and blushed, which nobody seemed to notice.

Raymonde had not yet met Riri's sister. She only knew that she existed. But she was reminded of the instinctive tenderness she felt for Pretty Riri. She was pleased by the sisters' new situation and very glad that her brothers had given back their fortune.

And thus, the car drove Raymonde quickly to Ville-d'Avray. Raoul and Robert brought their sister to the wounded Captain who was lying on the couch, bandaged and smiling with only a slight fever.

"Go on, Raymonde," Raoul said, "you can kiss him. He's earned it."

It was their first kiss.

"Thank you, Fabien," Raymonde said."

Then they made the introductions because Raymonde did not know Madame Laurent either. Raymonde remembered the recent shame, the late reparation and hesitated nervously. Madame Laurent understood her difficulty and held out her hands. Then she hugged her affectionately.

"Mademoiselle, for certain hearts the day they meet doesn't matter because they have always loved each other." Then turning to Riri and her sister, "My friends Riri and Marie here, who care for you so much and as long as I have… hug them, they'll be so happy."

They young ladies exchanged tender kisses.

But Raymonde, being very observant, had noticed the looks that her brothers gave Pretty Riri. She understood the drama that was playing out in their noble hearts.

"The poor boys," she told herself, "they're in love with the same woman."

She also saw that Raoul, despite the effort he made to control his love, was beaming. She saw the willpower Robert was using to hide his love for Riri from his brother… and the grandeur of this sacrifice touched her deeply.

And she guessed which of her brothers had stolen Riri's heart. She loved naïvely, simply and sincerely—Riri loved Raoul like she herself loved Fabien!

It was agreed that the Captain would a couple of days in the villa, a good excuse for everyone to see each other again the next day.

That evening since Robert was staying with his patient, Raymonde went to Rue Chalgrin with Raoul to the rooms that the two brothers shared at their mother's house. The first thing she did was to check all the rooms.

"It's to see if Marcelin is spying on us," she said. "That guy is always where he's not supposed to be."

"Oh, you noticed that too."

"Sure but I'm watching him… and correcting his faults." With no explanation Raymonde went on, "You know, Raoul, I'm really glad to know Madame Laurent and especially the two sisters Riri and Marie."

Raoul shivered as he wondered where his sister was going with this.

"Riri," she said, "is delightful. I know only one other who can compare to her, to her charm and grace, her beautiful eyes and her smile…"

"Who's that?"

"Irene de Valtours."

"That's true… yes, indeed…" Nervously Raoul asked, "Why are you telling me this?"

"No reason. Riri just made me think of it. I'm just talking, that's all."

"No, Raymonde, you're thinking of something. Go on, be honest, tell me what you want to say."

"Nothing."

"Come on, when you talk about a young lady like that to a man it's because you want them to marry."

"I guarantee you that I have nothing like that in mind."

"Well, let me tell you that I have no desire to marry… that I can't…"

"Why?"

"You know the mission we've taken on."

"What else?"

"Nothing else."

"Nothing with golden hair?"

"What?"

"And big beautiful eyes?"

"But…"

"A charming smile."

"I…"

"Riri of course… Pretty Riri?"

Raymonde squeezed her brother's hand affectionately.

"You can't hide the secrets of your heart from your sister, Raoul. Oh, yes, I know more about it than you can know."

"I don't understand."

"I know that you love Riri."

"I swear to you…"

"You love Riri… and Riri loves you."

"Riri?"

"It's so obvious… you love each other."

Raoul answered solemnly, "Well, yes, it's true, Raymonde. But I'm forcing myself to hide it. Yes, I love Riri with all my heart… and I'm sad, yes, terribly sad."

"Why?"

"Because, look, Raymonde, you know that Riri is a Menardier."

"So."

"So between a Menardier and a Montreil, the banker who ruined her, who killed her father and plunged her family into poverty, there's a huge gap, an abyss…"

"No, Raoul, you filled in that gap. You, Robert Montreil, not knowing who Riri was, you came to her aide because she was defenseless. You, a millionaire, loved poor Riri and you wanted make her your wife."

"That's true."

"Riri is rich today but only thanks to you. She loved you then and she loves you even more now that you're the poor one! Besides, with a girl like Riri money is no issue when it comes to love."

"You're speaking with your heart."

"Riri has the same heart, I'm sure of it."

"Marriage is impossible. It would look like I was trying to get back what our honor forced us to give away."

"You gave back Riri's fortune but you still owe her for years of suffering, poverty and unhappiness. You owe it to her to make her happy and she will only be happy at your side."

"But Raymonde…"

"I was talking about Irene because both of you are thinking about Robert's happiness now. I think he will find it with her, our adorable Irene."

The next day it was Robert who found himself alone with Raymonde broaching the subject.

"Have you noticed," he told her, "how Raoul looks at Riri? He embraces her with his eyes." He shuddered sadly when he said this.

"Yes I have," Raymonde replied. "So?"

"He loves her."

"Okay. And then?"

"Don't you think that Riri would be a perfect wife for him?"

"Do you think so?"

"I'm sure… since he loves her."

"And her?"

"Her? It's obvious she loves him too."

"Great. But look, Robert, the past… the Menardier affair…"

"Well, we righted the wrong done by our father. You can't fault Raoul…"

"If Riri finds out about it…"

"But she'll know everything and I'm sure she'll see how noble he was."
He'll be poor."

"Now that's something that won't bother Riri. She'll love him penniless like he loved her when she was poor. And she'll know that she's not being loved for her money. Anyway, Raoul's not so poor. First of all he'll manage the bank and he's got his law practice to boot. If need be I'll give him my share."

"What about you?"

"Me? I'm Dr. Robert, the doctor of the poor… I'm used to poverty.

"Don't you think about marriage?"

Robert shook his head, "No, I won't marry."

"Why not?"

"I'm devoted to my mission as a doctor. I'm not made for the love of a woman. Me, I was born to be an uncle… a doting uncle. You'll see. Anyway, I'll have enough trouble taking care of all the colds, coughs and measles of your children and theirs. My life will be plenty full, plenty… and my happiness will be seeing you happy."

Raymonde stopped listening to him. She put her arm around his neck and kissed him on the cheek. "You have the biggest heart of all of us!"

26. The happy villa

A few hours later Irene de Valtours arrived in Paris with her father for a long stay. Raymonde had a talk with her that could have been an extension of her conversation with her brothers.

"You know, Irene, that I want you to be happy, that I love you like a sister."

"Like a mother, too. Yes, my dear Raymonde, and you know how emotional I get when you start talking about my happiness."

"Shall I talk about my brother Robert? You know that he has a great reputation as a doctor and among the poor he's like a savior."

"Yes, I know."

"The name Dr. Robert is revered. The poor are relieved if the hospital tells them Dr. Robert will be taking care of them. They bring patients from all over Paris to see him. I've seen mothers kissing his hands like they used to do to saints before faith was replaced by science. This recognition from good people has something beautiful and grand about it... and well, this simple and sweet man who has earned these honors through his knowledge and kindness... I want to see him become your husband."

"But, Raymonde, you know that for a long time... you know my secret... I love Robert more than anything, but he who can see all the ills of the poor cannot see the suffering in me. Those eyes that can spot all the evil microbes in a microscope never bother to look at me."

"Well, we're going to force him to abandon his dear microbes and deal with this little pink and blonde butterfly that is you, my pretty Irene."

"You think it's possible?"

"Soon Dr. Robert will find his big heart too small to cherish you like he'll want, like you deserve."

"How can we do that?"

"You're going to get sick."

"Sick?"

"Yes. When a woman doesn't want to do something she starts by getting sick. She does the same when others don't want to do what she wants to."

"That's right. Okay, I'm feeling sick."

"You're going to ask for Dr. Robert and the rest is up to you."

"I see."

Every woman, even the purest, the most modest and honest, like Irene, is a born actress. The day after this meeting Monsieur de Valtours was alarmed by this daughter's sudden illness and summoned Dr. Montreil right away. Robert showed up in the afternoon.

The patient was lying on a lounge chair, dressed in gorgeous pajamas. She had loosely tied up her blonde hair with a wide ribbon. She looked lovely.

When Dr. Robert saw her he was really touched, even troubled. "Only Riri," he thought, "can compare with this beautiful girl."

For her part Irene kept her eyes half-closed and watched him like all women know how to do. She felt the same as he did, but even more emotional since she loved him. She drank in the charm of his man looking so serious and sad, with his gentle voice and the kindness in his gestures, the devotion in his clear, honest eyes...

Better than anyone she understood why everyone loved Dr. Robert and wanted to put their lives in his sympathetic hands. She gave herself to him completely, body and soul.

The love of two people is written in the book of fate from time immemorial. When those bound to love each other meet, it feels like they have always loved each other and they are no more surprised by it than nature is when the sun rises in the morning.

Now Robert was thinking, "A flower is blooming in my heart. I thought its name was Riri but in truth it is called Irene."

When she forgot that she was supposed to be sick and he forgot that he had come as a doctor, they began talking about the past... and the present. They were about to start on the future when they heard the voice of the Count de Valtours.

"Well, doctor, what's wrong with our patient?"

"Oh, right. Mademoiselle is sick, yes..." Robert babbled a few explanations and as he saw the father looking more and more confused he wrapped up with, "I'll write a prescription."

He scratched a few words for some Madeira wine mixed with quinquina and phosphate of lime, a harmless, fine-tasting concoction.

"A little drink before meals," he said on leaving. "I'll see you tomorrow."

When he left the Valtours Robert felt completely different. He had just had a revelation about Irene and was feeling the joy of a man who had suddenly discovered a treasure that he had passed by all the time. He kept hearing Irene's sweet voice, kept seeing the blue glint of her eyes... his heart was pounding. He needed fresh air. His soul was suffocating.

He was driven to the Bois, then to the house. He needed to talk to someone about his patient. He would find Raymonde... who was waiting for him.

At first sight Raymonde knew that her strategy had worked beautifully. Robert talked for a long time about his visit and thought (poor boy) that Raymonde had no idea that his heart was singing.

Now Dr. Robert divided his day into three parts. The biggest part belonged to his patients and the hospital; the most pleasurable was for Irene; and the third part was reserved for wounded man brought to Girardet's villa. This secret patient was none other than Paulin Broquet who had been transported there after the dramatic scene at Madame Verdier's. For his charming nurses he had Madam Laurent, Riri and Marie, sometimes helped by Raymonde and Irene.

The gorgeous villa that was once so sad now rang out with laughter. You could hear the strong, deep voice of Raymonde, the clear, golden voices of Riri and Irene, all of them singing for the sick as Raymonde's fingers or Madame Laurent's danced over the piano playing those beautiful works that comfort and console and make one think.

Madame Montreil sometimes visited with her daughters or with Raymonde and Captain Rennebois came whenever he could escape Fontainebleau. And this group around the sick man, around the wounded, this meeting of good people who had suffered in life and therefore understood it better, was something rare, touching and delightful.

Andre Girardet's story was simple, cruel and upsetting. As a young officer he loved a girl who found the tenderness and affection with him that she was deprived of at home. This girl's husband was hard, brutal and selfish, making her life unhappy. Andre and she adored each other and would have been happy to stay together and declare their love, but the husband would not hear of separation, let alone divorce. His fortune and livelihood relied on his wife's dowry.

Well, one day as the young lady was coming to meet Andre the stupidest accident befell her. Her car hit a big truck hauling stones. The girl was thrown under the truck and crushed, her bones broken along with her heart full of love.

Andre Girardet thought he would go mad! Under those stupid, cruel wheels his happiness was destroyed. He asked to be sent to the colonies. He tried to end his suffering in reckless adventures and acts of insane bravery. Death rejected him. But after many long years away, when he came back to France the pains he suffered in the swamps and the brush and one serious injury to his hip took away the use of his legs. Still young he limped around like an old man and lived alone in the world with his inconsolable mourning.

Madame Laurent had been a friend of the beloved girl, the accomplice of her secret love. She was the one, therefore, who carried flowers to the cemetery in Andre's absence. And that was why she kept in touch with Aunt Melie. She was wrong not to tell her husband, not to trust him with the truth, but for the sake of the dead girl's memory Andre did not want anyone else to know the tragic secret.

She felt it her duty to say nothing and we have seen how complicated this simple, touching mystery could be. Soon, however, things were going to work themselves out.

Raoul was in charge of the Laurent case. He was giving back the money that had been swallowed by the bank. Moreover, an engineer, a friend of Andre Girardet, had run the factory during Laurent's absence and it was doing very well. Then Laurent was going to get out of jail soon because his father-in-law, Monsieur Bilmat, was likely to drop the case. Raoul had guaranteed the mayor of Itonville that thief were not his son-in-law.

Now that Laurent knew the truth he renewed the trust and love of his wife. He was going to be with her soon and her friends who were keeping a place warm for him at the villa.

The fact that Paulin Broquet was in the happy villa, being cared for and healed, was due to the clever mind of his lieutenant Gabriel.

27. Just in time

When Baiter had made his report about Julie, after all the brandy got her talking, Paulin Broquet guessed the truth about the mysterious Madame Verdier. The fortune-teller ploy seemed the only way to get the poor old lady to confess what the detective needed to hear. As we saw it worked like a charm.

But we know that Broquet had enemies whom he knew were strong and influential. He had to have irrefutable proof. Madame Verdier was not only imprisoned, so to speak, from the world by her brother and son, the thieves were also watching her closely, always afraid of some indiscretion from this lady who knew too much.

Naturally, despite all of Baiter's precautions and skillful maneuvering, the so-called Baron Dupont and Count de la Gueriniere knew of Julie's weakness for brandy and snuff. Broquet knew that they knew. But he figured that after the battle in the hangar the Zs were badly hurt and as usual after a failure were off on their own, licking their wounds, probably not even thinking about the Verdier house. It was, therefore, the perfect time.

Broquet jumped in, playing the role of Madame Roulet, fortune-teller. But contrary to his expectations the Zs were watching.

When the fortune-teller was brought secretly into the Verdier house, the Baron and the Count were informed by their men. They came over as soon as possible.

Despite his wounded thigh Zigomar (whose extraordinary energy we have witnessed) wanted to be there. He was hoping to get his revenge in this new encounter. With the help of his uncle Baron Dupont he got to the Verdier home and forgetting all about his pain he leaped into the room where the pseudo-chiromancer was listening to the story of the sick old lady imprisoned by bandits.

We have seen how the session was interrupted, but Broquet had time to hear what he needed.

Zigomar also thought it would be good to split open his skull so that the memory of all his confidence would pour out with his brain. He figured it would be better to get rid of Broquet like this, very practically, at the moment when he was in total control rather than wait to kill him later with a sword or a gun.

His plan was simple: smash his head in and then dump his body in the street somewhere. People would think the old lady just fell off the curb but when they investigated and found out who the victim really was, that it was Paulin Broquet, the grief in Paris would know no bounds.

And Zigomar would make sure that everyone knew it was his decisive victory.

In fact, after bludgeoning Broquet he wanted to carve a Z into his forehead and then use a red-hot iron to brand his chest with another. Like the indelible mark left on his own chest Zigomar would leave a permanent, indestructible trace of his triumph.

Therefore, Zigomar clubbed Broquet and despite his fighting skills the detective could not dodge it. He was hit hard, but his skull was protected by the wig and hat and did not split open like the bandit hoped. And as Broquet was falling to the ground, bleeding from his nose and mouth, Gabriel and Baiter burst into the room and beat the Count and the Baron to a pulp.

Broquet had prepared his men. He had told to Baiter, "Tonight you're bringing over the fortune-teller you told your friend Julie about."

This was enough to understand that their boss was going to go it alone but hard-earned experience had taught them all not to leave him to the mercy of chance.

When Baiter and the so-called Madame Roulet had left, Gabriel and Simon followed at a distance. They were prepared for any eventuality. There was also a car parked nearby in front of a wine shop. The driver and his two passengers were ready to go into action at the first signal.

After Baiter brought the false soothsayer to Verdier he came out and checked the street. Confident that all was clear he went back up to share a drink with Julie. While sipping his brandy he listened carefully and kept on his toes. But he heard no suspicious noises in the house. Then suddenly he heard the Baron's voice boom out along with the Count's cry of victory. He ran to help his boss at the same time as Gabriel and Simon popped up.

The two lieutenants had, in fact, seen three or four men whom they had recognized on the street and followed into the house. The Baron and the Count were so sure of themselves this time that they did not even bother to put on disguises. Maybe also because when they figured out that Julie's friend was actually Baiter they were in a hurry to catch the detective off guard.

Logically they imagined that Broquet would believe his enemies were too disorganized to form a plan and would leave him alone. Anyway, he was unrecognizable in his disguise so would take fewer precautions than usual. In their view, Broquet had just walked right into the lion's den. It was too good an opportunity to pass up.

Therefore, they rushed into Madame Verdier's room just at the moment when she was confessing to the detective. The Count came in through a door behind Broquet and took aim at his head. He let loose his triumphant yell and swung as hard as he could.

Broquet fell. But as the Count was about to finish him off he was knocked away. Gabriel had punched him so hard that he was seeing stars, as they say in boxing.

As for the Baron, the clown kicked him in the back with no regard to his fancy clothes. When his nose smashed into the wall it started bleeding profusely.

This all happened quickly, silently, with such precision that when the Baron finally turned around, feeling his swollen nose, all he saw was his dead sister and the Count lying unconscious on the floor. There was no sign of the fortune-teller. Paulin Broquet had disappeared.

Gabriel and Baiter carried their boss downstairs and into the car that was now parked in front of the house. They slid in beside him as best they could on the seat that could fold down into a kind of bed. The driver took off for the center of Paris. He just wanted to get away. Later they told him where he had to go. Gabriel and Baiter had to discuss it first.

Should they take the boss home to Avenue Trudaine or to the house in Neuilly? They figured that Trudaine would still be watched but then again they did not want to take the chance that Zigomar could find out about the house in Neuilly... They thought about a hospital or clinic in Paris but they knew that after Julie told the police everything she knew there could be reporters swarming all around.

So, they came up with the idea of asking Andre Girardet if he would harbor their injured boss. He was more than willing. A simple phone call summoned Dr. Robert who was there in no time with his brother. This fortuitous idea turned out to be the best for everyone.

As soon Broquet was lying comfortably in the room Girardet had prepared for him, he was already coming around. By the time the doctor arrived, he was fully conscious.

Dr. Robert examined the wounded head. Thanks to the wig and the hat, thanks also to Broquet's thick skull, the detective was not killed by the blow...

It took a few for Broquet to recover fully, to feel the pain slowly dissipate so that he could go back on duty in Paris, coming back to the villa just to sleep.

Besides him there were also Madame Laurent, Riri and Marie the hunchback sleeping in the villa. They were afraid that Zigomar might strike again against Riri. It was possible that with several Zs in prison they would try to avenge themselves on Riri or kidnap her and hold her for ransom.

Broquet had assigned two of his men to watch Pretty Riri everywhere she went in Paris but it seemed easier and safer to have her in the villa at night where they could watch over Broquet as well. Anyway, it seemed unlikely that Zigomar would attack them there right away.

Gabriel had told Broquet that he thought he really felt he had seriously injured the Count when he punched him. And yet (something hard to believe) the old clown Simon who was still working at the club, as well as Baiter who was going to out to the shows, both swear that the Count de la Gueriniere continued to hit the town, sometimes at the club, sometimes cheering on Lucette Minois, out strolling the streets, eating with friends, living it up as usual!

Simon, who knew how strong Gabriel was, made sure to scrutinize the Count's face carefully. To Broquet's great surprise his face showed no trace of the blow received by Gabriel's powerful fist.

"Okay, okay," is all Broquet said. "Even though your Zigomar shows no trace of your little slap, my Count still has the indelible mark on his chest... we'll find him with that!"

28. Beet problems

Paulin Broquet was back to Avenue Trudaine and his daily routine when he thought it might be good to take in a show... to see how the Count de la Gueriniere was admiring pretty Lucette Minois like all of Paris. It happened to be the night when the performers were having a little problem, one of those minor issues that took on major proportions behind the curtains, as happens all the time in the theater.

For several days they had been unpleasantly surprised to notice the absence of Monsieur Mathieu, whom they called the Beet. Had the industrialist from the north lost interest in the show that he was so enthusiastic about before? Or had he suddenly become tired of his platonic love? These were the questions they asking in the wings, coming up with all kinds of answers. The most common opinion, for no special reason, was that he had gone back to his factory and they would never see him again.

However, from that first day of his absence a wonderful bouquet of flowers was delivered to Lucette Minois without any card to indicate the gallant sender. In theater even more than in life there are no secrets. Soon everyone knew about the mysterious devilries that seemed to surprise Lucette even more than her jealous comrades. But was her surprise real? Did she really have no idea who was sending the flowers? She swore that she knew nothing, nothing at all!

But in the theater they ended up assuming that the sender must be the Beet who was keeping precious memories of the star. There it was for her that he had been coming. The other girls paid her bitter compliments.

But what did the Count think of all this? What did he do about this romantic intrigue in the wings? So far he had said nothing.

As always in such situations he, the lover, was the last to know about it. Being a gentleman he did not give Lucette a hard time about getting flowers from a stranger. He did not forbid her to accept them since she was a celebrated artist. One day he would meet the admirer and thank him for the homage.

"Watch out," they said in the wings, "that'll be the day when swords are drawn."

And they felt sorry for the fat, friendly industrialist. They could not picture the Beet holding a sword, squared off against the Count.

Then all of a sudden on the evening that Paulin Broquet decides to go to the theater, the Beet shows up in his usual box, right before Lucette comes on stage. It was such a surprise that the singer forgot her lyrics... the comedian babbled nonsense... and the orchestra squealed.

Behind the curtain the news spread like wildfire. "The Beet is in the room!"

They told Lucette who came out calmly and sang as usual without any problems.

As for Monsieur Mathieu, called the Beet, he looked as friendly as always, smiling and cheerful. He seemed happy to be back in his box, in the theater. Without the least suspicion, as peaceful as a lamb, he made a sensational return.

The Count could see from his box but showed no sign of acknowledgement. He did not even turn his head to look. But during the intermission he left his box and went over to the Beet who was smoking a big cigar. The Count greeted him very politely and so as not to make a scene bent down and whispered, "Excuse me, monsieur, I'd like to thank you."

The Beet turned red. "Thank me? For what?"

"Allow me to introduce myself, since I haven't had the pleasure... I am the Count de la Gueriniere."

"I am Monsieur Mathieu."

"Wonderful. So, you like the arts?"

"Very much."

"Especially the artists... the singers?"

"That depends."

"You shower them with marvelous bouquets."

"When they deserve it."

"Wonderful. And no one deserves it more than Lucette Minois who you've been sending flowers to these last few days."

The Beet started shaking and stammered, "What's that? They told you? You know... it's artistic appreciation only, really."

"I have no doubt, monsieur. Except that Lucette is my mistress and I don't like when others show their... artistic appreciation."

"Believe me... I... just..."

"I understand. But trying to run into her wherever she goes in the city is going a bit far for artistic appreciation, don't you think?"

"It's just... I thought... monsieur..."

"You're not well acquainted with Parisian customs... that's your excuse. But you must know that sending flowers to an artist without a card is very pretty nervy. When it happens more than once it's downright rude."

"Rude?"

"When the sender shows up in a box to get noticed not only by the singer on stage, the object of his obsession, but also by whole audience..."

The Beet tried to defend himself, "Believe me, monsieur, I never meant to get noticed by the audience..."

"In that case, they won't notice when you leave."

"Leave?"

"Yes, because you're leaving right now."

"Why should I leave? I want to stay until the end of the show."

"I won't allow it. You're going to get out of here."

"But, monsieur, I'll look ridiculous."

"I don't care how you do it, just do it."

"This is some kind of joke. I won't listen to another word you say."

"In that case, two of my friends will have to see you tomorrow morning."

"For what?" the naïve Beet asked.

"They'll tell you. Here's my card."

"Here's mine but I'm not leaving this show."

"No need. I'll be going."

"I'm not making you."

"Obviously. But you can be sure that they day after tomorrow I'll be the only one coming." And the Count de la Gueriniere left with his friends.

The next day two of the Count's friends, Viscount de la Soulle and Baron Loiselet, showed up at the hotel on Rue de Rivoli and met Monsieur Mathieu. The Beet still did not understand why they had come.

The Viscount spoke first, "Monsieur, the Count de la Gueriniere has been gravely offended by you and will accept no apologies."

"But I'm not apologizing for something I didn't do."

"You sent flowers to his mistress."

"As an artist, yes."

"You tried to steal her away... was that also as an artist?"

The Beet had no answer but asked, "So what does the Count want?"

"That you find two witnesses to second you."

"A duel!" the poor man exclaimed. "A duel?"

"With swords."

"Swords? But that's impossible. Look, messieurs, for a few flowers... yes, I was fawning over Lucette Minois... because she's beautiful! But it's not so serious that you have to cut my throat."

"What's your decision?"

"The Count de la Gueriniere is a professional duelist. How many has he fought and won already? He's a hired killer. Me, I'm not a fighting man. I make sugar... and not with a sword!"

"Do you know how to hold a sword? Have you ever fenced?"

"Like everyone in school I played around but I don't know anything about fencing."

"We can't talk about it anymore. We'll be waiting for your seconds."

The Beet looked very upset by this ridiculous turn of events. But he had no choice. He was obligated to act against his will but he had to act. He went to find two friends: an engineer called Gelinert and a lawyer, Bradeau. They were business colleagues but they acted as his witnesses.

Since the Count was the offended party he could choose the weapons. He had picked the épée. The duel would take place the next day on some private land in Neuilly-Saint-James. The lawyer Bradeau knew that his colleague Montreil had a brother who was a doctor and asked if he would help the Beet.

As you can imagine, this encounter piqued the interest of the two brothers. They went to tell Paulin Broquet right away.

"I'll be there," the detective said. "Yes, we'll all be there."

"It'll be a murder by the Count."

"Bah! What's one more matter?"

"Can't we stop it from happening?"

"No! Do only what the poor Beet asks of you."

29. A hole in the chest

Messieurs Bradeau and Gelinert came right on time with Dr. Robert to pick up their client. The Beet was almost ready.

"Did you sleep well?" they asked him.

"Yes. I feel just fine."

Whatever he said, it was clear that he was worried. He must have felt like a man waking up on the day of his death sentence. But he was very brave to go up against the seasoned and (sorry to say) fatal sword of the Count de la Gueriniere. The duel was scheduled for 10 am. It was absolutely private. No public! No one! The Count insisted.

"They're accusing me," he said, "of being a show-off with these duels. I'm tired of it."

Raoul, however, was standing behind a curtain in one of the rooms in the house on the property. Other people he did not know, probably friends of the Count, were also there and in other rooms. Certainly Broquet and his men must have been hiding in the bushes or stables or somewhere…

The duelists had taken off their jackets and put on their cuffless glove. They were hoping that the Count might be kind for once, being faced with such an inexperienced adversary as the friendly industrialist, and for his honor only poke him in the arm. But only the Beet's witnesses were hoping this. Those who knew the Count had no such illusions.

The Count was the first on the field. As usual he looked splendid, relaxed, comfortable, maybe a little pale as was fitting, but smiling and self-confident.

The Beet arrived shortly afterward, very pale, almost white. Plump and pudgy he stumbled forward between his two witnesses with his head hanging down, very anxious, just waiting for that fatal blow. At his moment, no doubt, he would have told Lucette Minois and her charming smile to go to hell! He was probably thinking that the flowers he had sent her would lay on his coffin tomorrow. Not a pretty sight. Poor old Beet!

The shiny épées were handed to the duelists and the director—who was not the elegant Baron Dupont this time—asked the usual, "Are you ready?"

"Yes," the Count said firmly.

"Sure," the Beet blurted out.

"At your will, messieurs," the director announced solemnly.

The Count posed like an expert fencer, ready to play with his opponent before lunging to the finish as he liked.

The Beet looked a little wobbly, holding his sword like a votive candle and not really sure what he was supposed to do with it.

The smiling Count attacked right away but all of a sudden, obviously out of instinct, but with unexpected skill or luck, the Beet parried the blows and straightened out his épée. They saw then that the Beet could defend himself better than supposed... and the Count was not going to skewer him like a helpless little boy.

The Count attacked again, with a flurry of swipes. The Beet backed up, farther and farther, stayed out of range, his tip still held in a straight line. The Count could not strike him. Time and again some inept looking maneuver blocked his sword. Clumsy and timid, the Beet reacted admirably but refused to answer, to riposte. His épée was an impassable wall but it would not counterattack.

Now the Count was getting annoyed. He felt ridiculous, him the expert fencer being held off by this sugar-maker. He figured it was his own fault for holding back and just trying to nick his opponent's arm. Therefore, he decided to quit playing and be serious.

This time the Count attacked furiously. He was aiming at the body, trying for a mortal wound, but the Beet's sword remained impenetrable. It was like a steel shield blocking everything thrown at it.

The Count was in a rage. He tried moves that he only used on the most formidable adversaries, surprise moves, moves that forbidden by the code of honor... Nothing worked. Surprise, force, violence, everything rammed into the sword being wielded by an expert hand, apparently unaware of its true caliber. It was a miracle.

The Count tried a hold that nobody so far had been able to withstand. He grabbed the Beet, held him, leaned on him, then he stooped and lunged with his épée held out—he became a human arrow.

It was meant to plunge his steel all the way to the hilt in his opponent's chest. Indeed it produced a cry of terror. They thought the Beet was run through because the two men were now standing face-to-face, chest-to-chest. A sword fell to the ground... it was the Count's!

The Beet took one step back. He was holding his red blade in one hand and piece of the Count's shirt was hanging from the hilt. His épée had slid into the Count's right side.

The Count staggered. Before the stunned witnesses had time to react, to intervene, he fell on his back, his arms spread out and his chest bare. A triangular hole was leaking a stream of blood.

And on this chest, which the Beet was watching intently, there was no indelible mark that had been stamped by Paulin Broquet.

30. The dying wants to talk

There was utter bewilderment in Paris, which is so fond of arms, when they learned that the marvelous duelist, the unbeatable Count de la Gueriniere had been stabbed by the peaceable industrialist from the north, the sugar-maker!

To be beaten by such a wimp was a double defeat. And the Parisian joke never got old that said he would probably die of "beet stroke".

In the Count's house near Avenue du Bois there was a long line of friends and fencing partners and curiosity seekers waiting for news and leaving their cards because absolutely no one was let in.

The reporters were going crazy. It was a sensational affair, of the highest interest, very Parisian… and yet they could not get any details. The doors were shut tight. They could not interview the man who was probably on his deathbed.

It was no better for the industrialist. The Beet had disappeared. They had to go into the northern countryside to question all the manufacturers called Mathieu and as deep as they dug not a single beet.

But our Mathieu had not left Paris. He just wanted to escape being interviewed by seeking asylum with Dr. Robert and Raoul, the friend of one of his witnesses. The Montreil brothers very kindly put their rooms in their mother's house at his disposal. Thus he could keep some distance between him and his adversary and receive news from Dr. Robert about the injured man.

Robert had offered his services on the field of honor and was gratefully accepted by his colleague on the Count's side. The two of them were now at the watching over the gravely injured man lying in his bed. His life was hanging by a thread. Only his strong physique was keeping him alive. But it would take nothing to send his soul flying from his tough and brawny body.

The wound was very serious. Only by a miracle had the Count not died on the spot. A few inches more and the Beet's épée would have pierced the heart. It had entered under the right armpit because once again the Count had lunged with his right. By a fluke of luck, which often happens in duels, the épée had hit part of the lung then slipped under the shoulder blade, stopping short of the spinal column. If the steel had gone through the spine it would have pierced both lungs and undoubtedly reached the heart.

The wound was bad but not so dangerous that the doctors had given up hope. They were witnessing, therefore, a spectacular sight. Those who knew about the dramatic background could appreciate this curious tragedy. Dr. Robert had come here out of courtesy, out of obedience to his profession, and the young doctors had backed away. They watched Dr. Robert Montreil using all his skill to pull the dying Count de la Gueriniere out of death's grip. The situation did not lack grandeur.

At the moment the life of this man who had driven Robert Montreil into dreadful mourning was in the hands of Dr. Robert. And Dr. Robert was using all his medical skill to save this man whom he believed was his father's killer.

After a makeshift bandaging on the field they had transported the wounded very carefully to his home as the witnesses wanted. Robert wanted them to take him to the clinic but they refused. Besides, the Count's house was nearby and he might not survive a longer trip. The doctor yielded to their wishes.

He got his surgical instruments out of his car along with everything else he might need. All day long he stayed by the Count's bedside. After a new bandage was put on with great care the Count looked a little better. He felt the effects of the caffeine they injected him with and opened his eyes.

Did he recognize who was standing over him? Maybe. His eyes were fixed on Dr. Robert.

"Thank you," he murmured. "Sorry…" And he fell into a coma-like sleep.

Lucette Minois, the cause of the tragic duel, was quickly informed of the catastrophe. She came over as soon as she could to nurse him. She loved the Count like any stage girl loved her lover: because he was not mean and ugly, he had a nice name, he was fun, gave her money and made all her comrades jealous.

The Count loved Lucette Minois more sincerely than he imagined, more deeply than it looked. He was happy to feel her by his side.

The room was huge and richly furnished. It was not exactly the modern room of an athletic man but rather the cushy, comfortable room of a rich man who uses it to rest quietly, alone, a special room in his house. Thick rugs covered the wood floors, muffling the footsteps; heavy tapestries hung on the walls and doors to keep any sound from sneaking in.

In the evening the Count seemed to be regaining some strength.

"It's almost sure now that we've saved him," the doctor told Lucette. "Keep your hopes high."

The Count could even talk. By now he was clear-headed and awake. "Ah, you're here, Dr. Robert," he said. "Good. Give me a little more strength… Keep me alive another hour… I have to talk to you… I have to…"

"To me?" Robert was nervous.

"Yes, to you, Robert Montreil. And if your brother Raoul can come, I'd be even more grateful."

Robert did not know what to think or feel.

More weakly, almost in a whisper, the patient said, "But we have to be alone, doctor. Nobody else can hear… nobody…"

Robert was learning to be suspicious under Paulin Broquet's tutelage. He did not want to trust the Count's servant nor anyone else of his friends. Therefore, he was trying to find a way to warn his brother quickly and discreetly.

He had asked a young doctor who usually helped him to come with some extra equipment along with a couple of nurses. Now, one of these nurses was none other than Simon the clown. Instead of a servant it was him, naturally, that Robert trusted to tell Raoul.

Moreover, the whole house was feeling agitated. The master's injury, his impending death, apparently, could all explain the disturbance, but there was something else as well—comings and goings, hushed discussions between the servants and people outside and even though all access to the house was denied they still let in some strangers.

Robert stayed by his patient's bedside so he was unaware of all this. Still, he thought it best to give simple excuses to Simon for warning Raoul under the pretext of getting some new medication.

Lucette Minois wanted to stay by her lover but she had no backup at the theater and everything happened so unexpectedly that there was no time to find a replacement. She could not miss a performance so she had to go. Robert assured her that when she came back the Count would be a little better. So she went to the Lutetia after promising to return after the show.

Naturally, at the theater they did not see the Count but neither did they see the Beet! Nevertheless it was a full house. The curiosity seekers wanted to see Lucette Minois, the star they fought duels over, the cause of the all-new tragedy... The reporters had nothing to gain at the Count's house and could not find Monsieur Mathieu so they beat a path to the pretty singer. They besieged her dressing room and Lucette answered their questions as best she could, being both very worried about the state of her lover and also very content with the attention it was bringing.

Simon met Raoul at the Montreil house. He had come to see if the industrialist had any news. When he entered the room he was surprised not to see his butler Marcelin whom he had put at the guest's disposal.

"Don't worry about him," the industrialist said, "he's taking care of me. He's very good at his job. I send him out on some errands."

When Robert had asked Simon to bring back Raoul, he also asked him to bring some handkerchiefs, which he had forgot to grab in the morning. Raoul went to his brother's wardrobe but it was locked and the key was not in the lock.

"He must have taken it with him," Raoul said, "but he never does that."

The Beet responded, "He must have slipped it into his pocket without thinking."

"Probably distracted. I'll bring him some of mine."

The sugar-maker smiled behind his white beard and mumbled, "We are distracted sometimes... and sometimes surprised, very surprised."

The Beet did not want to impose on the Montreil brothers any longer and said as much to his host. So, he and Raoul left the house and went to get a quick dinner at a restaurant on Avenue de la Grande Armée. Then the young lawyer left the industrialist to go catch a train to return home in the north. Raoul went to meet his brother at the appointed time. See, the Count was resting and would not wake up until late in the night.

They did not make it easy for Raoul to get into the Count's little house. Robert's aide had to come and bring him back into bedroom. The Count was awake. The doctors were giving him food and stimulants.

"I'm doing much better," he told Robert. "At least I feel better... Give me some strength now, yes some strength... I need it."

When Raoul showed up he smiled.

"Thank you for coming, monsieur."

The two brothers looked puzzled at this man whom they believed had killed their father, this man who was the very image of crime for them, this tough guy who had fought tooth and nail against Paulin Broquet... and they saw with absolute astonishment a defeated, trembling, pathetic creature, sweating and shivering, barely hanging onto life.

Was it possible that the approach of death had done this to the renowned fighter and the man had changed? That no more energy, no more courage—as dishonorably sued as it was, sure, but still magnificent—remained?

Zigomar was beaten and dying feebly, not like they imagined—magnificently amidst the horror and rage and blasphemy... in a radiant apotheosis of crime! Here was a slaughtered lamb, not the tiger biting the spears in its side fighting with his final breath.

Or was this some clever act being put on by the wretch? Was he luring the two brothers to his bedside before giving up the ghost in for one last triumphant act of sinister vengeance like a true bandit?

31. I'm a wretch

The two brothers stood at the bedside staring nervously at this troubling man, pondering these disturbing questions now.

But the Count's eyes held no malice. And his pale face, except for some twitches of pain, showed no tension or treachery, no sign of double-dealing. After asking Robert's aide and the other doctor to excuse them for a moment, he slowly, quietly started talking to the brothers.

"Messieurs, if I live thanks to the skill and dedication of Dr. Robert... or if I die as would be just... I owe you a confession..."

Robert was giving a spoonful of cordial to the patient now and then.

The Count whispered on, "I wanted to have Paulin Broquet hear this with you... or a judge... but it can't wait. Time is not on my side and I have to speak. Listen to me. It's almost by magic, fortunate circumstances, that you are here at my death bed to hear me..."

After a short silence to catch his breath the Count went on.

"I'm a wretch! I deserve to be despised by every honest and loyal man... I'm a wretch, absolutely wretched... but I'm not the evil one you imagine. I'm not the murdered of the banker Montreil..."

"You didn't kill our father?" the brothers jumped together.

"No, messieurs, no. Believe me! Let me talk... I didn't steal the diamonds from the Baroness either. I didn't kill my friends held prisoner or the Count de Marnais and that other poor fellow to keep them from talking... I didn't burn that face to keep it from being recognized."

"Are you really the Count de la Gueriniere?"

"I am... but not the Count who is Zigomar! No, I'm not Zigomar!"

"You're not Zigomar? Then who's the crook who says he's the Count de la Gueriniere? And who are you?"

"I told you I was a wretch. Now listen and you'll understand." He breathed deeply again before continuing. "Paulin Broquet has made a serious investigation of me and can tell you about my past, my resources and my questionable way of life until the day that everything changed. I lived in this house and I lived a fast life as you have seen. But skip all that because time is precious and I need it, I need the strength for what's important."

He asked Robert for another spoonful of cordial and resumed.

"I did the worst thing a desperate man could do... I stole! Another found out about it... Baron Dupont. He could have turned me in, ruined me, but instead he showed pity on me and offered to save me. I accepted and here's why: I had met Lucette Minois and I was like I still am very much in love with her. To remain her only lover I stole... her gorgeous necklace... that I sold to a fence who happened to be a friend of Baron Dupont. That's how he got me. And then, to save myself, what the Baron demanded of me… He offered me this house and enough money to lead the life I wanted, to be Lucette's lover. In return I lent him my identity."

"Your identity?"

"Meaning there would be another Count de la Gueriniere in Paris doing as he pleased and I could do nothing about it."

"We understand."

"A friend of Baron Dupont was always by my side. He gave me orders every morning and evening. I had to obey on the spot without question. Besides, all I had to do was show myself very conspicuously in certain places at certain times… or disappear completely… while the other Count was operating."

"Okay."

"I should have refused, fought back, turned myself in and accepted the punishment… or just killed myself… but that life was so easy, so wonderful… and I loved Lucette Minois!"

"You didn't try to make amends?"

"No. But I have to say that I didn't know about the crimes they committed in my name. I didn't know that the Count de la Gueriniere was Zigomar!"

"Really? You didn't know he was Zigomar?"

"I only started to suspect it when I heard about your father's murder."

"What did you do then?"

"I was outraged. I wanted to go to the police but they locked me up here, kept me prisoner for days. It's Zigomar, not me, who Broquet came searching for here. It's Zigomar who saw your father. And everything had been set up for their confrontation, for the glory of Zigomar. Me? They kept me prisoner until the Count was declared innocent."

"And then?"

"I went back to my life of parties and pleasure. I was wrong, I admit, I should have told the police, but to reveal everything would have meant losing Lucette… and I wasn't strong enough for that. Of course after this affair the Baron and his nephew Zigomar no longer trusted me. I was a thorn in their side. I scared them. So, they sentenced me… to death… at the first mistake I made, any sign of betrayal…"

The brothers listened intently and intensely to the emotional tale.

"In my shameful contract I was supposed to fight—either him or me—when the Count was challenged. Sometimes when the adversary was harmless the Baron's nephew took the field. You know he is an expert in arms and know some surprising moves that never fail to succeed. That's why he thought he'd finish off Captain Rennebois. I refused to fight him, refused to kill him like they ordered, so it was Zigomar who went out to slay him."

"The wretch!"

"However, he left me Monsieur Mathieu, the industrialist, the Beet who was courting Lucette. The whole affair was my fault; I got carried away by the situation… You'd really think that in this apparently minor incident there was some iron will controlling events that the Baron and Zigomar were powerless to stop. Anyway, Zigomar had been gone for a while. They said he'd left Paris and was off on a new job with the Baron but I rather think he was hurt badly by Paulin Broquet and was licking his wounds, trying to get back on his feet. Whatever the case he got word to me that he was really upset with my actions. They ordered me to be done with the Beet quickly. I was hoping I could scratch his arm and call it a day but I found myself faced with a surprising adversary… and then, messieurs, I guessed the truth. I saw the trap and understood… I knew!"

"What did you know?"

"That the whole thing was a set-up. A beautiful set-up. They were counting on my jealousy. This Mathieu the industrialist never existed. The Beet was a tool, a partner… a Z! He was Zigomar's man!"

The brothers shuddered at this revelation, "A Zigomar man! What makes you think that?"

"Everything. The outcome, the acting… and my injury. He was sent to get rid of me, to kill me, to murder me without suspicious circumstances since it was a duel."

"It's possible."

"It's true! I saw it at the first touch of steel. This shy, peaceful man playing the good kid from the country was a dangerous swordsman. I saw right away that he wanted to kill me and I had to defend myself. But I couldn't ant they won. I'm going to die… the Count de la Gueriniere murdered by Zigomar."

Exhausted he fell back on his pillows mumbling, "To die… oh well… it's better for me… but I will be avenged… by you. The sons of the murdered banker Montreil, you who constantly cursed my name, you will avenge this wretched Count now that you know…"

Robert leaned over and said, "Be strong. You can be redeemed. I'm telling you that you won't die from the sword wound. You will survive. And in a few days you'll be feeling much better." Then he added, "Now stop talking. Rest. You just need some rest, some calm… and patience."

"Yes, save me! Oh, if only I could live… get my revenge… yes, I'll sleep, but please wake me up when Lucette comes back."

"Will do."

Lucette Minois showed up almost at that very moment. She was happy to see that her lover was doing better. "I'm going to stay here next to him all night long."

The two brothers carried a lounge chair to the bedside and she lay down. Watching her, smiling at her, the wounded man felt sleep overcoming him.

Raoul and Robert left feeling confused and upset. They went into the salon whose windows looked out upon a little garden separated from the street by an iron fence. They needed some fresh air to cool their feverish minds. They also wanted to talk alone and figure out how to contact Broquet as soon as possible about this strange turn of events.

Simon, who was playing the nurse, met them just then for a quick word. "The boss has set a trap. The house is surrounded. Probably catch the real Zigomar this time."

"The real Zigomar? So, Broquet knows."

"Of course. He wants me to tell you stay put."

The house was completely silent now. You could feel something serious, something tragic was about to transpire. And everything happened in the shadows, in silence. It was really intense.

All of a sudden someone screamed... in rage... howled in anger and almost right away gunshots rang out.

"Help me! Help me!" a voice yelled.

Robert and Raoul recognized this voice. It belonged to Paulin Broquet. It came clearly through the walls and tapestries from the Count's bedroom. For Broquet to call for help like this he must have been in real danger. Maybe he had been shot...

Against Simon's orders the two brothers ran to help their friend. Ignoring the gun that might be waiting for them in the room where the criminals had probably invaded they rushed in.

"Light! Quick, get some light!" Broquet shouted.

Robert was starting to know the layout of the place and quickly turned the switch. From the ceiling and walls light flooded the room.

The sight before their eyes was truly terrifying.

32. Again Zigomar! Always Zigomar!

Right after the brothers had left, as Lucette Minois fell to sleep almost immediately, understandably after such an emotional day, the Count de la Gueriniere started to doze off as well. Suddenly a man came mysteriously out from behind a tapestry that was hiding a secret door. Silently, carefully he snuck into the room. He listened closely, made sure that Lucette was asleep, then stepped over to the bed. He grabbed the Count's arm and shook it hard.

"Wake up. Come on, wake up," he said.

The Count slowly pried his eyes open. He was trying to wake up mumbling, "Is that you, Dr. Robert?"

But he did not see the doctor. He saw a man with a blonde beard whom he did not recognize and he almost jumped out of bed. His nerves snapped him awake in the blink of an eye. "Who are you? What do you want?"

The man put his finger to his lips, "Quiet. Whisper... Baron Dupont and the Count de la Gueriniere order you to say nothing, to reveal nothing about anything to anybody. Watch what you say. If the law comes keep up the role you agreed to play..."

"Or else?"

"Or else the law will know who the Count de la Gueriniere really is. They'll know who stole Lucette's necklace, who lied and cheated, who lived off the fruits of crime... how and why the Count de la Gueriniere sold himself."

A spark of hatred gleamed in the wounded man's eyes. "Too late!"

The man was startled. "You talked?"

The patient sat up and spoke proudly, "Yes, I talked! You can tell who send you, who I will get my revenge on, that I talked."

"It's not true. You didn't talk."

"I talked," he shot back. "Yes, I talked. You want to kill me, you creeps, but my death won't do Zigomar any good. I told them everything."

"Impossible. You're not strong enough."

"Dr. Robert gave me something, made me strong enough to tell him everything."

"You told... Dr. Robert?"

"Robert and Raoul. Both of them were here. They know everything and soon enough Paulin Broquet will find out..."

He did not finish. The man swore in anger and jumped on him. "You wretch! Now we too will have our revenge! You talked for nothing!"

The furious bandit tore off the bandages on his chest. He pulled out a knife to cut them and then put one hand around the sick man's throat, using the other to get the wound bleeding again. Mercilessly he watched the blood flow out, watched life flow out with the blood from the wound. And suddenly the crook

531

turned executioner was yanked off the bed, lifted up and thrown across the room.

But he jumped to his feet right away, holding a gun. He tried to run out the door but the man who had surprised him was on him and despite three shots from the revolver he caught him.

The two men were strong and both knew how to fight. There was a terrible struggle, extremely violent, that ensued in the room. They fell to the ground, rolling around and roaring like wild beasts trying to tear each other to pieces—a relentless duel.

It took only a few minutes for the end of the fight to come. There was a ghastly cry of pain, then a voice called out, "Help me! Help!" It was Paulin Broquet.

The brothers had heard this cry for help and came running into the room. After Robert had turned on the lights they did not see the Count at first. He was out of bed, lying on the floor in a pool of blood, showing no signs of life. The bandage that had been so expertly applied to the wound had been ripped off. Laid bare it was bleeding again.

On the lounge chair, motionless, Lucette Minois lay quietly. Maybe she was dead too…

But Paulin Broquet, who had called them in, was nowhere to be found. He had vanished into thin air.

Then the panting voice of the detective said, "Over here, my friends!"

Raoul rushed over as Robert went instinctively to the wounded man.

Simon came running in at this time, soon followed by Gabriel. Broquet was behind the bed, on the ground, which is why they did not see him at first. And he was not alone. He was grappling a man in a jiu-jitsu hold, a redheaded man with a white beard who was vainly wasting his last efforts trying to break free. He yelled out in pain and futile rage.

Gabriel and Simon grabbed him and pulled him to his feet, keeping his hands behind his back. Broquet got up afterward. At first with his back to the room, then he turned to Raoul.

The lawyer cried out in surprise, "Monsieur Mathieu!"

"The Beet in person, yes," Broquet responded. He pulled off his wig and beard and became Paulin Broquet again, but beaming with pride and joy now. "Enough of these fun and games, we've got Zigomar. Zigomar is finished!"

Someone burst out laughing. It was the prisoner answering the detective, "You'll never have Zigomar! Zigomar will never be finished!"

On a sign from their boss Gabriel and Simon carried the criminal over to a chair. Now Zigomar looked in really bad shape.

"Maybe I squeezed him a little too hard," Broquet said, "but with a guy as tough as him you need an iron grip."

Just then Robert turned around, saw the prisoner and cried out, "Monsieur de la Soulle!"

532

Broquet stepped over to this Soulle, ripped off his vest, then tore open his shirt, exposing his bare chest.

"There! See…"

On the prisoner's chest was a big, dark stain.

"It took a long time for me to figure out how to tell the difference between the two Counts we were dealing with whenever we faced Zigomar. Because I knew there were two of them from the start, but I needed proof. Every time I hurt Zigomar when we met was not enough. I needed better. So, the day the villain dueled with Captain Rennebois, I played the servant and put a vial in his pocket that made this mark when it broke. After that I just needed to run into him again. That's how I came up with the Mathieu character, the Beet in love with Lucette. The real duel was between Paulin Broquet and Zigomar. It was my last trump because this man is a wonder with the sword and would never give up… but I was dealing with the real Count and I have to admit I was fooled by the resemblance. I had to see my mark and I ran him through for it. Alas, he was not my man! He didn't have this mark here that's on the chest of de la Soulle, the other Count, and all the other characters he played, above all Zigomar."

Broquet grabbed a bottle of alcohol from the table. He used it to rub the prisoner's face and peel off the beard. Zigomar's face appeared. It was the spitting image of the Count de la Gueriniere except for the dyed moustache that was usually black. The prisoner and the patient could have been twins.

Everything made sense.

But Robert was leaning over the wounded man again, examining him. He looked up and said, "The poor guy's gone. Justice has prevailed… he's dead."

"Killed by this wretch!" Broquet growled. "This will be his last crime. I arrived too late to save this man I thought was Zigomar. But the real Zigomar came to shut him up, to finish him off, to keep him from revealing the truth. He, too, was too late because he'd already told us everything…"

"You heard?" the brothers rang out together.

"I was here during the confession. I left to set the trap for Zigomar who I knew was in the house. And the coward came in while I was gone to commit this murder."

With Robert's help Broquet lifted the Count's body and put it on the bed. He covered it reverently with the sheet.

"As for Lucette," he said, "don't worry. She's sleeping. This crook needed her asleep to commit his heinous crime so he got her to drink some tainted champagne. She's sleeping. Leave her alone."

The criminal or Monsieur de la Soulle or the Count de la Gueriniere looked in bad shape. "Drink!" he rasped. "Give me something to drink!"

Robert, who took pity on all suffering creatures, gave him a little water mixed with the cordial he had prepared for the patient who had just died. Zigomar gulped it down without blinking.

It did him good. He looked up, stared at the people around him, then burst out laughing. Loud, raucous, defiant, insulting laughter full of rage. This was truly the criminal Robert and Raoul had been expecting when they thought the real Count was Zigomar.

In a brash, arrogant voice Zigomar said, "Lemme loose! Come on, I'm caught. Look at all you, the house is full of cops, I can't escape. No need to break my arms like this." Then looking at Paulin Broquet, "I almost had you, eh? Well, now you got me. I'm all yours. Your revenge'll be sweet. But tell them to loosen up my arms. You know you already half broke them during the fight. And a winged bird, even with a good gun, out on the Quai de la Loire, you know, I'd never get away."

Broquet said nothing.

"Besides," Zigomar went on, "it does no good to hold me. In no time at all you'll have to let me go."

Then the detective waved to his men, "Take him away, boys."

"Not before I've talked to Robert and Raoul."

"Take him away!" Broquet raised his voice. "Now!"

Gabriel and Simon lifted Zigomar up and led him to the door.

"I want to talk about their daddy!" the crook yelled.

Raoul spoke up, "Stop!" He turned to Broquet, "My friend, we have to let him talk."

"No, no," the detective barked back. "It's useless. What can he tell us? Just lies!"

"The truth!" Zigomar cried out. "I'll tell the truth!"

After a short pause of uncomfortable hesitation Broquet sighed, "So be it. But brace yourselves for some painful truths."

They put Zigomar back in the chair and he looked at the two brothers for a moment. Then he spoke.

"You were trying to find out the document given to the banker by Bejanet and Grillard? I'll tell you. Let's go back... You've got yourself in trouble with the Zs. They could have killed you instantly, anytime. Do you wonder why they didn't? Sure, but you'll never guess. I'll tell you... You were also surprised to see the banker deny his previous allegation and declare the Count de la Gueriniere innocent, right? It's for the same reason. So, you have to know that the reason you're both still alive is that... you' re my brothers."

Robert and Raoul jumped. "Lies! You're lying!"

"My brothers! The reason Montreil declared me innocent is that I'm his son."

"It's not true!"

Zigomar started laughing. "The proof of it is what Bejanet and Grillard showed their banker friend."

"You're an impostor."

"Well, why don't you ask your friend Broquet there about what my mother told him… good old Madame Verdier in Menilmontant who the banker Montreil was sending money to for years, which is proven by that mysterious file you were so intrigued by."

Raoul asked the detective, "Is he lying? He's making it all up, right? One more vicious scheme of his…"

Zigomar laughed louder.

Broquet simply said, "I told you to brace yourselves for some painful truths."

Robert and Raoul were stunned, "He's really our brother?"

"Your daddy's son," Zigomar sneered. "Exactly. Your brother."

"It's awful! Absolutely horrifying!"

Zigomar felt Gabriel and Simon loosen their grip in their astonishment and took the opportunity to wriggle free and stand up. He took a few slow, painful steps forward. "Yes, I'm your brother… your older brother. There's no need for further proof. You already know in your hearts that it's true." After a heavy silence he added, "Now, let's see, my dear brothers… let's look at the situation like we should. Tell me if you want me to go to court. You've had enough trouble with your honor by trying to pay back the money that the banker Montreil—a worthy father of Zigomar—earned so profitably. Are you going to let me sit in that chair of infamy while my lawyer tells all these sordid stories to the judges?"

It was too much for Robert and Raoul. They broke down in tears. "It's so shameful, too shameful… too disgraceful!"

Paulin Broquet went to them and took their hands tenderly, "Be strong. Take courage."

Zigomar limped over to them. "Yes, Robert, yes, Raoul, talk. Are you going to let them take me to court? It's up to you. Are you going to send your brother to the guillotine?"

The brothers were too busy sobbing to answer.

Zigomar swung around. Behind him was a window that looked out upon the garden. He threw it open and said, "Broquet, You still don't have Zigomar! Zigomar is still not finished!"

He jumped… right out the window and into the night. But Broquet was right behind him at the window with his gun in hand. Just as Zigomar got to the open gate Broquet fired. Zigomar froze in his tracks and screamed in pain. Swearing loudly he teetered and fell to the ground, face down in the grass with his arms spread out.

Broquet shouted, "You see, Zigomar, you can't escape justice!"

Then he, too, jumped through the window. But he fell on top of a man standing underneath it. He rolled on the ground, leaped to his feet and started fighting with the man. In the light from the window he recognized him. It was Baron Dupont, the elegant Baron Dupont, armed with a sword.

As he was about to strike the detective he got hit on the head by a club and collapsed to the ground.

"It's me, boss," Baiter had arrived just in time. "It's a specialty of mine, knocking out barons."

"Let's get to Zigomar," Broquet ordered.

They ran but got caught in some rose bushes and it took a few extra seconds to pull free. When they finally reached the spot where Zigomar had fell he was gone. Broquet rushed to the gate but it was closed. Parked at the curb was a car with its engine idling, ready to take off. A man sat behind the wheel.

"Tom Tweak!" Broquet shouted.

He raised his gun but did not fire. Between him and car a young man suddenly appeared carrying Zigomar in his arms. He threw the limp body into the car and jumped in. And in that movement, from the lights of the car, Broquet and Baiter saw the reddish tint of hair under the driver's cap.

"Her!" Broquet shouted again. "The redhead!" And he lowered his weapon.

He could not risk hitting the woman by trying to shoot Tom Tweak. She had saved him from a horrible death at Zulma's and he owed her. He could not hurt this woman, the gorgeous beauty, the curious stranger, the mysterious redhead.

The car raced off carrying the body of Zigomar. And it seemed to Paulin Broquet and to Baiter as well, that over the roaring engine they could hear Tom Tweak shout out the rallying cry of Zigomar:

"Zalavi! Zalamor!"

Epilogue

The fashionable little house of the Count de la Gueriniere was now in the hands of the law. Broquet and his brigade searched it from top to bottom. One by one they arrested the Zs who were hiding there for the last hurrah or some other job to do. The elusive Zs got introduced to handcuffs and the paddy wagon that took them away to prison. It was a total victory for Paulin Broquet.

As for Baron Dupont, they took him into one of the rooms where Robert agreed to give him first aid. Even with the heavy blow to the head from Baiter's club, the stubborn soul refused to leave the body, although it was seriously damaged. After Robert had wrapped the Baron's head in a bandage, Zigomar's uncle, who looked dead, slowly came back to life.

"We can't imagine," Baiter commented, "how hard a life these criminals lead. After a blow like that most normal people would be dead. This guy's already getting better."

However, a few hours later the Baron was delirious. He muttered incoherent nonsense and babbled wildly. All of a sudden he sat up and shouted, "Montreil! So, you refuse... Montreil... You want to snitch... had enough of giving money to your son? Ha, you'll keep giving! No? Then I'll take it... we will take it... don't try to stop us... stop!"

As he talked he acted out the scene of the murder: his right hand grabbed the pillow and squeezed hard, as if it were strangling someone; in his left hand, holding an imaginary knife, he stabbed the pillow, killing the imaginary banker...

Paulin Broquet and the two brothers watched this scene.

"Here," Broquet said, "is revealed the secret of your father's murder and it should relieve a little of the horror that Zigomar's confession added to the tragedy. It wasn't Zigomar who killed the banker. Your unfortunate father wasn't killed by his unworthy son. It wasn't parricide. He murderer is right here. See, he's left-handed, stabs with his left, which confirms my suspicions in the initial investigation."

"My friend," Raoul said, "you're amazing. We can't thank you or congratulate you enough."

A few hours later when Robert and Raoul went back home Broquet told them, "I'm coming with you because I forgot a package in the room that you so graciously offered the Beet."

"We'll send Marcelin with it to you tomorrow."

"No, no, I want to get it right away."

The three of men went up to the room. Robert and Raoul noticed that their butler was gone. "He must have run away," Raoul said, "when he heard about his friends and Zigomar being defeated."

Broquet opened Robert's armoire, for which he had the key, and pulled out Marcelin the butler, all tied up. Marcelin the eavesdropper had been caught spying and was packed up by Broquet.

"He's the one," the detective revealed, "who warned Zigomar about your plans to rob the notary's safe. He's the one who stole the blade that wounded the Bejanet's night watchman to put the police on the wrong track."

Marcelin the butler went to join his friends in prison.

The most astonishing revelation of all was for Monsieur Mathieu, the Beet, when he woke up in the evening and found out that he had beaten the Count in a duel... and killed him. The Beet never knew anything because Broquet remained poker-faced and never told him that he had put him to sleep to take his place. Deep down the Beet never figured out what was true. He ended up accepting the compliments and enjoying the glory of being a killer in the world of sugar beets.

Now that the criminals are taken care up, let's see what happened to the good folk. Let's visit our favorite circle of friends.

Riri and Raoul were engaged to be married.

The Count de Valours was happy to accept Robert's proposal for the hand or his pretty daughter Irene.

Paulin Broquet was able to offer the mayor of Itonville solid proof that he had been robbed not by his poor son in-law but by professional thieves, by the Zs, by Zigomar. He told him that Monsieur Laurent had recovered his fortune and added to it. Therefore, Bilmat withdrew his grievance and went to Paris to embrace the couple.

Monsieur Laurent had learned everything and was happy to find his wife as good and generous and faithful as ever when he got out of prison. He went first thing to Andre Girardet to thank him for everything he did.

The young couples went to Orleans to attend the wedding of Captain de Cazeaumont and Alice de Brialle who spent their honeymoon in Paris to attend the weddings of their friends.

It was agreed that the three marriages of Raymonde and Rennebois, Riri and Raoul and Irene and Robert would all take place on the same day. Naturally Paulin Broquet, Gabriel, Baiter and even the clown Simon were all there to share the joy that was partly due to them. Andre Girardet was also brought to the ceremony. He wanted to be there. Besides, it was at his newly decorated villa that they had the celebration afterward.

Then the three couples went their separate ways... to return soon...

Marie the hunchback and Andre Girardet, the two who would never know love, felt united by their misfortune.

"To be happy," the hunchback told the cripple, "we should both talk about the happiness of those we love."

And the two of them, surrounded, pampered and cherished, had many stories to tell because there was a lot of happiness around them.

But Paulin Broquet was still thinking about Tom Tweak who had got away and shouted one last challenge at him: "Zalavi! Zalamor!"
He was also thinking of that beautiful redhead...

www.ingramcontent.com/pod-product-compliance
Lightning Source LLC
Chambersburg PA
CBHW030922020726
47498CB00001B/77